THE FORGOTTEN WAR

BOOK ONE: AUTUMN

THE FORGOTTEN WAR

Howard Sargent

First published in Great Britain in 2014 by

The Book Guild Ltd

Copyright # Howard Sargent 2014

The right of Howard Sargent to be identified as the author of this work has been asserted by him in accordance with the Copyright, Designs and Patents Act 1988.

All rights reserved. No part of this publication may be reproduced, transmitted, or stored in a retrieval system, in any form or by any means, without permission in writing from the publisher, nor be otherwise circulated in any form of binding or cover other than that in which it is published and without a similar condition being imposed on the subsequent purchaser.

All characters in this publication are fictitious and any resemblance to real people, alive or dead, is purely coincidental.

ISBN 9798396589810

Dedicated to both Helens, with much gratitude. Nug. (Special mention for the old codgers, too.)

BOOK ONE: AUTUMN

1

For three days solid the rain hadn't stopped. That was a rather superficial analysis to tell the truth. Sometimes it had reduced to little more than a feathery drizzle coating hair and clothes in a spidery mist; sometimes it was the more dependable type of rain – consistent, never varying – you knew if you left your tent and walked to the cookhouse or midden exactly how wet you would get by the time you returned. At other times, however, the skies truly opened, drenching everything in an unrelenting tide of freezing cold clammy wetness, making clothes stiff and heavy and sending everyone scuttling off like beetles, heads bowed, for the nearest shelter. That was just how it was now.

He was sitting in his tent, hands stretched out towards a hissing brazier as the rain drummed its frenetic tattoo on the canvas over his head. He was not a tall man, but stocky and muscular, someone used to regular physical work. Little else of him could be divined as he shrouded himself in a large black or dark-green cloak, but his face was clear enough – the hot coals illuminating it in a harsh red glare. It could be seen that he was a man in his middle years, maybe thirty-five, clean shaven, with a strong jaw and an almost aquiline nose. His eyes glittered like the coal itself, keen and intelligent, but behind that there seemed to be a certain weariness about them, almost as if he was mentally much older than the body he inhabited. And then there was the scar, livid in the flames, running from the left cheek across the throat... Even now he played with it, idly stroking it with his forefinger, even though it looked like it had been there for many years.

He barely moved, staring into the void, as inscrutable as a monolith. He was the fixed point around which everything else revolved. To him the rain, the acrid smoke of the brazier, the damp packed earth under his feet, the wind tugging persistently at the tent flaps – all these registered as little more consequential than the buzzing of a cloud of midges, or the high-pitched whine of a marsh mosquito as he strained his ears to catch the sound he wanted to hear.

Finally, it came – heavy boots sploshing through liquid mud

accompanied by the metallic clink of chain mail. Expensive leather boots, he had no doubt, and the mail would be patterned, maybe with the eagle-claw crest or even possibly the double serpent. He jerked his head leftwards as the tent flaps were opened.

'The Baron will see you now.' It was Sir Reynard, knight of the Eagle Order. He regarded the sitting man with a barely concealed look of distaste. 'Thank you' came the response. The other man got up and followed the knight out of the tent.

He looked at Sir Reynard in his polished silver mail walking over the sodden wooden planking as if daring the rain to bother him, blue cloak emblazoned with the yellow eagle claw hanging heavily from his shoulders. There was a time when this tall blond knight, his bearing the very quintessence of his noble birth, would have been off jousting at tourneys, downing goblets of the finest southern wine, and dazzling the spoiled, pampered ladies at the Grand Duke's court.

Instead he was here.

He was probably in his mid-twenties, which would mean he would have been fifteen or so when this whole sorry affair started. He had spent his entire adult life at war, then. For a noble knight this was no bad thing – reputations and honour are of course forged on the battlefield. If only this war had been like the glorious campaigns against the Wych folk, or the three-year war of imperial succession that had culminated in the Battle of Hawks Moor when the independence of the Duchy had been secured. And not this sordid, half remembered little war in which – after ten years of invasion and counter invasion, massacres of men, women and children, the slaughter of priests, the burning of towns and villages, public executions of traitors, deserters and minor nobility, and the transformation of hundreds of square miles of fertile, arable land into a morass of mud and thick, tangled grassland – nothing more had been achieved than a minimal redrawing of borders and the swelling of towns outside the warzone, bloated by refugees made to feel as welcome as an un-lanceable boil. No glory to be had here then, only an endless cold attrition.

He looked up – they were nearly there. The Baron's pavilion was much larger than the other tents around it. It had to be, for, as well as housing his personal quarters, it was where the military counsels were held, packed full of erstwhile commanders eager to have their say while the Baron looked impassively on. Above it flew the banner of the House of Felmere, the mace and shield, the mace being ironhand, wielded by Baron Rovik Felmere, founder of the house some three hundred years before.

He followed Reynard into the pavilion. The white fabric of the tent cast an eerie glow on to the great table at its heart, almost as if the moon was inside the tent shining its thin ghostly light on the proceedings. At the table's head was a great oak chair, intricately carved, and behind the chair part of the tent was closed off to give the Baron some privacy. Reynard turned to him.

'I will tell His Grace that you are here.' He disappeared into the private quarters. No servants were visible; presumably all were busy on errands at the moment – there were always a thousand things that needed doing here. A minute or so later Reynard returned, the Baron following close behind. 'It has been a long time, Morgan, has it not?'

'Indeed it has, my Lord.'

'Leave us, Reynard, I have much to discuss with this gentleman.'

Reynard's eyebrow lifted slightly at the last word, but he bowed slightly, turned and left, leaving the two men together.

As the Baron had said, it had been a long time since they had last met and that time had not been too kind on him. He had a slight paunch now and his eyes had the bloodshot appearance of a man too fond of his cups. He still had that presence though, that indefinable something that meant others would gladly follow him. Was it confidence? Assuredness? He did exude a self belief that Morgan often saw in those born to privilege, a certainty in the order of things that placed them at the top with everybody else bound to follow. Barons here were not necessarily noble born – the Grand Duke, among others, could appoint a trusted commoner to a high office if his deeds impressed sufficiently. Baron Lukas Felmere, though, was born to rule.

But there was a price, though, and Morgan could see it in the drawn features, the inability to settle in any one place for a period of time.

He wondered why they had bothered bringing the baronial chair all this way when he could never sit on it for more than a couple of seconds; and then there were his eyes, red rimmed and haunted. Most definitely haunted.

'What do you think of Reynard then?' His manner was as bluff as ever. 'A whelp when all this started ... couldn't even blow his own nose; now in the last year or so he has become my right hand. Without his knights last week we could have been pushed back towards the river again. I mentioned him in my last despatches to the Grand Duke.'

'We did not exchange two words, Baron.'

'What? Really? He does have a bit of the raging snob about him, like a lot of the younger nobility these days. Another six months in the field will beat it out of him. A good man though, promising. He is Roderick Lanthorpe's boy, you know, a good family. Their lands border my cousin Hardwick's – that's how I know him.' The Baron stood, walked a little around the table before returning to his chair. 'Anyway, Morgan, how are things? When I sent you down south to help out that fool Esric I did not think you would be there so long. He had lost more land in six months than we had gained here in the north in years.'

'There were spies in his camp and jealousy over his promotion to Chief Prosecutor of the southern war. There were several trusted retainers in the pay of his rivals and one lordling, a baron's son, receiving money from Arshuma. We set a trap and caught them in the act of betrayal. The information they had been giving the Arshumans up to that point was proving to be particularly ruinous.'

'I see,' said the Baron thoughtfully. 'And has the problem been resolved?'

'It has,' said Morgan succinctly. 'For now.'

'And this baron's son?'

'His head was returned to his mother. The heads of the other spies still decorate Esric's camp.'

This heartened the Baron. 'Excellent! We will win this cursed war yet, by all the Gods.'

'Your optimism must be heartening for the men to see.'

BOOK ONE: AUTUMN

The Baron narrowed his eyes. 'Not an optimism you share, I see.'

'You know me, my Lord. We go back a long way, so you know I have always taken a somewhat bleak view of things.'

The Baron opened his mouth to reply then checked himself before finally saying, 'You know, Morgan, this was not how it was meant to be. One glorious summer campaign and the Arshumans driven back past the Seven Rivers, our banners flying over the city of Roshythe, all our ancient lands restored...'

'And you and the other nobles basking in the adoration of the grateful peasantry.' Morgan's tone reeked of bitter experience.

Felmere growled threateningly. 'You know, Morgan, not many of my men could get away with speaking like that to me.'

Morgan smiled. The two of them did go back a long way – it was easy to be honest in the Baron's company. 'I thought my lack of sycophancy always came as something of a relief to you.'

The Baron nodded. 'Yes, I do tire of being surrounded by people convinced the sun shines out of my arse... Anyway, before I start telling you why you were recalled here, do you want a drink?'

'Thank you, but no.'

'Mind if I do?'

'Of course not.'

He called out to the unseen servants, one eventually emerging from the Baron's quarters to fill a goblet from a wine pitcher. The Baron drank deep and had his goblet filled again. He dismissed the squire.

'Now,' he said, 'to business.'

'First of all,' the Baron continued in his gravelly voice, 'I had better update you on the situation up here. Up until last week we had pushed forward further than we had for a long time, all the way up to the banks of the Whiterush River. However, the village of Grest – little more than a glorified hill fort but one that controls this section of the river – continued to hold out against us. We attempted to take it but, as you see, we got driven back. As we advanced, they had catapults up the hill in the village itself throwing rocks and bundles of burning furze at us. It spooked our light cavalry, making the whole line nervous. Worse than that, though,' he added grimly, 'they had a mage.'

'Really?' said Morgan, obviously surprised. 'How did they pay for one of those?'

'Who knows, until recently neither our duke nor their king wanted to spend money on this war. I remember nine years ago lining up to face them with seven thousand men and four mages and they had about the same. Today, without a muster and assistance from the other barons, I would struggle to put up half that number and the only mage we have is our healer in the main camp a day's travel away. That,' he said, grinning wolfishly, 'may be about to change.'

Morgan realised that the Baron was imparting a confidence and so let him continue on at his own pace.

'I have connections these days. Three years ago my little sister, Eda, married into the Hartfields of Edgecliff. They have two kids already so she wasted no time. Anyway, after having my whiskers singed by wizard's fire last week, I decided it was time to call in favours. I may not have the ear of the Grand Duke but the Hartfields definitely have. And finally, today' – he held up a crumpled letter – 'at last the dandies out west are doing something about it. Two mages they are paying for: one of them senior, with a makeweight thrown in. Hopefully they will be here by the end of the month. We need something, Morgan. I know you think this whole situation dipped into the furnace a long time ago but I know...' He emphasised the last word. 'I know it can be retrieved.' There was conviction in his voice, whether forced or genuine Morgan could not tell.

'I hope you are right,' he replied. 'Perhaps you are too closely involved to see things clearly, but a lot of people are saying that what we have is two exhausted armies, who, having fought each other to a standstill, are too proud to sue for peace but not committed enough to risk all in a full engagement, and so they hole up and glare at each other, daring their enemy to make the first move. And all the while they leave almost one-tenth of the country abandoned, full of ghost villages and ruined or burnt crops, haunted by bands of brigands or rogue mercenaries fighting over what little spoil remains. Some are even linking you to that priest massacre some months back.'

'It is a slander,' said the Baron wearily. 'I have enemies at court that would happily see me dead so they could fight over my lands when the war ends. What happened was this. Some mercenaries we hired – they called themselves "The vipers" and were all tattooed as such – well, we decided that we did not need them anymore, they cost too much and spent most of it on drink. I paid them up and told them to go. They weren't happy but left anyway. Some days later I hear the monastery at Frach Menthon, well behind our lines, had been burnt down and robbed with the priests hung on gibbets. One poor old sod survived and told a story about a bunch of drunken men with snake tattoos. I sent Reynard with some knights; he caught them, killed a number and drove the rest into the mountains where they will hopefully starve. Frach Menthon is on Baron Ulgar's land. You know the animosity between Felmere and Vinoyen so I imagine these rumours started with him.'

'You have some of Ulgar's troops with you.'

'Yes, but never enough that they could cause me trouble. I still watch them closely though, especially now.' He took a drink. 'Anyway, I am digressing. I have a job for you – I didn't summon you all this way for a chat.'

Morgan smiled. 'I rarely get hired for my conversational skills.'

'Neither do I, my friend, but if it is conversation that you want, the fellow I will be introducing you to will happily supply you with more than enough. Much more than enough! I had an hour with him last night and almost chewed through a tent pole in my desperation to escape.'

Morgan looked disconcerted. 'And what does this man have to do with me?'

'He is your mission,' said Felmere, smiling so broadly he showed his yellow teeth. 'His name is Cedric of Rossenwood, professor of something or other at the great university of St Philig's in Tanaren City. When you meet the honour will be all his, I assure you.'

'You want me to baby some academic? What on earth for? Surely someone else could do this?'

'Point one,' said Felmere, raising a solitary finger and obviously enjoying his companion's discomfiture. 'This man has quite a long and difficult journey to undertake and, without you and a few men I will furnish you with, he will have no chance of completing it. Point two: well, he arrived with a letter from the Grand Duke himself, expressing the urgency of his mission and that I should give it my highest priority, and so I sent for the best. You, Morgan, shall be his bodyguard.'

Morgan looked coldly at the Baron. 'So what you are saying is: I escort this man to Artorus-knows-where and in return you get your mages.'

'Purely coincidental. I summoned you here before I knew the mages were coming.'

'But not before you requested them,' Morgan said pointedly.

Felmere smiled disarmingly. 'You have me there. As I say, though, this mission is sanctioned by the Grand Duke himself. Completing it successfully will hardly lower your standing. I will make sure I mention your name next time I write to him.'

'That is of less than no interest to me,' Morgan grumbled. 'Is there any pay?'

'Fifteen crowns.'

'I am sure the Grand Duke could afford twenty.'

'Well fifteen is a fortune for a foot soldier, but you are right – I am quite sure he could manage twenty. I will let him know.'

Morgan nodded. He was not naturally a man covetous of gold but his lack of enthusiasm for the task he had been given had put him in a bad humour, though only temporarily so.

'Right,' said the Baron, 'it is time you got acquainted with the learned Cedric. Before we go though, there is one more thing.'

'Yes, Baron?'

The Baron looked grave. 'I trust you, Morgan, I really wish you had been noble-born so I could have you lead an army. I trust you more than any other man here and one day you may find out exactly how much. What I am trying to say is, don't bugger this up! It is important to me.'

Morgan was both surprised and mollified by the Baron's candour. 'I will do my best. You have my word on that.'

'Good. Now come with me. It wouldn't surprise me to see Cedric throttle himself with his own tongue if he goes without conversation for an hour.'

The Baron led him out of the tent – Morgan noticed the rain had slowed considerably – past rows of smaller bivouacs for the more humble troopers until he reached a covered wagon beside which two carthorses, free of their reins, were stoically munching the wet grass. Just behind the wagon was a larger tent with its flap pegged open. Here the Baron finally stopped. He turned to Morgan. 'In there.'

Ducking under a guy rope, he strolled inside. 'Ah, Cedric!' he barked.

'This man will be your escort.'

This tent, though comparatively small compared to the Baron's own, seemed to be packed full of chests, books and chairs. There was a folding table at its centre which seemed to be completely covered in scrolls and at it was sitting a man in the middle of perusing one such scroll when the Baron addressed him. He got up and approached them, hitting his head against a hanging lamp.

Morgan had not met too many scholars or professors in his time but this one seemed to be a perfect amalgam of all that he thought they should look like. He had thin, wispy grey hair and a medium-length beard of a similar hue which Morgan noticed had been waxed. His complexion was pale, as befits an indoor type, though there was a faint red flush to it, indicating yet another man who enjoyed his wine, though whether it was a past or present love Morgan could not be sure. He wore the expression of a man who appeared to spend much of his life in the act of concentration; his forehead seemed to be permanently furrowed over his wild, untamed eyebrows. His clothes, pale-beige shirt and black trousers, had seen better days, though they were obviously of a good make. Most curious about him, though, were his reading glasses of which Morgan had never seen the like before: two circles of glass in a frame of thick wire that balanced on his nose. As he stood up, he removed them, tucking them into a pocket in his trousers.

'So, you must be Morgan of Glaivedon – the Baron here has told me much about you, one of the most respected and feared men on this frontier of war. The honour is all mine, I tell you ... all mine.'

He proffered his hand, which Morgan took. 'Ah, such a firm handshake, powerful, decisive. A man of action indeed. The enemy must surely tremble when confronted by such indomitable spirit.'

'If only that were true,' Morgan replied. 'Alas, the enemy have their own share of indomitable warriors. Ten years on the front line will temper even the puniest milksop, if he lives that long.'

'May I ask, have you been fighting here all that time?'

Morgan nodded. 'Pretty much.'

Cedric seemed a little awed. 'Then I see you are the ideal man to aid us in our little ... undertaking.'

Morgan raised an eyebrow. 'Us?'

'Oh, myself and my assistant, Willem. The boy is running messages for the Baron but will be back shortly.'

The Baron piped in. 'Sorry, gentlemen, but I must be away. I need to see Reynard – the first of a multitude of sundry tasks to complete before night falls.' He nodded to each man in turn before hastily exiting the tent.

'Now then, my boy, take a seat and let us talk.' He offered him another chair at the table. Morgan noticed his voice had a rich, mellifluous quality, something. he realised, that would be required for a man who had to do a lot of public speaking. A professor taught students mostly, did he not? 'How much has the Baron told you of our little jaunt?' Cedric asked as Morgan seated himself.

"Next to nothing, I am afraid. He said that you would explain everything.'

'Right,' said Cedric thoughtfully. 'Right, now where to start?'

'Well, at least tell me where we are going.'

Cedric seemed surprised. 'He hasn't even said that? Well, you really are in the dark, my boy. Allow me to shine a little light on proceedings. What the Grand Duke has empowered us to do involves opening negotiations with potential allies to get them to fight in the war. Certain events have happened recently which leads me to believe that we have a fair to reasonable chance of success.'

Morgan seemed unimpressed. 'There are no "allies". If there were, they would have been hired by now. Every mercenary band between here and Anmir has been involved at some point and they cause as much harm as good if booty is not easily forthcoming. Anyway, I thought the war chest was empty these days.' His patience was wearing thin again. He had travelled a long way through dangerous country to get here – being sent off on some wild-goose chase was the last thing he had in mind. Cedric's leisurely obfuscation was not helping matters either.

'Oh, these people won't be fighting for money – money means nothing to them anyway.'

'Then for the love of Artorus tell me who these people are! Who would tread into this furnace on earth if not for coin?'

'I will tell you, my boy – we are heading north. We will be parlaying with the Wych folk.'

There was a stunned silence. Cedric leaned back and folded his arms; he seemed to be thoroughly enjoying himself. Morgan suspected that he had a great love of theatre and tailored his statements so as to be as dramatic as possible.

'Someone important has really lost it this time,' he muttered. 'Who on earth came up with this crackbrained lunacy?'

'I did, of course,' Cedric said blithely. 'And I have persuaded the Grand Duke as to the worthiness of the enterprise.'

'Then perhaps,' said Morgan, his teeth gritted, 'you can persuade me.'

'I shall endeavour to do so, but it will take some time. First of all, do you wish to give me some of your objections?'

Before Morgan could reply the sound of footsteps could be heard approaching outside and a young boy, probably in his late teens, entered the tent. He had a crop of unruly fair hair, striking pale-blue eyes, wore a simple peasant tunic and trousers, and was flushed from running. He carried with him some provender – bread, cheese and a pitcher of wine – something Morgan was relieved to see as he had been ignoring his complaining stomach for a while.

'Excellent, my boy, excellent. Please set the food down here, then you can sit in the corner and be quiet. This, Morgan, is Willem, a smart boy who I am sure will be a professor himself someday. His main failing is, well, is that you hardly get a word out of him, but then he does spend a lot of his time around seniors who love the sound of their own voice.' Cedric gave a little embarrassed cough at this point. 'In such surroundings the young can often be intimidated.'

Morgan nodded at the boy who grinned back at him before going to sit on a stool in an all-too-rare cleared corner of the tent. Cedric then got up and pulled the tent flap shut. 'Just to avoid prying ears.' Sitting back down again, he looked at Morgan. 'Now, man of Glaivedon, your objections.'

Morgan cut some cheese, before pulling off a chunk of bread and stuffing it in his face. A quick draught of wine from the goblet Cedric had provided and he was ready.

'Objection one: just getting to the Aelthenwood, going around the Derannen Mountains, could take many weeks, if not months, and it will be winter when we get there.'

'Around, my boy? Cannot we go over them? The Baron assured me you knew all the passes.'

'Mmmm, we could do but...' Cedric leaned forward, all eager anticipation. 'But we must be quick; we would need to get through before the snows come and, with all due respect, neither you or the boy look as if you are up to several forced marches.'

'Could we not take the wagon? Could not people rest on it in shifts?'

'We could but the horses would need rest, too. We could take two teams but then we would need more feed... The whole thing is fraught with risk. If the snows trap us up there, then we might as well leap from the highest peak to stop ourselves starving.'

'Risky but not impossible then,' said Cedric.

'Not impossible, no, just unlikely. Do you really want to put yourself and the boy through this? It would be terribly hard, even for a fit soldier in his prime.'

'Willem volunteered, just as I did, so the answer to your question is yes.'

'Very well then,' Morgan replied. 'But be aware also that there are ... creatures in the mountains as well as groups of brigands forced up there by the war and by the Baron's men. If we are encountered, I make no guarantees about what might happen.'

Cedric sounded confident. 'I have made a study of the dangerous creatures that lurk in the wild places of the world. No one knows more about what we might encounter than I.'

Morgan was not expecting such bravado. 'OK then, say Artorus and Mytha the war god see us through the mountains and we cross the plains and get to the forest, do we just walk in? How do we entice the Wych folk to speak with us without them killing us first?'

'There is a ritual. The river Taethen which borders the forest is usually quite shallow. There is an island in the river on which the summoning ritual can be performed. They watch the river constantly; it will not be long before they will come to see us.'

'And then they will kill us as they do with all unbidden visitors; their hospitality is legendary after all.'

'Ah,' Cedric nodded, 'I will concede that point to you. I cannot guarantee that they won't kill us, so we will be rather relying on my skills as a diplomat at that juncture.'

'You have skills as a diplomat?'

'Not really no, but what I have to tell and show them should be of great interest to them. It would be their loss if they kill us first.'

'That is comforting.' Morgan got the impression that nothing he said would make any difference to the old man. 'What if I refuse to go?'

'Then I will go alone. I am bound to try with or without the help of others.'

'Very well,' said Morgan. 'I thought you would say something like that. But tell me, why? Why the Wych folk?'

'Ah, now that is a tale in itself. Allow me to start with a history lesson.'

Morgan sat back in his chair expecting to be there a while as Cedric continued.

THE FORGOTTEN WAR

'Over eight hundred years ago in the east the empire of Chira was beginning to expand. Its old enemy, Anmir, had been subjugated and the people of the lakes paid it tribute. To the north and west lay great fertile plains on which it cast envious eyes but these lands were already occupied.

The Wych folk, Aelva or elves had been there for thousands of years, their light cavalry and skills with the bow making them perfect inhabitants of the plains, hunters of elk and herders of cattle. They were clannish folk, though, divided into many tribes all of whom held ancient enmities for each other; it was an odd thing but many of the Aelven tribes coexisted on far better terms with the humans of Chira and Anmir than they did with their own people. It was partly because of this mistrust that, when one day the Aelven Lutelia tribe immediately north of Chira was attacked by fellow elves of the Baetal tribe, the Lutelians approached Chira for help. It was the worst thing they could have done. This started the first war of the Aelva. It lasted twenty-four long years but by the end of it Chira held the lands of the Lutelia and the Baetal, both tribes ceasing to exist as separate entities as they were absorbed into human society.

'The retaliation wasn't long in coming. Just a few years later the Wych general Gellethon launched a stunning attack on Chira. Two great battles on the lakes wrested these lands from Chiran control and then, at the Battle of Lebethra, two-thirds of a Chiran army was destroyed in a day. The Aelven tribes, united for once, encamped outside the capital itself – it was Chira's darkest hour, one of humanity's darkest hours. But they resisted, refused to surrender and the tide slowly turned. Gellethon's great army started to dissipate and be riven by infighting. Then the Chiran general Kathan drew them into petty skirmishing which sapped their will and resolve even further. The Wych folk were not equipped for long sieges and so withdrew from Chira city itself back to the lakes where Kathan continued to harass them. And then...' Cedric made a flamboyant gesture with his arms '...came the decisive stroke. A young Chiran general named Tolmareon – later Tolmareon Aelvhassen – had a brilliant idea. While the Wych folk were occupied fighting humans in the lake country he struck directly at their homelands. Tribe after tribe fell to him as he carved through the plains until he reached the sea. It was at this time that his commander, Tanar, moved here and formed our own country of Tanaren.

'Gellethon reacted to this incursion, abandoning the lakes and moving north to meet the Chirans. They met at the plain of Shefom and, despite having a mobile army suited to fighting on open ground, Gellethon was worsted because Tolmareon had sowed the ground with stakes, ditches and other obstacles designed to hamper the Wych horsemen. It was a conclusive victory.

'The Wych folk hung on in a greatly reduced territory but their time was counting down. Nearly fifty years later Chira declared war on them on a pretext. There was some resistance but it was all over in two years. The remaining Wych folk fled into the forests or over the sea and Chira held the plains at last. The Wych folk of the Aelthenwood have been there for nearly eight hundred years.'

'And,' said Morgan as Cedric finally seemed to have finished speaking, 'because of all that they hate us and kill us on sight.'

'Not always, no. They fought with us at Hawk Moor in the War of Succession; their hatred of Chira overcame their hatred of us.'

'But Chira is not involved this time.'

'No, but Arshuma is a client kingdom of the Chiran Empire. If pressed, they could ask the White Empire for military aid but they will not do that as they know it will mean an end to what little sovereignty they have. Despite that, the spectre of the looming empire should be a powerful one for the Wych folk.'

Morgan still sounded sceptical. 'Yes, but in that case they have had ten years to join us but haven't. What by the Gods would suddenly convince them to do so now?'

'Two things, one of which I am not interested in but another that does interest me greatly. The first of this is iron and steel. The Aelva do not mine – they are creatures of nature – but this means they have very little iron weaponry that isn't antique. Their weapons are often tipped with flint or obsidian, though I have heard that they make use of metal from rocks that fall out of the sky. The Grand Duke feels that offering our ancient enemies iron weapons is more a symbolic gesture of trust than anything else. But he bade me make the offer to them. The second thing, however, is much more intriguing.' He drew himself forward, lowering his voice confidentially.

'In the far west of the country, in a bleak uninhabited place close to the sea and blasted by the wind, are some ancient ruins, possibly thousands of years old. In my capacity as a scholarly collector of antiquities and student of the ways of the Wych folk I have had occasion to visit there several times in my career and this spring I decided to go again, probably for the last time. I took Willem and a couple of other sturdy fellows ... and Alys, a student with a gift for drawing, my past sketches of the ruins not really being up to scratch. So when we got there we proceeded to slowly cover the place foot by foot, recording our findings in a scientifically acceptable manner. It is a most unusual place; I could recognise three different architectural styles and five phases of building...' He looked at Morgan, who was obviously drifting.

'Sorry, my boy, I shall get to the point. This place being on the coast, I think it was once a port, you know. Well, the land is unstable and prone to slipping and this is exactly what had happened since my last visit. A large portion of the cliff wall had collapsed into the sea. It was tragic to see the demise of something that had stood for many centuries but, as I walked through the rubble, where the land had fallen I saw something new. Stairs ... a stairway leading down a shaft cut under the hill. I cannot tell you the level of excitement that I felt; scholars such as I can go an entire lifetime without seeing such things. I was all for charging down there straight away until Willem pointed out the nauseous smell coming from the shaft and the dangerous broken nature of the stairs. We left it until the following day when the smell had disappeared. Torches lit, we slowly climbed down the shaft. I counted 198 steps, six times thirty-three, both significant in Wych folk mythology. The walls and ceilings of the shaft were all of vaulted stone, which had prevented its collapse, but the carvings on these walls! Some of the original colours remained – vivid blues, reds and greens with pictures of rearing stags, fierce bears and wolves. There were hawks flying on the ceiling as well as gentler animals, goats and oxen, all of which are spirits or deities in Wych mythology. But then, finally, I realised there was a beast whose long, thin body ran the entire length of the shaft, coiling over the ceiling, down to the walls and back to the ceiling again, until at last we were confronted by a frowning stone door on which the beast's fierce head was displayed. The head of a dragon!'

'Dragons are myths,' said Morgan unconcernedly as he finished off the food.

'Maybe, my boy, but what we were looking at was a depiction of the Wych creation myth and I quote, "The great black dragon opened its maw and out streamed all the animals of the Earth, but soon they sickened through cold and damp and so the dragon breathed again and thus gave the world fire." That is part of the annals of the Aelven. Before our second war with them the priest chronicler Adalferth travelled to their lands recording their histories and mythologies. After setting these things down in writing, he returned with other priests and tried to convert them. They were all killed, one of the catalysts for the second war. Anyway, we had to get this door open.'

'What caused the smell?'

'The dragon's eyes,' Cedric replied. 'On closer inspection we realised that his eyes were in fact spheres permeated by holes set into the stone. They were made of a strange red stone, inside of which was a powdery substance that smelled so strongly that even now, after all these years, it made our eyes water. They are still examining them back at St Philig's. The door itself, though, would not budge and I regret to say we had to force it. Once it gave way it collapsed backwards and shattered, a regrettable loss...'

'So, what was behind the door?'

Cedric's eyes lit up, like a beggar thrown a leg of mutton. 'Things you could not imagine. Straight away I sent one of the lads back to St Philig's to bring wagons, such were the amount of finds that were there. My theory is this: after the second war, many Aelvenfolk fled our lands by ship. If they sailed from these ruins, perhaps they gathered what treasures they could find and sealed them, hidden from human eyes, in this chamber.'

'But why not just take them with them?'

'I do not know. Maybe space on board was at a premium. Maybe they intended to return for them but for some reason never did.'

'And now you feel they want these objects back.'

'Indeed! Willem, fetch the trunk.'

'Yes, Master Cedric'

Willem sprang up from his sitting position and dragged a large black trunk next to him towards the table. He pinged open its clasps and lifted up the heavy lid. Inside, concealed in vellum wrappings, were half a dozen objects of indeterminate size and shape. Cedric lifted the first one out and delicately unwrapped it, a hungry look in his eye.

The first object was a statuette of a stag, maybe the size of a man's head. Morgan was about to agree that the delicacy of its features, its cocked ears, its large eyes and the finely carved tracery of its antlers marked it as a masterpiece of its kind, but then dully realised in the dim light that it was entirely fashioned from pure gold. He leaned back in his chair.

'Artorus's eyes!' he sighed softly.

Cedric grinned at him and unwrapped the other objects one by one.

The second was a falcon, each feather carved in the minutest detail; blue gemstones served for its eyes but, apart from that, it, too, was all gold. After this was a beaver, again golden apart from its rudder, which consisted of a series of tiny glittering amethysts held together by ... by what exactly? After this was a snake twisting and coiling in on itself, green gems set in its golden back.

'Two more objects,' said Cedric. He proceeded to unwrap what looked like a canine tooth, except that it was over a foot long. Its root was bound in gold and set with red gems. The tooth itself was carved with dozens of tiny delicate lines; it looked like a script but Morgan, a literate man, could not fathom a word.

Cedric saw his confusion. 'I think it is ancient Aelven; no human living today can know what it means.'

'You think they might translate it for you?'

'Why not? Can you imagine...' Cedric gasped in excitement. 'A cultural exchange ... with the Wych folk – what an achievement that would be!'

'And the tooth itself comes from what animal?'

Cedric shrugged. 'I hope it is long dead, whatever it is.'

The last object took the efforts of both men to lift it out. It was long, narrow and three to four times larger than the others. Cedric gingerly unwrapped it. Morgan's jaw fell slightly.

He assumed, correctly, that it was a dragon: a large reptilian head with red gems for its eyes, a long thin snake-like body, each scale rendered in gold, its tail lifted into the air, the claws on its feet studded in white stones. Its wings were vestigial and folded over its back. The worth of this piece must have been staggering. Cedric took note of his companion's numbed expression.

'There are six of these, and another of the teeth. Each dragon is different. Notice the wings on this one; on some of the others the wings are much, much larger. They are all individuals and they all represent ... something.'

'You don't know?'

'No. Not for certain. The mythologies are not clear. The dragon itself was worshipped as an elevated spirit involved in the creation of the world but other than that I am guessing.'

Morgan looked sceptical. 'And you are just going to ... give these back to them in return for their support in this war? You could buy Felmere's baronetcy for this, and his neighbours'.'

'Oh, there is much, much more than this. The Grand Duke has laid claim to the rest. Negotiations with him regarding the settlement of all the finds are on-going.'

'Well, one thing is certain.' Morgan sat back in his chair, a half smile on his face. 'We need to leave quickly. If the men get a whiff of what you are hiding here, your lives won't be worth an Arshuman groat.'

2

She sat back on the bench, closed her eyes and let the scent of the sea roses gently overpower her. The soft warmth of the late-afternoon sun felt good on her skin and in the near distance the omnipresent crash of the sea against saw-toothed rocks only enhanced her torpor. She had a firm belief that everyone should have a period of solitude every day, a time to be alone with one's thoughts and reflections. So, while the other initiates congregated in the main hall turning it into a hub of chatter and gossip before the evening meal was served, she instead retired to the bathhouse and, after ten minutes soaking in a tub scented with sage and lavender, she took her book and, skin and collar-length hair still damp, retired to the rose garden to keep her own company for a while.

The garden itself was walled on all four sides, access being through a warped wooden doorway which had a tendency to creak loudly on its hinges when opened. The bench (her bench she liked to think) on which she sat was situated in an alcove in the corner where the north and east walls met. It was one of the few places on the island where you could not see the austere sable black stone walls of the Grand College of the Magisters, the place she had called home for the last fifteen years.

She opened her eyes. Elmund, the lay brother who tended to the garden with a zealous attention to detail, was busy with his pruning shears, wisps of his white hair flying in all directions in the breeze. The garden being walled mitigated the excesses of the wind and salt spray, but as this was a small island surrounded by the slab-grey ocean its presence was always felt.

She gazed absently at the cracked stones of the path through which the weeds constantly tried to push before Elmund could notice them and pull them loose with a maniacal cackle, sending a spray of loose earth flying. As she did so, he finally noticed her. He slowly straightened his back, wincing slightly as he did so and made his way towards her, favouring his right leg. His left had been injured in a fall on the stone steps leading up to the college; they were high and uneven and many of the older brothers had fallen victim to them in one way and another over the years. He raised his hand in greeting.

'Good afternoon, Sister Cheris. I heard the gate but wasn't sure if it was you.' He was a sprightly old man, a bit deaf and always smiling.

'Oh come on, Elmund, who else would it be at this time of day? Fancy a pastry?' His sweet tooth was legendary and a quick detour to cadge something from the kitchens was almost obligatory on her way to the garden. His pale-blue eyes fairly gleamed.

'Ever so kind of you, Sister Cheris. Many of you youngsters never pass a glance at a lay brother, but if you don't mind me saying so, you have always been different. You've always shown consideration to those that keep this place running.'

'I know, I know!' she laughed. 'We owe our food, our water, our bedding and our warmth to the ceaseless labour of the lay brothers and yet we never give any thought as to how it is all provided. We live like the duchesses and baronesses of the mainland, taking every luxury for granted, never thinking of the work involved in filling our plates and goblets, washing our laundry and stocking the log piles.' This was almost word for word the speech he always made on her visits to this quiet, half-forgotten corner of the island.

'Aaaah, but as I said, Sister, you have always been a bit removed from the others.' He cast her a deferential look before shoving the pastry into his almost toothless mouth in one go, flakes of it fluttering around his chin before being taken by the wind. Cheris laughed again. The old man liked her, she knew, but then, didn't everyone?

Cheris Menthur – twenty-two years old, five foot four; jet-black hair cut short to her collar in a bob; keen, penetrating blue-grey eyes betraying her sharp intelligence – had never been an average pupil at the college. When she had arrived on the island at the age of seven her raw untrained abilities already surpassed those of pupils twice her age and since then her progress had continued unabated. It had left her slightly isolated at times – jealousy and, yes, fear in her contemporaries had made her early to mid-teen years difficult, but the gentleness and warmth of her character combined with a tendency towards self-deprecation meant that few of these problems existed nowadays.

Most initiates were deemed to have graduated by their mentors at around the age of thirty, for there were many tests to pass, all of which had to be performed perfectly under the unsparing glare of five different seniors. She had completed her final test just the night before and was waiting for her chief mentor, Brother Marcus, to summon her to his chambers to confirm to her what in her heart she already knew: that she could now officially call herself a mage, that is, a fully qualified practitioner of magic.

    She could discard the white (or, rather, off-white, she thought testily) robes of the initiate and don the dark-blue ones so coveted by her peers. It was the truest mark of status here. She could even teach others, though in someone so young she knew that would be seen as rather unseemly. Her province in that regard would likely be the smallest of the children, the newest arrivals, caught and shipped here as soon as evidence of talent was detected. All of which made the fact that she had not yet been summoned a matter of vexation to her. She turned back to Elmund, who had finished his treat and was looking at her like an eager puppy.

    'Was that nice?' she asked politely.

    'Lovely, thank you, I had better be getting back to the roses now.' He turned to go, stiffening and putting his hand to the small of his back. Cheris looked concerned.

    'Have you ever seen the healers about that?'

    'Oh no, Sister Cheris! They have more important things to do than coddle an old man.'

    'Do you want me to speak to them for you?'

    'You're very kind but no – to be honest, all they could do is take the pain away, not replace crumbling bones.'

    'But surely, being free from pain would help?'

    Elmund looked thoughtful. 'Yes and no. It would be nice certainly to work without discomfort but the pain is important. It tells you when to stop, you see, before you damage yourself further. Without the ache in my back I would continue working and, when the healing wore off, it would come back to kick me tenfold. The almighty Artorus gives us everything for a reason, even that which we would rather not have. Anyway, Sister, it has been lovely to talk to you but I must return to my duties. Weeds never stop growing, pain or no.'

He ambled back to his roses. She watched him for a moment, inhaling the flowers' sweet scent, then finally returned to her bench.

She picked up her book, The Abuse of Mana and Its Terrible Consequences, but decided she was not in the mood for another lecture on the dire costs of the hunger for power. She set it back down again and shut her eyes once more.

Where was Marcus? Granted, if anyone lived up to the well-worn cliche concerning the enigmatic behaviour of 'the older mage' it was he but her patience, she could feel, was draining out of her like water from a sponge. Perhaps she had failed the test? Unthinkable. Anyway, even if she had, he should at least do her the courtesy of telling her. She went over the test in her head for the thousandth time. How she had stood barefoot in the stone casting circle near the island's west point; how she had called the ball of lightning forth, held it in space four feet above the ground and ten feet from her outstretched arms, then gently commanded it to move, slowly, in a circle around her. How she had stopped it dead, then made it rise higher and higher into the evening sky, until it finally took its place among the stars, before bringing it back towards Earth once more and, with one imperious gesture, dismissing it from this world altogether, showing her complete control over the elemental forces she could summon. No, it had gone perfectly – there had been no mistakes – so where in the pits of damnation was he?

She sat there quietly a little while longer until the liquid blue sky started to deepen in colour and the increasing cold started to nip at her fingers and ears. Then, just as she was about to get up and head off to the refectory, the gate gave a loud creak. She stood up as Marcus finally came towards her.

He was a big powerful-looking man, probably in his mid-fifties (she had never asked him his age), black hair streaked with grey as was the short brush of his beard. His brown eyes were lined with red (a scholar's eyes, she had heard them called, caused by too much reading by candlelight or not enough sleep, or both), and as ever he exuded a barely discernible air of grandfatherly disapproval, of which she was usually the cause. His robe was long, blue and flowing, tailored for him, and completely unlike the one-size fits-all white initiate robes that caused so much grief and despondency among the younger female mages, many of whom resembled little more than a sack of meal once they had put them on. Catching sight of her, he harrumphed loudly before walking authoritatively towards her and seating himself on the bench. She remained standing until he gestured for her to sit next to him.

'Mentor,' she said, trying to keep both her impatience and irritation out of her voice, 'I have been waiting.'

'Ha!' he snorted dismissively. 'I do not doubt it!'

'Is there a problem?' she asked. 'I mean, did I fail in my task? I was only thinking earlier...'

He cut her short. 'Don't be foolish, child; of course you did not fail. No, I was delayed by other matters ... by business I had with the Chief Magister which I will discuss with you presently. When you return to your cell you will find your new robes waiting for you. Arbagast is preparing your staff even as we speak. From now on you have the full title of Magister. You may attend council meetings and...' He hesitated at this. '... You may go to the mainland on specifically sanctioned council business. Cheris, it is this last point which I wish to talk to you about now.'

'Wait!' she said excitedly. 'You are going too fast for me. I ...I have passed then...? What about the ceremony of induction? And the presentation of the Book of the Magisters? And the...'

'Yes, yes, all of that formal nonsense, too; you'll have all that to endure I am afraid.'

'And the presentation of the key? The key to the senior magisters' library?'

'All in good time.'

She bit her lip in frustration; something she had been working fifteen years towards he was treating like a mundane triviality. 'Now is a very good time! You know how the initiates feel about having knowledge withheld from them.'

'I don't know why! The senior magisters' library is quite possibly the dullest place on the island, worse than the house of Artorus during

Father Tomas's prayer recitals.'

'You know it is the allure of the forbidden, and you know how terrible I am at resisting temptation.'

'Yes, I know all about your feeble self-control, whether it is a library forbidden to the initiates or the chambers of Brother Mikel.'

He shot her a sideways glance, catching her flushing pink and glaring at the floor.

'Worry not, lass,' he said in a far kindlier voice. 'I have told no one and, besides, you are committing the oh-so-familiar sin of completely distracting me from the purpose of my calling upon you.'

'What!' she started. 'This is not about my graduation?'

'Of course it is, but surely you are not surprised to have graduated? It is something I have always seen as an inevitability. No, the reason for my preoccupation is another matter entirely.'

'What other matter?' she said, smiling. 'What can it be that is more important than that which I have spent most of my life in trying to achieve?'

'It is simply this,' he said. 'You are coming to the mainland with me. You are to fight with me, in the eastern war.'

They had left the garden and were now walking slowly along the stone path leading to the college. It was uphill, starting at a gentle slope but getting ever steeper until they came to the college stairs – some fifty high steps, cracked and worn, leading up to the great door. Behind them were the various enclosures for the herb garden, rose garden, and the garden of silence, which was a place many went to read, along with the pens for the animals and the grain stores. Past all these the island continued to slope downwards to the west, tapering all the while, a narrow winding path leading to the mages' stone circle where Cheris had been the previous night, until finally the island ended, still some fifty feet above sea level, its black cliffs patrolled by vociferous birds. From east to west the island was shaped like a giant teardrop that gave it its name – the Isle of Tears.

As one island ended, another began, smaller, flatter and almost circular. The gap between the two islands was little more than a gorge through which foaming waves crashed constantly. It was so narrow a bridge joined them. It was stone, some six foot wide with rails on both sides, but was rarely attempted on anything other than good days. The most popular way of traversing the isles was by ferry; the smaller isle had beaches and a low pier where the ferry itself was usually moored. The Isle of Tears was undercut by a cave on its eastern side, and a small harbour and mooring had been carved into the rock of the cave. A low tunnel with steps led directly up to the college's ground floor.

The smaller isle was called the Isle of Healing. It held a low single-storey building which had spread until it covered almost half of the island's surface. This was the great hospital of the mages where those on the mainland sent their sick and infirm, if they had the coin. Research and education were its other functions – many aspiring young doctors resided there including those who had no magical gift at all, as the college did not discriminate. Mages were so rare after all and it was only the more prosaic methods of healing that were available to most people. It also housed a small house of prayer dedicated to Meriel, goddess of healing, and an equally small chapterhouse of the Knights of the Holy Thorn, there to police errant mages. The chapterhouse in the Grand College itself was much larger.

Cheris and Marcus had not spoken since leaving the garden. Her mind was racing so fast that one question was immediately displaced by another before she had the wherewithal to ask it. They were about to go up the steps to the college when she seemed to come to her senses.

'Excuse me a minute,' she said. She then proceeded to extract a small bag which seemed to be concealed in a pouch in her robes. (Mage robes are voluminous enough to contain many pouches, the majority of which contained many rare and, to the common man, wondrous ingredients.) She turned aside from the path and called out in a clear ringing voice only slightly diminished by the wind 'Fidget! One-eye! Knocker!' A few seconds later she called again.

From somewhere over the other side of the hill three cats started running towards her. They were all large, well-fed, black-and-white cats. One had an eye missing.

BOOK ONE: AUTUMN

She opened the bag and emptied its contents, pieces of ham and chicken, on to the ground. As the cats tucked in she made sure that each of them had roughly the same amount of food, talking softly to them as she did so. 'Don't be so greedy, Knocker; let Fidget have some more, he is smaller than you. Come on, One-eye, tuck in! Here's some chicken; I know you prefer it.'

When they had finished she stayed a while stroking each in turn, then stood up to return to the path. 'Who will feed them now, I wonder?' she mused sadly. She rejoined Marcus, and they turned up the path together, climbing the stairs to the college and escaping the wind, which was picking up as the sun started to go down.

The great doors, dark wood bound in iron pitted by salt, were open just enough to admit two people. Two knights, in dark mail covered in white cloaks emblazoned with the symbol of a blood-covered thorn, stepped aside to let Cheris and Marcus in. Their eyes took a few seconds to adjust to the cool darkness but the surroundings were so familiar they could walk through them blindfold.

The Great College was fashioned out of unyielding black stone. There was little that was beautiful about it; rather, it was a building in which function was all important. The reception area was small, though flanked by two great staircases, partially carpeted, and lit, badly, by candles set in strategic alcoves along the walls. The windows, as they were elsewhere, were too small to make much difference, although now, as the sun began to set, they cast shafts of light, shot through with dust motes, on to the floor.

Through the next set of oak doors was the main hall, in which major meetings were held and dignitaries received. It made an attempt at grandeur; its walls were lined with tapestries with busts of the many former Chief Magisters filling the gaps between them, aping the Grand Duke's palace in Tanaren City. It also held four great chandeliers, which, though they usually held candles, could be fitted with many glass orbs that could be lit magically. The college, a place of austerity with many strict rules, usually frowned on the frivolous use of its arts, but if visitors needed to be impressed then rules could be set aside, if only for one night.

    Through the next set of double doors were the refectories, with the kitchens leading off them to the south and the lay brothers' cells to the north, and through yet another set of great doors was the initiates' library, one of the busiest rooms in the building. Teaching was done in very small groups or on a one-to-one basis so no teaching rooms existed, although the library had alcoves in which mentor and pupil could sit together. The library was not a place of silence. Quiet study would take place in the initiates' cells just off the library. These small, spare rooms just held a bed, chair, table and bookshelf. There was also a small wardrobe in which the initiate hung their robe, no other form of dress being permitted. Light came through a small grilled window which could be closed with a wooden shutter. A little shrine to the mage god, Lucan, stood in every cell along with the Book of Lucan, a holy book full of dire warnings concerning casual use of magic by the foolish or ambitious. Initiates were supposed to pray for guidance from him every night, but Cheris hadn't done so for years – she wasn't the only one.

    Up on the second floor were two great balconies, one facing east to catch the sunrise and one facing west for the sunset. The eastern balcony overlooked the cliffs on the highest part of the island, but apart from that there was just the white-flecked sea, endless and imperturbable, and the small patch of ground under which were housed the rarely used prisons.

    The western balcony overlooked both islands and it was here that, after taking a meal, Marcus and Cheris now stood, watching the light becoming ever more eerie, dappling the water and turning the unfussy buildings of the hospital into sinister blocks of shadow that seemed to absorb the light around them. About their heads great white seabirds swooped and screamed in their seemingly ceaseless agitation. These birds could be a problem at times and necessitated a canopy of sturdy sailcloth over both balconies. Other mages were gathered here – watching the sunset was a popular daily event.

    'I told you at dinner,' Cheris opined sweetly, 'I am no soldier. I cannot try to take another's life; I find the idea repellent. I don't even eat meat.'

'Yes, that is a strange habit of yours,' said Marcus with a smile. 'I am amazed the cooks put up with you.'

'Oh believe me, I have had a few frank discussions with the cooks over the years. They tolerate me these days rather than just glare; we have developed an uneasy truce. Anyway, you are ignoring my last statement, so I will say it again. Why do you wish me to go to the mainland to see the ugliness of battle and possibly be required to take life? This war is of no relevance to me; I see no purpose in my going at all. And why, by all that is holy, do you want me to go when there are plenty of others itching to leave the island?'

'It is not that simple and you know it.' Marcus was frowning, his tone almost wistful. 'Unfortunately, Cheris, or maybe fortunately, I do not know, Lucan has given you the rarest of talents. You could have been a healer or a conjuror of illusions, but we both know what you are best at. Your talent is one of pure destruction. No one at your age should be able to wield fire and lightning the way you do. Your power is one that would achieve full congress on the field of battle. Apart from that ... you are my pupil and no one knows your capabilities better than I, and believe me when I say that most of it has yet to be tapped. So there you have it: your potential simply demands that you leave here.' He looked her in the eye, emphasising each word. 'No one mage here, including myself, has the abilities that you could display. Believe me, to your foes you could become the god Xhenafa, the reaper of the dead.'

She looked uncomfortable. 'You see me as the god who takes the last breath of life from all of us, before leading us to our judgements? No, you are describing a demon ... a monster. Is that truly what I am? Is it the way you see me?''

'Not at all – a monster is savage, unreasoning. You, however, know how to exercise restraint. Your powers would be used to save the lives of our soldiers, lives that otherwise could easily be lost.' He saw her shake her head. 'And as much as you may deny it, they are our soldiers. You may have spent much of your life here, but you are a citizen of Tanaren, just as much as I am.'

She sounded derisive. 'Citizen of a country that sent me into exile as a child just because I am ... different.'

'If they hadn't done that, you would most likely be dead now; no one knows how many children the lynch mobs get to first. If you are lucky and your parents are the first to spot the signs, you get given to the authorities and sent here. If not, it is a rope or a pyre for you. I spoke with one of the knights here earlier on; he was a new arrival and told me his last duty on the mainland was to cut down the bodies of two children no more than six years old. On the mainland you are a witch and I am a wizard, and neither of those terms are ones of respect.'

'Then I say it again: these are not my people and I owe them no loyalty.' Marcus sighed. 'We have these gifts, Cheris; for good or ill we have them. As mages, there are many unpalatable truths that we have to face up to. All countries are the same – once our abilities are noticed we are sent into exile to learn how to harness and control our powers. From then on our exile only ends if our return is requested for whatever reason. Even then, once our job or period of service is completed, we have to return into exile again. On the mainland we have to wear distinctive red robes, though we may conceal them in battle. People, the common folk, are terrified, absolutely terrified of us. When we walk down a street it is to the sound of doors and shutters slamming, children being hushed into silence by their mothers – even the taverns go quiet. The Knights of the Thorn are with us constantly to protect us from them and them from us. It is the way.'

She laughed disdainfully. 'You are not making it sound any better.'

'No,' he smiled, 'I am not. Look, how long have you been here on the island?'

'Fifteen years.'

'Well, I have made many trips to the mainland for one reason or another. If I had never left, I would now be in my forty-fifth year here. I like to think I have a fairly active mind and I know you have, but if I had never left the island even for short periods I would now be on our neighbouring island in their asylum by now. If you don't leave now, you may never be allowed to. You may have another sixty years of life left; do you really think you can spend all of it here?'

She pouted. 'There are other reasons mages leave here, not connected with war. Things like council business, whatever that may be.'

'That is true but the council members who discuss our business with the Grand Duke are all my age or even older. I have been to a couple of council meetings but it is only as a junior member. For a young person to leave here there are only two viable reasons, either as a healer or as a warrior. And, alas, your healing skills are not your strong point.'

She looked downwards. 'I do not know battle or violence. I do not know how I would ... manage in such situations. I have never been close to peril before; I just do not know how I would react.'

'That is something we never know until we have to face it, but I will be with you and the knights act as protectors in the field. And, as for battle itself ... well, I believe you are far stronger than you seem to think you are. My first, second and third engagements made me physically sick but it is like anything else. The more you do something, the more used to it you get... Please don't think I am trying to force you; you can say no right up to the day the ship departs. It is just that we mages are limited in our choices: if you wish to leave here at all, then this is the only way open to you.'

She nodded her head slowly, her eyes sad and thoughtful. 'I see.'

He turned to face her. 'Do your parents still write to you?'

'Yes, I get letters once or twice a year. I write back but all my letters sound the same – "got up, studied, annoyed my mentors" – that sort of thing.'

'You are very lucky that they can read. Most people have to be taught when they get here. Where do they live?'

'In the capital, in the Loubian district; they are quite well off. Father is a merchant. He has some ships and does well out of the southern spice trade, or so his letters say. Are you thinking I might get to see them?'

'It would be difficult. I have already told you of the reception we will have, but the secondment is for a year, so I will see what favours I can call in. Perform well and it will become easier for us.'

'Thank you for that. If I choose to go, when would we be leaving?'

'A ship will be here in about four days. Say your goodbyes and don't forget to arrange a cat feeder. Let's go in.'

He went in through the doorway behind them leaving Cheris alone on the balcony. After taking a deep draught of the chill air she turned and followed him inside.

Night had set in. Most of the initiates had retired to their cells, save for the few who were gossiping in the library. Cheris, however, had gone to her room to find her blue robes waiting for her. She put them on and tried studying her appearance in a small mirror, her own personal possession, on the table.

It was impossible to see herself properly. Instead, she left the initiates' quarters and crept upstairs. The mage quarters were much larger with more luxuries allowed, a reward for a successful graduation. She pitter-pattered as quietly as possible along a dark, barely lit corridor, before arriving at a door in which candlelight was showing through the gap at its bottom. Ever so softly she tapped on it and, on hearing a muffled reply, she crept in.

The room was twice as large as hers. The bed was larger and more comfortable; there were many books on shelves and rugs on the floor. In a large high-backed chair near the shuttered window a mage was reading. He would have been about ten years older than Cheris, strong-jawed with a crop of well-tended jet-black hair that had the bluey sheen of crow's feathers. His eyes were grey, very pale, almost dissolute, but his mouth, which was almost always set in a permanent sardonic smile, dispelled any concerns as to a lack of moral rectitude. He had only one weakness, and a prime, healthy specimen of it was now standing before him, arms outstretched, showing him her new robes.

'Well? What do you think?'

'I would prefer a silk dress on you personally.'

'Oh, Mikel, so would I! It is a little big, to be honest, but still, I won't be wearing it for long.'

'Why not? Don't tell me you have been promoted to the council!'

'If only!' she laughed. 'No, it will be red robes for the next year. I am not sure red suits me, though.'

'You are off to the mainland? Already?'

'Yep, Marcus is taking me. I have a war to fight apparently.'

Mikel stroked his chin in surprise. 'I wonder why he chose you? You are not bedding him, are you?'

'No!' She spoke with false indignation. 'I was going to say, "Of course I am not, he is my mentor," but then that didn't stop us, did it?'

He looked thoughtful. 'But you going away will though, won't it?'

She stared at him, her eyes amazed but knowing. 'Don't you dare tell me that you will miss me, or that you will keep it in your robes until I return. I wasn't your first, or even your twenty-first. The second I leave you will be after somebody else. My guess is Elsa – pretty, quiet, needs a firm hand...'

He returned her smile. He had already spoken to Elsa that day; she was coming up for an extra tutorial on the morrow. 'I suppose I made my nature clear to you from the outset, although in my defence I was hardly your first either. I will miss you, though; that is the truth. There is nothing I like more than feeling the sharp edge of your tongue... Now, wait a second, where is it?'

He got up and pulled out a chest that was concealed under his bed. He opened it and rummaged through various scrolls and papers until he found a small leather pouch. Opening it, he pulled out two gold coins as well as some pennies. 'Two crowns, take them and here are some ducats. Money can be useful; you never know when you might need it. Oh and take this too.' He threw her a separate pouch. 'Spell components, iron filings, nitre and other stuff ... just in case.'

'Thank you.' She was surprised; altruism was not a notable characteristic of his. He sat back down.

'Not used to seeing money, eh?'

'Well, we don't need it here. I doubt if I have ever had more than a few pennies. Where did you get it?'

'My last trip over. I have been to the mainland three times now. I did a favour for someone. Anyway, do I get a reward?'

She looked uncertain. 'I should go back downstairs; you know how the knights prowl.'

'Then you had better stay here till dawn. I wonder how we will fill up the time?'

Her uncertainty seemed to dissipate immediately. Smiling, she walked up to him and kissed him gently on the forehead. 'I am sure we can think of something.'

He blew out the candle.

3

'Time to wake up, my Lady; your bath is ready.'
'Five minutes, Doren, just five more minutes.'
'As you wish, my Lady.'

Lady Ceriana Hartfield, buried under finest silk sheets, invisible save for a tousled mass of nut-brown hair, turned on her side and fell asleep again.

Five minutes later. 'My Lady, your bath is getting cold. I have fetched more hot water but even that will cool shortly.'

'All right, Doren, I will be there presently.'
'Thank you, my Lady.'

Ten minutes later she was reclining in a bath strewn with rose petals and heavy with the aroma of scented oils. Doren, a dumpy lady of early middle years, was gently pouring more hot water from a ewer on which the symbol of the House of Hartfield, a rearing white deer, was emblazoned. Lady Hartfield was tapping on the water with her big toe, looking idly at the rings the water was making. Then her leg started to ache so she sunk it back under the surface again. 'Is Father back yet?' she enquired.

'He has sent word that he intends to arrive on the morrow, just after dawn. It is a time I am not sure my Lady is aware of, though I can always call you then, if you desire it.'

Lady Ceriana's sharp features became even sharper. 'I swear by all the Gods you are the most insolent handmaiden a woman could have! I absolutely insist that you call me the second he is sighted from the Archer's Tower. Once you have done that you may leave my service; I am sure a more obedient girl can be found among the kitchen staff.'

'As you wish, my Lady, although I am not sure one could be found with the patience to stand idly by while my Lady decides on the dress she shall wear, or the perfume she shall put behind her ears, or what colour ribbons go best with crushed red velvet, while all the time the sun rises towards noon and her stomach rumbles ever the louder.'

'You think not? Oh well, I will keep you on a little longer then. Let it not be said that I am unkind to the elderly and infirm. Now, what dress shall I wear today?'

Doren grimaced, pouring out the rest of the water in one go.

The Hartfields were one of the oldest, most revered noble houses in Tanaren. They had been among the closest advisors of the Grand Duke for centuries and before that had even held that august office themselves, which only reinforced their reputation for justice, temperance and piety. Their estates comprised much of the land surrounding the great, seething mass of humanity that was Tanaren City itself, and all of the land was productive and fertile, bordering as it did both sides of the mighty river Erskon. Its rivers and lakes were full of fish, the fields full of golden corn and grazing cattle, and its woods full of deer. The Hartfield estates, then, made them possibly the wealthiest old family in the country.

They owned several houses, too. There was Loubian Hall in the capital city, not a thousand paces from the ducal palace. There was Erskon House on the river, which regularly entertained the Grand Duke with regattas and great feasts held on the Duke's own golden barge, but the spiritual home of the Hartfields was Edgecliff Castle, occupying a high promontory on the coast from which Tanaren City could be spied in the distance. It could be supplied from the sea at times of siege and had never fallen to its enemies, not in the half a thousand years of its existence. From its many towers, with the Archer's Tower being the highest, flew the Hartfield pennants, a white deer on a green background, all of them snapping and flapping in the wind. This was the place Ceriana counted as home.

She had one brother and two sisters. Her brother, Dominic, was First Commander of the Knights of the Silver Lance, the Grand Duke's own personal bodyguard. He had married into the Felmere family out east, slightly beneath himself if truth be told, although it had helped to strengthen ties with the ever surly eastern baronetcies. Her sisters, Giselle and Leonie, had married into wealthy families nearer to home. All three siblings had children, ever strengthening her family's political hand, and so the only eligible Hartfield remaining was herself. She was quite the prize.

She sat down at the top table in the great hall. It stood on a low dais and was covered in a rich red cloth filigreed in gold. The other tables on the lower floor faced it at right angles. There were some thirty to forty people at these tables, including a number of young men, many of whom looked at her intently. Sitting next to her was her mother, the Lady Margarete. They were the only two people at the high table. Bread and meat was brought along, with fruit both fresh and stewed. Wine was poured. Once everything was ready, Lady Margarete broke some bread, dipped it in the wine and ate it. This was the signal for everyone to start eating. A lively conversational hubbub started to fill the room.

'Why do they all stare so?' she moaned to her mother. 'They look as if they are catching flies.'

'You know exactly why, girl.' Her mother was a no-nonsense sort; if Ceriana was being honest with herself she still found her intimidating. 'Every unmarried man here wants you for his wife. And you have been promised to most of them at one time or another.'

'I really have no say at all, do I?' she sighed resignedly. 'I suppose I have been lucky to remain single until now.' She chewed absently on a rind of hard bread.

'Yes, you have been lucky not to be married off at thirteen; thank your father for that. And no, of course, you have no say, The very idea is preposterous. Anyway, your father is discussing this very question with the Grand Duke even as we speak. He will confirm your betrothed when he returns tomorrow. Personally speaking I would like you married off before the end of the year; you would make your mother very proud if that was to be the case.'

'As you wish, Mother, as long as it isn't "Baron Cuthbert of the missing teeth" I will be content.'

But, of course, she wasn't really content at all.

Later on that day she sat in a windowed alcove overlooking the sea in the Sailor's Tower. She had embroidered for a while before tedium had overtaken her and now she was pretending to read. Megan, the castle harpist, was playing for her and her young companion, Lady Catherine of Nevenn, was embroidering next to her.

'Do you know what she is playing?' Catherine asked.

'Yes, it is the Lay of Fair Isabel who was forced to send her true love away so that she could marry her father's choice, the fat and old Baron Magrin. Rather than submit herself to his lechery she cast herself into Lake Winmead and even today on moonless nights you may still hear her song of sorrow among the whispering rushes.'

'That is ever so sad,' said Lady Catherine. 'But surely by taking her own life her soul is condemned to walk the void between the heavens and the furnace of the underworld.'

'And that,' said Ceriana, 'is why you can still hear her.'

Catherine nodded knowingly and Ceriana thought of telling her that she hadn't a clue what Megan was playing and that she had made it all up, but decided that it wasn't worth the effort. She picked up her book.

Later, as evening drew on, she decided to clear some cobwebs and walk the battlements. She passed the occasional guard each of whom acknowledged her with a polite 'My Lady' and continued to walk until she came to the great barbican at the front gates. Before heading indoors, she looked out over the battlements, first at the motley collection of buildings close to the gates that comprised Edgecliff town itself, and then at the ground directly beneath her. Could she do it, she wondered? Could damnation of the soul be any worse than damnation of the spirit? It would be quick after all. Her mother would claim it as an accident; people did fall from such places surprisingly often, so she had been told. The world would go on without her. She stared at the ground intently for a while, wondering what it would be like to fly through the air, but then, suddenly, she turned away. Biting her lip slightly, she went through the doorway in the gate tower and headed down the stairs, all the time cursing herself for her abject cowardice.

'What is it, my Lady? Another black mood?' Doren had just made up the bed and was scattering fresh rushes on the floor as her mistress sat facing her mirror idly running a comb through her hair. A pale moonlight gleamed weakly through the leaded window. 'It is nothing,' she replied weakly.

'I know a lot will be changing for you, going to a place full of strangers and marrying a man you may not know at all, but...'

'No, it isn't that,' she interrupted. 'I am a nobleman's daughter; I have been prepared for this all my life – a marriage to further my family's interests is what I was born for. It is just...' She seemed to be searching for the words for a second before continuing.

'Remember my aunt, Augustine.' Doren's face fell at that name. 'I just remember it so vividly. I was seven at the time and was playing in the dayroom with my sisters when Mother came and told us to go to our rooms. We knew something was wrong but we did as we were told. I was sat on my bed when I heard the screaming. I remember my throat tightening, but there was something that compelled me to go towards the sound. I went down the stairs as quietly as I could. The sound had stopped but I knew where it had come from. By chance, a servant had gone into the room and left the door open, so I followed her in.' She stopped and swallowed hard. 'I swear by Camille and Artorus the almighty, there was not a square inch on that bedsheet that was not soaked in blood. Doctors, midwives, the Sisters of Meriel, were swarming around the bed but I could still see Augustine's face, bathed in sweat and white, ghostly white. I think she had already gone; she looked ... peaceful, if that was at all possible. Then someone saw me and shooed me out. It was ten years ago but it is still crystal clear in my mind. Both Augustine and the child died. Blessed Elissa did not help them on that day.'

Doren looked at her sadly. 'We all remember it, child; it was a terrible day. But these things do happen; it has happened in my family, too.'

Ceriana looked contrite. 'I am sorry, I was being selfish ... but ... when you had your children were you not frightened, too? We all die someday obviously, but I just don't want it to be ... like that.' She walked over to a table in a corner of the room. On it was a small carved figure of a woman in a cloak and small cape holding a swaddled bundle in her arms. On either side of it were two lighted candles. She touched the figure gently. 'Blessed Elissa protect me.'

Doren broke her reverie. 'Look at your sisters, my Lady, turning out children like rabbits. You have nothing to fear – the Gods will always look after the Hartfield girls, believe me.'

Suddenly the young girl laughed as if embarrassed by her sadness. 'Will you just listen to me! I remember there was a merchant, in the square, selling trinkets and ribbons. I had to look, so I went down there with Catherine. For some reason I started to debate with him the merits of temporal power over the supernatural, or rather the lack of them, and do you know what he said?'

'No, my Lady.'

'He gave me the strangest look and said. "You know, my Lady, beautiful and clever you may be, but I do feel that you may have too much time with nothing of substance to fill it. Most folk I know are too concerned with putting food on the table and only think of the Gods on a Sunday, or when something bad happens.' He is right though, isn't he? I am luckier than most. So do I then have the right to feel unhappy?'

'Yes, you do, my Lady; everyone has the right to feel every emotion the Gods have gifted to us. It is what separates us from the common beast, after all. Now, are you ready for bed? You are being called at dawn, remember?'

Ceriana climbed into bed, affecting a yawn. 'Dawn it is. Call me any later and...'

'"You will be released from my service",' they both said together. The girl laughed as Doren blew out the candles, bathing the room in the thin light of the moon. 'Good night, my Lady. The Gods keep you safe.'

'Good night, Doren. The Gods keep you, too. And thank you.'

She heard the door close softly and knew right at that moment that she wouldn't sleep a wink.

'My Lady, it is nearly dawn!' Doren was now reduced to shaking the comatose girl – my, how she snored! A nice surprise for her future husband indeed! 'Ah, at last you are coming round.'

'Xhenafa take you – it is still dark!' wailed the girl, desperately trying to pull the sheet over her head.

'The heralds have arrived; your father will be here in less than half an hour!'

She sat up. All brown hair and large brown eyes, her pale skin spattered with freckles – possibly the most despised freckles in the world.

'Oh!' she said, deflated. 'I suppose I had better get dressed then.'

'Yes, my Lady, and quickly!'

Twenty minutes later, after changing into a rich, dark-blue dress that probably cost more than Doren saw in several years, she stood in the courtyard by the gate, which was opened with the portcullis raised. She was shivering in the cold of the new morning. The sky was tinged pink and, although some fitful stars could still be seen, the night was in abeyance. The courtyard itself was still dark and shadowed but, as Ceriana looked up, the light caught the white pennants on the Archer's Tower and slowly began to slide down the grey, moss-covered stones towards them. Her mother was there, along with Doren, Lady Catherine and various assembled courtiers and knights. The seneschal, Berek, a vigorous grey-haired man with a hawk nose, was trying to arrange everyone into a semblance of order. He had had rushes scattered over where the ladies now stood as, given the propensity for geese (she could hear them now) and pigs to run freely over the courtyard, there was a good chance that one of them would ruin their expensive light shoes by stepping into something nasty.

Ceriana's hair was loose, falling almost to her waist; she had had no time to pin or braid it. When it came to matters of personal appearance she was most particular, not letting Doren or any other handmaiden do her hair, colour her eyes or cheeks, or put on her brooches and necklaces. She wore a brooch now; it had an ornate silver setting in which a large green gem resided. Her father had given it to her as a sixteenth birthday present; she wore it often and was determined to make sure her father could see it. She knew a green gem on a blue dress was not an ideal combination, but her father had no fashion sense whatsoever and would not pick her up on it.

'Don't slouch, child,' her mother said to her, disapproval oozing from every pore.

Ceriana stiffened her back immediately, trying to stand as erectly as one befitting her status should. As she was the last (and least important) of four children, the mother–daughter bond had never been particularly strong. Her mother had devoted most of her time to Dominic and Giselle, the eldest daughter, leaving Ceriana somewhat neglected and with plenty of time on her hands. This she filled with walks around the castle, wild romantic daydreams and the infernal embroidery which Catherine seemed to like so much. Her father, though, was another case entirely, doting on her whenever time allowed. She was a thin, slight girl, different to her sisters and he always seemed to think that she needed extra protection. Her mother frowned on all this, believing that indulgence was wasted on a girl whose only duty in life was to marry properly. This was why it seemed to Ceriana a slight betrayal on her father's part that he should be discussing marrying her off. She did understand that he would have to do something about it eventually but she had hoped for a couple more years before the inevitable happened.

She squinted ahead of her. The castle drawbridge was lowered as usual so the ditch surrounding the castle could be crossed; it could be filled with water in times of war, she had heard, although she had never seen it herself. Over the ditch the drawbridge connected to a cobbled road which ran straight ahead for nearly a mile; either side of it were many tightly packed ramshackle cottages. A castle supported a whole community of craftsmen, labourers, vintners, butchers, cheese-makers and other suppliers of goods and provender, and they all had to live somewhere. Doren's family home was among them, although she stayed in the castle most nights now her children were older. Eventually the road bent eastwards behind a low hill and it was here that most eyes were directed.

Then, just as Ceriana's fingers were so cold that she imagined them as stalactites in a cave, she saw them.

Two horsemen, mailed in bright silver, lances held high so their pennants flew proudly in the breeze, were the first people to emerge from behind the hill. More similarly attired knights brought up the rear of the column, but between them were other horsemen, not armoured but wearing rich velvet doublets of varying colour, partially concealed under heavy riding cloaks. At their head and becoming more recognisable as he drew nearer was a tall man in a black cloak, trousers and riding boots. His face was characterful, strong and stern, lined in such a manner as to give an impression not so much of age but of power and experience. His still brown hair and eyes marked him as a Hartfield, characteristics that had been passed on to his youngest daughter, though not to his son, who was altogether darker. As he passed by the houses lining the road, people, both young and old, came out and cheered; some women even threw flowers on to the road before him and so it was that Nicholas, forty-third Duke of Hartfield, returned home.

Ceriana ducked under her mother's restraining arm and ran towards the horses as they finished crossing the drawbridge. 'Father!' she called, her face flushed despite herself.

He reined in his horse, swung himself off the saddle and went to meet her. 'Ah, you are wearing your brooch, my little one.'

'Of course, Father, you know it is my favourite.' She inhaled the scents of horse, leather and sweat and thought them the best in the world.

'Oh well, if you already have a favourite, then there is no point giving you this.' He opened a gloved hand and held out his latest acquisition for her. There, dangling on a chain of pure gold, was a brilliant-blue sapphire. The sun, which now shone brightly on the courtyard, made its many facets glitter like the feathers on an Erskon kingfisher. She barely suppressed a squeal.

'Thank you, Father. That is so beautiful. Where did you get it?'

'A gift from Ludo Gerlig. His estates include mines in the Derannen Mountains where it was found.'

'Quite a gift, Father; I hope it didn't come at a price.'

'Everything comes at a price, my dear,' he said. Although she was still focusing on the gem, the look of regret that fleetingly crossed his face as he spoke did not escape her. 'Now, I have business to attend to with Berek and your mother. You and Lady Catherine can go back indoors and I will speak to you properly once I have eaten.'

Ever the obedient daughter she curtsied and left them, still clutching her present and all the while trying to forget the feeling that the executioner's axe hung poised above her neck.

She did not go down for the noon meal, feigning a headache. Instead, she retired to her room, but soon got fractious stomping around like a bear in a pen until her head really did start to hurt. She was just about to wander back down to the great hall, claiming a miraculous recovery, when there was a knock at the door. She bid the caller enter, knowing his identity without even looking up. 'Are you feeling better, little one?' Her father's tone had a sardonic edge.

'Um, yes, I mean no, not really.'

'We can talk later, if you want.'

'No, Father; please, if you have any news, tell it to me now.'

'Very well.' She was sitting demurely on her bed; he pulled the chair from her dresser so that he could sit facing her.

'Did you hear me earlier when I said I had to speak to Berek?' she nodded. 'Well, my discussions involved making preparations at Erskon House for a visit from the Grand Duke some six weeks from now.'

'I didn't know he was due to go there; he normally only visits in high summer, and that is now passed.'

'No,' Nicholas said, 'he doesn't normally, but this is different because I will be hosting one of the biggest events of the year.'

The axe had fallen; she spoke, knowing his reply long before it came. 'It is my wedding, isn't it?'

'Yes, my dear, I am afraid it is.'

'Well, then, I suppose you had better tell me all about it.'

'Indeed, now where shall I start? First of all, I had many things to discuss with the Grand Duke and had decided to leave your nuptials until the end of my stay; I had half a hope that it would be forgotten, what with the eastern war becoming a priority again, but it was not to be. The night before last we were at dinner, myself, the Grand Duke, Duke Edrington, Duke Marschall, Barons Duneck, Fillebrand, Gerlig, Richney and others, when out of the blue the Grand Duke spoke up, saying to me "What about that daughter of yours? Sorted a husband for her yet?" I replied that I get petitions for you every day and was in no hurry to arrange anything. There was a groan at this, half the barons at the table had a son they wanted to foist on me. At that point, though, Leontius, the Grand Duke, interceded. 'I am sorry my, friend; I would not normally do this to you without a private discussion first but it so happens I have a match for her.' Duke Nicholas stopped and looked directly into Ceriana's large eyes. 'I cannot tell you how my heart sank at this news. I was hoping to hold on to you for at least a year or two more, and now I was not even to get to choose a husband for you.'

She met his gaze steadily. 'Go on.'

'Leontius has been Grand Duke for nearly two years now, as you know. At first, knowing how well I got on with his father, he readily listened to what I had to say. Alas, this last year or so I have seen my influence waning. He is a young man and it is the younger nobility that mostly have his ear. For years, for example, I have argued for a negotiated settlement to this pointless and costly eastern war, Leontius, though, now wants a decisive victory without understanding that one is hardly possible without great sacrifice. It is frustrating – he has the makings of a fine ruler but the advice he listens to is, I feel, leading him down paths best left untrodden.'

'Water, Father?' Ceriana handed him a bowl into which she had just dispensed water from a jug on her bedside table. His voice was getting a little husky. He readily accepted, drank, and continued.

'Well, apart from you, the two main reasons why I was seeing the Grand Duke was to discuss reinforcing the war in the east, details of which I will not bore you with now, and to discuss the latest unrest among the northern barons. As you know, they are not native Tanarese but rather are descended from the men of Kibil who were given safe haven here when they fled from their Chiran conquerors some two hundred and fifty years ago. The northern territories are quite poor; the coast is rugged and rocky with many small islands, each of them a baronial holding in their own right. Recent harvests haven't been good up there and local discontent has been fuelled by many of the more outspoken barons. It is an odd situation. They would never openly declare against the Grand Duke – they are nowhere near powerful enough – but they may rebel in some other form, demanding more autonomy or more control over their taxes. We know that a heavy-handed response to any rebellion with ringleaders executed and troops sent in would only make the matter worse; force is at best an ultimate sanction only to be used when other methods have failed, and with the war in the east already draining resources a protracted struggle on two fronts is not what the nation needs.'

Ceriana could see what he was driving at. 'I am to marry one of them?' The Duke of Hartfield nodded.

'But, Father, the north is ... is the middle of nowhere. The people are poor and backward; some even say that brothers marry sisters there and all their children have six fingers and toes!'

He managed a weak laugh. 'Not all rumours are true. They are grim and stoic folk, yes, but they are not without honour. Indeed, they have so much of it they can be difficult to deal with at times.'

'So the Grand Duke wants to use me to ... to bribe these blackguards into behaving themselves. Am I not more important than to be traded off to a fisherman who has never seen the inside of a bath?'

'Alas, Ceriana, you are my fourth child and outside my castle and lands you are seen as nowhere near as important as my son, or even my other daughters. You are, however, important enough to be used to assuage the northerners.'

She raised her voice in frustration. 'But I will never see you again, Father; the north is an age of travel away – you never visit there!'

'On the contrary, Leontius is hoping I will visit regularly, backed up with a large quantity of knights and men at arms, just to show the locals the strength of his supporters.'

Her shoulders sagged; there was no point in fighting. 'Well, who is this husband to be then?' she asked tremulously.

'He commands the island of Osperitsan, the largest and most powerful of their baronetcies. His name is Wulfthram and he is seen as the voice of the north. His previous wife died three years ago – disease claimed her.'

'Does he have children? How old is he?'

'No children, no legitimate ones anyway. As to his age I am unsure, but the general reckoning at court is that he is about twice as old as you.'

'Twice as old,' she said, half to herself. 'Any more bad news? Have all his teeth fallen out? Does his breath smell like a village latrine in summer? Please do not say that he has six fingers.'

'I have met him barely and have no clear recollection, but Leontius speaks quite well of him, apart from his tendency to rebellion of course. Not your typical northerner were his words; he even shaves his beard apparently.'

'Sounds like you are trying to soften the blow,' she said. 'How is Mother taking it?'

'How do you imagine?' he sighed. 'He is not the husband she envisaged for you. I have spent the last hour feeding her wildthorn berries and trying to calm her down.'

'If you have any left,' she said with a shrug, 'bring them over to me! ... I have six weeks then.'

'Yes, you will marry at Erskon. The Grand Duke will use the occasion to size up the northern barons, then you will travel to Osperitsan the following morning. My first official visit will be some time after.'

'I imagine this Wulfthram is as unhappy about this match as we are.'

'Yes and no. On the surface it will be seen as an effort to rein him in, so I would expect a public display of reserved antipathy; however, in reality a northern baron has just been given a seat at the Grand Duke's high table. It is almost unprecedented. It is forcing him to tread a line between pleasing his fellow barons and pleasing the Grand Duke, which is of course Leontius's intention in the first place.'

There was silence for a moment. She stood up and looked out of the window staring idly at a lone goose pecking its way across the courtyard's straw-covered stone. Her world was falling in on her. 'Thank you for telling me, Father, for explaining everything. If this is my duty, I will not fail you.'

'Thank you, my dear, and I am sorry.' He came towards her, kissed her gently on the forehead, then turned and left the room.

Ceriana watched him go, down the narrow passageway leading

from her room then down the steps towards the great hall. She then shut the door, sat on the bed and rubbed her eyes, trying desperately to stop the tears welling up inside them.

She needed to get out of the castle. Being the daughter of a duke, however, this was easier said than done. Firstly she had to tell the seneschal who had to arrange an escort, check her route so any undesirables could be cleared out of the way, and organise wagons, supplies and the like. Once all that was done, she could proceed.

The coastline around the castle was all high cliffs and precipitous drops, but some two miles away a small river, barely more than a stream, cut a cleft through the hills before entering the sea. Where it did this there was a small rocky beach that could be accessed only via a steep path that was almost completely concealed by brakes of high ferns on both sides. This beach was a favourite spot of Ceriana's; it was quiet, with just the sound of the sea, the gulls and the wind whipping her hair into an unholy mess. The wagons had to be left at the top of the path and those retainers and soldiers who had no choice about remaining up there with them had to endure the steep climb down, burdened as they were with provender and other essentials required for a picnic on the beach.

She took a little guilty pleasure in hearing them cursing and sweating as they clambered over the soft earth and pebbles. The ferns made the air still and hot, and the cloying smell of the densely packed vegetation filled the soldiers' noses. At long last, at the bottom of the path, the ground levelled, the ferns suddenly fell away and they were hit with the shock of the sea air billowing around them, cooling the sweat on their faces, its exhilarating freshness bringing new vigour to tired legs. The journey back up the hill was another matter entirely but Ceriana would worry about that later. Now she was just standing looking at the waves as they broke on the sand and crashed against rocks, and wondering if she would ever see one of her favourite spots again.

Lady Catherine scurried up to her, her pinched face blotched red with exertion. 'I really wish you would choose somewhere more accessible for your walk, my Lady.'

'If it was easy to get to, then it would be full of people and hardly the same place at all. The effort to get here makes this a much more appreciable place, don't you think?'

'I don't think my legs will be appreciating anything tomorrow,' the girl groaned.

But Ceriana wasn't listening to her; she had already started to walk along the beach. Ahead of her a couple of soldiers fanned out, with more either side and behind her. Just clambering through the ferns were some servants, including some unfortunates bearing heavy hampers for the meal they would take on the beach.

Since the conversation with her father she had gradually come to terms with the fate awaiting her. The wedding was now only a couple of weeks away and, although she had always imagined that she would want to control all the minutiae of its organisation, she found herself surprised to find that she had no interest in it at all. Rather, she was content to let the myriad servants, courtiers and sycophants who had appeared at the announcement to get on with it. Instead, she contented herself with seclusion, being surrounded with as few people as possible and taking in the joys of reading, Megan's harp and even embroidery, although she was still terrible at it. She felt that she was a passive observer in her own life; it was a journey in which she was merely a passenger and she had no control of either the destination or the directions required to get there. If that was the way it was to be, she thought, then so be it. She could get married standing in a muddy puddle and wearing the hides of beasts if that was what they wanted. She had to content herself with small victories and today was one of them.

Berek came up to her; he could be quite a cold fish at times, although he was always so busy she never blamed him for it. He didn't need to come along really, but she sensed that he was just as relieved to get out for a few hours as she was. 'My Lady,' he enquired, 'is there any particular place you would like us to set up your picnic?'

'Oh, somewhere quite close to the stream, I suppose. Not too close, though; we don't want anyone falling in.' She giggled at this as though the idea of someone falling in was actually quite amusing.

'As you wish, my Lady. Just give us ten minutes or so to set things up.'

'Of course, Berek. In the meantime I will walk along the beach just where the waves come in.'

'Don't get your feet wet, my Lady.'

'I will try not to but I doubt if I will have any success,' she said impishly.

He smiled, a notable event in itself. 'Well, we have towels and clean shoes should they be required, my Lady.'

'Thank you, Berek. You think of everything.'

She left him and, along with Lady Catherine, meandered slowly towards the shoreline. The phalanx of soldiers still stood protectively ahead of her and behind her, although apart from their party the beach was deserted. She looked back to see Berek and a dozen servants fixing up trestle tables (who on earth had carried them? she wondered) and opening hampers, although the wind was doing its best to foil their endeavours. The early-afternoon sun was strong off the sea and when she looked ahead of her she had to shelter her eyes with her hand.

There appeared to be something of a commotion with the soldiers ahead of her. One was pointing to an object that appeared to have been brought in by the tide; another soldier was trying to get Berek's attention by waving and shouting in his direction. The wind whipped his voice away almost before she could hear the words –

'Sir Berek, a body, a body on the beach!'

Curious, she turned her head back towards the object in question and saw that it was indeed as the soldier had described it. It was too far away for her to make out any distinctive features but it looked like a man, a man in a black cloak and boots. She was about to go in for a closer look but at that point Berek stepped in front of her.

'No, my Lady, let the soldiers and myself deal with this; he may have been in the sea a long time.'

Thus stymied, she turned and walked away from the soldiers who were rushing to the scene, towards a large rock that stood up from the beach like a rotten tooth, shallow waves breaking gently against it.

Lady Catherine, having caught up with her, put her hand to her mouth. 'Oh, Elissa, how terrible!'

'Go to the servants, Catherine. Stay with them until Berek says otherwise.'

As Catherine left her, she realised that for once she was alone and not the focus of everybody's attention. Her pace quickened towards the rock, and she decided to explore it. It was irregular and had footholds; perhaps she could even climb on it before she was seen. Once she got there she looked around – she was still unnoticed. Quickly she pulled up her dress, exposing her ankles and calves along with her woefully inadequate soft shoes, and started to clamber on to the rock. She skirted around its edge until where she stood was actually overlooking the sea. They are bound to see me soon, she thought. She looked up and saw that the rock now completely concealed her from the soldiers as well as the servants. She would get such a scolding! The sea splashed at the rock, wetting her feet and legs. She would need her spare shoes after all. And then she saw it.

What by Elissa was that? She crouched down for a better look. Some six inches under water, caught in a cleft in the rock, was what appeared to be a ruby. The problem with describing it thus, though, was that it appeared to be nearly the size of Ceriana's fist. She put her hand into the water, soaking her lace cuff. The ruby or whatever it was was embedded quite firmly and needed a bit of a tug to get it free. It came loose in her hand but the effort required caused her foot to slip. She ended up on her backside, feet, legs and part of her dress in the sea. Then a larger wave covered the rock face on which she was balanced, drenching her face and hair. She did not care, though. Righting herself, she took a deep breath before regarding her prize.

It was a ruby... What else could it be? It had no facets, certainly, but an unpolished stone would not sparkle as brilliantly as this did. She held the jewel up to the light and found her face and neck bathed in a rich, blood-red luminosity. Yes, she thought, it has the colour of blood! As she stared at it she realised covetously that she did not want anyone else to see it, not yet – not until she had examined it properly herself. She took out the handkerchief that she kept tucked into her dress and used it to quickly wrap the stone; she then gripped it tightly in one hand so that it looked like she had just been using it to wipe sweat and water from her face and brow. She turned back, retracing her steps and with one last flourish hopped lightly off the rock.

Berek was not five feet from her with an expression as if he had just drunk a flask of sour wine. He held up something in front of her face.

'Clean shoes, my Lady?'

BOOK ONE: AUTUMN

4

After the rain came the frost. The night was unseasonably cold. The inky blackness of the camp was lit up by a smattering of red smoking braziers around which the shadowy figures of the night watch had congregated. Wispy tendrils of mist slithered between the tents, driving down the temperature. The dawn was coming. The ground was coated in brittle ice, and the mud, churned up in the wet, had frozen into a variety of contorted ropelike patterns. As the camp stirred in the glow of the dawn, the sounds of heavy boots, animal hooves and the wheels of the wagons crunching through this frozen sludge rose above the hoarse cries of the officers and the grumbling of the rank and file.

In many ways Reynard Lanthorpe was the Tanaren ideal – blond, blue-eyed, a well-trimmed flaxen beard – but even he had that barely perceptible look of a man who had seen more than he should, a look borne by many men who had fought in this war too long.

'Morning, Glaivedon.' he said brusquely as Morgan ambled towards him, frenziedly rubbing his hands together. 'I have to supply you with some men, I believe. I hope you don't want too many; there is only so many we can spare.'

'Not too many, no. Four or five should be sufficient. We really want to move as quickly as possible and not get noticed, though that may be difficult with the wagon we have to take. Whoever volunteers and is chosen needs to know that this is a job that carries many risks; maybe more than if they were to stay here war or no war.'

'Experienced men then! They are an even more precious commodity. I spoke with the men last night and we have some volunteers. I will go to speak with them again. Shall I mention your name?'

'You had better – it may help to thin the number of volunteers down considerably.'

Twenty minutes later Reynard returned to where Morgan was waiting outside his tent with some dozen or more well-built, surly-looking men.

Morgan recognised one of them immediately.

'Hey, Rozgon!' he called. 'Still avoiding your wife?'

A grizzled bear of a man, almost as broad as he was tall with a shock of white hair and a long, tangled beard stepped forward. He wore what looked like a wolf pelt over his studded leather jerkin and an ugly-looking axe swung at his side. He regarded Morgan fondly, only through one eye though, his left being white as milk.

'By Keth, which one?' He clasped Morgan in a grip as bearlike as his appearance. 'Here's me telling everyone you had died still owing me ten ducats.' He was renowned for never forgetting a gambling debt.

'Pah, the dice were loaded, and they were your dice, I seem to remember; either that or you had Uba's luck.'

'They were my dice, they weren't loaded and I don't need the God of Chance to beat you!'

'Do you ever lose with them? I mean, seriously? And what's with the stupid beard?'

'The good lady Britta, who does for me most handsomely in this blighted camp, says it makes me look younger.'

'I suppose at your age I would like to look sixty, too.'

Rozgon snorted and smiled. 'Cheeky whelp! If anyone else had said that they would be decorating their armour with their own teeth. Anyhow, what is this all about? The good knight says you have a job to do, one that could drive us all into the arms of Xhenafa.' Xhenafa was the god who carried the living to the world of the dead and their final judgement; soldiers would invoke him if they saw their chances of survival as dubious.

'He might be right, but I think we could all get through it. It is just a jaunt through Claw Pass. Want to come?'

'Claw Pass?' said Rozgon thoughtfully. 'At this time of year? Keth take me! If it gets me out of this shithole of a camp, count me in. The newer recruits have no respect here, you know. I was telling a few of them about our defence of Fort Axmian when one of them yawned. Yawned, I tell you! The little bastard, I had to dangle him upside down over the campfire before he apologised.'

'You were always a persuasive man; we should have sent you to negotiate with the Arshumans years ago.'

'Aye,' nodded the big man enthusiastically. 'They would have sued for peace immediately.'

'Only if you bored them to death by droning on about our defence of Fort Axmian.'

Rozgon laughed at this, a sound that startled even the warhorses. Morgan grinned himself. 'Now, who do you recommend out of this lot?'

'Well, they are all good men. What are you after? Bruisers? Archers?' Morgan nodded when he mentioned archers. 'Well, in that case the two boys at the end. Samson, Leon, step forward.'

Two much younger men advanced. Both were tall, spare and more lightly armoured than Rozgon. One had jet-black hair and a thin smattering of chin stubble; the other was as bald as an egg with thin watery blue eyes.

'Leon's the one with the head like a baby's arse,' Rozgon said tactfully. Morgan spoke to them. 'Growler here has recommended you. I need archers that can scout, hunt game, not waste arrows, and follow orders. It is a risky mission and we will be in the wild for much of it, so foragers are the sort of men we need.'

'You have described us both perfectly,' said Samson. 'We are handy with knives and short swords, too.'

Leon turned to Samson and they both smiled, as if sharing some private joke.

'Do the two of you know each other?'

'We are cousins, sir. Always competing with each other; one day Leon may even catch up with me. Anyway, that is why we both want to go – camp life has not offered up enough challenges as of late.'

'Very well, I will give you all the details shortly. First... Hold on, that's Haelward.' Morgan recognised another of the volunteers, although in truth he only barely knew him. He remembered noticing him in a skirmish with some Arshuman mercenaries where he had impressed with his blade. Though not as young as the two archers, Morgan would not say he was as veteran as himself; rather, somewhere between the two. He was quite a short and wiry man with no spare fat on him. He wore heavier armour than the other men – a lot more chain mail – and had metal leg guards, too. Slung over his shoulder was a plain circular wooden shield. His long sword was sheathed in a scabbard far more ornate than most of the men here carried. 'Hello there, sir,' the man said. 'I am surprised that you recognised me.' He, too, was dark haired, though it was curly and thinning on top.

'Not at all – I remember your abilities with the sword.'

'Abilities that get little enough practice here; I am more adept at putting up a tent and dice playing these days.'

'Well, if you want a more hazardous challenge...'

'Thank you, sir. I will be ready when you call.'

'Good man.' Morgan turned to Rozgon. 'Now all I need is someone who can handle horses.'

'I can help with that.' Reynard who had been listening at a respectful distance came forward. 'You should have one of the knights with you – to represent the Baron, if nothing else.'

Morgan readily acceded. 'Very well, I will let you choose. Everyone should settle up their business here today; we will be leaving tomorrow at dawn.'

And so they departed. The camp was on a slight hill with a good view of the open plain around it and was fed by a small stream, and it was the course of this stream that they followed. They took four horses with them, not the glorious chargers that the knights favoured but rather smaller, sturdier beasts built for hardiness. The knight selected by Reynard was one Sir Varen of Shayer Ridge, a town nestling in the foothills not too far from the pass they needed to take through the mountains. He was the son of the magistrate there and it would be the final civilised place they would be stopping at to resupply and get fresh horses if required. The choice of Sir Varen was a good one therefore, because, apart from him, only Morgan and Rozgon knew the route they were taking, so even if two of them were to die the mission could still continue. Morgan's only concern was the man's youth; he really wanted more veterans in the party but the handsome young knight looked like he had only recently been promoted from squire. Varen had forgone the usual knight's plate in favour of mail and studded leather, and appeared to favour the mace in the Felmere tradition, as one was strapped to his back, its blackened metal head giving it a particularly vicious look. Morgan himself favoured the long sword; it was his opinion that four feet of tempered steel had never let anybody down.

They were to follow this course westwards for two days until they came to the Vinoyen River. They would cross it at the bridge at the town of Tetha Vinoyen, turn northwards and two to three days further travel would see them at the pass. Of course, it also meant passing through Baron Ulgar's lands, a man whose hostility to Felmere was well known. Morgan hoped that his own close association with the Felmeres would not be too problematic.

After half a day's uneventful travel they came to a dirt road sheltered by a brake of trees on both sides. As they joined it, Morgan mused on the fact that they hadn't seen a soul all day. There was a time when many of the abandoned farm buildings they had passed would have been hives of activity. It was getting close to harvest-time and the fields would soon have been filled with many sweating men and women, singing and breaking their backs as they scythed and bundled the crops, pausing just twice a day to fill their bellies with bread, cheese and sweet cider. The farm he had grown up in wasn't too far from here. He remembered his father hoisting him on to his shoulders, carrying him to the fields where he could sit, play and be fussed over by the women as the line of labourers ahead grew ever smaller and more distant as more and more of the crop was felled.

It felt like a hundred years ago.

They paused briefly to take on water and chew on the unappetising soldier's rations they had brought with them. Rozgon got his dice out, eager to lighten the other men's purses. Cedric had sat in the wagon all day, presumably poring over scrolls and books. He had been surprisingly quiet. For the most part young Willem had walked with the men, Morgan had him pinned down as a shy lad and was pleased to see him and Haelward apparently hit it off. Morgan went over and spoke to him.

'Enjoying the journey so far? Haelward is looking after you, I see.'

'Yes, sir. It turns out that Haelward and I are from villages just a few miles from each other.'

'What villages exactly?'

'Oh, you wouldn't have heard of them. They were both farming villages on the lands of Baron Hartwig in Skonnetha, close to the Erskon.'

'The heart of the country.'

'Yes, sir, pretty much its geographic centre. Master Cedric has shown me many maps.'

Morgan's brow creased a little. 'So if you are not from Tanaren City, how did you meet Cedric?'

Willem spoke earnestly. 'I was lucky enough to join the house of Artorus at Skonnetha when I was twelve. At first, I was a lay brother working in the kitchens, plucking chickens or turning the spits. Well, at service one day one of the senior brothers noticed how well I rang and, thinking it would boost his choir gave me the chance to join the order proper. It turned out I had a talent for writing and reading and I quickly picked up on my studies, so much so that it was decided that I should spend seven years at St Philig's studying history and theology before returning to the monastery as a scribe. It was in a history study group that Master Cedric noticed me giving a short dissertation on the effects of the Black Plague two hundred years ago on the rights of rural labourers. He invited me to be his assistant and so now I am here.'

'So the monastery funds your education. Would they approve of you being here?'

'I doubt it, but even here Cedric insists on teaching me at least one hour a day.'

'How do you find Tanaren City compared to the country?' Morgan himself had only ever been there a couple of times as a younger man and remembered finding its sheer size intimidating.

'It took me a while but I got used to it; it has so many temptations for a brother of Artorus.'

Morgan grinned. 'Just stay away from the women on the harbour front and the Rose district and you will be OK.'

Willem looked a little downcast. 'It is not the women on the harbour that bother me.'

'Go on.' said Morgan intrigued. 'Is it the men?'

'No sir, not like that, sir.' He hesitated. 'Master Cedric the other day mentioned Alys, a lady with a talent for drawing.'

'Not just for drawing, I take it.'

'Well no, sir; we have become very ... fond of each other since our trip to the ruins. She is a little older than me but her talent has taken her a long way and she is as clever as she is fair.' 'And your religious instruction?' 'Exactly, sir.' He sighed.

'Artoran monks can marry, though.'

'Only at the behest of the Grand Lector and only then once a monk's studies are completed or he turns thirty, whichever comes sooner.'

'But your studies cannot be too far from completion.'

'At St Philig's, yes, but then I return to Skonnetha for ten years of religious instruction. I would have to wait many years before the Grand Lector could even be petitioned and I would not expect Alys to wait that long.'

'A lot of priests I know,' said Morgan slyly, 'keep a lady or a man at their side for many years unofficially, and no bolts of fire strike them down.'

'Not in Skonnetha,' laughed Willem. 'I had to leave it to realise how conservative it was.'

'I see.' said Morgan thoughtfully. 'And the monastery funds your education, funds which would have to be repaid if you abandoned your life with them.'

'Correct, sir. As you can see I am rather trapped by circumstances.'

Morgan searched his head for words of comfort. 'Many years have to pass before you reach the age of thirty, for both good and ill. It is too early to despair over things just yet. For example, I rather feel that Cedric enjoys having you as his assistant and would be loath to let you go.'

Willem shrugged his shoulders. 'Maybe you are right, though what Master Cedric could do about it I do not know. At the moment, though, there seems no way out.'

'Be patient. As I say, things may change. Listen, I wanted to ask you, do you have a weapon?'

'I have an eating knife.'

'No, that won't do. Here, take this.' He handed him a short dirk in a leather scabbard. 'Don't use it unless you have to, just in case something gets past us fighters.'

The boy's face lit up. 'Thank you, sir!'

'As I say, only use it if you have to. An untrained man with a weapon can be as much a danger to himself as to his enemies.'

Having eaten, they continued onwards. The road they were using was poorly maintained and they frequently had to avoid deep water-filled wheel ruts and loose stones. With the wagon finding things difficult it slowed their progress and in a few hours all of their boots were caked with liquid mud.

As the sun started to drop in front of them, they came to their first abandoned village. Most of the buildings had been burned; few had thatch remaining on their roofs. Nature had started to reclaim the place. Weeds and brambles poked through empty windows and shattered doorways. The tavern sign had fallen and lay unregarded on the ground ahead, and the stone surround of the well had crumbled. Just outside the village, though, as they left it behind them, they found something still in use. From the executioner's tree hung three gibbets, all containing some grisly remains – one looked as if it had been used recently. The corpse within it was eyeless and the flesh had partially putrefied under a heavy cloak of droning black flies. Some of it had sloughed off the dead man's body and lay in stinking, fetid gobbets at his feet, all of it crawling with maggots. Above the gibbet was posted a crude wooden sign with one word scrawled upon it: DESERTER.

As the territory here had changed hands two to three times over the preceding months, none of the observers could even tell which side he had deserted from. Rozgon made the sign of Xhenafa on his chest, though soldiers normally regarded deserters with little respect. The others followed suit, bar Willem, who was being sick on the side of the road.

BOOK ONE: AUTUMN

A mile later the stream they had initially followed rejoined them at the side of the road and it was here that they made camp. Samson and Leon disappeared for a little while and when they returned they were clutching three rabbits. 'I bagged two of them,' said Leon with the tiniest hint of triumph. An hour or two later, after a hot rabbit stew and a jug of ale, they prepared to bed down for the night.

'Where are we going tomorrow?' asked Willem.

'We follow the road,' Morgan replied. 'We will pass through more villages like the last one and in a few hours the road will broaden till we get to Tetha Vinoyen and the bridge.'

'So back the way I came with Master Cedric some days ago.'

'Yes, that will change once we are over the bridge, though. We will take the north road then.'

Rozgon had been listening. 'We also need to make sure that we don't fall foul of Ulgar's lackeys. Anything he can do to get at Lukas Felmere he will do, especially after that business with the monastery. We are Felmere's men, you see, and will need to keep an eye out.'

'It's a bit late for you, old one-eye; you weren't supposed to take that instruction literally.' Haelward showed admirable dexterity in ducking under the (empty) jug that was hurled at him.

Morgan and Haelward took the first watch. The fire was burning low, so Haelward prodded it casually, staring gloomily into its depths. Though they were now some miles behind the front lines, bands of horsemen from both sides often roamed this land with impunity. Morgan, though, had decided to take a calculated risk in lighting a fire, reckoning that they would hear horsemen long before they arrived. It was autumn and the nights were starting to get a little colder, even on a bright day like today. It would also keep away the wolves who had been greatly emboldened in recent years by the prospect of easy carrion in these lands.

Haelward yawned, looking over at Morgan. 'Have you ever seen one of the Wych folk?'

'No, never.'

'I have.'

'Really?' said Morgan curiously. 'When was this?'

'About seven or eight years ago. I used to serve in the Tanaren City garrison and, like I often do, fancied a change of scene. So for a year or two I joined the marines. It was at the time of the wars with the Kudreyan pirates who kept attacking our trade routes. I saw action at the Battle of Galpa where they were mostly destroyed.'

'You were at Galpa?' said Morgan; obviously, Haelward was more of a veteran than he thought.

'I didn't do much,' Haelward replied. 'My ship was held in reserve; we were merely involved in the final sweep picking off the last pockets of resistance. Anyway, before all that we used to escort trading vessels to the isle of Danathra. The Wych folk, or Aelves as they call themselves, are not allowed to trade in Tanaren due to ancient laws stemming from the wars against them. Instead, they have a port in Danathra and we go there to trade with them. It is some three to four days out of Tanaren, depending on conditions.'

'From what I have heard it is supposed to be a beautiful city.'

'It is quite small, not really a city at all, but yes. I have seen nothing else like it. Their buildings have high, needle-thin towers with walkways running between them that look as if they are suspended in the air, and the statues that they fashion, some out of the hardest granite ... well, it stunned me the first time I saw it.'

'And the Wych folk themselves?'

'Reserved and polite, no interest in mixing with us; we had a quarter of the city in which to stay but most of it was off limits to us. They were interested only in what we had to trade, not in what we were. I managed to pick up a couple of words of their language too.'

Morgan threw a damp mossy stick that he had been fiddling with into the fire where it smoked for a long time before igniting. 'What do they look like? Are they that different to ourselves?'

'No, they are quite like us really: thinner and slightly shorter; angular faces with vividly coloured eyes, mainly blue but sometimes gold or even a light purple.'

'And the famous pointy ears?' Morgan grinned.

'Exaggerated, the ears are a different shape, but then you could say the same about their noses, which are very thin. Even their eyes are slightly larger. There were only a couple of women that we saw but they were extremely beautiful, delicate-looking creatures; the men, the human men, were drooling over them but they wouldn't let us near. I must say though that those that live in the Aelvenwood seem to have taken a different path. They sound much more savage and unforgiving than the ones I met; perhaps they just haven't done as well as their mariner cousins.'

'Interesting.' said Morgan. 'Well, if they don't kill us on sight, I might let you try your Elven phrases on them.'

Haelward shook his head. 'I am not sure what use "My rudder needs repairing" will be in the circumstances.'

'Well, you never know. Why did you leave the marines?'

'After Galpa, what else was there left to do? The war down here was going badly at the time but, rather than join a group of mercenaries, I travelled here and enlisted in Felmere's army; it seemed more honourable somehow. Of course, by the time that happened we had recovered a lot of the ground we had lost to Arshuma and since I arrived we have got more and more bogged down.'

Morgan gave a short bitter laugh. 'This is not the place to seek glory.'

'Too true! I think Mytha God of War has determined that I am forever to miss out on parading through a city in triumph with grateful maidens throwing rose petals at my feet.'

'Don't believe all the old tales; the one time it happened to me after Axmian most of the "maidens"" I saw seemed to lack any teeth.' 'Ah well,' said Haelward wistfully. 'If you shut your eyes...'

Morgan threw another stick on to the fire.

5

'Tanaren City, Tanaren City, was there ever a jewel more radiant, any maiden so fair as thee? I remember my first glimpse of your proud beauty as I remember the birth of my only son; it is emblazoned on my mind with crystal clarity, a picture that will remain burned on my soul until the day Xhenafa clamps it to his bosom. 'Twas on the third day of midsummer just as dawn's fiery red had started to weaken, broaching the fine sea mists as we passed Heldaras rock, that my eyes first beheld thee in gentle somnolence, nestling on low sloping hills caressing the sea that lapped gently against the harbour walls.

I counted the hills, enclosed within the crenellated belt of its fortifications – five, just as the scholars had told me. I could even name them. The Loubian Hill, highest and fairest. From my ship I could see the white stone palaces that stood upon it, their towers and spires glinting in the emerging sunlight. And then, right next to it, lower and flatter, St Kennelth's Hill, home of the grand cathedral of Artorus, its great belltower the tallest outside of Chira itself, standing tall and proud. And it was true! The tower was covered in gold! They say that it can be seen for many miles out at sea if the city is approached from the south and, my friends, you will not find this humble soul disputing these claims.

And then there were the three lower hills: to the west, the Artisans' Hill where the world's finest craftsmen laboured ceaselessly to produce armour, clothing, glassware, brooches and necklaces for export around the world. Then there was the central hill, known as People's Hill, the largest, broadest hill in the city and home to most of its many thousands of people, and at its centre the grand market, trading in every conceivable item, foodstuff, spices, leather, animals ... all brought in from every corner of the world. You could buy barrels, wagons, wine, silver, gold, fresh meat slaughtered in the adjoining shambles that very morning. I remember walking the smooth worn cobblestones of that market, brushing up against sons of the Duke, merchants in bold livery, maidens in fair white dresses, toothless old crones, beggars, pickpockets, cutpurses, knights with rapiers, humble priests, tavern wenches and the vendors, red-faced with voices hoarse from shouting. Then there were the smells, spices, burning incense, cooking meat, fish and sweat all mingling into a heady fragrance.

And finally the last hill, Voyagers' Hill, the hill adjoining the harbour. The city folk call it the poor quarter but, my friends, its dockside taverns, the small closely huddled cottages, the fish market on the harbour front, the cry of the gulls, and the shanties of the sailors repairing their nets and stitching their sails, give it a character all of its own.

Our ship was docking now and, as it did so, I beheld the first of the city's many statues – the statue of Hytha, Goddess of the Sea was there before me, arms outstretched, both protecting and welcoming sailors returning to shore. Before the day was ended I would see many more statues, of gods renowned and obscure, of every grand duke and duchess, typically standing alongside the fountains that were a feature of every square, no matter how small, and for which this city is justly famous.

...And now I must depart. No sigh is deeper nor heart heavier, for I have seen that which is incomparable in mine eyes. No more shall my sleep be a peaceful one until the day of my return here is upon me.'

Marcus snapped the book – Travels of a Humble Priest – shut; he always read that passage before arriving in the city, although he had never quite shared the awe of the itinerant brother Wolper, the author of the piece. They had been at sea for just over a day and would probably be anchoring close to Tanaren City harbour that evening, so they could arrive early the next day. The ship was one he had been on before, an old-style galley with both oar and sail and around eighty feet long. It only had one cabin, nominally the captain's but, as Cheris was the only woman in a ship's complement of over a hundred, he had chivalrously surrendered it to her. Marcus had wondered if Cheris might have felt intimidated by this situation but, as it had turned out, she had other problems of her own. She was about ten feet away from his position up aft, voiding her stomach contents into the briny. She had been doing this for much of the voyage, much to the amusement of the sailors. Once she had finished, she turned to walk towards Marcus, and, as she did so, a sailor no more than a boy bumped shoulders with her. He apologised but then, as she passed him, turned and smiled.

'You know, my Lady, you would be a pretty girl if your skin wasn't so green.' She shot him a withering look, then, catching sight of her red robes, he seemed to remember exactly what she was.

His face fell. 'Sorry, my Lady. I meant nothing by it. Please don't explode my head or anything.' Many of the older sailors laughed at the boy. They were used to ferrying mages and did not have the fear of them that many others had.

'I will let you off, just this once,' she croaked and came up to Marcus. 'Xhenafa take me. How much longer must I endure this?'

'We will arrive at dawn tomorrow,' Marcus said cheerfully. 'We could be there by this evening but certain protocols have to be observed.'

She looked alarmed. 'You are not serious – what protocols?'

'They have to fly the red flag for one hour before arrival so all on land can see it. Then on land they sound a horn every ten minutes or so as a warning that there are mages arriving. This gives everyone a chance to finish their business and go and hide, if that is their wish. Then, after we've docked, the knights escort us through the city to their tower in the city walls. Once there, we will get into our furnished wagon and the knights will ride us to the battle front, all the while flying a red flag so that anyone we meet on the road has the opportunity to dive behind a rock somewhere and cower in terror.'

'If I didn't feel so wretched, I would laugh.' she said. 'Do we really provoke such fear?'

'Among many of the more ignorant common folk, yes. The more educated will not hide from us; some will even stay and talk, although they will be very guarded. Unsurprisingly, it is the people who see us most often, the soldiers, these sailors and the like who are the most relaxed around us. You will get used to it. Where are you going?'

'To the cabin for a lie-down. If I am not out in an hour, I have probably died.'

'Well, try not to decompose too quickly. Think of my sensitive nose.'

BOOK ONE: AUTUMN

The cabin was tiny – a low bed, a desk with drawers, a chamber pot and a small circular window summed up its contents. Her own trunk was on the desk and she opened it, pulling out her mirror. By Artorus, she looked terrible! She wondered whether or not to put some make-up powder on but dismissed the idea; the powder was quite rare and at the moment it would be like trying to camouflage a ghoul. She pulled the belt on her robe in a little tighter; Marcus often laughed at initiates' vain attempts to feminise their garments, but Cheris vigorously and vocally disagreed with him. She had taken a knife to both her red and blue robes when they were presented to her, trimming and gathering them in, so that they looked more like tight-fitting dresses than badges of office.

On the bed was her staff, presented to her at her induction ceremony three days before. It was made from black metal, light and easy to carry. It included a detachable blade at the bottom in case it needed to be wielded as a weapon and it had a white orb of crystal at its head. A wizard's staff was much more than a walking aid; it was a device that held a reserve of power which could be drawn on when required to give a final impetus to a spell, so avoiding the risk of frying a mage's overtaxed brain. Over-estimating one's ability and reserves of mental strength was a perpetual danger when magic was wielded and the staff served as a vital safeguard against the worst possible outcome. She took her staff off the bed and rested it against the wall; then, picking up her newly presented Book of the Magisters, a history of magic and its wielders, along with descriptions of the most common incantations, she lay on the bed and attempted to read.

They sailed until the evening, finally weighing anchor when the lights of the city could be seen. Cheris had dozed off and on all afternoon and was feeling a lot better. Above the captain's cabin was a small quarterdeck and she stood there now, leaning on the rail staring at those city lights. Marcus was with her.

'Nervous about tomorrow?' he asked.

'Yes,' she said wistfully. 'But it's not just nervousness; there's a whole lot of other things too. My parents are out there somewhere; maybe one of those lights could be theirs.'

'I wish you could see them tomorrow, but we will be out of the city pretty quickly.'

'I know.' She sighed. 'I have been trying to remember, you know – what it was like, living in a house, being in a family, but everything is maddeningly vague at best, like a vivid dream that you forget in the morning.'

'Do you remember anything at all?'

'I remember mealtimes. I have a brother, you know, and a sister who was born after I left. We would sit at the table and laugh; my parents could be very funny, I remember laughing a lot. And I remember one evening, too – I had a colic or something, my temperature was high and my throat was dry and rasping – I was in bed and Mother was there, passing me water to sip, telling me Meriel would look after me. She sang to me, too – "Meriel Watches over Me". Do you know it?'

'Yes, it is a popular children's song.'

'I suppose that is true.' She smiled and then in a plaintive and clear voice she sang softly:

Meriel watches over me, on the land or over sea
Pain she eases, fever calms
Always sleep gently in her arms
Meriel watches over me
Wherever it is that I may be Safe forever in her gaze
From now until the end of days.

She had forgotten they were not alone and started as some of the sailors applauded her. She turned crimson and assayed a generous bow.

'Do you know "The Captain's Sword is Bigger than Mine",' called out one voice.

'No,' she laughed. 'You will have to teach me.'

'By Artorus!' Marcus muttered. 'By the time we go back you will be cursing like a tavern wench.'

'I really hope so,' she said with an impish smile.

They took a light, simple meal – Cheris hoping she would keep it down this time – and then she retired for the night as the men slept under the stars. Tomorrow would be a day to remember.

Tomorrow finally arrived, clear and fine. Cheris was awake early enough, though, as she found out when she left the cabin and climbed on to the quarterdeck, not as early as everybody else. Above her, large pink-tinged clouds sat motionless in a limpid blue sky. The sea was so smooth it looked as if it had been fashioned in glass. There was hardly a breath of air. She looked at the main mast – a red flag hung limply from its highest point. Marcus, who was on the main deck talking to one of the knights she assumed would be accompanying them, saw her and strolled nonchalantly up on to the quarterdeck to speak to her.

'How long has the flag been up?' she asked before he could get his breath.

'About half an hour. The men are grumbling because it looks like they will have to row into the harbour. I have just been talking to Sir Dylan, the head of the knights here; he arrived by boat from the city not ten minutes ago. Normally, we get through the city as quickly as possible and leave within the hour, but it turns out the axle on our wagon is bust and won't be repaired for some time. We will be given rooms in the knights' tower and will leave tomorrow morning.'

'Really? What will we do in the meantime?'

'I don't know. You have your Book of the Magisters to read.'

'I have spent half my life reading books. Can I not go out for an hour? I could wear a cloak over my robes; I wouldn't speak to a soul.'

Marcus could not disguise his sarcastic tone. 'Why don't you ask Sir Dylan? I am sure he will be very accommodating.'

She was not giving up. 'I do not see that me, in a cloak, walking up to the market for half an hour is such a terrible, terrible thing.'

Marcus sighed. 'It is not going to happen, Cheris. The job of the knights is to keep us as well away from the non-gifted as possible; you will have to try to find your parents another time.'

'I wasn't saying that. I know which district they live in but apart from that I wouldn't know where to start looking for them. Anyway, perhaps this separation of the gifted and non-gifted isn't good for either of us. If we met and talked, maybe we could learn from each other; maybe their fear of us might diminish if they could see that we were just as ordinary as them in all respects bar the one.'

'Ah, but that "one" is fairly significant, don't you think? Most people cannot fry you with a lightning bolt if their drink gets spilled.'

'That's not funny.'

'I know... Sir Dylan is on his way up.'

The knight Marcus had been talking to was indeed on his way up to see them. Cheris was surprised at how young he was, probably only a few years older than her. He was obviously fastidious about his appearance, too, with his close-cropped brown hair and recently shaved jaw. His armour had a solid breastplate displaying the emblem of the thorn but apart from that it was all chain. His white cloak fairly dazzled in the low sun.

'Hello there, Marcus.' The young man spoke cheerfully. 'Have you told the lady about our little problem?'

'I have indeed, Sir Dylan, but allow me to introduce you both. This lady is Cheris Menthur, recent graduate of the College of Magisters and its most promising student for many years. Cheris, meet Sir Dylan of Mettenheath, knight prefect of the Holy Thorn.'

Dylan gave a small bow. 'The pleasure truly is all mine.'

She spoke carefully, in well-modulated tones. 'You are very kind, sir. May I be so bold as to enquire as to what arrangements will be made for us prior to our departure from the city?'

''We have several guestrooms in the knights' tower where you can be accommodated, I have assurances that we will be able to leave early on the morrow.'

'Then would I have permission to disguise myself for an hour and stroll around the city?'

Dylan looked askance. Marcus smiled to himself, shaking his head slightly.

'Why, by all the Gods, would you want to do that?'

She gave her sweetest smile – strong men had been known to

crumble under the force of it. 'Come, sir, I have spent over fifteen years of my life on an island whose perimeter you could walk in under an hour – no streets, no marketplace, no taverns, just a lifetime of studious austerity backed by the cries of a thousand gulls. I would say nothing, do nothing but observe; I would truly be the epitome of meekness.'

Sir Dylan looked troubled. 'As you can see, Sir Dylan,' Marcus interjected, 'all our time in isolation can change a person. Cheris is not the sort of woman you encounter very often on the mainland – educated, bold and outspoken. She is completely unaware of this herself, of course; she imagines all women to be as she is and not consumed all hours of the day with putting bread on the table for her and her family so she can avoid a beating from a drunken husband. She has much to learn about life outside our own cosseted environment.'

Cheris glared at him. 'That may be the case, but surely the best way for me to learn would be for me to actually mix with the women of whom you speak so disparagingly, however restricted the circumstances.'

Sir Dylan realised he was staring at her and turned away, looking at the sea as though jumping into it would be preferable to conversing with the two mages. 'No one has ever made such a request before. I am answerable to a chain of command and I doubt very much that they would approve. Bear in mind that the normal procedure is to forewarn people of your arrival, so that they may clear the streets should they so choose.'

Cheris was like a dog with a bone. Marcus looked ruefully at the skies – how many times had he seen her like this, especially when she felt she had a point to make?

'Surely,' she said, 'the procedure is to make people aware that mages will shortly be walking the streets and, as you say, give them the choice on how to react. Now, if I were to arrive at your tower and to leave again immediately, then anyone still around must be aware of the possibility that a mage could still be in the vicinity. I tell you what: why don't you accompany me? I would speak to you and only you and be utterly subservient to your demands.'

He stuttered. 'No, my Lady, no. You are persuasive but no, it would not be appropriate.'

Cheris's eyes shone. 'We are some half an hour from the shore, before our ship docks, yes?'

'Longer! They will have to row; there is no wind.'

'Excellent! Then that gives me plenty more time to work on you.'

Marcus looked at her animated face and that of the blushing, stumbling knight and realised that he had never felt more sorry for anyone in his life.

The sailors finally secured the ship in the harbour after an hour's hard rowing. The gang plank was put down and a couple of knights helped to carry the mages gear on to land. Cheris thanked a couple of sailors for their help, including the young lad who had spoken to her the night before, stepped lightly on to the gangplank and then on to the jetty. Thereafter it was up a flight of stone steps to get on to the harbour wall proper. Marcus was labouring up the steps behind her. She waited patiently for him flanked by two knights. In her bright-red robes she realised that she would stand out like a beacon.

'Do you want to lean on your staff, get your breath back after those horrible steps?' she said playfully when he was finally standing next to her. 'I can tell,' he said slowly, 'that today you are feeling a lot better.'

They started a slow walk along the harbour wall, behind Sir Dylan and the knights, who were pulling their gear which had been loaded on to a small handcart. Ahead of them, past the statue of Hytha, the harbour wall ended in a flight of steps which then opened on to a large flat area paved in stone that nestled between a shingle beach dotted with small fishing craft and a line of low tiny cottages – some whitewashed and salubrious; others looking far less favourable. This flat area was where the sailors worked at their nets, except in the mornings when the trestle tables would come out and the fish market was held. Between two of the cottages, some two-thirds of the way along the beach, was a cobbled street, Voyagers' Street, the main artery traversing Voyagers' Hill, cutting through it until it joined the larger People's Hill, where it took the name, unsurprisingly, of People's Street. It was towards this street that the knights now headed.

To Cheris's surprise, the area was not fully deserted. After

Marcus's dire warnings of the terror the mages provoked among the common folk, she had expected to see no one at all, but there were clusters of people, keeping a respectful distance, regarding them with what appeared to be only barely engaged curiosity. Some fishermen were still working on their boats, apparently oblivious to the strange procession close by them.

'Marcus,' she said, 'these people aren't bothered by us at all.'

'It looks that way,' he replied. 'But actually the harbour front should be teeming with people right now. We are holding up the fish market, you see; these people are waiting for us to disappear up Voyagers' Street so they can start to set up their wares.'

'So we are stopping these people making their money.'

'Yes.'

She swallowed, feeling guilty, seeing accusation in every local's glance. Fortunately, though, they soon reached Voyagers' Street and turned into it. Cheris's relief that they were no longer holding up the business of the day was immediately replaced by one of horror.

'By Lucan, the smell!'

Within a few steps it was like plunging into another world. The street with its smooth uneven cobbles was hemmed in on both sides by dark two-storey buildings that extended outward and above her, cutting out the light. It was almost possible, she reckoned, for neighbours across the street from each other to reach out and shake hands through the small, upper windows. Rank straw was scattered over the cobbles, and on either side of the road was a small trench that served as an open sewer, the source of the odour that so offended Cheris.

'It is a shock, the first time, isn't it?' said Marcus. 'A lifetime on an island with the sea filling your nostrils ill prepares you for this. Tanaren City actually has an army of night-soil men who work like beavers until dawn, but they concentrate their efforts in the better-off areas; somewhere like this might see them once a month. A few weeks back in high summer it would have been a lot worse.'

They continued onwards up the hill. Most of the hills in the city sloped gently upwards, the exceptions being Loubian Hill, with its palaces on the crest, St Kennelth's where the Great Cathedral was located, and the western fringe of the Artisans' Hill where it met the city wall, so progress wasn't too difficult for them. Now and then they would pass a side street, which was always narrower, even more ramshackle and ill-favoured and piled even higher with filth than the one they were proceeding along. Here they did meet no one, apart from the odd skinny feral dog cocking its leg against a wall, or a comatose drunk slumped in a doorway. However, behind these doors as they passed there were sounds – a crying child, a drunken argument, even some wild laughter – but nobody dared come out to face them.

Eventually they reached the top of the hill. Here they emerged into the light again, out into a small square in the centre of which was a statue of a man holding a book and a sword – the usual symbols, Cheris found out later, of the office of Grand Duke. Under the statue was a small tired-looking fountain opening out into a stone basin some ten feet across. The road continued downhill on the other side of the square, but it was not there that the knights now headed. Rather, they turned eastward to their right, towards a narrow street that also headed downhill. This street was a lot cleaner, brighter and better maintained. Along its length Cheris spotted a couple of bright tavern signs and some shops selling wickerwork and the like. There were even a few people in the street; some did disappear down side streets when they spotted the red robes, but there were others who blithely carried on with their own business. One, a large wealthily-dressed man in a red velvet tunic, even walked straight past them while wishing them a good morrow. He seemed to look at her with open admiration. Cheris smiled back at him – being so frankly appreciated by others made her pleased about what she had done to her robe. It was tucked tightly in at the waist, and the lacing at the front was tight enough to emphasise her figure; it wasn't too long, either, which was the curse of most feminine robes. In fact, at a distance she was sure it would pass as an evening dress.

'Can you spare a penny, my Lady?'

The child's voice cut into her thoughts. She stopped and looked to her right. A side street cut into the road they were on – it had the dark look and evil smell of the ones they had passed earlier. Sitting on the ground at the junction of both streets was a little girl of maybe six or seven. Her brown dress was dirty and ragged, probably riddled with lice; her bare feet were covered in filth and she had the large sunken eyes of someone constantly battling malnutrition. Instinctively, Cheris reached into the purse but as she did so one of the knights stepped in front of her.

'Sorry, my Lady, but you are not allowed to do that.'

She coloured. 'By all the Gods, why not?'

'People will think the money is magical. If the child dies, we will be blamed for it. It's not worth the trouble.'

She opened her mouth but no sound came out. Instead, she shrugged her shoulders and moved off, though slowly, letting the others get ahead of her. When no one was looking she turned to look at the child again, and, catching her eye, she surreptitiously let a penny fall on to the cobbles. No one heard it. A couple of minutes later she looked back again to see the child running off into the side street, clutching a bright penny in her hand.

At the bottom of the street the houses disappeared. Ahead of them was a broad space paved with wide slabs leading up to the city walls. Here, the wall was some twenty feet high with a parapet wide enough for two men to walk abreast. One of the city gates was here. The gate was opened and Cheris could see a drawbridge over a narrow ditch. On either side of the gate was a conical tower with arrow slits rather than windows; she assumed the gate towers housed the portcullis mechanism as well as a small garrison. As she stared, she realised that her entourage had turned left and was walking slowly uphill again. 'By Keth, not another climb.' She did not have to worry for long. They had gone barely a quarter of a mile before they came to another tower. This one was also circular, conical and built into the walls but it was much broader, had some windows of glass and could obviously accommodate a lot more people. Above it flew the flag of the thorn. Finally, they had arrived.

6

For Ceriana, the next few hours passed in a blur. They still took their meal on the beach but the food tasted like paper in her mouth. She listened to the menfolk discussing the body. It had been nibbled by many of the denizens of the sea and was putrefying, yet they could still make out that the man must have been strong and vigorous in life and that he had shaven all the hair from his body. He was clothed entirely in black and the clothes were of good quality, but to Ceriana for all the interest that the dead man held for her they might as well have been discussing the price of grain. She clutched her prize, feeling it hard in her hand. At the first opportunity, she had slipped the thing into a purse she had asked Berek for, but for some reason she kept being drawn to the thing, reaching under the table to touch it again and again.

The climb back up the hill was exhausting; her lungs tore at her chest and her muscles burned. By the time she was seated again on the wagon she was red, flushed, sweaty and encrusted with salt, but it caused her none of her usual consternation. Her mind was elsewhere. Doren, who had stayed at the top of the hill, chastised her for her bedraggled state, as did her mother when she returned home. She ran the gauntlet of frowning courtiers as she sped back to her room, caring not one jot. Shutting the door behind her, she sat on her bed breathing deeply.

She clutched at the purse, scrabbling to loosen its drawstring.

Pulling the object out, she gently unwrapped the stone from the handkerchief and gingerly held it up to the window. It seemed oval in shape but its base was slightly larger than its tip, almost like a water droplet. Its sides were glassy and smooth, but as she looked through it she felt she could see little imperfections, like tiny air bubbles deep inside it. She kept staring at it, squinting until her eyes hurt. Elissa's blood! Were these bubbles moving? She felt sure they were, though very, very slowly, as you would see with thick sugar syrup. And the thing felt warm, like it was generating heat. This was no ruby! What in the name of all that was holy had she found?

There was a tap on the door. It was Doren calling her. Quickly she opened her vanity desk draw, pulling out one of several jewellery boxes. She chose one with a key, opened it and shoved the thing inside, locking the box tight shut. She then opened the door for Doren.

'Please could you run a bath for me? I smell absolutely terrible!'

She dressed simply for dinner, in a white linen dress covered by a blue silk kirtle. Her parents were there at table when she arrived; she sat with her father to her right with her mother next to him. He spoke to her in a gently admonishing tone.

'My dear, I know you were probably distracted but you shouldn't wander off unattended. Berek and the guards completely lost you for a while today.'

'There was no danger, Father – the beach was deserted and I just had an impulse to go climbing on the rocks.'

'You could have fallen into the sea, child,' her mother chided. 'Even if you were unhurt, it is unseemly for a duke's daughter to do such things.'

Ceriana pouted a little. 'I am not made of porcelain, Mother.'

'You are about to be married; you could have caught a chill and a chill could lead to pneumonia. If I had been forewarned about your little excursion, I would have put a stop to it even before you had left.' Margerete realised she was bristling and tried to modify her tone. 'You are a thin girl and prone to bad humours; your good health is of the utmost importance until you are married.'

'Until I am married, but not after! Are you not worried about the reputation northern men have of using their women roughly? Is there no concern that the lack of meat on me will serve me ill at the hands of a northern bear?'

'Ceriana!' her father snapped, she realised she had spoken out of turn.

'Sorry, Father; sorry, Mother.'

'I am as unhappy about this match as anybody else,' her mother continued. 'More so in fact. I would much rather have kept you within one or two days' journey like the other girls, not the weeks it will take to visit you now. But this is a match the Grand Duke himself has proposed and it is your – no, it is our duty – to comply.'

'Surely no one has suggested that I will not do my duty?'

'No, my dear.' Her mother gave a rare smile. 'You are a Hartfield and a fine example of the line. None of us doubt you.'

Such praise was rare. Ceriana felt a little shame at her truculence. Perhaps her mother was more afeard of losing her than she let on.

'Thank you, Mother' was all she could manage to say before turning her attention to her meal.

In bed that evening she was restless – sticky, too, for the night was warm and close. She was tired. Catherine had been right – the climb up the cliff had been exhausting – yet she felt sleep was still some distance away. She kept glancing at her vanity drawer. She desperately, desperately wanted to tell somebody about the ruby that was not a ruby but there was something so ... odd about it that it was compelling her to silence. She hadn't realised it earlier but the longer she shared a room with it the more she could perceive the strangest feeling of ... wrongness about it, something unnatural that she couldn't quite shake off. Perhaps it had magic... She shuddered at the thought – even the educated classes held a deep suspicion of such things.

And whose was the body on the beach? She had barely given the poor man a second thought after making her find but on listening to her father speak of him at dinner he seemed almost as odd as the object in her jewellery box.

'We can only assume he was a shipwreck victim,' he had said. 'I have sent a dispatch to the city for any details of ships recently lost at sea. Some minor flotsam was reported as coming on shore a mile or two further up the coast, but no one is going to report anything of value that they could keep for themselves. As to the man himself, someone suggested that he had the malady that makes a person's hair fall out, but there were signs of stubble on his chin: his hair was shaved, not merely absent. His clothes were thick and would have drowned him pretty quickly; it seems like it was some sort of uniform, but the uniform of what order no one here appears to know. He had a ring on his finger, silver, depicting a double-headed snake that maybe the university could identify, but I fear that the answer as to who this man was will remain closed to us. I have written to the university in any case.'

Flotsam from the shipwreck. That there was a connection between this man and her find seemed fairly obvious to Ceriana. Why hadn't the stone sunk straight to the bottom of the sea though? The matter was getting ever more perplexing.

At length she could resist it no longer – she pulled back the covers and clambered out of bed, the night air cooling her damp skin. She pulled open the drawer, took out the box, turned the key, lifted the lid then took two steps back in horror.

The thing was glowing.

It was dark in the room but a light came from the stone, the deep-rich colour of blood. It wasn't a strong light but could be seen clearly – the mirror, the jewellery box, her face as she stepped back towards it, were all backlit by an eerie red glow. It was not a constant light either – one second the light would die, the next it would flare back up again. It did this for at least five minutes while all the time Ceriana stared at it, eyes like dinner plates, completely rooted to the spot.

Then suddenly, without warning, the light went out. She stretched out a nervous, trembling finger and gave it the lightest of touches. It was still warm.

Shuddering, she slammed the lid back on to the box, locked it, pushed it to the back of the draw and jumped into bed, covering herself with the sheets. Suddenly the wedding seemed to be the least of her worries.

The wedding day itself drew ever closer. The plan now was for the wedding to take place at the Grand Cathedral of Artorus and Camille in Tanaren City and for it to be presided over by Grand Lector Josephus XVII himself. This was at the instigation of the Grand Duke who wanted this most political of unions to receive as high a profile as possible. The only thing stopping it from being a full state occasion was that he had not declared the seven days of grand revelry for the populace, limiting it to a meagre three. Once the nuptials had been completed, they were to travel by carriage from the cathedral, skirting the base of the Loubian Hill to the Grand Duke's staging post on the river Erskon. From there they were to take the ducal barge to Erskon House, a trip of some three to four hours. Most of the other guests would have to ride there, a quicker journey but one that gave many of the nobles a chance to reacquaint themselves with each other and to enter into all types of politicking. Ceriana would spend her wedding night at the house before starting the long journey, of some ten days' duration, to her new home.

All these arrangements meant the rehearsals for the ceremony would have to take place within the cathedral, so, three days before the wedding, she was to travel to the city, where she would remain at Loubian Hall. Her betrothed was summoned to do likewise but would stay in the Grand Duke's palace as an honoured guest. Her departure from Edgecliff would therefore be sooner than she had anticipated.

There had been no reoccurrence of the incident with the stone. She had checked every night but it had remained cold and lifeless, much to her relief, and so it had been pushed to the back of her mind somewhat, although she had been careful to include the box in the list of items to take with her.

One day before she was due to depart to the capital, with the sun beginning to set behind the Archers' Tower, she sat pensively in her room chewing her lip to distract her from the butterflies in her stomach. Her sister Leonie, having travelled down from the country that day, was with her. She was a fuller version of her little sister with fewer freckles and a broader, homelier face. Marriage and childbirth had led her to put on some weight, a situation she found most disagreeable. Doren sat quietly nearby, almost unobserved in the corner.

'The doctor said I should forego cakes now,' her sister chafed. 'Cakes! At this rate I shall be eating little more than rye grass and water.'

'You haven't put on that much weight,' Ceriana replied for the umpteenth time. 'Besides you look healthy with a fine complexion. Mother always says I look one stage away from consumption.'

'Mother is always prone to over-egging the pudding. There, I have done it again! There is not one conversation I can have in which I do not constantly mention food! It is bad enough that whenever I host formal occasions these days conversation is usually accompanied by my rumbling stomach.'

'What does your husband say?'

'It amuses Morton terribly; he will often make a huge joke out of it, in front of guests furthermore! It is most humiliating.'

'You haven't done too badly out of him, though.' Baron Morton Lewengrun was well known for indulging his wife. 'And at least you knew him before your wedding.'

'He does spoil me, I know,' Leonie admitted. 'Now, to the purpose of my visit: tell me, do you know anything about your husband?'

'Nothing,' said Ceriana with a roll of her eyes. 'Father has barely met him.'

'Then let me tell you this: Morton is acquainted with him; he has some trade connections with the northern barons and on some occasions has to travel up there. They lack some of life's finer things, silks, spices and the like, so Morton supplies some of the baronial estates. It is a lucrative sideline of his.'

'Aaaand?' said Ceriana, impatient at her sister's prevarication.

'Oh yes, your husband, sorry, your husband-to-be. He is the chief baron on a large island; his estate is the best and largest Morton has seen up there. Many of the men there are a little rougher, coarser than those we are acquainted with, but Wulfthram is not like that. He is quiet and very self-possessed. You know the sort, the kind who speaks only when they absolutely have to. His first wife died of illness and they say he has never recovered from it fully. Imagine, a northern baron mooning over the death of a woman! He was very devoted to her by all that I have heard.'

Ceriana pursed her lips slightly. 'So he will probably resent me?'

'I doubt that. He is much older than you; you will probably seem little more than a child to him. Probably the only time you will spend in his company will be in the bedroom when the urge takes him. Make sure you never say no to that either; they can get most tetchy if refused.'

'I will do as you suggest; he would probably only force himself on me if I said no anyway.'

'Oh you do not know that. Sister, you are so very gloomy today! Think of the good things about this arrangement; think of the freedom it will entail! Here you cannot make a trip to the garderobe without being followed by courtiers wracked with concern as to the comfort of your seating.'

Ceriana nodded slowly. 'So I should take a good book with me then.'

'Indeed!' said Leonie enthusiastically. 'And do not forget your embroidery.'

'I would never do that.'

'Quite right, sister. Now let's see – I have imparted what little information I have on your husband, so the next thing to do is call on Mother. Actually, as I am soon to be her nearest daughter in the geographical sense, that may be something I should do more often in the future.'

The two women hugged and Leonie took her leave. Doren and her mistress sat in silence for a while before Ceriana spoke.

'You do not have to come with me, you know; I am sure this Wulfthram has staff he could spare me.'

'I have a duty to the Hartfields,' Doren said firmly. 'I will not abandon you.'

'Your family is here; your husband cannot leave his business and your children...'

'I will return for a few days here and there.'

Ceriana swallowed and set her chin firmly; she had already made her decision but hated the words as they came out. 'No. I cannot permit it. I am a selfish girl, I know, but in this case I must do the right thing. This time, Doren, I really am dismissing you from my service. Lady Catherine is to remain here as a companion to my mother and you will become her maidservant.'

Doren looked at her, her eyes moist. 'But what of you, my Lady? It will be so lonely for you.'

'If this is what the Gods have decided for me then I am ready. Besides, Father will be travelling up there quite frequently and Keth's furnace will freeze before I stop returning here whenever I can. This will always be my home.'

'Thank you, my Lady.' Doren sounded both grateful and upset. 'You are truly growing up before my very eyes; you have always been the daughter I never had.'

At that, Ceriana's poise and assurance broke, and the two women embraced each other, accompanied only by the sound of their own soft tears.

Ceriana stood in the centre of the Grand Cathedral. Behind her in the nave stood her parents, siblings and other family members. In front of her, stroking his saintly white beard, was Grand Lector Josephus XVII himself, the head of the Divine Pantheon, first disciple of Artorus, chief supplicant to the Holy Trinity and head of the church in Tanaren. Light bled through the stained-glass windows on to the central dais on which Josephus stood. In front of him, covered in a simple white cloth, was the great altar on which the rings of marriage would be placed, between the figures of the golden lion and silver dove, the symbols of Artorus and Camille. These represented the very ideal of marriage; strength tempered with mercy, impetuosity with reason, ambition with gentility. It was to these two gods that she would make her pledge tomorrow. Then the Grand Lector would bring forth the symbol of the hare, which was the attribute of Elissa, and ask the goddess to bless the marriage with children. Then the ceremony would be over.

Her groom, who had arrived in the city yesterday, was late. Apparently, he had arrived with an entourage of lesser barons and gone straight to his rooms – to drink as the palace gossips would have it. Josephus cleared his throat in mild irritation.

She drifted and tried to remember the depictions on the stained-glass windows without looking at them; she had been here many times after all, though never as the centre of attention. First, appropriately enough, there was Artorus, father of the gods, here depicted as the mighty veteran warrior, smiting his great enemy, the god Keth, into the underworld. There Keth, consumed by his desire for vengeance, created the furnace of the damned, upon which was forged an army of demons. It was here that those condemned by the gods, damned by lives of dissolution, were sent to labour for eternity, their spirits tormented by fire and a thousand other exquisite agonies. Then there was Camille, a lesser goddess in Tanaren but revered almost as much as Artorus elsewhere. The window depicted the tale of Camille and the prostitute Tamira. Camille had entered this woman's house disguised as a cat but then revealed her true form to teach Tamira – and the world – about temperance and modesty. The prostitute thereafter became her chief disciple, setting up the all-female Order of Camille whose stronghold was in the empire of Chira. Shortly after these events Camille became Artorus's consort.

    The next window depicted both Artorus and Camille holding Elissa, their first-born, in their arms, and after this was a window showing, appropriately enough for a city built on the sea, Hytha with his great axe, riding the waves as he continued his perpetual battle with Uttu, god of storms. Then there was Sarasta, goddess of the harvest. holding a basket of fruit and bushels of wheat. And then Xhenafa the withered, in his cloak of shadow, standing on a pile of bones; Mytha, god of warriors, who was shown as a great bear tearing apart the fiery demons created by Keth; Meriel, the Lady in White, bathing a crippled soldier in radiance and making him walk again, Elissa, standing before Keth the Deceiver, who had cloaked himself in a fair form in order to seduce the goddess but who unintentionally revealed himself when she asked him for his opinion on the greatest virtue and he stated it to be ambition rather than love. After this was Artorus again, tearing the Earth away from the underworld and creating the void between them, the home of the restless soul, and this was followed by Lucan, god of magic in his many forms – a being of fire, water, lightning, ice, earth and air. And so then to the final window, depicting the entire pantheon: Artorus at the head; Camille, slightly smaller next to him; Elissa at their feet, and beneath her the brothers Hytha and Mytha; Meriel, bathed in light, next to Sarasta, and under even them, hammering away in his furnace, Keth the ever watchful. Xhenafa, conveyor of the dead, never appeared in these depictions.

    She looked up at the windows and was pleased to see she had got them all right. She shuffled restlessly. She was standing in the cathedral's transept, both sides of which ended in an apse whose semi-domes were covered in gold leaf. Ahead of her, to the left and right, were the balconies that would house the choir which had finished rehearsing earlier, and directly ahead was the great apse itself, colossal in size, covered in gold and lapis lazuli and housing marble statues of Artorus and Camille. Its semi-dome depicted the dove and the lion and, most importantly, the staff of justice, its wood blackened by cleansing fire, the overweening symbol of both Artorus and the Grand Duke. An archway and tunnel at the back of the apse led to the famous bell tower.

Josephus cleared his throat again. 'Perhaps, my Lords and Ladies, given the time constraints upon us we can proceed with...'

At that, however, the great bronze doors of the cathedral ground open, admitting the bright sunlight that was bathing the city outside. Silhouetted against it were several figures all of whom were hurrying towards them. Ceriana turned her head back to Josephus and waited.

She felt someone stand alongside her but did not look as her cheeks had started to flush. She concentrated on the golden lion ahead of her, breathing deeply and hoping that would calm her down. Josephus had already started to open his mouth in admonishment when the man next to her spoke.

'Apologies for the late arrival, Grand Lector; we are unfamiliar with your city and badly underestimated the time required to get here. Have no fear: we will be on time tomorrow.' The apology sounded forced to her, made through gritted teeth. The voice itself though was deep and powerful and she couldn't dislike it as much as she wanted to.

The rehearsal began. It was Josephus, mostly, who spoke, telling all present of the wonderful and joyous event unfolding before the eyes of the Gods; occasionally the bride and groom would have a line, generally relating to their piety and humility. Bizarrely neither of the bride and groom looked at each other, Ceriana concentrating rigidly on the book of service that she held in front of her.

'Now both of you approach the altar.' Josephus had that voice that all priests, great or small, seemed to have within them, rich, well enunciated, perfect for making the audience hang on to every syllable.

They both complied.

'The rings will be present on the altar before you. Wulfthram. When I prompt you to take the ring, turn to Ceriana and place it upon her finger.'

The couple turned to face each other and for the first time Ceriana looked directly at the man she was to wed.

The northern barons were descended from the men of Kibil and she could see their characteristics in him immediately. His hair was black and his jaw firm-set, almost blocky in appearance. His moustache trailed over his top lip and hung down in plaits from either side of his mouth; she realised then that his hair also had a couple of plaits extending well past his neck. His eyes were a clear deep blue, darker than a summer sky but lighter than a sapphire, and they contrasted sharply with his weathered brown skin. As to his age, if anything, those who had said he was twice as old as she had underestimated it, for his eyes were finely lined as were the top of his cheeks; he seemed to be a man worn down with care to her, but apart from that his expression was unreadable. He spoke then, almost as if involuntarily: 'By the Gods, she is so young.'

Of all the things she could have heard him say, that was probably the worst. She turned beetroot in colour and glanced away. She mumbled her way through the rest of the ceremony, and when it was finished her husband to-be went straight to her father, apologised for his lateness again with an equal lack of sincerity, and was gone, his cronies following close behind him.

7

The night passed, clear and cold, and morning brought with it a light frost whitening the tips of the grass as though they had been lightly dusted with sugar. After a quick breakfast of hard bread, Morgan and his companions were on their way again.

They passed villages more frequently now and, although the first couple they saw were deserted, they were at last starting to see people, hardy souls willing to take the chance that their former homes would not fall under enemy control again. At one point they stopped to let some knights ride past heading eastwards; their pennants and cloaks bore the eagle claw so they were obviously going to join up with Reynard. Further evidence that the front line was being reinforced came as another body of troops marched past them. They were well equipped, too, some hundred men marching under the banner of a great white charger rearing above a waterfall.

'Baron Fenchard's men,' growled Rozgon. 'He controls the lands around Haslan Falls, south of Ulgar's estates; the two of them are supposed to be as thick as thieves. It is strange, though: Fenchard has been telling everyone he hasn't the men to spare.'

Sir Varen shrugged his shoulders. 'Perhaps he has been ordered to muster some at last; they are well equipped, so he certainly has the money.'

'Fenchard is one of the Aarlen family; rich and powerful, they control many baronetcies here and in the lands near Tanaren City. Money is not an issue but until now he has been very reluctant to commit men to the front line. I wonder what has changed his mind?' Rozgon spat on the ground as the last of the soldiers marched past.

'Is Felmere planning a final push before winter?' asked Morgan. 'He has said nothing to me.'

'Rumour among us foot soldiers is that he definitely is.' said Rozgon. 'He wants to take Grest, to push the Arshumans back over the Whiterush. He has obviously put out the call.'

'It will be a fiendishly difficult town to take.' said Leon grimly.

'When we last attacked it we had a mage to contend with and it wasn't just him – they had artillery and ballistae on the hill raining down death from the skies. We would need to outnumber them three to one and to expect damaging losses.'

'If he takes it, though, then what with winter coming will the Arshumans bother to respond?' Morgan wondered. 'He may well get the time to both build up the defences and call for reinforcements for a spring offensive.'

'From what I hear, though,' said Varen, 'the Baron is not one for reckless gambles. He never forces a conflict unless he is certain of winning it, a lesson Esric Calvannen in the south is slowly learning.'

'Which means that there will be more men to follow.' said Rozgon.

'Probably,' Morgan replied. 'There is definitely a mage or two on their way as well; something is definitely up.'

'So we are leaving just as things here are getting exciting.' Leon sounded disappointed.

'Do not worry on that score!' Morgan grinned at him. 'Ours is by far the more dangerous road; once we are in the mountains everything we encounter will want to kill us.'

Rozgon was right about further reinforcements following – they passed two further units before making camp; they both numbered just over fifty and were less well armed and equipped that the men of Haslan Falls, in leather and brigandine, with short swords, bows and slings. They carried no banners. On enquiring, they were told that they came from the Athkaril area. This was a key town on the west bank of the Kada, the first of the Seven Rivers going from west to east. Once a small hill town overlooking a bridge over the river, the war had seen its population swell to many times its original size with refugees fleeing the conflict. Many of them lived in squalor, in tents or tiny wooden hovels that had sprung up like a fungal growth around the old hill town. It followed, then, that many of these men had so little to lose that they were willing to risk their lives to recapture the lands where their homes had once stood. They claimed to owe their allegiance to Baron Wyak of Athkaril, but really that loyalty was tenuous at best. Baron Wyak had hardly welcomed them with open arms and seemed keen to furnish them with enough basic equipment to make them battle ready so that he could get rid of them. He had promised to look after the families they were leaving behind, although some of the men were concerned. 'If he goes back on his word, he will have a riot on his hands,' one of the men told them.

As they set up camp that evening under a knot of birch trees, Morgan sought out Cedric. The old man had been pretty quiet since the trip started, staying in the wagon most of the time – presumably studying his books. Morgan, like most soldiers, thought that scholars did little else with their day.

But this time, as Morgan climbed into the wagon, that was exactly what Cedric was doing – poring over a tome in the fading light close to the fitful glow cast by a pungent tallow candle.

'Why don't you use the lantern?' Morgan asked. There was one hung on a pole at the front of the wagon.

'Too much fuss, my boy – a candle and my reading glasses are perfectly adequate for the task.'

'Are you looking for anything in particular, or does travel bore you?'

Cedric looked up and peered at Morgan over the top of his glasses.

Morgan noticed that where they sat on the bridge of his nose they had marked the skin red.

'Not at all, no; I am just reading and rereading everything I have here relating to the Wych folk. I have, after all, to conduct a tricky and delicate negotiation with them and make sure none of us are killed in the process. Knowledge is everything, so they say, but unfortunately for us our knowledge on this subject is patchy at best.'

'Speak to Haelward; he met some on Danathra.'

'Their trading post? Well, that could be useful. Unfortunately, though, all the evidence I have here shows that since the folk of the sea and the forests sundered from each other they have diverged in many ways – culturally and linguistically to name but two. The folk of the Aelvenwood, I am afraid to say, seem much more savage, tribal and suspicious. Maybe I should just flatter them; perhaps that might be the best option.'

'If they are suspicious, they will see through that immediately. Better to stand up to them, show we are not afraid. Tell them we have come through great peril to see them and deserve an audience, if nothing else.'

Cedric looked thoughtful. 'Maybe, my boy, it is you who should talk to them.'

Morgan laughed. 'We have to get there first! It might be more worth your while looking up the perils of Claw Pass – if the snows don't get us, the bandits might; if the bandits don't get us, then, well, it might be something else. Worry about the Wych folk when we clear the pass, not before.'

'And worry about Tetha Vinoyen before we get to the pass.' Sir Varen, who had just finished tethering and feeding the horses had obviously heard their conversation and poked his head into the wagon to make his own contribution. 'There is little doubt that Ulgar knows we are coming; we may be on the same side against a greater enemy but the ambitions of the barons are never far from the surface. The land we are on now is disputed between Felmere and Vinoyen; their rivalry goes back decades. He will not openly oppose us but keep your eye out for a knife in the dark.'

'But he doesn't even know about our mission,' Cedric said.

'He knows Morgan, and he knows Rozgon, and he knows I am an Eagle Claw. To him we are all Felmere men and that is enough. If he can hamper us, he will; just putting one over on Lukas Felmere will satisfy him greatly. If you want my advice, get out of Tetha as quickly as possible and make for Shayer Ridge. It is my town, a Felmere town, and we will be protected there.'

'I agree in part,' Morgan replied. 'But I fear we may need to spend the night in the town – better surrounded by people than be caught alone in the country at night. That way we need only have one night out in the open in Vinoyen's lands.'

They left the wagon and settled around the campfire, a far

heartier affair than the one they had had the night before. Cedric was shaking his head, obviously chewing something over in his mind; Morgan asked what was ailing him.

'What the young knight was saying earlier, about the petty conflicts between these barons. I will never understand people who put their own personal ambitions above all other things.'

'Ah.' said Morgan, 'but to such men their ambitions are never petty.'

'Which brings me to the other thing troubling me, Morgan – how does this baron associate you with Felmere?'

'That is a long story,' Morgan replied. 'It would have started about seven years ago at Fort Axmian, the great river defence to the west and south, which these days is in Vinoyen's lands. Now, back then, Arshuma held Tetha Vinoyen and Ulgar was a baron in exile. If Axmian fell to Arshuma, his entire baronetcy would have been lost. At the time Felmere held only a rump of his original lands outside of his own city so both barons were fighting for their own territories, to preserve their own existence as nobility. Both Felmere and Vinoyen attacked Axmian together, to try and relieve the siege, but were forced back. Inside the fort, amongst the defenders, were me and Rozgon. We had water – the fort is on a river after all – but the food supplies were thinning and if the siege was not broken then the outcome would be inevitable. So we in the fort took the big risk of sallying out to try to catch the Arshumans in a pincer movement – us on one side, Felmere and Vinoyen on the other. Fortunately for us all, it worked – we broke the Arshumans and the knights harried them all the way back to Tetha Vinoyen, their base, which was now the most westerly point of their advance.

'Ulgar was all for attacking them there immediately, so keen was he to reclaim his baronial seat, but Felmere argued against it. The men were exhausted; we had been under siege for eight weeks and in no condition to try and storm a defended position. The chances were that we would have been cut to pieces, losing all the gains we had made. Ulgar was furious; he saw Felmere as holding out because it was not his lands that we would be restoring. He immediately earmarked Felmere, and the commanders at Axmian of which I was one, as traitors and enemies. I had only been promoted during the siege as so many ranking men had been killed and within weeks I had a baron as a mortal enemy.' Morgan laughed softly. 'Anyway, we wintered at Axmian, reinforcements arrived and, as soon as the first shoots of spring were showing, we attacked Tetha Vinoyen by surprise, storming it immediately and forcing the Arshumans back for so many miles it meant Felmere was able to reclaim nearly all of his lost lands as well as Vinoyen. Ulgar has never forgiven us.'

Cedric looked puzzled. 'Perhaps you weren't the best choice for this mission then?'

'I agree!' Morgan was perfunctory. 'I would rather have stayed in the south hanging traitors, but Felmere offered me a large bag of money and told me he trusted me. What else could I do?'

'Don't listen to Morgan, scholar.' Rozgon gave a wicked smile. 'The reason Felmere asked him to guide you here is because he is the best man for the job. He also underplays his hand at Axmian; the battle could well have been lost without him. We had charged into the unguarded rear of the enemy but they outnumbered us and rallied quickly. Our standard-bearer was cut down before us and we were wavering. Then Morgan picked up the banner and carried it to a small hill, calling us to join him. He stood there alone for a while, killing any Arshuman who dared challenge him, despite his wounds, until we all got to him and counter-charged. The Arshumans saw him with the banner and fled. Morgan is known to every veteran soldier around here thanks to that– he is the hero of Axmian and I will bet there are a few in Tetha Vinoyen who would as soon side with him as with his baron.'

'Bold words, my friend,' Morgan replied. 'Tomorrow will see if there is any truth in them.'

In the first four years of the war, Tetha Vinoyen had been lost and recaptured six times. A large part of it had been burned and nearly all of it looted and ransacked. Since then, although at times the enemy had got within ten miles of it, people had returned and, displaying the extraordinary resilience of tough frontier folk, had slowly rebuilt the town.

Its most prominent new feature was a fifteen-foot stone wall guarding that part of the town on the eastern side of the river. Its two gate towers were dotted with archer slits and were always fully garrisoned by Ulgar Vinoyen's men in their green and white surcoats. The town itself was unremarkable; on its western side, after the low stone bridge had been crossed, it had a large square which held a weekly market for the farmers who had returned to tend to their lands again. Leading on to the square on its northern side was the Ferry inn (it had stood there since before the bridge was built). It was a tavern with extensive stables and a large front yard which held on one side the gallows and the stocks and on the other a cockpit. This was a popular place on weekends and was always packed out, as the professional gamblers made themselves a tidy profit at the expense of the well-oiled patrons. The inn itself was looking a little shabby, as though there were neither enough staff nor guests staying in its rooms to warrant its full maintenance.

    On the southern side of the square were the large wattle-and-daub buildings of the town's more well-to-do inhabitants, and on its western side, facing the bridge and the river was the baronial hall. Baron Ulgar had a country residence but spent most of his time in this building. It was a large, white; timber-framed building with northern and southern wings and was entirely surrounded by a five-foot wall. Although its wide gate was always open, it was constantly policed by many of the Baron's handpicked men who were loyal, well paid and always vigilant.

    After five or six hours' travel, as the weak and pale sun started to dip a little ahead of them, Morgan and his companions arrived at the eastern gate. The gate was open but the way was barred by two stout fellows carrying halberds and wearing the green-and-white quarters of Vinoyen.

    'State your names and the business that you have in the city,' stated one of the men brusquely and not without a modicum of relish.

    'Certainly,' said Morgan courteously. 'I am Morgan of Glaivedon and need to pass through your, um … city to complete some business that has been made incumbent on me by none other than Grand Duke Leontius VII. With me are Cedric of Rossenwood, an eminent scholar, his assistant Willem, and several soldiers fresh from the front line of battle.'

'I see.' said the man suspiciously. 'Wait here for a minute.'

The man ducked behind the gate and into its northern tower. He emerged some minutes later, but not before a small boy had come running out of the same door heading for the bridge.

'Message for the Baron,' Rozgon murmured to Morgan.

'You may pass,' said the guard when he eventually re-emerged. 'But I warn you, this is an orderly city and we brook no trouble from anybody, Grand Duke's business or no.'

'Worry not.' said Morgan. 'I have no intention of causing any.'

They headed towards the bridge. The eastern side of the town was barely a quarter of a mile across and seemed to be reserved solely for the military. It had stables, blacksmiths, armourers and weapon smiths aplenty, all working like Keth's demons. Horses churned up the muddy ground and ostlers and stableboys cursed loudly as they tried to control them. The air smelled of leather and metal. They attracted little attention as they walked through, armed men being the most common sight on the road here after all. The bridge when they got there was broad enough to take three horsemen abreast. It was a sturdy affair, its three arches spanning the Vinoyen River, fast and deep, a real defensive barrier which served only to highlight the strategic importance of this place, the only sure crossing for horses, carts and wagons that the river had this far north. They were halfway across the bridge when Sir Varen nudged Morgan.

'Look, we have a welcome party.'

Morgan had already noticed that a group of horsemen had assembled ahead of them in the square. They were still too far away to be recognised, but two of the horsemen held banners, one displaying the green-and-white quarters, the other the white horse and cataract. There was no avoiding them, so Morgan led his men straight up to them. As he did so, he invited Cedric to join him and it was these two that approached the horsemen, with the others following a few steps behind.

Baron Ulgar Vinoyen was at the head of his men. He was a darkskinned, dark-haired man of about forty years and a living testament that high status or privilege was no protection against the ravages of smallpox.

His face was covered with the deep-pitted scars that the disease left on its victims and, despite his attempts to mitigate them by growing a large beard and moustache, they could never be fully disguised. Next to him and slightly behind was a much younger man. He had long sandy hair and pale-blue eyes and wore a suit of dazzlingly polished plate armour that obviously had never been within a country mile of a battlefield. He was clean-shaven and Morgan suspected that his eyebrows were plucked regularly; this was a man more at home with a full-length mirror than a sword.

Morgan inclined his head slightly. 'Baron Vinoyen.'

'And to what do I owe the pleasure?' The Baron's voice was higher in pitch than might have been expected in a man of his appearance. 'Morgan of Glaivedon returning to the city that he so abjectly abandoned seven years ago!'

'And helped to reclaim six years ago.' said Morgan. 'I am here at the request of the Grand Duke and am escorting the learned scholar Cedric of Rossenwood who has business that takes him through your city and beyond.'

'And here I have the Duke's letter of authorisation bearing his seal.' said Cedric, holding a sheaf of paper aloft. 'It compels all those loyal to Tanaren to assist me in my endeavours, as this man of Glaivedon is currently doing. I am engaged on a matter that is directly related to this war and hopefully may expedite it in our favour.'

Don't say any more, thought Morgan. The last thing we need to do is pique his curiosity.

'We intend to remain in your city for one night only,' Morgan continued. 'If the inn has any rooms, that is, and we shall be long gone ere tomorrow ends. I assure you that my presence here will be a fleeting one only.'

'Make sure that this is the case,' the Baron replied firmly. 'You are not a friend to me or the city. I shall not hinder you, if the Grand Duke has given you his blessing, but you will receive no aid from me either.'

'You are too generous, Baron!' The man at his side finally spoke. 'If I had been so slighted in the past, then this churl would have been whipped and dragged out of the city tied to my saddle.'

Ulgar smiled. 'Allow me to introduce Baron Fenchard Aarlen of Haslan Falls. His father passed away last winter and I am instructing him as to his baronial duties. As you can see, he has not yet acquired my temperance and moderation.'

'They are skills that are acquired only through time and experience,' Morgan replied. He turned to face Fenchard. 'I remember your father well and was sorry to hear of his passing. He was a fine warrior and a generous man. I hope he has taught you well.'

'My father was all that you say he was.' Fenchard's tone was sneering. 'But he was prone to being over-indulgent towards his subjects. They must always know where their loyalties lie. Where do your loyalties lie, Glaivedon? With the Grand Duke? Lukas Felmere? Or just your own purse.'

'Loyalty is not a simplistic issue, not a question of black or white, and yet ultimately my loyalty is to Tanaren, and always will be.'

'Many a traitor has used such words in the past and still they never escape the disembowelling knife of the executioner. Be wary, Glaivedon! I am watching you – one slip and a silver tongue will be no defence against me.'

'Then I am forewarned and will be wary. I have no desire to be held down and subjected to the ministration of your eyebrow tweezers.'

The men behind Morgan sniggered as Fenchard started in his saddle. His eyes blazed with fury and he made to ride towards Morgan, but Ulgar put out his hand stopping him.

'Patience, Fenchard! The man's tongue will be his own undoing one day and on that day you have my permission to nail it to the nearest privy door.' He looked at Morgan. 'It is the scholar and his letter that has saved you here. This time tomorrow I will make for the inn. If you have not left by then, I will set my men on you; they can have the pleasure of slapping you in those stocks.' With that he spurred his horse and turned back to his manor, his troops following. Fenchard lingered a second more, glaring at Morgan, before he, too, turned to follow the Baron.

'Keth's flaming balls! Who was that jumped-up snotty little turd?'

Rozgon had come forward and was now standing next to Morgan.

'A jumped-up snotty little turd who dares speak only because he has soldiers beside him and the patronage of the most powerful Baron this side of the river. We saw his men on the road yesterday; undoubtedly he has many more. He's not really the sort of enemy I was looking to make.' Morgan did not take his eyes off the Baron's party until they were behind the walls of the manor house.

'You had no choice. The boy was spoiling for a fight; he obviously wanted to impress Vinoyen.'

'Maybe. Couldn't you just smell his ambition? Oh and Cedric, thanks for producing that letter; you had hardly any time to retrieve it from the wagon.'

'You are right,' Cedric replied. 'I had hardly any time at all. This letter is actually...' he unfolded the scroll '...a letter from Professor Hartwinge asking me to attend his lecture concerning physical depictions of the divine.'

'Did you go?' Morgan asked.

'By Artorus, no! If you think I can talk, then you should sit and listen to one of Hartwinge's three-hour lectures. I saw Claw Pass as a preferable alternative.'

'I think I would prefer a three-hour session at the inn.' said Rozgon hopefully.

'I am afraid we will have neither.' said Morgan. 'We get a room, we get some food and we hide out until tomorrow. That is the plan.'

'Maybe you, the Professor, and the boy should, but it might be a good idea for a couple of us to look around town; there might be something worth hearing.'

'Fair enough.' Morgan nodded his agreement. 'We should pick up some supplies as well if at all possible, I imagine the inn has plenty of space; I cannot see there being too many commercial travellers in this part of the world.'

8

Their rooms were of a good size on the ground floor, their small windows looking directly out on to the city. The bed was large and a lot more comfortable than what Cheris was used to back in her little cell on the island. She went to Marcus's room, which was at the other end of a narrow, semi-circular corridor, and told him.

'I am feeling rather tired. All the excitement has rather worn me out – I think I will get some sleep.'

'I understand completely; the sea air doesn't help either. We will be eating in our rooms. so call me when you are ready and I will organise some food.'

She returned to her room. Leaving the door slightly ajar, she lay on the bed and shut her eyes. After a few minutes came the sound of barely perceptible footsteps on the stone outside. She felt the door open, then close again soft as a whisper. Without opening her eyes she said quietly: 'Well, Sir Dylan, did you get it?'

'Right here,' he replied in equally hushed tones. 'I have to be back on duty in one hour, so we need to move quickly.'

She opened her eyes at last and looked at him. He had removed his helmet and was wearing a mail shirt covered in a rich blue surcoat. His breeches and high boots were of black leather. In his hands he held up a simple white linen dress, laced at the front, along with a brown kirtle to fit over it.

'Don't laugh but I have never had a dress before. Where did you get it?'

'A couple of the scullery maids live in the tower; one of them ... likes me so allowed me to borrow it.'

'Could I buy it? I have a crown –would that be enough?'

Sir Dylan nodded. 'Enough to buy several of them I would imagine; I will speak to her about it... Now hurry!'

'Patience, I have never put one of these on before.' She started unlacing her robe.

Sir Dylan looked uncomfortable. 'I hope by the Gods you are not asking me to help you. I will wait outside.'

'No!' she giggled. 'I can manage, and don't be so silly about waiting outside; someone might see you. Just turn your back to me.'

Five minutes later she was every inch the peasant girl, although her delicate hands and long nails betrayed her little subterfuge. 'What now?'

'Just follow me and be quiet.'

He led her through the corridor, past Marcus's room (she didn't dare breathe) and on to a small landing housing a spiral stairway lit by sputtering torches. Instead of going up the stairs, though, he led her through a narrow opening in the opposite wall, down a dark and dank unlit corridor and through a doorway of oiled wood. Now they were looking at a narrow black iron gate which opened out into daylight and the world outside. The city wall was to their right and a high curtain wall green with moss hid them from the houses to their left. Dylan produced a key. 'Servants' entrance,' he said. A minute later they were outside, where Sir Dylan stopped behind the sheltering wall and turned to speak to her.

'If I am caught, it means probable dismissal and maybe even some time in prison. I still cannot believe I have been so gullible as to fall for your imprecations, but no matter we are here now. So we go to the market, spend five minutes there and return. You speak to no one but me. Understand?'

'Completely,' she said. 'And thank you; I will find some way to repay you one day.'

He looked at her – those eyes afire with excitement, her small pointed nose, her perfect teeth framed by her delicate lips – and cursed himself for his weakness. 'I am sure Artorus will see to it.'

And then, with her following not two feet behind, he led her into the city.

They made good speed, him with his long firm stride and her half running, half walking, turning her head hither and thither, eyes like saucers marvelling at every belching peasant or merchant in hose two sizes too small for him. She was like a child witnessing its first dawn or a small bird who not minutes before had escaped its nest at last. She tried to miss nothing – every wagon piled high with barrels, every gapped-tooth townswoman arguing with her landlord, every urchin running hard, head down to escape the switch from his parents, was a source of wonder to her. Every couple of minutes she would look for Sir Dylan who was getting further and further ahead of her and run to catch up with him. She was aware that she looked like his servant, so her following him in this way seemed like a perfectly natural thing to do.

They headed back up the street where earlier she had seen the little beggar girl to the square, which was now a lot busier than when she had first visited it. She saw a tavern in one corner that she hadn't noticed earlier. Outside it was a gang of ruddy-faced young men all holding tankards and laughing with each other. She made sure she didn't catch their eye. Sir Dylan ignored them and plunged down the side street on the right, the one opposite the road to the sea that they had climbed up earlier. This street was also narrow with overhanging buildings, but the night soil men had obviously visited here recently as it was a lot cleaner. They were going downhill now and she had to be careful not to lose her footing on the uneven cobbles while avoiding bumping into people in what was the busiest street she had witnessed so far. At one point she even had to wriggle past a man pulling a team of three horses, all in single file. Dylan's pace was unrelenting, so in the end her burning legs made it necessary for her to speak to him.

"Lissa's blood, slow down! You are taller than I ... I cannot keep up!'

'Can't you fly or something?' he said mischievously.

'Only Gods can fly,' she harrumphed. 'I even detest running.'

'Well, what can you do then? What is it that makes you so terrifying?'

'You haven't seen my temper yet,' she said. 'But keep this up and you just might.'

'I told you we had to hurry, and see ahead – Duke Bernardus Bridge. This leads to People's Hill and the market.'

He was right. Ahead of them was a sturdy, wide bridge with high parapets, its flagstones worn smooth by a thousand passing feet. As she crossed it, she looked over the edge, under them was a long level road running along the low part of ground where the two hills joined. She saw straight away that this was where most of the wagons and mounted traffic passed, avoiding the narrow streets and hills. Fronting this street were large buildings with broad double doors. Dylan noticed where she was looking.

'Warehouses,' he said. 'The traders use the wide roads at the base of each hill, or the one that encircles the city. They store their goods here and then just have to transport them up People's Street ahead.'

She looked ahead past an imposing statue of (presumably) Duke Bernardus and saw that there were wide spaces either side of the bridge for horses and wagons to climb up from the road beneath. The thoroughfare before her was much, much wider than anywhere else she had seen and the houses were built of beams and brick, rather than wattle and daub. They, too, were large with many glass windows. Cheris whistled softly.

'Such fine houses! Is this where the rich live?'

'No, that is further on. These are mainly trading guild buildings, not private dwellings; you would see many similar buildings on Artisans' Hill. Keep walking.'

She did as she was told, noticing that the street was so broad that either side of it was paved with large flagstones for those who wanted to avoid the jarring cobbles or the risk of being trampled to death by panicking livestock. The sewage trenches here were pretty spotless; she guessed they were cleaned every night. Then, almost without realising it, they were there.

And she saw how unprepared she was.

The market was rectangular in shape, its widest point being at least half a mile long. At its further end she could see Loubian Hill climbing above the market rooftops, its white palaces close enough now that she could see their fine arched lancet windows. Ahead and to the right the golden bell tower of the cathedral dominated. But it was what lay directly ahead that focused her concentration. She had expected a crowd something like the grand congregation in the College of the Magisters when the main hall was full for a meeting or religious service but this was something else altogether. There was not a square foot in the market that seemed unoccupied as people bustled about their business apparently oblivious to their neighbours and surroundings. And the lack of order! She had never seen such jostling, barging and pushing as all present jockeyed for position, desperate to pore over each vendor's wares. Most there were dressed as simply as she was – small-scale buyers looking for a slab of cheese or loaf of bread – but intermingled with them were others of a grander kind. One lady garbed in a rich purple velvet dress trimmed with silver was being escorted by an armed guard and a couple of well-dressed servants. There were men dressed just as Dylan was, in surcoats and mail, and others in brightly coloured tunics and breeches. Some even wore extravagant hats, great wide-brimmed floppy caps adorned with feathers.

And from these people rose such a tumult that she was amazed any of them could understand each other, whether they were grumbling, gossiping, haggling, swearing, or singing... Amid the uproar she caught only small snatches, alternately of negotiation – 'I'll go no lower than seven ducats ... Six it is then,' – confrontation – 'I bought this jerkin here last week and the lace holes have perished already' – and flattery – 'Madam, it is almost as though this hat was made specifically for your shapely little head.'

The whole scene was chaos. Beautiful, captivating chaos. Cheris did not know where to begin.

Dylan noticed her consternation with a certain wry amusement.

'Come on,' he said, 'just follow me.'

She walked behind him slowly; they appeared to be in that part of the market that sold food. There were half a dozen cheese vendors; others selling bread and fruit, great sides of meat, butchered that morning, and already attracting the large, dozy, heavy flies that had not yet died off in the autumn chill. To her surprise, after the initial shock she found herself adjusting to her surroundings. She stopped at a pie vendor's to gaze at the rich pastries with their gigantic crusts, then at a ladies' stall that sold sticky cakes. How delicious everything looked!

'Can I tempt you with one, madam?' The vendor, a lady of middle years with a wide handsome face, was looking at her.

'Oh, thank you, no,' she said demurely and moved on.

Dylan turned to her; she knew her five minutes were probably up. 'Come on, Cheris, it is time to go...'

'Dylan! Sir Dylan! It is you, you old dog. Come and say hello.'

A man was saluting them, frantically waving his arms as he came towards them.

'Say nothing,' Dylan growled to her through gritted teeth. He then launched into a convincing fake smile.

'Sir Adnan, you are looking so well. Have you put on weight?'

'Am I fat, you mean?' He seemed a man preternaturally disposed towards jollity. He slapped his stomach. 'This is what two years of guarding merchant caravans does for you – minimal risk of violence, maximum risk of gout!' he laughed. His round face was somewhat reddish, especially his cheeks. Then he noticed her.

'Well, Dylan, you old... Come on then, introduce me.'

Dylan hesitated. 'Oh! This is ... is...'

'My name is Miriam, sir.' Cheris made a vain attempt to look coy and maidenly. 'In service to Sir Dylan and the Knights of the Thorn.'

'I am enchanted, Miriam.' said Adnan. 'But let me tell you: Dylan is a man of piety and honour and as a result earns much less than I do. If you ever feel the need to find out what really fine living is about, look no further than me. Some flowers need a lot more care and attention than others and I see a no more delicate bloom around here than your good self.' She caught the lascivious look in his eye and wondered how many hapless serving girls he had tried that line on before.

'You are too kind, sir,' she said, looking shyly at the ground. 'But, alas, you are mistaken. I am far more the salt-resistant rose, which can grow even by the sea so impervious is it to the elements than the fragile delicate flower you just alluded to.'

'Well bred for a serving girl, aren't you? Family hit on hard times, eh? Well, I would not expect Dylan to be slipping it to any old slattern, eh, Dylan, eh?' He nudged Dylan, whose smile was weakening by the minute.

'If you ever change your mind, Miriam, come to the Armourers'

Guild on Artisans' Hill; mention my name and you will have a job with half the work and twice the pay. And other benefits!' He pointed to his crotch, laughing uproariously.

'Adnan,' said Dylan, at last finding his voice. 'We really have to go; I am back on duty very shortly. I will come round and see you when I can. I am sure you still owe me an ale.'

'I owe everybody an ale!' he laughed. 'But come on round by all means; we can discuss your recent development of an incredible taste in women!'

'I will do that. Now farewell, Adnan. The Gods keep you.'

Both Dylan and Cheris turned to start back the way they came. She stiffened in shock as she felt a hand impacting firmly against her rump. 'See you both soon. Very soon!' She turned in shock, enraged.

Adnan winked at Cheris before disappearing back into the crowd.

Dylan looked sheepish. 'Sorry!' he said. 'He is more an acquaintance than a friend.'

'Just be grateful for him that I am under your protection. Otherwise, he would just be a greasy puddle on the floor.'

They headed back down People's Street, but when they got to the bridge Dylan went to its left, down on to the broad street between the hills where the warehouses were. 'Busier...' he said, 'but quicker. Keep your eye out for carts and horses.'

They hugged the side of the road, keeping to the thin shadows thrown by the warehouses. Dylan was right; they made excellent progress amid the clattering of wheels and hooves on the stone, as barrel-laden carts and barrows raced past them in both directions. Eventually, they reached the city wall and turned southward; they could see their tower not five minutes away when Cheris stopped dead.

Opposite them, by the small grassy bank that hugged the city wall, a horse had collapsed. It was still tethered to the wagon it had been pulling, which was laden, overladen even, with trunks and barrels. The horse was something of a bony old nag and did not look as if it was up to pulling such a heavy cart in the first place. And over the horse stood a man sweating profusely; he was swearing at the horse and in one hand held a cruel-looking switch that he was using to thrash what little life was left in the beast out of it. Cheris walked slowly towards him leaving Dylan standing.

'Get up, you little bastard, get up! I will sell your useless carcass to the glue man. Fuck you! Get up!' He started hitting it again.

'Can you not see that the horse is sick, man?' Cheris said calmly. If you keep hitting it, it will die, and what happens to your precious goods then?' He swung round to face her, his face a mask of anger and amazement.

'And who in the name of Keth's rancid guts are you? You think I am going to listen to some silly little serving tart? Stick to what you know – bending over for your betters...' he indicated Dylan who was walking slowly towards them. '...and leave my business to me.'

She coloured but remained calm. 'I will say it again: leave that horse alone; it needs to be freed from that wagon and then we can see if we can help it.'

He snarled at her. 'Piss off, slut!' He turned to the transfixed Dylan. 'You, man, learn to gag your little whore and teach her that her mouth has one use and one use only.' He turned back to the horse, raising his arm to strike it again. Cheris dug her nails into her palm.

'Hit that horse one more time and you will be sorry.' Her calmness was evaporating; there was steel in her eyes.

'You know what?' The man's voice was hoarse from screaming. 'I think I will stop; I would much rather use this thing on you.' He raised his arm to strike her.

'Stop!' Dylan shouted, but it was too late.

Before the man could land his blow Cheris raised her hand and said something almost under her breath. Immediately the man was thrown backwards, slamming violently against the side of his own wagon, Dylan heard his head crack against the wood. Groaning, he slumped to the ground, leaving a thin trail of blood against the wagon. Cheris stood over him, as he regarded her with horrified, uncomprehending eyes.

'All actions have consequences,' she said. 'I hope you have learned that. I will send some men to help you with the horse.' She felt Dylan bristling beside her as he took her hand roughly and pulled her away from the scene. 'For Artorus's sake, come on!' He sounded panicky.

By the grace of the Gods there appeared to be no witnesses to the incident. The buildings overlooking them were empty warehouses and the few wagons that passed took no notice of them. The sound of the wagon wheels pounding the cobbles meant that the man's shouting was heard by no one and the men driving them were seemingly intent on their own progress, giving an injured man and a lame horse barely a second glance. Once they were sheltered behind the curtain wall, Cheris spoke, her heart full of misgivings.

'You will send some men to help that poor horse, won't you? And the man for that matter.'

He put his face right next to hers. 'We were that close!' he said angrily, gesturing with his thumb and forefinger. 'We might still be in the mire; just pray that there are no witnesses and that no one believes the man's words.'

'He slipped and banged his head,' she said. 'His concussion made him see things.'

Dylan breathed. 'Maybe!' he said tersely. 'Maybe... Now let's get back.'

Dylan opened the gate, leading the way as they shot along the dark corridor and up the stairwell until finally they stood outside her door. Nobody saw them.

'Stay there while I get changed and give the dress back to you; I won't be a minute.'

She slipped into her room and shut the door. Leaning back against it, she was about to let out an enormous sigh of relief when she saw the chair by the bed. Marcus was sitting on it.

She had never seen him looking so furious, but before he could speak she raised her hand.

'Say what you will, but please let me change first. Dylan is waiting outside.'

He grunted and turned his back; she was back in her red robe faster than she thought possible. When she had finished she opened the door, handed Dylan the dress and bade him on his way.

Time to face the storm.

'I don't know where to begin with you!' His voice was angry, though controlled. But it was not that which disconcerted Cheris the most, for his words were shot through with something else. Disappointment... disappointment in her. 'Do you have any idea what trouble you could have put that man through in your stupid, selfish hot-headedness? He could end up in prison, disgraced... even disowned by his family, and, yes, you could see that he came from a good family. That is partly what made it so easy for you to make him dance to your tune. He has been brought up to always try to give a lady what she asks for.'

'It's OK; we weren't seen or caught,' she said, not entirely truthfully; she had already decided not to mention the incident with the horse.

'Well, if you weren't, it is down to the grace of the Gods and no other reason, and what about you? You could have ended up dancing on a gallows if people knew what you were; one man could not stop a lynch mob. Was all this to try to see your parents?'

'No, mentor, I just wanted to see the city as a normal person would.'

His voice was all cold fury. 'Get this into that rock between your ears.' He stood and came over to her. She backed away a little; she had upset him many times in the past but never like this. 'You will never, never be a normal person in the eyes of the people here. To them, you are a freak, a dangerous aberration; you spoke lightly about being a monster to me the other day; well, to them that is exactly what you are. You are the demon that haunts men's souls, a night horror...'

She swallowed. 'That is a bit unkind; not all...'

'Is it?' he said. 'Think about it, why are you here? Is it because you are a graceful dancer, or have a lovely singing voice, or is it because you can kill men effectively?'

Her mind flashed back to the look of horror on the man's face after he had crashed into the wagon. It had been easy, too; she barely had to concentrate to do it.

Marcus sat back down again. 'And now you have drawn that poor boy into your web; we were his first major command, you know; most of the senior knights are out in the country chasing mages. I have told you before: the knights exist to keep the people and ourselves apart, to keep the hanging crews from us and to stop us frying them in fear, or in temper. Instead, the two of you traipse off hand in hand into the city like two lovebirds going on a picnic. If this gets out...'

'I already said that no one found out.'

'That is fortunate but beside the point. He has been brought up into a world where the ladies of his class are taught to blush demurely and be meek and coy. And then this boy comes across a woman who is smart, beautiful and, for once, even better educated than he. And of course she is extremely manipulative. I should have seen the danger signs a mile off.'

'He is a grown man; perhaps the fault is partly his?'

'Oh, I do not doubt that, but he is not my responsibility – you are.'

'Are you saying that I was too forward with him?'

Marcus rolled his eyes in exasperation. 'Of course, I am saying it! This is not the island, and he is not Mikel!'

'But, mentor,' she said softly. 'I am sorry, yes, but I had no idea my behaviour was really that untoward.'

'Untoward!' he snorted. 'If he gets out of this in one piece, you owe him the biggest of apologies. Perhaps I should have listened to the others about you.'

Cheris screwed up her forehead. 'What do you mean?'

'When I told the Grand Magister I was taking you with me, he and some of the other senior council mages tried to talk me out of it. 'It is folly,' they said. 'She is too young and has no idea of life in the outside world. Her head will be easily turned; you may not think her flighty but the mainland changes people. It would be like finally giving a child the key to a sweet shop that he or she has spent years looking longingly through the windows of.'

She stared miserably at her feet. 'I am sorry I have let you down.'

'I am glad you can see it. Do you know what the punishment is for breaking the rules here?'

'No, mentor.'

'You would be put on the next ship back to the island under guard and upon arrival you would serve a time in solitary confinement as determined by the Grand Magister. You should never be allowed to leave the island for the rest of your life.'

She felt her cheeks burning and her eyes watering. She respected Marcus more than any other person and the shame she felt in letting him down so badly was finally beginning to register with her. When she spoke her voice was hoarse. 'Is that what you intend to do to me?'

'Believe me,' – his voice softened a little on seeing her tears – 'I was sorely tempted, but, if I do that, your good friend the knight will be implicated in your disgrace. It is possible that a knight with such poor judgement deserves it… But then I thought better of it. If people never make mistakes, how will they ever learn, and that applies to both of you.'

She looked at him, brushing tears from her reddening eyes. 'What will you do then?'

'The plan is unchanged, but you owe me, my girl… You owe me a lot!'

'Thank you, mentor. I will learn from this, I promise.'

'I know,' he said gently. 'Tell me: was your transgression worth it?'

'Yes, I suppose so. We went to the market – it was like nothing I have ever seen.'

'You went to the most populous place in the city? Even I am forced to admire your boldness. Now come.' He lifted a cloth covered object off the bed and pulled the cloth away to reveal a platter with bread, cheese and apples. She noticed a goblet on the dresser. 'Your food – it is why I came here in the first place.'

She thanked him. 'What is happening on the morrow?'

'We leave early,' he said. 'Be ready at first light. One thing, though,' – he looked at her guardedly – 'I did speak to the knight in charge here; I told him that you and Sir Dylan had become … close.'

'And?'

'The result is, he will no longer be travelling with us; he will be replaced by an older, hopefully uglier, knight. The commander assured me there was no disgrace in this; it would be put down to an administrative error; he will be sent into the country to investigate reports of newly discovered mages and will be assigned to another mage ship in the near future.'

She nodded, a little downcast at this news. 'I see.'

Marcus got up. 'I will leave you to your thoughts for now,' he said. 'Enjoy your food then rest awhile. If you wish, we can speak later.' He walked out, shutting the door.

She did eat, and greedily. The wine made her feel heady. In her room was a copy of the Book of Artorus and the Divine Pantheon, the standard book of prayer issued by the church. She hadn't read it in years but found herself browsing its thin, leafy pages. She read some passages about the danger of excessive pride and the cautionary tale of the man with the great mansion house by the sea; how he used to invite people around to show off the grandeur of the mansion but then was never content with it, believing that it could be even better. So he added another wing, and another, and another. In the end it grew so large the cliff could not support it and it collapsed into the sea, leaving him with nothing. She shut the book.

She undressed and lay on the bed in her thin white shift, constantly replaying the day's events over and over in her mind. She thought of Uba, the god of fools, and how he now had one extra convert to his cause.

Chief among her thoughts was the ease with which she had hurt that man. He was horrible, yes, but his livelihood was stuck on that road – if he couldn't shift his wagon, she was sure there were plenty of cut-throats who would help themselves, and then there was the other thing. The disturbing thing, the feeling inside her when she looked at his face. She had enjoyed seeing his fear. The separation of mages from the people was something that had always vexed her – could they not learn from each other? – but now, for the first time, she was having doubts. Did merely having this power make her the monster of which Marcus had spoken? It was not her fault that she possessed these abilities, but within an hour of arriving in the city she had used them ... and badly. No wonder they killed mages here and elsewhere.

She sighed and thought of Dylan. Please don't let him be in trouble, she thought.

She felt tired. The wine did its soporific work and she drifted unawares into sleep.

Suddenly she snapped to. There was a tap on her door. It was dark outside; she had slept longer than she had intended to. Assuming it was Marcus, she went and opened it.

It was Dylan, back in uniform, carrying a bundle. She gestured him in, forgetting she was only partially dressed. In the dark, though, he didn't seem to notice.

'I am so, so sorry,' she whispered.

'It is all right.' He smiled wanly. 'Nobody noticed us; everyone had thought I had gone to the market in my off-duty time anyway. Only they thought I had gone alone, an assumption I did not challenge.'

'What about the man? And the horse?'

'Oh,' he said, 'I mentioned I had seen a man and a horse injured when I got back and our farrier and a couple of knights went to have a look. The man was dazed; he said he remembered shouting at some woman and that he must have tripped and fell. He wasn't badly injured; he was patched up and the wagon righted.'

'And the horse?'

'I am sorry. It was too far gone; there was nothing anyone could do. We lent the man a horse to take his goods back to his warehouse.'

She sighed. 'Poor horse. Have you heard about tomorrow?'

'The change of command? Of course I have. It was inevitable, I suppose; knights should not get too friendly with mages. You are a dangerous lot, you know.'

'I am sorry,' she said again. 'I have made so much trouble for you.'

'Forget it!' He smiled. 'I fully intend to go and see Sir Adnan and make him insanely jealous.'

'Yes, tell him that the lady Miriam is utterly, utterly devoted to you and that her heart belongs to no other. Tell him she realises her status is too low for you to wed so she intends to keep you by using every wile known to women in the bedroom. Tell him she has studied the Tarindian ways of lovemaking and practises all of them on you, and, finally, tell him she would rather lay with a suckling pig than a red-faced man with gout.'

They both giggled. She was close to him, and he could feel her breath on his face; it smelled sweet, like a breeze from a meadow full of spring flowers. 'What is that?' she asked, pointing to the bundle.

'Oh yes.' He opened it – inside was the dress she had worn earlier. 'She is quite agreeable to parting with it.'

'Wonderful!' said Cheris excitedly. She took a purse off the dresser and handed him a crown. 'I am ever deeper in your debt.'

'It is costing you a lot more than it is worth.' 'No matter! It is worth it to me.' 'I had best be on my way.' He turned to go.

'Oh Dylan, I am so sorry for today. Never listen to such a stupid girl again.'

'Life is a learning process, and the last thing you are is stupid.'

She leaned forward, kissing him lightly on the cheek. 'Thank you, my friend.'

'Goodnight, my Lady. I hope and trust in the Gods that we shall meet again.'

'Goodnight, Sir Dylan. I hope that day will come soon.'

He nodded to her, his cheek warm with her kiss, and then he was gone.

She looked after him, thinking hard, then at the dress he had given her. She lifted the lid of her trunk and folded it gently inside. Perhaps it had all been worth it after all.

BOOK ONE: AUTUMN

9

It was a fine clear night and a full moon sat heavily in the sky under its carpet of stars. Now and then a thin wisp of cloud would float tentatively in front of it, fragile and ephemeral, a delicate strand of gossamer, until it had traversed its ghostly face and disappeared into nothingness. The air was crisp, brittle. As she breathed, she exhaled gouts of smoky-white air into the velvet blackness. Where was she?

She looked about her. She stood on a narrow parapet atop a great tower, an impossibly tall tower, and by the light of the moon she could see that it was sheathed in gold. It was the bell tower of the cathedral. Looking down confirmed this for her. Under her feet was the cathedral's sloping roof framed within its own spires and surrounding it the cathedral square, its colossal flagstones hardly visible in the cloaking darkness such was her height above the ground.

She kept looking down without ever wondering how she had ended up here in the first place. It would be so easy, so, so easy, just to throw out her arms and then, while still cruciform, just to lean gently forward, little by little, inch by inch, until her momentum would be unstoppable and she would be ... falling.

Falling, so she was, she was falling, arms outstretched, wind coursing through her uncombed hair, buffeting her face and ears, as, eyes open, she beheld the ground, its enormous rectangular flagstones rushing towards her. She idly and quite dispassionately wondered which one she would hit. It would be any second now ... any ... second.

But no, she hadn't hit the ground; rather, she was moving upwards, the moon getting closer, the roofs of the houses getting smaller and smaller. She was flying.

Where was she now? The momentum had stopped. She was still, alone in a pool of night in which nothing, not even silhouettes or shadows, could be seen. All there was was the sound of water, a steady drip-drip-drip into a large body of water close by. It was probably a lake. There was a cavernous echo to the sound – was she in a cave? She felt cold; there was a glacial bone-deep chill inside her. She felt like she wanted to move her heavy, stiff limbs, but she just couldn't, just couldn't. Was she paralysed? It certainly felt like it. And then she understood why all was darkness about her; it was that her eyes were shut firmly. She couldn't open them either; her eyelids felt like two great, lead shutters, impossibly heavy, like the rest of her body. She felt frustration building inside her, real frustration. Whenever this sort of thing happened to her as a child, she would get redder and redder in the face until at last she emitted something that sounded like a great sigh or an angry sob without it being either. She was going to do it now, she could tell. With an effort of will she thought barely possible, her mouth opened; her frustration was building from her stomach, up her throat and into her mouth. And then she ... roared. Not a sigh, nor a sob, or even a howl, but a full-throated animalistic roar powerful enough to send stones falling from the cave roof. The roar of some ... monster.

Ceriana sat bolt upright in bed, dripping in sweat, mouth open but unable to scream. Tears welled up in her fear-haunted eyes.

The door opened and in walked Doren. Sunlight filtered through the great windows of Loubian Hall, where she had the second bedroom.

'Morning, my Lady, no time for nightmares now; I will run a nice bath and myself and the other ladies can get you ready. You will never look more beautiful than you will today. It will be a wedding to remember.'

Ceriana stared uncomprehendingly for a moment then slumped back on to the bed. Wedding. The top of the bell tower had never seemed more appealing.

It was a clear, bright day with the merest hint of autumnal chill in the breeze sweeping the cathedral square. Noon had passed and a crowd had gathered behind a line of blue-liveried city guardsmen. As it was not a full state occasion many people were still working hard in the market, at the seafront, or in the halls of the artisans, but there were still enough of the idle and curious to swell the crowd to a respectable size. Quite a few street vendors had moved from their usual pitches to try their luck here – the people selling scarves or leather goods doing less well than the food vendors roasting nuts or strips of meat and fat over braziers, or doling out jugs of mead or ale to those with a thirst. Many had been there quite a few hours and quite a party atmosphere was developing.

'Did you see her go in?' a matronly lady in a white bonnet said to a friend whose silver hair was covered by a black shawl. 'I reckon it was samite, white samite studded with jewels. I heard others say it was silk but, well, I guess they never saw samite before.'

'Put a ducat on it,' replied her older companion. 'That tall fella over there, he's taking bets on it, you know.'

'I'll put one on for both of us, and I'll bring you back a jug of ale, too.'

'Half a jug! You know how my bladder plays up.'

'Drink it all, then you can use the jug! I'll be back in a minute.'

After she returned with the ale her companion took a deep draught and said. 'She is a tiny little thing, isn't she? You would think with all that money she would be as fat as the barman in the old Crab Pot. If I was as rich as that, I would eat and eat and eat.'

'Well, one thing the likes of us can do is choose who we marry, though even then it is easy to make a mistake. That poor lass gets married off to Elissa knows who and has to get carted off to the middle of nowhere as well! I am amazed her father let it happen.'

'Rumour is that he didn't,' said a tall thin man in a stained yellow jerkin standing next to them. 'As I heard it, he didn't want her married at all, but the Grand Duke overruled him.'

'And how would you know that?' said the matron scornfully.

'I has a cousin that ostlers in Edgecliff; he heard the servants talking. They say she is a sad lonely little thing but the apple of her dad's eye. It's not good when you think of it, not good at all – the two most powerful men in the country falling out like that.' He smiled, expelling ale breath over a maw of cracked and discoloured teeth.

'You best be careful what you say, sir, with all these guards about.' said the old lady. 'I remember when one of her sisters married here, someone said something untoward and one of the guards dragged him out and put him in the stocks. He was there till next day – ever so sorry for himself he was.'

'Especially when you emptied that bowl of rancid cabbage over him,' the matron laughed.

'Well, he insulted nobility; I have no truck with people like that.'

'And you never miss one of these occasions either.'

'Not in fifty years; I have seen them all, every one.'

Suddenly the chimes started. In the bell tower an army of priests were straining on the ropes letting out a paean to the happy couple. A spontaneous cheer came from the assembled throng who pushed against the restraining guards eager to catch sight of the great doors being opened.

And suddenly they were, their great hinges groaning as the doors slowly pulled apart like the mouth of a great whale devouring a shoal of fish. As the crowd watched open-mouthed, out they came, the great and good of Tanaren society. When the familiar figure of Nicholas Hartfield emerged there was a great cheer; when it was the Grand Duke's turn it was a little more muted – seemingly the general populace were as ambivalent about him as the Duke of Edgecliff himself. Then, finally, out came the bride and groom. The matronly lady nudged her friend knowingly. 'Samite.'

Lady Ceriana Osperitsan-Hartfield looked positively radiant. Her pure white samite dress bedecked with red and blue gemstones and thin golden tiara nestling on her rich brown hair sparkled in the sunlight, drawing gasps from her appreciative audience. Her hair, as befitting a woman on her wedding day, was gathered up into a white hennin trailing a sheer veil over her otherwise exposed milk-white neck. Her dress had a long train flowing behind her, as she descended the cathedral steps and made for the open gilded carriage that would convey her to the ducal barge that nestling on the quayside at the bottom of Loubian Hill. There was confetti and shouting, applause and many expressions of good health and happiness from the crowd. Ceriana walked towards them to wave briefly, an action that elicited the biggest cheer of all. The groom, clad mainly in white with his ceremonial sword in its gold-encrusted scabbard, was barely noticed; he was as good as a foreigner to most of the crowd, who had little knowledge of the lands from which he came.

Once she was seated in the carriage, Ceriana acknowledged the crowd once more, waving enthusiastically to them, and with that they were off. Knights of the Silver Lance provided the escort and her parents, the Grand Duke and other dignitaries followed in slightly more modest carriages behind them. It was a breathtaking spectacle in the early-afternoon sun, one not even remotely spoiled by the barely noticed sight of an elderly lady relieving herself into a jug as they all thundered past her.

The sun was almost down by the time they arrived at Erskon House. Berek was waiting at the jetty ready to escort them from the river to the evening feast, along with an honour guard of twenty handpicked Hartfield men resplendent in the livery of the Duke. For Ceriana, the day had passed in something of a whirl; she had had little time to think or catch her breath, which in all fairness was probably the way she wanted it. Everything to her surprise had gone exactly to plan, even she had to admit that the dressmakers and fitters had done a very good job on her and for the first time in her life she felt she could look in the mirror and not criticise. Even her freckles seemed unimportant such was the loveliness of the dress, its jewelled inlays and the fancy gems of the necklace and tiara offsetting the shimmering white cloth perfectly. The ceremony had gone without a hitch; the rehearsal had been invaluable on that score and, to her ears, the choir had never sounded better. Her groom had been courteous if distant and her parents and sisters had spent much of the time grinning happily from ear to ear. The only slightly sour note was that her brother, who was almost as protective as her father towards her, was not able to be there, the Grand Duke having dispatched him and a contingent of Silver Lances to the war in the east. The Grand Duke himself was with them on the barge dressed resplendently in a trimmed red velvet jacket and black breeches and boots of the supplest leather. He was only a few years older than Ceriana, handsome in a dark saturnine way, with a thin waxed moustache and a sliver of a beard. She wondered if the rumours were true, of his excessive womanising and overly close relationships with the Barons Fillebrand and Richney. He had actually announced earlier that day that he was making Fillebrand a duke, a title held by only five other people and the first to be raised to such a status since the founding of the country; it was a move with huge constitutional implications for the country and certain to raise ire in many quarters, but as the wedding was the only thing that mattered at that moment it was all but forgotten. The arguments could be left for another time.

As for Ceriana and Leontius, she had hardly said a word to him in her entire life but was informed earlier that he would be sitting next to her at the top table. She was hardly relishing the prospect.

Erskon House was every inch the traditional baronial country estate, a long rectangular two-storey affair, its wattle and daub newly whitewashed. Several wings led off the main body of the building, newer additions to the original construct; one held the servants' quarters, another the new kitchens, and there was an entire wing built specifically to accommodate the Grand Duke, a frequent visitor, though not as frequent as his father once was. It was originally a hunting lodge and was indeed still used for that purpose, as could be evidenced from the various sets of crossed antlers and boar heads and tusks that adorned the walls of the great dining hall. As at Edgecliff, the head table was raised on a dais with the guest tables at right angles to it. As the Grand Duke took his seat at the head of the table, above him and to his right was a gallery that housed the musicians who had already been playing for some time and were already well into the swing of the evening celebrations. As everyone took their seats, the mead and wine started flowing immediately, served up as it was by a silent army of servants gliding from table to table working so efficiently they were barely noticed by the revellers.

Ceriana sat down and glanced around, taking in the seating order. To her left was her husband, then a certain Baron Einar who seemed to be a close associate of his, and then her two sisters. On her right was the Grand Duke, her father, mother, and then Lady Catherine, who had already taken up her new role as her mother's companion. She felt a little isolated sitting as she was between two men she barely knew, but before any conversation could start out came the food.

And what a feast it was. There was fish – salmon, trout and herring from the sea – all flavoured with various fruits – apples, pears and woodland berries. There was pork, roasted, with quince and chestnuts. There was swan and other smaller game birds, pies filled with eggs, vegetables and jellied meats, loaves upon loaves of luxury white bread. Side dishes of cabbage, garlic, onion and frumenty, cheeses both soft and hard, there was duck, goose and stork flavoured with pepper, mace and galangal, and, of course, a suckling pig served for the delectation of the Grand Duke alone. All this was washed down with wine imported at great expense as well as mead, although Ceriana stuck with the sweetened almond milk that she had always preferred. Once the main meal had been devoured, out came the desserts – crepes, fritters, sweet custards, pastries and tarts flavoured with rose petals. It was a meal remembered by everyone for months, nay years, afterwards.

Ceriana, however, ate like a bird and realised she would have to force herself a little so nervous was she. As she helped herself to a thimbleful of salmon, the Grand Duke turned to speak to her. She tried not to blench.

'This is quite the feast, is it not? I fear it will outdo even the best efforts of my own kitchen in the city.' He had an easy charm about him but at this stage of the day, like most of the men here present, he was well into his cups.

'Yes, my Lord, Father wanted to make it special what with losing his daughter and all that.'

'Well, he may not lose her for ever,' the Duke replied cryptically, lowering his voice so her husband could not hear him. He, however, was oblivious to such matters, being deep in conversation with Einar.

'Whatever do you mean?' She forgot to address him formally such was her surprise.

'Well, as you probably know, I – as Grand Duke – am the secular head of the church in Tanaren. This means that in some rare cases I can grant divorce petitions, although it is a power hardly ever used; my father never needed it and never wanted to as it would mean crossing swords with the Grand Lector. I, however, am quite happy to use it, or any other of my powers, should circumstances render them appropriate.' He leaned towards her a little more so that their faces were but inches apart. 'You,

Lady Ceriana, are still a sought-after woman. I married you to Wulfthram because at this moment it is the right thing to do politically. Politics and allegiances can change swiftly, however.'

'I see. I had heard, my Lord, that I was marrying because you want to temper the rebellious spirit of the northern Barons.'

'Not all of them are rebellious, no. Most are loyal, just like your husband. My spies, however, tell me that some sort of rebellion is brewing up there and I am hoping that your marriage to the North's most powerful man will strangle any such sentiments at birth. I really do not want to send troops up there permanently. Anyway, I am digressing. What I meant to say is that Duke Nicholas's youngest daughter is still a target for marriage for many of our noblemen.'

She exclaimed incredulously, forgetting for a second to keep her voice quiet. 'But I cannot be expected to marry them all!' She put her hand over her mouth and continued to speak a little more quietly. 'You would have me divorce then? Wouldn't the same barons whose behaviour you seek to curb be slighted by this?'

'In a few years there will be alternatives; Marschall's and Duneck's daughters will be of age then. My plan is for you to divorce him and for Wulfthram to marry one of those girls instead.'

'Do you have someone lined up for me then?'

'Not directly, it will depend on who is most favoured at the time. I have not even ruled out taking you for myself.'

She coloured and hurriedly drank some almond milk, turning her top lip white.

'Links between my house and that of the Hartfields have always been strong,' he continued. 'But there has been no intermarriage between us for a few generations. It would be a logical step to bolster our alliance in such a way.'

'But what if I have children by him?'

'I hope you do.' He smiled. 'The barons of the north will have a blood connection to us; it should ensure their loyalty without there being too close a rival for my position. No one down here would accept a half-northern child as Grand Duke.'

It all sounded plausible to Ceriana, but surely so many people would be annoyed by such a move? She resolved to ask her father about this sometime. 'And what of my sisters?' she asked. 'Will you do the same to them?'

'No, I only have this right over marriages sanctioned by me and under my rule. It is not something I intend to do every five minutes. Oh and it goes without saying...' he nodded his head, indicating Wulfthram, '...that you mention this conversation to no one else.'

'You are testing me, are you not?' she answered coquettishly. 'If I do say something, I will be shown to lack character and loyalty and certainly not deserving of your hand in the future. Yet I will also be expected to keep a secret from a man with whom I will be spending most of my days and to whom I now owe a bond of loyalty, too. You are making my position invidious.'

He smiled knowingly at her. 'Yes, you could say that.'

She spoke firmly. 'You have sworn me to discretion and so that is something I will honour. I would rather not discuss my divorce on the day of my marriage, however; Elissa's breath, I have not even had my wedding night yet!' Did her father know of this? Her mother? No, her mother would not know, but her father? Could he keep something like this from her? Her head was swimming.

'Good,' Leontius replied. 'I will speak no more of it. You have comported yourself most admirably today; I will be keeping an eye on you.' With that, he feigned a slight bow to her and turned to speak to her father.

She was hoping to excuse herself, saying she needed the latrines, whereas in truth she just needed a walk to clear her head, when to her surprise her husband turned to her, his conversation with Einar presumably at an end.

'Well, my Lady.' He spoke curtly but politely. 'I suppose it is time we conversed on matters other than the exchanging of rings.' She could tell he had been drinking a lot, too, but he seemed able to handle it much better than the Grand Duke.

'I suppose you are right,' she replied. Why did he make her so nervous? She found him more intimidating than the Grand Duke. 'Is there some question you wish to ask of me?'

'How about this one?' he said. 'You are obviously intelligent and far better connected than I. I am also old enough to be your father. Is there anything in this marriage to make you happy?'

She was thrown by this. Did he feel sorry for her? She swallowed, suddenly uncertain. 'My family has always done its duty, but I ... I...'

His smile was sardonic. 'Yes?'

'Well, I get the impression that you are faintly embarrassed by the whole situation. I am not sure, though, whether your embarrassment is caused by being forced to marry a spoiled, privileged child from the south or by being dragged into the Grand Duke's politicking and co-opted into the old ruling class of this country.' She hadn't really meant to say so much; her tongue was running off with her again.

He looked at her. Some of her hair had come loose under her tiara and there was a stubborn defensive look in her eyes. His response was measured: 'There is a little truth in both those statements; maybe more than a little truth. The ramifications of this marriage will become more apparent to you once you arrive in Osperitsan. You will be made most welcome by the way and treated with the respect your status accords. We may not have as many luxuries as you have been used to and you may grow weary of the taste of fish – Osperitsan being an island after all – but I fully intend to give you as good a life as possible. There will be a welcome reception for you on arrival. It will be attended by all the barons that matter – so you can meet them; and they you of course.'

'Will the rebellious ones be there?' Another statement she regretted and she hadn't even been drinking. She determined to remain silent after his reply.

He stroked his chin thoughtfully. 'Everyone down here has a rather simplistic view of us; we all have to be for or against, black or white, night or day. In a way I wish it was like that; it would be easier, then, to round up the troublemakers and this marriage would be as unnecessary as the Grand Duke's spies.'

'You are right, of course; I cannot come to judgement until I see your lands for myself. I have spoken quite ill-advisedly and I apologise for that. People do have a tendency to jump to conclusions based on the scantest of evidence. Down here we do tend to see you as ... well, as a little barbarous and unrefined.'

Einar caught her words over the din of the music and laughed uproariously. 'Well, Wulfthram, you have wasted no time in upsetting your new wife. It is daily baths for you from now on!'

Ceriana giggled. 'Scattered with rose petals, of course.'

Wulfthram gave a slight smile. 'I do not bathe any other way.'

As the night went on, she talked to many other people. Einar was a giant of a man with an infectious laugh, to whom she warmed immediately; she spoke briefly with Barons Duneck and Richney, who both wished her well. She noticed something in Richney's eyes as he spoke to her. It was as though he knew every word of her conversation with the Grand Duke earlier. Finally, as things were winding down, she spoke to her father.

'I think I will retire now, Father; it has been a very long day.'

'Yes, my dear, and I believe your husband wishes to start off early tomorrow.'

'I will miss you, Father. I fear I might get quite lonely.'

'I will miss you, too, little one. It seems like only a few years ago you were a babe in arms and I was presenting you to the staff at Edgecliff. You were the only child that never cried; you loved being held and shown the outside world, the sea and the cliffs and the ships bobbing in the harbour. Wulfthram is a good man, if a little dour; we have talked much over the last few days and I know he will do well for you. Settle in over the winter and hopefully I will be up to see you in the spring.'

She wanted to ask him if he knew of the Grand Duke's plans but her head felt too heavy. Instead, she kissed her father goodbye and retired to her room, completely failing to notice the lecherous roaring of the crowd of drunken men behind her as they saw her go.

Doren was waiting for her, sitting in a chair by the dark wooden bed.

'Right, my Lady, allow me to prepare you for your new husband. If you need the chamber pot, use it now so that I can wash you down there; men can be quite particular about such things...' Her words floated over Ceriana's head.

So that was how Wulfthram found her some time later, laying on the bed in a thin shift, hair beautifully combed spread out on the sheet underneath her, a light citrus perfume dabbed behind each ear, between her breasts and legs, make-up on her eyes and cheeks and ... snoring like a drain. He laughed silently to himself; perhaps she was going to be more interesting than he had thought...

BOOK ONE: AUTUMN

10

'Father!' No reply.

'Father!' Still nothing.

'Father, A heron is eating all the fish!'

It was true, on the bank of the river a stake had been driven into the ground; a rope of thick twine connected it to a large wicker fish trap, weighted at the bottom, whose open end protruded above the water. Hovering intently over this trap was an old silver-grey heron that was eating his fill from its contents. The bird was not so engrossed, however, as not to notice the stone hurtling towards it. However, he was an experienced hand at this game – before the stone had found its mark he was away, propelling himself upwards with slow powerful wing beats, his belly sated till the next morning.

The hurler of the stone ran towards the trap, passing two small urchins, neither of them more than four years old, sitting on the bank pointing their fingers at the heron. Stepping into the water, he lifted the trap. There were still fish in there but in a greatly reduced number, though enough for a meal for three or four. He groaned, dropped the trap and walked towards the children.

He was quite a young man but in that short lifetime exposure to sun and wind had left his skin brown and ruddy; his hair was jet black, short and plastered to his head. He wore breeches but no shirt, and on both pectorals there appeared to be deliberate scarring in a pattern of a coiled rope reaching up to the base of his neck. His eyes, of a gentle brown, regarded the children fondly.

'We still have enough to eat tonight and there are other traps for tomorrow. Come, it is time to return home.'

He gently picked up the smallest child, a little girl, and strode off; the boy, a year or so older, scampered after him. There was another stake and rope here, but this time it was attached to a small circular flat-bottomed boat. The man deposited the girl inside then held it steady so the boy could clamber in. He then returned to the trap, emptied out the fish, swiftly dispatched them, impaled them on a sturdy-looking skewer and returned to his boat, leaving the trap in the river .He climbed in, freed the rope from its mooring and pushed off from the bank using a broad-bladed paddle. He began to propel the boat forward using broad sweeps of his muscular forearms. The round boat started to glide forward, the paddles' blade breaking the glassy, peat black surface of the water.

If a great seabird had the mind to fly northward, starting at the infinite broad sweep of the great Mothravian Delta and ending at the southern part of the Land of the Seven Rivers where Baron Esric Calvannen was fighting nobly for the cause of the Grand Duke of Tanaren he would have traversed a vast, broken land of water and marsh scattered with occasional eyots of land, known simply as the Endless Marshes. This is where the Seven Rivers, getting ever more sluggish, stumbled into each other like drunks in a crowded room. They ceased to have either direction or definition in this land, diverting themselves into ponds or lakes or rolling incoherently between patches of land dotted with trees. Sometimes, they would come to their senses again and resemble a river once more, their purpose regained, heading determinedly towards the sea, but this impetus never lasted long. Sooner or later the momentum would dissipate, the river would split into dozens of streams, which in turn would sputter into deep lakes, or broaden into shallow treacherous marsh choked with weed and lily pads. Men of more civilised lands rarely, if ever, ventured here, a land of mosquitoes and quagmires and other beasts the nature of which would only be discussed by hushed tavern gossips well into their drink.

Yet people did exist there. In tiny numbers, certainly, but the Marsh Men were there practising their own culture and traditions, only venturing up the Seven Rivers to trading posts where some of the more exotic plants and animals could be bartered for iron or leather or even livestock. All the marsh villages kept a small herd of goats on the little scrap of dry land they were built on – goats, after all, could eat anything – and their milk supplemented a diet that consisted mainly of fish, birds and their eggs, and the edible marsh plants, when they could be found. To live in the marsh was to experience warm-to-hot summers punctuated by frequent thunderstorms, and winters that varied from mild to freezing, when whole lakes would ice over and snow would cover this broad flat land in a blanket of silence. Silence defined this country in any season, though; often little could be heard above the sounds of gentle winds sighing through the reed beds, or the slow metronomic wing beats of skeins of geese flying overhead, or the gentle 'plunk' of predatory fish breaking the water's surface in pursuit of low-flying insects. It was a timeless land, savage yet beautiful.

At length, they returned to their village. Here, the black river broadened into a small lake and at its centre was a green island bordered by reeds. Surrounding the island were half a dozen one-room thatched shacks built on stilts, straddling the land and water. On the edge of the lake, where the bank was fringed with trees, were a few dozen more, also mainly built over the water. Standing slightly apart from these and completely over the lake itself was a much larger structure. It had no walls and was thatched with rushes; and from each of the roof's support posts hung a grisly display of skulls – gleaming white and fleshless and grinning impassively over the brooding stillness. This was the great house that could hold upwards of fifty people, where the elders and other inhabitants of the village would meet to discuss matters of import.

The man stopped his little boat at the island, hauled it ashore and helped the children get out. They followed him up the bank and on to a narrow wooden walkway leading to one of the houses. The side of the house facing the island had no wall; a rush screen partly covering the roof could be lowered in bad weather and a wicker screen, normally used as a fence for the goat pen, could be leaned against it in freezing weather and insulated with squares of turf cut from the bank. Now, however, neither was needed. The island itself was low and flat, with its grass cropped close by the small herd of goats that wandered round untethered by day, though they would be penned in at night. Thin columns of smoke drifted up from some of the houses and the smell of cooking fish was all-pervading.

He stepped into his shack. A large hammock was strung in the corner next to a couple of rush-covered cots. A pot was suspended from a roof beam above a raised fire pit which sat under a central chimney that was nothing more than a small hole in the thatch above. A couple of wooden spears and a simple bow leaned against another wall and from the ceiling hung some thin lines of gut from which were threaded various bone implements, hooks, needles, arrowheads and the like. Some wooden bowls and small bone knives lay by the fireplace. Apart from all that, the shack was bare. Well, not completely, a woman was there. She was short and slim with long jet-black hair and skin that was paler than the man's, though it, too, was weathered. She wore nothing except a woven skirt dyed in blue and slippers made out of some soft leather. Like the man she was bare-chested. On seeing her, the children yelped excitedly.

'Mama, we saw a heron; it started eating all the fish until Papa chased it away!'

'We still have enough.' he said, handing her the skewer.

'You will need to go out again tomorrow,' she said, taking it from him. 'Winter is coming; we need to prepare. And Dumnekavax has called a council for this evening. Hunters have returned with news; I don't know what exactly but it didn't sound good. It was even suggested that he may call on the spirit world to guide him.'

'Truly?' the man replied. 'I wonder if I will be called upon? If the elder needs me, I will ask my brother to check the fish traps tomorrow.'

She frowned and admonished him. 'Cyganexatavan, my husband, why would you be called upon? You are no longer a callow boy eager to prove himself. You have children now. Do not rush foolishly into danger when there are younger, eager warriors with no responsibilities who would happily do so in your stead.'

He nodded. 'Of course, you are right, Vaneshanda; my blood no longer has the heat of youth anyway. I will be content to listen and defend our home if necessary.'

She looked at him as if she didn't quite believe him. 'Honour that promise. Come, help me with this fish; then you can eat it with the stew before you have to go.'

'As you wish. The children enjoyed themselves with me today. The boy was eager and quick to learn. It will not be long before his naming ceremony.'

'By the spirits, you do not know!' She looked distraught. 'Poor Shettevellanda's youngest boy, he was found dead today!'

Cyganexatavan looked up. 'He has died? When did this happen?'

'Shortly after you left, he was found still in his cot; his spirit must have left quietly in the night. She has three other boys but is obviously grieving. All of the women have taken turns to sit with her, including myself, but it is still a sad time for her.'

'I will go see Fasneterax, her husband. If I am able to check my fish traps tomorrow, then I shall do his also; he should remain with her for a while.'

'I believe he has had many offers of this kind already,' she said. 'But it is right that you speak with him.'

'Perhaps this is a part of the bad news of which you speak. Anyway let us eat and by the morrow we should all know a lot more.'

When Cyganexatavan took to the water again the sun was sitting close to the western horizon, its dying rays casting a violent-orange flare across the lake. Over at the great house the rush torches had been lit, the summoning horn being sounded not five minutes earlier. Shadowy figures could be seen moving around on its floor and more and more people could be seen arriving. Round boats, scuttling like giant water beetles, dotted the lake's surface as they all converged at the same destination. There was a long, narrow jetty outside the house where the boats were secured. Once they were tied up, their passengers could either haul themselves up on to the floor of the house directly or use one of the several short ladders provided for the same purpose. Obviously, the younger element in the gathering made a point of never using the ladders.

Cyganexatavan was one of the last to arrive. The fish stew had been delicious and he had made sure he had as much of it as his stomach could handle. After securing his boat he climbed up to the great house, making sure that he took the ladder. It was a male-only affair; people were circulating, talking to each other, before the Elder formally called the council together. As Cyganexatavan got his bearings, a man, similar in size and appearance to himself but with a withered leg, hailed him, 'Cygan, my little brother, I wasn't sure you made it back in time.' He came towards him, hobbling and supporting himself on a sturdy walking stick. They embraced each other.

'I had the children with me; I wanted them to see the fishing grounds for the first time, so I couldn't stay out this evening.' As he spoke, the wind seemed to pick up and the torches sputtered. Cygan's brother spoke again 'The weather is changing; it will rain tonight for sure.'

'The spirits are good to us, Uxevallak; a little rain keeps the midges away.'

'But when it stops, they come back tenfold,' replied his brother who was seemingly the less sanguine of the two. 'Listen, have you seen Fasneterax yet?'

'No, but I have been told what has happened. I was hoping to see him tonight, to ask if he needed assistance with anything.'

'He won't be coming,' his brother replied in hushed tones 'The Elder went and spoke to him earlier and told him all the news the rest of us will be hearing tonight; apparently the Elder might be wanting volunteers for something, for a few people heard Fasneterax declare "Whatever it is that needs to be done, you must include me." I myself am unsure if sending a grieving man on some errand is a wise decision – it can cloud their judgement – but it sounds as if there will be no stopping him.'

'Intriguing – it seems as if the Elder has already determined on a course of action. I wonder what has made him...'

He was interrupted by a sharp hissing sound. At the back of the room was a large brazier, one of the few metallic objects in the village. As Cygan was speaking, a man dropped a mixture of leaves and powders into it, causing it to flare up into a riot of pinks and purples. It hissed loudly and a pungent white smoke filled the room before being caught by the stiffening breeze. This was the signal for the meeting to commence. Everyone present proceeded to sit cross-legged on the floor, bar the man at the brazier, who now turned to face them.

This man was easily the oldest person there. Thin, wiry, with a shock of white hair that fell over his shoulders and halfway down his back, he had no beard or moustache unlike a lot of the men who favoured both (Cygan was another exception) and his nose was prominent and hawk-like.

BOOK ONE: AUTUMN

Standing in front of the brazier, he was cast in shadow, though his eyes still glittered like coals, and behind both him and the brazier, on a shelf against the walls, were a row of skulls that glowed red in the fire, an audience of the dead joining the audience of the living. At length, when everyone was settled, the man spoke in a voice deeper and more vigorous than might have been expected in a man of his years.

'I have called you all here for two reasons. The first is to relay to you for those that may not know news of the passing of Fasneterax's youngest boy. A child who like so many others did not reach his naming ceremony. Ukka, the spirit of the underworld, has taken him. Her great spirit has joined with his lesser one, making both of them stronger. Together they now travel the Great River that joins the Earth to the Heavens. By day he will be with Cygannan of the skies only to return to Ukka's side at dusk as, of course, we must all do one day. Tomorrow, before we hold the funeral feast here, we shall walk the path to Lake Meshallax where we will let Ukka claim him. Let your grief for the child be short, for he has gone to a place of radiance and enlightenment beyond our humble imaginings, where he will be taught the way of the spirit world; once he has joined with Ukka he will be in every tree, every bird, every fish and beast that walks, swims or flies upon this world. He will be with every Elder that has preceded me, every warrior, every huntsman. Where our words and thoughts and dreams pass as smoke in the wind, he will have an eternity of peace, free of pain and torment. Our mortality is brief, a mere water droplet along the course of the Great River itself. He is now ahead of us in the great journey along that river and on the morrow we will commend his spirit to Ukka and ensure his passing to her side is a smooth one. Praise Ukka.'

'Praise Ukka,' they all said as one, heads bowed. Many of them had lost children in similar circumstances so there was no artifice in their utterance. A distant rumble of thunder could be heard and a fresh wind whipped around them, pulling at their hair and their clothes. Dumnekavax, the Elder, looked at them, his expression grave.

'The second matter is one that you will not hear from my lips. Rather it is Vengefarak here who will tell his tale. He returned today from a visit to the Jagged Hill tribe, some three days' journey away. They are a tribe who live close to the sea where the water starts to taste of salt. Once he has told his tale, we must all decide what to do.'

Vengefarak, a dour man of middle years, powerfully built and scarred on his chest as all the men were, stood and faced his audience.

'It is as the Elder has said. The purpose of my visit was to arrange a dowry for the wedding of my daughter as she has had her fourteenth summer this year. They are not so numerous as ourselves and the son of their Elder had recently come of age. For those who have never been there, I will just say that they live some two to three hours from the sea on a small rocky hill in the midst of a broad flat lake. The water is always choppy for they have little protection from the wind blowing in from the sea. They fish the lake using wide nets and constantly have to protect their catches from the large seabirds. They also need to boil their water as the lake can get quite salty, though like us they collect rainwater in large butts to see them through the dry times. The lake never freezes, though the winters there can be extremely bitter; the trees bordering the lake are low and twisted by the wind. The people there are fairer than us and this would be the first marriage between our peoples. Both Elders sanctioned it some time ago and, as I have said, I had to travel there to finalise the details.'

He stopped, wiping his mouth on his arm; he was evidently unused to speaking in front of a large audience. No one interrupted him. After swallowing deeply, he continued.

'My journey down there by round boat was uneventful. I saw no one on the way, even though I passed quite close by some other villages. The land changes as you approach the sea; there are fewer trees and broader stretches of water, the days can be hotter and the nights colder. It is a strange land. Nevertheless, I made good progress and on the dawn of the third day of travel I espied their jetty on the hill and made for it. I was expecting the Elder to formally welcome me as we would do here, with pipes and music and a small exchange of gifts; instead, when I got there, there were armed men waiting for me. They bundled me out of the boat and propelled me to the great house at the centre of the hill. At this point

I feared for my life but looking at the faces of the other men I saw something unexpected. Fear.

Nearly the whole tribe were in the great house, including the Elder who greeted me warmly and apologised for the reception I had been given. Naturally, I asked him why they were behaving like a frog that has seen a grass snake. He looked at me and said that earlier that day two men were out on the lake fishing when one of the boats capsized and the man who was steering it was pitched into the water. The other went to aid him when he saw him being pulled underwater. The man stopped and hesitated before continuing. What this man saw was his companion being pulled underwater by the Malaac.'

A shocked silence filled the great house as Vengefarak stopped for a second. Then everyone started talking at once.

'The night devils, just three days away?'

'Pah, they are a myth! The man's eyes were addled by the sun.'

'They go for the children; they eat the children first.'

'We must form a war band – no one's safe!'

The babble continued for a good minute until Dumnekavax threw more leaves on to the brazier causing it to hiss and smoke violently again. Everyone stopped talking. Another rumble of thunder was heard, slightly closer this time.

'I heard someone say the Malaac were a myth,' said the Elder. 'If only that were so. The Malaac are Ukka's abandoned children, the night devils, an amalgam of amphibian, reptile and man. They normally live in the Forbidden Zone, in the Lake of the Eye, where no man will live as the dangers there are so great and a quick death almost certain. That they have moved such a distance northwards and westwards from there is disturbing. That they have attacked a grown man by the light of day is remarkable.'

Vengefarak continued: 'This fisherman saw his companion surrounded by three or four Malaac; they were pulling him under to drown him. He had his spear with him and tried to get them off the man. He stabbed two of them but they were relentless. The man disappeared under the waves and was not seen again.

'I volunteered to stay and help them see out the night. The Malaac only venture on to land at night as their eyes are sensitive to too much light. The village was already fortified by a stockade, so it was just a matter of reinforcing it, seeing it was in good repair and then waiting. I had my bow and spear and was asked to defend the women and children at the great house. All the women there are like our own, well practised with sling and dart, so they, too, were not defenceless.

Night came. The sky went from red to blue, from blue to deepest purple, and then to black. From the lake came the strangest noise, a mournful whooping cry, from one voice, then two, and then many more joined the chorus. Everyone's blood was chilled. And then the attack came. From my position I could make out little, just shapes trying to scale the stockade and being repulsed. The flaming torches outside the great house made vision even worse if anything. It was chaos – the cries of men and the howling of the night devils – I had my bow in my hand but could see nothing to aim at. Eventually, the men at the stockade drove them back but it was only a brief respite.

In total, they attacked seven times that night. After the second or third attack I joined the men at the stockade. They are terrifying foes, fast and strong, slimy, with green lizard-like eyes that shine in the dark. I wounded a couple and I think I hit some with my arrows. They did break through in the end, but the women aided us pelting them with stones. Just as we were weakening, dawn broke. In total, six men were lost, with many more injured. Their bite has a poison to it that slows the healing of wounds; the Elder tried healing them with mud poultices but with limited effect. We don't know how many of them we killed; they took the bodies of their dead with them. I have heard they cannibalise their own. I spoke to the Elder and the other wise men. It was decided that they would reinforce their stockade and send all of the older warriors that could be spared to other villages to ask for help. It was agreed that I should return here for that same purpose, so, about one hour after the break of dawn, I departed and reached here after just over two days' hard rowing and taking barely any rest. And I now humbly present the entreaty from the Jagged Hill tribe for aid, whether through warriors or just supplies. We do not know if the Malaac will attack again or if they will move elsewhere, but if they continue to attack this tribe every night they will not withstand them for long.'

With that Vengefarak bowed to his audience and returned to his sitting position among them. The Elder spoke again.

'When I first heard this news I and the Circle of the Wise...' he indicated a group of four or five men sat in the front of the assembly '...concluded immediately that we need to do something. As to what, I am unsure; if these creatures do move on, then we need to look to our own defence. No one is safe from them. There is also another matter that concerns me. I have been waiting for some days for an emissary from the Twin Snake tribe. As you all know, last year there was trouble between us concerning hunting territory; there were two or three skirmishes in which, though no one was killed, several were injured on both sides, Vunatax here can confirm that.' He looked at a young man who, on closer inspection, had several fingers missing on his left hand. 'We were going to settle the dispute and discuss recompense for the injuries done on both sides. When I last visited them they said they would arrive on the day of the next new moon, and yet it passed some seven days ago and there has been no news of them. I am troubled by this, for when an Elder gives his word to another tribe it is never broken unless some cataclysm has occurred. Vengefarak's report has obviously heightened my concern.'

'The priority has to be our women and children,' said one of the audience, a tall man with red hair who stood out from the rest of the tribe who were almost universally dark. 'Of course, the women can fight, but it is the job of the menfolk to see that they don't have to.'

'True enough, Raduketeveryan. Would everyone be agreed that we follow our normal course of action for when the camp is threatened? That is, withdraw everyone to the central island, surround it with a stockade and sharpened stakes, arm everyone with at least a sling and stones, keep our food and livestock penned in the centre, along with our most vulnerable, and cede the rest of the village, stripped of everything of use, to the enemy.'

There was a murmur of approval and a voice at the back shouted,

'We only need do this at night, for that is when they come.'

'Agreed,' said the Elder. 'Everyone in the village is to assemble on the island before dusk, bringing their weapons and valuables. Tomorrow, after the funeral feast, we will construct the stockade. The Malaac dislike fire so we will keep several burning when night falls. Now, what of the other issues?'

One of the Circle of the Wise, a man almost as old as Dumnekavax but even thinner and wirier stood up and addressed the audience.

'It is the opinion of the Circle, of which I, Mutreverak, am the spokesman, that a force of men is sent to the Jagged Hill tribe to proffer aid, whether through fighting, evacuating the wounded, or repairing their defences. The number of men we send need not be large, but enough to be effective. We were surmising anything between ten and twenty men.'

'Twenty is too many; we need a large force to stay here,' said several people at once.

Order broke down at this point with people arguing about numbers or whether any men should be sent at all. This time the Elder let everyone have their say until they tired themselves out. The noise started dying down when a flash of lighting was seen southward over the marsh, followed very soon afterwards by a slow rumble of thunder. It was apparent that the storm was growing ever louder and closer. After everyone had finished the Elder spoke again.

'I believe that a force should be sent, even if it does nothing more than discover further information about the threat we might face. If you feel we should send a force, then say so now.' At least two-thirds of the men present got to their feet shouting 'Aye!' over and over again. Clearly the majority were in favour. Cygan stood but did not shout; he was as worried about the storm as anything else.

'That is good – a force will be sent then,' announced the Elder. 'I propose three longboats carrying some eight men; this gives enough room to carry supplies and evacuate some of the wounded, if we fit five or even six to a boat. I also propose that we send one longboat with four men to the Twin Snake to discover the reason for their silence. Once they have completed their task, they will then travel on to the Jagged Hill and meet with the other boats there. Twelve men, a reasonable force and one we can afford. Does anyone disagree with this proposal?'

There was a lot of head shaking and murmuring – the Elder saw this as affirmation of his proposal. 'Then that is what we will do. The two parties will depart after the funeral tomorrow; they need not attend the feast. Does anyone wish to put themselves forward for these tasks.'

People stepped forward and hands went up again; Cygan was one of the few not to do anything.

'That is a good response.' The Elder gave a grim smile. 'I propose Vengefarak return to the Jagged Hill with Raduketeveryan as his second. The choosing of the six followers I will leave to them. And, as for the Twin Snake, I feel that I alone should decide on those to go, as it is as much a diplomatic visit as an investigative one. Firstly, I will send Fasneterax, for he has specifically requested that he prove himself for the tribe again and I could not refuse him in the circumstances. Secondly, I will send Tevagenek, the youngest of the Circle and still a doughty warrior. Representing the youth of the tribe, I will send Cerrenatukavenex, one of our most promising young warriors. And, lastly, to assist Tevagenek when he mediates with the Twin Snake, I will send a wise head on relatively youthful shoulders – Cyganexatavan shall go.'

Cygan stood still as a stone as simultaneously the thunderstorm finally hit. A brilliant white flash of lightning was followed almost immediately by a ferocious crack of thunder. He could hear people around him calling it an omen. And then the rain started to fall. The wind whipped it in all directions so there was no shelter in the great house. A torch guttered and went out. Someone whispered in fear: 'Ukka is angry! She has sent the Malaac and has persuaded Cygannan to send thunder. Ukka is angry!' the man cried. It was taken up by others until at last the Elder was forced to do something to placate the dozen or so wailing men.

'Silence!' he said, his voice commanding. 'Tomorrow, after the moon rises and we are safe on the island, I shall drink the nectar of the Gods and walk the divine path. I will discover what the Gods need in order to be appeased. Now return to your homes and we will meet shortly after the light breaks to send the child to join with Ukka.'

Cygan didn't hear him; he was already on the jetty stripping the cover off his boat. The rain stung his eyes; steering the boat would be very difficult in the driving wind but he didn't care.

All that concerned him was how to tell Vaneshanda.

She was lying in the hammock with the children in their cots. The screen at the rear of the house had been pulled down and secured. (He had to loosen then retighten its fastening to get in.) The fire hissed angrily as streaks of water came through the chimney and spattered upon it. Despite the rain and howling wind and the sound of the screen being whipped in all directions, the house was perfectly warm. Cygan wiped his sore eyes and brushed some water out of his hair. He removed his sodden clothes and hung them close to the fire. With great dexterity he climbed softly into the hammock next to his wife's warm body. He hoped she was asleep, despite the storm, but as he lay back she stirred softly and moved under his left arm.

'So what happened?'

'I will tell you in the morning, but I am afraid you won't like it.'

He felt rather than saw her eyes open. 'He is sending you away again, isn't he?'

Cygan sighed his affirmation. 'Uxevallak will look after you. He will go around the fish traps and gather the food, for you, for Shettevellanda or anyone else that needs help. He may not be able to fight and travel like many of us, but he is always there in a crisis. As for the Elder, his mind was made up before I even reached the great house.'

'You know he sees you as a future Elder, or at least as one of the Circle. This is why he always sends you out. Whether it is to the north to trade with the Taneren, or elsewhere to talk to other tribes, it is always you, always you.'

'I am the only one that speaks the language of the Taneren, that is why I go north. But you are right. I shall speak with him in the morning and try to persuade him to keep me here.'

'Cyganexatavan, you will do no such thing. He has bestowed upon you an honour. You cannot refuse without losing face.'

'I would if you asked it,' he replied softly. Overhead crashed more thunder, louder than ever. Their little daughter began to cry. 'Go see to her, make sure she is all right. What has happened to Shettevellanda has made me even more determined that not even the most vengeful God will ever stop my children from having their naming ceremonies.'

Vaneshanda picked the little girl up and climbed back into the hammock with her. Cygan held them both, trying to keep them warm as the storm raged outside.

11

They managed to secure a room at the inn, which was, as Morgan surmised, largely empty. The landlord regaled them with tales of times before the war when on market day there would be ten to a room and how in the largest room downstairs people would pay a penny to spend the night sleeping by leaning against a rope that he had tied there some three to four feet from the ground. They ordered some food to be brought up to their room in an hour or so, and Sir Varen went to check the stabling for the horses and the storage of the wagon. The gear that the wagon held the rest of them took to the room themselves.

It had a small, low bed which Willem and Cedric would share; the rest of them arranged their bedrolls around it. It had one window, which overlooked the square. Once settled, Samson, Leon, Haelward and Rozgon decided to go and reconnoitre. Beside the main square, the rest of the town consisted of under a dozen streets, most of which hugged the main north and south roads out of the town, so Morgan did not expect them to take too long. After twenty minutes or so Sir Varen returned.

'This place is practically deserted,' he said 'If you take out the soldiers and the people who supply them, there is hardly anyone here. And I am pretty sure we are being watched. The stable wing overlooks the river and just across it was a man pretending to take a stroll up and down the bank, but he barely stopped looking at what I and the stable lad were doing. I gave the boy a ducat to let us know if something suspicious happens.'

Morgan went to the window and after gazing out of it for a short while he said, 'You're right; there is a man walking around the cockpit who keeps looking up this way. Surly-looking fellow, with a pointed beard and wearing gloves, possibly doeskin. It is not surprising – Ulgar will want to know where we are. We need to stay alert, though.'

'All this cloak-and-dagger stuff is beyond me,' said Cedric. 'What on earth does anybody hope to achieve with all this?'

'Maybe nothing,' said Morgan. 'Or maybe they are just watching in case I shout at the tavern keeper, or haggle too aggressively over the price of cabbage. Any excuse to clap me in the stocks.'

'Then make sure you do not give him that excuse,' said Cedric.

Samson handed over the money. The four of them had located a couple of traders off the square and behind the mansion house; it not being market day the town was very quiet, with little to buy, so it was with some relief that they had discovered somebody selling vegetables and other basic foodstuffs. They bought some bread and enough vegetables to make a potage and decided to go back to the tavern. As they were about to turn left to go back into the square, Leon said, 'You have all noticed him, yes?'

'Yes,' said Rozgon. 'Let's carry on down the south road here for a while.'

Walking not more than twenty paces behind them was a man dressed in Ulgar's green and white. Although he appeared to be following them, he appeared to make little or no attempt at secrecy.

'Artorus's teeth!' said Samson. 'Leon's seven-year-old could make a better job of spying on us. What's this fellow's game?'

'Perhaps he feels he has too many teeth of his own,' said Rozgon. 'Maybe we should loosen a few of them for him.'

They continued down the rutted path that hugged the eaves of the tiny thatched cottages till they came to a turning leading to a small cobbled square with a well at its centre. They walked into the square. The man following blithely behind them did the same – at least, until he got to the square. At that point he stopped as Rozgon's arm around his throat held him fast with a grip of iron. Leon put a dagger to the man's face.

'I take it you fancy having an extra mouth?' Leon pushed the dagger on to the man's cheek, drawing a drop of blood. The man tried to talk but Rozgon's throat hold meant that only a choking sound got out. Haelward spoke.

'Loosen it a little, Growler; he's going nowhere till he talks to us anyway.' After Rozgon, to an extent, complied, the man spoke.

'You've got it all wrong. I am not following you – I just wanted to talk,' he gasped.

'Well, now is your chance,' said Haelward. 'Be quick about it; none of us is a patient man.'

'I just wanted to warn you – a gang of the Baron's hired thugs and killers are after you. They will try and attack you tonight; if they can't, it will be tomorrow after you leave here.'

'I see. So one of Baron Ulgar's lackeys is coming to tell us that Baron Ulgar is trying to kill us. We are not all touched by Uba here, boy.' Rozgon tightened his throat lock again.'

'No, not Ulgar – Fenchard! It is Fenchard you need to watch here.' The man's voice was a strangled gasp.

Rozgon let the man go. After putting his hand to his throat and breathing deeply for a minute, he looked in turn at each of the stony faces of his audience, then continued: 'I am one of Baron Ulgar's armourers. After they returned from seeing you all earlier I went to an anteroom where we have some equipment stored when he stormed in with another man. I shrank against the wall so theyt couldn't see me. Fenchard was ranting about being insulted by a common thug – no one, he yelled, gets away with saying things like that to him. I am sure you are not surprised to hear that he is as popular among Baron Ulgar's staff as a dose of the pox. Anyway, he finished by saying, "You know what I pay you for – tonight or tomorrow, see that it gets done. Let's give Felmere a kick where it hurts by killing his men.'

Rozgon shoved the man in the back. 'How can we trust this fellow? He could be setting us up; everyone knows Vinoyen and Fenchard are close. It could be a ruse to lure us into trouble.'

'No, no, that's not the case,' said the man. 'Baron Ulgar has no love for the man of Glaivedon but he will always respect the Grand Duke's wishes. He is very loyal in that regard. Fenchard, though, is different entirely; he is only loyal to his own interests. He also has come into an awful lot of money; no one knows where it comes from but it is enough for a sizeable army and for him to hire all kinds of brigands to do his dirty work... And, well, I was at Fort Axmian; I saw who led the counter-charge and broke the Arshumans. You were one of them, too.' He nodded at Rozgon. 'You saved my family that day. I owe you and have always vowed that I would repay you somehow.'

'Well, if what you say is true, then you have done just that,' the big man replied. 'But, if I find out you are lying...'

'I am not! May Xhenafa take my wife and children if I am not speaking the truth.'

'Off you go, my friend, before your boss notices your absence,' said Haelward.

'Thank you, sir – just watch out tonight.' And he was gone.

'If we stay in the room,' said Samson, 'there is not a lot they can do.' They had returned to the inn with the news and were discussing their next move.

'You are right of course,' said Morgan, 'but that would probably just mean they will pursue us out in the open when we leave tomorrow. We could find a decent defensive position but it could take time and we need to be at the pass three days from now.'

'Then the only other option is to confront them here.' Samson seemed nervous at the prospect.

'I am afraid so. Sir Varen, you stay here tonight and guard Cedric and Willem. The rest of you, let's take a quick walk outside; we need to chat. After that I will speak to the innkeeper, I may need to part with some coin to keep him sweet, looking at the trade he is getting I am sure he will be grateful for it and more than willing to turn a blind eye to what we have to do.'

There were still a couple of hours before the sun went down. Morgan took the opportunity to visit the stalls where the others had bought their supplies earlier; he took just Cedric with him. While he was there he bought some turnips and some apples on the turn – 'For my horses. I will be sleeping in the stables with them tonight; you have to be wary of rustlers after all.' They strolled back to the inn, taking plenty of time, and Morgan slowly explained to Cedric that all horses loved apples and that he would slowly feed them all to them through the course of the night. He spoke loudly and repeated himself many times over, just as the rest of his men were doing at the same time in the tavern. They seemed carefree and oblivious to the shadowy figures lurking in doorways or slowly following ten to twenty paces behind them…

The night was crisp and cold. The weak waning moon cast little light on to the courtyard at the rear of the inn, on one side of which stood the stables; only a solitary lantern, hanging from a bracket over the inn's rear door, cast its pallid yellow glow over the straw-covered cobbles. There were ten stable doors in all, facing on to the courtyard, then on to a slippery greensward that separated the courtyard from the river, a river swollen by the recent rains. The river could be heard but not seen and only the occasional lantern illuminated the far bank. The bridge could just be noticed poking out in the distance from behind the inn's east wall. In contrast to everywhere else, it was well lit with lanterns and flaming torches that turned the dark waters under its arches a churning crimson. Apart from the constant rush of water, no other sound could be heard.

Suddenly, a figure emerged into the courtyard from behind the last stable. He was cloaked in black and hooded. Almost noiselessly he scampered past the stable doors until he reached the fourth one from the inn. Halting there, he put his fingers to his lips and gave a low whistle like a calling bird, and within seconds he was joined by five other men, all cloaked but not as quiet as the first man – the distinctive sound of metal against metal could be heard; it appeared some were wearing chain mail. They all congregated around the same stable door.

Then another man joined them, also cloaked, and wearing soft leather gloves. He appeared to be the man in charge as he immediately started hissing instructions to his companions. A wooden bar secured the lower stable door and a bolt secured the upper. Slowly, silently, one man slid the bolt free, keeping a hold on the upper door to stop it opening; another, crouching down next to him, started to slide the wooden bar free from its housing. It came loose; there was the sound of metal against leather and the glint of steel in the moonlight as weapons were drawn. The two men by the doors readied themselves to swing them open as the others readied themselves to charge in. The tension was so thick it could be tasted on the air.

Suddenly a noise broke their collective concentration. As one, they turned to face the inn. Its rear door had swung open and standing there, looking almost like pale ghosts in the pallid light of the lantern, were four men, their leader being an absolute giant of a man, one-eyed, clad in a wolf pelt and fingering an axe.

'Now, fellas,' he said, 'you wouldn't be waking our horses now, would you?'

Chaos broke loose. Rozgon closed the ground between himself and the enemy in two bounds, slamming his axe foursquare into the face of his nearest foe. The man went down instantly. Leaving the axe where it was, he swept out a brutal-looking hammer concealed under his cloak, shoulder charged the next man to him, before bringing the hammer to bear on the side of the man's head with a sickening thud. While he was doing this, Haelward next to him was thrusting his sword clinically through an enemy's throat. With a half-twist of his blade, the sword was free to engage another foe, leaving his first victim thrashing desperately on the floor as he tried vainly to staunch the flow of blood on to the cobbles. Samson and Leon both loosed arrows, sending another man tumbling.

The two men by the stable door were standing at the ready, gripping wicked-looking knives, when suddenly the upper door swung violently open. It caught one of the men on the back of the head, sending him tumbling. The other had just enough time to get out of the way but dropped his guard to do so. It was enough time for Morgan. He leapt out of the stables, sword raised, before swinging a deadly blow at the man's neck. It did not quite sever the head but he was killed instantly, jets of arterial blood shooting in all directions. The man sent flying by the stable door lasted only a brief moment longer, as Leon's arrow pierced his throat, its barbed head pushing through the back of the neck. This left one man, the man with the gloves. Seeing the ruin around him he turned tail and ran. Samson let loose an arrow, which stuck in his leg; he went down for a second but continued to desperately try and escape, now limping badly. He was slowed so much, though, that Haelward and Morgan caught up with him on the grass by the riverbank. Haelward brought the pommel of his sword down on the man's head, knocking him to the ground. He held the sword to the man's throat, forcing him to lay still. Rozgon, walking armoury that he was, was dispatching the wounded with a knife. His task completed, he, Samson and Leon came and joined the other two men by the river.

The whole battle lasted much less than a minute.

Such was the ferocity of the ambush that most of the men had gone down with barely a sound, and no alarm was raised, no hue and cry. Six men had died unnoticed, accompanied only by the sound of the swollen river.

The surviving man was forced to stand and Rozgon was given another chance to use his headlock. He was a well-groomed man, dark-haired with a trimmed pointed beard. Morgan sheathed his sword and drew his knife, which he placed close to the captive's face. 'Your name, and who you are working for,' he said succinctly.

The man smiled and spat at him. 'I am telling you nothing, Felmere man.' Morgan looked at the man impassively. He had avoided the man's spittle and instead appeared to be looking at a small tattoo the man had on the collar line.

'Why not?' he said. 'You have nothing to lose.'

You won't hurt me,' he sneered. 'The hero of Axmian would be above such things.'

'Your ambush was incompetent,' said Morgan. 'Only seven men? All of you attacking together in a mob? Your employer will be greatly displeased. I imagine he paid you quite well.'

'You know nothing!' hissed the man. 'I may have failed but there will be others. Oh yes, he who pays me can afford many others.'

'But I am afraid that that,' said Morgan, 'will no longer be your concern.'

With that, he thrust his knife deep into the side of the man's neck before pulling it outwards, opening the windpipe and causing a stream of gore to spurt forth, hitting Morgan in the face with greater accuracy than the man's spit had done earlier. He nodded to Rozgon who dragged the almost-dead fellow to the water's edge before pitching him in with a gentle splosh. Morgan's last image of the man was of his frozen, startled expression before he disappeared into the dark waters.

'Was that necessary?' Haelward said in a low voice. 'We could have just sent him back to Fenchard.'

'Who would have had him killed anyway.' said Morgan. 'Only more slowly and painfully, if what we have heard about Fenchard stands up. A failed assassin is a dead assassin. Besides, what did you notice about him?'

'I don't know,' said Haelward. 'It was rather dark.'

'Firstly, and this is a minor point, did you see his beard?' Morgan was cleaning his knife on the grass. 'He was well dressed, some expensive gear, yet his beard was hardly Tanarese high fashion. Few people here wear their beards in such a way, and secondly and more importantly I noticed a small tattoo of Mytha just under his throat.'

'We all have them,' said Samson. 'How is that unusual?'

'Yes, of Mytha the bear, but our religion is different to other places. Women here venerate Elissa above Camille and for us Mytha is a bear. This man's tattoo was of Mytha the bull. That and his beard led me to believe that he was...' 'Arshuman,' whispered Haelward.

'Exactly,' said Morgan, sheathing his knife. 'An Arshuman that has lived here for a long time, judging by his accent, but an Arshuman nonetheless.

Now let's get this mess cleared up.'

'Why hire an Arshuman killer?' Rozgon enquired. 'It makes no sense.'

'To be honest, I can't be doing with thinking about it now. One thing is for certain, though: Master Fenchard keeps some very strange company.'

The other bodies were collected and faced the same fate as the Arshuman victim – that of being dumped into the river. Haelward busied himself with a bucket and did his best to sluice the cobbles clean of blood. Rozgon was about to throw the last body into the river when he noticed something and indicated for Morgan to come over.

'Look at this one,' he said, indicating the man's hands.

On the third finger and little finger of each hand the nail was missing, and instead the skin had grown thickly to form a fleshy pad. With a little difficulty – the muscles were already beginning to lock – Morgan forced his mouth open. The same two incisor teeth on each side of the mouth were missing, too. 'They have been pulled.' said Rozgon. 'As have his fingernails.'

'The man has been tortured,' Morgan mused. 'And a while ago, judging by the way the skin has regrown on his fingers. Has Fenchard been emptying his dungeons? Kill us and get your freedom maybe?'

'Who knows?' Rozgon replied. 'But your explanation is as good as any.' 'Well, it doesn't matter now; we had better pack up and leave before dawn. I am sure Fenchard won't be up before noon, but we might as well be on the safe side.'

'One question,' said Haelward, setting down the pail, 'why did you leave Sir Varen behind? His mace would have been useful; you could have moved the professor and Willem to another room and locked the door. They would never have been found.'

Morgan stopped and looked at him. 'Because Sir Varen is a knight and an honourable man. Honour would not have best served us tonight; I wanted no one reporting back to Fenchard before we were able to leave. I know you're not happy with what I did it – and it might surprise you that neither am I – but the fact is our mission takes priority and the Baron's grudge against me is not important when compared against it. I reckoned you had a better chance of understanding that than Varen.'

'You didn't kill him just because he was Arshuman then.'

Morgan smiled at him and walked back into the inn.

They left as soon as they could, while it was still dark. Sir Varen gently propelled the horses forward, his face showing yellow by the light of the wagon's lantern. As soon as they passed the baronial hall, they took the road northwards and very shortly they were clear of the town and into the copses and fields of the surrounding countryside. The road narrowed to a smaller dirt track at this point and veered slightly eastwards until it was closely hugging the river. The birds slowly started to find their voice as dawn slowly broke and a pale light started to show through the pink-tinted clouds above. They met nobody and spoke little themselves being content with their own thoughts and the smell of fast-flowing water coming from the river as it bubbled and sang alongside them.

Looking ahead it dawned on Morgan how familiar he was with the approaching mountains. They had been there with him pretty much all of his life and generally he took as much, or as little, account of them as he did of his weather-worn boots or the dagger he had had since he was eleven years old and which he still polished and whetted every day. Looking at them now, though, it was as if he were seeing them for the first time.

He had heard stories of the great Dragon Spine Mountains in Chira whose tallest peaks soared upwards, past even the highest clouds; of Mount Kzugun in northern Koze, part of the Gnekun range, which was supposedly the tallest mountain in the world; and even of the Red Mountains, Chira's northern boundary and the longest range known to man, running for thousands of miles west to east, joining the Western Ocean to the barely explored Sea of Squalls, reputedly home to many fantastical creatures – but the Derannen Mountains ahead seemed formidable enough on their own – a broad, bluegrey array of spikes, at some points over a mile high and fringed with snow. The pass they sought cut between Mount Deraska in the west and Mount Baenarran in the east, both just under a mile in height. The pass was slightly less than half the height of these two peaks, so it was under the snowline but of course not immune to heavy falls of snow itself, which blocked it permanently for two or three months a year. They were beginning to travel gently uphill already and within a day or so they would be in the pine-clad foothills, inhaling the smell of resin and walking on the spongy carpet of discarded brown needles as they made their way to Shayer Ridge, the mountain town the enemy had never conquered. Then they would veer westwards to the Tower of Hayader, which guarded the narrow mouth of the pass. After that ... well, after that, they would be on their own.

They proceeded northwards for a good while, wanting to put as much space between them and Tetha Vinoyen as possible, and did not stop for a meal until the middle of the afternoon. Morgan wondered about the wagon again; it definitely slowed their progress and, although the pass could accommodate a wagon, it would still be painful-going as the snow clouds gathered above them. It had to be taken, of course, as it bore the gold for the elves, among other things, so there was little point worrying about it. Also Cedric could never walk the pass unaided. And what of Cedric? He had barely emerged from the wagon since they had started their journey. It was odd for such a garrulous man. And did he know of the unspoken dangers of the pass? Attacks by animals or worse. He had stated that he had made a study of such things. Morgan decided to climb into the wagon and chat to him.

The wagon itself was full of clutter but a central space had been cleared where Cedric sat on a trunk with a book opened in front of him. Willem was not there; he was eating with the other men. Morgan was about to greet him when he noticed something odd. Cedric's left side was facing him with his hand resting on his knee. Except that it wasn't resting. It was shaking, quite violently, and uncontrollably. Morgan identified it immediately.

'The shaking palsy?' Cedric looked at him grimly, nodding as he did so. 'At least you have heard of it,' he said. 'I knew I would have to tell you all eventually but I just couldn't work out the best way of doing so.'

Morgan smiled sympathetically. 'Not all of us soldiers are brain-addled killing machines. My grandfather had it. When did you first start to notice it?'

'Oh, about three or four years ago now. I was reading a tome – I am not sure I can recall which one, possibly something relating to the sightings of fell horrors in the Morrathnay Forest – when I noticed the little finger on my left hand had the tiniest of tremors. I tried to stop it but I just couldn't. After that, it began to happen quite frequently and always slightly worse than before. Ultimately, I checked with the university's healer, who confirmed what you have just told me yourself. It is not too bad ... yet. I get stiff and have difficulty walking some days, but other than that I get by. Willem is as much my carer as my student, I am afraid.'

'Why didn't you mention this earlier?'

Cedric looked at him quizzically. 'Would you have undertaken this task if you had known?'

Morgan smiled again. 'Surprisingly enough, yes. As I have said, my grandfather had it and it will change nothing when we go over the mountains. I would have kept you in the wagon regardless. We just need to make sure you have an extra blanket. That is all.'

Cedric snorted. 'Please, no special treatment. It will be some years before I am confined to a chair or bed and I have no desire for that to happen to me until my ague absolutely forces me into one. I suppose now I will have to tell the others... Do you think any of them will want to turn back?'

'Not a chance. None of these boys strike me as the lily-livered type. And don't worry about telling them. I will do it.'

Cedric seemed grateful. 'Thank you. By the way, how poorly is your grandfather now?'

'Poorly in the dead sort of way, I'm afraid. And it wasn't the illness that did it – just the Arshumans, in the first year of the war, when they forced us back to the river Kada.'

'I am so sorry to hear that. Was he the only family member you lost?'

Morgan looked grim. 'Let's put it this way, if you look for the village of Glaivedon on any map drawn up in the last ten years, you will not find it.' Cedric bowed his head. 'You have lost much, I see.'

'I am not the only one. Many villages have been destroyed in this war. Rozgon is another to lose those close to him. We were all farmers or craftsmen once; none of us here became warriors for any reason other than necessity. It just so happened that some of us are rather good at it.' He decided to change the subject. 'Now, the creatures that live in the mountains, you know of them?'

Cedric perked up at this. 'Oh yes, now they are very rare, because food up there is so scarce. This makes them especially savage of course, especially to those caught on the mountains in winter. You may find frost giants, though personally I believe that they are extinct in these parts. Ettins, trolls, snow wolves and others I can't recall do exist here, however. The best defence against them is fire. None of them is familiar with it and, as all these creatures have fur or thick hair, it may be an effective deterrent to anything that sees us as a meal.'

Morgan nodded. 'Good point. I shall see what we can pick up in Shayer Ridge. Now get yourself comfortable and I will fetch you some food. Willem is not doing his job, I see.'

'Oh, that is not the boy's fault. It is a nice change for him to have some younger company. Food will be welcome, though, however unappetising' Morgan laughed. 'Unappetising? You can have Artorus's own personal guarantee that it will be that.'

'So,' said Samson, lying in the ground with his back against a tree, 'what is it that you really dislike about the Arshumans?'

'Their silly little pointed beards, and the fact that they all seem to grow them,' said Leon. 'How can a hundred people all want to look the same?'

'Those beards are catching on over here now though,' said Haelward, while chewing some dried meat. 'I have seen a few people with them. Morgan was wrong when he said that man's beard made him an Arshuman.'

'The tattoo was pretty conclusive, though,' Samson countered. 'Mytha as a bull? Utter bollocks.'

'Fair point,' Haelward conceded. 'Where is your tattoo? Mine is on my forearm'

'Same here,' said Leon. 'Some of us have no imagination.'

'Me,' said Samson, 'on my chest. Artorus's flaming teeth, it hurt! Growler, where is yours?'

Rozgon was whetting his knife. He put it down and looked at them. 'I have two. One' he slapped his left shoulder, 'here.'

'And the other?'

The big man grinned. 'For that, my friend, you will have to ask my wife, or a couple of the friendlier ladies back at the camp, or that girl who tended my wounds after Axmian or...'

'Mytha's claw,' exclaimed Haelward. 'I hope for their sakes it was dark.' They all laughed.

'Cheeky dog,' said Rozgon affectionately. 'Anyway, back to the Arshumans. There is a lot to hate about them but what really gets me is their obsession with all things yellow. They all wear it, the little snots. If it's not in their armour, it's in a silly little scarf, or in a feather in their cap. Facing them in battle is like squaring up to a flock of canaries.'

'It is their national colour, though,' said Varen, who had just joined them. 'And don't we just know it. I mean, we are not like that. Our colours are blue and white, with some grey for the mountains if you are from this neck of the woods, but aside from our main banner we don't feel the need to display them everywhere.'

'I do wonder, though,' Varen replied, 'if it helps with their discipline. Seeing everyone wearing the same colours maybe makes people pull towards the common goal.'

Leon looked up at him. 'Nah.'

Samson cut in: 'They have a king who rules by fear. I have heard not wearing yellow into battle is a flogging offence. Thanks, but I would rather stand foursquare with a bunch of friends as determined to watch my back as I am theirs than be driven into battle under fear of the lash.'

Haelward nodded. 'Well said that man; anyhow, how can a country that regards snails as a luxury dish be possibly called civilised.'

'They eat snails?' Willem had just joined them.

'Yes, said Haelward, 'pickled in vinegar and wild garlic. When we fight them they never use their swords; they just breathe on us. It's very effective.'

'Hey, Willem,' said Leon with a glint in his eye, 'why don't you get a tattoo done when we get into the town tomorrow. Just a small one, on your arm maybe?'

Willem looked sheepish. 'I am not sure the monastery would approve.'

'Nonsense!' barked Rozgon. 'Ex-soldiers join the church all the time; besides, you are one of us now and we have all got one. We'll sort one out for you in Shayer Ridge; you will get some God-given courage then when we get to the pass.'

'All right then. Why not?'

'Good man!' Rozgon slapped him on the shoulder and went off to see Sir Varen who was watering the horses.

Leon got up, too, stretched his back and pulled off his gloves – three fingered leather ones, as worn by a lot of the archers – and stretched out his hands, bathing them in the cool air. He had another tattoo, on the back of his left hand. Haelward asked him about it; it was a name, though he couldn't make out whose from where he was sitting.

'Miriam, my good lady. We have been together since we were fifteen.'

'Any kids?'

'Two – a boy and a girl, seven and five years old.'

Haelward laughed in surprise. 'I had no idea. You have never mentioned them.'

Samson chipped in. 'They do not fit in with the dark and moody persona he likes to portray. Fact is, they are the most devoted couple I have ever seen and he can't wait to finish his army service in two years so he can get back to them. He has only come on this little jaunt because I wanted to and we always fight together.'

'That's not true,' his cousin replied. 'I needed to get out of camp as much as you. Sitting there waiting for Artorus knows what was making my head explode, and yes Haelward, I do miss my wife. Compare this to my cousin with his countless bastards, probably one in every town in the east. You have no idea how many times I have had to save him from irate, axe-wielding cuckolded men.'

'What can I say?' replied his cousin. 'Can I help it if women love me? Especially if they have dull, tedious farmer types for husbands whose conversation extends no further than the price of pigs on market day?'

Leon looked at Haelward. 'Samson was always the spoiled one in the family, the one they could afford to educate. Little did his parents know that the only use he would put it to would be to talk gullible women out of their petticoats.'

'Nonsense, I make them laugh, feel important. Show them there is more to being a brood mare for some rock-brained bumpkin...'

'Then run off and leave them.'

'Nonsense, I would marry them all if I could. And I often return to see them again ... if their husband is away.'

'And if you didn't know Miriam and me, would she be fair game?'

'No,' said Samson emphatically, 'I only bother with women who are obviously unhappy, and Miriam is not one of those.'

They stopped as Morgan came to join them. He called Rozgon and Varen to him and when everyone was present, he spoke. 'Right, lads, I have something to tell you about our esteemed scholar...'

They camped that night on a hillock covered in trees and light shrubs. During the day Morgan had dropped back from the party on several occasions to listen for any signs of pursuit; hearing nothing he allowed a small fire, which was doused once everyone had settled down for the night. He took the first watch, sitting motionless as he faced southward listening to the soft breath of the wind in the trees and the calls of the owls looking for scurrying mice on the forest floor. Rozgon took over from him after three hours and Haelward after that. The night passed peacefully; evidently the two barons were so discomfited as to consider pursuit not worthwhile.

The following day the path stopped hugging the river and instead plunged uphill into the pine forest. They trudged wearily through these gloomy woods for a while as the path twisted and turned before them. Later, though, it rejoined the river, which was now a fast-flowing stream chattering and gurgling as it sped downhill over jagged rocks and pebbles worn smooth and covered in weed. Some time after noon they arrived at Shayer Ridge.

Perched on a flat-topped, sharply sloping hill, it was easy to see why the town had never fallen to the enemy, despite undergoing a two-month siege at one stage of the war. Joining the rock face to completely surround the town was a fifteen to twenty-foot-high stone wall, with the only access being through a great door of wood and iron. Over it hung a wooden machicolation, a crenellated wooden platform attached to the main battlement, full of murder holes used to spring nasty surprises on any attacking enemy. Through a stone culvert in the wall protected by an iron grill spilled the river, which passed down the hill and into the enclosing pine forest on their right. Shayer Ridge was a mining town; little agriculture was possible here, so it imported its grain, storing it in large silos, and exported what it found deep under the earth. This included many precious gems that all too often were found adorning the wealthy and opulent of Tanaren society. This was Sir Varen's town; he was the son of the local magistrate and it was he who would take charge of their provisioning for the journey through the pass.

'I know most of Baron Felmere's lands are the other side of the river,' he said, 'but Shayer Ridge is his town as well. Both Baron Vinoyen and Baron Lasgaart have lands around here but we declared for Felmere decades ago, as we were fed up of the Lasgaarts stripping the wealth from the town and giving nothing in return. He tried taking the town by force but that ended badly for him. If you all wait at the gate, I will arrange things for us.'

He was as good as his word. Within the hour they found themselves housed in the magistrate's hall, the finest building in the town. Baths were prepared and once they had cleaned up, a large feast including chicken, pork, meat and fruit pies as well as bread and stew was prepared for them, all washed down with a strong ale.

'Eat as much as you can,' said Morgan. 'Only the Gods know when we will have such a feast again.'

They spent the night in the private wing of the mansion, sleeping on feather mattresses close to a roaring fire. Then, as the cock crowed to herald a leaden dawn, every one of them awoke to realise that the real journey was about to begin.

After a quick trip to the latrines, Morgan headed into the courtyard. It was a raw morning and his breath showed in white plumes. Everyone was assembled and looked ready to depart. Sir Varen was standing at the head of the horses, talking to an older man finely dressed in a green velvet cloak. The family resemblance was immediately obvious to Morgan – both had the same strong jaw and sandy hair, though the older man's was flecked with grey. He went up to them.

'I take it, my Lord, that it is to you we should convey our thanks for the more than generous hospitality we have received since our arrival.'

'No thanks are required,' said the older man. 'I am Vanek the magistrate here and Varen is my boy, as I am sure you know already. I am sorry I was not here when you arrived yesterday but rents have to be collected, and a lot of local villages often need to be visited and persuaded into fulfilling their obligations to myself and the Grand Duke.'

'Times are hard for us all,' said Morgan. 'I must say though that the two of you look very much alike. Sir Varen is a credit to you by the way. Far too noble a gentleman to keep his present company.'

Varen laughed. 'On the contrary, sharing a journey with two of the heroes of Axmian, and another who fought at Galpa, is an honour well in excess of what I deserve.'

Vanek looked at Morgan. 'Take care of my boy. He is brave but young, and so far has had little experience of warfare.'

Varen looked annoyed. 'I can acquit myself as well as any man here,' he said.

'There will be little opportunity to nurture anyone along on this trip,' said Morgan, 'but I will keep an eye on him, as much as I can. Varen, have you stored some brushwood on the wagon?'

'I have indeed,' said Varen, 'lots of it. I think poor Cedric is making a bed out of the stuff.'

'It is time I took my leave,' said Vanek. 'May Artorus protect all of you and see you back safely.' With that he gave an abrupt bow and left them alone.

Morgan looked at Varen. 'He means the best for you. In my experience an over-protective father is better than no father at all.'

'He has high expectations yet does not wish me to take the risks involved to achieve them. He has had duties here which have kept him away from the battlefield, except for the siege when he managed the logistics of the operation as opposed to manning the walls. I fear he rather wishes to live his thwarted ambitions through myself.'

'Well, as far as I am concerned he has looked after us well and we could not be better provisioned for the journey ahead. By the time you return it is highly probable you will have fulfilled all of his ambitions for you anyway. If you are not dead, that is. And do not worry. There is no possibility of me keeping you out of any trouble we might get into; there will be no passengers on this trip.'

'Yes, I quite realise that. I wouldn't have volunteered otherwise. Have you seen Willem yet? Whatever you do, don't slap him on the arm. Rozgon has had it tattooed!'

Shortly afterwards they moved off. The western road to Claw Pass hugged the mountain side, with a sheer drop into the pine forest on its left of some twenty feet or more. This meant that they were rather exposed to the biting wind, causing them to pull their cloaks tightly around their ears and their noses to run uncontrollably. Morgan laughed at their discomfiture.

'This is just a taste of what is to come.'

After travelling for some hours the road dipped under the tree line, providing some relief from the wind. They took advantage of this, stopping to eat a brief lunch and waiting for their ears to thaw. With the horses, progress was disappointingly slow and Morgan realised that they wouldn't get to the pass until the morning. Having resigned himself to that, he decided not to force the pace too much and camp for the evening quite early, all the better to conserve their strength for what was to come. Eventually the road dropped so that it was now level with the floor of the forest. Little light filtered down through the high branches of the trees, and the ground, carpeted with needles, was light and spongy underfoot. Not a bird sang in the trees and no animal was seen excepting the occasional squirrel scampering into the high branches, eager to build up its store of winter food. This was a rarely used road at this time of year and they met no one on it all day. The silence cast a pallor over everyone, making them reluctant to speak or stray from their own thoughts.

They made camp, lit a fire and Samson regaled everyone with tunes on his flute; he was quite the virtuoso and before too long they were all singing around the fire, even Cedric and Willem, who had a thousand requests to bare his forearm and show off his new tattoo. The frivolities were cut short, however, as the wind picked up and they were pelted with bursts of short squally rain. Those that could not fit into the wagon slept directly under it. In this fashion they passed an uneasy night.

In the morning they started off early. Within half an hour they passed a fast-flowing mountain stream, small enough for the wagon to cross it without difficulty but enabling them to fill all their water skins. The road veered north shortly after and started climbing again, leaving the forest behind, and less than an hour into their journey they reached the Tower of Hayader, which marked the starting point Claw Pass. It was an unassuming grey stone tower that did not serve as a barrier to the pass, as the west road they were on and the south road which joined it here both gave it a wide berth before climbing upward into a U-shape cleft in the rock. It was inhabited though; a couple of men in the red livery of Baron Lasgaart come out to speak with them.

'Hail there, friends,' said one. 'Are you seriously going to attempt the pass before springtime?'

'We have no choice,' said Morgan. 'We are on urgent business on behalf of the Grand Duke and Baron Felmere.'

'Then it is not for me to stop you, but I warn you: if the snow starts before you get to Jeremiah's Saddle, turn back. The pass will be impossible to clear if that happens. There are tales of people resorting to eating each other after they had got themselves trapped up there.'

'Don't worry!' Morgan indicated Rozgon. 'If it comes to that, he will see us through winter, spring and summer.'

The man laughed and passed a wooden box up to Varen, who was leading the horses. 'Iron rations, meat and fat. You may need it on the journey ahead.'

'Thank you,' said Morgan. 'I will mention you to Baron Felmere if we return.'

And with that they passed the tower and started to climb the wide road that led into the gaping maw of the pass.

12

It was a different type of dawn chorus for Cheris. The raucous cries of seagulls had been replaced by the chatter of a great variety of smaller birds, some musical, some less so. Add to that, the early rumbling of wheeled traffic on the road outside her room and she had no problem getting up and being ready for the next part of her journey. Marcus had got what he wanted – the new knight in charge of their escort was both older and uglier. He had a large red birthmark that covered his right cheek and went by the name of Sir Norton. As she waited in the frosty dawn air for the horses to be fixed to the wagon that she and Marcus would be sharing, she cast her eyes about hoping for a glimpse of Sir Dylan but with no success. Her heart sank a little.

There were four knights going with them in total; apparently there would be a further twenty or so at the army camp, all of whom were employed to look after the healer mage, a lady called Anaya. Cheris remembered her well, a striking lady some ten to fifteen years older than her with bright-red hair held in a bun. She was quite a serious woman, not prone to outbursts of laughter. Cheris made a mental note to act accordingly when she met her.

One of the knights was a very young lad, probably not even in his twenties, who went by the name of Roland. It turned out the reason he was on this trip was that he was very good with horses, having grown up on a farm. He would be the one driving the wagon for them and made a beeline for Cheris when he saw her. He explained what he would be doing on this trip, which prompted her to ask:

'Have you finished all your knightly training? Please don't think I am being rude or anything, but you look as if you have barely started shaving.' 'No, my Lady, I am but a squire who has barely embarked on his studies. It will be several years before I can call myself a knight. Rather, I am here to tend the horses and clean the knights' armour, weapons and so forth.' He looked at her as if unsure of what to say next.

'Pardon me, my Lady, but I have never met a mage before, I am ... curious as to the nature of your powers. I know I will be trained in as to how you use your abilities, but this will be only from a knight's perspective. I wonder if, as we travel, you could try and explain magic from the position of one who wields it.'

Cheris looked surprised. 'I was not expecting such a request. I fear it will be difficult if not impossible for me to convey the complexities of our powers but ... yes, I will try. I suppose it is a long journey and this may help alleviate any tedium.' She was painfully aware that Marcus was stood not ten feet from her and the last thing she wanted to do was give the impression of flirting with yet another young man. She decided to try and treat him as a younger brother, so as not to give off the wrong signals.

Sir Norton called to them. 'Everything is ready. If you could both climb into the caravan. We loaded your stuff on board earlier.'

At this, Roland gave her a hand up as she climbed the small ladder into the back of the caravan and clambered inside.

It was a solidly built affair with wooden sides and a canvas roof. On either side of it was a long couch that would also double as a bed. It had two small windows and at the front were their trunks, sitting alongside a set of drawers that held cooking utensils, lamp oil and the like. The only access to the caravan was at the rear, where the wooden panel had been fashioned into a lockable door. Marcus climbed in after her, carrying what looked like a white sheet. 'The knights have given me this. There are hooks here and ... umm ... here that we can hang it from to give us privacy if required.'

'Excellent, I hope you don't snore.'

'I don't really know; I am always asleep at the time.'

They pottered around for a while and rigged the sheet up folding it over itself for the time being. Cheris got out her mirror and a small bottle of scented water, and dabbed a little behind her ears. As she sat down, she heard a cry from the knights and felt the caravan slowly lurch forward. They were off.

For this, the first, part of the journey she got on to her knees on the couch and looked out of the window, ignoring Marcus comment of 'No need to get so excited, it really is quite unremarkable out there.' She saw the wagon bathed in shadow as they passed under the walls, out of the city gates and over the drawbridge, and then it was all rolling grassland dotted with the occasional tree or small copse. They were going gently downhill and as she craned her neck to look back she could see the imposing grey city walls, crenellated, with many conical towers getting smaller in the distance. The sky was a leaden colour studded with ominous low-lying black clouds; it looked like it would be a rather nasty day.

'If you come over this side, you can see the sea.' said Marcus.
'Thank you but no. I have seen enough of the sea in my lifetime.'
'Yes, I suppose you have; it will take us about two to three weeks to complete our journey. Early tomorrow we will cross the Red River, a branch of the Erskon and then it's ten days or so through a green country, full of farms and small villages, until we reach the Kada, the first of the Seven Rivers. You will see things change then; it is a military frontier after all. After that, we should get to the army's forward camp within a few days, depending on where it is of course – the battlefront is constantly changing.'

'I don't really want to think about war or battle, not just yet anyway; I just want fresh air and peace for a while, and no one shouting at me of course.' 'And what am I to do for my amusement if I can't shout at you?'

'See, I only misbehave to keep you happy.'
He sighed wearily. 'It's going to be a long, long journey.'

The knights stopped at about noon where they took a lunch consisting of a hot wheat porridge washed down with some rather nasty weak ale. They stood under a low canvas pavilion that they had attached to the rear of the caravan – the rain had started to come down quite heavily. Lunch over, Cheris went and sat with Roland at the front of the wagon. Its canvas roof extended over them to keep them dry and Cheris covered herself with a blanket to keep out the cold.

'Now then, young Roland, what is it you wish to know?'
'Oh, where to begin?' He tugged the reins, called to the horses and they were off again. 'Well, basically what makes you all so special?

How are you able to command these powers? Do the Gods give them to you?'

She laughed. 'That's a lot of questions to begin with. Hmmm, it could take some time to answer. Let me see...' Her mind went back to some of Marcus's early lessons 'What do you see ahead of you?'

'Well, there is the road, a couple of houses, Sir Norton and Sir Werner, the red flag, the horses, what else is there?' He sounded puzzled.

'You are right, of course; all that is ahead of us. But look at Sir Norton, for example. What if I were to tell you there is another world, a world that occupies the same space as our own but one that exists under completely different rules. A world of energy, where nothing is corporeal or solid. Sir Norton on his horse is occupying the space taken by this energy; it runs over him, under him, inside him and through him, and we, as mages, have the ability of "seeing" this world in our minds and drawing power from it. We can cross the divide, the barrier between these worlds and, with practice, can control and shape what we take from it to our will. We all have different abilities: some of us are stronger and can take more power, or mana, from the Plane of Lucan without risking any of its concomitant dangers.'

'What dangers? And can you actually "see" this world?'

'No, not as you or I see Sir Norton. Lucan has given us the ability to let it into our minds – there and there alone is where we can picture it. And, as for the dangers, well, think about it: we are using our minds to shape and redirect energy; get it wrong, lose control of that energy and you could be in enormous trouble. At best, you forget what you are doing, lose control of yourself for a moment; at worst, your brain can literally fry.'

'Have you ever seen this happen?'

'At the college we are brought on very very slowly. We spend years doing mental exercises, incantations, focusing ourselves through the use of things like hand gestures, all of which helps to give us full control over what we wish to accomplish ... but, yes, things do go wrong. Some of us have too much ability with too little mental discipline and that is when things can get messy. There was a boy of about ten, I remember; I had only been at the college a few months and a group of us younger initiates were practising some basic summoning when the poor lad started screaming. Our mentors ran to help him but it was too late. Blood started pouring from his nose, his mouth, and his eyes and ears. Then he stopped screaming and collapsed, dead. It was horrible. None of us would try anything for a while after that.' She stopped, peering reflectively ahead through the rain and gloom.

'Are you able to just ... um ... stop using your powers, so that that sort of thing doesn't happen to you?'

'Theoretically yes, but it takes an awful lot of self-discipline; your mind is always in touch with that magical part of it and the temptation is always there. At the college they recommend occasional, supervised, low level use of magic – lighting lamps, starting a fire, in a fireplace of course, just to keep the urge to use our powers in check. The best analogy I can think of is that it's like making love; you don't ever have to do it but it releases a lot of stress and tension when you do. Oh Elissa preserve me, I've embarrassed you, haven't I? I am so sorry, I just forget where I am sometimes.' She put her hand over her mouth – the poor boy was scarlet!

'No, no, my Lady,' he mumbled. 'Everything you are saying is very interesting. This other world you describe; does anything live there?'

'Yes,' she said slowly, 'creatures of elemental energy, fire, lightning, ice and the like. They are like the forms you see Lucan take in the Scriptures. They are capricious and can be quick to anger, so our training enables us to spend as little time as possible in their world so as we do not attract them to us. We are an alien presence there, you see; they could be friendly or hostile, but it is better for us never to find out.'

'You are talking about demons, yes? Are there not forbidden arts that enable you to call them into this world?'

'Not all these creatures are demons, and I believe it is your job to stop any mage who even contemplates summoning one of them into our world. They are incredibly dangerous once they cross the divide. There are tomes at the college that concern this subject as well as others in the universities in Tanaren, but the ones at the college are kept under lock and key by the Grand Magister and Sir Benedict, the head of your order on the island. They both hold half of the key, so one cannot open it without the other. Needless to say, I have never seen these books.'

'Why, by Artorus, would anyone want to get involved in such a thing if it is so dangerous?'

'I do not know,' she said, shrugging her shoulders. 'The desperate or those seeking power might try, I suppose. If we sense a demon being drawn to us when casting, we have to abandon our attempt at a spell for they will attack us immediately. If somebody can first summon and second control a demon in this world, then they control a sentient being of great destructive ability. A demon cannot survive long in our world and to prolong its existence it has to feed on life energy. So for it to survive it has to kill and kill again. It will seek out mages first, as we are more attuned to them and our power can sustain them for longer, but thereafter anyone is fair game. If a mage can control one and direct its killing power towards its enemies, then he is only a little less than a god for the time that it lives. It is all hypothetical, though – the power and ability required to summon and control such a creature is beyond all but a handful of mages that have existed since the colleges were founded hundreds of years ago. At least, this is what I am given to understand; as I have said, I have never read any demonological work and have no intention of starting.'

Roland nodded gravely. 'Yes, demonology and the control of mages who have such powers are a significant part of our teaching, or so I am given to believe. Thank you, my Lady; you have given me much to think about.'

'It was a pleasure, Roland. Now if you could stop the caravan for a minute while I go back inside, I would be most grateful. If I get any colder, you could snap me in two.'

She lay on her back on the couch. It was a horrible night with the rain spattering against the caravan, making it difficult for her to sleep. The dividing sheet was up but she could sense that Marcus was having the same problems as herself.

'Marcus,' she said.

'What is it?' he replied languidly. So he was awake.

'Was it really necessary to spy on me like that? I could sense it, you know; you using mana to hear what I was saying to Roland.'

'Ah, but I knew that you would know that I was using it, so "spying" hardly seems to be appropriate in the circumstances. I am sorry for doing it, Cheris – it was only for five minutes – but after your escapades in the city I had to be sure. I won't do it again.'

'He is hardly my type. You know I prefer older men. You are in more danger from me than he is.'

'Then I consider myself duly warned,' he laughed softly.

'On a related topic, how are things with you and Gilda? I haven't seen you two together for a while.'

'Things are fine. We have been... um ... very close friends for longer than you have been alive. Just because you haven't seen us in one another's company for a while doesn't mean that there's anything wrong.'

'Pfff, you older people!' she snorted. 'How can you be so dispassionate? If I had met the love of my life, I would want to spend every day in their company.'

'You do know that strictly we are not allowed to have relationships, don't you? Let alone marry. Discretion is a common-sense path to take sometimes, though that may be a difficult idea for you to grasp – you wouldn't know common sense if it came up towards you and hit you over the head with a brick.'

She laughed and affected a 'grumpy old mage' voice: 'Oh, the impetuosity of youth! Why is it that wisdom comes only with great age!'

Marcus groaned and put a blanket over his head. 'Go to sleep!'

Cheris continued to smile. 'She is a nice lady, Gilda; you are very lucky to have her. It is very difficult trying to maintain a relationship without the knights noticing; the fact that you have done it over so many years is a credit to you both.'

'The fact that the knights turn a blind eye a lot of the time is more pertinent in this case, I feel. I hear that some of the colleges in Chira are a lot stricter and transgressions are punished with imprisonment. I heard a story years ago about a mage couple who had a child. The child was taken away and exposed and the man was castrated. The girl was imprisoned and went mad. I don't know if it was true or not.'

'By Elissa, that's monstrous!' she said. 'Anyone could have an accident... I know we have ... ways of ending an early pregnancy but even so...' She trailed off. 'Did you ever want children, Marcus?'

'Of course,' he said, 'but even if we could conceal a pregnancy, we cannot conceal a child. It would have been taken away from us and sent to an orphanage, and monitored of course for signs of the gift. If it did have talent, it would be sent to college a long way from our own. Gilda has been pregnant, you know – years ago – on a couple of occasions but we had to end it. They were very sad times.'

'I am so sorry; I didn't know.'

'It has happened to a lot of us,' he replied. 'It will probably happen to you one day. Don't be tempted to keep it. Our college may be more tolerant but the prison is there for a purpose. I don't want to see you in there one day. Now go to sleep.'

The days passed and the caravan rumbled ever onwards through a land patchworked with hedge-enclosed fields, streams, copses whose leaves were turning ever browner, and the occasional small village that usually consisted of nothing more than a few thatched cottages hugging the road, a tavern which would be the largest building present, and a small stone chapel, often graced by a weatherworn statue of Artorus outside the porch.

Her conversations with Roland had continued. She had adopted an almost Marcus-like approach with him, that of a teacher with an almost maternalistic concern for her pupil. They had been travelling for well over a week and were now only a couple of days from the river Kada, close to the war zone. She was sitting with him now, as usual, as he steered the horses.

'Do any of you try and extinguish your talent,' he asked, 'so that you can join ordinary society? Is there a way to do this?'

'Not that I have heard of,' she said. 'Actually, that isn't true. I have heard of some fanatics who cut out their tongues or break all their fingers so they cannot cast, but I cannot say whether this is true or not. And in the empire of Koze far to the south I hear they "experiment" on mages by doing unspeakable things to their brains, leaving them unable to speak, but again I don't know if this is true either. We are stuck with the way Artorus or Lucan has made us, I am afraid. Just as you cannot determine your hair colour, the shape of your nose, your height, so I had no choice as to my ... gift, as Marcus calls it.'

'Would you remove it if you could?'

'Oh Roland, that is an impossible question. This has been with me all my life and I cannot imagine being without it. You adapt to your circumstances. The Isle of Tears is my home and that is that. I am actually quite fond of the place. What is it?' She saw him looking at her with a wary glance. 'Some other question?'

'No,' he said in a low voice. 'It was something Sir Norton said but I cannot ask you about it.'

'Why ever not?' She looked at him with a pert smile. 'Am I that frightening?'

'No, but it is something a gentleman should not ask a lady.'

'Now you have really piqued my curiosity,' she laughed. 'Come on, just ask it before I turn you into a rabbit.'

'Very well,' he said, keeping his voice low. 'Sir Norton says that mages, when ... in the throes of passion, can lose control of their abilities and ... er ... set on fire the object of their affections...' He finished by staring fixedly to the ground.

This time she really did laugh, a high, musical sound that drew glances from the other knights. 'Really! You don't seriously believe...!' She started laughing again.

He started smiling, too. 'I take it that's a no then.'

She calmed down. 'A very big no, Roland. From what I have been told, we are no different from anyone else in that respect; however, it is possible to use a little electrical magic at certain times during the act. It can be extremely stimulating for both parties. But I am letting on to mage secrets here; I had better be quiet. Hang on, what's that?'

They had just turned northwards, the dirt path they were on circling a small copse which had obscured the view ahead. They were actually on the crest of a hill. In front of them the path dropped gradually until it hit a broad flat plain dotted with fields and the occasional farm building. In the distance to the north, partially obscured by mist and crowned by low white cloud, lay a belt of grey mountains, while to the east Cheris could discern a broad silver ribbon of a river, its course undulating this way and that until it finally passed them snaking off into the southern distance. Some way ahead, maybe about five miles away, the river looped westwards towards a low sloping hill not dissimilar to the one they currently occupied and on the crown of this hill was a settlement enclosed by a low crenellated wall. It had a gate in its western side from which a road ran. It was actually the same road they were travelling on; she saw it run like a bootlace from the town until it eventually reached their position and of course continued ever onwards until it reached Tanaren City itself. Surrounding the town ahead, covering the hill and spreading into the river valley below, were a motley collection of small, dark, irregular shapes, closely packed together .She asked Roland for clarification.

'Yes, they are shacks and tiny one-room buildings fashioned out of wood, turf and sods of earth. This is Athkaril, the main destination for refugees fleeing the war. By all accounts there is much friction between the locals and newcomers. We will not be staying there long. In fact, I think Sir Norton will camp soon and just drive through there on the morrow.'

'How do they all make a living I wonder?'

'Well, some of them have a trade which they can practise here, though they often get less than the going rate; others join the army to feed their families, and the rest, well, they just do what they can to avoid starving.'

The following morning she saw that some of them were barely avoiding that terrible fate. A sense of growing unease led her to stay in the wagon rather than sit with Roland and, as they skirted the hill Athkaril was built on and made for the bridge near its eastern gate, she was glad she had made that decision. Surrounding the dirt path to the bridge were these shacks she had been told about; they could barely be called dwellings, fashioned as they were from whatever material came to hand. Many did not even have doors just a pulled-down piece of dirty cloth concealing a dingy enclosed space containing whatever goods these people had managed to spirit out of their former homes. People sat outside the entrances in front of small fires heating their cooking pots. Many thin ribbons of blue smoke trailed upwards to the sky.

The refugee village must have contained hundreds, probably thousands, of these buildings. Channels had been dug from the river to divert water to people's homes but these had been long clogged up with filth and rubbish. Cheris could smell the place even from her secure position; in high summer, she thought, it must be unbearable. Was there any city that did not have these terrible places? Worse was to come, though, for as soon as they passed the first two or three buildings they found themselves swamped by children, their pale thin bony arms outstretched as they begged for money. The filthy rags they wore, their large hollow eyes and thin pinched faces were just like those of the girl she had given money to in Tanaren. But she couldn't give everyone here a coin – there were dozens of them, pleading with the knights in their high, reedy voices. Eventually Sir Norton threw a handful of pennies into the air which landed behind them. They immediately lost interest in the knights and dived on the money. There were fisticuffs and tears until finally the lucky few who had grabbed a coin or two ran off into the maze of buildings and were lost to view.

Shortly after, they crossed the broad stone bridge over the sluggish river and gradually left that unhappy place behind. They were now in the Land of the Seven Rivers and their destination, the camp of Baron Felmere, was only a few days away.

Cheris stayed in the wagon more frequently now. Roland had run out of questions for her and she could feel the tension inside her building up as their journey neared its end. Marcus helpfully reassured her that she was definitely the junior partner here and would be kept out of trouble as much as possible, but this didn't help her sleep, which was often troubled. A couple of times she became aware that she was crying out loud in the midst of an uneasy dream; Marcus must have heard her but would never say anything the following day.

Three days out from Athkaril they reached the next river and the town of Tetha Vinoyen where the bridge was. While the horses were being watered, Marcus went for a stroll, accompanied by Sir Norton, while she stayed indoors. She noticed here that people were more blase´ about the presence of magic among them. Despite Marcus sticking out like the proverbial sore thumb in his bright-red robes, everyone else went about their business almost oblivious to him. When he returned to the wagon he seemed quite agitated.

'The town here is buzzing! The city watch have spent most of the day fishing bodies out of the river. It appears there was a fight at the inn last night involving some bandits and a group of Baron Felmere's men. The bandits definitely came off worse. Some people are saying the bandits were Baron Vinoyen's men; there is a feud between him and Felmere, you see. You will pick up on all of this over the next few days.'

'How close to the camp are we now?' Cheris couldn't even feign interest.

'Felmere has two camps. His main camp is just over a day away. It is where Anaya, the healer, is stationed. We will stay there one night then move on to his forward camp where the Baron himself is quartered. So, to answer your question, we will be at the first camp on the morning of the day after tomorrow and the second camp the day after that. We are almost there – one more night in this wagon and the luxury of a tent after that.'

She looked pensive, then gave out a huge sigh. 'I wonder what fate Artorus has in store for us?'

'None that can be seen clearly. In Koze in the south they have the great Temple of the Auguries and thousands of priests and mages desperately try to fathom out their emperor's dreams and predict the future. If they get it badly wrong, some are put to death. The truth is that no mortal can read the minds of the Gods; for us the future is unwritten. All we can do is to face it with courage and a true heart.'

She looked at him with clear eyes. 'Your words are very noble, but inside I feel like jelly. I fear I am little more than a quivering mouse and hardly the great all-powerful mage you seem to think I am.'

He then did something unexpected. He put his arm around her

shoulder and hugged her to him. 'Fear not!' he said boldly. 'Sometimes the truth about ourselves is kept from us and only others are able to see in us what we ourselves cannot. I have every confidence in you, my girl. Now, let us eat. I have just purchased some rather delightful-smelling cheese. Let's have some with some bread.'

And so their journey drew to a close. They crossed the river after eating and after passing some villages inhabited by the brave and hardy entered a country filled only by soldiers and camp followers. She noted the stillness of the place after the bustle of the towns and villages they had previously passed. Even the birds sounded mournful. She had never seen mountains before and when she first espied them on the approach to the river Kada she had dismissed them as something of a disappointment. Now, however, as they drew closer to them and she could get a better idea of their scale and grandeur, she had to revise her opinion. She had read many stories involving mountains and the beasts – the eagles, bears, giants and griffons – that supposedly lived in them and now that she was close to them, their whitecapped peaks soaring above the pine-clad foothills, she found herself much more inclined to believe them. The ancients had even believed the Gods lived in them rather than the heavens, and she had to admit they did seem like a fitting home. She imagined standing high on one of the snow-capped peaks looking down at the world below, seeing people no bigger than ants scurry about on their business. How petty the dealings of men, their wars, their feuds, their empires would seem from somewhere so high. How insignificant she would look – little more than an insect to be stepped on and forgotten. She had often even wondered whether the Gods themselves were little more than a construction of the human mind, something put there to give importance to a life that was difficult, painful and all too brief. She had even voiced this opinion once, to Father Barris, one of the senior Artoran priests on the island. He had dismissed her argument and spoke to her instead of the importance of faith to the human soul, how its nature nourishes and enriches and enables us to see that which we cannot see, hear or touch but which was there all the same. Cheris wasn't convinced – she apologised to the father but kept her true thoughts to herself. What would he think if he stood atop that mountain?

The following day it rained. Nothing heavy, just a fine misty drizzle, but it was enough to chill her bones and dampen the spirits. Oh for the soft cushions and open fire of the college's common room! The heads of the mountains were covered in heavy grey cloud which seemed to drain the landscape of its colour, leaving it bland and anaemic. She sat with Roland for a while and watched as he swung gently northwards along an uneven side road where the wagon's wheels and the horses kept throwing up liquid mud until everything within two feet of the ground was covered in its soft brown mess. To Cheris, the day both dragged and went too quickly. The countryside provided little of interest or that she had not seen before and yet she did not want to make camp – their last camp before joining the army the following day.

But, as no mage yet had invented a spell that could stop time itself, camp was made, bunks were slept in and the dawn of the next day arose pink and fine. The rain had stopped but the seasonal chill in the air persisted. Roland had a spare weathered dark cloak which he gave to her and she hugged it close as he spurred the horses on one last time.

'So you will be staying at this main camp while we move on to the forward one,' she asked him, although she already knew the answer.

'Yes, my Lady, we will part ways tonight. I would like to thank you, though. I have enjoyed our conversations and learned much. Please keep that cloak. I have another and with winter coming you may well need it.'

'Thank you; I do tend to feel the cold. Maybe it's because we are close to the mountains but I haven't felt warm in days.'

'Just wait till the winter! The other knights tell me you can get ferocious snowfalls around here with great drifts some ten feet high.'

'Well, that just sounds terrific,' she moaned. 'On the island we rarely saw snow; apparently being close to the sea means a lot less snow for some reason. I will ask Anaya, the healer, if she has any spare petticoats. It would be ironic if I were to travel all this way to fight only to be killed by the chill.'

The journey continued. Now and then they would pass abandoned villages in various states of disrepair. One in particular looked like it had been deserted many years ago; the houses were blackened shells with walls barely a foot high, and trees and shrubs had recolonised the place. On the dirt road through it she saw some blackened bones that looked like they had been tossed into the air and left to fall randomly. She remarked on this to Roland.

'They have probably been moved. The wolves around here are much bolder than they used to be and there are other carrion feeders that could have done this also.'

'Like what?' she said dully.

'Oh just rumours! Some say ghouls, pale monsters that feed on the dead, still exist around here, or anywhere where death is commonplace. They hide in dark places during the day and only come out to feed at night. They have a special fondness for the drinking of human blood, or so you will hear if you frequent any tavern in wilder parts of the country.'

'Hopefully they will remain just rumours,' she said, shivering slightly. 'What happened to the people that lived here, I wonder?'

'We probably passed them in Athkaril living in the squalor there. Or maybe they went all the way to Tanaren and are doing well for themselves. Artorus knows – I hope the latter.'

At length the sun reached its noonday zenith and Cheris at last started to feel a little warmer; the air, fresh and clear, was beginning to make her feel drowsy. She could feel her head slipping on to her chest when Roland cut in. 'Here we are, my Lady.'

Ahead of her was a broad field dotted with shrubs. A small silver ribbon of a stream cut across it, winding hither and thither on its journey westwards to the Vinoyen. Behind all this she could see the pine uplands sitting just below the jagged mountains, the sun turning their snowy heights a deep burnt orange. Where the stream became a barrier ahead of them was a broad wooden bridge with a small tower at each corner. Over the bridge the road widened and continued north-east for some half a mile. And there it was ahead of them – a fort constructed entirely of logs, square in shape, with the stream flowing just past it on the right forming a natural barrier. On its other three sides it was surrounded by a ditch laced with sharpened wooden stakes, blackened at their tips and pointing outwards. There were three towers on each wall, except for the wall that held the gateway directly ahead of them, which had four including one at each side of the gate. Each tower had a crude wooden crenellation at its top and was protected by a roof of brushwood covered in hides. From the gate towers flew many flags and pennants. One, which flew higher than the others, was a plain blue-and-white halved banner bordered by gold which even Cheris knew was the standard of Tanaren. Others she could make out had a mace, a bird's claw and a great silver lance, and there was a plain green-and-white one similar to the Tanaren banner. Another had a waterfall, another a striking snake and another a snarling wolf. Last of all she noticed the banner of the thorn. She reflected on its history. It had reputedly come about because St Elysa, founder of the order of knights whose purpose was to protect practitioners of magic from others and from themselves, was challenged by the then emperor of Chira to prove she was not a heretic in thrall to demonic powers. To do this, she recited verses from the Book of Artorus while a rope made of thorns was passed through her tongue. She recited them all clearly without hesitation and so the emperor declared her pure in soul and elevated her to the ranks of the saints – those humans whose devotion to the Gods elevated them to quasi-divine status. Divine or not, the tale always made Cheris wince.

They arrived at the bridge. Sir Norton briefly spoke to one of the halberd armed guards that approached him, who then waved them on. She could see men patrolling the wooden ramparts of the camp, the sunlight gleaming off their metal armour, and as they got closer she could hear voices – officers barking orders at the guards on the gate, she supposed. The gate then opened to accept them. Then they were in.

The camp itself was structured in a highly regimented manner with a road running north to south bisecting a similar one running east to west. Where they met at the centre of the camp was a square used for drills or for announcements that the commanders needed to give to the men. She expected the camp to be a mainly tented affair and, although tents indeed took up much of the room there, there were also a number of hastily constructed wooden buildings – grain stores and the commander's quarters, according to Roland. The place was a bustle of men and animals; she could hear a blacksmith at his anvil and smell the large pots of stew that the cooks were preparing nearby. Over many of the tents were hung flags or banners denoting the affiliation of its inhabitants. She guessed that Sir Norton was heading for the flag of the thorn, and after they had reached the central square and turned west she could see it, near the end of the road on the northern side. However, just before arriving there he stopped at a large pavilion bearing an all-red flag with a white heart shape at its centre. Sir Norton came to speak to her. 'The hospital tent. You may wish to get Marcus, as I am sure he wishes to speak with the healer. If you go with him, head for our tent after you have finished. You will be quartered there.'

She thanked him and, after telling Roland she would see him later, hopped lightly off the wagon and went behind to speak to Marcus.

'We're at the hospital tent – do you wish to see Anaya?'

'Indeed I do – it has been some years since I saw her last.'

'How long has she been out here?'

'Six years. It is something of a sore point; our secondments normally last for a year, two at most, but there have been no other healers wishing to attend here. It is a theatre of war, after all.'

'Why ever not? What better place to practise their craft?'

Marcus sighed. 'You would think so, but the truth is the healers have an easy life on the island pampering the wealthy and living in far nicer accommodation than the cells you are used to. Why risk life and limb when everything is so easy for you?'

'Well, it seems very unfair on Anaya.'

'Indeed it does and it worries me.'

He said no more but instead walked over to the tent, ducked under its flap and entered. Cheris followed hearing Roland spurring the horses onward behind her.

It was quite dark inside, although some light came from lanterns hanging from the tent's supports. She could see a lot of low beds, mostly unoccupied, although a couple did contain prostrate forms lying motionless. At the back of the tent was a partition and sitting in front of it on one of several chairs positioned there was a woman whom Cheris recognised as Anaya. Marcus called to her and she got up and embraced him fondly.

She had changed: whereas Cheris could remember a tall green-eyed redhaired woman with a friendly if no-nonsense demeanour, the person she was looking at now was drawn, with pinched features and weariness behind her eyes. Her fine red hair was now streaked with grey and held in a severe bun. For a woman in her mid-thirties she looked much more like a contemporary of Marcus than of herself.

'Marcus, old friend, I heard you were on your way; how do you fare? How is life on the islands?'

'As unchanging as ever,' he replied genially. 'You remember Cheris, don't you? She will be assisting me this time around.'

'Of course I remember. She has grown up a bit, I see.' She turned to Cheris. 'How are you coping with being Marcus's great protégé these days?'

'Well, it's never easy but I get by. I think Marcus has all but given up on me, bless him.'

'You are evidently being too hard on yourself. It is obvious Marcus thinks a great deal of you. Come, the nurses here can deal with the patients for now; let us retire and have something to eat.'

She led them behind the screened part of the tent. It was a cluttered area full of shelves, each of which was packed full of bottles and bowls – liquids of every conceivable colour, powders, dried leaves, even dead insects... There were open trunks full of fresh dressings and surgical instruments and a couple of stoves on which to heat them. There were also a couple of low beds and a table and chairs where they now sat down. A nurse in a simple white dress acknowledged them and, after putting some bread and cheese on the table, left the three of them alone.

'May I speak frankly?' Marcus said to Anaya.

'You always do, and I have never heard you ask for permission before,' Anaya said archly, with the thinnest of smiles.

'Very well. Let me just say that you look tired, my dear. I really think you have been out here too long.'

Anaya sighed. 'There was a time I would have argued vehemently with you over this. But you are right, I am tired. Last winter was very, very cold and I came down with a fever from which I don't think I have fully recovered. Ironic, isn't it, a healer laid low with illness? I felt so weak I was unable to use magic and I have found the fighting season here very taxing.'

She was about to continue when Sir Norton appeared from behind the screen.

'I am sorry, Marcus, but Sir Reynard and Sir Dominic wish to meet with you urgently.'

'Artorus's beard, I have barely sat down. Please excuse me, ladies; I will see you both later.'

They both nodded to him as he went. Cheris and Anaya were now alone. 'It is good to see Marcus again,' said Anaya. 'He was my very first mentor before I was sent to the Isle of Healing. Irascible, but kind. And now he has you. He has spoken highly of you on previous visits. I knew he would bring you eventually.'

Cheris cleared her throat. 'I just don't want to disappoint him. In a way I wish I was a healer. It is far nobler to save life rather than to take it.'

She was surprised at the older woman's reaction. She snorted derisorily and said harshly. 'I used to think that, too. I thought being here would help me grow as a person; increase the nobility of my spirit. But the opposite has happened.'

'How?' said Cheris softly.

'In the fighting season, when men are brought here in their dozens you have to make some terrible decisions. Last summer, for example, two men were brought in here at the same time and both were losing blood quickly. It could not be staunched by normal means and so I had to use magic. I then realised that I would only have time to save one of them, that I would have to let one of them die – and do you know what I did? I saved the best-looking one. A man died because I was possessed by a womanish whim. It turned out he had a wife and three children; she is probably selling herself to some tavern drunk in Athkaril now to stop them from starving. Nobility of the spirit indeed. What a joke, what a terrible joke.'

'I am sorry Anaya, but you are still saving people here.'

Anaya ignored her. 'The other thing is, because you have magic, people think you can practically make the dead walk. I am sick of telling people that I can stop blood loss but cannot reattach limbs; that I can stop pain, but can't always remove its cause; that I can reset broken bone but cannot remove splinters; that I can stop further infections but cannot heal putrefied flesh. The list goes on and on.'

'Too much is being expected of you. Your hair had no grey when I last saw you.'

'Oh that! It is part worry, yes, but also it is because in summer I use our powers every day. You know there is a price to pay for that, a drain on our bodies from which both time and rest are required for recovery. If you get neither, well, you can see what happens.'

'Of course,' said Cheris sympathetically. 'Look, when my year here is up, I will go with Marcus to the healers and insist they replace you.'

Anaya smiled. 'Thank you. It is not all bad here. In winter I get a lot of freedom. I have been to St Delph's University in Tanaren a few times to study in the library there and Baron Felmere has even given me a cottage, near to a place called Shayer Ridge, where I can relax away from everyone. If only I could see an end to this Keth-accursed war, a decisive stroke that would end all the suffering, I would be happier. Unfortunately, I think it will last for many more years yet.'

'We don't know that. I hear the Grand Duke is putting much effort into resolving things.'

Anaya looked motherly. 'Aah, child, you are so naive; all these men of war think they have the ability to do something here. In reality, they are the problem, not the resolution. There is no resolution.'

Hearing footsteps, they stopped talking. Marcus walked around the partition.

'Sorry, Anaya, but I must take Cheris from you for the moment. Sir Reynard Lanthorpe and Sir Dominic Hartfield both wish to meet her.'

13

'My dearest Leonie,

It seems such a long time since I have seen you! I hope all is well with you and your husband and that that waistline of yours is not giving you too much concern (although the way you attacked the custard at my wedding feast gives me reason to believe that this may be something of a forlorn hope). It was lovely to see you and Giselle that night – who knows when I shall see you both again?

I am settled here now. The journey from Erskon House took an absolute age, although it was interesting to see the country change. You plunge into the Forest of Morrathnay, climb up and around Mount Talman, then travel down into western Tanaren, a land of small fields enclosed with stone walls, hills scattered with fluffy white sheep, swift foam-flecked rivers and small copses full of trees stunted by the wind. It is a rugged land with few people, all housed in stone buildings – for stone is more plentiful than wood here.

Eventually we entered a small port town Vihag or Vihaga (I have heard it called both) where we took ship and a day later landed at Osperitsan, an island very much like the land we had just left. Two things I wish to convey to you. The first is a source of minor irritation – why is it called the north here when all the maps show it to be in the west? North-western would be a far more accurate expression and that is the one I shall use from now on. The second point – something I am sure you will agree with – is to the utter remoteness of where I now am. It does feel like a different country here – the life of the people here is as far removed from life in Tanaren City as it would be from life on the moon! Did you know there was a famine here barely five years ago? Many of the elderly and the young perished here and yet I knew nothing of it.

The baronial hall is similar to Erskon House with the exception that it is built purely in stone. Other than that, it is long and low and has two storeys, although its enclosing wall has towers and battlements – once necessary apparently, as they had great trouble with the Kudreyan pirates until we defeated them.

The Baron, that is my husband, has been courteous and respectful to me, probably too respectful; he is not the first person to think I am made of the finest porcelain. Hopefully he will learn in time. He arranged a reception for me on arrival which was attended by most of the local nobility. It seems you only need to own a cabbage patch and a one-room house here to call yourself a baron. There appeared to be hundreds of them; I ended the evening more confused than ever. I like one baron, Einar, who is my husband's closest friend and who appears to have taken a shine to me. He has been a great prop to me as I adjust to my new life.

And with that I shall finish for now. I have a new handmaiden called Ebba. She is a sweet girl, much nearer to my age than Doren. She has already said she will arrange delivery of this letter along with the others I have written to Father and Giselle. Mind you, by the time I finish signing my name the winter's snows may be over and we will be looking at the first bluebells of spring.

Take care and love as always,

Lady Ceriana Osperitsan-Hartfield, Baroness of Osperitsan and the Far Reaches, Keeper of the Ancient Traditions of Kibil (I jest not – I do not even know what they are!), Scion of Tanaren and the North… (There is more but I will desist at this point.)'

Ceriana folded the parchment and applied the wax seal of Osperitsan, twin axes surmounting a wolf's head. She then put it with the two other letters she had written earlier. Once that was done she sat back in her chair, peered out of the leaded window and let out an enormous sigh.

She had been one week in her new home. She had her own quarters and they were comfortable, filled as they were with dark wooden furniture that would have been considered old-fashioned in the higher echelons of Tanarese society but which seemed perfectly suited to her surroundings here. The windows were small and faced north, overlooking a cobbled, straw strewn courtyard and a cluster of outbuildings that nestled against the modestly high battlement. Thin wisps of smoke trailed upwards from their chimneys dissipating into the watery blue sky over which thin straggling beards of white cloud drifted slowly. It was colder here than it was back in Tanaren City, or even draughty Edgecliff castle, which accounted for the blazing fireplace in her room, a constant feature since her arrival. Beyond the external wall lay the cluster of low stone buildings which made up the town of Osperitsan. All the buildings were small with no more than two rooms, with the exception of the house of Artorus and house of Meriel, both of which stood slightly apart from the town itself, in their own square. She had discovered that the people here made a living either through employment in the baron's service or from the myriad of smallholdings scattered over the nearby hills, all of which were surrounded by the dry-stone walls so prevalent in the area.

Not that she had been out since she had arrived; it had seemed far easier for her to keep to her own rooms rather than stepping out into the unknown. Einar had been kind to her but he had left for his own lands in the west of the island. She had learned that the island itself was divided into three baronetcies – a Baron Thudig held the lands in the south. Her husband had spent little time with her; he admittedly had been busy since his return but seemed to have little inclination to seek out her company other than to assert his marital rights over her on a couple of occasions. Even then she felt he was doing it more out of a sense of duty than anything else. She obviously disappointed him in pretty much every respect, but what could she do? The marriage had not been her choice either.

'Ebba!' she called – Artorus's teeth, she even felt self-conscious raising her voice! From an anteroom a tall dark-haired lugubrious-looking girl entered; she was maybe five or six years older than Ceriana with a pallid face and large hawk-like nose. Baron Wulfthram's choice as her new handmaiden.

'Ebba, I have completed my letters; you said a merchant is leaving for Tanaren City tomorrow.'

'Yes, my Lady.' She took the letters. 'He delivers letters there for us all the time.'

'How much do you need to give him?'

'A crown will suffice, my Lady.'

Ceriana unlocked a wooden box and passed the money to Ebba. 'He is not one of those to pocket the money and burn the letters, is he?'

'Certainly not, my Lady.' Ebba sounded most put out. 'He is a man of integrity and, besides, you are far too important for him to lose your letters. It is hardly something he could get away with doing.' Ceriana felt humbled and a little guilty.

'Oh I am sorry – my words were badly chosen. I did not mean to imply anything untoward. You will soon learn that my mouth runs away from me at times. Please don't think any the worse of me.'

'Of course not, my Lady. I will take these letters to him and return presently. What do you wish of me on my return?'

'Perhaps you could run a bath for me, a hot one if possible; I am feeling cold again, I am afraid.'

'As you wish, my Lady.' Ebba nodded and was gone.

Ceriana looked out of the window and watched Ebba as she emerged into the courtyard and headed for an outbuilding. She picked up a book – *A History of the Baronetcies of Northern Tanaren, Their hierarchy and Organisation* – which she had been perusing avidly since her arrival and continued from where she had left off earlier.

The following morning she felt the need for spiritual guidance. The manor house had its own small private chapel situated to the rear of her own quarters. It had a small pulpit and seating for about ten people over two small pews. The father of Artorus who tendered to it was a decrepit octogenarian by the name of Sidden who had been retained in his dotage since the chapel itself was barely used. He greeted her in a frail but kindly voice.

'Hello, my dear, do you wish to share a small prayer with me? Your company will be most welcome. It does get rather lonely at times here.'

'Yes, Father, I would like that very much. We can both be lonely together.'

'Very well, my Lady, then let us read the Prayer of Artorus right at the front of the holy book.'

She bowed her head, opened the book and read, even though she knew the words by heart. Her clear plaintive voice married with his tremulous high-pitched one in the oddest of duets.

'Oh Artorus, father of the Gods, creator of the Heavens and the Earth and all its multitude of creatures therein, guide us, your most humble servants, to follow in Thy divine path, to show mercy even to the most undeserving, to show generosity even to the most avaricious, to show kindness even to the most cruel and temperance even to the most dissolute. Let us show, through our own supplication and self-sacrifice, the qualities inherent in both Thyself and in Camille, Thy divine consort, and let us purge ourselves of the unclean desires of vanity, pride, greed and idleness. I dedicate my life to Thou. I dedicate my heart to those whom I love, family and neighbours all. I would gladly sacrifice my body to honour Thy glory. Please give me the strength to always honour Thee, for now and for eternity until Xhenafa claims me for his own. As it must be. For ever.'

Father Sidden stopped at this point but Ceriana continued with the Prayer of Elissa:

'Oh Elissa, protector of all women, provider of our virtues of modesty and strength of mind, of our qualities of endurance and forbearance, of our loyalty and steadfastness to others even if they deserve it not, unlike Thee who deserveth it more than any mortal man, imbue me with Thy light, make my heart stronger than those around me and fill me with Thy love and divine spirit so that I may show to others the best that my sex has to offer. Endow me with your gift of fertility and enable me to nurture my own progeny with both strength and gentility. Protect me and my family from Keth and the furnace and make me immune to temptation, for now and for eternity until Xhenafa claims me for his own. As it must be. For ever.'

Father Sidden waited patiently for her to finish, a look of gentle concern on his face. 'What troubles you, child? Has it been difficult for you to settle in?'

She looked at him, unsure as to how much she should tell him.

'Everyone has been very polite, Father. Really, really polite. I am frightened to say anything so as not to offend and this is from someone brought up in the courts of Tanaren city.'

'Your lineage goes before you; you are seen as someone far more important than Baron Wulfthram. Nobody wants to offend someone so close to the Grand Duke, at least not openly.'

'But I am not important,' she said exasperatedly. 'The fourth child is never important, yet even my husband seems to think I am some sort of spy for the Grand Duke or at least a close confidante.'

'Does he treat you as the others do?'

'Yes, he is worse if anything; he seems to do anything to avoid my company.'

The old man stepped down from his pulpit and sat beside her.

'You need to understand that the Baron loved his late wife a great deal. He, if truth be told, is still grieving for her. The situation is very, very hard for you and it will take some time for him to accept you fully. But please do not despair over this. I see a lot of similarities between Sofie and yourself; you are even physically similar to the way she was and you share her kindness, humour and generosity of spirit. You need to pray to Camille for the virtue of patience. If you do that, you will be rewarded in the future – I believe Artorus will show Wulthram the way to you. Be patient, child; it will happen.'

'Thank you, Father. It may even be that I have been avoiding him as much as he has been avoiding me. I shall go and speak with him as soon as I can. Maybe after I have eaten.'

He looked at her with mild surprise. 'Maybe not today, my Lady. He is meeting with the Northern Council.'

She tried to affect forgetfulness. 'Of course, he did tell me earlier; my head is like a sieve. Having said that, Father, he did not actually explain what the Northern Council is.'

'It is the three-monthly meeting of major barons here, along with other people important in local politics. They discuss anything of significance in the region and determine what to do about any problems. I believe your father has been invited to one early next year.'

So the local priest in his dotage knew more about events than she. She gave him a sideways glance. 'It is being held here, isn't it?'

'Of course, my Lady; it always is.'

'Thank you, Father. For everything.' She went to go. When she got to the door, however, she stopped and, turning back to the priest, said, 'Did Wulfthram's wife ... sorry, I mean the Lady Sofie ... did the Lady Sofie ever attend these meetings?'

'I believe she did, most of them anyway. I do not know how big a part she played in them.'

'Thank you, Father.' Ceriana bade him farewell and shut the door.

It was a large door, panelled in dark wood, and she had been looking at it for some ten minutes or so, clasping and unclasping her hands, smacking her lips and exhibiting a dozen other symptoms of agitation. It was the door to the main hall, where the barons were, where the Council were currently meeting, and all that she had to do was open it and walk through. Except something was stopping her. Instead, she stood in the dark stone windowless corridor, lit only by a couple of flaming torches, guttering in their brackets. Above each was a small open grill in the roof, built to release the smoke. Not that they did a good job. The acrid taste of soot stuck in the back of her throat, drying it even more. She could hear the harsh cry of a crow; it must have been on the roof right next to of one the grills. It sounded as if it were mocking her.

'Come on, you foolish girl; what would your father think of you? All you have to do is open the door and take your rightful seat as the wife of the chief baron of the north and daughter of a duke. Just walk through into a room of total strangers, all of whom see you as the child you undoubtedly are judging from current behaviour.' She had changed into one of her grander dresses, a rich purple velvet one embroidered in gold thread, and perfumed herself with rose-water, to try and bolster her feeble resolve. It still wasn't working, though. Artorus's eyes! All she needed was a little courage, just for a couple of seconds. The alternative was to spend a lifetime hiding in her room, in a land full of strangers. It suddenly seemed quite enticing just to turn around, return to her own room, and sit in her favourite chair watching the light drizzle fog up the window she read by. Enticing indeed! Then she slapped her hands smartly to her sides, cleared her throat, muttered something like 'Damn me for a fool' to herself, strode forward and opened the door.

Unlike the corridor, the great hall had large, very grand windows, taking up as it did the entire front section of the manor house. It took her a second or two to adjust to the sudden brightness. When her eyes could see again she hesitated, ever so slightly. The east and west walls – it was through the door of the latter that she had just entered – were covered in beautifully coloured tapestries depicting the various events with which the region was associated; the latest one (you could tell it was so from the fact that many of the others were slightly faded) depicted the naval Battle of Galpa in which the Kudreyan pirates had been finally defeated. Aside from the tapestries. the room otherwise held only several beautifully carved long wooden tables that admittedly had seen better days and the chairs to seat those dining from them. Only one of these tables, the central one, was now occupied. There were maybe just under twenty people, all men, all well dressed, sitting at it. And all of them were now looking at her.

'Good day, gentlemen.' Gods, her voice sounded so small. 'I apologise for the lateness of my arrival; I was just taking morning prayers with Father Sidden. I hope and trust I have not missed too much of importance. I have promised my husband after all that I will be most attentive to matters here. A wife who does not interest herself in the affairs of her husband is no wife at all, as I am sure you will all agree.'

Wulfthram was sitting at the head of the table and was fixing her with a look she found difficult to describe. It wasn't anger, though; she felt relief at that at any rate. Surprise? Yes, possibly surprise.

Einar was sitting close to her husband, facing towards her. 'Good to see you, my Lady. I was wondering when you would arrive. The Lady Sofie, Camille bless her and keep her at her side, always sat next to Wulfthram at these meetings and I see he has kept the same chair vacant for you. Isn't that right, Wulfthram?'

Wulfthram said nothing but pulled the chair back for her to sit on.

It was of black wood, heavy and noisy, as he pulled it over the stone floor, but it was padded and comfortable. He beckoned to her in the most understated way possible to come and take her seat.

'I believe all of you here have met my new wife, the Lady Ceriana, however briefly. I very much doubt that she can remember all of your names so please, when you speak, introduce yourselves.'

One of the barons, a younger man with sandy hair, broke in immediately.

'I would just like to say, my Lady, that the meeting has only just formally opened and you have missed nothing of great import. I am Baron Jon Skellar of Thakholm, an island south of here. We only had the very briefest of meetings last week, so allow me to reiterate the welcome I gave you then and to express my hope that you are gradually settling in here.'

'Thank you, Baron Skellar, I can assure you that everyone here has been the very embodiment of courtesy itself. It is I, I fear, who needs to show that I am worthy of such courtesy. I hope the ensuing months will go to show that I am, for it will not be for the lack of endeavour on my part. May I also ask you, Baron Skellar, how the construction of the new jetty on Thakholm is proceeding? I believe it is being enlarged to accommodate the mightiest ships in the Tanaren navy in order to provide a capable deterrent to any future pirate incursion.'

He looked at her with something only a little short of wonder. 'It has just finished, my Lady, a grand affair three times larger than the original. May I formally extend an invitation to visit us and see it, as soon as your schedule allows.'

'Thank you, Baron Skellar. I of course would be delighted, if my husband permits it.'

'I permit it,' said Wulfthram with a gleam in his eye. 'Now let us begin. Each of you in turn give your reports from the area you represent...'

The meeting continued as each baron spoke in turn, giving Wulfthram their dispatches. Ceriana was glad she had read up on the issues that concerned these people primarily. There was a genuine fear of famine here as the land was so poor. Her husband had gone some way to mitigating this by setting up a series of grain silos in which the excess in good years could be stored and set against any years in which the crop failed. Also, there was the threat of brigandry; the Kudreyan pirates might be no more, but many of them, fleeing Galpa, had landed in the remoter areas of the north, from where they continued to harry the local people. As to the barons here present, there appeared to be some form of hierarchy, though all of them deferred to her husband. Principal among them appeared to be Baron Farnerun of Slemsholm, a long coastal area in which fishing was important. It held many ancient Elven ruins and had a reputation of being haunted. Then there was Baron Rosk of Taksgat, an island east of Osperitsan, and Baron Fyrdag of Thetta, a large area in the south. The other Osperitsan barons, Einar and Thudig, also seemed important as well as Baron Tragsmann of Vihaga, the port from which she first took ship to her new home. It was Fyrdag who was now speaking.

'In the southern part of my lands and in that of my neighbours it is virtual bandit country. People are living in fear and I do not have enough men to be everywhere at once. The latest way these bastards are making money is through kidnapping. They are taking young girls aged from about thirteen years upwards from their parents. We believe that they are being sold on to brothels in Tanaren and other southern cities. They hide out in caves in the broken hills and move around frequently so they are almost impossible to catch. Short of evacuating whole villages and abandoning farmlands I am not sure what to do.'

'What if we call the muster?' Wulfthram said. He turned to his wife. 'A muster is called in emergencies like this one. Every one of the northern barons is required to supply one man in every ten of their men-at-arms throughout the spring, summer and autumn.' Then he turned back to Fyrdag. 'Perhaps a show of strength might be what is required.'

Fyrdag looked doubtful. 'A muster would help in the short term, I feel, but you know a council majority is required to organise one. And I am not sure if everyone here would give my problems full priority like you do.'

Wulfthram scanned the faces of those present. 'Well, you heard the man. Does anyone here object?'

A couple of people shifted uneasily in their seats and then Baron

Rosk, a tall spare man whose skin was drawn so tightly around his face that he seemed to be little more than a talking skull, broke the silence.

'The problem we have, as you know, is that we are not just here representing ourselves. As well as Taksgat, I am here for three other barons who hold smaller islands near to my own. And I know for a fact that trying to persuade them to part with ten in a hundred men to go traipsing round some barren wilderness, leagues from their home, will be nigh on impossible. If the council agrees to do it, I can force them to comply, but in doing that it would only stoke up problems for the future. The last thing I want is some petty rebellion. If I put it down with force, then I would be ruling over an unruly populace and sleeping with a knife under my bed. If I couldn't put it down, then you would be speaking to someone else this time next year. Couldn't these threatened villages bolster their fortifications in some way?'

'Of course,' said Fyrdag, 'but in most cases we have done that already. These people are farmers or traders and cannot spend their lives cooped up like chickens. The bandits get them when they are outdoors and vulnerable.'

Wulfthram looked at them, his forefingers resting on his chin. 'Nevertheless, I feel something needs to be done. If we do nothing, we will be seen as weak, which will only encourage and embolden these brigands. The problem we have is that between us we represent well over fifty other barons. Keeping them all happy is a task not even a god could manage. 'He looked around the table. 'Give me an idea, everyone; if I call a muster, who would agree with me.'

Some hands went up, others stayed down – the room looked evenly divided. Wulfthram could barely conceal the disappointment in his face. He looked at Fyrdag. 'I think it's a slight majority, but really I need about two thirds with me to carry this.' He spoke to the room in general. 'What about concessions? Say I could negotiate a small reduction in taxes for the Grand Duke for a year. Would that change your vote?'

Baron Thudig, Wulfthram's southern neighbour, a man well into his fifties who retained a shock of dark hair which seemed far too youthful for his mottled red face, spoke. 'Do you really think you could arrange this? This Grand Duke does not seem the type to reduce taxes for nothing. He has already made one highly aggressive move against us. I would vote for this muster only if you could guarantee some sort of reduction.'

Ceriana barely stopped herself from reddening when she realised that the 'highly aggressive move' he was referring to was the planned visit of her father with his troops the following year. She was beginning to see the juggling act her new husband must have to perform regularly just to keep these men in check.

'My new father-in-law visits here next year and will attend the spring council. It would be interesting to see if I could squeeze anything out of the Tanaren nobles and get them to help us for a change. Fyrdag, would you be happy to see the vote deferred until then?'

Fyrdag nodded. 'I am content.'

'Very well,' said Wulfthram. 'The matter is settled for the time being. Now for...'

Ceriana interrupted him. 'This muster of which you speak, would it be predominantly foot soldiers?'

'Almost entirely,' said Wulfthram. 'Only I and Einar and a couple of the other barons retain any standing cavalry up here.'

'But to chase down these bandits, cavalry would be useful, no. Even if the terrain is poor they would still travel faster than men on foot, yes?'

'Yes,' said Wulfthram. 'But there is very little cavalry available.'

'My brother is a knight of the Silver Guard,' she said with no little triumph. 'I am sure both Father and myself could persuade him to release some men to aid you. Even a small force of, say, thirty men would help, wouldn't it?'

Silence. Some people looked at their feet; others picked their nails. Einar spoke to her gently. 'There would be a lot of resentment against the fine knights of Tanaren riding in to solve our little problems. It would appear that we are incapable of resolving issues on our own, and may encourage further and closer interference from the capital on other matters. It is one of those times when what sounds like a fantastic idea in theory becomes a much more troublesome one in practice. In itself, though, it is a very good idea and I am sure everyone here is grateful that you are trying to help.'

'Forgive me,' she said, 'I am still getting used to the concept of you all seeing yourselves as a country apart. I was not aware that outside interference from the capital would be seen as a mark of hostility.'

Baron Thudig looked at her with pale watery eyes. 'May I speak frankly, my dear?'

Ceriana met his stare. 'Of course, Baron.'

'Very well. I know it is not your fault but there are a great many barons who resent the way your marriage has been imposed on Baron Wulfthram. It smacks of the high-handed arrogance that we have come to expect from Tanaren and, though I have not heard it directly myself, there has even been talk of armed rebellion, not against the Grand Duke, but against your husband. It would be no idle threat either; over here barons are deposed regularly if they are seen to be failing. There are no shortages of ambitious men here in the north.'

'Enough Thudig!' Wulfthram said harshly. 'If you have heard rumours of treachery, then see me afterwards and tell me what you know. What you do not do is insult my wife to my face. If you...'

Ceriana took his arm. 'It is all right, my husband. I invited the Baron to speak frankly and he did just that. I am sorry that I have put you in such a difficult position. But please be aware, Baron Thudig, that the imposition applies to both of us.'

Wulfthram looked at her and for the first time she saw sympathy in his eyes. 'You have not, and you have nothing to reproach yourself for. Let us take some lunch and we will continue the Council in an hour or so.'

He signalled to one of the servants and shortly afterwards some food was brought out and set down on the table. People did not remain at their seats; rather they got up and mingled with each other in small groups, a routine that obviously happened each time a council was held. For the first time since she walked into the room Ceriana felt awkward. Wulfthram and Einar were speaking to Thudig, and so she felt no inclination to join them. She was about to excuse herself and leave the room until lunch was over when Baron Skellar came over to her.

'My Lady, I think you have surprised and delighted a lot of people here today, including myself. My invitation to visit us at Thakholm is a genuine one; it might be nice for you to tour a few of the outlying areas, just to get a feel of the country you have ended up in.'

'Thank you, Baron, but I don't feel my presence has been as universally welcomed as you seem to think.'

'Ah, ignore Thudig, if bullshit was a currency he would be living in the lilac palace in Koze and sleeping on a bed of solid gold. If he was to smile, his face would shatter. Nobody expected you to join us and be so charming – dare I say it, least of all your husband.'

She laughed softly. 'I gave him no warning that is true, but then I didn't really know I was going to attend either. I am sure he will have something to say afterwards.'

As she spoke Wulfthram noticed the two of them together and came over to join them.

'Well, Jon, when do you want my young bride to come and visit you?'

'At your convenience, of course, but the sooner the better as far as I am concerned. A couple of the great warships in the Tanaren navy should be arriving in a couple of weeks; perhaps a formal welcome from the Chief Baron of the North might be appropriate.'

'A good idea indeed, and one I have already looked into. Unfortunately I am otherwise engaged at the time. However, I believe the Chief Baroness is available. What say you, Ceriana? It could be your first official visit.'

'Of course, I would be honoured.' She looked him directly in the eye but as usual could read nothing. 'When should I leave?'

'It's a two-day trip by land and sea, so perhaps you could leave in about ten days' time. You could arrive a day or two before the ships arrive and Jon could show you around the island.'

'That won't take too long,' Baron Skellar said, laughing. 'But I am content. I shall await your arrival with both trepidation and excitement. You will have the place of honour at the head of the table.' With that he bowed and took his leave.

'Are you angry with me?' she blurted it out, seeing as the two of them were alone together for once.

'Why should I be? I did consider asking you to come but thought it might be a bit early for you, seeing as you keep to your rooms most of the time. Mind you, it was obviously time well spent. Everyone here seems impressed by your attempt to get a grip on the problems we have here.'

'Thank you; I am resented by some, though.'

'As am I! And ignore Thudig; we are all used to him here, as you will be soon enough. Baron Skellar seems enchanted anyway. He is a single man, so be on your guard when you see him. He already has a reputation with one or two of the other baronesses.'

'Oh, you surely don't think ... not with me?'

'I do think,' he said with a smile, 'I know him of old. Don't worry, though; I have every faith in you. All you have to do is follow him around and approve of everything. I am sure you had to do that plenty of times back at Edgecliff.'

'You have never spoken a truer word. I have a great tolerance of the mundane and dreary, all of it stemming from attending my father's inspection of the soldiers every week as a child.'

'I bet you never knew how useful that would be as you got older. Spend just under a week with him – that is the average length of an official visit – then hurry back home. You will have my flagship at your disposal and I shall ride with you to the port and see you off.'

'Thank you, my Lord; I would like that.'

The meeting resumed shortly afterwards. Baron Farnerun of Slemsholm was speaking.

'If I may, I will continue with the problem of brigandry, for it does seem endemic in our lands of late. We were obviously all relieved when the Kudreyan pirates were defeated, giving us some respite from the constant raids on our shores, on my shore in particular. But it would be wrong to say such attacks have stopped completely. They still have some ships and are still making surprise attacks by sea. I don't know how but there seems to be a rump of these people still operating on our coast. Where they base themselves I know not, but there have been two attacks on my lands in the past week. The fact that they were unexpected made it worse as they raided a couple of villages with impunity before making off with their spoils, gold from the churches and the homes of the magistrates. I was hoping that Baron Skellar could ask these ships from Tanaren to do a sweep of my coastline; maybe they could at least find out where they are based, if nothing else.'

'I do not control them directly,' Skellar replied, 'but I shall certainly ask them when they arrive.'

'I will speak to their commander if need be,' said Wulfthram. 'And again I shall mention it to Duke Hartfield when I see him. Perhaps some sort of regular patrol can be organised; I can't see there being any objection to that.'

The meeting continued and ploughed into what was obviously familiar territory for most of those present – local taxes and grain supply and allocation. As they delved into its intricate minutiae and baron horse-traded with baron, Ceriana sensed herself drifting. The mental effort required to force her into the meeting was tiring her out. She was thinking longingly of her soft bed and a jug of warmed almond milk when she heard her husband summing up. Evidently things were drawing to a close.

'So, most of what I have to do involves speaking to my father-in-law when he arrives. Is there anything else anyone wishes to say before we finish up here?'

'One thing,' – it was the grey-bearded Baron Tragsmann of Vihag – 'something I should have mentioned earlier maybe. Baron Fyram of Clutha, the next town north of mine, is dead. He has been replaced by Vorfgan, his cousin.'

'And the significance of this is?' questioned Farnerun.

'It might be of no significance at all,' said Tragsmann. 'Fyram was killed in a hunting accident pursuing boar in the northern Morrathnay Forest. His brother, the next in line, died six months ago in a boating accident in which there were no survivors. Vorfgan still isn't the next in line but Fyram's son, who is thirteen years old, has not been seen since the accident. The version Vorfgan is telling us is that he has taken sick and is confined to bed. A bed in Vorfgan's mansion. As I say, no one outside of

Vorfgan's immediate circle can claim to have seen him and Vorfgan has claimed the protectorship until the boy gets better.'

'It sounds suspicious but I am guessing there is no proof of foul play, and in all honesty it could all just be coincidence anyway.' said Wulfthram.

'Indeed, but then Vorfgan is a very ambitious young man, one who needs to be watched. And did I mention the arrow that killed Fyram by accident belonged to one of Vorfgan's men? I am not suggesting he should be deposed ... yet. But as I said he should be watched, intently.'

'Thank you for that, Tragsmann. If I can find the time next year, I might just pay a visit to Clutha. What is Fyram's boy's name?'

'Dekkan, a quiet lad, easy to manipulate.'

'I shall write to Vorfgan enquiring as to the health of young Dekkan then, see what he has to say for himself, and let him know I am watching him. Now let us conclude this council. Thank you all for your time and we shall reconvene in three months after Winter Festival Day. Syvuhka watch over us.'

'Syvuhka watch over us,' they all solemnly echoed before rising from the table. Ceriana had heard the name before but didn't quite know what it signified so when she had the opportunity she asked Einar.

'Syvuhka?' he said. 'It is all to do with keeping our history and traditions. In Kibil we had the same gods as you but we knew them by different names. Syvuhka is the old Kibil name for Artorus and we invoke it when we want to remember who we once were. Ironically, hardly anyone in Kibil uses the name now. It has been part of the Empire for so long that its gods are now their gods. In fact, if you want to see how Kibil used to be, your best bet would be to watch us. We keep some of the old language, religion and festivals. In fact, the festival of Logammasnat, when we set fire to a wooden boat on the ocean, will be observed in a couple of weeks' time. As with all great Kibil festivals, we all get drunk to insensibility afterwards.' 'Drink is an important Kibil tradition, I take it?' she laughed.

'Well, it can get arse-numbingly freezing up here. Sometimes it is the only way to keep warm.'

'You never got round to discovering fire then?'

'We did, but lighting a fire is nowhere near as much fun.'

The barons mingled and talked until the sun had long gone down. They would all stay in the mansion house that night before journeying home tomorrow. Ceriana tired quickly and excused herself early on. On retiring to her rooms, she asked Ebba to bring her some bread and milk and resolved to have an early night. Once she had eaten, she dismissed Ebba, put on her nightclothes, blew out the candles and climbed into bed.

She couldn't remember her dreams; she felt so warm and woozy. She had been so cold since her arrival; it felt like such a pleasant change. She felt like she was melting into her bed, dissolving into the sheets, into nothingness. Just her and the warmth she felt within her...

Elissa's breath she was hot! She sat bolt upright in her bed. Her chest and the back of her neck were soaking. Outside she could see the moon, its pale light filtering in through her window. It was the dead of night. She had slept for hours. She drew her knees up to her chin, noticing that the fire had gone out. How could she feel this warm without the fire? She went to put her face in her hands when she stopped. What was it this time?

She looked at her pale forearms in turn. The only light source in the room came from the moon. But there was no doubt about it. The thin tracery of veins in both arms was glowing, shining luminously through her milk-white skin. She groaned. It must be that Keth-accursed stone! She hadn't looked at it since she left Edgecliff but she knew exactly where it was. Getting out of bed, she went to a drawer in her dresser, pulled out the jewellery box and opened it. She already knew it would be glowing before she looked at it and, sure enough, there it was, pulsating exactly like before. Trying to keep her panic in check, she went over to the full-length mirror next to the room where her clothes were stored and pulled off her nightclothes. What she saw only compounded her nausea.

It wasn't just her arms; she could see the pattern of veins in her body travelling through her arms, her shoulders, and her torso and into her legs. The only places they weren't shining through her skin were at her extremities, hands, face and feet. She was sweating profusely, both through the unnatural heat and through the fear she felt rising within her. A drop of sweat collected at the tip of her nose before falling and splashing on to the wooden floor. It was followed by another. And another.

'Dear Elissa, help me, dear Elissa help me, dear Elissa help me!' she whispered to herself again and again. She had no idea what to do so; she just watched herself, naked and translucent, glowing with an inner light that came from Elissa knows where. Her hair was plastered to her back and forehead, and sweat dripped over her nose and chin before sliding between her breasts and on to the floor, where a pool of tiny droplets were gathering.

Then, just like before, everything stopped abruptly. The stone's light went out and she was just an unclad pale young woman again. She squatted slowly on to the floor, shivering in the cold air as the sweat dried on her skin. 'I need help,' she said to herself. 'I need help *now*.'

Shortly after dawn, Ebba found her still on the floor, staring into space and shivering. Suspecting a fever, she sent word to Wulfthram and the mansion's doctor. She carefully lifted the girl up, put her nightdress back on her and placed her gently back into bed. In all this time the stone in the box went completely unnoticed.

BOOK ONE: AUTUMN

14

 The storm had blown over, leaving the morning bright and crisp. On the bank of the lake, just past the last dwelling that bordered it on the south-eastern side, the land broadened out into a small circular plain. It, too, was fringed by dwellings and it was here that the whole tribe, well over one hundred strong, now assembled. They waited patiently for the Elder to arrive by boat from the great house. When he did, he was accompanied by his fellow elders and some younger men, one of whom beat a solemn tattoo on a drum held in the crook of his arm while others blew through pipes fashioned from wood and reeds. In front of all of them, though, were the bereaved couple, the stocky Fasneterax and his wife, her face pale and drawn. Between them they held a small bundle wrapped tightly in white cloth. They walked ahead of the rest of the group and down a dirt path leading directly away from the village, the elders and musicians walking behind them. Keeping a respectful distance everybody else started to follow.

 The slow procession continued for a mile or more, winding along through small knots of trees and past extensive beds of reeds and bodies of still water covered in lilies, iris and marsh marigolds. Eventually they stopped at a lake almost circular in shape whose waters were as black as ink. Built on to the water was a large wooden platform built on piles driven into the water. Trees had been cleared from this section of the bank, though they surrounded the rest of it, pressing close to the water's edge. The elders, musicians, Fasneterax and his wife stood on the platform while the rest of the village took up positions on the high bank overlooking the deep, impenetrable waters.

 The elder addressed the crowd, telling them that they had arrived at the sacred lake, one of the few places where Ukka, god of the underworld, could access the land of mortal men. He then stated that today would mark the joining of the child's soul with those of the Gods and the beginning of his journey along the Great River. He then threw some woody sticks on to the brazier, which smoked heavily and gave off the sweet smell of incense. He raised his arms to the crowd, entreating

Ukka to accept the child to his side. 'Ukka, accept the child!' the crowd responded.

When this was done the Elder gestured to Fasneterax, who moved forward gently placing the bundle at the Elder's feet. Two of the musicians then placed it on a small wicker raft and took it to the water's edge. Some women holding baskets then stepped forwards scattering flowers and garlands on to the lake. Dumnekavax then made his final address.

'Oh great spirits, ensure that our grief is assuaged by the certainty of your acceptance of this innocent child into your world. Protect him for eternity and ensure that he is there to greet his parents when they, too, are called to your side.'

The two men then placed the raft on to the water. Taking a large pole each they gently propelled it out on to the surface of the lake. The drummer and remaining musicians played a slow, solemn tune as the raft and its contents got smaller and smaller until, finally, the water overcame the raft and both it and the child it held disappeared silently under the surface.

Everyone stood still for a moment, showing their respect, then the Elder, head bowed, left the platform, to walk slowly back to the village. The other villagers walked behind him until at last only the bereaved couple were left. They held each other and stared silently at the sacred lake, lost in their thoughts and memories, until at last even they turned from the lake and began their walk back. Behind them two swans swooped low over the water landing on it almost noiselessly and began craning their necks against each other.

The great house was a hive of activity. At its centre, space had been cleared and wooden bowls of varying sizes were being placed there by the village's womenfolk who were scurrying around like ants. There were bowls of goat's milk, cheese and flatbread, of edible seed pods and rough cereals. A goat had been killed earlier that day and its cooked remains formed the centre of the feast. Elsewhere, there was every type of denizen of the river, small fish pickled in a local vinegar, fish cooked in wild garlic, prawns and crayfish boiled till they turned pink, and some ducks and geese plucked and cooked in their entirety. Children milled around trying to steal titbits, before they were caught and cuffed around the ear. The men stayed away until the summoning horn was sounded giving the signal for the feast to commence.

A lot of them were on Cygan's island, starting the work required to put up the stockade. Some had already started to dig a ditch using crude picks while others were sharpening stakes.

Cygan was not assisting them. Rather, he was sitting outside his house working on a small fire, which was heating a pot containing a black, viscous liquid. When he was satisfied with the fire, he went to inspect the rest of his equipment – a water skin; a leather bag containing strips of dried fish, hard cheese and berries; a flint and some light tinder; his bow, quiver and some twenty hunting arrows; along with his bone knife and spear. He had his thicker shirt on, along with a cloak which could double as a blanket and his shoes that had been freshly oiled and waterproofed. His wife, wearing a blue shirt with her skirt as befitted the colder weather, was behind him.

'Vengefarak and the others have left for Jagged Hill,' she said. 'Your party will be waiting for you at the great house by now.'

'I just need to finish this,' he indicated the fire and pot in front of him. 'Then I will join them.'

She went and stood in front of him. 'Please be careful.'

'I will. I will be back within the week.'

'You shouldn't make promises you may not be able to keep.'

'No. No, I shouldn't. Look after the children. And my brother. His leg pains him, though he would never admit it.'

'I will. I have my knife and my sling if required. I should go and join the children. They are already at the great house, probably trying to steal food.'

'Yes, you go. Tell the others I will be there shortly.'

'Dumnekavax walks in the spirit world tonight. It troubles me greatly. It is said that he could see the spirits of the dead and those about to die. What if ... if he sees you there?'

'And what if he doesn't? I will return. And that is a promise I will definitely keep.'

She looked at him intently, her large brown eyes conveying more in a glance than a thousand words could. Then she turned away, climbed into her round boat and was gone.

Cygan's eyes followed her for a moment, and then resignedly he turned back to his pot. Satisfied with its contents, he lifted it from the fire, wrapped it in a soft goatskin and prepared to leave his house behind.

A funeral feast was always a happy affair, a celebration of the life of its subject, however short, and it was against a background of laughter, the high-pitched voices of excited children and the banter of men well into their grain beer and honey mead that Cygan and his three companions pushed off from the jetty in their longboat expertly fashioned from a single log.

None of the men spoke as they made their way, almost silently, out of the lake and on to the black river heading southward. Before they had left, Dumnekavax had presided over a traditional ceremony. 'Here is Genexetan, wisest of the Elders – may he guide you in uncertain waters!' With that he placed a skull on the prow of the boat, fixing it on to a wooden prong that had obviously been carved there for that purpose. The long-dead elder would be the fifth member of the crew, there to impart his knowledge to them as they dreamed.

Cygan was second oar on the boat behind Fasneterax, a stocky dour man at the best of times, but whose intense stare seemed to have magnified tenfold since his son's death. Sitting directly behind him was the elder Tegavenek, rowing as assuredly as the rest of them despite having at least twenty years on them all. Behind him, by contrast, was the youngest member of the party – Cerrenatukavenex, or Cerren, as he was known, a young lad of barely eighteen years. Despite that, he was big and strong, taller and broader than the others, and a lad who always seemed to have a smile on his face. This was his first major trip out of the village.

As they paddled on downriver, the river, which by normal rules should have grown broader, grew narrower and narrower until the high banks of reeds almost closed in upon them completely. It also got more and more sluggish until one could see the clouds of midges hanging in the air, buzzing in their ears as they drove the boat through them. At one point Cygan inhaled at exactly the wrong time, causing him to choke and splutter uncontrollably as he took in a lungful of the little monsters.

Despite the slow pace of the river, they made good progress. In the early afternoon they stopped for a brief meal before continuing their journey. Shortly afterward the river opened into a broad shallow lake choked with lilies, marigolds and pondweed. After casting around for a little while, Tegavenek extended his arm.

'There!' he said.

Following his instructions they came to a narrow creek, one of the lake's outlets, and into it they rowed. It was barely ten feet wide, and its banks grew higher and higher, almost blotting out the pale sun. Many birds nested in these banks and they saw dozens of swallows and kingfishers as they progressed. Cerren was getting impatient.

'Is there an end to this stream? It doesn't just disappear under the earth, does it?'

'Patience,' said the Elder. 'We will be out of here soon enough.'

He was as good as his word. Shortly afterwards, the creek veered eastwards and, with the sun behind them, they entered another river, as broad as the black river but with clearer water and higher banks. Tegavenek spoke again.

'We will be staying on this river until we arrive at the Twin Snake. We will camp shortly, away from the bank to avoid the mosquitos, and should arrive at their village before late afternoon tomorrow.'

And this is what they did. Before dusk arrived and the midges and mosquitos came to hunt, they hauled the boat on to the bank and looked around for somewhere to camp. The ground was extremely marshy, however, and they had to be content with settling down inside a small knot of trees where, although the ground was still spongy, at least it wasn't sodden. The mosquitos were still a problem, though, so Cygan pulled what looked like a gnarled root out of one of his storage bags, cut off a piece, divided it into four and shaved off the barky skin. He handed a piece each to his companions and all proceeded to rub the exposed areas of skin with it. It gave off a faint whiff of citrus. Tegavenek ate the root once he had finished. 'It will sweat through all of my pores,' he said.

So as not to sleep on damp ground, they cut some branches off the trees and laid their boat on them. The boat was big enough for four of them to lie in with reasonable comfort. They also managed a small fire, although once their tinder had burned off it was quite smoky and gave off limited warmth.

They ate some of the supplies they had brought with them and settled down for the night. Cygan took the first watch.

Cerren, the biggest of the four of them, was having difficulty getting comfortable. Eventually he sat up straight and sighed with exasperation.

'Can't sleep?' Cygan said.

'It is not easy; my legs are too long for the boat. Perhaps I should try the ground.'

'No, it is too damp; you will end up with fever and find parasites have laid their eggs in your skin. We would have to burn them out of you.'

'Suddenly the boat seems very cosy indeed,' said the young man. 'Cygan, may I ask you something?'

Cygan nodded. 'Go ahead.'

'Why do you not have a moustache? We all have them, or at least try to grow them.' It was true, Cerren was very proud of his long moustache that drooped down past his chin.

'Well, I used to, just as you did. But then my father, who didn't have one, took me to trade with the Taneren. He used to scout for them in an old war and had learned their language, which he then taught me. They are very different, the Taneren. Their homes are dry, by which I mean they can be nowhere near water, and they ride animals over long earthen roads. Unfortunately, they regard us as barbarians, uncivilised creatures whom it is their spirit-bound duty to short-change when bartering. And one of the things they have contempt for is our moustaches. They call us the "long faces"; it is a joke to them. So, after my first visit to them, I shaved it off. When I returned to their country the following time, they knew that I knew their opinion of us and any attempt to leave us the worse off after any trade would not work.'

'They are numerous, the Taneren, aren't they?'

'Yes, Cerren, as numerous as tadpoles in the summer. Their lands are vast beyond reckoning. They leave us alone only because they find the country we live in hostile and unfriendly. It is best, I feel, that our contact is limited to bartering a few times a year; our differences would only lead to conflict otherwise.'

'Do they have warriors?'

'Yes, they are always fighting. Our ways are far more peaceable than theirs. If they had had a few skirmishes with the Twin Snake, it would end up as full warfare with hundreds killed on both sides. Whereas we attempt to resolve our differences as soon as we can.'

'But is it not the way of the warrior to seek glory in battle?'

'Only when the battle is a just one and there are no other ways to solve the problem. Unlike the Taneren, there are very few of us, so every life is valuable. Lives should not be wasted without good reason. It is frustrating for a young warrior like yourself; I remember having the same feelings at your age. Then came the war with the Sand Warriors who used to live on the coast and I had plenty of opportunity for glory. All you can do in the meantime is serve your village as the Elder sees fit and uphold your honour. In any respect, if what Vengefarak says is true, you will get your chance soon enough.'

They started off again the following day as soon as the pale light of dawn started to shimmer over them. In this vast flat land the sky was all-encompassing, reaching over them and behind them, constantly changing with a thousand shades of blue, grey and white. It could be leaden and oppressive, like a heavy stone lying on one's chest, or cerulean and playful, full of song and laughter. It was always capricious, though; it could change so quickly that only a fool travelled without a sturdy cloak, even if the sun at its zenith baked the reed beds dry. At night it was a different beast altogether; then the heavens seemed almost within touching distance, star after star after star, one for every spirit lost to the mortal world – spirits who now sat above them, looking down on the barely significant world they had left for good, a world created by the seed of Cygannan, the great progenitor, he who oversees the world from above, just as Ukka views it from the dark underworld below. The wonder of the night sky, especially on cold nights when it was crystal clear and as palpable as morning frost, had always captivated Cygan, and always would.

It was a warmer morning, causing a dawn mist to hover over the river. The area they were now approaching was a low-lying area and therefore swampier than back at Black Lake. It had a lot more trees, too – tall black spindly trees that hugged both banks of the river, supplanting the reed beds. The clean smell of running water was replaced by the dank one of moss and decay. Crows frequented their branches, their harsh voices not helping to allay the feeling of unease hanging over the party. It seemed like an effort to even speak but eventually Tegavenek cleared his throat and tried talking to the others, never an easy task when in a longboat.

'The village is not far. Like our own dwellings they are spread out over a distance. We will pass outlying settlements before reaching the village proper.'

Noon was fast approaching, the sun making everyone hot and clammy, when Cerren let out a cry. 'Buildings! Where the river bends!'

His eyesight was good. The river ahead continued in an almost straight line for a great distance before curving eastwards. Where it started to turn was a small knot of three or four shacks built on stilts, so far away as yet they looked like child's toy houses. The first sign of the Twin Snake tribe.

Tegavenek spoke again. 'We have made good progress. Let us speak with them and inform them of the purpose of our visit.'

Putting on a spurt with their oars, they rapidly closed the distance to the dwellings. Cygan kept looking up to see if anybody there was out hailing them or even manning their own boat to row out and meet them, He saw nothing.

The first house had a landing for boats jutting out into the water. There were a couple of round boats tied up there but still no one came out. 'It looks deserted,' Fasneterax said, breaking his silence.

Tegavenek called out, 'Hail the Twin Snake! The Black Lake comes to parley with you!' He was answered only by the crows and the sigh of leaves in the wind.

They tied up their boat, and arming themselves with spear and bow, went to the first house. Tegavenek called out again, louder this time but with the same response. Cygan entered the house, Fasneterax behind.

It was a regular marsh house, single-roomed, adorned with hammock and cooking utensils, but it was deserted. They then went to each house in turn and found no one. Every house looked lived in until very recently.

'If they have abandoned these dwellings, why leave all their possessions behind?' Fasneterax said holding up a small carved wooden longboat, obviously a child's toy.

'Perhaps they are out hunting,' said Cerren unconvincingly.

'What, the women, the children? That is no hunting party I have heard of. Hold on, what is this?' Cygan bent down and picked up a bone knife lying, unseen till then, on the floor of the last house. He held it up to the light.

It was a standard-looking knife, with a wooden handle attached to a bone with its edge sharpened. Such tools, though of limited use and quickly worn out, were commonplace among the marsh folk. However, as they looked at it they could see its blade was covered in a translucent green black slime with the consistency of honey. As Cygan held the knife up, some of the ooze dripped off the knife's tip. He wrinkled his nose.

'It absolutely stinks,' he said. 'Black mud and bog gas.'

They exchanged glances; no one spoke or dared mention that which was preying on their minds. Then Tegavenek, who had been outside on the bank looking into the trees, joined them. Cygan showed him the knife.

'We need to move on' was all he said. 'There will be more houses further downriver.'

They returned to the boat and cast off. This time, however, weapons were readied. Within twenty minutes they espied the next clutch of houses, again located on a curve of the river. This time, though, it was bending westwards.

As they approached them, Tegavenek spoke.

'Let us land the boat here and approach the houses over land.'

'Won't that look suspicious to the villagers, especially if we are now armed?' said Cygan.

'Leave it to me. I will be ahead of you and will convey our good intentions.'

They did as he said. They left the river some half a mile from the houses, pulling the boat on to land and concealing it with hastily cut branches. Then, with Tegavenek leading the way unarmed, they walked through the trees to the houses.

There was a small clearing in front of the houses and they crouched down just outside it, concealed by the trees, watching for signs of life. After five minutes or so Fasneterax whispered, 'Nothing. No fires. No children or women. It has been abandoned.'

Tegavenek nodded. 'Let's see if you are right.'

He stood up and strolled into the clearing, hailing the Twin Snake just as he had done before. It was soon obvious that no one was here either and he signalled to the others to join him. Cerren gave him back the spear he was minding for him.

'Everyone fan out and search. They must have left some sign as to what has happened here.' He headed for the first house.

The jetty here was separate from the houses and raised a good three to four feet above the water, the better to cope with rain surges. For some reason Cygan felt an urge to walk along it and look at the river. It reached a good ten to fifteen feet into the water and when he was at the end of it Cygan looked round.

The river here was broad and flowed smoothly. The riverbanks themselves were pretty uneven with many trees almost stretching into the water, their twisted roots exposed by the flowing current. Flotsam, weed, branches and other debris collected around these roots until dislodged by the tidal flow. Cygan was looking at one such tree. It had been undermined by the river to such an extent that it lurched at a crazy forty-five degree angle over the water; surely it was only a matter of days, hours even, before it collapsed and was swept away. But what was that at its roots?

It wasn't a branch nor did it look like any natural debris. It was pale, maybe two feet long. He decided to walk along the bank to get a closer look when the river did the job for him. The object came loose and drifted gently in his direction. As it came closer he saw exactly what it was. He suddenly felt quite numb.

There was no mistaking it – it was a child. One still in its infancy. It was naked and a boy and quite dead. Its, or rather his, features looked quite peaceful, almost as if he were only sleeping. Cygan realised that the boy would drift by the jetty and so dipped his spear in the water, to direct the poor creature against the wooden pilings where he could crouch down and haul him out. He braced himself as the boy was a matter of feet away.

Suddenly he was aware of something being wrong. The water here was greenish and quite dark, but under the boy it seemed even darker as if a shadow was being cast there. But it was a shadow that moved.

As Cygan watched he saw a hand and arm come out of the water to claim the boy, but it was the hand of nothing he had ever seen before. The fingers were long, impossibly long, and thin and ended in a claw. There was no thumb. Both hand and arm were a green–black colour and covered in scales. Between each finger was pale-green webbing. The hand held the boy, arresting its progress downriver. Then in a moment he was pulled under. Cygan had a quick glimpse of two pale eyes with vertical slit-like pupils and a brief smell of the same rank odour he had detected on the knife. Then the boy and his captor were gone.

He stood on the jetty, his mouth agape. He studied the water closely – could he see two, or maybe three, more shadows drift past his gaze? He could not be sure.

Well, he had his answer. The mystery of the abandoned dwellings was a mystery no more. Walking back along the jetty he saw his companions, lifted his arms and called out to them. 'Malaac!'

THE FORGOTTEN WAR
15

*'To the Professor of Ancient History and Arcane Studies
University of St Philig's, Tanaren*

Dear Sir,

I have occasion to write to you on a matter both perplexing and disturbing which is affecting me personally and causing me a good deal of consternation. Some weeks, possibly months back, my father, Nicholas Hartfield, Duke of Edgecliff, forwarded to you a ring taken from the body of a man washed up on a beach near to Edgecliff Castle. I believe the ring depicted a double-headed snake. I am wondering whether or not you have drawn any conclusions as to the nature of this find, with regard to either the meaning behind this symbol or possibly the origin or nature of its wearer, a man clothed in black with all hair shaven from his body. Here, I must be frank with you.

There was another artefact found at the same site, the description of which I am reluctant to divulge in writing until I have had some acknowledgement at least of your receipt of this letter. I know not if this second artefact is connected either to the ring or the man but, in my opinion, the possibility is a strong one. It also appears to have some magical properties which may be affecting my health adversely. I apologise if I appear to be unforthcoming but until I hear your thoughts on the ring in your possession I will not disclose any further information.

I thank you for your attention in this matter and hope to hear from you as soon as is practicable.

Yours,

Lady Ceriana Osperitsan-Hartfield, Baroness of Osperitsan and the Far Reaches, etc. etc.'

  The man finished reading the letter, put it back down on the desk, rubbed his nose and yawned. He was a man in his early sixties with a shock of silver hair that looked like it had never been combed. It partly obscured his face, although his prominent hawk nose could never be hidden. Much the same could be said of his dark glittering eyes and bushy eyebrows which were actually slightly darker than his hair. He grunted to himself, a habit he could never get out of whether in polite conversation or lecturing a room of uninterested students. It was dark outside; the autumn moon was showing through the small leaded window overlooking the desk which otherwise was lit only by a solitary candle. It was a not a large room but every corner, every shelf, every surface, was cram-packed with clutter, books and papers, all piled on top of each other with scant regard for order or organisation. That part of the floor that could be seen was covered in a fine layer of dust. It was a room that contrived to be used frequently and be seriously neglected at one and the same time.

The man was not alone. Standing opposite him facing the desk was a young woman with a pinched face, large blue eyes and mousy-brown hair tied in a bun. She fidgeted nervously in his presence.

'Keep still, girl, I will never finish here if you keep distracting me.'

She looked at the floor. 'Sorry, Professor Ulian. Shall I wait outside?'

He grunted. 'Actually I have a job for you. Go and fetch Professor Dearden from his room and bring him here. Tell him it is important. Then you can wait outside.'

'Yes, Professor.' She left as fast as her legs could take her.

Ulian stood up, stretched his legs and looked out of the window. He could see the lights of the city reflected in the broad sweep of the river Erskon, which passed pretty much directly outside, though some thirty feet below. He could see the Grand Duke's barge sitting at its landing immediately next to the magnificent stone building in which Ulian had lived, studied and taught in for the last forty years and out of whose window he was now observing the world.

The University of St Philig's was the oldest university in Tanaren, predating the upstarts at St Delph's by some twenty years. Ulian thought it the most aesthetically pleasing building in a city full of them, all elegant arches and quiet colonnades, leafy squares with fountains at their centre, grand halls with enormous windows and, at its heart, the great library, repository of some of the finest works ever produced, not only by Tanaren, but by the world's great empires, Chira and Koze. It even had tomes reputedly written by the Wych folk and the stout Folk under the Stone, unseen for millennia, as well as even older, more mysterious writings, whose preservation was a matter of the highest priority for such houses of learning.

There was a knock at the door and in walked Professor Dearden, a small, slightly hunched man; younger than Ulian but one for whom the troubles of the world seemed constantly to press on his stooped shoulders.

'Take a look at this.' Ulian handed him the letter. Dearden read it then handed it back.

'The correspondent says little. Do you think it worthy of a reply? Shouldn't it wait until Cedric returns? It is in his room and is addressed to him after all.'

'Didn't you read who sent it! One of Duke Hartfield's daughters! We have to look into it as a matter of priority. Cedric may not be back for months. Do you know anything of this ring she is alluding to?'

'I shall check with the artefacts manager to see where it is stored and have it retrieved for you tomorrow. Might I also suggest you speak to Alys who is waiting outside? It is likely she has copied its design on to paper.'

Ulian picked up a sheet off Cedric's desk. 'Here, she has already provided it.'

Dearden looked. 'Definitely Cedric's field. Its design reminds me of ancient barbarian jewellery, or even of the Wych style before the wars.'

'I thought the same. And what of this man in black? Where does he come from exactly?'

Dearden shrugged. 'The shaving of the head is often ritualistic, related to religious orders, or orders of warriors. Other than that I cannot say.'

'Artorus's beard! Where to start? There must be a book here with the answer. And that is not the only thing. The Hartfield girl mentions health problems. We cannot let this be; one of us is going to have to visit her, as soon as possible, too!'

'I would gladly do so,' said Dearden, growing ever the more oleaginous. 'Alas, my back prevents me from making journeys of any distance these days.'

'These days!' harrumphed Ulian. 'The last time you left this building the Grand Duke was not even a glint in his mother's eye!' He sighed. 'I will go, but do me a favour, please. Try and contact Cedric. It won't be easy, I know, but we do have an idea of where he is going.'

'I will write and send our best messengers; I will pay the highest rates with a further bonus given a successful outcome.'

'Good man. Now I had better reply to this letter and inform her of my intentions.'

'So be it,' said Dearden and with a small bow he took his leave.

Ulian picked up a blank sheet of paper and dipped his quill into the well of ink. 'Alys!' he called.

The girl came in.

'I will be travelling to Osperitsan in the back end of nowhere in a couple of days.'

'Yes, Professor.'

'I say a couple of days because it will take me that long to find any books in this Keth-cursed mess of a room that might explain the drawing you gave me earlier.'

'Oh, Professor, but they are over there.' She pointed to some shelves behind him 'Marked "Ancient Religions: their practices and rituals". Professor Cedric was always talking about them.'

Ulian's eyes gleamed hungrily as he made for the books. 'So he was always talking about them, was he? Alys, do you feel a change of scene might be beneficial for you?'

Margarete may have been many, many miles away but Ceriana felt as if she was being mothered to death. Since Ebba discovered her in her distressed state over a week ago she had been confined to bed, watched and pampered almost every minute of the day. A doctor had visited her. She had been leeched and forced to swallow antimony, which made her sick as a dog. Wulfthram had written to the mage healers, asking them to send someone, despite her imploring him not to do so. The fact was, aside from the doctor's poisonings, she felt fine.

She had hidden the stone before Ebba or anyone else could see it and it had given her no more trouble. They had allowed her to write letters, which she had done with great vigour producing almost a dozen, the real purpose of which was to render the letter to St Philig's, the only one she had really wanted to write, inconspicuous.

And then there was her scheduled trip to visit Baron Skellar, which was supposed to take place in two days' time. Wulfthram had all but cancelled it, but she felt so hemmed in at the present time that the need to break out and do something else was strong in her. Also she wanted to make her mark here; having her first official visit cancelled on health grounds could not be borne.

Ebba was sitting with her as she lay in bed, feeling an utter fraud. At one point she even fed her soup with a spoon. Ceriana, though, had warmed to her somewhat; she had been genuinely distressed at seeing her mistress on the floor all those days ago and her concern since was obviously not affected. 'Ebba,' she asked, 'are you married?'

'No, my Lady.' Ebba looked at her. 'I have a good man, a fisherman who spends many days at sea but we have never got round to be officially wed as of yet.'

'Is that not seen as scandalous?'

Ebba smiled. 'A little, my Lady, especially among the more religious folk, but with the necessity of providing food, a house and my father's limited means in providing a dowry it has just not been able to happen.'

'Is there anything I can do to help? If you need money...'

'No, my Lady, you are kind, but it would not be seemly for you to help the likes of me.'

'Why ever not? I really would like to help you. I have my own means separate from my husband's so I need not ask his permission.'

Ebba looked at her; she was evidently wavering. 'I will speak to my betrothed if it will make you content, my Lady.'

'Please do so; it would make me very happy.'

At that point the door opened and her husband walked in. Ebba curtsied and left the room. He looked at Ceriana.

'How are you feeling today?'

'Oh, Wulf, there is nothing wrong with me! I had an episode and, yes, I was upset and frightened but I am over that now. I need no healer or doctor and would like nothing more than to get out of bed and take my place at your side. In fact, I am quite happy to demonstrate for you now how fit, active and healthy I feel.' She had a gleam in her eye as she took his hand and placed it on her breast.

'Meriel works quickly I see.'

'Indeed she does, especially with the righteous.' Ceriana pulled him on to the bed next to her, putting his hand to her face this time. She stared at him, making her brown eyes as large and soulful as possible. 'I wish to be as good a wife to you as possible, whether it be now, in our private time, or in fulfilling the more public duties...'

'Like visiting Jon Skellar in two days' time?' He gently withdrew his hand.

'Would it be so very wrong of me to do so? How would you feel if at the very first opportunity you had to prove yourself as First Baron of the North you took to your bed with an ague?'

'You are young and thin as a wand, and the winds outside are getting colder.'

'I am as Elissa wishes me to be. Can I not wear a cloak, or even those smelly furs you people here are so very fond of? Let me show how very grateful I can be.' She put her head to his chest opening his shirt and kissing him.

'I am not happy, but maybe if you shortened your stay with him...' She stopped, looked at him and moved her head lower, then lower again. He closed his eyes.

'Very well have it your own way. Return after just five days though. One other thing ...'

She stopped again and looked up. He felt her silky hair against his bare flesh as her hands loosened his breeches. 'Yes?'

'You called me Wulf. Only my mother and Sofie have called me that.'

'I am sorry. Shall I stop?'

'No, don't stop. Don't stop at all.'

She was the beast again. She could feel the power in that massive body, even though the bitter cold pervaded its flesh, rendering it torpid and sluggish. She could still hear the water dripping from the roof into the lake and the echo as an eyeless fish breached its surface before settling back into its nameless depths. There was a difference, though. Difficult though it felt, she knew it could open its eyes. She felt it doing so, felt the struggle to move its massive lids upwards. Her lids. It was done. She knew they were open, even if she could still see nothing. She sensed it was deep underground, deeper than any man had travelled. The underworld.

Could she move? All concentration and energy were focused on the right forelimb. When her mind was here before it felt like it was cast in stone but not now. There was a pain, like the pain one felt after sleeping on one arm for too long and one had to wait before it could be moved – but slowly, inexorably, one felt life return to it. She felt the limb slowly lift and the digits clasp and unclasp, as life energy gradually seeped back into them. This was done for each limb in turn until all was ready for the next step.

With trepidation (she could feel the beast's trepidation as it were her own) she felt it starting to walk. As each foot came down, the ground trembled slightly and she could hear stones slide down unseen walls. Then it stopped, exhausted, needing a further rest. There was just enough energy to do one more thing. She felt the head raise itself and breath exhale from the body. As she stared ahead, a long gout of flame spurted from her. Suddenly the cave could be seen. It was vast! Cathedral-sized, its roof still shrouded in blackness, its walls reflecting the glitter of a thousand faceted gemstones. Then it was dark again. Exhausted but content, both she and the beast slept.

It was difficult separating the skyline from the horizon. Both were slate grey and brooding, pensive and ominous. Slabs of white-flecked ocean rolled landward before crashing against the harbour wall, dashing salt and spray into the air to land on Ceriana's upturned face. They had arrived not one hour ago and, although conditions were far from perfect, she had been told that the ship would depart very shortly. Servants were loading her luggage on to the war galley that would take her to Thakholm after just under two days' sailing. It rose and fell with the swell of the water and she could hear its timbers creaking as the elements did their worst. One thing she was enjoying about living on the island was the freedom she was given to ride a horse. Back at Edgecliff more often than not she would be forced to sit in a wagon and be driven to her destination, but here it was just assumed that she would be riding herself. Wulfthram had an idea that the best way to see his country was to experience it in the raw, on a wild day such as this one, an idea she readily agreed with. And so, after an exhilarating three-hour ride southward through moorland, westward over rugged highlands pierced by a thousand icy streams, with the wind tugging at her clothes and pinching her nose and cheeks till they were pink, she felt completely stimulated and alive and excited about the journey ahead. Wulfthram was standing next to the boarding plank, talking to the ship's captain. When he had finished he came over to her. 'You may go aboard now if you wish; they will be leaving very shortly.'

'Very well.' She was smiling. 'Tell me about where I am headed – what is this island like?'

'Rocky,' he said, phlegmatic as ever. 'And small. Its most important asset is its sheltered harbour, a haven for the ships out here. The Baron's residence is an interesting place, too; it is perched on a lip of rock jutting into the sea so you are surrounded by water on three sides.'

'I grew up in a castle with a similar aspect. It will probably seem very familiar.' She hesitated a second. 'Thank you for letting me do this.' 'There is no need for that. You made it clear that this is what you wanted.' He kicked a stone into the sea and paused before continuing. 'The problem I have with you is that you look so young. You have no meat on you at all, have never left your parents' side before and, yes, sometimes you behave like you have had just eighteen summers. Other times, however, you seem closer to my age than your own.'

She didn't want him to stop, so rarely was he open with her – so she just nodded silently.

'Sofie was some ten years younger than I. At first it was noticeable – to me she seemed frivolous and shallow and to her I am sure I seemed dour and grim. Over time, though, an understanding developed and by the time she died, well, we ... were more like very close friends than husband and wife.' Ceriana stared at the waves. 'I am sorry for your loss, truly.'

Neither spoke for a minute. They both stood there watching the ship moving slowly and listening to the gulls crying their frustration as they battled the headwind.

'What is the island's name again?'

'Thakholm.'

She laughed. 'Your accents are so funny, very up and down all the time. Thaaak-hoolm,' she mimicked, deliberately exaggerating the pronunciation.

By the Gods, she made him smile. 'At least I don't sound like I spend all my time with a peach in my mouth.'

She looked amazed. 'Do I sound like that? Honestly?'

He looked at her. 'With an accent like yours you could never be anything else than royalty.'

'Well, I never knew!' she exclaimed. 'I wonder what I will sound like after a few years here.'

'Your father and mother will never recognise you, especially if you cover yourself in our – what was it? – our smelly furs.'

'Yes and maybe I would have got used to that poisonous ale you drink round here and I will have a blotchy bright-red nose all drinkers seem to have.'

'Not a bad idea!' he said. 'A nice contrast for those freckles.'

Her bony elbow dug him in the ribs. 'I suppose I had better go.' She sighed.

'Yes, ' he said, 'it is time. Don't let that rogue Skellar try and get his hands on your stays.'

She snorted contemptuously. 'I think you will find, my husband, that it is only the older or somewhat overweight woman that needs to resort to corsetry. I never wear them. I would have hoped you had noticed that by now. And Baron Skellar won't be getting his hands on anything of importance, I assure you.'

The captain waved over at them. Sailors were buzzing over the decks now – departure was obviously imminent. Ceriana made to move.

'Goodbye, my husband. See you in a week or so.'

'Indeed. Have a pleasant journey and enjoy yourself.'

'Thank you. Farewell for now.'

She smiled a soft smile at him and walked up to the ship. The captain gently took her hand and guided her over the gangplank. She followed him as he led her below deck where she was lost from view.

Wulfthram stood and watched as the mooring ropes were cast off and the vessel was pushed into the harbour's main channel. Under the power of its oars, it was slowly manoeuvred out to sea and clear of the headland. Once it was there, the oars were withdrawn and a single sail raised. It caught the wind almost immediately and sped out to sea, the flag of Osperitsan flapping proudly from its main mast. He continued to watch until it was barely discernible against the horizon. Then he suddenly turned, climbed on to his horse and was away in an instant.

THE FORGOTTEN WAR
16

Marcus walked quickly towards the parade ground at the centre of the camp, leaving Cheris struggling to keep up with him. When he got there he turned right towards the front gate. She huffed and puffed behind him until at last she had had enough. She pulled his sleeve and stopped dead on the road.

"Lissa's blood. I am not moving another step until you talk to me.'

Benignly he stopped and turned to her. 'What is it, my dear?'

'Why on earth should these people want to see me? What by all the Gods have I got to say to them?'

'You are a mage. That is enough. You will be privy to all war councils and strategy meetings because of your talents. We may be feared elsewhere but the only thing a good general likes more than having a mage in his army is having two mages. It's like the Winter Feast celebration has come early for them.'

'I rather thought,' she said archly, 'that I would be able to hide behind you in all these matters.'

'And so you shall. They still want to see you, though. Dominic Hartfield is a knight of the Grand Duke's personal bodyguard and Reynard Lanthorpe of the Eagle Claw is pretty much Baron Felmere's second-in-command here. I have a feeling they will just want to size you up. Whenever a mage turns out to be a woman, it makes them a little wary. Women on the battlefield are an ... odd concept for them.'

'Well, if they want to send me home they are more than welcome. Come on then, let's get this over with.'

Marcus continued onwards. Amid all the tents and pavilions was a low building constructed hastily out of logs. Its doorway was little more than a sheet of canvas, currently being held open by a fastening hammered into the wood. Without hesitating, Marcus strode inside. Cheris stopped, rolled her eyes a little and plunged in after him.

The structure was just a single room, windowless with a bare earthen floor. Light was provided by a couple of lanterns which were barely up to the task. From what she could see there were two other men in the room, both in full armour. One was fair-haired and bearded, and the other had short dark hair and was clean-shaven. Aside from that, she could make out little in the gloom. Marcus spoke.

'Sir Reynard, Sir Dominic, allow me to introduce Cheris Menthur, a lady of not inconsiderable talent, whom I have had the pleasure of mentoring these last fifteen years.'

Both men bowed curtly to her; she, being unsure of how to respond, did the same. The blond man spoke.

'Pleased to make your acquaintance, my Lady. As you are probably aware, this war has been bogged down rather nastily for the past few years. However with your arrival and that of many other troops including Sir Dominic's here, Baron Felmere is poised to make a decisive push against the enemy before winter sets in.'

Sir Dominic broke in. 'Most of this camp will be moving forward over the next couple of days to join the main army. Then the forces will be mobilized for a strike on the town of Grest, on the river Whiterush. If we take the town before winter, then we can use it as a forward base from which to further advance on them next year.'

'There will be battle then? Very soon?' Cheris tried to sound casual.

'Most definitely,' said Reynard. 'The Grand Duke is determined to give this conflict fresh impetus and to prosecute it with vigour until the enemy concedes the land he has taken from us. That is why your talent has been employed.'

Dominic spoke. 'Marcus tells us this is your first military deployment.'

'Indeed it is. It is actually my first time off the island since my childhood.'

'There will be a lot of pressure on you to display your Lucan-given talent. Are you not afeard of buckling under everybody's expectations?'

Cheris felt her hackles rise – she could question her own abilities, Marcus could question them, but for a layman to do so was little more than barefaced cheek. Perhaps a demonstration was in order.

'I am terribly sorry, Sir Dominic, but the light in here is terrible and

I would rather see the face of the man accusing me of being a flake. If you don't mind?'

She made a quick gesture with her hands and said something under her breath. Instantly the room was illuminated with a soft white glow emanating from her upturned palm, picking out the startled expressions of the two young men. She could see they were both ruggedly handsome, tall, with a determined set to their jaw. She didn't bother looking at Marcus; she knew his disapproving expression only too well.

'There,' she said breezily, 'is that not better?'

Suddenly Dominic laughed. 'Exactly the response I was looking for! Reynard, we will have to watch this one. Bit of a change from the sycophants we usually have to deal with, eh?'

Reynard looked at her. With the light she could see his keen blue eyes piercing her like a lance. 'Indeed, my friend, though she will have to be aware that the Arshumans, too, have a mage who may not be as impressed with this as we are.'

Marcus spoke. 'I have heard of this mage. In battle we can seek each other out like beacons; we can sense when our opponent is trying to draw energy from the Plane of Lucan and can travel there with him and so try to nullify his powers. I will have to deal with him.'

'That's as maybe, and it will be both your jobs to stop him raining havoc down upon us like he did last time,' said Reynard.

Dominic, still smiling, made towards the door. 'In two days' time Baron Felmere holds a council of war at the forward camp. You will both be there, and then we will see how our fortunes will fare. I bid you both good day.' He bowed and left them.

'Yes,' said Reynard, 'sleep here tonight and the three of you can join us there tomorrow. Things are moving quickly now. By the spring we may even have newer, more exotic allies, but I cannot speak of this further at the present time.'

Cheris asked him, 'Have you been out here long?'

'Yes,' he said, almost ruefully, 'almost since the beginning. No one will be happier to see a rapid and successful outcome than I.'

As he left, Cheris dropped the light spell; it was showing up far too many spiders in the corners of the room. She followed Marcus outside.

'Sorry for the cheap parlour trick.'

He laughed and started walking back to the healer's tent. 'Don't be! I thought it was rather effective. Imagine, two seasoned warriors doubting the powers of a twenty-two-year old girl.' He laughed again.

She was chasing after him again. 'Are you mocking me?'

'Not at all. But don't let your cleverness go to your head. As Lanthorpe pointed out, there will be a mage facing us. A mage duel can be a frightening thing. We can get into each other's minds, sense our opponent's moves; he can try and disrupt our attempts to cross the divide and we can do the same with him. As I said earlier, leave him to me.'

Cheris screwed up her brow. 'If we can sense him so strongly, why can't I do that on the island? Magic is used there constantly.'

Marcus looked at her knowingly. 'But you can. You are just never interested enough to focus on it properly. It is nearly always a question of low-level spells cast by initiates there; powerful spells are rarely employed and there are shielded rooms on the upper floor of the college set aside for them. Think of your room in Tanaren City. The first few minutes there I bet you thought: "My! Listen to all those carts and wagons going past." But I bet after a few hours it barely registered with you. It is still there, but it has become mundane, and so it is with magic on the island. Now, when a single mage close by is drawing a lot of power and wishes to use it to kill you or your allies, then you will most definitely notice it.'

She nodded slowly and changed the subject. 'So Anaya is coming with us?' 'Of course, you cannot have your healer some miles behind the battle.'

'I fear for her. She has seen too much death and suffering. She needs to leave all this behind, at least for a while.'

'I agree. I can do nothing about the current battle, but when it is done perhaps we can take her back with us. She needs to appreciate the tranquillity of island life again.'

The Knights of the Holy Thorn had partitioned a small room off for them in their pavilion. It had little more than two low camp beds with blankets and a table off which to eat. After a quick meal Cheris fancied a walk around the camp, only to be told by Sir Norton that even here there were restrictions on mages' movements.

'But what if I want to use the ladies ... facilities?'

'Anaya and the nurses have a private tent for such things.'

Thus stymied, Cheris spent the rest of the day reading. Soon her magic would be called upon like never before, so she needed to be prepared. When her brain began to ache and the light of the candles ceased to be effective, she lay down to sleep. It was a hard bed but she was used to it. Marcus had been here and there on business, but eventually he, too, joined her. Her last memory before drifting off was of him turning this way and that, trying to get comfortable on a bed that was too short for him.

The next day, the beginning of the next stage in her journey. she spent the morning helping Anaya to pack her bottles and equipment, fold down some of the beds and load the healer's wagon. Only a couple of nurses were to be left here with minimal equipment, so the logistics of the move were considerable. By noon it was done, however, and Cheris saw the healer off through the main gate, Anaya sharing her wagon with the nurses and some of the Knights of the Holy Thorn. She was not alone. Many of the soldiers had gone already and some were even now marching just behind Anaya's wagon on the way to the front. Looking round, much of the camp was stripped bare, with bruised grass and mud showing in areas that had previously been blooming with tents. As she looked round, she saw her own wagon come towards her, driven by Sir Norton this time, as Roland was staying behind.

When he got to her he stopped.

'It is our turn to go now, my Lady. Marcus is already in the back.'

She nodded to him and climbed into the wagon. Together they headed towards the last camp before battle.

This camp was much more like what she had expected of a military encampment. Unlike the calm organisation of the place she had just left, this one was full of chaos and bustle – men armed and armoured chasing this way and that; horses steaming and sweating as squires struggled to control them; carts and wagons carving great ruts through the mud; men shouting, barking, cursing and laughing, and the smells of sweat, leather, smoke from the campfires and mud and wet grass. She had taken the opportunity when they had broken for a meal earlier on to sit up front with Sir Norton. He said little but she was not in much of a conversational mood herself. And now, as he steered the horses to the knights' tent, she felt a strange sense of what could almost be euphoria. Everyone here knew what was soon about to happen and she could feel the nervous energy and excitement of the men, all poised to bring their inactivity to a close and all with a deadly purpose.

Presently, they stopped at the knights' tent. Inside it was the same arrangement as before – a space partitioned off with two beds and a table. She sat down with Marcus opposite her. He remarked on the bustle around the place.

'Yes,' she said, 'you can sense the anticipation in everyone here. It is hard not to get caught up in it all. I never thought people could get so enthusiastic over a battle in which they could get hurt or killed.'

'I think you are misreading the situation,' he said. 'Getting the blood pumping and the aggression flowing is the best way to banish the fear over what is to come. A battlefield is a terrible place – you will see soon enough – and if your nerve breaks when you fight you are practically cutting your own throat. As for us, we cannot have the luxury of a drink or a battle song before the fray. We have to stay controlled and focused and deal with our fear in other ways.'

'What other ways?'

It may sound arrogant but we have to have faith in our own abilities. Our self-belief can be our strongest weapon. Never think that anything you face is deadlier than you are, because most of the time this is the truth – we are the deadliest weapons of all. We can command nature against our foes. All men have an innate fear of us and it is that we can exploit to our advantage. I will show you this if I can.'

'Should I stick with the abilities I am most familiar with?'

'Yes you should – just stay with that which gives you confidence. One thing, though: pay special regard to your skills at nullifying another's power. Stopping the enemy is just as important as dealing death on your own account.'

Sir Norton came round to see them, holding a large bowl whose contents were steaming.

'Some potage – vegetable only of course,' he said, looking at Cheris. 'Eat your fill, then come and see me. I will take you to the grand pavilion where the barons' war council will start in an hour or so.'

Cheris started eating the stew but for some reason had trouble swallowing it, although it tasted good. "Lissa help me, I am so nervous.'

'Nervous as in frightened or excited?'

She looked at him, her grey eyes sparkling. 'I am not frightened.' He nodded at her and continued his stew.

The nights were drawing in now and, as a pallid sun lay low in the western sky, Sir Norton took them to the war council. The grand pavilion was easy to find, being the enormous tent at the centre of the camp flying the pennants and flags that represented everybody present, with the blue, grey and white of Tanaren flying above them all. The pavilion was crammed with men standing cheek by jowl and, lit as it was by dozens of braziers and lanterns, it was also pretty hot. She could not see another woman there and in her red robe she felt not a little self-conscious. They stopped at the back of the crowd, from where she could see nothing – a situation she was quite happy with – but then Sir Norton started into the crowd.

'Make way for the mages.'

To her surprise, everyone immediately stood aside for Marcus and her. She followed the two men through the avenue of bodies until finally they were clear at the head of the room. There, sitting at a table, she recognized Reynard and Dominic, the two knights she had met earlier along with another dozen or so other men, all of differing ages, but all armoured and bearing various insignia. At the centre of the table in a great chair and sporting a breastplate displaying the emblem of a mace was a man of middling years with red rheumy eyes – this, she assumed, was Baron Felmere. To her horror, she saw Sir Norton go around the table and indicate two chairs behind it for them to sit on. She followed Marcus as he complied, making sure she sat at the very edge of the table. Sir Norton sat between Marcus and another knight wearing a red-and-white surcoat. They waited for ten minutes or so until everyone was settled and then Baron Felmere spoke.

'It is good to see you all here. Many of us have worked long and hard trying to assemble an army such as this, one of the largest I have commanded in the last nine years. And, my friends, we are all here for a purpose, for within the week we will be sitting in the baronial manor at Grest looking down at the Whiterush and drinking the finest wine the north has to offer!'

Most of the men cheered at this. It was the sort of thing they wanted to hear. After waiting for the noise to subside, the Baron continued.

'I am sure we have many doubters here who remember the last time we tried to take the town, how their artillery and their mage had us running backwards in no time. Well, let me assure you that will not be happening again.'

A man in the crowd, bald, middle-aged and with a spade-like beard spoke.

'There is a larger force here for certain. But scouts tell us that the Arshumans have also swollen their numbers and the difference between us and them will not be that great. How can you be so confident that we will be successful this time?'

'A good point, Kenvor; you are right of course – they, too, have been reinforcing themselves. But there are two major differences between then and now.' He stopped and scanned the eyes of the men facing him. 'The first thing, as you can see, we have two mages to counter their one.' He indicated Marcus and Cheris and there was a general murmur of approval. 'I am sure the veterans here recognise Marcus of the Isle of Tears and are well aware of his capabilities. With him is his protege, a lady called Sherise who Reynard assures me is of equal competence.'

She felt all eyes turn to her; she didn't really care about the mispronunciation of her name, but however briefly she was the centre of attention and she was not sure she liked it. The Baron spoke again. 'OK, lads, no leering over the mages; there are other women in camp who would happily accommodate you afterwards. Their job here is to neutralise the mage opposing us. And they have another task...' He stopped again. 'Well, written orders will be handed out to you all this evening. The final contingents of men will arrive tomorrow. The day after this we march for Grest.'

'But what of the artillery in the town?' The man in red next to Sir Norton spoke. 'This will be a major difficulty for us to overcome.'

'Ever the cautious one, Lasgaart,' laughed the Baron, 'but I have a plan for that. Grest was never an Arshuman town. Most of our people fled it when the war started but some still remain there. The Arshumans believe they have all switched allegiances but this is not the case. What if I was to say that three days from now when dusk falls the gates will be unlocked? That if we deploy for battle at that time the enemy will be looking at us, not at their own artillery, and that a small force should be able to break into the barely defended town and destroy the catapults and ballistae based there.' He paused, letting the observers digest this information. The murmuring became a crescendo. Felmere raised his hand for silence. 'Any questions?' One man stepped forward.

'Ostark?'

The man spoke. 'Two questions. Baron: the first is how can you be sure there is not a double betrayal going on and the gates will remain locked despite the assurances you have been given. The second is: why not capture the catapults and use them against the foe rather than destroy them?'

'To your first question: well, you can never be wholly certain but I am as certain as it is possible to be. Like you, I have been here long enough to know bullshit when I hear it and the people that have ... come forward have been promised much in return. But you are right, insurance will be required. The men going up the hill will be volunteers only and Marcus the mage should go with them.' Marcus started at this but let the Baron continue. 'As for your second question, in order to target the Arshuman deployment, all the artillery would have to be moved substantially, and we will not have the time or manpower up there for that. So what I propose is that they are all burned so that the fire will rattle their troops and give us the attack signal. All this will be in your orders.'

'May I speak, Baron?' It was Marcus. The Baron nodded at him. 'It may be not such a good idea to split the two of us up. My colleague is every bit as capable as I, but this is her first engagement and I was rather hoping to show her the ropes, as it were, rather than plunge her in head first.'

'I appreciate what you are trying to say, Marcus, but the mission to destroy their artillery is the absolute priority here. The men going there will need all the protection they can get just in case something goes wrong, so as far as I am concerned a mage has to go, and it should be the most experienced. Does your colleague feel this will be a problem.' He looked directly at Cheris for the first time.

She swallowed. Her throat was dry. 'No, it will be fine, Baron. Marcus should go with your surprise attack.'

She didn't hear the next few minutes of the council. It was decided then! Despite Marcus's reassuring words about looking after her, she would be on her own. The Baron had spoken and she could see he was not going to change his mind. Still, she didn't feel frightened. Nervous, yes, and her throat was dry and raw in the heat from the braziers and dozens of closely packed bodies, but she was not frightened. In a way, it might even be better for her to be on her own, making her own decisions. She switched back to the council. Felmere was speaking again.

'Now, as for numbers, I will be providing a thousand foot soldiers, many of them experienced men; Lasgaart here has three hundred, as has Vinoyen. Haslan Falls have sent five hundred, Athkaril two hundred, Barons Maynard, Bruchan and Sowden two hundred between them. The heavy cavalry has Reynard's Eagle Claw – two hundred strong – with an additional fifty from the Serpent Order. The real bonus is Sir Dominic Hartfield's fifty Silver Lances. The elite cavalry of Tanaren, their banner alone will make the enemy quail. As for light cavalry, I, Lasgaart and Maynard have rustled up some one hundred between us. They will have spears and short bows and will deploy to protect our flanks. We are looking at some three thousand men here, much more than our usual complement.'

'How many archers?' said a voice from the crowd.

'I have two hundred good men; Wyak of Athkaril has sent a hundred; Lasgaart and the others have supplied a hundred or so between them. That, if my mind is not addled, gives us some four hundred archers and cavalry, plus the two thousand regular troops. The finalised battle deployment you will get on the day of the battle.' He stroked his chin thoughtfully.

'One other thing. The people of Grest are our people. We want them on our side. When we take the town there is to be no violation of its womenfolk. Failure to comply will be punishable with twenty lashes, no exceptions. Do I make myself clear?'

One of the soldiers spoke up. 'They would do it to our women. A lot of the troops see it as their right, the spoils of war.'

'Not any more,' said Felmere. 'We need to win minds here. A man whose wife is spoiled by our soldiers will never join our cause. This sort of thing has gone on long enough and I should have stopped it earlier.' He put his hands behind his head and stretched.

'And that, my friends, is that. Tomorrow the advance guard will move out, with everyone else following the day after. It is the day after that when Artorus and Mytha will determine our destinies. And remember, we need a nice slow deployment with as much fanfare as possible; we do not want them to focus on anyone but ourselves; they need to be looking at us and not the town or its catapults. Now, unless there are further questions, we can call these proceedings closed.'

Cheris remembered little else of that day; Sir Norton escorted her back to her bed with Marcus joining her a little later. They did not speak, Marcus' sensing correctly that this was not perhaps the right time. All she could recall afterwards was that before sleep took her she prayed to Elissa, to Lucan and Artorus himself, as well as to all the saints she could remember, for the first time in many years.

The following morning, though, she was on form. Seeing Marcus sheepishness she sensed a kill.

'Any words of comfort for me, O great protector?'

He sighed, expecting no less. 'I am as happy as you about this; I did not want us split up. The only one with the authority to tell us what to do is the Baron himself and unfortunately he has done just that. I will return to you as soon as I possibly can, I promise.'

'And how can I trust anything you say anymore?'

He groaned exasperatedly. 'Don't be like that, Cheris! How was I to know what was going to happen? If I had known, I would have brought someone else. As I said, I will get to you as soon as I can.'

'I will probably be dead by then.'

This time he snapped at her. 'No, you will not. Whoever this mage facing us is I know two things about him. The first is that he is not more talented than you, and the second is that he is certainly not cleverer than you. He may be more experienced and know how to rough you about a bit, but ultimately you will be more than a match for him.' He left her and went over to talk to Sir Norton.

Cheris watched him go with pursed lips. 'I hope you are right. As Elissa watches over me, I hope you are right.'

17

It was an opulent room. Its walls were panelled in dark wood and hung with heavy cloth tapestries. The drinking vessels on the richly carved table appeared to be made out of silver. Velvet-clad servants secreted themselves as discreetly as possible into darkened corners. The windows were large and wide and admitted shafts of mid-morning light. Through them could be seen an impressive view, dominated by a waterfall with a drop of some twenty feet, around whose broad circular splash pool were cluttered some low stone houses interspersed with trees. Nearer to the windows, occupying an elevated position on a flat-topped hill, was a house of Artorus with its conical spire built in the same grounds as a house of Xhenafa, a small box-shaped stone building overlooking a cemetery. Both religious houses occupied a sward of level ground between falls and hill and were surrounded by the town's more humble dwellings. A man clad in a rich green-and-gold surcoat was standing at the window at this moment, mesmerised by the fall of the water into the pool and the cloud of spray that constantly hung over it. It never changed, he thought. How unlike a man could that be? Could it not see how change was dynamic and positive, how it threw the deserving high into the air to stand over the weak, the foolish, the gullible. Some people lived to be led, to feed like a dog on scraps thrown at them from the high table while all the time braying their gratitude at the thrower. He could never live like those people – by Artorus, he was change's fiercest instrument. The next few months would see to that.

A servant, all wariness and deference, sidled up to the man. 'Baron Fenchard, the man you wished to see has arrived.'

'Show him in, and fill up two goblets.'

He went and sat down at the head of the table in a high-backed chair whose carvings were hidden by cushions. The servant poured the wine, which he drank immediately; it was too early really but Keth himself wasn't going to tell him what to do.

The door opened and in strode a man who looked like he was born on a battlefield. Six feet of hulking muscle, almost as broad as he was tall, clad in tarnished plate mail bearing no insignia. He was bald with dark merciless eyes that glared at Fenchard over a broad grey-black beard. His right ear looked like it had been partly chewed and a long-healed white scar lined his right cheek. He smiled at Fenchard, showing some missing teeth – the ones remaining were blackened and irregular. He spoke, with a voice so deep it seemed to emanate from somewhere underneath the nearby cemetery:

'Of what do you wish to speak?' The man's presence was unsettling.

Unnerved as he was, Fenchard was determined not to show it. 'Sit down.

The wine is poured; drink your fill.'

The man sat but did not reach for his goblet. 'I do not.'

'Very well. I asked you here, Sir Trask, after Baron Ulgar mentioned you.' 'What did he say?'

'Many things. That you were a knight expelled from the order as your methods were. unpalatable to them. That you have since become a freebooter, fighting for both sides and for whoever pays the most. That you are utterly ruthless and determined and that nothing gets in your way.'

'Ulgar is well informed. I deny nothing.'

'Good. How would you like to work for me?'

'You had better be persuasive; I have had my fill of fops in this war.'

'I guarantee I will pay more than anyone else you have worked for.'

'A good start, what else?'

Fenchard took another draught from his goblet. 'I have powerful friends. I cannot tell you who they are yet but I guarantee that in under a year I will be the most powerful baron in the east – Keth's furnace, maybe in the whole country. Even the Grand Duke will fear me.'

Trask's face looked as if it were carved in granite. 'Your ambitions mean nothing to me. If I am to work for you, I will need something more concrete than that.'

Fenchard leaned forward, warming to his subject. 'Think about it — if all goes to plan, I will have access to the gem trade here, the income and taxation from nearly all the lands east of the Kada will be mine, and you, my fine fellow, will be the first beneficiary after myself.'

'Fine words, but words when spoken are just air. They mean nothing. How do I know you are not just some rich pretty boy with his head where his arse should be? Thank you for your time but I will be going now.' He stood up and made to leave.

'How will a hundred crowns as an advance do?'

Trask stopped, fixing the younger man with a cruel stare. 'Show me.'

Fenchard got up and went to a lockbox on the floor by the windows. Opening it, he drew out a large leather bag which was obviously quite heavy. It clinked as Fenchard lifted it up, causing Trask's eyes to glitter hungrily. Fenchard then upended it on the table, allowing its contents to spill out — gold coin after gold coin clattered on to the table. Trask ran his hand through the pile and whistled softly.

'You may have just talked yourself into a deal, boy. What is it you want?'

Fenchard smiled to himself — gold, such an easy way to procure the service of lesser, simpler men. 'I have men out at the front to fight Felmere's war for him. I have a further six hundred here waiting to march out tomorrow. You will lead them and whip them into a fighting force. Tell their current leader, Bakker, that he is demoted and answers to you from now on.'

'I will do that now.'

'One other thing, do you know a Morgan of Glaivedon?'

Trask grinned — his expression was that of a wolf who has just sighted a lame deer, alone and helpless. 'Our paths have crossed, yes.'

'He killed some of my men the other day; their bodies ended up in the river. They were only prisoners and lousy sellswords but that is not the point.

If you see or hear from him, I want to know — understand?'

'Nothing would give me greater pleasure.' He turned to leave.

'Before you go.' 'Yes.' Trask grimaced.

'Is it true what I've heard ... your nickname?'

'The Finger Man. Yes, it is true.'

'Why exactly...'

'Is it not obvious? I cut the fingers off those I kill and wear some of them attached to a thin rope around my neck. When they blacken and rot I replace them. It scares the shit out of those who have no right to be on a battlefield.

Will you be riding out to join us at the war front?'

Of course, in a week or so.'

'Good, I will see you then.'

Fenchard watched him leave, musing over whether a hundred gold crowns had ever been better spent.

Morgan held out his hands and put them close to the fire. Their first day of travel along the pass had gone well. The road they had been travelling along was an ancient one. Carved into the mountain side; it was broad and flat, and the climb, though noticeable, had been gentle. Even Cedric had walked with them for part of the journey, using a stick as a prop, one that Samson had carved for him on their last night in the forest. They were walking on the shoulders of Mount Deraska at the western end of Claw Pass. Mount Baerannan, the higher of the two peaks, was in the east and between them was a deep gorge that once held a flowing river, but now just knifed between the two mountains and was full of loose treacherous rocks pockmarked with the occasional tarn as it broadened out further up the pass. To slip off the edge of the road here was to invite certain death; anybody so unfortunate to suffer such a fate would provide nourishment for wolves, bears and the other denizens of the mountains.

Occasionally, along the road, the mountain side would fold in on itself, creating little sheltered nooks and crannies where a camp could be made out of the ever-present wind. Such a place was where they were now, as a bitter night pinched at the ears and the tip of the nose. Inside the wagon were Cedric and Willem; there was also room for one other. Everyone had agreed that each of them would take turns so that all could, at some point, get a night out of the wind. It was Haelward's turn tonight. Morgan was on first watch.

There was a creaking noise and, as Morgan looked up, he saw Cedric climb out of the wagon, stretch himself and come over to join him by the fire.

'It is strange to be here, isn't it? Sitting at my desk at St Philig's planning this journey is one thing but sitting here in the darkness hearing the wolves howl in the gorge is something I never thought possible, if truth be told.'

'You mean you never thought this journey would ever take place?'

'Well, there have been so many obstacles – getting the Grand Duke's approval, my own health and so forth – I never really believed all this would actually happen.'

'We can always go back, if you want.'

'And disappoint the Grand Duke? The man who wants responsibility for the first human–Elven alliance for generations? Hardly an option, I fear.'

'I was not being serious. I am almost as curious about seeing the Wych folk as you. Almost as curious.'

'There is a long way to go first – the pass and the summoning ritual.'

'What is this ritual exactly?'

'It has to be performed; otherwise they are at complete liberty to ignore you or just kill you. An island in the centre of the river Taethan has a magical statue; you speak an incantation, burn some herbs and leaves at its feet, and it should shoot forth a column of blue flame which stays permanently until one of the Wych folk nullifies it. It is an ancient agreement dating from the time when they first moved into the forest and the people here were sympathetic to their cause. If you ignite the blue flame. then they have to come speak to you, though they are not obliged to help.'

'And I take it you have the herbs and know the incantation?'

'Well, I have a book that gives me the incantation. I hope my pronunciation of ancient Aelvish is up to scratch. As for the herbs and leaves; I have some dried ones in the wagon. The same book is old and partially damaged, so it is not clear on the amount required, but I think I have enough.'

'It had better be! Imagine travelling all that way and failing because we don't have enough leaves.' Morgan was grinning.

'Exactly, my boy; the Wych folk should kill us if we are that stupid, or kill me at any rate.'

'We will defend you to the death, my friend – stupid or not.'

'That is comforting to know,' smiled Cedric. 'How long is your watch?'

'Oh, there is a couple of hours to go yet, it'll be Leon's turn after that.'

'Then I shall leave you to your reverie, if things go well how much longer should we be in this pass?'

'Given the terrain and our rate of progress, some four to five days. I have only been through it a couple of times myself, so I am not exactly certain.' 'And this Jeremiah's Saddle? When will we get there?'

'Two days or so; it is the high point in the pass – a narrow cleft in a great outcropping of rock, barely wide enough for the wagon. A prime ambush spot, and one you don't want to be halfway across when the snows start.'

'So the real dangers are yet to come?'

'Definitely.'

The next day brought some consternation to the party.

'Look at the sky,' said Samson. 'It is white.'

'It is certainly carrying snow ,' said Rozgon, who was swathed in furs, making him look even bigger. 'Hopefully it will just drop it over the mountain top.'

'May I ask something?' piped up Willem.

'Of course, boy, what is it?'

'Who in the name of Artorus uses this pass? It seems so remote.'

Samson answered him. 'It is, but it is used a lot in the summer and early autumn. As you saw, Shayer Ridge and the other towns near it do not make enough food for their people. On the other side of the mountains is Zerannon, the nearest city to the Aelvenwood. It is a port and has many fertile fields. So they trade grain for gems and coal; both do very well out of it. In population and wealth Zerannon is probably only second to Tanaren City.'

'A distant second,' said Rozgon.

'Of course, but it is an important place all the same. Hence the significance of this pass.'

'And the fact it is crawling with bandits.'

'Not likely at this time of year. Only complete idiots would try to cross it now.' Samson bit into a piece of dried meat he was holding, so it was impossible to tell how serious he was being.

They continued to climb; it was a steeper walk today and the road was narrowing. Now and then Willem would look over the edge – the gorge had widened. Clumps of tough, spiky grass grew on its sides, and now and then small groups of mountain goats or sheep could be seen, picking out the precipitous pathways to their next meal. The drop had increased considerably and he could only look down for a short period before feeling nauseous. Sometime after noon he drew their attention to the top of Mount Baerannan. 'Is that snow over there?'

It was true enough. Although its white head was shrouded in cloud there was definitely more snow on the peak than earlier in the day. The group regarded it stoically. 'We move on,' said Morgan.

They camped in a similar sort of shelter to that of the previous night; the wind had picked up and it was colder, too. The air was also thinner. Little conversation was made. The next morning the air was raw and their breath was expelled in smoking white plumes. The sun shone bright and clear above them, tingeing the snow on the mountain tops rose pink, but it gave off no warmth. They lit a fire and had some hot stew for breakfast, but soon afterwards they were off. They wanted to be at Jeremiah's Saddle as soon as they possibly could. After less than two hours' walk, though, Haelward, who was walking ahead of the rest called a halt. Morgan went up to see him.

'Up ahead,' said Haelward, 'Is that blood?'

BOOK ONE: AUTUMN

The road climbed steeply at this point; at its crest, turned black by the sunlight, was some kind of smear, or stain standing out against the rock.

'Let's go and look.' said Morgan.

The two of them slowly climbed the slope, and at its top the road straightened. Ahead of them, barely discernible in the distance, they could see the mountain side extend further into the gorge, which now became little more than a narrow slit as the two great peaks almost touched. Where the road hugged the mountain side, it was riven by a smooth, if narrow, cleft. It was difficult to tell how long the cleft ran through the road from where they were. That was not what concerned then now, however. Where they stood was a large dried pool of what was unmistakeably blood. Further along the road scattered here and there were other bits and pieces of gore, discernible as dark patches in the sunlight.

The two men exchanged a telling look. 'Human?' said Haelward.

They had their answer soon enough. Further down the path they came across more substantial remains – the upper part of a man's body, a head, part of a torso and the left arm. The clothing had been torn off it and the face had been partially chewed. There was also impact damage as if it had fallen a considerable distance.

'Well, I never,' said Morgan. 'So this is what happened to the vipers.' The tattoo was clearly visible on the arm.

'Vipers?' Haelward asked.

'The mercenaries, forced up here by the baron's men after the massacre at the monastery.'

'Oh them, bad soldiers and troublemakers all, no loss to anybody.' Haelward scanned the remains further. 'It has been dropped from further up the mountain. Maybe whatever did this fought with another of its kind and they lost it by mistake?'

Cedric was alerted as to the find and came over to peruse it; he stiffly crouched for a better look. 'Poor man,' he muttered.

'Don't waste your sympathy,' said Morgan. 'All this man was known for was slaughtering monks and despoiling churches. Artorus's bones, just look at that!'

'Elissa's great milky tits,' hissed Rozgon.

From somewhere inside the denuded ribcage Cedric pulled a yellow incisor tooth. It was cruel, sharp and some four inches long. Almost as one, they all looked up the mountain side as if expecting to see its owner charge down towards them.

'What we are looking at here,' said Cedric, 'is either an ettin or a troll.' 'What exactly is the difference?' Willem was white as milk.

'Oh, by the Gods, there are many, boy. The first difference is size. Trolls are larger but thinner. Their fur may also be of any colour while an ettin's is always white. Trolls have long arms and claws that grip the mountain side enabling them to climb it; however, they are not social animals and would not casually toss a meal off a cliff. What I believe we have here is an ettin pack. They are about eight to ten feet tall and have large eyes and black faces with a broad nose, which gives them an acute sense of smell. Their claws can be a foot long or more. Their feet have large splayed toes to make it easier for them to climb and retain a grip on precarious surfaces.'

'And how many make a pack?' asked Morgan.

'Oh, for hunting the males band together and take kills back to the females. I believe the average hunting pack has around ten individuals.' 'And with their sense of smell they probably know that we are here.'

'Their hearing is very good, too. I have no doubt they know about us'

'Well, this gets better and better,' said Leon. 'We have four more days in the mountains with ten of these things after us?'

'Well ..., yes,' said Cedric, 'but it isn't nearly as bad as it sounds.' 'Would you care to ... elaborate?' said Morgan sardonically.

'Well, they are incredibly stupid and cowardly. They attack in a mob, but if one is killed or something frightens them you will not see them again. And don't forget fire – it really will unnerve them.'

'OK – Varen, can we keep a torch burning for the next four days and have fuel for more if we are attacked?'

'It will be touch and go, but we should be able to.'

'Right, light a torch now and keep it on the wagon. If they are watching us, it should make them think.'

'Right away,' said Varen, scuttling off.

'Leon, those double-pronged arrowheads the archers use to bring down horses and large animals – do you have any?'

'About a dozen; I shall fix them to the shafts now.'

'Good, six each for you and Samson then. Cedric...'

'Yes, Morgan?'

'Into the wagon with you. Willem, do you have your knife?'

'I do, sir.'

'Then guard your mentor with it; in the wagon with you, too. Rozgon, stay behind the wagon; Haelward and I will march ahead. Let's get moving. I want us past the Saddle by this time tomorrow.'

Thus chivvied, they moved on, Varen having fixed a flaming torch to the bracket at the front of the wagon. Fortunately, the horses were well trained and weren't spooked by it. Leon sat at the back of the wagon fixing the new arrowheads – that is, when he wasn't verbally sparring with Rozgon as he marched behind the rest of them.

After less than an hour they got to the Saddle. It was much larger close up than many of them imagined. It was difficult to tell if it was a natural feature or man-made; Morgan suspected a little of both. Here, if a cross-section of the rock could be taken, it would look a little bit like a horizontal S shape – sheer rock on their left climbing into the clouds, the cloven walkway, maybe ten to twelve feet across, and the bulge of rock to their right, taller than their heads, before the final drop into the gorge below. One thing comforted Morgan, though: whereas a group of bandits could plant traps and lay in ambush for them, a mob of hungry ettins, lacking that subtlety, could only rush them from ahead or behind. He wondered how fast they were – whether they would have time to light up torches or fire off arrows before they were devoured. Camp tonight would be an interesting affair that was certain.

Once in the Saddle, it warmed up a little bit as there was some shelter from the bitter, freezing wind. The noise they were making – the turning of the cart wheels, the gentle clop-clop-clopping of the horses and the steady trudge of booted feet – rebounded off the walls, amplifying them so that even their breathing seemed abnormally loud. Despite the cold, Morgan found himself sweating and he suddenly noticed how sore his feet felt against the hard rock. Hours passed, with little to break the tedium. When they stopped for a brief lunch he managed to break even playing dice with Rozgon. No birds broke the silence, just the occasional slide of loose rocks down the mountain rattling their way into the gorge.

'What a desolate place,' said Haelward.

They had been climbing steadily for some time and weren't far from the highest point of the pass when something brushed Morgan's hand. Then his face. Something wet and cold. He looked up into the sky and his worst fears were confirmed. 'Artorus's teeth!' he grimaced under his breath. It was snowing.

It was not a light shower either; it was settling and the narrow confines of Jeremiah's Saddle were perfect for it. Morgan stopped and called everyone to him, including Cedric and Willem.

'We are going to have to march through the night,' he said. 'Otherwise the snow will trap us in here. In the winter months it can fill this damned Saddle completely. We will have to carry on until we are clear of it; otherwise the wagon will be trapped and the horses will freeze to death.' 'What about these monsters after us?' asked Samson.

'Well, I have seen neither hide nor hair of them yet. We will march in shifts, one of us taking a break for an hour to lie in the wagon. It will be slow progress but in about six hours from now we should be back on the broad mountain path again and be going downhill, which will be even better. Keep the blankets on the horses and the wheels of the wagon turning. Having to stop to dig us out is the last thing we want.'

They continued on, as the light left the sky and night closed in. No stars could be seen, smothered as they were by the cloud blanket below them. And still the snow kept falling. It was over a foot deep now and Haelward had borrowed Varen's mace to clear the snow from in front of the wheels. Morgan used his hands, but even with his thick gauntlets the cold and wet seeped through. Everyone felt thoroughly miserable.

'Everyone needs to stay alert. Varen keep that torch going.'

As he spoke, wolves started howling some way ahead of them.

The sound carried, amplified by the rock, mournful and sad. Then, as if in answer, there came another sound, a deep guttural cry followed by a series of short barks as others joined in. The stillness of the night was shattered by the ever-rising cacophony. If anyone in the company was drifting off, they soon snapped out of it.

'Ready your weapons. Let's get some torches burning. Samson. Leon, get those arrows ready.'

Fires were lit and weapons readied. The two archers walked ahead of Rozgon, Morgan and Haelward, who each now carried a flaming torch. Slowly and deliberately they moved forward, breath steaming in the freezing air. The barking continued. Suddenly Haelward gave a hiss. 'What in the name of Mytha is that?'

They had thought the mountain side to their left unscaleable, but there must have been the slightest of ridges there, enough for a skilled creature to get a foothold, for coming towards them and some thirty feet above them was such a creature. It was white, bear-like and shaggy, and was traversing the mountain side using powerful forearms tipped with pitchfork-sized claws while gripping on to the nearly sheer surface with its broad toes. It glared at them with large black eyes, each seemingly bereft of an iris, and opened its mouth to bark at them, thereby displaying its brutal yellow fangs dripping with saliva. It gave out a cry that froze their marrow. Then on the path ahead they could see other white shapes, much more distant but definitely loping towards them, four or five at least. The horses started rearing in terror. The snow kept falling. Rozgon felt his axe blade and roared back at them.

'Come on, you bastards. Time to taste some Tanaren steel!'

THE FORGOTTEN WAR
18

The island was ringed with stakes and fire. Every ten paces stood a man holding a spear and carrying a bow. It was a still, breathless sort of night, muting even the birds, though clouds of midges still took their time to torment its inhabitants. At the centre of the island under a hastily constructed shelter were the womenfolk who were employed with the nigh-on impossible task of getting dozens of excited children to sleep. The goats were tethered next to them, along with the villagers' most precious possessions, and next to all that sat the Circle of the Wise and its leader, Dumnekavax, who sat crosslegged opposite them flanked by two posts on which skulls had been placed. Before him was a bowl sitting over a fire, its contents acrid and steaming. Dumnekavax spoke to his companions.

'It has been decided following what has happened lately and the apparent anger of the spirits that I shall walk with them tonight to try and determine their intentions and ask the best way to propitiate them. The path is dangerous, and only I and my appointed second may walk it. If I do not return, Mutreverak will become your Elder and my head should be prepared so that it can join my predecessors in the great house.'

Having spoken, he took the bowl in front of him and put the hot bitter liquid to his lips. The other members of the Circle watched him intently. Suddenly he gasped and fell backwards on to the soft ground, his eyes wide, staring blindly at nothing.

He was a great white hawk swooping over the marshes. Its rivers far below ran like liquid silver, running into each other, slicing the soft land into a mosaic of tiny islands. He flew higher, then higher again, as the carpet of stars grew nearer and nearer, their light cutting into the back of his eyes. Then he saw it, the river of night, invisible from the ground but now here before him, a blackness within a blackness, a void stretching into an infinite maelstrom of nothing.

Now he changed. He was a fish. A majestic pike powering his way through the Great River back down towards the underworld. The Earth below him grew again; he recognised the village but he did not go there.

Instead, he plunged into the dark eye of the sacred lake and went deeper and deeper until the light of the moon was extinguished. As he looked around he saw other ghostly white presences, He passed Fasneterax's little boy, who turned and smiled at him. He saw many other spirits there, people half remembered or long forgotten – all were smiling and happy. Then he saw his father, who embraced him, and his mother, who took his hand and spoke in her soft voice, one he still heard in his dreams. 'Come, my son. I shall take you to Ukka.' Still further they went. The void was black but not cold. He held his mother's hand and stared ahead. And then he realised that Ukka was now before him. The spirit could be either male or female; Ukka alone chose which form he or she took. Tonight she was female, standing proudly before him, impossibly tall, severe yet kind, with eyes that beheld him with both compassion and indifference. As with all the spirits she was not there to protect man, but rather to ensure balance and harmony in all things. In order to obtain her benison, a price had to be paid. She spoke to him, her voice deep and sonorous.

'Dumnekavax of the Black Lake, you come before me again. Do you think we spirits have the time to listen to you and your petty concerns? Know you this: I will allow you one question only. Ask and return to your people, but understand I already have your spirit in one hand – maybe shortly I will have it in both.'

Dumnekavax prostrated himself. 'Oh Ukka, mighty and illustrious goddess of the underworld, I beseech you to make me understand why your children the Malaac have been unleashed upon us. What supplication do you require to call them home to the Lake of the Eye and ensure that they do not leave again to make war on us?'

'You misunderstand the Malaac as you misunderstand me. They are spirits of anger doomed forever to swim the Lake of the Eye. But there has been a great and terrible disturbance in your world. A new power has been unleashed there which even the Malaac cannot withstand and so they have broken free and must terrify those who summoned this power forth. Your kind have dabbled in things you do not understand and broken the covenant with the spirits. Your punishment is self-inflicted and must be borne as such. However, if you wish your village to be spared, your case must be made before me. Send me an emissary, young fit and strong. Let him deal with me directly and, if your case is good and just, the tide of the Malaac may avoid you as I will it. Go back to your village and tell them this and I shall await the response of your people. Go.'

Mist formed before Dumnekavax's eyes. He could no longer see the spirits around him. He called for his mother, his father, but received only a stony silence. All around him the light grew ever stronger until finally the mists began to disperse...

Suddenly he was back. He stared comprehending nothing for a moment, his mind a blank. Then, slowly, his mind returned to him. Above him was a pale sky flecked with light cloud. Closer and looking down at him were faces of men, beards shot with grey, concern in all their eyes. He realised he was on his back. Slowly he sat up and then the other men helped him to his feet. 'Are you all right, Elder?' said one of them. 'You were travelling the path all night.'

'I am fine, Mutreverak. And furthermore I now know exactly what we must do.'

The four of them stood on the jetty, looking intently at the river and trying to count shadows.

'There, there's another one, there,' said Cerren, pointing at a patch of water where a tell-tale patch of darkness briefly appeared.

'How many does that make now? ' said the ever-grim Fasneterax.

'At least five, maybe seven,' said Tegavenek 'They are waiting for us to take the boat out.'

'So they can tip it over.' Cygan gripped his spear.

'We are stuck here with nowhere to go then,' said Cerren. 'Where do these woods lead?'

'It is bounded by water on all sides,' said Tegavenek. 'We could find its centre and stay there, but sooner or later we will have to venture out. These creatures may be patient, may just wait for us.'

'Then we have to drive them off,' said Cygan. 'We have no choice.'

'And how exactly do we achieve that?' Fasneterax said. 'Grow some gills?'

'No, at night they come on to land; we lure them up here and kill enough of them to make them think again. Let us bring the boat down here; it has our equipment. There will be things there that can help us.'

They followed his suggestion and half carried, half dragged the boat until it stood some ten feet from the dwellings. Cygan then reached in and pulled out the vessel containing the black substance he prepared before they left.

'Coat your spears and arrowheads with this,' he said. 'It doesn't work quickly but if they are in water when it starts to work it could well drown them.'

'We need a position we can defend,' said Tegavenek. 'Somewhere they cannot get round and flank us.'

'Unless we dig a ditch and surround it with stakes the best place to defend would be one of the houses. We block off the rear entrance, so they can only come at us through the roof or a window. They will have to tear down the rear screen or a wall, which should give us enough time to pepper them with arrows.'

'But surely then we are inviting them to swarm us,' said Cerren.

'If you have a better suggestion, I will happily hear it,' said Tegavenek.

Cygan smiled at the young man. 'It is time to prove yourself as a warrior, my friend. In this house we can at least guard each other's backs and in a confined space it will restrict the numbers that can attack us at once. Hopefully, if we kill or wound a couple of them, the others will run off.' 'Vengefarak said they attacked many times during the night,' said Fasneterax. 'I doubt they will be put off that easily.'

'All the more reason to prepare our defences now,' said the elder. 'We can sleep in shifts until nightfall. None of us will sleep when the sun goes down.'

And this is what they did. They fixed the screen to the rear of the house, tying it securely. It was still the most vulnerable part of the defences; a clawed hand could tear through it fairly quickly, but not before an arrow could find its mark. They then set to poisoning their weapons and eating some of their rations. Cerren settled down to try to sleep and the others sat on the floor and busied themselves with their own thoughts. Fasneterax was checking the tension on his bow; Cygan watched him absently for a while, then decided to ask him, Why did you want to come out with us? Why not stay with Shettevellanda?'

'I would be no help to her now. The womenfolk know how to comfort her far better than I could. Your lady has been one of the kindest to her. I will not forget that.'

'Dying out here won't help her either. Not that we knew about the night devils before we left.'

'She would find another man. The tribe looks after its own. Besides, the same could be said about you.'

'You have me there!' said Cygan. 'Although you volunteered for this, whereas I was nominated by the Elder. It has worked out well for us here, though; there is no doughtier warrior in the tribe.'

'We go back some years, do we not? It will be like fighting off the Sand Warriors again. Maybe we will reap another harvest of enemy heads. Remember them piled high in the great house waiting to be boiled down and stripped of flesh.'

'I remember the smell. It was a hot summer. It was good to defend the village. They did many terrible things to other tribes. There was no room for mercy in that final battle.'

'It was another example of outsiders thinking they could enslave the barbarians of the marsh only to end up skewered on our spears.' Fasneterax sounded grimly satisfied. 'Maybe one day they will learn.'

'I doubt that,' Cygan said. 'One thing my contact with people outside the marsh has taught me is that they always see war as a reasonable option when they can't lie or cheat to get what they want.'

Tegavenek interrupted: 'You have such a low opinion of the dry landers.'

'I do, yes. To be fair, I have only met and dealt with traders. Maybe I would think differently if I met others of their kind. But that is not likely to happen soon.'

Fasneterax looked at Tegavenek. 'If we drive off the Malaac

tonight and the river seems clear, what do we do then? None of the Twin Snake are here, do we mount a search for them, or do we just return home?'

'These are just outlying settlements, most of the Twin Snake tribe live on a river fork, half a day's journey away, but with the river full of these creatures it will be nigh on impossible to get to them. Our instructions from the elder were to visit the Twin Snake to find out why they did not arrive at mediation talks with him. We now almost certainly know the reason. We are not enough to free their village on our own, so to continue up this river seems pointless. We were then told to visit the Jagged Hill to aid Vengefarak and the people there. We should still do this if we can.'

'According to Vengefarak, these creatures can tip over our boats and drown us. We should spend as little time on the water as possible.'

'This is true,' Tegavenek said, 'but remember he was talking about a single man in a round boat on a large open stretch of water, not four men in a larger boat on a river. I may be wrong but that may not be typical behaviour for them. Perhaps they were driven by hunger or something else making them equally desperate. Everything is speculation with these creatures. Why did they leave their home lake? What has driven them to attack us? Are they controlled by an individual or is their behaviour completely random? All of these questions need to be answered if we are to fight back against them.'

'It is important you get back to the Elder with news of the events that have happened here,' said Cygan. 'We will take you to the Jagged Hill if we can, but your safety has to be a priority now.'

'Nonsense,' said Tegavenek. 'Any of us can talk to the Elder; we have all seen the same things. No one of us is more important than the other. Besides, as far as he is concerned, you are already the main contender for the next addition to the Circle. You would be a grievous loss to the tribe.'

'I am surely too young. There are older more deserving people for that honour.'

'Dumnekavax holds great store in your knowledge of outsiders and the skills you have earned as a diplomat. The Taneren are not going to go away and to be able to deal with them may be important to the tribe's future.'

Cygan looked doubtful. 'All that I care about is providing for my family. Nothing else is as important as that.'

'Undoubtedly, but remember duty and responsibility can find you even when unlooked for.'

The sun outside was starting its descent; they all sat and waited listening to the sound of rushing water and wind sighing in the trees. Across the river the crows had settled in one particular tree and their harsh calling could be heard constantly. Tegavenek and Fasneterax were sleeping uneasily. Cerren was awake, with one eye looking out of the building's one narrow square window, which faced the river.

'We should block this before nightfall,' he said. 'I am sure they will attack the screen mainly but they could put their arms through here and surprise us.'

'We will do; we have wood enough here for that.'

'I wonder where the night devils came from; I mean how they were made. We are the children of Cygannan, the sky creator; surely they are not of the same stock as me or you?'

'They are not. You heard the Elder say they are part reptile and part amphibian. They are the children of Ventekuu, the great snake spirit, herself one of the progeny of Ukka. The tale as the Elders tell it is that, shortly after Cygannan made the world and the creatures of the surface, Ukka grew jealous. On looking at the world he saw that the world was unbalanced containing as it did no great predators, no insects and no creatures of the water. Ukka then set to work to rectify this. Ventekuu was his first creation, a snake five hundred paces long. After this, Ukka created the fish, then the midges and blood-sucking insects, the leeches and lampreys. Ventekuu saw all this boon of life and wondered, "Can I not create my own creatures, those that would serve me?" In thinking this she was deluded, for she had no power to create life and failed to understand that Cygannan and Ukka's creations were not their servants, but devices to bring balance to all things, to see that as one thing died, another was born, that for every hatched bird that survives another must die to feed a snake or an eagle or a pike. And so Ventekuu fled to the Lake of the Eye, the deepest lake in the marsh. Angry that she could not breathe life into air, she tore off her scales, cut herself on a rock to make her bleed, took the great spirits' creations the frog and the lizard, and used their life force to create the first Malaac.

'Cygannan and Ukka saw this and conspired to punish Ventekuu. Ukka told her that she could make many Malaac until her desire to create was sated but they could never leave the confines of the lake. And Cygannan put all his power forth and created man, the balance against the Malaac, to show Ventekuu the full potential of life, one that her own mean and evil attempts could never match. And so it came to be that we have the marsh and they have the lake, a balance that could only be broken by the anger of the spirits at their creations, or by powers outside the marsh – the men of the dry lands blundering and interfering in matters they do not understand.'

'Then it is true,' said Cerren. 'The gods have been angered by something and have sent the Malaac to punish us.'

'Either that or the Taneren or other outsiders have done something stupid.'

'Possibly,' said Cerren, 'but that may be out of our control. Maybe, though, we can do something to placate the Gods, to show that our errors, whatever they may be, were accidental and can be put right.'

'That is Dumnekavax's responsibility. He will tell us what to do when we see him.'

Then it was Cygan's turn to sleep. Despite the straitened circumstances he managed surprisingly to do so well, flitting into and out of dreams featuring eagles and owls hunting rats and mice. Then as he looked the talons of the raptors became black claws and the toes became webbed and slimy. Then the birds opened their beaks and started to howl, a most unbirdlike sound. It was a long-drawn-out noise, high-pitched and tremulous, disturbingly unnatural. It was a sound that froze his marrow and turned his blood to ice. Suddenly someone was shaking his shoulders. It was Fasneterax.

'Listen, the Malaac are gathering.'

Cygan realised that the noise was a real one and not a figment of his imagination – out on the river the Malaac were calling. He realised that the sun had almost gone down; the half-light would dapple the river, tricking the eye as it threw out chiaroscuro shapes and confusing perceptions of size and distance. In half an hour it would be dark.

The others had set a fire in the fireplace, which sent out a comforting deep red glow. There was no point in concealment at this time, as they were trying to tempt these creatures into a rash attack. Cygan picked up his bow. It felt good in his hand. He knocked an arrow ready to fire. Any time now, he thought to himself. They all strained their ears against the river and the wind. 'There!' he hissed.

Out to their left was a sound like that of an animal scrabbling over wood, but it was a heavy animal, no waterfowl or young goat. He could hear its feet now as it moved on to the damp earth. It was trying to be quiet but it was coming ever closer. Fasneterax drew his bow, and the muscles in his arms corded. The howling continued from out on the river. Suddenly the screened wall started to rattle and Cygan saw a black four-fingered hand force its way through the gap in the screen and side wall. Fasneterax's bow twanged. His arrow punched through the screen where he guessed the creature's body would be; Cygan's arrow followed a second later. There was a cold sharp hiss and the hand was withdrawn. Shortly after they heard a splash, the sound of a man-sized body falling into the water. The howling cut off immediately. Cygan's heart was pumping, his blood rushing in his ears.

Still they waited. Dusk turned into night. The glow of the fire flickered around the room casting eerie shadows against the walls and floor.

'Perhaps they have gone.' said Cerren.

As if in answer, there came more scrabbling, much louder this time.

'They are climbing the wall.' said Cygan.

The noise moved upwards. They raised their heads, realising that the creature was on the roof. They saw a shadow pass over the chimney hole.

    Fasneterax loosed his bow again but this time the arrow stuck in the roof missing its mark. A hand came through the hole and started to tear off lumps of thatch. Cerren threw a dart at it but it was too dark to see if he was successful. Then it was Cygan's turn. They heard the impact of his arrow against a solid body. There was an angry howl. More footsteps could be heard outside. The screen started to shake as several creatures started pulling at it. Tegavenek rammed his spear through the screen impacting into a muscular body. Cerren followed suit. Parts of the screen started to disintegrate as black-scaled clawed hands punched through it. The creature on the roof was still there tearing a larger hole into the ceiling; others of his kind joined him up there. Cygan and Fasneterax fired off arrow after arrow, then seeing the perilous situation they set down their bows and took up their spears. They exchanged a grim look. It would be a matter of seconds.

    A creature plunged down from the roof between the two of them. Two or three simultaneously burst through the screen. One got two hands on to Tegavenek's throat. He went down.

    'For the Black Lake!' screamed Cerren, ramming his spear into the creature attacking the Elder. Black ichor spurted from the wound, splashing his face. Cerren pulled out his knife and stabbed the creature again and again. It howled and thrashed in its death throes, but Cerren didn't stop even when another of the beasts dived on him, sinking its teeth into Cerren's shoulder.

    While this desperate fight was going on, Cygan was duelling with the creature from the roof. It was too dark to make out its features clearly; he could see its rows of pointed white teeth and the pale-green luminescence in its eyes; the rank smell of the bog filled his nostrils. It dodged his first spear thrust, and his second. It then ducked under his third and barrelled towards him, knocking him backwards against the wall. Cygan let go of his spear and pulled out his metal knife, a precious object bartered from the Tanaren. The creature was on top of him, its fetid breath in his face as it made to bite down hard on the exposed vein in his neck. In an act of near desperation Cygan twisted his body, freeing his right arm. Then he sank his knife into the creature's neck.

It didn't die easily. It thrashed around on top of him, its claws rending his arm as he protected his face. Cygan kept a grip on his knife, holding it firmly as his enemy's blood, sticky and black, oozed over his hand. Then it was still.

Kicking the dead thing off him, Cygan sprang up knife in hand, ready to deal out more death. The screen, he saw, was in shreds. Fasneterax was holding one of them at bay with his spear. Cerren was rolling on the floor with another of them, limbs flailing everywhere. Tegavenek's spear was impaling yet another of the monsters; he was leaning against the wall gripping it tightly, but Cygan could see his strength was failing. He swept up his spear and finished the skewered creature off.

Then the Malaac broke and ran. He saw four, five, maybe six, shadowy figures abandon their attack and run from the shack. He heard their heavy feet in the mud of the bank and the breaking sound of the water as they plunged back into their native habitat.

Cerren went to run after them.

'No!' said Fasneterax. 'We stay here.'

And that is what they did. They retook their positions in the shack, spears in their hands, waiting for the next attack. The moon sank behind the trees; they still waited in abject silence. The light started to break, the crows started to call, then thousands of other birds joined with them in a cacophony painful to the ears. The four men still stayed where they were, waiting for the noise of claws against wood or bare feet slapping against mud. But the Malaac did not attack again.

Eventually, in the wan light of the morning with a light drizzle gently fogging the river, they emerged. Cerren had a nasty bite on his shoulder and Tegavenek had claw marks scoring his chest and left arm. There were ingredients in the boat that could be made into a poultice for these wounds but it would take time. In the shack and on the earth just outside it lay the bodies of four Malaac. In the light of day Cygan could see they were dark green rather than black; their scales were actually quite lustrous and had an almost metallic sheen. They had a couple of small near-transparent fins on their back and one behind their head, as well as some feathery gills either side of their wide mouth. Apart from that they were exactly as others had described them.

Cygan pulled the healing herbs out of the boat, together with a wooden mortar and pestle. They would need a binding agent; he wondered if the mud here was suitable. Behind him, Cerren was kneeling over a fallen Malaac; he appeared to be doing something to its corpse. As the other three watched him, he turned around to face them, triumphantly holding the creature's head high in his right hand, its black blood dripping and pooling on to the floor.

'Behold,' he said, 'the head of the Malaac. I, Cerrenatukavenex, have taken its power for my own. Am I not worthy to be called a warrior?'

Fasneterax went over to him, putting his arm around the boy's shoulder.

'Your bravery is not in question, you have more than proven yourself, but I have a feeling you will get many more opportunities for this over the next few weeks.'

Tegavenek slumped down, leaning against the boat. Cygan saw him. He decided to bark some orders.

'First we patch the two of you up. Fasneterax, check the water; see if the Malaac are still out there. Unless the Elder wishes to return home, I want us at the Jagged Hill within the next three days.'

THE FORGOTTEN WAR
19

'Good afternoon, my Lady, allow me to welcome you to Thakholm.' Baron Skellar was courteousness itself as he gave her a low bow.

The location of his welcome was hardly auspicious, standing as they were on the great harbour wall, its implacable grey stone sweeping outwards into the bay, The harbour was sheltered on both sides by great promontories of rock that curved into the sea until they almost met each other, the gap between them being just large enough to admit one great ship at a time. The wind here, however, could still be treacherous, and it was like this now, whipping past their heads as it seemingly blew in all directions at once.

Ceriana had been advised by Ebba to leave her hair loose, saying that no power on earth or in the heavens could keep it in shape in these conditions, and now, as the Baron stood before her, great strands of it were flicking into her face, making it difficult even to see him.

'Thank you, Baron.' She raised her voice so he could hear her. 'The harbour is impressive indeed.'

'Yes, it is. There has been an army working on it all year, mostly from the mainland. Now they have gone, the island feels deserted. Did you have a pleasant journey?'

'I must admit I am not overfond of sea travel, but, yes, the journey was passable enough.' In fact, as travelling by ship goes, it was almost luxurious. It was one of her husband's ships and her cabin was quite large, with a long velvet seat that doubled as a bed, a window to watch the ocean go by, and even her own privy. There was room for Ebba, too; she slept on cushions on the floor.

'What do you think of the warships? I suppose you have seen them many times before.'

'Not that many.'

They had moored quite close to them, two of the Grand Duke's great war galleons, their blue-and-white gold-edged pennants flapping noisily from their high forecastles. A contingent of marines was drilling on the quarterdeck of the nearest ship and sailors could be seen on both of them, scrubbing decks and coiling ropes. A piece of Tanaren City a long way from home.

'We have been invited to officially inspect them tomorrow; a Baron Richney has travelled with them as the Grand Duke's representative. He is currently enjoying the hospitality of the manor house, as, my Lady, should you be. Come, your carriage will take you.'

He took the hand she presented to him and led her towards land. There were a couple of gaudily painted wagons waiting for them. The wind subsided once they climbed off the harbour wall and Baron Skellar spoke to her again in a confidential tone.

'I do not know if you saw his carrack in the harbour but we have another guest, too, and not one I had expressly invited. Do you remember at the council them discussing Baron Vorfgan of Clutha? Well, he is here; getting to know his neighbours, so he says. I am sure it is no coincidence that he arrived the day after the warships.'

'Do you not mean the Baron Protector? He was administering those lands while the former Baron's son recovered from illness, I believe.'

'I am sure he will tell you himself, but young Dekkan, alas, did not recover. Xhenafa claimed him over a week ago. Vorfgan is now officially the baron of that land.'

'I see. I wonder if he knew I was coming.'

'Undoubtedly, it was discussed openly at the council. In any event, all barons have their spies in other camps, so I am sure the news reached him pretty quickly, by whatever means.'

With his assistance, she and Ebba climbed into the carriage. Baron Jon took the one behind. Thakholm was a busy little harbour town, all cobbles and small brightly painted stone fisherman's cottages. The road they took wound through the centre of the town along a road that broadened into a wide square with its houses of Artorus, Hytha and Meriel all standing side by side.

'At least it's not market day,' said Ebba, 'or we would never get through.'

Once clear of the square, the cobbled road narrowed and started to climb uphill. Ceriana's impression of the northern towns being somewhat grim and colourless was put to the test here. She could now look over the bay and saw it filled with ships and boats, most of them small cogs or other fishing vessels and most spectacularly painted in reds, blues, yellows and greens. In keeping with an old seamen's tradition, the eye of Hytha was painted on many of them. Many of them, however modest their size, bore bright flags and pennants. She remembered from her book that Thakholm was called the 'Rainbow Isle'. Fishing was at its heart because the land here was poor, most suited for sheep, goats and smaller, wilder strains of cattle. As they cleared the town and continued to climb, she looked back and could see the island was fairly treeless and dotted with smallholdings all the way up to the outskirts of the town. The land was also fairly uneven and hilly – hills that seemed to increase in height as they got to the island's heart. They crossed, via a low stone bridge, a small silver river, one of several watercourses that discharged into the harbour; she followed its path as it danced playfully over greasy rocks before skirting the nearest houses of the town and entering the sea through a culvert in the harbour wall.

Ahead, the road ceased to be cobbled, changing into a dirt track. It wound upwards still and turned towards the sea. She realised then that they were going towards the northern promontory, one of the two great arms that swung into the sea protecting the harbour. Craning her neck, she saw that atop this finger of rock was the mansion house. Its outer wall was a low one, following as it did the great cliff edges that bounded the house. Through necessity, the house itself was long and narrow, built of stone and roofed in slate, which she believed was quarried here somewhere. It was single-storied, though as it followed the contours of the rising ground, the rear of the house was somewhat higher than its front. She imagined what it was like living there in a fierce winter storm. They passed some cottages before accessing the mansion, dwellings of the staff, she imagined, also noticing that they were far less colourful than the houses in the main town. The iron gates were opened and two guards clad in green and blue saluted as the carriages halted before the building's main door. It was a large door of dark wood hinged in black metal, flanked either side by a rectangular window – reminding Ceriana somewhat of the face of one of those lugubrious hunting hounds some nobles kept that always seemed to live under a pallor of sadness.

Baron Skellar led them through the doors into a narrow reception room and great hall. Passing the kitchens and storerooms, they climbed a flight of stairs and headed towards the guest rooms. Eventually they came to a door which, Ceriana assumed, could not be far from the very rear of the mansion house.

'For you, my Lady, the master guest bedroom.'

She was right – this was the last room of the house. In each of its three walls was a large picture window: through the left window she could see the harbour; through the right, the rugged green headlands of the island; while straight ahead was the sea, and nothing but the sea, grey and violent and shrouded in cloud.

'I thought you might like it here, as you come from a castle on the coast. On a good day you can see Osperitsan, though this is not one of them unfortunately. The windows have curtains, lest the light keep you awake.'

'Thank you, Baron, the room is lovely; you have been very considerate.'

'I am glad you like it; we take an early dinner here, probably in two to three hours. A servant will notify you nearer the time. I am sure the other barons will be eager to meet you. A servant is on her way to show your handmaiden her quarters. Until dinner then. I shall take my leave.' He bowed and closed the door.

Aside from the windows the room was comfortably furnished – she was especially pleased to see a full-length mirror in the corner. With horror, she regarded the straggling bird's nest that once was her hair and she also detected a pink tinge to the skin on her face, a legacy of the strong winds that blew so frequently up here. Among nobility even a hint of ruddiness to the skin, with its implication that its possessor worked outdoors in a manual occupation, could not be borne. It also seemed to make her freckles even more prominent. I look like a farmer's wife, she moaned to herself.

Within the hour she was transformed. Ebba returned to her and combed her hair thoroughly until it was silky soft and looked like liquid honey. She washed and freshened up before donning the rich red velvet dress she had brought specifically to make an impression. It had long wide sleeves and was embroidered in gold thread. In her hair Ebba placed an emerald-studded comb and she also wore a simple emerald necklace her father had given to her. She idly noticed her hair had grown and now reached down to the small of her back, so she decided to leave it loose. She perfumed herself with rosewater and applied some make-up to her face, dusting her lids and around her eyes, hopefully making them look bigger. Thus prepared and backed by Ebba's assertion that she looked 'every inch the Grand Duchess', she strolled to the main hall for her dinner.

She was the last to arrive (something she had counted on). The tables were laid, one, it seemed, for the lesser members of the household and one for the barons. Baron Skellar noticed her and beckoned her over.

It was only the three barons at the table. Richney she knew – one of the Grand Duke's closest confidants, a young man with extensively waxed moustaches, he always dressed ostentatiously, even by Ceriana's standards. Today was no exception – he wore a rich golden, extensively embroidered surcoat over a black shirt and leather trousers. He wore a rapier at his side; she knew this was only for show, as he had probably never used such a weapon in his life. Ceriana had heard the derogatory phrase 'perfumed warriors' applied to such men; those born to a nobility they had never earned and who eschewed the responsibilities inherent in such an office, preferring to pay others to do the work in their stead. Her brother had followed the family tradition, joining the Grand Duke's knights and so earning the respect of the people he would one day rule over. Richney obviously felt respect was his by right.

She had already drawn up a mental picture of Vorfgan – tall, bearded and grim, like so many of the men up here. The last thing she expected was the smiling, blue-eyed flaxen-haired man standing before her. He was cleanshaven and relatively simply dressed in a pale-blue shirt and brown leather breeches. He was also quite tall; she was taller than the average woman herself but was aware that she was having to tilt her head quite pronouncedly to get a good look at him. Baron Skellar introduced them both.

'Hello, my dear,' said Richney. 'I see the healthy northern air is working wonders on you. Your father sends his fondest regards.'

'Thank you, Baron. Any news you have of my father would be greatly appreciated. We do correspond but letters can take a long time to travel between us, as you can imagine.'

'He has actually given me a letter to deliver to you. I was going to find a ship going to Osperitsan and deliver it that way, but I see that that will no longer be necessary. I am actually returning to Tanaren City on a fast caravel the day after tomorrow, so if you wish to pen a reply I will happily give it to him.'

'Thank you. I do not know if I have the time to pen a reply, but if I do manage it, I would be happy for you to take it to him.' She didn't entirely trust Richney, he had been one of her suitors and, in line with her discussion with the Grand Duke, might still have designs on her. She could see him quite happily reading any letter trusted to him.

'And this,' said Baron Skellar 'is Vorfgan, Baron of Clutha.'

'May I say what an honour it is for me to meet a daughter of Duke Hartfield.' The man was courtesy personified. 'Although, if I may be so bold, it was never explained to me what a great beauty she actually is.'

'Jewellery and expensive clothing can make anybody look impressive but I thank you for your compliment.'

'You may not believe me but when I made that statement I hadn't even noticed that you were wearing jewellery.'

She laughed. 'I am not sure I believe you but, as it is our first meeting, I will give you the benefit of the doubt.'

They all sat down. The food was meaty and rich, with gravy and bread for dipping into it. There was ale and wine, which she avoided, and almond milk, which she drank thirstily. Richney explained that it was his first trip to the north and that the Grand Duke was keen to foster both closer and friendlier relations between them and the capital. He felt that it was his purpose to bring the various disparate elements of the country closer together, especially as it was his desire to resolve the conflict in the east as soon as was practicable.

'Fine words indeed,' said Vorfgan. 'Unfortunately, the problems we have here can be a little more complex. Loyalties can shift easily; some barons are unfailingly loyal to the Duchy, others less so. There are even some who advocate total separation and the establishment of New Kibil, what with the North's differences in culture and religion.'

'Bear in mind,' said Richney, 'that the Grand Duke has not held his position that long. He is determined to get to grips with the problems here. Tanaren is Tanaren, not Kibil, not Arshuma, not a Chiran client state. He will be inviting several of your barons to the Tanaren Spring Council next year, so grievances can be aired and problems hopefully resolved.'

She was sure she noticed a strange gleam in Vorfgan's sky-blue eyes at Richney's remark. What is he thinking? she wondered.

'I am sure most of the barons here will welcome such a gesture,' said Baron Skellar. 'I can see where the next problem arises as every baron up here will want to come down. May I suggest he looks at the constituents of the Northern Council and hand-picks individuals from the various regions to speak before him? That does not include me by the way; I am not a great traveller. Osperitsan is the limit of my horizons, I fear.'

'And what of you, Baron Vorfgan, would you like to speak before the Grand Duke?' said Richney earnestly.

'I am barely established as a baron following the sad death of young Dekkan, and my lands are not extensive enough to establish me as one of the major nobles up here. My neighbour Baron Tragsmann would be a more fitting candidate. He is far more experienced in circles of diplomacy than I.' 'So be it,' said Richney. 'I shall convey all of this to the Grand Duke.'

'The Tanaren Spring Council is held after the northern one I believe.' Ceriana felt the need to speak. 'In which case I am assuming the barons summoned to Tanaren will return there with my father.'

'I had not considered that,' said Richney. 'But it makes perfect sense now you mention it. Would you be travelling, too? If your husband is called south, it would make perfect sense for you to come as well.'

'That,' she said, 'would be a decision for my husband.'

They continued to eat. A band of musicians had started playing in the gallery above them. She was unfamiliar with the tune and asked Baron Skellar about it.

'It is an old Kibil song, the "Lay of Gudrun and Ahnvehr" and the story of their doomed love for each other. I can tell you the full tale later if you want, though. I am sure you can guess it didn't end well for them.'

'How very sad,' she said. 'Is there any nation that does not have songs telling tales of doom and misery?'

'There are happy songs, too,' said Skellar. 'I think you will find that for a nation to consider itself a mature one its cultural breadth must be broad indeed; both happiness and despair must be chronicled in song and verse, for there are always times when a man seeks recourse in one to the exclusion of the other.'

'And a woman,' said Vorfgan, flashing Ceriana a dazzling smile with a full mouth of pearly white teeth. She acknowledged him, their eyes meeting for a brief but lingering moment.

'Is it true,' she said, 'that every man in my present company is single?'

Skellar laughed. 'I believe so! My advisors want to pair me off with a fat widow from the mainland. So far I have resisted their machinations. How about you, Vorfgan?'

'When it happens, it will have to suit me politically ,' he said. 'If only Syvuhka would allow us multiple wives.'

'Some of the nobility in Koze in the south do just that, I believe,' said Richney with a smile. 'I, too, am waiting for the most advantageous moment to wed. The Grand Duke has someone in mind for me, I believe, but now is not the right time.'

Ceriana wondered whom exactly he meant, but after admonishing herself for her paranoia she decided to change the subject.

'We are inspecting the ships tomorrow, Baron Skellar? What does such a task entail?'

'It is merely ceremonial,' he said. 'The captain has had his men scrubbing desks and painting wood all day. He will lead us around; all we have to do is observe.'

'Will you be asking him to patrol the coast, to see where these pirates are based?'

'That I will, my Lady.'

'I thought our troubles with pirates were at an end?' said Richney, his eyebrows raised.

'It is never the case with pirates,' sighed Skellar. 'They are always here, maybe in fewer numbers, but they are never completely eradicated. What exactly are the three of you planning to do after tomorrow?'

'Alas, I have to return to Tanaren,' said Richney. 'There is a fast caravel waiting in the harbour.'

'And I have to continue my tour,' said Vorfgan. 'Baron Rosk is waiting for me.'

'I thought you were here for at least another three days?'

'Alas, there has been confusion with my schedule. I was going to tell you earlier but the opportunity did not present itself.'

'Then, may Hytha speed both your journeys,' said Skellar. 'Lady Ceriana, what do you wish to do?'

'I was hoping to see more of your island?' she said hopefully.

'Of course,' he said with a laugh. 'But I doubt it will take that long. Apart from Thakholm itself, there are a few other fishing villages and Gvernur in the high hills where they quarry the slate.'

'Any beaches?'

'Some small ones, but you would need to be on horseback to get to them, not in a carriage.'

'Excellent,' she said. 'We will do a riding tour, and you can show me your beautiful island. Can we do it in a day?'

'Most definitely, my Lady. The matter is settled.'

She slept well that night; she put it down to the great draughts of sea air she had been breathing over the last few days. The next morning she was up bright and early (for her), dressed herself in a plain white dress with paleblue kirtle and decided to walk the grounds of the manor. Stepping through the front door she noticed how the wind had dropped; it looked like it would be a milder day all round. The next thing she noticed was what appeared to be two men fighting in the main courtyard ahead of her; she heard the clash of wood and a shout of triumph and decided to investigate.

Barons Skellar and Vorfgan were duelling each other with quarterstaffs. They were both stripped to the waist and sweating profusely. Both men's torsos bore ugly red weals where their opponent had already found a mark. She noticed how lean they both were, with not an ounce of fat between them, how the muscles corded in their forearms and shoulders, how tight their pectorals were as they circled each other looking for the next strike. A small circle of servants and guards were watching them, a circle she quietly joined.

Suddenly Baron Skellar noticed her. Raising his arm to his opponent, he lowered his staff and walked over to her, Vorfgan following.

'I was not expecting such auspicious company for our little morning exercise,' he said. 'Tell me, my Lady, which of the two of us impresses you more?'

'I joined the crowd barely a minute ago,' she replied. 'Certainly there has not been enough time to see who has the advantage. I was actually going to do a circuit of the manor house, so I shall proceed with that and wish you both the very best with your endeavours.'

'You would disappoint us terribly if you did not stay but a little while longer,' said Vorfgan with a smile. 'Come, Jon, let us start our duel from scratch and let the Lady Ceriana judge the winner.'

'I am sorry, gentlemen, but I have no knowledge of this type of combat. I have been to tourneys before and seen men duel with lance, sword and mace, but I really do not feel able to judge the winner between the two of you.'

Vorfgan, however, was not giving up easily. 'Worry not, this is not a serious competition; we will treat it all in the light-hearted manner in which it is intended, so it barely matters as to whom you call in favour of.'

'Very well,' she said warily. 'Just as long as you see it as a trifling thing then I will play along.'

'Excellent,' said Vorfgan emphatically. 'What say you, Jon, a duel of no import with ten crowns from the loser to the winner.'

She was about to raise an objection but the two men were already crouched, circling each other. Vorfgan licked his lips, a hungry smile on his face, and lowered his guard. Skellar aimed a blow at his head which he dodged easily. Vorfgan assayed a counterstroke, which Skellar parried. The game of punch and counter punch continued for some time. Ceriana grew bored; she had no idea who was the better of the two and had even tired of admiring the impressive physiques of both men. She didn't even know if it was appropriate for a married woman to be watching such a display. She was about to try and stop both of them and declare a draw when Skellar caught Vorfgan's leg with a lightning blow, tripping him and sending him flying. The ever growing crowd cheered and booed in equal measure; evidently most of Vorfgan's entourage were here.

He got up, spitting out dust. 'Good blow!' he said to the other.

The fight continued. She noticed, though, Vorfgan's mask of absolute concentration and sensed his determination not to be caught again. Skellar attempted a similar trick but this time his opponent leapt over the blow, landing firmly back on his feet. He was smiling. 'You are quite the master, Jon,' he said. 'but you haven't stopped me yet.' Skellar made another attempt at him, missing by quite a margin, but in doing so he left his guard open. Quick as lightning, Vorfgan countered, the edge of his staff catching Skellar square on the temple. There was a loud 'thwack' and the hapless man was flat on his back, his staff rolling free, to land at Vorfgan's feet. He groaned as his servants rushed to attend him.

Vorfgan walked up to him. 'Are you all right, Jon?' He received a feeble croak as a reply.

'Good, I will see you later for my ten crowns.' With that he handed his staff to a retainer and strolled confidently back to the manor, followed a minute later by four servants bearing the limp form of the house's owner.

When Baron Skellar was struck Ceriana let out an involuntary squeak and put her hand to her mouth. Although she was relieved she would not have to decide between the two men, it was such a fierce blow she was genuinely concerned for his welfare. Once he had been back in his room for ten minutes or so, she decided to pay him a visit. He was sitting in a high-backed chair with two female servants either side of him; one was applying a damp cloth to a nasty swollen red welt on his forehead. He looked groggy.

'Are you all right, Jon? That was quite the blow you received.'

He stared at her, his eyes glassy. 'It will heal; the blow to my pride, however, is probably terminal. And the one to my purse, for that matter. Still, it will teach me to go to ridiculous lengths to impress a lady.'

'And which lady was that, may I ask?'

'You of course; alas, I now look quite the fool whereas the Baron of Clutha has all the glory.'

'I am a married woman, you know,' she said, smiling. 'Men are so prideful and foolish to think a lady would be so impressed by the winner of a stick fight. As much as it is worth, I regard you as a friend and a good man. Now relax and let these ladies look after you. We can inspect the ships without you easily enough.'

'Artorus's teeth, you will do no such thing. I will be there even if I have one foot in Keth's furnace.'

'Very well, I will leave you now to recover.'

'As you wish, my Lady. And thank you, I will take your friendship any day of the week.'

She left him to his misery but made little progress down the hall before bumping into the victor of the duel.

'My Lady, how is the invalid? I was just paying him a call myself, and not just to collect my winnings, I assure you.'

'His pride is as bruised as his head. But he will be well enough to join us at the harbour.'

'Good.' Vorfgan's smile was dazzling. 'My blow was a lot firmer than I meant it to be. I hope you do not think me a vicious brute.'

'Ha!' she laughed. 'Two men duel each other and both come out of it feeling sorry for themselves. Fear not, you both went into it with eyes wide open and I think none the worse of either of you. My opinions of you both remain unchanged.'

He looked at her intently, eyes holding her transfixed.

'As I am completely unaware of your opinion of me prior to our little engagement, I am unsure as to whether you have just paid me a compliment or not.'

She felt unable to look away from him. Something burned in his eyes, something she just couldn't fathom.

'Believe me, sir,' she said quietly, 'it was definitely a compliment.'

He bowed slightly, walking past her and into Skellar's room. She went to her own, aware of a strange tingling in her cheeks and hands.

As official inspections went, this one was pretty seamless. Ceriana and the Barons (Baron Skellar sporting a bandage round his head) were led by the captain first around the Pride of Hytha and then on to the Indomitable. She had never been on such large warships before and found herself rather enjoying the experience. They were led below decks to look at the captain's and surgeon's quarters, passing through the hammock-filled deck where the crew and marines slept. She was then led to the aft castle where one of the ship's catapults was based and shown its workings, together with the hollow clay pots that were filled with incendiary substances before being fired at the enemy. Then she was shown one of the ship's many ballistae, used to thin enemy numbers before boarding. It was explained to her that these ships could work with oar-powered galleys that could be equipped with rams. They could hole an enemy ship while the galleon kept the decks busy fending off missiles and putting out fires. If boarding was required, the galleon could work with the smaller, high-castled carracks to bring numbers to bear and overwhelm the enemy.

'We must have the most formidable navy in the world,' she told the captain. 'More formidable than those of the land powers of Chira and Koze.'

'Indeed, my Lady. It is one of the reasons for our security and independence. But as to the most powerful, well, I would say that the Sea Elves could outmatch us. Marvels their ships are, faster and more manoeuvrable. They sport vessels with two, even three, hulls and many tall sails. They do not hit as hard as we do, but they can move close, rake you with ballista fire and be away before you can even respond. Their larger ships have rams that can split a hull in two. It is as well they are our trading partners and not our enemies.'

The visit over, Ceriana returned to her carriage. On the way back to the manor house she fell deep into thought. Richney had given her the letter from her father. He had expressed his affection for her and how she was missed at Edgecliff. He mentioned Dominic fighting on the front lines in the east, and recalled his own days in the Silver Lances before the outbreak of the war. He mentioned her sisters: both were well; Giselle was pregnant again with her third child. Lastly, however, he mentioned this...

'I have been informed by the Master of St Philig's that you have contacted them regarding the mystery of the man washed up on the beach that day. I do not know why the matter interests you so, but the university are sending someone to Osperitsan to discuss the matter with you. It is not the scholar you requested (he is actually away on a matter of business for the Grand Duke), but he is still a learned gentleman with some knowledge of the subject in hand. His name is Professor Ulian and he should be with you fairly shortly.

She felt she should be pleased at this news but rather found herself viewing the professor's arrival with trepidation, rather like the man not wanting to see the doctor in case he was told there was something wrong with him. It rather spoiled the rest of the day for her; she was full of false smiles and fake bonhomie at dinner, and took to her room as early as was expedient. She opened her jewellery box to look at the stone (she had not dared to leave it behind), but it was dead and lifeless. Or was it? Just for a second she saw it glow softly in her hand, a brief pulse of light and her mind caught a glimpse of the great head and glittering yellow eye of the beast of her dreams. Suddenly a thought occurred to her. She went and stood in front of the full length mirror – her hair was loose and windblown, her nose sharp and slightly reddened by the wind and sun, her brown eyes large and curious. She regarded the stone again. Immediately it started to pulsate, though only slightly, highlighting the veins in her hand as she grasped the thing tightly. There it was again. She could see the creature; it had been slumbering but obviously something had awoken it. Was it the stone? Was it her? The creature raised its head and put out its long forked tongue; it was seeing something, trying to sense it, smell or hear it. She knew exactly what had brought it to wakefulness.

It was seeing her.

She held the stone close to the mirror – the creature's eyes widened, curious. She then realised that as well as seeing it, experiencing its experiences, there was something else. She was beginning to sense its thoughts. At the same time it was obviously sensing hers.

With an effort of will she slammed the stone back into the box and locked it. She no longer had any concern about meeting this professor – let him come and tell her what madness was happening around her.

A couple of days later she was on horseback. Vorfgan and Richney had departed on their respective ships, so it was just her, Jon Skellar and a half-dozen armed men on the road out of the manor, heading north eastwards along the coast. It was a bright, dry day, the wind was in her face and an excited flush was turning her freckled cheeks pink. She would never be allowed to do this back in Edgecliff.

'So, Baron Jon, what are we going to see today?'

'There are a few fishing villages and small coves and beaches on the road out,' he said. 'On the way back it is, well, exactly the same, unless you want to visit the slate quarries, but there really isn't a lot to see there. Thakholm is just about the harbour really; if it wasn't for that, I would not be sitting on the Northern Council.'

'It is a very pretty harbour, though. I watch it from my room. So many different types of ship, painted so boldly, too.'

The Baron was sporting a livid-purple bruise on his temple but after an initial enquiry as to his health she decided not to mention it. He had been quite subdued since losing his duel and she didn't want to hurt his pride any further. Her horse was a beautifully docile grey mare, a couple of hands shorter than Skellar's stallion but perfect for her. She even wondered about asking to purchase it from him but decided that she didn't want to subject the beast to a sea voyage back to Osperitsan.

The road was uneven, a broad dry mud track that became cobbled only when they passed through one of the many villages that dotted the coast. Whenever they passed through a village a small crowd would gather, mainly ruddy-faced women trying to control an unruly gaggle of small urchins who would run hither and thither, their faces encrusted with dirt and dribble. They would wave at the crowd, who would wave back enthusiastically. She put the absence of men down to the fact they were probably at sea.

The road wound in and out from the coast, passing occasionally through knots of trees already stripped of leaves, their bark grey and wind-blasted and their twisted naked forms showing starkly against the bleached-white sky. She felt a little saddle-sore but would never let on, seeing as it was she who had asked for this trip in the first place. She was glad, therefore, when they stopped for a bite to eat in one of these stands of trees. She asked the Baron for an idea of the time.

'It is early afternoon, my Lady. Please don't feel pressured to do a complete circuit of the isle; we can turn back whenever you like.'

'No, I am fine to continue for now. May we review the situation in an hour or so? I am enjoying myself; your island is very pretty and rather reminds me of home in a small way.'

'I am glad to hear it. I must admit my head still aches a little, so I will be perfectly happy with whatever you decide.'

'Then you stay and rest, Jon. I will ride on alone for a while and when I return we can go back.'

He looked alarmed. 'Don't you want a guard to go with you?'

'I will not ride on far and will be back before you notice it. I will turn back if I come to a village, so have no fear that any of your people will rob me.'

'Very well, my Lady, but return promptly.'

She nodded to him, gently spurred her horse and was away.

Ah, the freedom of being on one's own, she thought, as she trotted back towards the coastline. Had it ever happened before? Of course, it had – it had been when she had found that accursed stone. But she dismissed that from her mind. The coastline here started to dip a little towards the sea; indeed, if she got off her horse she could walk down to the seashore with little difficulty. She passed one tiny beach, strewn with sharp rocks, and another; the salt tang of the sea was filling her nostrils. The road then turned inland through a small copse before curving back towards the sea where it seemed to dip a little further still; it would surely be at sea level soon.

'I will just ride past that bend to see where it leads, then I must return,' she said to herself.

The grass was tall and thick either side of her, the stems sharply pointed and glossy. Down the path she went, around the bend in the road, then she pulled up short.

Ahead the path continued to dip, leading towards a broader, more secluded beach with much fewer sharp rocks, and there in the bay barely forty feet from the shore was a small ship. It was a single-masted vessel carrying no sail at the moment, but apart from that she had never seen a design like it. It had a broad high prow with a giant figurehead carved to resemble that of a great lizard. No, not a lizard, a dragon! At the vessel's stern above the rudder the creature's tail had been carved, so that head and tail put together almost equalled the full length of the ship's midsection. There were small wings, too, carved into the side of the hull above the rowlocks. What sort of ship was this? She had heard that elves sometimes incorporated dragon carvings on to their vessels, but judging from what the ship captain had told her the other day this was no elf ship. Then she saw the figures. There was a small landing craft pulled on to the beach and, standing close to it, were three men. She was too far away to make out what they were doing but that didn't matter to her. What she could see was that they were men and that they were wearing cloaks which flapped around them in the stiff breeze. Black cloaks. And, yes, the men were all shaven-headed. There was a lump in her throat as she pondered her next move. She didn't notice the figure in the grass walking purposefully towards her until he was on the path not ten feet away. There he stopped, letting her focus on him. His eyes were dark as coals and his skin pale and waxy. He was hairless and swathed in black also. His polished boots glistened with the moisture from the grass. He beheld her as she stared at him dumbly; then he spoke, in an accent she had never before heard, thick and guttural.

'We have been looking for you. It is time for the thief to return what she has stolen from us.'

She turned her horse quickly and spurred it, not so gently this time, galloping away from the man as fast as it could possibly take her. Behind her the man regarded her for a minute, his face as impassive as granite. Then he turned on his heels and strode back towards the beach.

20

'Where shall I put these jars?'

'On the third shelf, next to the citrus leaves.'

Cheris was helping Anaya. They had moved to the forward camp earlier that day and she was arranging the medical supplies in the hospital tent. There were a lot more nurses here as well as some men clad in dark leather. She asked Anaya what their purpose was.

'Oh, they are the surgeons. They pull pieces of metal out of people and perform amputations. The big man holds them down and one of the others uses the saw. They have to cut the flesh around the limb in a circular manner exposing the bone. Then they saw through that. I help to staunch the blood flow and try and control the pain. We use tincture of thadmion, a herb from the Endless Marshes that can knock out a bear. The main problem, though, is shock; that alone can kill a man I am afraid.'

'Will there be many amputations after the battle'?

'That,' said Anaya succinctly, 'depends on how the battle goes.'

'What happens to the men once they have recovered; I take it they can no longer fight.'

'No,' she said with a dry laugh. 'If there is a job they can do in the army, then they do that. You may have seen a few of our former patients around the camp. If there is no job, then they are paid whatever wage the army can afford and cut loose. What happens to them after that I do not know, I'm afraid.'

She stood back to look at the shelf she had just stacked. 'Sorry Cheris, every time we talk I do nothing but lower your spirits.'

'No, you're not like that at all. I find what you have to say very informative. There are books in the college library that I read as a child regarding our wars. They were full of tall knights with silver-tipped lances and giant chargers swatting aside the cowardly enemy and covering themselves in glory. No amputations or even blood for that matter.'

Anaya looked straight at her. 'You fight tomorrow; you will see plenty of it for yourself.'

Cheris did not answer, rather busying herself with emptying

another trunkful of exotically coloured jars.

'I will pray for you tonight,' said Anaya. 'My time here has sorely tested my faith, but I will ask Elissa and Meriel to watch over you. I hope they will listen.'

'I hope so, too,' Cheris said, trying to laugh lightly. 'But thank you, I will take any divine help I can get. Hopefully we can talk in two days' time after a victory.'

'I have seen many victories and defeats here. No matter what the outcome I will be happy to see you come back in one piece.'

Once Anaya was satisfied with the way the hospital tent was being organised, Cheris made her excuses and walked out into the fresh air. With battle imminent, the noise and excitement of earlier in the week had subsided. People were grimmer now, more focused, as the day of destiny loomed before them. She had been given a large black hooded cape, to cover the red robe on the battlefield where it would make her an obvious target, and she wore it now as she was feeling the chill.

There was a large gathering of people at the centre of the camp where there were no tents, used as it was as a parade ground. It had a high wooden platform at its centre on which a couple of figures were standing, preparing to address the crowd. One was a dark-robed priest of Artorus; the other in her full-length white-and-red robes was a priestess of Meriel. She then saw other priestesses walking among the throng, swinging censers full of smoky incense. The incense, it was believed, helped confer Meriel's protection against injuries. The priest spoke first.

'Warriors of Tanaren, you stand here before me ready to prove your worth in the eyes of the Gods and to defend your country from the ravages of the enemy. Know you this, Artorus stands with you in this fight; he sees that the cause is just. Did he not say unto us in his divine proclamations "Unto the men of Tanaren, in perpetuity, I giveth the lands of the rivers of the Derannen to sow and reap in the name of my sister Sarasta. It is theirs to protect and nurture as long as they remain true to my word and my teachings." And so it is, my brothers – march into battle with those words ringing in your ears and know that, even if Xhenafa should call you to him in the fight, you will stand at Artorus's side as one of those privileged few who have sacrificed all to make his word good. The blessings of Artorus and his consort Camille upon you.' He then started to recite the Prayer of Artorus with his audience joining him.

As she finished reciting the prayer, Cheris noticed Marcus at the back of the crowd, a little way from her. She sidled along towards him, just as the priestess of Meriel was beginning her address. She idly wondered if the line in the prayer about showing mercy to the undeserving was appropriate but concluded that the prayer should be taken as a whole; it was more about making oneself a better person in the sight of the Gods than anything else. She had put her questions of belief to one side for the time being. As the large crowd showed, when one's own life is in jeopardy, belief becomes a sturdy prop indeed.

'Divine Meriel,' said the priestess, 'protect the lives of your humble servants who march into battle in the cause of justice. Give them strength for the fight ahead, ease their pain and heal their wounds. Remember the story of the soldier of justice who, after fighting for many good causes, succumbed to the rigours of time – his beard turning grey and his strength greatly diminished. He went and stood on the banks of the great river Balkhash, removed his armour and cried out in anguish to the Gods. "Where art Ye, O mighty Gods, for I have fought many battles in Your name, have won many great victories to further Your purpose and yet here I now stand, frail and helpless, unable to carry a sword. Why have I been forsaken and forgotten, left to die in the mud of the river." Hearing no answer, he jumped into its watery depths and waited for Keth to claim his soul. But it was then that Meriel came to him, lifting him above the waters and setting him down on the bank. "Oh warrior," she cried, "all of the Gods know of your victories. Why do you claim We have forgotten you?"

'"Because I am old and frail," he replied, "and can serve You no longer."

'"No," said Meriel, "You serve Us merely by being. Not just in battle is Our glory reflected. For every man, woman and child that obeys Our teachings and practises Our virtues our purpose is served. Now go home, and honour the span Artorus has given you."'

'And so my friends,' continued the priestess, 'if you honour the Gods, not just in battle, but in every aspect of your life, then Meriel will protect you from harm. Even if Keth the wicked casts a plague among us Meriel will be there.'

Cheris reached Marcus and nudged him in the ribs. He beckoned her away from the crowd and up an incline to the mages' tent. 'I have been told,' he said, 'that I will be leaving tonight.' 'Tonight?' she said, her eyes wide.

'Well under cover of darkness anyway; we have to get to the hill, which is heavily wooded and hide there until the gates are unlocked tomorrow.'

'Can't you just get to the hill tomorrow night when all our troops are deploying?'

'They have deemed it too risky and have changed the plan; we go in tonight and hide. Look!' He pointed. 'You can see the hill from here.'

She followed his finger to the flat-topped hill that she had seen many times that day without making the connection that it was the objective of their enterprise. It was less than ten miles away, she reckoned; the hill and the ground around it were steeply wooded and the surrounding fields were strewn with copses. 'So that is Grest,' she said absently. 'It doesn't look that important from here.'

'Oh but it is, the hill controls the river and the land around for many miles. The soldiers I am travelling with are grumbling because they will miss Mytha's ceremony tonight.'

'What is that exactly?'

'You will not see it. It is for warriors only; there will be several ceremonies at the various army tents. They pray to Mytha to make them great warriors; they are anointed with bear's blood and have to eat raw flesh, so I am told.'

'Charming!' she said. 'So I am keeping company with men who eat raw flesh and think nothing of violating the enemy's women. Such circles you have me moving in these days.'

'These are warriors, Cheris; war and the dangers it holds can terrify even the bravest. It provokes behaviour from men that they would normally find unthinkable.'

She nodded. 'May the Gods protect you tonight.'

'And may they protect us both tomorrow.'

They returned to her tent and Cheris went over the powers she would use tomorrow. 'You need not use many, but you must know their workings by heart,' Marcus had told her. She read and reread the incantations, even though she knew them all word for word, until she felt tired. She shut her eyes and had a little nap.

She felt a tap on her shoulder. After stirring grumpily, she saw it was Marcus leaning over her. 'It's not dark already?' she asked.

'It is, Cheris. I have to go now. The other men are ready.'

She swung her legs over and stood up. He was clad in black; she noticed he had even camouflaged his face with some paint or other. She kissed him lightly on the cheek. 'Lucan protect you, Marcus.'

He gave her a sad smile. 'Just make sure you are here when I return. I shall admit now that I am doubting whether I should have brought you. I fear my head ruled my heart in this case; I know you can shine out here but you are so young. I am more worried for you than I am me.'

'Head should always rule heart,' she said. 'I am proud that you have such faith in me. It is not the time for regrets or recriminations. We are all in the hands of the Gods now.'

'I do have faith in you. More than I have in myself, if truth be told. Remember, I don't know who the other mage is or where he comes from, but he is just a man not a god, and not more powerful than you. Believe in your abilities and you will prevail.'

'I will, Marcus. See you in two days.'

He hugged her, took one last look at her and was gone.

She went to the opening exit of the tent to see him strolling away from her with long purposeful strides. How many times over the years had she had to run to keep up with him! He disappeared behind another tent, maybe gone for ever. She was about to go back inside when a group of young men strolled past her; they were soldiers, obviously in high spirits, laughing and joking with each other. Despite the half-light, she could see that their hair and faces were covered in sticky blood. It was drying on their skin in the cool air. She looked at her feet and closed her eyes. Then, shaking her head slightly, she turned and went back into the tent feeling very small and alone.

On the morrow the wagon was out again, preparing to move her with the army. She had slept fitfully and had barely managed to eat her breakfast. Now she had butterflies doing somersaults in the pit of her stomach. Despite that, she asked Sir Norton if she could sit up front with him; maybe watching the army mobilise would distract her somewhat.

It was a fine bright morning and signs of activity were everywhere. Many of the tents had been taken down and loaded on to the army's baggage train, dozens of large six-wheeled wagons due to be pulled by sturdy, shaggy horses that were now placidly grazing the bruised grass, grabbing a quick meal before being put to work. The camp followers – cooks, civil servants and the medical teams – were to remain here, guarded by a nominal force; everyone else was on the move. Felmere's infantry were the first to mobilise, the largest block of men in the army. She could see they were seasoned men by the way they calmly went about their business. While the others were still sorting out their armour or cleaning their blades, they were hoisting the banner of the mace and the great banner of Tanaren and marching off singing one of the many battle songs of Mytha. She knew little about such songs, but all of them sounded the same, stirring and powerful when sung by dozens of young men with the light of battle in their eyes – the sort of songs that would unsettle all bar the most fanatical of enemies.

As they left, she caught sight of the Silver Lances, easily the most visually impressive contingent she had seen – clad as they were in full suits of silver armour, their helms sporting high crests of blue feathers, their great steeds clothed in blue-and-silver barding, and a great banner of two crossed lances on a blue-and-white background flapping above them. Enough to make a girl weak, she said to herself, not without irony. She could certainly imagine the impression they would make on the pampered ladies of the Grand Duke's court. The Serpent knights with their green crests and then those of the Eagle Claw rode with them, both a sight to behold, although they were maybe not quite as impressive as the Silver Lances.

The light cavalry, with their smaller, nimbler horses, leather armour and short bows and spears, were a much more mundane sight and did not ride as a single unit; rather, they spread out ahead and to the flanks of the main body of troops, screening them from surprise attack. After all these came smaller contingents of men. She could not remember them all: some wore red and white; others green and white. The men of Haslan Falls she remembered, as their banner gave their origin away. They were towards the rear of the column, their armour polished and looking like it had never been used in a fight – not until now anyway. Finally, she saw the contingents of archers, one of which, marching under yet another Felmere banner, carried crossbows, the heavy-hitters of the missile troops. Each section of the army had its own drummers and horn blowers, the horns blasting the signal to start marching and the drummers beating a steady, leaden tattoo to give everyone a rhythm to follow. She watched them all go; it took over an hour for everyone to leave.

'Impressed?' Sir Norton asked.

'It is a lot of people, indeed,' she replied. 'So many people. See how far into the distance they go.'

'Three hours and they will be at Grest. They have been told to arrive with as much fanfare as possible so as to distract the Arshumans' attention from the town itself. They will be ready and deployed shortly before the sun goes down. The enemy will have to rush to match them.'

A small contingent of men carrying a banner displaying a golden sun marched past them, looking around she realised that that was it, the whole army was on the move.

'And now,' said Sir Norton, 'it is our turn.'

He tugged the rains and chivvied the horses, jolting them into life; six other Knights of the Thorn rode ahead of them. Above, the pale sun climbed towards noon; her time had almost arrived.

Several blasts on the horns told the army to stop and rest. They had barely been going for two hours, following the wide Grest road, but as

Sir Norton pointed out strength had to be conserved for the battle tonight. Men everywhere were stopping, talking, and breaking open their water flasks or field rations. It was army policy for a soldier to always keep three days' field rations in his supplies in case he got separated from his unit for some reason. Above them was a fine autumn sky, a pale-cyan colour flecked with grey tinged clouds. The air was also quite humid and close, and Cheris pulled at her collar to let a draught of cooler air pass under her clothes. She asked Sir Norton if she could hop down and stretch her legs; he consented and a minute later she was walking over the tussocked grass drinking from her own flask.

A building some two hundred feet away had caught her eye. As she got near to it, she realised that she was approaching another ruined village standing slightly apart from the main road. The building she had noticed was obviously the old house of Artorus; it was the only building left that had not been razed to the ground. All that remained of the rest of the village were blackened outlines where once walls had stood. A few of the crossbowmen were here, sitting on the grass or lying on it; a couple were leaning against the wall. She sidled past them, excusing herself, and stood at the front entrance. The door had gone; only a blackened part of the frame remained, but some trailing ivy hung down over the gaping hole as if trying to replace what was missing. She brushed it aside and entered the building.

It was a small house of worship, typical of those found in villages; she guessed it could hold some thirty to forty people if they packed inside. The narrow windows had long gone, though some of the leaded frames remained, and above her parts of the ceiling were missing, allowing shafts of light to break through. A rural building such as this would only have had a packed earth floor and it was now covered in yellow grass and weeds. The small stone pulpit was cracked and lay on its side and the single remaining pew had mostly disintegrated. A bird sang forlornly from one of the roof beams. As she looked up at what remained of the ceiling, though, she noticed that fragments of its original artwork remained. She was looking at a painted sky of royal blue, together with a carpet of silver stars surrounding a pale full moon. Above where the pulpit used to be were crude but colourful paintings of the Trinity, Artorus, Camille, and Elissa, staring benevolently down at their long-vanished flock. There was some bold writing underneath them which said simply: 'Artorus defends and preserves. Camille teaches and protects. Elissa nurtures and loves.'

She stared up at it for a minute or more, lost in her thoughts, oblivious to the idle chatter of the men outside or the strengthening wind tugging at the ivy at the door, then she turned slowly, took one more gulp from her flask and left the building for ever.

For the rest of her journey she remained inside the wagon. She read, reread and read again the relevant pages in her tomes of magic until she could replicate them word for word in her head. After less than two hours the wagon stopped. It was still light. Shortly afterward Sir Norton knocked at the rear door.

'We have arrived, my Lady; the army is deploying for battle.'

'Thank you. How long have I got?'

'Oh at least an hour, I would say; where would you like to stand?'

'I haven't the faintest idea – what would you advise?'

'There is a low hill to the right of the deployment position; from the looks of things some of the light cavalry are lining up close to it. If we stand there, we should get a decent view of the field. That will be very important for a mage; you do need to see what's going on.'

'That sounds sensible enough; I will stand there then.'

'We will be with you – that's six of us and four who arrived earlier. We will stand around you in a circle to protect you from assassins and other targets. You understand mages are prime targets.'

'Yes,' she said airily, 'that seems to be the case. I will prepare myself for now. Can you call me when it is time?'

'Of course, my Lady.' He nodded to her and shut the door.

She lit the lantern and pulled back its hood, letting the light flood into the wagon. She went over to her trunk and fetched her staff, something she had almost forgotten about. Gripping it firmly, she felt its power comforting her greatly. Opening the trunk, she pulled out the staff's blade and attached it to its base. She tried some practice swings with it against an imaginary enemy but only succeeded in upsetting the lantern which swung crazily, throwing light and shade around the wagon's interior.

'Behave, you idiot!' she admonished herself.

That task done, she pulled out her mirror. Her hair had grown long. Taking up a small knife, she carefully cut the offending strands until her hair barely covered her neck. Contorting herself into various ungainly positions with the knife and mirror, she tidied her handiwork up until her bob looked respectable. Satisfied, she opened her small make-up box. She took some dark powder and blackened her eyebrows and lashes. She then dusted her lids and around her eyes with a deep-blue colour, then her cheeks ever so lightly with red. She then painted her lips, trying to make them look even richer and more sensual than they actually were. She flicked her tongue over them and picked up the mirror. Perfect.

Before she had even landed at Tanaren, Cheris Menthur had decided that, if she was going to die, then by Elissa she would look damned good doing it. Picking up her staff, she opened the door and found Sir Norton by the horses. The light was fading and the stiff breeze carried the scent of warm grass and earth.

'Actually, Sir Norton, I am ready now. Please show me where I am to stand.'

21

'Get the brushwood in the wagon and the lamp oil. Lay it here in front of us.' Morgan barked out the order; they had very little time. The loping shapes in the distance were getting bigger all the time. They would be upon them soon. One good thing, though – the creature hanging on the mountain side appeared to have come to a dead end. Its footholds or handholds had obviously disappeared and it now appeared to be looking around to see the best way to climb into the Saddle. Leon stood next to Morgan, one of his arrows readied. It was one of the special, double-pronged arrowheads used to fell large beasts.

'As soon as one gets within thirty paces it's going to run into this,' he hissed.

Varen came out, his arms full of brushwood. 'Where shall I put this?'

'Along here.' He indicated the ground in front of Leon. 'Come, I will give you a hand.' Hastily he tried digging a trench in the snow, with limited success. Varen dropped the brushwood into it. Rozgon, Willem and Haelward brought more and did the same. Samson, Morgan and Varen brought out the remainder.

'The lamp oil, quickly!' said Morgan.

Varen had it. He started to douse the wood. 'Shall I use it all?' he asked. 'We will probably have to. We don't want the snow putting the fire out.'

'Won't we need some tomorrow?'

'At this very moment in time, none of us is seeing tomorrow!'

Varen complied; Samson stood next to him with a torch. The monsters were getting ever closer and they could distinguish individuals now, their breath expelled in powerful white jets and their barking getting louder and louder. They ran on all fours, with great loping strides that ate up the ground. They would be on them in under a minute. The climbing monster had managed to scrabble down the mountain and joined his fellows in the rear.

'Willem!' Morgan called. 'There are some bandages in the wagon.

Tear some strips off them and wrap them round some arrows. He nodded at Samson, who pulled some shafts from his quiver and held them out for Willem to grasp. 'There is some brandy in the wagon; soak the bandages in that first.'

'Give me two minutes,' said Willem and scurried off.

The ettins were some thirty seconds away. Scenting human flesh, they started lifting their heads to the sky and braying ferociously. Morgan looked at Samson: 'Now!' he said.

Samson lowered the torch to the brushwood. To Morgan's relief, it caught immediately. A river of flame leapt from one side of the cleft in the rock to the other. He saw the ettins slow their pace somewhat, as if suddenly hit by doubt.

'Here's something else to think about,' said Leon. letting fly his arrow. It sped through the flame and slammed into one of the creatures, hitting it full in the chest. It stopped for a second, looking dumbly at the shaft protruding from it. Then it swept its claw against the arrow, snapping it but leaving the head still stuck in its body. It bared its teeth and let out a howl of pain and anger. The ettins were finally at the flame barrier and they stopped dead. Although it was in truth a flimsy barricade that could be dislodged with one bold sweep of a great claw, they did not seem to grasp this. Morgan assumed they had never seen fire before, as they had stopped behind it and just stared, apparently confused.

Willem came out with an adapted arrow; Samson took it and put it to the torch, which he then gave to Willem. The arrow started burning with a blue flame. Samson smiled and loosed the arrow, hitting a monster full in the face. This time the creature did not howl; it screamed. A cry of agonised terror left its throat. It turned tail and fled, scooping snow over its wounded face. It took no account of its direction, hitting one rock face, then lurching in the opposite direction only to hit the other. A couple of the remaining creatures were already starting to slowly back off when Leon fired again. Then Samson. Then Leon.

It was enough for the rest of them. Frightened by the flames, some wounded and burning, they all broke and fled howling this time in fear and desperation. The men cheered their triumph as the ettins grew smaller and smaller until the night finally swallowed them. Morgan kept watching them till he was certain they had disappeared, thinking all the time that it had seemed a little too easy. The flames were starting to go out already. He wondered if any of the wood could be salvaged. The wolves started to howl again, a sound he found strangely comforting.

'Hey,' said Willem, his cheeks red and a stupid smile on his face. 'It's stopped snowing.'

Morgan looked at the skies. A couple of stars were peeking out from behind the cloud; even a ghostly moon could be seen casting its chill glow on to Morgan's upturned face. He suddenly felt the cold again.

And the boy was right about the snow.

None of them slept that night. Although only two of them were supposed to be on watch, none of them could rest, the cold and their parlous situation was making them too tense and nervous. The brushwood fire didn't last long and they all feared the ettins would notice that and return. All of them kept a constant eye on the pathway, half expecting to see the loping white shapes appear in the distance, but to their relief nothing else happened all night.

Nothing except the cold, that is. After an hour or so waiting and watching, Morgan realised his hands and feet were numb. Hurriedly, he exhorted everyone to get moving and stamp their feet, warning them all in graphic terms about frozen digits and amputations. That got them moving soon enough. He went to check on Cedric. Despite being in the wagon and smothered with blankets, his fingers were stiff and white. He forced some brandy down him and dragged him outside. After that, he gathered some of the remaining brushwood and the tiny quantity of lamp oil that remained and started a fire. They managed to keep it going till morning, at which point Cedric pronounced himself a lot better before retiring to the wagon to sleep.

Morgan did not let the others rest. They were down to three horses now; one had bolted in fear during the night and he wanted to get out of this damned rock cleft as soon as possible. As soon as they had devoured a quick breakfast and salvaged the remaining wood they were on their way.

Progress was slow. The snow had frozen overnight and much of it had to be moved before the wagon could be moved. Nevertheless, they noticed that the lip of rock to their right was getting lower and lower and was now little more than a couple of feet high, low enough for them to see over it into the ever deepening gorge. They were all sweating hard. There was only one shovel between them, which Rozgon used while the rest just had their weapons or even their feet, kicking the snow out of the way in great sprays. Sometime after noon they finally left the Saddle behind them and they were standing again on a broad shelf of rock, with the sheer mountain side to their left and a steep drop to their right. Below them were snow-clad pine woods that sloped down into the gorge, where they could see a shallow meltwater lake like a thin silver mirror. Evidently it was a little warmer hundreds of feet below them.

'Two days and we should be as good as out of here,' said Morgan.

'Right now, I will be happy never to see snow again for the rest of my life.' said Rozgon, wielding his shovel with aplomb.

'It's the damned cold that gets me,' said Haelward. 'I hate the cold.'

'Last summer you were moaning because it was too hot!'

'What can I say? I am a heartlander; I like it mild. Mild does it for me.'

'So there are only about two weeks in a year when you are happy.'

'Not if it's raining.'

Rozgon hurled the snow in his shovel at him, hitting him with a white spray.

'Were you like this in the marines?'

'Of course, those blasted ships never stay still when you want them to.'

'And no one was tempted to throw you overboard?'

Haelward laughed. 'Of course! They were lining up. It was a flogging offence though, so none of them were bold enough to try. They knew I was better with a sword than them as well – even with the short swords they use for close-quarter fighting.'

'Well, just keep that sword handy now; I am sure we are not

through this yet.'

They could tell they were going downhill now. This heartened them even when it started snowing again. It was just a light flurry and when they looked back at the saddle they could see it was a lot heavier back from where they came.

'It will be nigh on impassable back there now,' said Morgan 'We have got through with less than a day to spare.'

'Then perhaps the Gods are with us,' said Samson.

'Say that when we have left Claw Pass behind.'

They came to a spot where the mountain bulged out into the path, and traversing it they found that behind it the mountain folded back in on itself, forming a very shallow cave. Delighted with their luck they decided to set up camp. The wagon would not fit inside so they kept it as a barrier guarding the cave mouth. The horses and the rest of them had enough room to fit inside, where they lit a small fire. More iron rations followed and then they settled down for the night with two of them on watch at any one time.

It was the dead of night and Varen and Leon were staring gloomily into the fire. The animals, sleeping men, and fire made the cave the warmest place they had been in days and they were finding it hard to stay awake. Suddenly, though, Varen snapped to.

'Do you hear that?'

Leon strained to listen. 'Barking?'

Varen nodded. 'Ettins – a long way away, but they are still out there.'

'Should we wake the others?'

Varen thought for a second. 'Not yet, let them come a little closer first.'

They continued to hear the noises but if anything they got fainter until they finally stopped altogether. Samson and Rozgon relieved them and finally daylight found its way past the wagon and into the cave.

One more day and they would be almost in the foothills and clear of the pass. This spurred them on and they made much faster progress than in previous days. The night before had not been as cold and the snow was much easier for even the wagon to move through. There had been a fairly strong wind, though, and occasionally on the path they would come across drifts of snow formed into small hillocks that they had to move around. Getting the wagon stuck in one of them would not be a good idea.

Samson and Leon, close as ever, were singing the marching song of Saint Rheged, patron of travellers everywhere, quietly at first but gradually increasing in volume as they grew more confident. Haelward and Rozgon joined in, then shortly afterwards everyone was singing it. The volume was impressive, although the choir of St Kennelth's Great Cathedral had little to fear from them:

> *There is nothing better than a long road ahead*
> *There is nothing warmer than a traveller's bed*
> *No music exceeds the stomp of my feet*
> *And there are no better fellows than the people I meet*
> *So let's raise a glass*
> *To each tree that I pass*
> *For as the sun hails the new morn*
> *To the horizon I'm drawn*
> *And each day is a new start*
> *Something to capture my heart...*

Cedric explained to Willem how Rheged had been a common man who travelled thousands of miles to bring people the word of Artorus until he was finally eaten by the six-eyed monster Keyanocorax in the Red Mountains while preaching to the barbarian North Men. The trip over the mountains had been very difficult for the scholar – the cold had caused his joints to stiffen and his shaking had become a little more pronounced. Even climbing out of his bedroll in the morning had been a major undertaking. But he was not going to tell anyone of this; it was solely down to his folly that they were all here in the first place. So he would put up with the aches and pains without complaint. It would not be long now.

Willem was sitting at the rear of the wagon, trying to put the books in order. Cedric spoke to him: 'My boy, I would like to speak to you about a matter that concerns us both.'

Willem moved towards him. 'What is it, sir?'

'I am getting older and this cursed illness is not helping matters one little bit.'

'Not to worry, sir; there will always be someone to look after you.'

'Will there, my boy? That is not the matter I wish to speak of anyway. What would you say if I took over the sponsorship of your education from the holy brothers? It would mean leaving the church, of course, and taking up the life of secular study. It's as cloistered in its way as the life of a monk and demands as much devotion to study and diligence. So I would not consider it as an easier option. What it does mean is that you remain at the university, with me as my apprentice. There will be exams and lots of work, but I feel that you are clever and curious enough to succeed me one day. What do you say?'

Willem tried not to sound excited. 'Won't it cost you a lot of money personally? The fees of a student are a considerable expense.'

'Oh, I have saved enough over the years. I have been corresponding with the church over the matter and they are happy with the remuneration I am offering.'

'But what about the Island of Healing? I always thought you would go there in your dotage.'

'To get there you need more money than a humble scholar earns in a lifetime. That or the recommendation of a senior mage, and seeing as I don't know any of them, going there is hardly a viable option. Anyway, I expected you to be overjoyed at the news! Especially as your studies would bring you into contact with a certain lady artist that we know.'

Willem looked sheepish. 'Of course, sir, there is that. But I did not think my affairs mattered to you.'

'Ha, it is not as if I would get nothing out of this. I would get a bright and promising young scholar at my beck and call!'

'Thank you, sir. It will take a long time to repay you, but I definitely will.' 'I do not doubt it,' said Cedric. 'Now back to your books.'

Outside in the snow the men were still singing. They had moved on from Rheged's walking song and were now on 'The Lay of Sweet Rosie' – something the St Kennelth's choir would never attempt. The road ahead curved eastwards to their right and started to drop steeply. In the distance they could see the two mountains drawing close together, the path they were on diving between them.

'And that,' said Morgan, 'marks the end of the pass.'

Samson next to him smiled. 'Artorus's holy breath, will I be happy to get there! Are you ready, Leon – There is nothing better than a long road a...'

He started to sing in a full-throated voice, Leon joining in, but suddenly something unexpected happened. To their right were a couple of large drifts of snow. Rozgon was passing one when suddenly the snow exploded upwards and outwards. Everyone turned in horror as the ettin hiding behind it bore down on the big man. Before he could sweep out his axe, its giant claw raked across his chest. Blood sprayed on to the ettin's fur as it hit him again with full force, sending him flying off the path and rolling down the steep mountain side until he impacted with a pine tree. There he lay still, a bloody trail stretching behind him in the snow.

'Mytha, give me strength!' yelled Haelward. He was behind the creature and putting everything into the blow. He slashed his sword at the creature's stocky foot where he guessed the ankle would be. The blade bit deep and the creature's dark blood spurted freely. Hamstrung, it roared its agony as it sank to one knee, trying to grab at its wound. Then Morgan was on him. With a two-handed thrust he forced his blade into the creature's open mouth puncturing its brain case and killing it instantly. The giant beast toppled over, taking Morgan's sword with it before he could twist the blade and pull it out. As they all stared at the creature, dumbfounded, there was more roaring and two other creatures bore down on them from the path ahead.

'Shit, they're fast!' said Samson, loosing an arrow. The creature it hit stopped for a second, looking at the arrow sticking out of its chest dumbly, then continued its charge. Varen took the torch from the bracket on the wagon, then ran at the nearest creature holding it out in front of him. At that the creature did stop. Varen noticed its face had a fresh wound – evidently it was a survivor from the first encounter two nights before. He had his mace in his other hand and the two of them circled each other warily. The second ettin joined them, manoeuvring to get behind Varen. Haelward joined Varen; they stood back to back, an ettin glaring at each of them. Morgan was struggling to get his sword out of the dead creature's mouth. Samson and Leon had their bows strung, ready to fire at whichever monster made the first move. Suddenly a new figure entered the fray – not Willem, who was frantically trying to calm the rearing and bucking horses, but Cedric. He was holding a sack in one hand and a rush light in his other. Morgan at last freed his sword and called to him.

'Get back, Cedric – they will kill you!'

Cedric ignored him. He put the light in the sack, which ignited instantly, then bracing his legs he hurled it at the nearest creature striking it square in the back. It merely bounced off the creature and fell burning to the floor, but it broke the ettin's concentration, making it turn round. Seeing the fire, it growled and backed away slowly. Seeing that it was disturbed, both archers let fly at it simultaneously. It was enough for the creature. Varen's torch, the burning sack, the keen-eyed men with swords and the bowmen out of its reach decided its course of action. It turned and started bounding back the way it came. Its companion, now isolated, barked ferociously at its onlooking foes, then turned tail and followed closely behind, going at great speed with its loping strides.

Everyone stood stock still, staring at the curved white backs of the monsters as they disappeared into the distance. Haelward finally turned to Cedric.

'Books!' said Cedric ruefully. 'Soaked in the last of the brandy.'

As he spoke, the wind whipped at the fire in front of him, sending some blackened smoking pages into the air. 'Where is Morgan?'

Morgan had disappeared. Haelward sighed 'I know where he is.'

Wearily he walked off the path on to the steep pine-clad slopes of the gorge.

Morgan had already scrambled a good way down, kicking up fountains of snow as he did so. There, lying flat against a tree and soaked in his own dark blood, was Rozgon. Morgan saw immediately that he was not dead – he was expelling ragged white plumes of air – but as he drew nearer he could see how badly wounded he was. The ettin had ripped open his chest, exposing the bone, and veins and arteries were visibly leaking blood on to the snow around him. Morgan knelt down beside him, gently cradling his head. The wounded man weakly opened his bloodshot eyes.

'Come on,' said Morgan gently. 'Me and the boys will get you on to the wagon.'

Rozgon gave out a weak, wheezy laugh. 'Don't be more stupid than you look; we are hardly first-year warriors. I am not leaving this spot and you know it.'

Morgan didn't know what to say. 'What can we do for you?'

Rozgon tried adjusting his position but quickly gave up. 'Fuck, it hurts! Do me a favour, Morgan – I don't know how long it will take me to die, but I don't want the last thing I see to be one of those bastards starting to eat me. Finish it for me now – as a friend.'

Morgan couldn't look at him; he looked at the trees to his left and right and swallowed hard. 'Don't ask me to do this.'

Rozgon smiled weakly. 'It won't be so bad; I will be with the Gods after all. And I will be with Greta and the girls again.' He lifted himself on to his elbow, wincing at he did so. 'Who knows, I may even see Lisbeth and little Erik.'

Morgan met his gaze this time. 'If you do, if they are there, say hello from me. Tell them I will be with them again, probably not before too long. Say I always think of them.'

'I will, my friend. Now do it for me, please.'

Morgan took out his knife; he had sharpened it that very morning.

'Xhenafa bring you to Artorus's side – there never was a truer warrior.'

'One last thing, leave me here. My body will keep those monsters interested and away from you for a while. It is only flesh; I care not what happens to it.'

Morgan nodded. All those who followed the Church of Artorus

saw the body after death as unimportant; it was nearly always burned. Gripping his knife firmly, he leaned over the man he had fought countless battles with over the last ten years, whom he had always looked up to as he found his own feet as a soldier.

And then he did what he had to do.

Haelward joined him a minute later. Tapping Morgan on his shoulder, the two of them turned and made the steep climb back to the path. Behind them the crows were already descending.

They continued their journey. Nobody spoke and the speed with which they had travelled earlier slowed. The one spare horse they had had fled, leaving them with just two. The worst of the journey was over, though. They didn't make it out of the pass that night, but now that the path was flanked with trees it was easy enough to gather plenty of dead wood and make a large fire. The snow had fallen here, too, but much less copiously and only one to two inches of it covered the ground. That night they heard the wolves and the braying of flocks of mountain deer but nothing else.

The following morning, the mountain path petered out into an upland of pine and spruce. The sun shone fitfully upon the travellers and a bright mountain stream spilled joyfully over rocks as it bounded down the wooded hillside. They followed it until it crashed over a lip of rock, creating a waterfall some twenty feet high. After finding a gentler route down they came to the splash pool where they filled their flasks and stopped to refresh themselves. Ahead was a broad grassy plain, dotted with bushes, low hills and similar streams to the one they were following. To their left they could see a wide dirt track heading west and north – the road to the city of Zerannon; to their right in the far distance was a belt of mist shrouding a low green smudge that stretched out into the endless distance. Nobody needed to be told that that was the Aelvenwood. At least the mountains were behind them now.

A large press of men stood facing two others. Between them was a large wooden fire. One of the two was standing on a low table which was so rickety that he had to keep moving his feet to keep his balance. His hands were bound behind him and a rope was round his neck, its other end being looped around a solid branch of a great oak tree next to him. The other man stood facing the crowd, the flames of the fire casting dark saturnine shadows over his bald scarred face. His black eyes could have belonged to Keth, god of the underworld, such was their implacable coldness, their lack of mercy. In turn, he held each of the gazes of the men facing him; none of them could stare back for long. Then he spoke, with a voice like gravel sliding into a bottomless cavern.

'All of you know me by now. You know my name, you know I command you, but it appears a couple of things still need to be made clear...

'I expect nothing less than complete loyalty from all of you. When I tell you to do something, you do it; you don't ask my reasons, you do not question me. This man, Bakker,' he gestured to the man on his left, 'failed to understand the consequences of doing such a thing and now faces punishment. If you follow his path of disloyalty, then you will face the same degree of retribution. You fight for me now. Forget that fop Fenchard; all he does is supply the money. You fight for me and you follow my code of honour.' He stroked his bearded chin. 'Honour – you may have heard of this as having something to do with knights in polished armour or velvet-wearing daddy's boys who take to the battlefield brandishing a perfumed handkerchief to banish the smell of guts, shit and fear. Then let me tell you, I have trod on more corpses of these snivelling little nobodies than you have squeezed spots on your baby-soft skin. I see what you all are – farm boys, chancers, craftsmen who make things that nobody wants anymore, and I imagine you all need ... clarification as to exactly what honour actually is.'

He took two or three steps to his right, then back to his left, and with a swift gesture kicked the table from under the other man's feet. Oblivious to the swinging jerking figure he continued. 'Honour is not about bowing to your opponent or waiting for him to stand if he falls over. Honour is about survival; it is about winning; it is about killing your opponent without mercy and taking his money, weapons, house and woman. There is no honour in lying cold in the mud with the crows plucking your eyes out as the worms wriggle through your grey flesh... But there is honour in drinking that man's wine and spending his coin while his grateful widow kneels willingly before you. Follow me without question and all this honour shall be yours. No more hungry bellies for your families, no more being spat upon by fat merchants as you sell them your under-priced goods and they sell you their overpriced ones. Follow me and see the fear and respect in the eyes of those that once loathed you. Sir Trask will make you the men you always wanted to be.'

The jerking of the man next to him had nearly stopped. As with all victims of hanging he had soiled himself, and urine was dripping from his boot on to the soft grass below. There was a flash of steel as Trask suddenly took hold of the man's arm. For a few moments his audience could not see what he was doing, as he had his back to them, but then he stepped in front of the fire. By its fierce light he looked like one of Keth's demons returned to this world ... and then they saw it. It was a rope of thin wire and attached to it, like the charms of a bracelet, were a selection of human fingers, some blackened and swollen, some white and bloodless. Bakker's finger was there, too, dripping blood on to Trask's armour. He addressed them again.

'Show your enemies the meaning of fear. If they fear your attack, then they cease to think rationally and your knife is already at their throat. Make them fear you and you will have all the honour in the world.'

As one they raised their fists and weapons into the air and called out hoarsely, 'Sir Trask! Sir Trask and Haslan Falls!'

Their cries echoed deep and long into the night and none who heard it failed to tremble.

22

Ceriana had been fitful and restless during the entire sea voyage back to Osperitsan. Ebba watched her as she would fidget in her cabin, stand up, sit down and stalk around its narrow confines. Oftentimes she would give an exasperated sigh and go up top to the quarterdeck where she would spend some time scanning the horizon almost as if she was expecting to see another ship following them. Then when night came she would toss and turn and make little whimpering noises as if in the thrall of an upsetting dream. Ebba had tried to ask her what the problem was but was met with uncharacteristic truculence and surliness. Once Ebba had caught her alone in the cabin with her head in her hands rocking back and forth in her seat. She sat up abruptly on hearing the door open and Ebba could see wetness in her eyes, something which her angry 'Knock before you enter next time' could not disguise. The journey home had therefore been a difficult one.

Still, it was over now – the ship was moored in Osperitsan harbour where Wulfthram was waiting to greet his wife. She bowed to him and he asked her how her trip went.

'Well enough. We toured the island and inspected the ships; Barons Richney and Vorfgan were there also for a couple of days; I enjoyed it ... mostly.'

'Good,' he said. 'Tell me more later. You have a couple of guests waiting for you back at the hall. I was going to give them short shrift and send them packing, but they showed me a letter you had written to them so I have put them up in the guest's quarters for now.'

She was taken aback. 'They are here? Father wrote to inform me they were on their way but I only received his letter in Thakholm and so have been unable to let you know about them.'

'I imagine the second they saw you are a Hartfield they stopped whatever they were doing and came here as fast as a horse could carry them. You forget the weight your name carries.'

'But I never even got around to telling you about them. I thought they would write first.'

'No, you didn't tell me. So perhaps you could furnish me with an explanation now.'

She could sense the disapproval in his voice and her heart sank. Was there anyone she could turn to?

'It is ... complicated. I was going to tell you about it when I knew they were either coming here or had written back. As it stands, I need to get some answers before I can tell you what I know. I am sorry it has happened this way, but I am asking you to trust me in this, please.' She hoped she didn't sound too desperate.

He seemed to accept this. 'I am disappointed that you feel unable to tell me, but no matter. Meet these people and talk to me afterwards, if that is what you wish.'

She felt the chasm between them that had narrowed in recent weeks yawn open again. She realised she did not know what to say to him and so kept silent.

Despite her wealth and status, all her life she had battled her own feelings of worthlessness and inadequacy. Doren called them her 'black moods' and knew to keep her distance when she was in one. Since her encounter with the black-robed man in Thakholm she had slipped into a miasma of torpid listlessness where she had wanted to do nothing more than lock herself in a room and blow out the candle. She had managed to keep up a front of restrained cheer to Baron Skellar, but once on the ship she had been ghastly to Ebba and could never shake off the sensation of being watched or followed. How had they traced her? Was it the stone? And who were these people anyway? Well, at least she might find out soon. Then maybe she could tell her husband before she was reduced to requesting a formal audience with him like everybody else.

They arrived back in silence under a leaden sky carrying the threat of rain. Wulfthram courteously bade her farewell and she headed to her room via a tradesman's entrance, thus avoiding the main hall. Her baggage was in her room when she got there and Ebba was busying herself with unpacking it. Ceriana decided to speak to her.

'I am sorry for my behaviour the last couple of days. Things have been worrying me of late and like the witch I am I have been taking it out on you. It has been wrong of me to behave this way; my old handmaiden Doren understood what I could be like but you, poor dear, have been thrown to a tetchy she wolf without any foreknowledge at all. I hope you can forgive me.'

'Of course, my Lady; I can see that you have been under some pressure of late. I reckon it has something to do with your recent illness; you have been a little ... different since then. You shouldn't, of course, give a fish wife's curse for what your servants think of you.'

'Oh but I do, Ebba, of course I do; especially as you have been so helpful since my arrival. I will humble myself before you a little more later on, but right now I have to see these people waiting for me. After the distance they have travelled it would be discourteous of me not to see them immediately; we will speak more once I get back.'

Her guests were the only people in the main hall. The servants had left them with some simple foods – bread, cheese and apples along with some weak beer. There were two of them: a distinguished, silver-haired man who exuded an aura of dusty academia and a girl, about Ceriana's age, wearing a severe bun and who was all demure passivity. They both stood as she approached them.

'I thank you both for coming; I really was only expecting a written reply so I hope your journey was not too arduous. I am Ceriana by the way, but I am sure you have already guessed that.'

The man bowed. 'I am Professor Ulian, my Lady, and allow me to introduce Alys, my assistant in this matter. I can assure you our journey was most uneventful; the horrors of the Morrathnay Forest are greatly exaggerated. We obviously departed as soon as was practicable upon receipt of your letter. I must confess I travel little and have found the new surroundings most stimulating.'

'And I trust the accommodation is to your satisfaction?'

'Compared to the rooms at St Philig's it is opulence indeed, although at first I feared we may be reduced to finding a bale of straw to bed down in.'

'Ah, the misunderstanding on your arrival. Entirely my fault, I am afraid. I have been away for a few days and did not inform my husband of my correspondence with your good self so he was not expecting you. I obviously apologise for my oversight.'

'No need at all, my Lady; it was all resolved quickly enough, Now shall we get down to the matter at hand.'

He had a powerful voice and was obviously used to speaking in front of a crowd. Ceriana decided to try and involve his companion in the conversation.

'Indeed, I am most anxious to hear your conclusions, but first my I ask the Lady Alys as to how she became involved in the academic life? It is so rare to see a woman in a scholastic profession after all; you must be very proud of your achievements.'

The girl looked directly at her. Unlike Ceriana, who had spent her entire life preening herself with a host of make-up powders, scented oils, exotic herbs and flowers and expensive jewellery, she was simply dressed in white linen with the well-scrubbed appearance of a farmer's wife. Her large blue eyes, however, gave her a natural gentle beauty to which Ceriana felt she herself could never aspire.

'My role is but a small one,' she said shyly. 'Master Cedric, another professor at the university, happened to see me sketching portraits in Tanaren market one day and engaged me on a freelance basis to reproduce many of the artefacts in his collection on paper. Since then I have become a more or less full-time assistant of his and have even accompanied him on field trips.

It is I who sketched the ring you yourself mentioned in your letter, my Lady.'

'Yes,' said Ulian. 'I had better clarify the situation as quickly as possible in order to assuage your disappointment. I am not the professor to whom your letter is addressed; he, Cedric, is engaged on some errand for the Grand Duke. We are attempting to contact him but until we do I am afraid it is my humble self who will have to serve in his stead. I can assure you that I work closely with him and Alys has been extremely helpful in furnishing information for me, but, yes, this is more his field than mine.'

'I see,' said Ceriana. 'How do your fields of study differ?'

'Cedric deals with the history of the Wych folk and Tanaren itself, whereas I am more concerned with the founding and history of the empire of Chira and its wars of succession and especially in its interactions with us. With regards to your circumstances, it is the histories of the Wych folk that appear to be the most pertinent.'

'Please sit down both of you and tell me what you know.' They complied. Ulian drank some ale and started to speak.

'Let us begin with the double-headed serpent, so ably depicted by Alys here.' He unfolded her drawing on to the table. Ceriana, of course, had never seen it and so eagerly drank in all the details. Alys was a very able artist – that was obvious. Every scale of the serpent was rendered in full detail, and it had fins, too ... or were they tiny wings? Its two heads appeared to be conflicting with each other; both had their mouths open and were facing each other as though engaged in a battle for supremacy. The ring was not a regular circle either, the serpent's tail folded and coiled in such a way as to make the ring somewhat uncomfortable to wear, at least that's how Ceriana saw it. She turned her attention back to the professor.

'This design is common in Wych folk jewellery. It depicts the great Black Dragon, Azhanion, the first creature to be given life in this world – that is in Wych lore obviously. Please note that my references to Wych mythology should in no way be taken as heresy on my part; I am merely quoting their beliefs here. Their religion has one god only, Zhun; he gave life to all things and in his first creation he wanted to reflect the eternal conflict in all things and how it was necessary to bring balance to the world. Hence the two headed dragon attempting to devour itself.'

'But why would a man take to wearing such a thing?' she asked.

'A good question. A degree of supposition is required here, but millennia ago the Wych folk lived much closer to many human societies; there was even trade between us and trade can also involve exchanges of beliefs and ideas. Why should it not be that some men adopted the beliefs of an older, wiser civilization? But there is more to this than that.' He signed to Alys, who opened a book that had been sitting on the table in front of her to a certain marked page.

'A man in black who shaves his hair? A strange creature indeed. This set me to looking at Cedric's tomes concerning ancient religions, cults and their practitioners. I must confess it was something of a frustrating dead end until Alys discovered a page Cedric had marked in a tome called Cults of Death and Believers in the Great Cleansing, written by a Brother Merkel around the time of the Wych Wars some eight hundred years ago.'

'The Great Cleansing?'

'Oh it is a reference to the end of the world, something that transpires in a spectacular and unpleasant manner of course. Unlike ourselves, who believe that we are on a path to ultimate enlightenment when all the secrets of the world will be laid bare for everyone to understand, these cults often see mankind as a repository of all that is evil in this world, whose sin and wickedness can only be purged through fiery destruction. They see themselves as catalysts for such an eventuality.'

'What? They think they can bring about the end of the world? So they are nothing more than mad heretics then?' Ceriana was incredulous, her eyes wide.

'Deluded rather than mad, I fear. Anyway this brother Merkel was a ship's priest who travelled extensively in the south around the steaming jungles and volcanic islands of western Koze; I shall quote this passage from his book:

'We were detained on this island, one which arises out of the azure ocean like a great jagged tooth, bereft of trees and almost sheer-sided, accessible only through a cave in which there is limited mooring for some three fishing vessels. Once the ship was secured by lines one of the inhabitants of this isle led us back out of the cave on to a stairway that climbed like a thin white line to the very summit, traversing the cliff side, into the crevice of the tooth where their temple was constructed. The steps numbered in their thousands, with no guide rail to protect against a slip and fall into the buffeting waves beneath. We were told later that only those judged worthy survive the climb, though he did not specify who was doing the judging. It took us some hours before, exhausted and breathing heavily, we broached the final step. Ahead of us, hewn out of the rock, was

a stone temple. It had two great towers, the crown of each being carved into a gaping reptilian maw. Between each tower, on sheltered land, was a green stretch of trees and gardens surrounded by water butts where herbs and vegetables the like of which I had never seen before were grown. We were greeted there by a man who, like every other man there, wore a black robe with every follicle of hair having been removed from his body. He proceeded to explain the tenets of his religion.'

'Their ships,' Ceriana asked earnestly. 'Does he describe their ships?'

'Um, somewhere.' Ulian glanced up and down, flicking over the page. 'Only briefly, unfortunately – 'dragon-prowed and winged...'; that is it, I am afraid.'

She sat back in her chair. The professor was on the right tracks, it seemed.

'Continue, please.'

'Ah yes, now where was I? ...

'He welcomed us to the Isle of Xvirra, a secluded place where the study of the ancient true religion could continue unabated. I asked him what the goal of that study was exactly. His reply was as portentous as I had come to expect from such cults – the destruction of all false gods and their unholy followers and the re-establishment of the ancient beliefs as taught to them by the Aelves. When I asked him how such a thing could be achieved he smiled knowingly and whispered "Wouldn't you like to know."'

Ulian looked at Ceriana. 'There is a lot of waffle about how he was shown their temple and watched their religious services and even looked at their books of lore, which had been either stolen from or bequeathed by the Aelves, but nothing more that pertains to your situation, I fear. The man you discovered was a priest of Xvirra. What he was doing at Tanaren, I am afraid this book does not say.'

'Why wear black? Why do they shave themselves?'

'I believe they wear black in honour of the Black Dragon, and they shave themselves as a sign of purity – they believe hair to be unclean. The Wych folk have no hair except that which they have on their heads. They are attempting to be even purer than the Wych folk so it seems.' He grunted, involuntarily.

'And now, my Lady, I have to ask you as to the second artefact you have discovered, the one that affects your health as your letter relates. Maybe there is something in this book that may explain it.'

Ceriana nodded. There was a servant waiting by the door. She beckoned him over. 'Can you ask my husband to attend us here; he is probably in his quarters.'

While they waited, she asked, 'So these people worship the Black Dragon?'

'Yes, and its subordinates, the five other dragons created after the first.'

'What dragons were these?'

'They represent some of the major elements – earth, water, fire, lightning and ice. All of them are immortal. Once they acted as the custodians of the world, but then things went wrong, as they always do, and now they sleep, for ever.'

She wanted to ask more but at that point Wulfthram entered the room. Once he was seated, she placed the jewellery box that she had carried with her on the table.

'You saw the letter,' she said to him. 'So you know about the discovery on the beach. What is in here is my own discovery, one which no one has seen until now. It may be completely unrelated to the man we found, but somehow I doubt it.'

With great care she opened the box and pulled out the stone. Its touch repulsed her but she let it nestle in the palm of her hand as she showed the onlookers.

'Beguiling, isn't it?' she said drily.

'May I?' said Ulian. She let him take it from her, though to her surprise she felt a slight reluctance to do so. He held it up to the light. 'Artorus help us!' he said softly.

'You know? You know what it is?' she asked earnestly.

'It is just a stone,' said Wulfthram. 'Too large to be a precious one at that.'

'Look closely, Wulf,' she said. 'It seems to contain some viscous liquid and yet there is no sign of a seal.'

'I do not know exactly what it is,' said Ulian, 'but there are references in some ancient myths that may be relevant here. How exactly is it affecting you exactly, my Lady?'

Ceriana explained the strange occurrences that had taken place since she had acquired the stone. 'Another thing,' she said, 'it seems to give me some strange dreams, in which I am some great animal hidden underground. The dreams are vivid – I can feel the cold in its cave, smell the damp stone, detect the weariness in its limbs. I can even feel an alien presence in my mind, like this dream creature exists and is inside me. It is very difficult for me to explain to one that has not experienced it.'

'I cannot give you definite answers,' said Ulian, 'but there is a passage in this book that may help to explain it.' He thumbed through a couple of pages before finding the section he sought.

'They wish to awaken the ancient dragons from their slumber by discovering the dragon stones, hidden throughout the world and holders of the very essence of these creatures, taken from them when they entered their eternal hibernation countless millennia ago. They believe that the bearer of a stone, if possessing a sensitive mind, can form a link with a dragon and even cause it to awaken. Over time the link becomes stronger and stronger and the two beings become inseparable, their minds coming together so that they become almost one being. The control of a dragon of great power can therefore be used to bring about the Great Cleansing of which they are so fond.'

'Does it say how such a link is broken?' Ceriana's heart was pumping.

Ulian scanned the book, turning more pages and looking up and down each intently. He looked at her. 'No' was his final response.

'You do not know that this object is the stone referred to in the book,' said Wulfthram. 'These people are obviously insane and they adhere to beliefs that would get anyone here tied to a stake and torched. there has to be a more rational explanation; maybe this stone is just poisonous or causes hallucinations.'

'I agree,' said Ulian. 'What I am reading here is an ancient account relating to a bunch of fanatics. It ends with them sparing the priest but throwing his crew from the top of the mountain into the sea. They then maroon him in the jungle where he is rescued by a passing Kozean flotilla – a miracle, or so he described it. I think this object needs to be taken from you and studied. The Baron's theory is a plausible one. We really need to look at this stone further. It is a fascinating object without doubt but one to which one of a thousand explanations could apply.'

'And yet it was found close to a man in black robes... There is something else I have yet to tell you.' She related her encounter with the man in Thakholm and then concluded: 'They at least seem to believe that I have found one of these stones.'

'And your dreams of the creature,' said Alys, 'seem so closely related to the dragon bonding mentioned in the book. Surely the evidence is mounting?'

'We cannot jump to conclusions,' Ulian said. 'Let us take this stone to St Philig's and inform you of our findings in due course.'

'But what puzzles me is where would they could have found such a stone in Tanaren,' Ceriana mused.

'Maybe in ancient Aelven ruins?' said Alys. 'There are plenty on the coast here.'

'And more in the Morrathnay Forest,' said Ulian.

'This is what I surmise,' said Ceriana thoughtfully. 'These people discovered the location of one of these stones; they collected it; one of them sought to locate the creature through it but on the voyage home their ship was wrecked and the man drowned. I happened upon the stone and now they want it back. Whether or not it has these powers and I am turning into some sort of dragon woman is immaterial. What matters is that they think it is the stone of which their religion speaks. This puts its possessor in danger. I am secure here surrounded by guards but if you were to take it back to Tanaren City you could be attacked and killed.'

'I could supply them with an escort,' said Wulfthram. 'I think the further away from you this stone is the happier I shall be. It is obviously not good for your health, whatever it is.'

'This Cedric – would he know more about this stone? Perhaps he would know how to combat its effects?' Ceriana was looking at Ulian.

'Very probably. No man alive knows more about the ways of the Wych folk than he.'

'Then perhaps we could send out messengers and ask this man to come here. More than anything else I want these strange things happening to me to end. Professor Ulian, thank you for coming all this way to talk to me, but I cannot burden you with this thing until I have a greater understanding of what is happening to me. You are both free to leave if you wish, but I will not be surrendering this stone at present. I will not be responsible for you being hunted down and killed far from home.'

Wulfthram looked at her sternly. 'I could command you to give it to him.

My offer of troops still stands and I will repeat my belief that you will be much better off without it.'

'You could command me, yes. I am grateful for your concern for me but bear in mind that these people are fanatics; they will try anything to get this thing and will not want it to be taken to Tanaren City.'

'Yet they let you go easily enough in Thakholm.'

'They have a plan,' she said. 'They can track the stone somehow. They let me go because they know its whereabouts. As Ulian said, they are deluded not mad; they have their wits about them.'

'You have no evidence of this outside of your own suppositions,' said Wulfthram 'The stone will go to Tanaren under escort. My word is final.' She was about to let fly with an angry retort when Ulian stepped in.

'Perhaps a compromise could be reached here. I have no wish to cause friction between the two of you. Perhaps if we could prevail upon your hospitality for, say, about six weeks, giving time for messengers to go out and return, then maybe – if we have not heard from Cedric – we should return to St Philig's then.'

Wulfthram thought about it for a second. 'Very well, six weeks it is then, but no longer. I hope and trust your stay here will be a comfortable one.'

'Thank you, Baron,' said Ulian. 'With your permission I will retire to look at these tomes further; it is always possible that I have missed something.' The two of them stood, bowed to both host and hostess, and left the room.

'Angry?' Wulfthram asked her, his eyebrow raised quizzically, as soon as the two of them were left alone.

She was flushed but didn't care; her temper was controlling her. 'What does my opinion matter to you? You will decide whatever you want without my advice – that much is apparent.'

'And if I told you that I was acting in your own best interests?'

Her hackles rose even further. 'What do you know of my interests?' Her voice was rising; she hated how, as it got thinner, she sounded like a raving woman.

'All I know is that, if you feel this stone to be the cause of your malady, then we are best rid of it.'

'You know nothing!' She stood up, staring at him with her eyes blazing 'I rather suspect you don't even believe what I am saying. You probably see me as a spoilt child prone to fantastic hallucinations, that I'm doing this to get the attention that I used to get at Edgecliff.'

He looked at her without answering. She was beyond self-control now. 'That is what you believe, isn't it? You ... you cold evil bastard!' She went to strike him but he blocked her thin arm easily.

'If you were me, what exactly would you believe? Think about it.' His dark eyes held her in its grip; her shoulders heaved as she considered his words.

'Fine,' she said, regaining her composure slightly. 'Then lay with me. Stay with me through the night, though it may be abhorrent for you. Eventually something will happen and you will be forced to reassess your opinion of me.'

'Very well,' he said. 'From tonight then.'

She was calmer now. 'From tonight.'

'And you are mistaken – it would not be abhorrent for me; I rather thought that it would be for you.'

She was thrown a little. 'No,' she said, shaking her head, 'maybe we have been at cross purposes. Stay with me, see what happens, see that I am not the needy child you think I am.'

'I will. I am prepared to learn. Perhaps we both should be.'

He turned and left the room. Ceriana remained motionless, her fists clenched. He would see... Yes, he would see. The thought that she was perceived as a child annoyed her more than anything else, except the thought that she enjoyed sharing her bed with him. She seized a remaining apple from the visitors' meagre lunch and took an angry bite, before heading to the main door leading outside. Fresh air would cool her temper and she needed it cooled before facing her husband again.

23

They rowed with all the strength they could muster. This was their second day on the water since their battle with the night devils. They had seen nothing of them since that night but their nerves were still frayed. The prow of their boat still held the skull of the Elder but the stern now held another trophy. Cerren had affixed the head of the creature he had killed to it, its dead eyes staring sightlessly at the boat's wake. There were only three of them rowing. The elder, Tegavenek, had not recovered sufficiently from his wounds to help them; the healing poultices had assisted him to a degree but the wounds on his shoulder and arm had not healed. The other wounded man, Cerren, had brushed off his injury; he was the youngest and strongest there, but even so his wound was still open, too.

They had been travelling east and south and watched the landscape change. The trees had thinned to be replaced by high grasses and banks of reeds and rushes. The river and water courses they travelled along were wider, heavy with brown sediment, and more open to the wind, making the waters choppy and difficult to navigate. Light reflected off them in shifting dappled patterns making it hard to see too far ahead. The crows and small woodland birds had gone, too, replaced by gulls and cormorants sunning themselves on whatever river perches they could find.

'We are on the right river,' Fasneterax said from the stern rowing position. 'It is difficult to judge, but we can only be a short distance away. The sea is close by. Can you taste the salt?'

Cygan had noticed this a while back. As the rivers approached the sea, a large delta was formed, all mud and sand bars. Sometimes they enclosed great lakes such as the one housing the tribe they were now seeking. If a great sea storm arose, it could cause giant waves to crash over these spits of land, sometimes opening these lakes up to the sea or sometimes reshaping the lands to create new lakes. It was anything but a permanent country here and could be treacherous for those unfamiliar with the surroundings.

The land here though was very flat and when they stopped for a brief midday meal they climbed the bank and attempted to see what lay ahead. Cerren pointed through the bright sun.

'There, he said, 'I can see a rock sticking out from the water; we could be there in under two hours.'

'Then we need to make haste,' said Cygan. 'We need to see our tribesmen and help the people here if we can. If the worst has happened, then we need to make our own preparations for when night falls. We do not want to be attacked again.'

'Like we did last night?' said Cerren gloomily. They had seen no Malaac but had spent the night being eaten by midges and mosquitos.

'If need be,' said Cygan. 'Come, let's get moving again.'

They continued their journey. The river was so wide here that great flocks of seabirds would sit on it in massive clumps, bobbing up and down on the water, then rising as one with disgruntled shrieks as Cygan's boat approached them. The weather changed quickly here and they watched with some consternation as slabs of grey cloud came scudding towards them and the wind got fresher causing small waves to come crashing into their prow. The waves were sending plumes of spray up across the boat and soaking Cerren who had the foremost rowing position. After nearly an hour of this he called to the others.

'Boats! On the river, coming towards us!' 'How many?' said Cygan.

Cerren stopped rowing and shielded his eyes. 'Six, maybe seven; all longboats and all of them full.'

He was quite right. There were seven of them with about six to each boat. As they drew closer they could see the heads of children moving around between the rowers, there were women there too.

'Is that Vengefarak?' said Cygan 'On the lead boat?'

'Yes,' said Cerren, 'And Raduketeveryan on the next boat. Hoy! Radu!'

His boat pulled up to theirs, and both men grabbed the prows of the other's boats, pulling them together. Vengeferak trod water next to them. They greeted each other as warmly as possible given the precarious circumstances.

'We are evacuating the village,' said Raduketeveryan. 'It has become too dangerous, The Malaac attacked last night and breached the defences; several were killed. I see you have had similar problems.' He indicated the head resting on the boat's stern.'

'We never even got to the Twin Snake's main settlement,' said Cygan, 'we were forced back. Tegavenek is injured.'

'We lost Adevenek,' called out Vengefarak. 'The Gods here are angry indeed.'

'Is the village empty now?' asked Cygan.

'There was no more space in the boats. In this water any more on board and we could capsize. There are several tribes here; they are taking the evacuees back to their own villages,' Raduketeveryan replied, not actually answering the question.

'The Elder and one of the Circle remain,' said Vengefarak. 'There were no more boats and they decided to sacrifice themselves to ensure that the others escaped.'

'Then we will go and get them,' said Cygan 'We can take two more.'

'Cygannan watch over you then. We will see you back at Black Lake.' Vengefarak spurred his boat onwards and waved them goodbye.

'Farewell, my friends,' said Raduketeveryan. 'You may even catch us up. One boat moves faster than seven.' He released the prow and the refugee boats continued on their way.

The Black Lake party watched the seven boats until they became indistinct lines on the horizon, then pressed forward.

The river continued to widen. The reeds gradually disappeared, exposing high banks of mud through which the thick roots of tough marsh grass showed – the only thing preventing rapid erosion of the banks here. Now the water was like a brown soup rising and falling in waves which pitched their little boat up and down so that it was now shipping water. Tegavenek stirred himself and did what he could to bail them out. Cygan, though, was thinking how much worse it would get when they started rowing through the lake with two extra bodies on board.

He did not have to wait long to find out. Suddenly the great muddy buttresses of the banks vanished altogether and they were pitched four square on to the lake. Immediately the wind whipped up, flapping at their ears and driving the boat to the right. The waves, too, increased in ferocity, lifting the boat high then slamming it back into the water, kicking up a ferocious spray. Within seconds all four of them were soaked. Tegavenek started scooping out the water with a renewed vigour, fighting the wind and tide as the three other men struggled to right the boat's course – for directly ahead was the black rock that gave the Jagged Hill tribe its name.

It was under a mile away – it was not a feature of great height, but one that stood out against the low country around it. They could make out the stockade and various dwellings constructed of wood and reeds but little else until they got closer. It was not too far to row but in the difficult conditions it took an eternity. They were fighting waves, wind and tide and, although all three of them were at the peak of fitness, they were soon exhausted. But, little by little, the island edged closer. They could now see the stockade had been flattened in parts and that thatch and wood lay strewn over the open ground. The great house, in the centre of the village, had partially collapsed – its front roof supports lay on the ground and thatch was strewn everywhere and was being whipped up by the wind in great clouds.

As they pulled up alongside the jetty, they started to be hit by large warm droplets of rain driving in from the sea. This, Cygan guessed correctly, lay less than half a mile distant. Cerren leapt out to secure the boat while Cygan and Fasneterax grabbed their spears and headed into the ruined village.

They found the two men sitting inside the ruins of the great house. Skulls, pots and wall hangings lay idly about them. At first they raised their spears and started their battle cries until they realised that the new arrivals were rescuers not enemies.

'I am Cyganexatavan of the Black Lake. We have one boat and can bring the two of you back to our village. We need to leave quickly so, if there are any belongings you wish to take, get them now and do not tarry.'

'I am Denekavaxan, Elder of what once was the tribe of Jagged

Hill. I thank you for your arrival but if you think you can escape the easier without us then do so. We are happy to give our lives defending our village.'

Fasneterax spoke: 'We did not come here to tour your lake. We will leave with both of you and, if the Gods allow it, we shall all return to our village together.'

'Very well, stranger, then let us depart.'

With all the haste they could muster the four men returned to the boat. As it gathered strength, the rain slapped mercilessly against their shoulders and the back of their heads. With little ceremony they clambered inside, the two new arrivals in the boat's centre. The Elder took up an oar while his comrade readied a bowl to scoop out the water. As Cygan expected, the wind and tide were with them this time and the boat fairly shot out from the jetty. The difficulty now was in keeping the boat under control, to stop it being pushed past the mouth of the river. They drew their cloaks around them as much as they could as the elements assaulted them from all sides. The river mouth approached. Never had Cygan seen anything so welcoming. Denekavaxan, sitting just behind him, turned to take one last regretful look at his former home.

'By Cygannan and all the Gods, do you see that?' Cygan turned and almost dropped his oar.

He saw the rock, black and keen amid the roiling brown water, yet just ahead of it and to the right there was something else. In normal circumstances he would have called it a coiling water snake, but they never grew as long as this! Three coils he discerned – three arches standing out in the water, the central one standing higher than Jagged Hill itself. He reckoned four men standing one on another could fit comfortably under its great span. He could see its scales, green-black, almost iridescent, quite beautiful in their own way, but each of them large enough to make a warrior's shield. As he watched, two of the coils disappeared under the waves, but emerging from the water came the neck and head of the great creature. He had expected a snake's head but it seemed more reptilian, arrowhead-shaped with a fin at its centre. Even at this distance he could see its teeth, many teeth, all needle sharp and maybe up to a foot long. As they watched, its mouth opened and a great hiss came out, like a storm-force wind over jagged rocks, then the whole apparition plunged into the water once more and was gone.

Denekavaxan gasped, his voice suddenly hoarse: 'Ventekuu, Ventekuu is among us. What can we do now? What can we do?'

Cygan wasn't listening; he was too busy frantically rowing towards the river.

Three days later they limped back to their village. As Cygan expected, the great house was packed – nearly all the village was there. After leaving the still-sickly Tegavenek with the other elders, he sought out Dumnekavax.

'You have heard the news, yes? Vengefarak is back.'

'He is, Cygan, yes; he got here barely two hours before you.'

'How have things been here? Has the village been attacked?'

'Not as yet and, if the Gods are with us, it won't be either. I have walked the spirit path and Ukka has instructed me. You, my friend, have a part to play in the resolution of this problem. Tell me your tale afterwards; right now I have an announcement to make.'

Cygan wondered what exactly 'his part' actually was but his pondering was cut short as the Elder called everyone to order. Cygan sat down with everybody else, feeling rather miserable if truth be told.

'You have been waiting for me to talk to you all following my journey into the world of the spirits. There I had the honour of being addressed by Ukka herself and guided as to the course of action that we should take. It is not an easy course but it is one in which great honour can be achieved. If we do this correctly, then our village should be spared.' He let the murmur of the crowd subside before continuing.

'Before I tell you the task that has fallen to us, let me welcome the Jagged Hill tribe to our village. They have withstood nightly attacks from the Malaac for many days and their bravery can only be an asset to us here at the Black Lake.' There was some applause at this, which Cygan participated in. 'Now as to what we need to do. Firstly, these disturbances are not caused by any failure on our part; we here have done nothing to anger the Gods. Rather, the cause lies with the people outside the marsh who have meddled in things they do not understand and upset the balance of life here. We need to find out what they have done so I propose sending our ambassador Cyganexatavan to the dry lands of the north to find out the cause of the problem.'

Another roar of approval and Cygan saw the way things were going; there was no point in fighting the inevitable. Wearily, he stood up and addressed the crowd.

'I accept the charge laid upon me and will leave when the Elder advises.'

Dumnekavax nodded to him. 'And now for the second task: Ukka needs placating. She has requested an emissary. Someone young and strong, eager to serve both his village and the Gods.'

Instantly every young man present got to their feet shouting at the Elder, imploring him to choose them. Dumnekavax stared impassively at them.

'Very well. I have chosen. Cerrenatukavenex will be the emissary. He has slain the Malaac and proven himself a warrior. There is none here more fitting.'

Cerren beamed at all and sundry. Honour indeed would be his for eternity.

24

If he was being honest with himself, he had never seen a river like it. Two days travel from the mountains through ancient oak woodlands and wide grasslands had brought them here, the river Taethan. They were just north of the point where the Taethan Falls crash on to the plain and spread outwards, to form the wide shallow river that flows down to the sea. They had journeyed along its course for a whole day and never at any point did the river seem to get any more than four feet deep; indeed, it rarely seemed to be any deeper than two along most of its length. The water itself was crystal clear as it ran over its stone bed, fronds of river grasses dancing gracefully as they swayed in the fast current. Morgan lost track of the fish he saw; most of them did not swim off either, but rather hung in the water regarding the unfamiliar interlopers with a bored curiosity. They river was dotted with many eyots rising out of the shallow depths; all were crowned with trees and had a thicket of shrubs and bushes at their base. Many birds perched in the high branches, calling defiantly to the humans passing below as if they perceived their very presence here as an affront. The river was very wide but everyone in the party could not help but glance frequently at the far bank. There sat the Aelvenwood. If ever a forest could glower, then this was the one. Impenetrable shadows gathered under the closely entangled branches of the densely packed trees. The whole place looked like light never pierced its inky depths, that it existed out of time itself, that it had looked like this a thousand years ago and would still do so a thousand years hence. As they walked alongside it with only the river separating them, they constantly expected something evil, an army of night horrors or a pack of slavering Agnathi beasts to emerge and bear down on them, all teeth and glowing red eyes. But nothing came aside from the wind in the trees, the calls of the birds and the chatter of water bouncing over sand and rock.

Cedric sat at the front of the wagon next to Varen, looking out for the island from whence the signal to the Wych folk would be sent. Morgan walked alongside them.

'Do you have any idea where this island could be then?' he asked.

'No,' said Cedric. He seemed a lot better for being off the mountain and colour had returned to his cheeks. 'Just keep your eyes out for a statue, probably covered in leaves or ivy. It has stood untended for many years after all.'

'It would not do to walk straight past it. We are already some three days from the sea; I don't want to get there and have to turn back and retrace our steps'

'And miss it again?' said Cedric.

Morgan groaned and looked back across the river.

As the river was so shallow, the banks were pretty marshy. They camped that night therefore a few hundred yards from the river, sheltered by a crescent of gnarled oak trees. They lit no fire as all of them had the uneasy feeling that they were being watched and the last thing they wanted was to draw unwelcome attention. None of them slept well that night. They lay on their backs, weapons in hand, watching the clouds scud across the face of the waxing moon.

The following day after some two hours' travel they found it.

Varen it was who gave the signal, pulling the reins up to stop the horses.

'There!' he said, pointing to an island nearly half a mile ahead of them. As they drew closer, they could see it. It looked like every other eyot they had passed, an island not fifty feet square that held some tall trees and shrubs. And a statue. Its natural stone colour had a greenish tinge and it was festooned with ivy, but it was unmistakeable. A statue of a man, some twenty feet high, holding aloft a spear with a shield in his left hand.

'That is Culmenion, founder of the city of Zerannon and friend of the Wych folk – possibly their last human friend. When they were driven here after the wars with Chira, he acted as their protector and the two peoples swore to defend each other's interests. This statue was put here so the Wych folk could be summoned in times of dire need; oaths were sworn and they were set to be allies in perpetuity. Then Culmenion died in suspicious circumstances, and the Wych folk blamed the humans and vice versa. After some bloody skirmishes they withdrew into the forest and have hardly been seen since.' Cedric looked at his audience, a look of triumph in his eyes.

'Hopefully that will change now.'

Morgan could see a low hill some distance from the bank.

'We camp there. Cedric and I will travel to the island and stay there; the rest of you stay at the main camp. If you see a bunch of pointy-eared maniacs swarming and killing us make sure you escape, get to Zerannon and sit out the winter there.'

His instructions were carried out. Once the camp was set up, Haelward helped Morgan with the trunk of golden artefacts. Struggling manfully, they stepped into the river with it, Cedric following with his walking stick. The shock of the cold water made them all recoil. The water seemed shallow enough until it was stepped into and by the time they got to the island they were all shivering. The ground was completely overgrown but they managed to beat a large enough area flat to set both the trunk and themselves down. Haelward bade them farewell and made to step back into the river. Morgan caught his arm first.

'Take charge of the others. I meant what I said. If something happens to us, don't rush to our rescue. I don't want anyone else lost on this trip.' 'We all volunteered for this,' Haelward replied. 'Don't blame yourself for what happened on the mountain. It was a miracle only one of us was lost. But I will do as you ask.' And with that he plunged back into the river.

Morgan found enough dry wood to start a small fire; they dried their soaking feet, not caring if the fire drew attention – the cold drove away any fear of the Wych folk for the time being. Once this was done they moved towards the statue.

At the statue's feet on the plinth the stone had been shaped into a bowl, cracked at the edges but still serviceable. Cedric ran his fingers over it. 'The herbs go here, I presume.' He opened a small pack he had slung around his shoulder and pulled out a soft leather pouch. He pulled open a flap and emptied its contents into the bowl. Morgan watched as a variety of leaves, some yellow, some waxy green, others black and crumbled, fell out. 'Lamb's foot, spitweed, yellow heartphlox and blackleaf, all rare and difficult to find. Wych magic is different to ours and closely tied to the earth. I just hope we have enough of these herbs here.' There was still plenty of room in the bowl. 'Now, the incantation. I just hope my ancient Aelvish is up to the mark.'

He opened up a book he had taken from his pack, turned to the right page, took a deep nervous breath and started to read.

> 'Vyaza culeth, shenia azha tulevaa
> Vheznia ule sylvazh azha nyava
> Meon al eona sea vavanaa Tesha
>   Ve nesteron ate.
>
> Tune oro tune voto kele mushedron
> Tutonos enae hashara thenestron
> Azha eliath ezho con eonon
>   Ve nesteron ate.
>
> Cucaniele kele zhuro beniath
> Cantele oliath nesterenta azhuntath
> Ze voto branate, strakate onherath
> Ta luno conemeon
> za fenosen azharath
>   Ve nesteron ate.'

A shower of autumn leaves twisted around them, carried by the swirling breeze. In the trees a bird was giving full voice to his song while all around them the river splashed, gurgled and foamed. But nothing else happened.

Cedric looked disconcerted.

'Ummmm...'

The leaves sat still in the bowl, protected from the wind. He reached in to pick them up, to start the ritual again. As he did so his trembling fingers brushed the cold stone of the bowl's lip.

Suddenly the leaves ignited with a cold blue flame. Cedric barely had time to get his hands out of the way, but in doing so he slipped backwards on the wet ground and would have fallen but for Morgan catching him in time. They both watched the statue.

The flame moved rapidly upwards, covering the legs and torso and then swathing the head. The flame was a vivid blue, not the blue of a cold fire, but of a blue so intense that it could only be magical. It sprang from the head on to the arm holding aloft the spear, whence it climbed until only the spear itself was wrapped in its radiance. From the tip of the spear the flame shot upwards into the sky. There it remained, the spear covered in its flame, a flame seemingly sustained by the air. The two men stood watching the pyrotechnics.

'Quite the sight,' said Morgan, whistling softly. 'No more than you deserve after reciting that verse. There can't be many men who can speak that language these days.'

'I would be foolhardy if I said I could speak it; it's written here – I learned it by rote. The language of the Wych folk has changed since this was written, not greatly, but like all languages it evolves. Hopefully I have enough of their tongue that I can communicate with them when they arrive.'

'I hope so, I would rather not conduct delicate negotiations through mime.'

'Ha!' laughed Cedric. 'That would be something to see. Come, let's eat; we can do nothing now but wait.'

And wait they did as day turned into night. As the light faded the flame grew ever brighter, its cerulean radiance seeming to bathe the island and making sleep difficult for its two human occupants. The flame gave no warmth, so they huddled in their blankets as the leaves fell around them.

'I am sorry about your friend,' said Cedric. 'As Haelward said, though, you mustn't blame yourself. If it is anyone's fault, it is mine. None of us would be here without my instigation.'

'No, it is no one's fault. We all volunteered for this... Actually, no, we are all being paid, but it was I who selected him. When you serve in an army your colleagues become very close to you; the bonds you forge are very strong. You all depend on each other in a fight, you know; you watch each other's backs. Rozgon was an experienced man when I joined up. He showed me the ropes, looked out for me until I knew which end of a sword to hold. I should have seen that ambush coming; I thought those creatures were too stupid even to do that, even though I thought it seemed too easy the first time we drove them off. They had obviously decided then to ambush us further down the road, when there was no fire to stop them. My carelessness did cost us, whether or not I am directly responsible for his death.'

'You got the rest of us through. As an academic man planning this trip, I gave no consideration to the sweat and suffering required to get us here. I am in debt to all of you, including Rozgon.'

'He was from the next village to me. I farmed; he was a soldier before the war. I knew his wife and kids before the Arshumans took them. He would send money back but for day-to-day things we all kept an eye on them, slipped them food, fixed their roof ... whatever was needed. It is what you do for a family in the army.'

'So you knew them for a long time then.'

'Yes,' said Morgan, looking up at the flame. 'Like so many, though, they were lost in the first year of the war.'

'Indeed, the dispute over Roshythe.'

'Yes, I believe our baron claimed the city and the Arshumans were looking for a pretext to start a war anyway. The fool of a man attacked them without permission from the Grand Duke and they responded by swarming the Seven Rivers with thousands of troops. Within weeks Athkaril was our eastern outpost. The damage done in those weeks was colossal. So many died, including Rozgon's family.'

'And your grandfather.'

Morgan stared fixedly into the flame. 'Yes, and my grandfather.'

Sleep did eventually claim him; it was not relaxed or comfortable but it was still sleep. When he awoke dawn had been and gone and the sunlight glinted through the branches of the trees.

The flame was still burning. Morgan eased himself up, stretched his legs and emptied his bladder. He saw Cedric standing at the northern tip of the isle, on bare ground, facing the forest.

BOOK ONE: AUTUMN

'Morning, Cedric. Those Keth-cursed Wych folk seem reluctant to show themselves, eh?'

'Not that reluctant,' said Cedric, pointing out across the water.

Morgan followed his finger. There, on the bank of the river directly opposite them, he saw three, no four, figures on horseback. He could make little else out; the sun reflecting on the water made it difficult to see, but he could see at least three of them carried spears.

'Oh, by Artorus's and Mytha's bleached-white bones, are we in trouble now!' He felt his sword in his scabbard, and his knife at his waist; it was the one he had last used on Rozgon. He shivered at the memory and released his grip.

'They are coming; they are in the river.' Cedric walked back up the bank towards the statue. 'We will receive them here. The trunk is there ... that's good. Right, Morgan, leave all the talking to me. Artorus only knows what will happen now.'

'I am happy to oblige you.' He stared fixedly at the approaching figures, their horses sending up plumes of water as they came across the river. He was starting to make out details. Three were cloaked and hooded in dark green. They all carried spears but the lead figure, riding a white horse, was different. Morgan saw at once why. It was a woman.

The other figures sought to conceal themselves but she was doing the exact opposite. She was tall, slim and carried a bow, and she was covered in dazzling gold. He could see a torque around her neck and a belt buckle that seemed to be made of nothing else. Suddenly the gold objects in the trunk seemed a little less splendid or indeed important. It was not a comforting thought.

They were here now. Two figures remained by the bank, their horses ankle deep in the water, but the woman and her remaining companion continued on to the island, riding through the scrub with seeming little thought for it. Then they, too, were by the statue and Morgan could see them properly at last.

The one with the spear had thrown back his hood; it was a man, pale skinned with eyes as blue and cold as arctic snow. His hair was inky black with a bluish sheen; his ears, as Haelward said, were nowhere near as dramatically pointed as he expected but were better described as 'gracefully curved'. He wore armour of hardened leather and Morgan quickly noticed his spear was tipped with obsidian glass. He regarded them icily. Morgan switched his attention to the girl.

Her hair was a similar glossy black colour to the man's and was held in a ponytail behind her by some golden cord. It reached down far beyond her hips, maybe even down to her knees, and periodically it was secured by further cords running down the length of her hair like bands. She had a single braid, too, that crossed her forehead where a small white gem was fixed to it at the centre. Her ears, graceful and delicate, had at least half a dozen small golden rings through the lower lobe. She wore leather, too; at first Morgan thought it black but then realised it was the darkest of greens. Both her jerkin and breeches fitted her like a second skin; he could not even see where her pointed boots joined the trousers, such was the closeness of the fit. And the belt buckle, like the thin torque around her neck, was gold – not chunky but carved delicately into a shape not unlike a coiled rope or a twisting snake. Her arms were bare and, apart from her head and neck, this was the only skin she displayed; unlike her head and neck, though, they were covered in tattoos. Not the clumsy efforts sported by soldiers; these were a fine, elegant tracery, coming together to form shapes like leaves, spider webs or thin branches, running up her arms on to her shoulders where they disappeared beneath her clothes. He thought of the crude tattoos he bore; it was like comparing the brush strokes of a great artist with the daubs of a five-year-old child. But it was her face that held him most. He had seen many fragile beauties in his time but they were forgotten in a trice here. Her skin was the palest translucent white, clear of blemishes, contrasting sharply with her coal-black hair. Her nose, thin and retrousse´; her cheekbones high without being angular; her chin pointed without being sharp; her lips thin and of the deepest burnt red, and her eyes, soft and almond shaped and a pale violet. That threw him momentarily but, yes, that was the colour they were; just as Haelward had mentioned. He then realised that for all her physical delicacy she was regarding the two of them with just as much icy hostility as the man. He suddenly realised that he had been seduced by the legendary beauty of the elves and pulled himself together immediately; this was no time to lose concentration.

She rode a step or two ahead of her companion and with a liquid grace slid off her horse. There was no saddle. Morgan also noticed a curved metal knife at her belt and his heart sank further. So they had iron, too. Her movements reminded him of a cat as she stepped towards Cedric who held his arms open in a welcoming gesture.

'Satala Aelvazharath ve tafalla ate co mhezhia sea Hemenestra.'

Cedric spoke in the voice Morgan knew he used for public speaking. There was no change in either expression of the elves. Then the man spoke. *'Zuke te nesteratse Aelveth nestezho vuto zheke voto iozho thenessate.'*

Cedric looked at Morgan. 'I believe he is asking for reasons why they shouldn't kill us; I had better make my reply a worthy one.'

The girl who was standing directly in front of Cedric raised her hand.

'Fesna! Tiavon. Al brachian olea uva tafal drezhemekh.' Her voice was clear, pure and commanding, reinforcing Morgan's belief that she was the one in charge here. She slowly circled the silent Cedric. She appeared to be smelling him as well as looking intently at every detail of his clothes and hair, even of his reading glasses. Then, when she was face to face with him, she spoke again.

'How did you know this ritual?' She indicated the statue.

'You speak our language, my Lady! That is good to know.' Cedric sounded flustered. 'Let me introduce myself. I am Cedric of Rossenwood, a scholar who has attempted a study of your people, albeit a poor one. This book has details of the ritual in question; I had no idea that it would work.'

If the girl understood him, she gave no indication. Rather she walked up to Morgan and stood face to face with him, not two feet away. She was his height, if not a little taller. She stared directly into his eyes, Morgan refused to blanch or change expression; rather he stared right back into those deep pale amethysts. He heard her sniff, quietly. She circled him now; she could easily pull out her knife and drive it into his back but he didn't move. She faced him again, her expression had changed slightly, and he could almost discern a certain wry amusement in her.

'You are a warrior, yes?' Her accent was soft, almost slurred, her voice like honey pouring over warm bread. 'Yes,' he replied stiffly.

'So here we have a sick man and a warrior who know a ritual forgotten in time. What could they possibly want with us, I wonder?'

Cedric turned to her. 'You know of my illness?'

'It is obvious, is it not? You come here seeking death? You may find it anyway.'

'No,' said Cedric. 'Aid, not death.'

'That, sick man, is not for you to decide.'

She was still looking at Morgan, her nose wrinkling. He decided to sniff her back, as loudly as possible. To his surprise, she did have a scent; it was like water. Not like the shallow river that surrounded them but rather a deep watercourse flowing swiftly, heavy with black sediment and autumn leaves; a clear fresh smell of clean air redolent of wood bark and pine resin. When he sniffed, she regarded him anew.

'Your name?' she asked.

'It is Morgan, Morgan of Glaivedon. And yours?'

'I am called Itheya. Itheya Morioka of the clan Morioka. The man who wishes to kill you is called Tiavon. He, too, is a warrior.'

'And you? Are you a warrior?'

'Of a kind,' she said. She was still barely two feet from him, her breath was on him and her gaze never moved. Cedric decided to break the impasse; he turned and walked towards her.

'My Lady, shall we get down to the business of why we requested your presence. I...'

She raised her hand again. 'Not so fast... I do not speak your language every day. Slowly, if you wish to be understood.'

Morgan asked her. 'How did you learn our language?'

Her eyes narrowed. 'You hemenestas, humans, come to our forest sometimes, to steal our gold, or preach the word of your gods. We kill most of them but one of your god men stayed with us a while. He taught me.'

'And where is he now?'

'Dead.'

'Did you kill him?'

'Do you wish I had?'

'Perhaps.'

Her long eyelashes fluttered slightly. 'No, I did not kill him.'

She reached out with her fingers towards his chin where there was a two-day growth of stubble. *'Vheyuzhe, Vheyuzhene Hemenest!'* she called out to her companion. She seemed amused.

'She is calling you hairy, a hairy human,' said Cedric.

'We have other names for humans.' said Itheya. 'Vheyuzheke, "the hairy ones", is one of them. It likens you to the mindless creatures of the mountains or the distant anthropoids of the southern jungles. It is not complimentary. She stroked his chin again, a light gossamer touch, almost tender.

'Fezhaye camma na Vheyuzheko, Itheya! Em olea brusha thitroska!' Tiavon shouted angrily at her.

She turned to him, her retort equally abrasive: *'Hashara coth ve ne, Tiavon! Teo pabran atan zhelen! Kileta ton ve crizhona te fesnath eonona tafall hlem ata eme!'* She stalked away from Morgan towards Tiavon and the two of them carried on a hushed conversation in angry tones. Cedric sidled towards Morgan.

'I think he came close to calling her a slut for touching you. She told him to know his place, so she obviously has some status among them. The two of them also seem to be more than just acquaintances; I think she forgot for a second that I can understand some of what they say.'

'Are you saying that I made the Wych man jealous?' Morgan couldn't suppress a smile.

'I believe that is exactly what you did, my friend; just keep smiling at her.'

The two elves separated. Tiavon remained seated on his horse but looked a little less hostile and a little more humble if that was possible. Itheya came back to the two of them; she stopped for a second as if collecting herself.

'What do you wish to discuss with us?'

'How someone who has barely met anyone that speaks our language knows the word "anthropoid".' Morgan couldn't help himself; he gave her the slightest of smiles.

She returned it, but it was laced with sarcasm.

'This man who taught me had travelled to these places; he used the word a lot. If that is all you have to say, we are leaving. If you have not gone by tomorrow at dawn, we will come back and kill you.' She turned to mount her horse.

'Wait!' said Cedric. 'We require your aid. There is a war and we need your help.'

She stopped, her back stiffening. Slowly she turned and approached Cedric. Morgan was again reminded of a prowling cat; her expression now was one of cold anger.

'We know of your war. There are passes in the mountains you know nothing of and we watch you. If you think we are going to risk the lives of our people in your petty little arguments, you are madder and stupider than I thought. You people are nothing to us. I have changed my mind; you have two hours to leave. Then I will return with fifty others and your heads will decorate the ends of our spears. Goodbye!' Her voice rose as she spoke, her fury barely contained. As she turned again, though, Morgan spoke to her – what was there to lose?

'Our heads would stick a lot firmer on iron spearheads rather than stone, don't you think?'

She stopped again, the sunlight dappling her white neck either side of the ponytail. Ignoring Tiavon, she pushed her face inches away from his, their noses almost touching. 'What are you saying?'

Cedric spoke: 'Our Grand Duke, the Mhezhen of our people, wishes to offer you iron weapons in return for your assistance in this war. Would this not give you an advantage over the other tribes in the forest?'

Itheya craned her neck slightly in his direction. 'If you really knew our people, then you would realise that such weapons would be distributed equally among us in order to retain the balance between tribes that has stood for aeons. You need to go back to your studies, sick man.'

'My resources for learning about you are limited,' he said; his voice was calm, measured and reasonable. 'There are little written records about you; as you said yourself, humans who come into contact with you often end up dead. Personally, I would love to learn more of your ways. Maybe it would foster a better understanding between our peoples.' Cedric's earnestness was disarming. Even Itheya stopped and thought for a second.

'Your intentions seem good, even if you are happy for our people to die for nothing in your wars. Your Mhezhen has offered us iron before, in the distant past; it did not convince us then and so it is not enough now. You have men that fight for gold. Pay them instead.'

'I did not think it would be enough, and so I have other things to show you.' He went towards the trunk, and Itheya and Morgan followed. Slowly he opened the trunk, letting Itheya look inside. She was silent. One by one she picked up the smaller objects – the snake, the beaver – lifting them to the sunlight, looking at the way the light played on the gemstones. Tiavon leaned forward, trying to get a better look.

'Where did you get these?' she whispered.

'There are ruins, old buildings of your people, close to the sea. I discovered them there, not a few months ago, and thought you had better see them.' 'Atem Sezheia,' she said quietly.

'City of light – yes, I believe that is what you called it. These things were all there, in a tunnel, secured behind a stone door.'

She delicately lifted the dragon. 'What is this, I wonder?'

Morgan was surprised. 'You don't know?'

'These come from a time before our wars with your empire; only a few of us would know all of the details. We thought our people over the sea had taken everything with them and that Atem Sezheia had little of value in its remains. And what is this?'

She replaced the dragon and pulled out the tooth. After scrutinising it for a second her expression turned to one of astonishment. 'Tiavon Dragan, Moliea Dragan!' Tiavon did not reply; he appeared to be equally shocked by what he saw.

'Even I cannot read much of what is written here,' she said to them. 'But this find,' she lifted the tooth, 'could be more precious than all of the others put together and multiplied by a hundred. Were there any more finds there?' 'Yes,' said Cedric. 'Including another of those teeth and another five of those dragons; each dragon appears to be different from the others.'

Tiavon spoke again: *'Thenessek azha tiehe co darahenezharon.'*

Cedric smiled. 'He really wants to kill us, doesn't he?'

She looked at him. 'You are human; it is reason enough.' She then turned back to Tiavon.

'In han meru deveken. Za spetu olea ial em dea tonu cantelevened per z'ezhed mustoen. Za meruzha olea ial em codosh neto celza desena. Ve teshele tafalla nesteretsava uven Foron. Voe, Wyatha onatazh polek.'

At this, Tiavon bowed, turned his horse and joined the two elves in the river. Itheya turned back to the men.

'My father is Mhezhen of my tribe. I will need to speak to him of this. The fire here will remain burning. While it does so, none of our people will kill you and take the objects for themselves, as it would not be honourable. Stay here until I return. I will put out the fire then.' 'And what then?' asked Morgan.

'I know not,' she said, springing on to her horse. 'Maybe we kill you; maybe not.'

'Wait,' said Cedric. He handed her the serpent. 'Take this as proof of our trust and goodwill.'

She looked surprised. 'It is not necessary. But if you wish, I will take it. I will return in a day or two with my father's reply.'

Without a second glance at them she skilfully turned her horse and was gone with the others. They heard the splashing of the river as the four of them rode, finally disappearing under the eaves of the dark forest.

25

She stood on the low hill looking at the dusk. To her right, by a knot of trees, a group of rabbits were feeding and playing, chasing each other into the underbrush. Above her, small birds darted and flitted against the darkening sky. No, not birds, bats feeding on the night insects which she already could feel brushing her face and hair. The air was warm, sweet and heavy; she drank it in like wine. She was surrounded by a ring of knights, and when she took her position they saluted her: 'Hail Cheris, mage of battle.' She didn't know how to reply so bowed to them, glad they couldn't see her blushing.

She was facing eastwards, the hill being at the southern point of the field. To her left, the army of Baron Felmere was deploying. She had expected much more noise but what they did was done with a quiet efficiency that impressed her. Ahead of her, a mile away, possibly less, was a copse; she could see men lining up there. As she moved her head to the left, she could see torches and the banners of the Arshumans as they lined up in response. To the far north and east, the field was bounded by the hill on which stood the town of Grest. The hill was covered in trees; she hoped Marcus was safely ensconced in them somewhere. The high ground provided a good defence for the city, but it still had sturdy stone walls. Squinting, she could see the catapults and war machines perched on them. She guessed that there was maybe an hour of light left; something had to start soon.

At the other end of the field, in the position of honour on the left, Lukas Felmere sat with Dominic Hartfield and the Silver Guard. Their banners flapped above them, though their heraldic insignia were difficult to see in the murk. Normally, the signalmen with their flags would sit with them, ready to display the orders visually to the soldiers, but they had been dispensed with that night. All orders would be transmitted via the cornets and drums of the musicians. Things could go wrong that way – if something was misheard for example – but there was obviously no choice here.

'There was no way the town gates could have been opened in

daylight?' Dominic asked. 'So many things can go wrong in a night attack.'

'No,' said Felmere, 'our agents are risking much as it is; they were too frightened to betray the garrison by day.'

As he spoke, a clear horn sounded from the dark block of Felmere's men. 'Ah, my men have deployed. Once the rest of the infantry have lined up –and it won't take long – we will get the archers to fire off a few volleys while they can. Then they can withdraw.'

'The light horse will protect them and if they get charged Reynard's knights will see the Arshumans off.' Dominic nodded at the Eagle Claw, positioned just ahead of them.

Felmere looked at the younger man. 'I have seen so many battles; every time I hope it is the last one, the key one to finish this damned broil. May Artorus let this be it. I am getting too old to sit in the saddle anymore. In five years my son will be of age; it would be good to bequeath him a stable, peaceful land.'

'I truly hope Artorus will do it for you,' said Dominic. 'But now is not the time to get wistful about it. See – Vinoyen and Haslan Falls are set.'

Felmere looked over the field. 'Indeed, signal the archers!'

From behind him the trumpets sounded. They stopped for a few seconds and then repeated the signal. Felmere's charger's ears pricked; it was a horse born for battle and its excitement was easy to read, even through its thick barding.

The knights watched as a thin line of dark-clad men emerged from the ranks of the troops and quietly crossed the field until they had the range of the enemy. The Arshumans still had not finished their deployment; quite a few were holding fiery torches, providing an easy target. Their broad yellow banners, stretching the width of their battle line, were easy to see, too. As the two men watched on, the archers let fly. Some three hundred bowstrings sang, the shafts released briefly darkening the sky before dropping on the unprotected Arshuman lines. This happened a few times until Felmere noticed the enemy cavalry preparing a charge. They had more cavalry than the Tanaren forces, including mercenaries – they always held the advantage in this respect –

so the Baron had the retreat signalled. As the archers withdrew, their own light cavalry rode out to screen and protect them. The Arshuman cavalry thought better than to advance and so held their ground. It was first blood to Tanaren.

Cheris watched this early skirmishing and felt her mouth go dry. Across the quiet field she could even hear the screams of men as the arrows fell upon them. As the archers withdrew from the field, running through the ranks of the infantry, the men of Tanaren let out a roar of triumph. The quiet was not about to return. She was still wondering whether or not to start casting her spells – and indeed which one she should choose and where she should cast it – when she felt something – a presence, something crackling in her mind, a frisson of electricity that made her shudder and tingle. Someone was out there, trying to read her. She scanned the darkening horizon, trying to sense the cause of this intrusion. Her eyes alighted on the copse. He was there, no doubting it, under the trees, surrounded by knights. They were almost directly opposite each other. How ironic! Lucan's humour was legendary after all. As she detected him, she felt him reach out to her. It was strange, this touching of minds; it was like having a shard of cold ice worming its way through her brain. One thing, though, there was no hiding now. Her staff hummed in her hand and she decided a touch of flamboyance was required. A quick word, a gesture, and the staff was covered in a blue nimbus of light which flickered up and down its length and crackled in her hand. Hopefully that will send him a small message, she thought, digging the staff into the soft ground. She decided to wait and see what this man could do, so she could try to counter him and gauge his power. The sky was indigo now, clouds splashed across it like dagger thrusts. The pale moon was finding its strength and the bats were still out; she saw one skitter across its luminous surface.

Suddenly there was a great throaty roar to her left. The soldiers were shouting, clashing their weapons against their shields and waving them at the enemy. The top of the hill was on fire.

Baron Felmere was grinning from ear to ear. They watched the flames move from catapult to catapult, turning them into great burning torches. The light from them illuminated the sky, throwing shapes on to the city's high towers. One of the great war machines pitched over the wall on to the hill below, where it ignited a pine tree. The tree burned, sending showers of sparks into the air. The fire was nearly certain to spread, Felmere thought, hopefully throwing the Arshuman lines into chaos.

'Signal the general advance.'

Trumpets sounded and the drums in the field answered. Slowly the blocks of infantry advanced, the largest, Felmere's own men, in the centre, flanked by Lasgaart's, Vinoyen's, Fenchard's and Maynard's men. The light cavalry flanked them on both sides. From their vantage point they heard the drummers beating out a steady two-four pattern.

'Watch out for their horse archers,' Felmere growled. 'They have haunted my dreams for years. It is the main way they outmatch us. We have tried mercenaries against them, heavy cavalry, long spears, but still they punish us. I have tried deploying archers between the infantry blocks here; it probably won't work but hopefully it will make them think.'

As if in response, the curved brass horns of the Arshumans sounded from across the field and their infantry slowly started to move forward, five blocks of men each numbering three to four hundred, the front ranks holding their yellow kite shields waist high, giving the appearance of a single entity such was their well-drilled precision. Their speed was glacial, though it gave time for the thin line of cavalry to form up in front of them, the lightly armoured horse numbering some three hundred or so. They started off at a gentle trot but gradually started to pick up speed as they advanced, soon leaving the footmen far behind them.

'And now we reach the next stage,' Dominic muttered under his breath.

Cheris watched the men advance, hearing their mailed boots on the soft grass and the clanking of metal armour and chain mail. The hoarse cries of the captains goading the men on, organising them, encouraging them, rose above the general cacophony. She gripped her staff with a clammy hand, finding its coldness reassuring, and then she realised that her opponent was up to something. She felt him reaching through the divide, pulling its power towards him. How could she thwart him? She shut her eyes trying to close the breach, stop the flow of energy he was drawing upon, but her heart sank as she realised she might well be too late. She could sense him, sense what he was doing, but getting into his brain and stopping him was another matter – he already had enough power for what he wanted to do.

'Shit!' she cursed to herself.

Her eyes opened and she saw it. In the copse she saw it glowing, a patch of incandescence among the trees. It rose into the air blotting out the emerging stars, a mini-sun standing out against the moon and the burning hill. It arced upwards and then started to drop, a ball of fire plummeting towards the rear ranks of Felmere's troops...

With mounting horror and feeling utterly helpless, the Baron watched the sorcerer's fire dropping on to his men. He saw the rear ranks scatter, desperately trying to get out of the way, but it was too late for some. The fireball crashed among them, exploding in an inferno of red and white flame that threw people ten feet into the air and immolated other poor souls who just happened to be in the wrong place at the wrong time.

'Mytha's claw!' the Baron growled. 'How many did we lose then? Twenty? Thirty?'

'About that,' said Dominic. 'But the men are regrouping; they are made of strong stuff... It could have been a lot worse.'

'Maybe. But it was just as well it didn't get Fenchard's or Maynard's men; I have serious doubts about their quality. We probably wouldn't see their arses for dust if it had hit them.'

'If they get through this, they will be the stronger for it. See, the line is moving again.' Dominic spoke with some satisfaction; Felmere was not nearly so happy.

'Where was our damned mage then? Is she dead? She was supposed to be stopping this.'

'I don't think she is dead. Maybe naive and unused to battle. Maybe she should have gone up the hill instead of Marcus.'

'No, the catapults are blazing; at least we don't have them to contend with.'

Dominic jerked his head in the direction of Grest. 'But look at that fire; he is probably trapped up there until it dies.'

'That is battle, my friend. You can plan for months but always the Gods will throw the unexpected at you. And now it's the horse archers; see, they have hidden their yellow colours so as not to leave a mark. They are coming.' The Baron spoke through gritted teeth.

Night was almost upon them, but the fire on the hill threw a bloody crimson glow on to a battlefield dominated by long shadows and crepuscular shapes. The horsemen were riding at the front ranks of the army of Tanaren, releasing deadly volleys from their half-sized bows, then turning around and riding away, before the archers protected by the shieldmen about them, could draw a bead on them.

But, despite all that, the infantry still advanced, stepping over and around the dead and wounded, leaving them to be stretchered off by the orderlies hovering behind the battle lines, risking their own safety by trying to save what lives they could. The drummers still beat out their rhythm and the infantry of the enemy drew closer and closer.

Cheris was angry and embarrassed. The Arshuman mage had hoodwinked her entirely and men were dead because of it. Part of her wanted to run off and sob behind the nearest tree, to curse the Gods for putting her in this situation, but another part of her, that competitive part, the one that hated losing even at the games of pitch stones she played as a child against the college walls, was being awakened.

Don't be angry! she told herself. It leads only to bad decisions and mistakes – be cold, be frosty! Marcus is trapped on the hill, so it is down to you and no one else. Think girl, Think!

Rather than going for the spectacular, she decided on a different tactic. Moving closer to the knights protecting her so that she wouldn't inadvertently hit them, she assayed a flowing gesture with her left hand, pointed her staff forward and whispered, *'Cuveatanu parissima!'*

The language was that of the Arcane, words of power from ancient sources such as the earliest Kozean or the elves of the plains. Potent words, a vocalisation of that energy touched across the divide, designed to focus the mana she was drawing from the Plane of Lucan, that magical realm that maybe only one person in ten or even fifty thousand was capable of reaching or seeing.

From her staff a blue-white bolt shot forth. It was aimed in the general direction of the Arshuman lines but that was not important. What was important was how her enemy responded. The bolt was just short of the whirling Arshuman cavalry when it disappeared, dispelled by the enemy mage. Cheris tried another and another, each one with the same result. She aimed a slightly more powerful one above the heads of the horses, only for it to disappear in a shower of green and red sparks like a Tarindian firework, causing a couple of the horses to be spooked and throw their riders. To all outward appearances, this mage was countering her every move.

But she was satisfied. He was drawing on his staff's power to stop her, not on his own; the fireball had obviously drained him for a while. If she kept doing this, eventually his staff would be drained, leaving him with only his own resources to fall back on. Then she would have him.

'Pretty, isn't it?' said Dominic, watching Cheris's pyrotechnic display. 'But is it actually doing anything?'

'Actually yes, it is,' said Felmere. 'It is keeping their mage busy. She may not have his power but we will get no more fireballs while this keeps on going on.'

'But what if he kills her?'

'It will be regrettable, but she is serving her purpose at the present. The Grand Duke has approved another mage for us. I was going to give him to Esric in the south. The troops involved in the southern war are much fewer and a mage could make a bigger difference there, but if we lose one here we have a ready replacement.'

Dominic nodded at this news, then saw the latest development in the battle below them. 'The horse archers are withdrawing; they will sit on either flank of their army from now on.'

'And now we are coming down do what really matters in every battle I have ever fought.'

'The press of men?' asked Dominic.

'The press of men.'

On both sides the troops had stopped marching. They stood facing each other, not a hundred yards apart. To the Arshumans' right the hill still burned. The Tanarese captains watched their enemy – their shields locked together, spears held forward above them, their broad yellow banners bearing nothing else but the number of each unit, one to five. There was no denying they looked more cohesive than the Tanaren army, the blue of Felmere and Tanaren, the green of Vinoyen, the red of Lasgaart, but it was heart that won a battle, not colours, especially where numbers were evenly matched like this. The signal came from the hill behind them and to the left where Felmere was stationed. At once the cry went up.

'Shield wall!'

The men drew closer to each other locking the edge of their shields over that of the man next to them. They had each been provided with a spear, which, like the Arshuman soldiers, they now held over the shield, pointing it outward towards the foe. Although they had their regular weapons, which they would use as soon as was practicable, the spear was always the first weapon used when shield walls clashed. Up and down the ranks the men were encouraging each other.

'I am with you, Tarek.' said a man with a broad grey beard to his companion, a man almost identical in every respect except for a bleeding wound on his scalp.

'We stand with each other' was a common imprecation called out by many captains on both sides.

'Those yellow dogs won't push us back,' cried a man in the front rank. He was young and was shouting to overcome his nerves, exhorting himself as much as anyone else.

'Mytha is with us, friend. Fear is for the enemy, not us.' That from his captain who stood not ten feet from him, trying to sound as reassuring as possible.

Then came the second signal, the one they had waited for. The captains called out.

'Advance!'

As if in reply the Arshuman horns blared out their own chorus.

Slowly, keeping rank discipline, the two sets of men moved over the soft earth towards each other.

Cheris stopped for a second. It would take all night to drain his staff in this manner, she thought; maybe another approach was in order. Options raced through her mind and she had decided on trying something a little more powerful when she sensed him again, earlier this time.

He was trying another fireball.

She looked ahead and to her left. The infantry was closely packed, preparing to engage the enemy; a fireball in the front ranks now would be devastating. She knew what she had to do.

For the first time that night she drew on the power of her staff. She saw the other realm in her mind, could see her foe, as before, attempting to pull power from it to fuel the conflagration he wished to inflict upon her battle brothers. Not this time, she thought. Not this time.

She put herself between him and the divide. The power he was drawing she pulled into herself, and as it entered her mind she felt numb and shocked, as though she had shoved her head into a bucket of ice water. The power itself was unfocused – because it was not her who had called it forth, it was too amorphous for her to shape and use, so she released it into her staff whence it shot forth in a spectacular display of blue, green and white light, exploding among the stars above her.

Across the field in the copse a ball of fiery red that had been growing slowly for many heartbeats sputtered and went out.

She suddenly found herself leaning on the staff, her legs felt weak; draining his power had cost her a little, after all. She collected herself, breathing heavily. She remembered Anaya talking about how the constant use of her powers had a price; she needed a minute to gather her strength. Seeing her straitened condition, Sir Norton turned and faced her.

'Are you all right, my Lady?'

'Fine,' she gasped. 'Thank you, I am fine.'

She consoled herself with the thought that the mage facing her had tried two fireballs; he would hardly be full of vigour himself. The battle between the two of them would be as much a war of attrition as that about to take place in the plain beneath her.

There were barely twenty yards between the opposing factions. The baiting between them was in full swing.

'Come and get your moustaches trimmed!' a young joker in Vinoyen's ranks called out.

'You can't hold a spear with six fingers,' a man in the Arshuman first company called back. In Arshuma the men of Tanaren were often seen as rustic or inbred.

'My grandma could take on you lot, and she's been dead six years!' A Felmere man, better armoured than his companions, an obvious veteran with a poor opinion of his enemy.

'Get some of this, you snail-eating sacks of shit!' A man in the Lasgaart front ranks, lofting his axe. He was clean-shaven and weather-beaten with the broad musculature of the farmer; obviously a man not educated in the language of the biting satirist.

'I am gonna wipe my arse with your baby-blue banner!' A young Arshuman in the Fourth Company, wearing the conical helmet so favoured by his companions. He was referring to the banner of Tanaren, whose colour matched the traditional one of the first gift given to a male new-born back in his home town.

The pace of the drumming had got more frenetic as the sides moved closer, but then suddenly, with barely fifteen yards between them, it stopped. Just for a second, apart from the crackling of burning wood and the mournful hoot of a single owl, silence reigned. They were close enough to see the faces of their enemy and fleetingly they saw how young they were, how small, how nervously they held the spear wavering before them, how the sweat stood out beaded on their faces, plastering hair to their heads. They could see their stubble, their blackened teeth, their breath frosting in the crisp night air. They imagined their personal effects, mementoes and letters from their family, small carved wooden figures of the Gods all secreted as close to their person as possible. No one wanted to die unremembered, after all.

Then – as the horns sounded the charge.

Shields locked, spears gripped before them, they obeyed. And they shouted and roared, a bestial roar from the bottom of their primeval souls as the battle lust overtook them.

From their vantage point Dominic and Felmere heard the shock of the shields clashing, wood and metal hammering against each other as the great push and shove of battle began. Ahead of them, Reynard Lanthorpe and his resplendent heavy cavalry started to move into a flanking position supported by the light cavalry.

'We will move down shortly,' said Felmere 'We need to see what their cavalry does first.'

'They have no heavy cavalry to speak of, which is good; at least there will be no lances riding into the backs of our men.'

'Nor into theirs unfortunately; their cavalry protect them too well. Our job is to wait for a break in their ranks and to try and push a wedge through them.' 'It may take a while,' said Dominic. 'Their discipline is as strong as ours.'

'Not to mention, their general watches out for the weak links in his men so that he can execute them afterwards. Felmere indicated with his arm: between the copse holding their mage and the furthest south of the Arshuman infantry blocks was a small, rocky hill. Perched on it under a yellow-and black-banner was the Arshuman general, mounted, surrounded by some thirty heavy cavalry, the only unit of its type that they possessed.

'That's King Aganosticlan for you, a man who thinks nothing of his subjects aside from what they can do for him.' Dominic's tone was deeply disapproving.

'Yet a formidable foe nevertheless; he must have drained his treasury many times over to keep this war going, and he refuses to negotiate a peace of any kind.'

'Nor should there be one, while Roshythe and Lake Winmead are in his hands.'

Felmere sighed. 'I have to admit, I no longer care. We have not held either of them for ten years and they are still a long way away from here. Sound the withdrawal.'

The horn signal came and the tired ranks, burnt out after a few minutes of desperate pushing and spear thrusting, withdrew from the fray, retreating until there was a gap between the armies of some twenty to thirty feet. The wounded were left in the no-man's-land writhing and crying pitifully. Ranks were redressed and everyone waited for the next signal.

Cheris watched the on-going conflict; she was feeling a little stronger now and her eyes were set on the Arshuman cavalry, which was effectively cocooning the flanks of the army, keeping them protected while also being poised to try and outflank the Tanaren soldiers should the opportunity arise. Her mind was racing with the things she could possibly do when she heard a swish and felt a draught as something flew inches past her nose.

'Get down!' shouted Sir Norton. He ran and stood in front of her as she crouched down to her knees. Some of the other knights ran off into the trees where shadowy figures could be seen starting to run from them. 'Assassins!' he said as she got up again. 'An arrow can kill you just as easily as it can kill me. My men will get them, don't you worry. Are you all right?'

'A little shaken,' she said, and she was too – her hands were trembling slightly. 'It never occurred to me that I would be targeted like that.'

'You have rattled them.' He smiled at her, itself a rare occurrence. 'They never expected you to be here.'

'Then I had better start doing something,' she said. She stopped the flame running up and down her staff. 'A silly vanity. I will not be doing that again.'

She saw the other knights return. None of them had been lost and blood smeared some of their surcoats.

'Dealt with?' Sir Norton asked.

'Yes, sir. They will not be coming back.'

Silently, they resumed their positions surrounding her. She breathed heavily, sensing the responsibility on her shoulders, took one look at the stars and made her next move. Pacing in a small circle she raised her staff and, facing inwards, recited over and over again:

'*Emiteverian luda tamrotos melian, emiteverian luda tamrotos melian.*'

At the centre of the circle, out of the air a ball of crackling blue light started to form. She continued to circle and recite the words as the ball grew larger, first the size of her fist, then the size of her head. The power inside her made her senses tingle; small strands of her hair started to stand upwards and wave about on their own account.

She knew it was going to happen, but suddenly she felt him inside her head. He was trying to do what she had done earlier – to take the power she was drawing from the other world away from her to send back into the void. She hardened her will and resisted. He then started drawing on his staff's power and it grew harder and harder for her to fight him. The ball was half the size of her now and she judged it to be enough, any more and he would nullify her spell. Before he could drag the power from her she raised both her arms high into the air. The ball – which had morphed a little and was now cylindrical in shape, sizzling and popping with bolts of blue and white effervescence – followed her arms in an upward trajectory. She held it there as her opponent made a final attempt to stop her short. He used so much power it almost knocked her off her feet and drew the breath from her body, but still she resisted. Planting her feet into the ground she fought hard to ignore the alien presence in her mind trying to siphon off her power, twisting all ways in its attempt to wrench the spell from her grasp. But he was failing. Pointing her staff at the horses, she had just enough inside her to utter a final croak – '*Ptaresass!*' – before slumping to her knees.

The cylinder changed again into a bolt of darkest cerulean, then in a shower of sparks and electricity it crashed into the cavalry on the Arshuman left flank.

'The girl learns fast,' said Felmere, impressed despite himself. The two men watched as the spell slammed into the light horse throwing riders from the saddle and terrifying the horses that started to run in all directions. In vain, the commanders tried to get them reorganised but many of them were as much at the whim of their panicked steeds as the rank and file.

'The flank is exposed,' said Dominic. 'She didn't kill that many but they are running all over the place.'

'Now is our chance! Signal Reynard and the light cavalry to keep the enemy's right flank busy and you and I shall try the left.'

'Let's hurry then,' said Dominic, pulling down his visor, 'before they regroup.'

From the perspective of a man in the front lines, little of these developments could be seen. Three times they had closed with the enemy, thrusting their spears at ankles, heads and arms and three times they had withdrawn with no clear advantage gained. A few men had thrown down their spears, either because they had shivered or because they weren't comfortable fighting with them, and had drawn swords, axes or maces to deal closer damage. This threatened the integrity of the shield wall as such men needed to swing their weapons rather than stand or push, but so far the wall had held. Most of them had grown up with derring-do tales of brave courtly knights and upright soldiers who dispatched their black-hearted enemies with a contemptuous swish of their blade. Nowhere in these tales did it say how hard it was to kill a man. He could be slashed, stabbed, hacked at; his bones could be crushed by a spiked mace; his blood vessels opened by sword or axe, but his breath would not stop – he just became more desperate and dangerous. One man who had lost his weapon and whose shield arm was crushed and limp fended off sword thrusts with his bare hands, eventually grabbing his assailant and turning his own blade against him. They continued to fight, wrestling on the ground, blood soaking their surcoats even when the lines withdrew. No quarter was asked between enemies who knew each other so well and none was given in return. The front ranks, many carrying wounds ranging from scratches to deep cuts and gashes that were leaking blood, had been mostly relieved by the rear ranks. The fresh ranks were preparing for their first engagement when the word started to spread:

'The Arshuman cavalry is routed – they have quit the field!'

The rumour flew around the troops like the fire on Grest Hill and at once the men started to roar. The men of Haslan Falls and Maynard's who had been hard pressed and were beginning to quail gained fresh heart. They beat their weapons against their shields, a deafening noise made worse for the Arshumans because the hill threw back an echo of it making it sound as if they were surrounded. The sense of the battle starting to turn was compounded further as they heard the trumpets of Baron Felmere and the Silver Guard, not from behind the Tanarese lines but to their right. Being few in number the shock cavalry only deployed when a decisive blow was in the offing. The shields were beaten even harder, and the men invoked the names of Tanaren, Felmere, Mytha and Artorus. Then the charge sounded perhaps for the final time.

Cheris was feeling smug. It had taken only a few minutes for the queasy feeling to subside and the jelly in her legs to firm up again. She felt tired but strong, and watched with satisfaction as the Arshuman cavalry was scattered to the four winds and was probably beyond regrouping. She was worried some of them might head her way but saw that a line of crossbowmen had come across to protect them – they appeared to be having a great time peppering the confused horse with well-placed quarrels. She watched as the lines came together again for another bloody push and shove, and saw the shock cavalry of the Silver Guard and Baron Felmere himself plough into the unguarded Arshuman flank.

If they thought the unit would crumble, though, they were to be disappointed. This was the first unit, based on the left flank, the Arshuman elite. They buckled heavily as the horse and the infantry of Maynard and

Fenchard engaged them, but they did not give ground and flee. She felt a little helpless – one of her destructive spells could not be targeted while the troops were in combat for fear of injuring her own men. She had to wait and sit it out.

She realised the whole battle was in the balance here. If the Arshuman first unit held, then the Tanaren reserves had been spent in vain. The Arshuman General had joined the conflict with his bodyguard; if the infantry of Fenchard could be pushed back, the whole Tanaren line could fold in on itself, collapsing like a pack of cards. What could she do to help? She sensed a strange prickling in her head. What was that exactly?

Suddenly she pitched to her knees, dropping her staff. She felt as if she was lying flat, a heavy door being pressed on her chest, and desperately she gasped for air. A crushing spell. A mage killer! A spell used to directly target an enemy spell-caster, it was tantamount to an assassination attempt. She had only a cursory knowledge of such spells, never thinking that she would need or encounter one of them. Such an omission could be the death of her, she realised. She desperately tried to inhale but no air reached her lungs. She clawed at the earth, a line of dribble fell from her opened mouth, tears slid down her cheeks. In a flash she thought of her family whom she would never see again, of Marcus, of Sir Dylan, of Mikel and the friends she had made at the college. Her head pounded and blood started dripping from her nose. She rolled on her back in a foetal position clutching at her chest. Her ribs were pushing inwards – soon they would stab her lungs and it would all be over. A figure loomed over her. It was Sir Norton, concern writ large on his face. For all that, he could do nothing to help her, for she was totally in the grip of her opponent. He had bested her, he was bending all his power on her, including all of that in his staff. If she could but survive, hold off the deadly assault, then he would be vulnerable.

She stared glassily at Sir Norton, small droplets of blood forming in the corners of her eyes, a thin line of blood-flecked drool running from the corner of her mouth. Using every ounce of strength, every sinew, every muscle available to her, she managed to barely gasp the following two words;

'My ...... staff.'

He understood immediately – picking it up and clasping it into her right hand. Her head felt it was about to explode, like one of those melons the jousting knights would practise their skills on in the Summer Festival. But then she felt the staff. It was damp from the wet grass and she was unsure if she had ever touched metal as cold as this, but she forced herself to open her mind, to let its power flow through her and so counteract the vice that was squeezing her into oblivion. It rushed through her like a blood supply. Soon she could use it to ease the pressure on her. There was a sharp crack as a rib snapped, and she screamed with the pain; it should have been an agonised, piercing shriek but instead only a hoarse gasp came out.

'Focus, Cheris, focus, use its power, ease the grip upon you.' And slowly this happened. Almost imperceptibly, the tiniest wisp of air slipped through her bloodied nose and into her damaged lung. The wisp grew into a trickle, and then a stream, and then a strong river, as strong as the Vinoyen. She felt him try and reassert his authority over her but this time she held firm. She used her staff against him until he stopped; there was still much power in it, enough to return warmth and feeling to her fingertips. She knew he was spent, his staff drained. She rolled on to her knees and drank the air as a man in the desert drinks when he finds an oasis. Her shattered rib pushed into her like a dagger thrust and she screamed again, this time a shrill full-throated scream, as her colour returned and she regained control over her wracked body. She spat a gobbet of blood and spittle on to the ground and indicated to Sir Norton to lift her to her feet. As he assisted her, he looked directly into her face and took a step back, surprised by what he saw there. There was pure devilry in her blue-grey eyes.

'That bastard!' she whispered in cold fury. 'He won't get the chance to do that to me again.'

She was on her own two feet, a little wobbly, but her anger overrode any exhaustion she was feeling.

'Fireballs, my friend, so you like fireballs.' She opened her arms in front of her.

'*Tera lakassa etu vidomatis.*'

Before her a small white flame appeared – how it danced between her palms as it slowly grew in size! She did not need the staff anymore, she sensed, and so had dug it into the ground behind her. Her revenge on this man would come from her own inner powers and not from any other devices. The flame had grown to be the size of her head; she could grow it further but she didn't really need to. She had to catch him before he ran. She placed her right arm behind her and gently assayed a throwing action while whispering the word –

'*Atulatesta.*'

Sir Norton looked up as the fireball sped high into the air before dropping, arcing downwards, as it sought out its target. The copse.

It illuminated all before it and he saw the terrified desperate figures under the trees turn and flee for their lives, but they were way too late.

The fireball crashed under the trees, igniting their branches until they were a crackling crown of flame. Under the trees there was an inferno. Cheris sought out her opponent's mind, trying to pin him down, seeing if he had anything left to face her with. All she felt was a brief second of terror and agony. Then nothing.

'He is dead,' she said to Sir Norton.

'Good, do you wish to retire from the field? You have done enough. The fire is nearly out on the hill and Marcus will be here soon.'

'No,' she said. 'There is one more thing left to do.'

It was desperate on the field. The men of Tanaren had the advantage, so it seemed, but the Arshumans refused to give way. They had reformed their lines and repulsed the cavalry assault, a colossal achievement in itself. Their units had dropped from five to four after reorganisation, their general was at their side, and their right flank, where Lanthorpe was having Keth's own time trying to pin the opposing cavalry down, was still protected. Both lines had withdrawn again, and thousands of exhausted, sweating men stared at each other, summoning the strength for yet another push. The euphoria among the Tanarese troops had gone, their wounds were hurting and their arms felt limp at their sides. It was the dead of night and the Arshumans still held the town and were not budging. For all Baron Felmere's promises, it was beginning to look as though they would be driven back and would spend the winter on the same patch of ground they had moved up from three days ago.

Some of the men looked up, as if searching for divine inspiration. The nearly full moon was strong now and the carpet of stars shimmered under its light. Then one of the men pointed. 'Look! Look there!'

As the men looked, they could see it was not a celestial object. It was spherical, a pale icy blue and it was growing in size. It was also directly over the centre of the Arshuman troops. It was plain that they had seen it, too. Men were pointing, looking nervously above them. The object continued to grow.

Back on the hill Cheris was chanting softly to herself. This was her favourite destructive spell. She had practised it many, many times, but the ball of lightning she conjured was never allowed to get larger than the size of her head, a standard measurement for the supervised initiate. This time there were no restrictions and no one to stop her and she wondered, just using her own powers, just how big the ball could get. It kept growing, now it was the size of her, and then of the horses standing by her caravan. The Arshumans underneath it were beginning to back away, forgetful of the discipline that had previously held their ranks so tightly together.

Now it was tree-sized, now it was house-sized, a colossal ball of fizzing blue energy. She lowered it a little, so it stayed not fifty feet above the heads of the enemy, the people who had left her crushed and bruised. Many of them were ignoring their commanders and were turning to flee. She saw this and decided it was time.

'*Meliotoris!*' she said, making a small downward gesture with her forefinger.

The ball dropped like a stone on to the upturned heads of the Arshumans.

Felmere sat on his charger, mouth agape. He almost felt sorry for them. As the ball crashed into the Arshuman line, it disintegrated, releasing a thousand forks of lightning. Some were azure, some turquoise, some green and some white. All of them shot through the bodies of the soldiers, leaping from one to another, hissing, sizzling and popping as they fried their screaming victims. In unison, the entire army broke and fled as the lightning died sputtering, its embers glowing green as they slowly disappeared leaving dozens of burnt corpses smouldering on the ground.

    The Tanaren knights put the gagging aroma of roasted flesh to the back of their minds as Felmere signalled the charge. Against hundreds of fleeing men with their backs turned it was a massacre, Arshumans fell like rain, as lances, spears and swords struck home again and again. They were pursued to the river where without a second thought many of them jumped in to be swept away by the current. The Arshuman general, having lost control of his steed, could only watch in horror as his horse plunged over the bank, dragging him in his full armour down into the foamy depths.

    In less than half an hour it was all over. Those who weren't dead or wounded, or who weren't lucky enough to cross the river (barely a hundred in number), were being rounded up as prisoners by the victorious troops. Baron Felmere, with Reynard Lanthorpe and a hundred knights, entered Grest shortly afterwards, encountering no resistance.

    And Cheris? As the lightning ball crashed to the floor exhaustion overtook her. Feeling as weak as a new-born and losing all control in her muscles, she crashed face down on to the ground. The last thing she remembered was the smell of wet earth and the moisture from the grass against her face.

BOOK ONE: AUTUMN
26

It was market day in Osperitsan village. Ceriana, Ebba and Alys were out shopping for a new dress. The range available was not spectacular but they were well-made sturdy dresses, good for ladies working in the fields or the wives of fishermen. There were one or two more expensive ones for the ladies of the court and Ceriana purchased one of these, a fetching green velvet affair with silver buttons on the sleeves. After handing over the money to Gudrun, the dressmaker, she turned to Alys.

'For you,' she said, 'your clothes are far too severe.'

Alys spluttered and went crimson. She was always getting embarrassed, that girl, thought Ceriana.

'I am sorry, my Lady; I cannot possibly accept this – it is too much.'

'Nonsense, it is a present, a thank you for coming all this way to help me.'

Alys assented, knowing she wouldn't win an argument with the proud, thin, upright woman next to her and they continued their trip around the market, until an outburst of squally rain drove them back to the carriage and then finally back to the baronial hall.

The three ladies had bonded somewhat in the two weeks since Alys had arrived. Ebba had been ordered to look after both of them and Alys had been moved into rooms next to Ceriana's. As the days passed, they had formed something of a trinity, spending a lot of time in each other's company.

As far as her husband was concerned, it was inevitable that nothing strange had happened since he had agreed to spend the nights with her. She found herself actually wanting to wake up in the dead of night covered in glowing red veins and dreaming of dragons, but of course nothing like that happened. All she got was her husband grumbling about her snoring and digging her in the ribs when she took too many of the blankets. She didn't care that relations had cooled between them; she had been forced into this arrangement as much as he had and had her own life to lead. She had settled here a lot more now and often went out riding over the bare hills and narrow walled paths of the island until she arrived at the sea. There she would uncover her head and let the biting wind make her ears go numb and pinch her nose red. Her nose would run, too, and she loved that – Lady Ceriana Osperitsan Hartfield, Snot Queen of the Islands – how the ladies of the court would bow to her then! Einar popped along to visit for a couple of days; he had some news – Vorfgan was up at his hall continuing his tour of the islands, and he and Wulfthram would be returning to visit him, Einar's hall being only a couple of hours away.

'What do you think of him?' she asked.

'He's like every baron I have ever met; he has his own agenda which is never out in the open. He has some charm as well, which is lost on me but never goes amiss with others.'

'Why is he visiting everybody like this? I never found out when I saw him in Thakholm.'

'It is not uncommon for a new baron to do such a thing, especially if he is in need of friends. I've known him for a while but he is a mystery to a lot of people, especially to those on the islands. Wulfthram will work him out pretty quickly; he has a gift like that.' 'With men maybe,' she said archly.

'Still frosty between you? Do you want me to knock some sense into him?'

'As long as you don't hold back,' she said with a smile.

'Are all southern girls so vicious?'

'Only when slighted – an apology though and I am quick to forgive.'

'I will tell him then, though I can never remember him apologising to anyone. He did to me once after upsetting my ale, but I am not counting that. In my opinion, he listens too much to his womenfolk. My wife has never argued with me in twenty years of marriage and six surviving children.'

'And what is the secret then?'

'Never to talk, of course. No conversation, no arguments. She has her handmaidens for company and me when she needs a bull in the bedroom. A happy arrangement all round.'

'Bull, is it? Does that mean you sweat a lot, smell terrible and can be led by the nose?'

He thought about it a second. 'That's one way of looking at it, I guess; not quite the way I meant but she would probably agree with you. Your husband will be back with you tomorrow night suitably chastised.'

'Tell him I await his return with breathless anticipation. By the way, tell Vorfgan not to duel anyone with sticks again; we can't have all the barons here walking round with bells ringing in their ears.'

'That sounds like a story I should hear sometime – but I should be on my way right now. Until we meet again when hopefully things will be better between you both. Farewell.'

Although her husband's absence was for one day only, she was now mistress of the hall with all its concomitant responsibilities. This included listening to petitions from disgruntled locals with an axe to grind. Ordinarily, she would send them away and ask them to come back on her husband's return, but she was in a bloody mood and decided that this time she would hold court herself.

She soon regretted her decision; the first petition was between two fishermen disputing ownership of a boat. The older man had been ill for some time and had leased his boat out on the proviso of the catch being shared equitably; the younger man stated that the boat had been sold to him and had written proof from the other of this. Two simple questions later and it was obvious that the 'seller' could not read or write so she found in the older man's favour, warning the loser that he would be flogged if he tried something like this again.

The second petition was against the proprietor of the local brothel: a couple of the women that worked there accused him of brutalising them if they made insufficient money or threatened to leave and work elsewhere. They displayed the red marks on their wrists, where they claimed they were restrained by ropes while they were beaten; there were no marks on their bodies, they said, because it would damage their ability to earn. The proprietor, a burly lump of muscle and bone called Cragvan, was a former sailor and prison guard who certainly knew how to injure without bruises; he used thick ropes on them among other things.

The man's defence seemed to be little more than that they were whores whose word could not be trusted. He appeared stunned when he saw it was the Baroness holding the hearing.

'So how did they get the marks on their wrists?' she asked him.

'Self-inflicted, my Lady; they have a grudge against me because they think I take too much of their earnings, but with the rent on the place they work I have no choice.'

'I see.' To her annoyance this was trickier than she wanted it to be; it was little more than one word against another. She called over Wulfthram's seneschal and right-hand man, a grizzled fellow in his sixties called Bruan. 'My husband would let him go, wouldn't he?'

'With a warning, my Lady; he would send the guards round to visit occasionally, to make sure nothing like this was going on again.'

'But the girls would be too frightened to say anything, and if he leaves no marks...'

'There is no real evidence against him and so, if he is punished too harshly, questions may be asked as to the wisdom of your justice. A brothelkeeper often has a wide net of contacts and could use that to bad-mouth you in the town and surrounding area; it could well prove detrimental to your husband's attempt to govern these lands in the long term.'

'You're not happy with me taking this court, are you?'

'It is entirely your decision, my Lady, though Baron Wulfthram's first wife never sat in judgment on others.'

'Well, hopefully Camille will guide me to show some little of her wisdom. Tell me, how much do these girls earn?'

Both women had seen better days. They were probably in their thirties but looked older; they had the large haunted eyes and sunken cheeks of women that had fought hunger for many years. The one woman had an ugly red welt on her forehead in the shape of a W where she had been branded, a punishment for prostitution.

'These two? They are not the best he can offer; they probably pick up a ducat an hour of which they would keep thirty pennies or so; so for eight hours' work they would get two, maybe two and a half ducats.'

It was a pitiful amount – barely enough to feed them, let alone any children they might have.

'I didn't know Wulfthram branded the girls up here.'

'He doesn't. She must have received it elsewhere; only thieves and felons that injure people get branded. He doesn't see whores as criminals.' She spoke to the branded woman.

'Do you have any children?'

'Two, my Lady. One works on the boats helping to mend nets and sails; the other is little more than a babe.'

'Your older child is...?'

'Seven, my Lady.'

'Seven.' She turned to the other woman. 'And you?'

'I have five children all under ten, my Lady. My husband works the land for you and the good Baron Wulfthram.'

'Thank you.' This wasn't getting any easier; she shut her eyes praying silently for divine inspiration. Suddenly something did come to her and she called Bruan over again.

'Their wounds, how long will they take to heal.'

'Two to three weeks I would guess, my Lady.'

'Very well.' She stood as she was supposed to in giving judgment. 'It has been decided that there is not enough evidence to convict Master Cragvan of damaging these ladies.' She avoided looking at their faces. 'However, it appears that they have received injuries that would impair their ability to work while the marks are still visible. Master Cragvan is deemed to be responsible for their welfare while they work for him and so he is required to pay compensation to them until their injuries heal in about three weeks' time. He will pay them each sixty ducats, plus a further ten to cover costs and expenses incurred in bringing this case. Seneschal Bruan will ensure that the premises are visited regularly so no further injuries are sustained by his staff. The petition has been heard.'

The ladies gasped with delight while Cragvan's eyes burned into her. The guards led them out of the hall.

'You know,' Bruan said, 'it would be a very stupid man to beat women without leaving a mark only to neglect injuries caused by wrist restraints. Why tie them up when they only needed to be held down?'

'Are you implying that those injuries were self-inflicted?'

'I imply nothing, my Lady; only that justice has been seen to be observed.'

'I hope so; he underpays those girls anyway. What is the next case?'

'One more case, my Lady; an odd one, too. Some fishermen and their families from Baron Farnerun's lands have fled here and settled themselves in Roten, the large fishing town in the north. They are eating into the locals' catch and compete successfully with them on market day. The petitioner is a local magistrate who wishes them to return home but they say they are afeard to. I don't know why.'

'Right, send them in.'

In they came. The magistrate was a tall thin man with a large crooked nose dressed in a faded red velvet jerkin and breeches; the exiles were represented by a stoutly built man in oilskins and a small shrewish-looking woman in a well-made though slightly threadbare dress that would have been quite the fashion twenty years ago. The petitioner spoke first.

'My Lady, I am sorry to take up your time like this, but this is a matter that cannot continue without some resolution. Some three months ago six small fishing boats arrived here from the town of Oxhagen on the coast, where Baron Farnerun has his lands. Since then they have purchased two houses in Roten and have set up in business here. In our town everyone has their own delineated fishing grounds from which they deviate only with permission from the family in whose waters they wish to fish, but these outsiders' fish where they like and furthermore undercut our fish prices in the market, pulling trade away from families who have fished here for generations. When I asked them why they have moved here in the first place they give us some Uba-driven nonsense about running away from ghosts! I humbly beseech you to tell them to return home.'

'And what do you have to say about this?' She turned to the other man.

'My Lady, I know I am the outsider here but I beg you to hear what I have to say. When we arrived we asked the magistrate to be granted some fishing grounds, however remote or poor. We were refused. We have also been refused access to the market and so have to trade from our homes half a mile away. Selling the fish cheaper is the only way to attract custom, even if it means we barely make a profit.'

'So how did you purchase your houses?' Bruan asked brusquely.

'Our life savings, sir; we now have nothing left and live three families to a house.'

'If things are so bad here, why leave your home town? What is this ghost tale that frightens you so?' Ceriana asked.

The man looked sheepish, so the woman spoke instead; she sounded like someone who would not be argued with.

'My Lady, as my husband' – she dug him in the ribs – 'seems to have lost the use of his tongue, allow me to speak on his behalf. We lived in Oxhagen, a fishing town that lies in the shadow of some ancient ruins, built by people long dead. Everyone says they are haunted but we's as lives there laughs at such talk. My family has lived there for hundreds of years and has never seen or heard anything scarier than a night owl screeching. Well, some three months ago, maybe four, my youngest, Moris – he is seven he is – well, he was playing in the ruins with his friends. Close to the ruins is a small cove – Pedens Cove; it is sheltered and has a beach and a steep path leads right up to the ruins it does. Well, Moris was chasing his friends around and mayhap catches sight of the cove below, and what do you think he saw, my Lady?'

Ceriana shrugged; she imagined the woman's husband spent as much time at sea as possible. 'I do not know. Please tell me.'

'Two ships.'

'Ships? In a cove? Hardly unusual, surely?'

'Are but these were ships built like no others anyone here has seen.'

'What do you mean?'

'They were built to look like monsters they were – great snake's head, with wings port and starboard and a long tail.'

Ceriana was suddenly all attention. 'Go on.'

'Well, my boy and his friends hid and watched, and from the boat men came climbing up the path to the ruins.'

'Could he describe these men?'

'Yes and no, my Lady. No – because they all looked the same. And yes – because they were all bald and wore black cloaks.'

The magistrate cut in. 'Preposterous! My Lady, do you even wish to hear more of this twaddle? I can have them both flogged for wasting your time, if you wish.'

'No,' she said quietly. 'Let them continue.'

The woman, who looked momentarily fearful after the magistrate spoke, carried on.

'The boys watched them disappear into an old stone tower; they were gone a long time, so my Moris, brave lad that he is, snuck up to this tower and looked in.'

'What did he see?'

'A great stairway going down into darkness – one that no one that has lived there years like me had never seen before. He started to go down them but when he reached the bottom there was lots and lots of branching tunnels. The poor lad was already petrified, so he climbed back up the stairs and legged it back home to tell the rest of us.'

The man butted in. 'None of us believed him, a boy and his wild imaginings, but to satisfy our ladyfolk' – he looked balefully at his wife – 'some of us went up there to have a look.'

'And were the tunnels there?'

'Yes, my Lady; it was as the lad said. Three of us armed with cudgels and carrying torches went inside. The tunnels twisted and turned and we were soon unsure as to where we were. The walls were covered in strange carvings and they were damp to the touch. After walking for some half-hour I turned and Byran, one of our number, had vanished!'

The magistrate sighed and shook his head. 'I would imagine her Ladyship would like to hear the end to these ramblings before Winterfeast.'

'Yes,' said Bruan, 'finish your story.'

'We retraced our steps, but took a wrong turning somewhere. While we were trying to find the right way out, I stumbled over something in the dark. I fell and bloodied my chin. When I got up my companion, Garthen, was standing over something with a torch.

It was a man, as my boy said, wearing black and with no hair, but he was covered in white frost, almost solid, his face and lips cracked. We thought him dead but then his eyes opened and he spoke to us.'

Ceriana looked intently at him. 'What did he say? It is very, very important that you remember the exact words.'

'Well, my Lady, his accent was strong and it made no sense – to me anyway – but it was something like "We have what we came for but we have awoken them." "Awoken who?" I asked. "The guardians," he whispered. I tried asking who they were... "Your death!" and then he laughed. I shook him for more details but he died there and then. Garthen and I looked at each other, wondering what to make of it all when we heard a scream, a terrible scream. We followed it through the tunnels and turning a corner we saw Byran. He was stood against a wall and was surrounded." The man swallowed; he looked frightened. 'The things surrounding him were ... shadows, dark men shaped things with glowing blue eyes. Byran was screaming and the frost was all over him like the other man. Then the shadows turned and saw us... Artorus help me, but we ran. We left Byran and ran. The Gods were kind for we found the exit quickly and we did not stop running till we got home.'

'And so you fled the village,' said Ceriana.

'No,' said the woman. 'There is more. Two days later my husband was waiting by the boat, waiting to go out, but Garthen, the first mate, didn't turn up. Impatient, he went to his cottage and found...'

'Garthen, his wife and children, all dead. Frozen to their beds. The man was white.'

'And so the entire family, cousins and all, decided to leave before it was our turn,' said the woman.

The magistrate gave a derisive snort. 'I cannot believe you have wasted our Lady's time with this nonsense.'

''Tis true as Elissa is my witness,' said the woman. 'The Gods strike us dead if we tell a lie.'

'Wait,' said Ceriana, 'I have decided. This matter needs to be investigated. Until these enquiries are concluded these families are to be giving grounds to fish and a place in the market. In return for that, they must charge normal prices for their fish. If there is no substance to this story, they are to leave the area immediately and return home.'

The magistrate blustered. 'My Lady, I must protest!'

'Your objection is noted; the case is for the moment closed.' She waved to the guards, who used their halberds to shoo the petitioners out of the room, the magistrate continuing to grumble to anyone who would listen.

After they had all left Bruan came up to her. 'You should not have angered the magistrate. Like the man before he could whip up local resentment against the Baron.'

'Then Wulfthram can smooth things over with him. I have done the right thing. It seems that everybody could whip up resentment if they so chose; it is impossible to keep everybody happy.'

'As you say, my Lady.'

That night Wulfthram returned. Ceriana was in her room dressed for bed and combing her hair when he walked in.

'I hear you have been taking petitions today,' he said drily.

'I have listened to my father's judgments many times. I used to sit in on as many as I could, even if only to remind me of how lucky I am in never wanting for food and warmth. I have always fancied myself as a bit of a judge; it was much more difficult than I thought, though. I take it I have annoyed you again?'

'Not at all. However, I would rather you didn't do it again without warning me first. I know most people around here and how to keep everyone happy.'

Bruan was impressed anyway.'

'He was? I wish he had told me. I felt like a naughty child.'

'Well, you are perhaps wilful rather than naughty and a young woman rather than a child. Bruan sees me as a boy, though, so there is not much we can do about it. It is all a matter of perspective, I suppose – Bruan sees me as young, I see you as young, but we are both capable in our own way.'

'Were you happy with what I did?'

'Yes. I would have flogged the brothel-keeper, though; he treats those girls abominably.'

'Oh, I wanted to as well. He got away lightly then.'

'You hit him in the pocket though; he won't like that.'

'And the fishermen? What shall we do about their story.'

'Nothing,' said Wulfthram. 'I shall ask Farnerun to investigate the tower.'

'Didn't you listen to what the man said? The men in black got what they came for. Perhaps all I need to do is return the stone there, if that was what they were referring to. This whole mess could be cleared up easily.'

'And these guardians? What if they kill you first?'

She snorted, climbing on to the bed. 'I have to do something!'

He looked at her, her dark eyes brimming with frustration 'Maybe. I am tired; it has been a long day. Let me sleep on it; we can talk tomorrow.'

'How did you find Vorfgan?'

'Untrustworthy, like everyone else. He avoided all questions about how he acquired his baronetcy and then told me that the Baron immediately to his north had retired to the country and given Vorfgan his title. He was in his seventies with no heirs and his lands were small, though they include a port and a small gem mine ... but even so, Vorfgan's hand continues to grow. He is one to watch ... closely. Right, I am sleeping now and do not want to hear from you till the morning.'

She looked him in the eye. 'Sorry for calling you a bastard.'

He laughed. 'I spoke wrongly to you. I was only thinking of your safety.

As I said, we shall discuss it in the morning.' She looked at him impishly. 'Was that an apology?'

'No,' he said. 'Goodnight. Artorus keep you safe.'
'Good night. And Syvukha keep you, too.'

Light. She could see light. She was surrounded by stone. She could sense it; it enclosed her on both sides and the darkness was almost complete. But ahead, there it was. She felt a pain in her eyes as she looked at it, a shaft of purest white lancing its way through the void. As she walked towards it, she felt the ground shake under her claws. Just how big was she?

She snorted and two small jets of flame leapt skywards. Yes, the flame illuminated the dark stone of a tunnel; she sensed she had been crawling through it for many days and that without a doubt it lead upwards. She – it – was close to the surface. The shaft broadened as she got nearer. As her eyes got used to it, she could see it was not one shaft but several, all fairly close together and positioned so their narrow beams joined each other, making a large pool of radiance that broadened as it filtered downwards. Positioned? Was this a natural feature or had these shafts been punched through the mountain by hand. And if so, why?

Her pace increased and suddenly she felt space. The walls of rock either side of her and above her had disappeared. Ahead of her was a broad flat ledge whose lip fell away into nothingness. In the light she could see she was looking at a colossal cavern, the size of which she could only determine by stepping up to the ledge and looking over.

To her surprise the creature she inhabited stopped. It was exhausted and needed to rest, but the ledge was only twenty feet away. To her surprise she felt herself saying:

'Go on, look over the edge – rest later.'

And the creature responded. With a supreme effort it hauled itself upward and crawled to the lip ahead of it. And looked over. Where, by all the Gods, was this place?

To call this a cavern would be understating it to a ridiculous degree, for below her was a fall of hundreds of feet into a bowl-shaped cave the diameter of which must have been well over a mile. She saw that the light shafts she had seen initially were not the only ones here; they were clustered about the rock above her so that the entire cavern was illuminated. She saw a dark river that spilled out of a shaft halfway up the rock, falling as a waterfall and crashing into a broad plunge pool. It then regained its course and neatly bisected the cave, before it disappearing through a dark chasm almost directly underneath her. But it was not that that had caught her attention.

For either side of the river was a city.

The majority of its buildings hugged the river and all of them seemed to be of a gigantic size. They were constructed not out of bricks but of great stone monoliths, skilfully jointed together so that no mortar or binding substance seemed required. She could see parapets and plazas, buildings crowned by battlements and others climbed via external zigzagging walkways. Low stone bridges crossed the river and there were vast waterwheels, too, presumably used to power machinery. And, in the plunge pool of the waterfall, sitting upon a colossal stone plinth, was a statue. A hundred, no possibly two hundred, feet high, it was a figure bearded and mailed, its two gnarled hands clasping the haft of a great double-headed axe. Atop its head was a great battle helm, flat-topped and fringed with geometric stone shapes giving it the appearance of a crown.

Despite the grandeur of the city, everywhere there were signs of neglect and abandonment. A waterwheel had come loose and lay on its side in the river, piles of dust silted up the open doorways of buildings, and loose stones and rocks lay strewn about its once-grand roads and squares. Nobody lived here now and the aura of faded opulence, of glory long fled, cast a melancholic aura over the black eyeless windows and the long shadows cast by the high edifices beneath her.

She suddenly felt vigour return to the creature's body. The vista beneath it had obviously given it a new excitement and purpose – though perhaps it was deriving it from her? It was she who had asked it to move earlier and it had done so; now was it drawing strength from her curiosity, her wonder at seeing this mysterious city?

The next thing it did, though, was definitely not prompted by her. She felt it stretch its long body and dig its claws into the dust. She heard it hiss. She heard the beating of great leathery wings, the sound pounding in her eardrums, making her head throb. Then she saw as the creature cast itself off the ledge and into the air...

For a few terrifying moments she felt it plummeting towards the river, its churning grey waters getting closer and closer, then it levelled out and started to gain altitude. It was flying.

She could feel the thrill running through its body, the blood pumping fit to burst a vein, the stale air rushing over the skin. It flew high, close to one of the light shafts and through it, briefly, she caught a glimpse of high cloud and the pale sliver of the moon. So it was moonlight that filled the chamber!

The dragon – for there could be no doubt of the creature's nature now – followed the course of the river, swooping past the high crowns of the buildings left and right, disturbing dormant clouds of dust that billowed into the air. Then it landed, coming to rest on the crown of the great statue. Despite the size of the structure, it still had difficulty finding the space to set down its great legs. Once it had, though, it threw back its great head and roared. A jet of flame sped forth like nothing she had ever seen. It almost reached the ceiling of the cavern and, when it finally died, she saw its smoke filtering through the light shafts and escaping into the outer world.

And then it was answered. As she looked around, she saw, emerging from the buildings or from unseen shafts in the cave walls, other creatures, all winged and serpentine. They were smaller than the creature she was sensing, though, and she realised they had no forelimbs, just powerful taloned legs. On the ground they walked clumsily, or withdrew their wings and legs and slithered like a primitive snake. In the air, however, they moved seamlessly. And that was just where they were taking to, for now a great flock of these monsters was flying above her. There were dozens of them, maybe more, and they croaked, hissed and swooped around her in a great circle as though welcoming an old friend. Maybe, though, they were recognising a master. A master who had finally returned home.

Wulfthram grumbled in his sleep and turned over, pulling the blanket over him. Instinctively he reached out for the slight figure who should have been next to him.

But she wasn't.

Sighing deeply, he forced open his sleep-filled eyes, trying to focus on the room around him, to see where in the name of Keth she was. Suddenly, with a shock, he sat bolt upright in the bed. He was awake now all right.

At the foot of the bed facing him was Ceriana. Her arms were outstretched and her head was thrown back and flushed with excitement. Her large eyes were euphoric. Her large red eyes.

Through her thin nightdress he could see the thin tracery of veins running through her body shining like liquid metal. Her blood was luminous and glowing, rendering her skin translucent. He could see her blood running through her ears, her lips and behind her eyes. She seemed oblivious to what was happening, though. She saw him and spoke, her voice tremulous and ecstatic.

'Oh Wulf, can't you see? I'm flying!'

In a couple of bounds he was out of the bed and pulling the box in which she kept the stone out of the drawer. As he opened it, its fierce glow filled the room, turning his face crimson. He went to touch it but recoiled in alarm; it was fiery hot and burned his fingertips. In the draw was a handkerchief. He grabbed it, folded it round the stone and dropped it into the water jug she always kept at her bedside. A pillar of steam shot forth from the jug as the stone sizzled. Then the glow rapidly abated.

He grabbed his wife and held her close. Her skin, her veins, were as normal again, although she was feverishly hot. With a pathetic whimper she subsided into his arms, tears flowing as she realised what had just happened.

'It's all right, little one ... Don't you worry, we will take care of it,' he said, trying to sound soothing, although it was obviously something that did not come naturally. He looked at her nightdress and felt his spirits lower even further.

It was covered in thin, black scorch marks and they were still smoking.

THE FORGOTTEN WAR
27

'No no, you lose this time. Four ones beat two fives and two fours.'

'But my score is higher than yours.'

'That only applies where no one throws a double.'

'Artorus's beard, I have studied all of the fifty-seven known wedding songs of the Wych folk – how each song applies to a different set of circumstances and how changing one letter in them turns high praise into an insult – but I have never encountered anything so intractable as dice gaming before. And why is this game called Killer anyway?' Cedric stroked his chin in frustration.

'Because it generally turns the loser into a killer,' said Morgan laconically. 'Go on, give the dice a shake; you should be good at that with your illness... Now roll.'

The dice sped over the muddy ground coming to rest at the base of the statue.

'Ha!' roared Cedric triumphantly. 'Three threes! Beat that.'

Morgan picked them up and rolled. 'Three fours, my friend. Have I cleaned you out yet?'

'Almost,' grumbled Cedric. 'Go on take another penny.'

'I am six pennies to the good,' said Morgan with a smile. 'Much more of this and I can buy a loaf of bread.'

'Well, I can't stay crouched like this much longer. I need to stretch my legs before I continue. How long have they been gone now?'

'The Wych girl? Just over two days.'

'Odd little thing, wasn't she?' Cedric walked slowly towards the river, stretching his stiff limbs.

'If by "odd" you mean murderously inclined and supercilious, then I would agree.'

'Now you see, I didn't get that from her; from him, yes, but she seemed a lot more reasonable than I expected. She seemed to take a shine to you, too.'

'I think it's all in your head, Cedric. I read nothing but hostility from her.'

'Let's bet on it then. My six pennies say that you two end up friendlier in a week than you are now; in fact, I should say friends rather than friendly, for I am sure that will be the case.'

'And how, by all the Gods, are we to judge that?'

'It will be obvious surely. If you can swear on whatever you hold dear that you two will feel greater enmity towards each other in a week than you feel now, I will stake another six pennies that you will not – enough for a loaf of bread and some salted meat. Is it settled?'

Morgan looked at him appraisingly. 'Settled.'

'Good. Speaking of salted meat let's have something to eat.'

They sat and did so. The statue still burned, blue fire licking up and down the haft of the spear. Everywhere the autumn leaves fell around them, leaving the trees naked, their splayed branches reaching up into the cold grey sky. The forest over the river, though, was still relatively green. And silent.

Later that day Morgan was about to start a fire, using only the dead branches of the trees as Cedric advised, when the older man called out to him.

'She is coming back!'

Morgan joined him looking across the river. Itheya was crossing the river on her own. Huddled under the branches of the trees were other figures, obviously with orders to stay where they were for now. She was followed by two other horses, following without reins, one of which was nearer pony sized rather than a full-sized warhorse; the other seemed a twin of her own charger. As before, her horse clambered on to the island and she slid gracefully off the animal to face the two men. Morgan noticed that she did not carry her bow.

'Have you spoken to your father, the Mhezhen?' Cedric asked politely.

She nodded. 'You are to come,' she said, 'with me to meet my father.'

Morgan turned to Cedric. 'Well, you have your answer, my friend. I would guess the smaller horse is for you.'

'You are correct,' she said. 'She is a good mount, obedient and patient; if you are taken ill, she will understand.'

'I am surprised that you are allowing a warrior into the forest,' Morgan said to her.

'Your sword is to be tied to your scabbard, as is your knife. Do you have any other weapons concealed on your person?'

'Yes. You are not going to search me, are you?'

She looked at him balefully. 'If I have to.'

He laughed. 'It won't be necessary. I have a knife in my boot and one hidden in my belt. I will leave them with our friends over the river.'

'Do so. As for your friends, they must leave here. The fire will be put out now and after that they will be seen as targets by some. Return your weapons to them and tell them to go immediately. There is a human city three days away. It would be a good place for them to go.'

'Pardon me for saying so,' said Cedric, 'but is something wrong, my Lady? You seem a little ... distracted.'

She shot him a dismissive look. 'No.'

'Then forgive me for being presumptive.'

'No,' she said, 'it is I who should apologise. There have been ... differences between us as to how you should be treated. There is great curiosity about the things you have with you, but some want them returned unconditionally and others are prepared to listen to what you have to say. Also, there is resistance to having a human warrior among us.'

Morgan spoke. 'I can go with the others if you wish – as long as you promise to look after Cedric and return him safely for us.'

'No, I have told them that you look after him. I have ... vouched for you. If you behave badly in the forest, I will be punished for it.'

Morgan was stunned. 'You really didn't have to do that.'

She shrugged. 'It is nothing. Just do as I say and do not insult or upset anyone. You are my responsibility now.'

'As you wish.'

She brought his horse to him. 'She is a strong girl but not wilful. She will carry you well.'

'I have got to get on her first,' Morgan grumbled. He was not the tallest man and hated riding anyway. To him, the mare, however stoical and patient, presented a challenge. It took several attempts before he could swing his leg over the damned thing; once he had finally managed he looked at his companions. Cedric was beaming from ear to ear. Itheya was trying to look as distant as ever, but he could see she was close to smirking at him. He looked at her directly.

'Yes? Have you something to say?'

She covered her mouth with her slender fingers. 'No, do all humans ride as you do?'

'Most are considerably better,' he said through gritted teeth.

'Really? I hardly thought it possible ... anthropoid.'

He was about to unleash a cutting rejoinder but the horse was already carrying him over the river where Haelward was already standing on the bank.

'You have to leave,' he told him. 'Only the two of us are going in and once that happens you will be fair game.'

'We will make for Zerannon then,' said Haelward, 'and await you there.'

'There is an inn there called the Spectral Goose. The keeper is called Ham; he knows me. Give him five crowns and ask to stay until I arrive. The beds don't have too many fleas and the food is passable. We will see you all there. If we are not there in, say, six weeks, consider your part in this mission over. Return to the front or do whatever you see fit from then on.'

'As you say. See you in a few weeks.'

'Yes, and thanks – if I don't see you again that is.'

'You will. Artorus will see to it.'

Morgan nodded to him and swung his horse around, heading back to the island.

Upon his return, Itheya busied herself with strapping his sword inside its scabbard using a strip of leather. She had to stand close to him to do this, her head craned over to see what she was doing. Her ponytail was held high, exposing the alabaster skin on her neck.

'Your friend tells me you are brave, that you saved his life in the pass fighting the Kergh, which you call ettins. Is that the right word – ettins?'

'Yes, it is the right word, and Cedric was very much over-emphasizing my role in crossing the pass; he saved me as much as the other way round.'

'This war, you have fought in it a long time?'

'Too long!' he said. 'And not through choice. I used to live in the area being fought over; I just got caught up in the fighting.'

'And your scar?'

'It happens in war. I have others on my body; getting wounded is part of the job.'

'Sick man Cedric believes that you are not naturally a man of violence and I can see what he is trying to say. Our people ... well, we are in tribes, yes, and tribes cannot agree on anything. We fight often, usually over nothing; we are often violent without reason. It is a failure in us, I feel.'

'Not just in your people, I am afraid, and you are wrong, I am a man of violence – my actions defined me long ago.'

'Well, in that case I will ask you to control your urges to kill until you leave Seyavanion, with or without our help.'

'As you wish, but how will I release my murderous frustrations, though?'

'I will find you a prisoner or something; he might be difficult to kill without a weapon, though.'

'I will use my bare hands; I am very good with them.'

'I do not doubt it, though your horse might disagree. There, I have tied up your weapon.' She stepped back from him. 'Now for the knife.'

She busied herself with his knife. 'This won't take long.'

'Your tattoos, the markings on your skin, what do they represent?'

'The khazoeth? They are our spirits. We have one god whom we do not depict. The spirits, though, they carry out his instructions on this Earth and we are free to display them on our bodies, this one is Etheren. She is a bird with a beautiful song. And this is Gharaghanann the spider –

she eats the male after mating, you know, and this one' – she pointed to her shoulder – 'is Lhuzhenna the willow, a sad tree and beautiful.'

'They are very intricate, and delicately drawn, the work of an artist really; how many do you have?'

'Many, I am the Mhezhen's daughter, so am allowed a lot. They are on my arms, back and legs; most only have them on their arms or back. The more khazoeth, the higher you stand in the tribe. We have specialists in our tribe who draw them on our skin. It is painful – your skin swells and burns for a while, but the ability to endure it is the mark of a warrior. There, the knife is done, you are now a warrior without weapons. This is good. You are fit to enter Seyavanion.'

'Thank you. Now where is Cedric?'

'He is trying to get on his horse. Do not try and help him; he is proud.'

'And braver than me; few men with his illness have attempted so much.'

'I think he is proving something to himself – that his sickness will not hold him or stop him doing what he wants. I have seen it in others; it is important to them – to still be vital despite it all.' There was a brief silence between them, then Morgan spoke again.

'What did your father say about the carving Cedric gave you?'

'They are intrigued. He wishes to know more, especially about the tooth.'

'Why the tooth? It is not as beautiful as the other models?'

'But it is the oldest. If it is what I think it might be, then, well, I had better say no more until Father sees it, but it could be very, very important.' She looked at him. Morgan thought she could almost be smiling.

'You ask many questions, do you not?'

'I am curious, that is all. I shall be quiet if you wish.'

'No, I am instructed to answer whatever you ask.'

'Do you have any family other than your father? Who will lead the tribe after him?'

'I have a brother, Dramalliel. You will find him less friendly than I;

he was against your coming. Tiavon is a friend of his; they share similar views of you, hemenestra. They were difficult to win over. As for the tribe, I am the eldest, so I will succeed when Father dies. But with us things can get ... complicated in that regard. You will learn more in due course.'

'Is Tiavon still trying to get us killed?'

She looked at him with her clear strange eyes. 'Yes, he may even succeed; it will depend on you and your friend, on what my father and Terath our lore master think of you when you meet. They are both reasonable people; you would have to do much ill to bring them to violence against you.'

'I see,' said Morgan, clucking his tongue. 'Cedric thought you and Tiavon were ... involved with each other, but if your views differ so strongly perhaps he was wrong.'

She did laugh then, a light musical sound. 'You do speak plainly. I like that; it is rare to find in my brethren. There is no man with whom I am involved. I have lain with him, yes, on several occasions, but I have done this with many of our warriors. It is an honour for them to be with a Mhezhen's daughter. If they have been brave, or have helped me or the tribe, I may choose to reward them. It is normal with our people; you humans are different I believe.'

'Yes, as a rule anyway. What of pregnancy, don't you risk having a child that you do not want?'

'Of course not! A rare foolish question, warrior man.'

'The name is Morgan.'

'I know, I may even call you it one day.'

At that point Cedric burst into the clearing. He was flushed and sweating but was astride the horse and looking triumphant.

'See, my boy, you have nothing on me. Ten minutes that took and now I just want to get off and sleep.'

'No, no sleep,' said Itheya. 'We travel now; we will go gently but will be at our village in just over a day. We have some daylight left and need to use it.'

'What of the trunk?' asked Cedric.

'I have people waiting on the bank. When they see us leave they will come and collect it. It will not be stolen from you, you have my word. When you meet Father it will be there with you. Come, the air is freshening – there will be rain soon.'

She was right. Overhead the sky was darkening and the cloud was thickening. A swirling wind sent up showers of leaves that caught in their clothes and hair. Morgan remounted his horse, finding it a lot easier this time, while Itheya walked to the statue. She said some words that he could not make out, then cast some sand or dirt over the bowl. The blue flame diminished, turned a pale-yellow colour and finally went out. Cedric had been right about her – she did seem sadder or more troubled this time while also being friendlier and more open with them. Perhaps not having Tiavon hanging over her shoulder made a difference. She walked to her horse, mounted it lithely, then spoke to them both.

'I will take you to Father then. My responsibility for you' – she faced Cedric – 'will end there. My responsibility for you, though' – she glanced at Morgan – 'continues till you leave the forest or are killed.'

She gave her horse the gentlest of kicks and moved off ahead of them. They struggled to follow her. Seeing this, she waited for them in the river.

'You,' she said to Cedric, 'remain next to me so I may help you if need be; your friend can follow if he is able. If he falls off' – she shot Morgan a backward glance –'we leave him, though we are allowed to laugh at him first. Come.'

The three of them ploughed through the water. Morgan briefly looked behind him. Already, Haelward, Leon, Samson, Willem and Varen were distant figures, going in the opposite direction. He wondered when and if he would see them again. Ahead the forest loomed large. Great thick-trunked trees overhung the water, packing close together, their broad roots showing through the mud of the riverbank. Under the leaves all was darkness. Itheya led them to a stretch of bank where the land sloped relatively smoothly down to the water. Without stopping, she climbed on to it and under the trees, taking Cedric with her. Morgan heard the splash of water as the other Wych folk went to collect the trunk, then, after taking a deep breath, he followed Itheya into the darkness.

28

They were back at the sacred lake; its black waters a veritable fissure into the underworld. The sweet, smoky aroma from the incense burners shrouded the onlooking villagers. The women watching were singing softly, and many of them had garlands in their hair. The men; grimmer in aspect, had painted their faces with charcoal-black stripes. They gripped their spears in honour to the warrior emissary standing on the platform. Cerren stood there, his faced also painted, his expression euphoric. Some hours before he would have eaten the spirit meal, a mash of grains containing the same substances Dumnekavax had used to contact the spirit world some days before, and its effects would now be working on Cerren's mind. He could probably see Ukka waiting to speak with him, tantalisingly close, but still too far apart. They needed to be brought together and that was Dumnekavax's job.

He prowled around behind Cerren swathed in the smoke of the incense. In his left hand he brandished a stick over which was threaded many closely packed shells secured with twine that rattled as he shook them. In his right hand was a thicker wooden cudgel with a bulbous metal head formed roughly into the shape of a skull. Cerren himself was flanked by two burly villagers, one at each side, both of them staring across the lake.

Dumnekavax addressed the crowd:

'People of the Black Lake, omens and portents have been seen that show us how the Gods have been displeased and now we have been told how Ventekuu has awoken and is free in our world. Although we have food aplenty and the harvest was good, it will be just a matter of time before this changes for the worst.

'We have been told that none of this has been of our making, but even so we are threatened with destruction, for the night devils prowl. Therefore Ukka is to be sent an emissary to plead our case. Cerrenatukavenex is to be that man.'

'Cerrenatukavenex!' shouted the men, slamming the butts of their spears into the ground. Some of them were passing round jugs of mead, which the men and women seemed to be drinking in equal measure. This had been going on for some hours and many people there were definitely the worse for wear.

There was a pause as the musicians struck up their instruments; the air was filled with the trilling of pipes and the heavy beat of goatskin drums. The younger girls, who wore the garlands, started to dance on the earth before the wooden platform, skipping playfully around a man whose entire face was charcoaled and was shrouded in a dark-green robe – the representation of Ukka. They twirled about him, bowing their heads as they passed his face. They wore skirts only, their heads, breasts and torsos dusted with a blue paint that represented the waters of the underworld in which Ukka resided. As the dance continued, they formed a circle around their god, drawing closer and closer to him until they were totally surrounding him – a sea of flailing arms and swishing hair – then, as one, they raised their arms to the heavens before collapsing to the ground around the man, breathless.

The musicians continued playing as the dancers returned to the crowd and were given mead as a reward for their efforts. Shaking his shell rattle, Dumnekavax drew the crowd's attention.

'It is time, O brothers and sisters, to honour our emissary. His name will be carved on to the tablet of honour in the great house, joining that of former emissaries. The last was Manaketenak, who spoke to the Gods during the invasion of the Sand Warriors, granting us victory against a terrible foe. Let us honour the emissary.'

'Honour the emissary!' There was something of a party atmosphere in the crowd. All were fearing attacks from an enemy out of legend and this was the way they were to be stopped. For that they had to be grateful indeed. Cerren himself, although facing the lake, raised his arms to acknowledge them. The crowd roared its response, clashing spear to shield, chanting and whooping. Cerren's parents were there, too, and they joined in with the raucous cacophony. It was a proud day for them.

Once the noise had died down, Dumnekavax raised his arms.

'And now at last it is time. Ukka has commanded and it is our place to respond. I hereby commend Cerrenatukavenex to you, O Ukka.

He is our emissary, and he will plead the case for our tribe. Hear him and be merciful in your response!'

He was now standing directly behind Cerren. After uttering his final exhortation to the god of the underworld he turned towards the lake, lifted the stout cudgel he still brandished in his right hand, and with all his strength brought it down squarely on the back of Cerren's head.

It was such a fierce blow that many in the front rank of the crowd saw the man's head partially cave in. The crowd roared in excitement, and the musicians played frantically as Cerren staggered drunkenly across the platform. The two men flanking him had him though; grabbing his shoulders, they forced him to his knees. More mead was passed around as the onlookers' anticipation grew.

Dumnekavax stood before them, his arms raised. He had set down the cudgel and stick and held up to them a stretch of rope, knotted in three places with a wooden handle affixed to each side. Spears were raised as this was seen. The women were singing softly.

As the men held him, Dumnekavax passed the rope over Cerren's neck, and locking the wooden handles together he proceeded to turn them, twisting the rope and so tightening its grip around Cerren's throat. Not even the musicians, the singing or the other noises of the crowd could hide the strangulated gurgling coming from their emissary. This went on for some time; many of the audience were standing on their toes, leaning forward for a better view, when Dumnekavax signalled his two assistants. They then, with difficulty, stood Cerren up and turned him to the crowd.

His face was bright red, his wild eyes were popping out from their sockets, the whites prominent. The crowd dismissed any notion that there might be terror in them; spittle ran down his chin, along with blood from where he had bitten his swollen tongue, which was now partially lolling out of his mouth. All the time the music and singing continued.

With great ceremony Dumnekavax showed the crowd the final instrument he would use – a long thin knife. It was a metal one, a thing of wonder in itself in these parts, with a delicately carved bone handle. As the crowd watched open-mouthed, he skilfully and swiftly drew the blade across Cerren's throat.

BOOK ONE: AUTUMN

The results were spectacular. A fountain of arterial blood shot from the man's neck, spattering the front row of the crowd. The cheering grew to near hysterical proportions as the wooden platform became covered in the gore from the man for whom life was now a very tremulous flame indeed. Finally he slumped to his knees, at last on his way to the underworld. As the music played and the happy blood-soaked crowd laughed, drank and danced, Cerrenatukavenex was carried by the two men to the edge of the platform where his body was placed gently into the water. His woollen clothes, weighed down by stones sewn into the fabric, ensured that slowly and inexorably he was carried down into the murky unfathomable depths. For a moment he hung there, one white hand breaching the surface. Then his body drifted down into the underworld, to the sound of the party carrying on beside the shore.

On returning to the village, Cygan sought out the Elder. He, as expected, was at the great house speaking to the Circle of the Wise. On seeing Cygan, though, he excused himself to them and came towards him.

'Cygan! I wanted to see you. What did you think? I thought it went very well. The young man is strong and brave; Ukka cannot fail to be impressed.' His face, beard and clothes were still heavily spattered by the man's blood. Washing it off was not the done thing as a little of Cerren's power had been passed to him that way.

'Yes, it did; Cerren's parents could not be happier for their son. First a Malaac slayer and now an emissary – the musicians should be composing a song in his honour as we speak.' In truth, alone among his people, Cygan had his doubts. His contact with the outside world had coloured his perceptions of the supernatural. The Taneren he had spoken with had their own gods and who was to say who was right? He hoped that poor Cerren had not died in vain.

'And now,' said the Elder, 'to your departure – when are you planning to leave?'

'Within the hour, if at all possible, although I am unsure as to exactly what I should be doing.'

'Let us talk about this. None of us here know much about the lands to the north or of what lies over the open sea. What you need to do is to find the nearest elder of their people and warn him about what is happening here and that if things are not stopped the trouble will spread into their lands. He must know someone who can point to the cause of the spread of the Malaac and the rise of Ventekuu.'

Cygan looked unconvinced. 'The lands beyond the marsh are vast, far beyond anything you or I can imagine. The chances of me finding the people responsible for causing this chaos are too small for reckoning.'

Dumnekavax looked grave. 'Nevertheless, it is something you have to attempt. The very survival of our people is at stake. Do you wish to take anybody with you?'

'No,' sighed Cygan, 'everyone is needed here to defend the village. Give me a month or so; if you hear nothing, by all means send someone after me.'

'Of course. One other thing, if leverage is required, we will give you some items that may be traded. The marsh plants that the northerners crave – spore fungus, blackroot, wet cap and spirit grass, slime moulds and white allium.'

'If they take all of that, they will be in the spirit world for the rest of their lives – which wouldn't be that long of course,' said Cygan with a laugh.

'You will take all our stock. Tell no one there about it until you have to, otherwise they will kill you and take it all for themselves. All of these ingredients have great worth in the lands of the north – for healing, killing or walking with the spirits. With that you should be able to access the important people of the north.'

'Very well, Elder, I will do this for our people. Tell me, how is Tegavenex?'

'He is still sick, the poison in the Malaac's bite is still in his blood. It will take him a long time to heal, as he is very weak. We have tried everything we can think of, but the effect has been limited. We will continue to do what we can.'

'Then keep at least some of the healing herbs. Do not give them all to me; I will need but a little.'

'As you wish. May Cygannan go with you on your journey; all our prayers will be with you.'

Cygan left the great house under a lowering sky. He steered his boat between groups of geese and ducks, bobbing on the water as they fed on clumps of weed brought into the lake by the river. On the bank he could hear the villagers still drinking and celebrating. The mood of the people had lifted considerably since the events of earlier that day. Surely the Gods were with them now. People were even stripping off their clothes and diving into the water for a swim, something common in the summer months but which had stopped since the rumours of the night devils had arrived here. Arriving back at his island, he walked into his house, now outside the defensive circle of stakes and stripped of what few possessions it had; they had been taken into the heart of the island where the villagers now spent each night. The cooking pot was there, though, and his wife and children and his lame brother Uxevallak were all sitting on the floor eating a fish stew out of bowls. Cygan helped himself to a bowl. It was quite delicious. He spoke to his brother.

'You will take care of everyone here while I am gone? I do not know how long I will be.'

'Of course, brother. Not even the night devils will stop me inspecting the fish traps every day and keeping everyone fed.'

'Just be careful. The waters may be treacherous; nowhere is safe here now.'

'It is you who needs to be careful,' his wife said. 'Will I ever see you again?'

He kissed her. 'Just pray for me. I do not know how things will go for me when I leave the marsh, but it will be my thoughts of you and the children that will sustain me at all times. The thought of never seeing the three of you again will be too much for me to bear. I will come back; I feel it is my destiny to return, no matter what.'

His meal finished he crouched down and called the children to him.

'I will call you Deravellak, the strong heart,' he said to the boy.

'You will be as wise as the Elder and as strong as Fasneterax the warrior, and you' – he held his daughter close – 'will be Atanananda, the gentle reed, standing supple and proud and never breaking even in the heaviest of storms. I see your mother in you already and that is no bad thing; she is both the strongest and the gentlest person I will ever know. You all make me very proud.'

He kissed all three of them and embraced his brother heartily. Vaneshanda cried briefly but only briefly. After this she wiped her eyes and smiled at him.

'You are the bravest and kindest of men. When you return we will increase the size of our family, for I know our tribe will be safe in your hands and the future is assured. Cygannan keep you, my husband; all our prayers go with you.'

Shortly afterwards the elders arrived, bringing with them a securely tied basket in which was held the various items that Dumnekavax had mentioned earlier. Cygan stored it safely in his round boat, along with his knife, bow, spear, fish hooks and strips of dried fish and berries, as well as his cloak and water skin. He looked back at his house where his wife stood watching him.

Raising his arm in farewell, he pushed his boat into the water and clambered into it. The sun was beginning to descend into the western sky, casting his wife into silhouette. Both his children were at her feet. As he started to paddle, they waved to him. He swallowed and forced himself to turn away, steering the boat across the lake and on to the river. As he got to its mouth, the sun flared, turning the waters ahead scarlet. A flock of swift-flying swallows swooped low over the river, chirruping and arguing with each other as they helped themselves to the swarms of insects hanging over the water. As their black forms diminished over the riverbank, he saw a fish break the glassy surface to feed, leaving concentric rings spreading over the water. He took one last look behind him. Many boats were arriving at the island where they were to spend another night of vigilance, secure behind the newly built stockade. He saw his house, insignificant and small in the distance, and fancied he still saw a small figure standing next to it still watching him as he faded into the distance. One more sweep of his paddle and the riverbank hid the village from view. He looked ahead where the river seemed never to end, and with a sigh – maybe of regret, maybe in anticipation of what was to come – he spurred his boat onwards. He wanted to cover a good few miles indeed before night descended on the marsh.

Several days to the south and east, where sand bars and spits of land held the marauding sea at bay, a jagged rock stood out defiantly in the midst of a brown turbulent lake. Upon this rocky isle were the remnants of what had once been a village built mainly of wood. Stray logs and supports lay loosely over the stone, covered by ragged strips of sodden thatch and straw. No building remained standing here. Chaos reigned supreme. As the sun traced its fiery path downwards into the west, figures started to emerge from the water – they were bipedal, green-scaled and finned; some even had vestigial tails. Slowly they moved to the centre of the isle where something impossibly large lay slumbering on the stone. Its arrow-shaped head lay still and motionless, its wormlike body coiled behind it, its clean scales glistened in the glow of the setting sun.

Slowly the Malaac surrounded the creature. They were quiet and almost seemed in awe of the creature in their midst. They stood around it, their heads bowed. The only sound was the wind on the water as it lapped against the island's shore. Then another figure came into view, walking up to the creature's giant head from behind its powerful coils. It was a man, clad in a black cloak which had become so ragged and tattered that it hung in loose strips about him. There was a growth of a couple of days' hair on his head and chin and a ghastly pallor to his face. His skin was sweaty, flour-white tinged with green around the lips and eyes. The eyes themselves were large and round and hardly ever blinked, and the lips appeared to be almost black in colour. He ignored the Malaac as he strode past them, and they in turn ignored him. He stopped at the creature's neck, just behind the head, and with one bound clambered upon it, standing on the creature's spine. He sat astride the great beast, one hand clutching at the small bony fin that ran the entire length of its body.

Slowly, he unclasped his other hand. There, in the shining wetness of the palm, he beheld it – the dragon stone. His mad, staring eyes gazed at its vermilion beauty, watched the liquid inside it, thick and viscous as it moved around almost imperceptibly, and then finally he held it up to the light, directly against the sun, letting its colour wash over his face and hand. The Malaac around him hissed excitedly as they beheld it; they, too, seemed transfixed by its power. The man gave out a strange guttural croak, his mouth wide open, his gums and tongue almost black, the colour of bruised and decaying seaweed. His eyes leaked at the corners, not normal tears but streams of water that moistened his face and neck. Just for one second reason seemed to prevail in him; there was horror in his eyes as he brushed the water off his face and tried to comprehend what had happened to his body. Then the madness returned. He looked at the stone again, bending all his thoughts towards it. Slowly it started to glow. As the light got stronger, it pulsated in his hand, and the stronger it became the more water discharged from his body – from his ears, his nose, his mouth.

And at last the creature stirred. It flicked the tip of its great tail and slowly swung its head back and forth. With a great hiss, a cloud of green smoke was discharged from its nostrils. The Malaac started their night cries and one by one they started to dive into the water, heads bobbing as they watched their master stir.

Its legs were small – it was as much serpent as dragon and its wings were barely man-sized, folded as they were against its back and never used. So it took some minutes before it could gain leverage against the rocky surface and, using its legs, push its head into the water, its body slowly following with a powerful splash. The dragon disappeared under the water for a full minute or so, before its head broke the waves again, the man still clinging to its back. His clothes were soaking, yet his waxy face and skin were no wetter than they had been on the land. He went under again and rose once more, still none the worse for his submergence. All around him the Malaac whooped and cried, excited to be swimming with such a great beast. And follow it they did as the great dragon swam, its powerful tail propelling it ever closer to the river ahead.

29

'Hello, can you hear me?'

The words floated into her head, clear and tinged with concern. Was she dreaming? All she could feel were her bruises and a sharp but receding pain in her left side. She couldn't focus. When she tried to think, her thoughts seemed to float away from her, drifting in the formless space surrounding her. All she could get from them were faint echoes, fragments half remembered before nausea drove them away again.

'Hello, Cheris, are you awake?'

There was the voice again; it was sharper this time, more concerned. She forced herself to react to it. She had to open her eyes, make herself respond. The fog was starting to clear at last, There was light and a dim, blurred image swam ahead of her.

'What? Am I in the field?' Was that her voice? It sounded so weak.

'No, silly, it's Anaya. You are in my tent.'

'Tent?' It was Anaya; she could see her now. Without thinking, she tried to lever herself on to her side, only to collapse backwards as her pain intensified; it felt as if she was being stabbed with a pitchfork.

'No no, you mustn't move yet; you are much too weak. I will let you try again tomorrow but no sooner. You must rest; it has been an ordeal for you and you need time.'

She could see a bit more clearly now. She was on a bed in Anaya's quarters, separate from the soldiers. She had blankets over her and a small feather pillow under her head. 'What happened to me?' she croaked.

'You collapsed after your last spell. I could see it in the sky all the way from the healing tent. You must have put everything into it. Shortly afterwards the knights carried you here. You poor thing, you must have lost control of everything when you fainted; you had a bit of an accident down there, but don't you worry. The knights didn't notice and I have cleaned your robes since. They are drying now.'

'O 'Lissa's blood, I am so sorry! And embarrassed. Very embarrassed.' She realised that under the warmth of the blankets all she was wearing was a thin nightdress.

'Don't be! I deal with that sort of thing all the time. Men are far worse believe me. Marcus wants to see you, but I said I would check with you first to see if you were up to it.'

'I am,' she said. 'Weak and bruised but I can talk.'

'Bear in mind, I have used magic on you to ease the pain, on the rib especially. It will hurt more later on, but really the best medicine you have now is time and rest.'

'Thank you, Anaya. When did the battle end?'

'Last night of course. We are well into the afternoon now and it is wet and miserable outside. The best place for you is right here. I have to go – I have other patients after all – but I will send Marcus in to see you.'

She left and Cheris lay back on her pillow, eyes half closed. She remembered everything now – how the mage tried to kill her, the panic she felt and her murderous response, not just against him but against the whole opposing army, whose soldiers, individually, had done nothing to her. She felt sick but fought the feeling. Even breathing normally caused discomfort; she dreaded to think how it would feel if she became excited or anxious.

She listened to the rain on the canvas; she was glad she wasn't outside in it, but here, under the blankets, it was a soothing sound. Suddenly there was a flash of a red robe and Marcus fairly bounded in, relief writ large on his face.

'Hello, Marcus,' she said. 'Whatever you do, please don't hug me.'

'No fear,' he said, beaming. 'Anaya has told me of your injuries, so tell me, how does the Heroine of Grest feel?'

'Terrible!' she said, honestly. 'Weak, sick and tired, and please don't call me such a silly name.'

'It is the name the soldiers have given you,' he said. 'That and the Queen of Storms. Everyone has forgotten my name now; the soldiers have let a beautiful young warrior into their hearts instead. Felmere wants to give you a title: Battle Mage of Tanaren. It means, once your tenure here is over, if he is ever able to re-engage another of our kind in the future, it is you he can request.'

She groaned. 'I have had enough already. Can I refuse to accept this "honour"?'

'Refuse a title bestowed by one of the most powerful barons in the country? Unprecedented. Technically you can but you would never leave the island again.'

She tried to turn to face him, but was only partially successful.

'Marcus, I found things out about myself last night ... dark things. When that man hurt me, and I would have died if Sir Norton hadn't given me my staff, when I had recovered, I ... I wanted to kill him. Even worse, I felt satisfaction when I did; I was just so angry. And even after that I wasn't sated. I felt so detached when I cast the last spell. I gave no consequence to the havoc I would wreak on those men; it was a technical exercise for me, one to see just how powerful I could make the lightning, and I know that, if I hadn't have been so exhausted and hurting, I could have done so much more with it. The lives that I took meant nothing to me ... then. It is not till now that what I have done is dawning on me. It is a worse feeling than the pain in my ribs.'

Marcus looked sympathetic. 'Let it go, girl, They would all have killed you without a second thought. You have to be detached anyway; it impacts on your effectiveness if you get involved emotionally. I think what is upsetting you is how chillingly effective you were. You are beginning to realise just how powerful you can be, and possibly it is that that is bothering you.'

'I don't know; it was my desire for vengeance that frightened me. It was so strong. I hated the man for what he did. I have an evil streak when I am pushed. How is it that I have always wanted to help where I can, be liked and friendly with everyone and yet here all I am good for is murder, mayhem and bloodshed. Does everyone end up turning into whatever it is they despise?'

'To some extent,' said Marcus. 'Life is a long road and sometimes you are forced to take a path contrary to your nature. You cannot travel its course without bruises; the Gods have a reason for every pitfall on the path and sometimes it takes years before you understand the reasons as to why they are there. Sometimes they are never apparent. What you did last night does not fundamentally change what you are; maybe it just informed you better as to the darker aspects of human nature, no more than that. Just bear in mind that a mere ten yards away outside this tent you are a heroine to many people. Your actions saved many lives as well, you know. I was stuck up that hill and couldn't see a thing. Without you the battle could have gone on for hours more and the death toll would have been much, much higher.'

'So you are saying that men died so that others could live?'

'Precisely, it is one of nature's more fundamental rules. Is it not sad when a falcon plucks a sparrow out of mid-flight? The sparrow dies but the falcon's chicks feed on it and grow strong. And there are many more sparrows out there.'

She tried to laugh, a feeble wheezy effort. 'I am not sure I understand your analogy but thanks anyway; I do believe you are cheering me up.'

'Good.' He paced to and fro, stretching his legs. 'Anaya is refusing to let you out of bed until tomorrow but I think Felmere wants you running about as soon as possible, so he can show you off.'

'Well,' she said, 'I don't want to lie here for ever; I will see how far I can walk tomorrow, if Anaya allows it.'

'Good. I will help support you, if necessary.'

'Thank you.' She was perking up by the second. 'Marcus, what happened on the hill anyway?'

'Never have someone my age hide flat out behind a tree for twenty-four hours. When the time came to sneak through the gate I could barely stand up, let alone walk. Anaya has given me a liniment to rub on my joints. By the Gods, I needed something! Apart from my decaying body, though, everything went as Felmere hoped. The garrison was watching the events in the field, the gate was opened for us, and the only thing that went wrong was the fire. I was a little over-zealous when I ignited the catapults and a couple of them collapsed on the hill, setting the trees on fire. The knights and I tried to join the battle down on the plain, but the flames and smoke meant we couldn't get out of the gate. By the time it died down and we could leave the town, we were only just in time to see your lightning show. As for the town itself, things were turning ugly when we left – the townsfolk were turning on the Arshumans. Retribution seemed to be the only thing on some people's minds; they were rounding people up and herding them to the town square.

Hopefully the soldiers will be able to restrain any excesses from the locals.'

'Well, I am hardly the one to lecture them on the evils of revenge,' she said. 'Has the army moved into the town yet?'

'The barons are already there and they are rebuilding the bridges the Arshumans destroyed when they took the town. When you are fit and well you can move up there with them. The rumour is that Felmere is not finished with pressing the enemy and may prosecute the war into the winter. But for now just think about getting better. Nothing will happen for a while yet.'

'More fighting?' she groaned.

'Don't complain about too much fighting,' said Marcus. 'Many people here have been slogging away for ten years and there is still no end in sight for them.'

'I don't know how they can bear it,' she said. 'It isn't even the physical punishment that troubles me. You know how it is – the first time you cast a light spell you spend weeks practising, exercising your mind for it; you are nothing but nerves when you have to perform under the eyes of your mentor. The hundredth time you cast it, it is of no more import than scratching your nose. Seeing people, friends suffering in front of you all the time, death becomes just another mundane occurrence little different from slaughtering a pig for Winterfeast. It just seems ... wrong somehow.'

'Imagine the First Aelven War or the one-hundred-and-fifty-year war between Koze and the kingdom of Hracja nearly two millennia ago. People were born and could live a hundred years all under the spectre of war, never seeing its beginning or its end. Just imagine that the next time you are called into battle.'

She tried sitting up again and managed to prop herself up on her elbow.

'Am I moaning again? Sorry. I would like to say you were right about one thing. I am glad I have left the island. I could never spend my entire life there without going mad, watching the supply ships coming in and then leaving, wondering where they were going, what these countries looked like. I was worried sick about fighting, but, now it is over, I would like to thank you. If this is the only way I could leave, then it is as Artorus wills, and I am glad I have come here.'

Marcus smiled ruefully. 'It is unfortunate that we come here to kill, I know, but a mind such as yours could never be constrained by our home. I will let you rest now; I will see you in the morning. See if you can remember how to walk.'

He left her then and, despite all his news, she felt an inexplicable wave of sadness wash over her. She couldn't escape the feeling that last night's conflict was merely the precursor of something greater and more terrible to come.

BOOK ONE: AUTUMN
30

The droplets from the silver fountain caught the bright noonday sunlight and cascaded into the pool in a spray of rainbow-coloured mist. There were several of these fountains in the oval pool, constantly refreshing the water for the large golden carp that shunted along in its depths or occasionally peeked out from underneath the olive-green lily pads and water iris that decorated its surface. The pool had a marble surround carved with recesses and these housed a variety of dark-green waxy-leaved plants that needed constant watering. Overhanging the pool, supported on four exotically engraved ebony-wood poles, was a sheer-silk pavilion that let in the light while keeping everything under it unseasonably warm. There were benches for those who didn't wish to stroll around this courtyard and one giant fountain behind the pool whose rose quartz base was cunningly fashioned in the shape of intertwining leaves, branches, vines and ivies. This fountain, however, was not in use at the moment and sat gloomily overlooking the courtyard as though in a deep sulk. The courtyard itself was tiled, walled in brilliant-white stone with heavy black doors at its front and rear. On the high and broad walkways surrounding the inner walls were planted several trees, with thin silver grey trunks covered in broad leaves that smelled of sharp but sweet lemon. Despite the time of year, not a leaf had fallen from them and an army of small garrulous songbirds greeted the new day from their branches. It was a haven of tranquil serenity.

Not that King Aganosticlan VII, ruler of Arshuma, was feeling the serenity at the moment. He loved the pool and would spend many hours strolling past it, throwing titbits to his fish. No, there was nothing wrong with the pool at all. Rather, it was the company he was keeping at the present time. The King himself wore a long purple silk robe, embroidered in gold and black, with wide sleeves and a broad collar, both encrusted with tiny gems. His hair was long, black and lustrous – combed to a fine sheen it spilled behind him like one of the legendary black rivers of the south. His pencil-thin moustache, hiding under his high-bridged nose and his small pointed beard were trimmed and waxed so that not a single hair was out of place. His fingers were encrusted with gold rings and kohl framed his large brown eyes giving him something of the appearance of an owl. He positively dripped opulence.

The figure walking alongside him, however, could not have been more of a contrast. Everything about him was severe, from his close-cropped grey hair and hard-chiselled face to his keen grey eyes that burned hard and merciless. His tunic, though well made, was a simple red colour, his black breeches and weathered boots were of good quality but severely utilitarian. At his belt was a simple ceremonial dagger, more a badge of office than a useful weapon, and although he wore soft black leather gloves, it could be seen that two fingers were missing from his left hand. What was apparent was that being in the company of a king overawed him not one whit; in fact, it was the other man who seemed unnerved by him. As Aganosticlan absently threw black bread for the fish, his companion spoke to him, his voice stern and uncompromising.

'The news of your latest defeat has reached the ears of the Emperor. Needless to say, he is displeased. For ten years he has allowed you to pursue this war as you have seen fit. Now, however, his patience wears thin. He desires to know if indeed you have a plan to bring victory to your people or whether or not you will be approaching Grand Duke Leontius to negotiate a peace; this, at least from his position in the Imperial Palace in Chira, seems to be the most sensible of solutions.'

The King looked uneasy. 'Ambassador Hylas, before entering into your current honourable profession, you served with distinction in the Imperial Army for many years. You should be as aware as anyone then that this was not a decisive defeat. A setback, yes, but little more than that.'

The Ambassador stopped walking; the other man followed suit.

'How many men did you lose in this battle?'

'About two thousand, along with the mage you so kindly supplied for us.'

'So I heard.'

Hylas sat down at a bench. The king clapped his hands and a young serving girl, clad in a white tunic that skirted the bounds of decency, stepped forth bearing a beautifully fashioned silver plate which held a variety of fruits. The Ambassador took an apple; the King waved the girl away. Taking a bite out of the apple with a satisfying crunch, Hylas spoke again.

'His Imperial Majesty has asked me to remind you of both your status and your responsibility to the Empire. When he ascended to the grand office of Emperor fifteen years ago Ucarioth decided to fix the boundaries of the Empire and to halt the policy of constant expansion, drain as it was on the Imperial coffers and detrimental to the wellbeing of its citizens. To that end, he offered all nations bordering the Empire the status of client kingdom, with the promise that there would be no war or invasion of these nations as long as they were prepared never to act contrary to the interests of the Empire and to supply an annual tribute amounting to seven per cent of each nation's calculated wealth. This meant that, for a small price, kings such as yourself could continue to rule your lands free from our interference – unless of course that interference was requested.'

'I am aware of my responsibilities to the Empire,' said the King haughtily.

'Are you? As I recall, you baited a fool Tanarese baron to attack one of your cities, using his attack as an excuse to launch a full-scale invasion of that nation, an attack that stalled and petered out within a year. Tanaren is not an enemy of the Empire's; it has a powerful navy and is a key trading partner. Your invasion of its territory therefore technically constituted a breach of your contract with the Empire, acting as you did in a manner contrary to its interests. The amount of work I had to do to convince the Emperor, the generals and the first citizens that you had not lost your mind and had not abused your client status will live with me to this day.'

'And for that, Hylas, my gratitude is still strong.'

Without warning, Hylas grabbed the King's shoulders, pulling him close so that the two men's faces were barely a foot apart. He shouted at him, his spittle spraying the King's face.

'Is it? Is it? Ten years later and we are having the same poxy arguments about it. Well, I am here to give you a final warning. You have one year. One year! If there is no peace or victory in that time, our boys will be marching through the passes and pissing in your pool before you can say annexation!'

King Aganosticlan retained his composure. 'Believe you me, Hylas, within a year the war will be over and I will be drinking the finest Tarindian wines in Baron Felmere's mansion.'

The other man seemed placated, to a degree. Though his eyes still burned with anger, he released his grip on the King and joined him strolling about the pond.

'One other thing, Your Majesty,' (the honorific was practically spat out) 'you are still hiring mercenaries and presumably you will be replacing your recent losses. How exactly are you financing yourself? The pecuniary assistance I negotiated for you ended some three years ago. Surely that money has run out by now?'

'I have other means, Hylas. I am no pauper and my nation has its own wealth. I am working the gem mines to capacity, though these days I have to use forced labour – prisoners and the like. So you see, it is in my interests, too, to end this war swiftly, my coffers may not be yet exhausted but they are not bottomless after all.'

Hylas looked grim. 'On my way here I passed through villages where everyone was saying how the food stocks would not last through the winter. You may be confronted with an unpalatable choice. Feed your people or fight this war.'

Aganosticlan stroked his beard. 'Pah, peasants! They live to serve the nation, as, indeed, do I.'

Hylas looked at him with little love. 'Odd is it not, that your service to the nation seems so much more lucrative than theirs. Anyway, I have delivered my message, I will leave now; a day's hard riding will see me over the border and back with the army. If you are not aware of it, we are camped just the other side of the eastern Derannen Mountains, within a few miles of your nation.'

'I am aware of it. Fare you well.'

'You too. Artorus deliver you victory.'

The great black doors swung open and Hylas was gone.

Aganosticlan did not bother watching him leave; he had already turned and was heading indoors to his palace.

The throne room was a long rectangular affair clad in white stone and colonnaded with marble. The King of Arshuma sat on an ornate wooden throne covered in gold leaf and carved in the likeness of a lion, its forearms acting as the armrests and its head, with the mouth open in a terrifying roar, looking over the top of the throne glaring at the King's subjects as they approached him. The room's high windows, arched and graceful, illuminated the red-carpeted walkway to the throne, while keeping the throne itself in relative darkness, which was probably the reason for the burning braziers located to its right and left. There was a certain sterility to the room, a cold remoteness which the King liked. It gave a certain frisson to his less popular judgements, something to make the common populace quail when they heard his words.

Not that he cared about that now. Entering the room, he stormed towards his throne like a bull chasing a farmer. Hurling himself on to it, he rang a small gong placed at its feet. A black-clad servant approached.

'Get me Obadrian. Now!'

The servant scuttled off and Aganosticlan impatiently drummed his fingers against the throne's armrest. Shortly afterwards, through the open door came a man in his early fifties with long silver hair. He was clad in black and carried a large staff of a similar colour, symbol of the office of Lord Chamberlain. The King barely let him finish his low bow before venting his spleen.

'I cannot believe the way that jumped-up politician talks to me! I am a king, and yet he, a man little more than the Emperor's wiper, comes in here laying down the law and threatening my person and my very office! I should have sent him back to his precious army in tiny pieces.'

'His army being the Western Army of the Chiran Empire, Your Majesty, that would hardly be an advisable course of action.'

'Advisable or not, it would be a strong warning to all those who think nothing of baiting a king! He has given me a year to finish the war, Obadrian; I must have Keth's own luck. Can you not find me a general that can at least point the army towards the enemy and not have them run back here at the first sign of trouble! Ach, my head hurts so.' He paused for breath. 'How many survivors of the battle were there anyway?'

'Some three hundred men have returned, Your Majesty; it appears the enemy deployed devastating magic against us.'

'Yes, we have to neutralize their wizardry if we are to make further progress, and quickly, too. As for the men, execute fifteen of them; keep them in gibbets to show what happens to cowards who would rather soil themselves than fight. Then get another two thousand men enrolled; see what mercenaries we can hire, too. This war continues through the winter.'

'As you wish, Your Majesty, though our coffers may not stretch to too many mercenaries.'

'Nevertheless, see what you can find.'

'Of course, Your Majesty.' He shuffled uneasily. 'Your Majesty, that delegate, the one you wanted kept away from Ambassador Hylas, shall I send for him now?'

'Yes, bring him before me. Keeping him in chambers outside the palace was hardly ideal but there was no way Hylas could see him.'

'Your Majesty, do you really think speaking to him is such a good idea? Playing both ends against the middle like this is a risky manoeuvre.'

Aganosticlan left his throne and walked the short distance to the room's back wall. There, displayed on wooden panels were a variety of finely crafted weapons – swords, daggers, maces – many encrusted with jewels, nearly all gifts from other countries.

'We have no choice, Obadrian. If we are to deliver victory in a year we need their money, especially since Hylas stopped sending us the stuff. The concessions they want are painful, but ultimately it will be a price worth paying.'

'If the Chiran Empire finds out, Your Majesty...'

'Do not question me! Now go and get him.'

'As you wish, Your Majesty.'

It did not take long. Aganosticlan was still dreamily looking at the weapons on his wall when he heard footsteps on the carpet.

'Your Majesty, I bring salutations and the warmest affection from the Eternal Empire. Koze and Emperor Gyiliakosh are delighted to include you among those nations friendly to its cause. I hope our meeting will further strengthen the burgeoning ties between our peoples.'

If Hylas style of dress contrasted sharply with the King's, then HemKhozar, emissary of Koze, could have been his darker-skinned cousin. His green and black silk robes flowed elegantly behind him; his beard, long, braided and waxed, reached down to his belt of silver and gold. His hair was as long as the King's, although it was greying at the temples and his skin, olive coloured and soft, told the tale of a man used to sunnier climes. He smiled warmly at Aganosticlan, showing a mouth full of gold-capped teeth.

'And greetings to your good self, Hem-Khozar. I hope and trust your voyage from the far south was a smooth and pleasant one.'

'Indeed it was. Although the storm season is almost upon us, we kept ahead of the worst of the weather and a following wind brought us here in good time.'

Aganosticlan shook the man's hand and embraced him, kissing him on both cheeks, the traditional greeting for a man from the ancient empire of the south.

Koze had once been merely a powerful city state, but some three thousand years ago it had started to expand, first swallowing up the surrounding islands and then the deserts and jungles on the mainland. It was as much a trading empire as a military one, forging ties with the barbarian human kingdoms of the north and, in a more profitable enterprise, with the elves of the plains and the sea. There were even tentative links with the underground peoples, with their iron, gold and gems.

For two thousand years now the Empire had grown and flourished. The first Emperor who in later times came to enjoy a semi-divine status among his people, started the construction of the vast Lilac Palace, a royal complex, designed in imitation of the dwellings of the Sea Elves, that spread across several islands linked by thin graceful bridges. It had a great lighthouse, the largest construction of its kind in the world, and included the High Tower of Kolosta, the seat of the Emperor himself. Built of quartz, marble and gold, its thousand great rooms were home not only to the Emperor and his thousand strong harem, but also to the Remorseless Guard, the Emperor's elite troops, and the Strekha, his all-female bodyguard, fanatical assassins who rarely left his side and whose name spread terror among the downtrodden populace. These early years of the Empire had produced the first great human mathematicians and philosophers, the likes of Bratenas and Callathenatash, whose exhaustive tomes were still the first point of reference for students, as well as artists like Erfenetas, poets like Tantanaemash and engineers like VanKenefesh, architect of the Lilac Palace and the great coastal fortresses of Kengigh and Manakefron. It was the Eternal Empire, the Land of the Divine Firmament, a force for human civilisation in the world. It would endure for ever, glorious and invincible.

Then, however, it had all started to go wrong.

The decline coincided with the emergence of another city state in the north. Like Koze before it, Chira arose from humble beginnings. The Emperor, sitting in his great tower, barely blinked as Chira conquered its neighbouring state, Anmir, and gradually assimilated the people of the lakes. Then, however, came its conquest of the elves and too late the Emperor awoke from his complacency.

Whereas Koze prided itself on all spheres of its achievement, Chira had one great asset and one alone. Its army. A Kozean army of seventy thousand marched on Chira. Its general even engaged a poet to write of his great victory before he had even left his palatial barracks. Two months later only his severed head returned with barely two thousand uninjured men. Suddenly, their folly – as witnessed by an over-reliance on mercenaries, generals picked for their connections rather than their ability, a surly rebellious populace ground down by centuries of excessive taxation and harsh treatment, and a dependence on a single man who might be a fool or mad, or both – was laid bare before them. Within a year they were forced to negotiate a peace with Chira, which exacted a terrible price.

Nearly a thousand years later, riven by centuries of rebellion, defeated in several wars and after the loss of many trading partners, the Eternal Empire was a shadow of its former self. Barely a third of its original size, it had had to considerably rein in its ambitions. Chira was top dog now and all Koze could do was watch and seethe, and fester in its bitterness.

The latest Kozean Emperor, though, although a libertine whose sexual excesses were already something of legend, was fighting back. He was trying to use his gold to reopen links with nations long forgotten and, through them, to curtail the Chiran juggernaut by chipping away at its frontiers while avoiding open confrontation. Hence the appearance of his trusted ambassador in the court of this minor king.

Aganosticlan directed Hem-Khozar to a space between the columns where a cushion-strewn divan was situated. Hem-Khozar reclined upon it, but the King remained standing. 'I take it my eastern counterpart has departed?' said the ambassador, adjusting a cushion for greater comfort.

'Yes, he has, after issuing many threats and ultimatums. I apologise if I seem out of sorts, but I am still angry with the way I was spoken to. They have no respect for status; anything that isn't part of their precious empire is only fit to be spat upon.'

'Indeed, my friend, we have had many centuries of experience of such treatment. I take it, though, that you cannot yet openly oppose them?'

'Keth's furnace, no!' spluttered the King. 'The Western Army could roll in here within two days! I may hate them, but I have no choice but to keep in their good graces, and to do that, I have just been told, I need to win this war within a year.'

Hem-Khozar looked at him, his eyebrows raised. 'Do you really think you can achieve this?'

'Not without your support. I have just suffered something of a setback and need fresh troops to proffer a response, and for that' – he paused for effect – 'I need money.'

The ambassador stroked his chin. 'Why not sue for peace?'

'I – the Gods curse me for my weakness – was actually considering it, but after losing that last battle it is Duke Leontius who holds all the bargaining chips. I will not sacrifice any land east of the Broken River but Tanaren wants Roshythe and that is tantamount to admitting defeat. And after ten years I will never accept that. Never.'

'It seems then that your best options are to negotiate a peace on favourable terms; a strong Arshuma, acting as a brake on Chiran ambitions, is in both our interests.'

'And for that,' said the King, his face animated, 'I need a victory.'

'Indeed. Let me convey to you the wishes of the Emperor. Firstly, and this is the bad news, there will be no further funds available for the time being. This is because a shipment of coin headed for another country was waylaid by a Chiran war galley; they now know we are financing their enemies and, just like yourself, we are not yet ready for open war with them; some of our borders would not have the strength to resist a full Chiran assault.' Seeing the King's downcast face. he continued hastily: 'You have used the money we have given you wisely, and have paid the right people. I would take advantage of your enemy's overconfidence and lure him into a fight where he will get the surprise of his life. It is not too late for you to end this year in control of the direction of this war.'

'A winter battle? It is something I have been thinking about. This may sound strange but last night Artorus gave me a vision, a dream. In it I saw a battle with frost upon the ground. A great blue dragon fought a yellow one. The blue had the early advantage but in the end the yellow was victorious, ripping out the throat of its foe. I was there. I stood in the field holding the heads of my enemies up high, Felmere and that boy of a grand duke.' He grew excited. 'Do you believe in destiny, my friend? Perhaps this dream was a portent; I can raise the troops; they do not have to be the best quality, as you say, and I have the plan to surprise Felmere and his men. The seeds are already sown for this.' His spirits raised, he clapped his hands: 'Wine! Wine for our guest!'

Hem-Khozar smiled. 'We, too, believe in the power of the divine manifesting itself in dreams. We have a temple dedicated to the god of dreams and I am sure the priests there would interpret your dream in a similar way. I will take it as an omen of your inevitable victory. However, there has been a slight change in our conditions of support.'

Aganosticlan's shoulders sagged and he bit his lip – this ambassador could deliver the poison of a serpent clad in words of pure honey. 'Go on, what are they?'

'The lease you have promised for the Isle of Tredum is to be for one hundred years not fifty, and our cut from your gem mines is to be twenty per cent, not fifteen.'

The King started pacing to and fro. 'You drive a hard bargain, my friend – the island on which you can base your ships close to Chira's coastal cities and increased access to the mines which made my country rich. And yet, I see no additional concession on your part – no money, no troops. Why should I change terms I agreed with you on our last meeting?'

Hem-Khozar stood and faced the King. He signalled to the chamberlain who was standing at a respectful distance. 'Send in the gift from the Emperor!'

'What gift?' asked the King.

'You will see, my friend. It is the role of the diplomat to never fully play his hand on first meeting.'

The King retired to his throne and Hem-Khozar joined him, standing at his side. Within a minute Obadrian returned, strolling up the red carpet with his staff held across his chest. Behind him was another figure – tall, lithe, black clad and hooded.

'Emperor Gyiliakosh himself has sanctioned the loan to you of one of his most valuable assets. In the past men have bequeathed kingdoms and surrendered nearly all their personal wealth in return for what is given to you freely in order to cement your forthcoming victory. King Aganosticlan, allow me to present one of his deadliest servants, trained to kill from ten years old, recruited from the foothills of Mount Kzugun, and never defeated in battle.'

The figure was now at the foot of the steps to the throne and Aganosticlan beheld its lissom form. The newcomer was armoured completely in black, and the gauntlets, vambraces and leg guards were equipped with small but lethally sharp outward-pointing spikes; there were straight and curved daggers at the waist and still more strapped to the thighs. The King watched as the visitor threw back their hood and the light from the braziers fell on the cropped blonde hair, throwing dark shadows into the pits of her eyes. HemKhozar spoke again.

'My king, I give you Syalin, Strekha of the emperor, first of The Ten, elite of the elite, his bodyguard and his most beautiful and deadliest assassin.'

The woman was at the top of the stairs. She bent on to one knee and bowed to both men. Aganosticlan was never to see her bow again.

BOOK ONE: AUTUMN
31

She had been right about the rain. They had been travelling through the forest for about two hours when it broke. Despite the protection of the trees, they became wet and cold in a very short time. Seeing Cedric was in some discomfort, Itheya called a halt.

'We will rest here tonight; our journey will still finish tomorrow. Some food and sleep may be a good idea.'

She led them under the spreading branches of a great oak. Little rain got past its broad branches and the earth by its trunk was still dry. Once they were settled, she set to lighting a fire then disappeared for an hour. 'I will get food,' she said. After watching her go the two men huddled close to the fire, doing their best to get comfortable.

As soon as he plunged into the wood, Morgan had seen how old it truly was. There was not a branch uncovered by moss or lichen, not a bank of earth uncovered by ferns. Every tree seemed to have a massive trunk and a great shaggy head with few leaves browning despite the time of year. Great roots sprang out of the ground like the gnarled fingers of the dead and everywhere was the damp smell of earth and wet leaves and the sad sigh of the leaves in the breeze. To Morgan's surprise, though, the forest was not trackless; they had followed a broad dirt path almost as soon as they entered the place. There was no grass on it, no dangerous roots or damp moss; it appeared to be well used or at least frequently cleared.

The other Wych folk carrying Cedric's trunk passed them quite early on. Itheya said something to them and they replied good-naturedly. 'They said, "See you there,"' she told her companions as they saw the trunk and its bearers disappear into the trees ahead.

After about an hour she returned with three dead rabbits. Without speaking to either of the men she skinned the rabbits, cleaned them and made up a crude spit, which she placed over the fire. As the rabbits slowly cooked, she sat between Morgan and Cedric staring at the fire.

'That was very impressive,' said Cedric. 'You caught them in no time.'

'No,' she replied, 'it took nearly an hour.'

'I was speaking relatively. Yes, it took an hour, but an hour to catch rabbits is a fairly quick time, I believe. Or am I wrong?'

'You are wrong. I should have been quicker. I should not have left you alone for so long. The forest is not without danger.'

'We were fine,' said Morgan. 'Cedric here was telling me of his youth and how he met the great love of his life. You came back just as it was getting interesting.'

'Then do not let me stop you. Continue, if you wish.'

'Maybe another time,' said Cedric. 'It wasn't that interesting anyway.'

Morgan laughed. 'Company not appropriate?'

Itheya's brow wrinkled. 'What do you mean?'

'Cedric is a gentleman, Itheya. There are some things he would dare not repeat in front of a lady.'

'Why ever not?'

Cedric broke in: 'In human society the conversation between men and men and men and women is different. There are topics which are best avoided when a man speaks to a lady. It is a question of taste and decorum, women being of a more delicate and sensitive nature than men.'

'Sick man Cedric,' she said, 'do you know many women?'

'Oh let me see – there is Alys, of course, and Grana the old lady, who cleans my rooms, when I allow her, and then there's ... there's...' He stopped and looked at her. 'No, I don't know many women.'

'I thought not,' she said and went back to checking the rabbits.

Shortly after, they ate. Itheya divided the rabbits into equal portions and rubbed some herbs on them that she had taken from her pack. They devoured it all hungrily. 'Delicious, quite delicious,' said Cedric.

The rain became heavier and the conditions colder. They huddled in their blankets close to the fire; well, the men did, Itheya seem fairly oblivious to the cold, and she just sat there licking the fat off her fingers. 'Waste nothing,' she told the men.

Once they had finished she passed round her water skin. 'Nothing stronger?' joked Morgan.

'Well, I have some zhath in my pack.'

'And what by the Gods is zhath?'

'The wine of the elves' There was a sardonic tone to her voice. 'Used to clean wounds and deaden the skin for kazhoeth. You can even drink it, if you are brave enough.'

'I seem to recall you telling me how brave I was earlier on,' said Morgan. 'If you have some to spare, I would happily try some, if only to keep the cold at bay.'

'Very well – you are welcome to as much of it as you want.'

She pulled a smaller skin from her pack and gave it to him. With a little trepidation he took a sip. He had a taste of spring flowers and pine needles and then his throat started to burn. Once his eyes stopped watering, he passed it to Cedric. Cedric drank without thinking and was soon spluttering helplessly. She regarded them with some amusement in her eyes. 'Our melian, our children, can handle zhath better than you two.'

'Then show us how it is done.' Morgan handed her the skin.

She drank, more deeply than the other two and showed no reaction to the drink at all. With an air of triumph she handed it back to Morgan.

The zhath was passed round several more times with no one refusing its potent contents. Morgan certainly felt warmer as well as a sense of euphoric happiness as the zhath took a grip of his skull. Itheya gave the impression that it did not affect her at all, but he could discern a certain pink tinge to her skin and the tip of her nose which hadn't been there before. The effect on Cedric was a little more obvious.

'Let me tell you both...' He swayed a little – both Morgan and Itheya were poised to steady him – but he managed to right himself. 'What an honour ... yes, honour. What an honour it is for me to ... to ... Did I say it was an honour?'

'Yes,' said Morgan, unable to suppress a grin.

'Yes, an honour indeed for me to have the company ... of the company I now have. You, sir, are a warrior with humanity and you, madam, are a lady ... a lady of great, er ... great elfanity and I thank you for allowing me ... us ... into your august realm. It is my considered opinion...' There was no more from Cedric as he slumped on to his back and started snoring loudly. Before Morgan could do anything Itheya was pulling his blanket over him and adjusting his head so that he would be more comfortable.

'Concern for a human?' Morgan was still grinning.

'For this human, yes. He is important. If it was you, I would just take your blanket for myself and roll you on to those tree roots.'

'Oh-ho. Now you are just being cruel.'

She ignored him. 'I do not know how humans react to the zhath. He will be all right, yes?'

'Well, he might be a bit sick in the morning and may need propping up on his horse, but apart from that, yes – just make sure he has plenty of water.'

'I will.' She gently pulled some hair back from Cedric's brow and brushed his forehead tenderly. 'Sleep well, sick man.'

'Does he remind you of your father?'

'In some ways – how did you see that? I am sure humans are the same but we respect our older people. Their knowledge is important, even if they are frail physically.'

'Some humans respect the elderly; others would sell their fathers for a crown – their children, too.'

'Really? You would describe your own people so savagely?'

'As with everything, once you scratch the surface, it is a lot more complicated than that. Many of us are like Cedric, would help our neighbours, attempt to better themselves as the church exhorts. I, however, have spent a large part of my life seeing the very worst that people can do. There is no greater instinct than that of survival and, to survive, people will do anything, absolutely anything. But there is something worse than that. There are people who would do anything not out of necessity, the need to survive, but for profit, to enrich themselves at the expense of others, and for people like that the word "savage" is far too mild.'

Itheya came over to him, crouching down to face him.

'Something has happened to you, yes? In the past, something bad. I could sense sadness in you when I first met you. You are a fighting man who dislikes fighting. Why is that, I wonder?'

'I think, my Lady, that I have said enough, especially to one who regularly threatens to kill me. My troubles are not for offloading on to others.'

'As you wish.' She turned away from him and started warming her hands over the fire. 'Cold, is it not? It will soon be time for winter clothing – effective, but unflattering, at least for a woman.'

'Well, here I am wrapped in a blanket and you just stood there in your thin leather.' He took the blanket off himself and held it out for her to take.

She did so. 'The leather is not that thin, but thank you.' And then to his surprise she went and sat down right next to him putting the blanket over them both.

'Like this, yes? We can keep each other warm.'

And warm she was. The bare skin of her arm brushed, feather light, against his hand. She pulled herself even closer to him so that they were in full contact. He had the sweet smell of the river in his nostrils again. She spoke, as if such intimacy was incidental.

'I believe that you both can make a good impression with my father, and with loremaster Terath. Please do not be flippant with them as you can be with me.'

'My flippancy annoys you?'

'No, it is just unusual for me to be spoken to that way. I am used to it now but Father will not be.'

'What about your mother? You have never mentioned her.'

'She is dead.'

'I see. I am sorry.'

'It is all right. She died bringing my brother into this world, so I never really knew her. Father misses her, though.'

She stretched out and lay flat on her back, 'I have drunk too much. Zhath doesn't get you at first – it takes time – and then when you do not expect it, it hits your head like a charging bear.'

'Do you all drink this stuff often?'

'Only at festivals and on great occasions. I think meeting you two counts as a great occasion. At the Festival of High Summer we drink all day and usually wake up next morning lying next to someone with whom we have never exchanged two words before.'

'Sounds like the old Glaivedon harvest feast.'

She giggled, an enchanting sound even to his own dulled senses. 'You know, if you weren't human, I would probably end up lying with you.'

'Does my being human make a difference?'

She looked at him, her wide eyes incredulous. 'Yes, the very idea; to lie ... with a human?' She collapsed into a fit of hysterical laughter, rolling on to her side and pulling the blanket over her. Morgan found himself joining in, lying flat under the canopy of leaves and branches, listening to the rain and the crackle of the fire. After some minutes she stopped and turned to him, wiping tears from her eyes.

'*Crizhonat ke Vheyuzheke,ve ne tulteth, em ozhotin oro benefe. Stavena vono.*' On seeing Morgan's look of incomprehension, she put her hand to her mouth.

'Sorry, wrong language. I may not see you after tomorrow, but if I do I will teach you some of our words – if you still live. I am sure you will still live, but you never know.'

'Why not teach me some now?'

'Because I will be asleep soon.'

'Go on, just a couple of words.'

'Very well, now say after me: *Presh kulk azha thenestra.*'

'*Presh kulk azha thenestra.* Now what does it mean?'

She started giggling again. Morgan slowly realised what she was up to. 'You are teaching me bad words, aren't you?'

She nodded, still giggling. '*Stavena vono,* Morgan, forgive me; I couldn't resist it. I will sleep now; tomorrow will not be as funny.' She lay back and was gone in a trice. Morgan pulled the blanket so that it covered them both and was asleep within a minute.

He was awoken the next day by the sound of Cedric coughing and spluttering into a bush. Itheya was stood next to him, her arm around him as he was doubled over. 'Do you feel better now? Drink some water when you can.'

Morgan sat up, rubbing his sore head. Itheya shot him an unfriendly look.

'You said he would be all right. Can't you see? He is poisoned.'

'No, no, I am fine,' said Cedric. 'One half-hour and I will be able to ride. It has just been many years since I have drunk anything of that nature. I knew what I was doing. I used to drink far more than what was good for me. I am old enough to make my own mistakes.'

The rain had stopped and it was warmer than yesterday. Morgan's head felt like Keth was inside it, hammering away at his furnace. Itheya looked fresher than them both. He was dimly aware of feeling her next to him that night – indeed, he was pretty sure that at one point her head had been resting on his chest with her arm around him – but aside from that he had been as close to unconscious as it was possible to be. He certainly could not remember when she had got up.

'Big day today,' he said to her.

She nodded. 'I hope he will be well.'

'He will. He has been working towards this for a long time.'

She went into her pack and passed him something resembling flatbread.

'I will help you as much as I can, but be aware that there are many of us who would happily see you to your death. Be respectful at all times. Both my father and Terath speak your tongue as does my brother, so watch everything you say.'

'Cedric is the important man here. I will just sit back and let him impress them.'

'That would be good, but I suspect you may be called upon more than you think. You are a curiosity to us; we may be hostile to you but we may also wish to know of the world you come from. Even I have many questions that I have not yet asked and may never get the chance to.'

'You should have asked them yesterday.'

'The zhath was talking more than I. I apologise if I acted

inappropriately.'

'You were fine. I apologise to you for the same thing, although personally I feel there is nothing wrong in a little inappropriateness from time to time.'

She smiled. 'You are strange human. I am glad I have met you.'

He smiled back. 'And I, you. Come, let's get moving.'

A swift walk, some fresh air, a draught of water and a mouthful of bread later, Cedric declared himself fit and well and able to continue. Shortly afterwards they were all mounted and on their way. The forest looked different in the fitful sunlight, all warm greens, yellows and browns. The leaves were falling more swiftly now; great swathes of them would swirl about the riders before settling on the ground and, as they rode, their thoughts were frequently drowned out by the chorus of birdsong coming at them from all directions. They passed a couple of small lakes, almost hidden by the trees, and just now and then from the corner of his eye Morgan was sure he could see figures watching them from behind the trees. When he turned to look, though, nothing could be seen.

Noon came and went and the afternoon sun started to sink behind them. Morgan was hot and saddle-sore and rather fancied stopping to rest awhile; he was about to suggest this when Itheya stopped ahead of them.

'Ahead and just after the bend in the road – Atem Morioka. My home. See, we will have an escort.'

He saw them. Four figures on horseback patiently waiting just where the road curved northward. As he looked, he fancied seeing a flash of silver through the trees – was it water? He realised he knew nothing of the place they were going to.

Itheya was riding slightly ahead of the men. As they approached the escort, one of its number rode out to meet her. He, too, was dark-haired and sharp-featured and wore a dark-green cloak that covered most of his body.

Morgan could see his tattoos extended up his neck and his eyes were a more garish violet than the girl he was greeting.

BOOK ONE: AUTUMN

'Satala, Itheya. Ta'zhena ne an atan pekha.'

Morgan saw Cedric blanch slightly but control himself almost immediately.

Itheya spoke to the man. *'Satala, Dramalliel, zhur sessala ezho seazha nesteratsen araelveth.'*

'I care not,' said the man. He faced the humans. 'I am Dramalliel, Itheya's brother. I have met few humans and most of them I have killed. And do not trust my sister; she has killed more than I. Follow me.'

His grasp of the language was not as comprehensive as Itheya's and his accent more pronounced. Itheya shot both men an unhappy look before following her brother down the path. Cedric leaned over to Morgan.

'He called us grubs, or worms; obviously another uncomplimentary name for us. Prepare yourself – we will be walking on egg shells from now on.'

They trotted around the long sloping bend and slowly Atem Morioka revealed itself to them.

As Morgan suspected, they were facing a broad still lake, bordered by trees, at least a mile wide. The wind had subsided and barely a ripple disturbed its tranquil surface. Before the lake, starting at the point they now stood, was a broad green lawn covered in thick fresh grass. Pitched upon it were a series of tents, or rather pavilions, in a variety of colours. For some reason Morgan expected everything to be green but nothing could be further from the truth, for their coverings were coloured in blues, reds and golds. Some had two colours running down them in broad stripes; others were plain. Large flags hung limply from the tent poles, many of them green and gold in colour, leaving Morgan to guess that these were the colours of the tribe.

Cedric asked Itheya what the tents were for.

'Various things – the craftsmen work here; horses are stabled here; some store food or other goods such as medicines or dyes. There are two other places like this at other places on the shore. Some people sleep here but most of the village is on the island ahead.' She gestured ahead of her.

As they passed the tents, they fully beheld the lake. Close to the shore, less than two hundred yards distant, was the island of which she spoke. It was large and like an irregular rectangle in shape and, although trees still grew there, it was covered in wooden buildings. From what Morgan could see, each building was a perfect circle, although the size of each varied. However, it was the building at the centre that dominated the others. As well as being the largest building, it was the only one over one storey high. Three storeys it must have been, each storey dotted with small windows that could be closed off with shutters. A series of hide-covered diagonal posts made up the roof of each building. But the most notable feature of each building were its flags.

Even the most humble construction was dwarfed by its flagpole and the colossal flag attached to each one. With the wind dead, the full effect could not be seen, but it was obvious that this was not a place desperate to conceal itself. The central building had half a dozen flagpoles surrounding its roof, pointing outwards like spokes, with an additional one upright at its centre. That one was flying the green and gold.

'Just how large is your tribe?' Morgan asked. To his surprise, it was Dramalliel who answered.

'We are over four thousand strong and can put nearly a thousand warriors in the field with just an hour's notice. This is our major settlement but there are others close to the lake. Our father is waiting for you in our main building on the island.'

Morgan suddenly became aware that any work in the tents had stopped and a crowd had gathered behind them. He could hear the words *vheyuzheko* and *pekha* being whispered and curious children asking questions of their parents. He turned and gently waved at them. Most of the children ran and hid behind the adults, but a couple of them responded in kind, smiling shyly as they did so.

Nestling against the shore were several large log rafts covered in planks. Several elves armed with large poles stood waiting to punt them to the island. They dismounted, leaving the horses to be led away, and climbed on to a raft. Itheya stood next to the men as two elves pushed the raft into the water and proceeded to steer them gently onwards. During the short journey Morgan noticed many elegant sailing vessels gracing the water, becalmed at present, waiting for the wind to pick up. This was obviously a prime location in the forest, belonging to an important tribe. How important he was yet to find out.

The rafts came to rest on the island. Itheya and Dramalliel led them between the smaller roundhouses to the grand building at the centre. Morgan noticed all the houses were decorated with painted wooden carvings, detailed depictions of horses, birds, wolves and stags. He wanted to stop and look, but he was already being left behind so he put on a spurt and rejoined the others.

'This is Zamezhenka, the leader's house,' said Itheya. 'You are welcome here and no harm will be done to you while you remain; no weapons are allowed to be drawn inside it.'

They were in front of it now. It was a colourful building, its walls painted in pale blues, greens and golds. From the second floor, poles jutted out at a right angle to the walls carrying banners displaying the animals of the forest – deer, bears, wolves, eagles and herons – all richly painted and shown engaged in various activities – running, rearing, flying... Unlike the smaller houses, the window spaces were teardrop shaped and the frames were carved in the shape of animals, their heads jutting out at the bottom, leering and growling at passers-by. At length they came to the great double door. It was all black wood with a great carved wolf's head at the centre of both panels. A loose stone path led to the door on either side of which were more banner poles flying the green-and-gold banner of the tribe. Guards attired in livery of the same colour and carrying spears stood at the open door and ushered them inside.

Morgan was expecting a packed earth floor and a dark room lit by torches. Instead, he walked into a light and airy circular inner courtyard open to the sky with a white tiled floor patterned in blue with depictions of trees, birds and waterfalls. Looking up, he saw that the central floor sections of the second and third storeys had been raised using a pulley system and that the hides on the roof had been pulled back to allow the light in. Surrounding the courtyard were entrances to several rooms, their doorways closed off by hand-painted sheets made out of a thin white fabric. A citrus smell was heavy in his nostrils, fresh and invigorating. Cedric was already in the midst of the courtyard, casting his eyes about him.

'The animals you have seen and this painting on the tiles tell stories,' he told Morgan. 'There are many elven fables and legends. Storytellers here are much prized, and there are day-long festivals in summer and winter for the children when they are told the history and mythology of their people. The elves hold a lot of festivals.'

'We do,' said Itheya. 'We actually have the festival of Armentele two days from now. Preparations are going on in the pavilions on the shore. That is why it seems so deserted here.'

Dramalliel was ahead of her, standing at a wooden stairway to the next floor. 'This way,' he said curtly.

The second floor was laid out like the first, though without the tiled courtyard. They came to another set of steps and climbed them, Morgan allowing Cedric to lean on his arm. Itheya excused herself here. 'I will change and join you shortly,' she said, before disappearing behind a curtain into one of the rooms.

They were left with Dramalliel, which was not heartening. Ascending to the third floor, the first thing Morgan noticed was that were no rooms. He then realised that they were in some sort of audience chamber. Even though the central floor section was raised there was still a lot of space here. Following Dramalliel, they passed a few open, unshuttered windows and stood finally before the man they had travelled all this way to meet.

The open roof and windows covered the room in a patchwork of light and shade. However, the high throne they faced would have been in darkness had it not been surrounded by a series of smooth polished stones held in circular bowls on wooden supports. These stones all glowed, giving off a soft red light and a mild warmth which Morgan could feel against his skin even several strides away. In brackets against the walls were lemon-coloured candles whose orange-blue flame was responsible for the citrus smell he had noticed earlier. The throne was made of tastefully gilded wood, carved into which were various abstract shapes –

whorls, circles and spirals. Upon it sat an elf clad in black and gold with long silver-white hair spread about his shoulders. He wore a thick golden torque around his neck and each finger held a thin golden ring. His robe was studded in green and white gems and he wore a thin crown of gold with a colossal diamond at its centre. He sat on the throne leaning on his right arm; his right foot bore a boot of supple black leather but his left was unshod and instead rested on a cushioned stool. Morgan could see it was slightly misshapen and a broad bandage was wrapped around his calf. To his left on a smaller, far less ostentatious, chair was another man, also silver-haired and clad in simple brown. His intense blue eyes fixed both men intently. Dramalliel went and sat on a chair to their left, slightly removed from the others. The figure on the throne looked from Morgan to Cedric with soft violet eyes that were not unlike Itheya's.

'Satala, humans. Welcome to Zamezhenka, the palace of the Morioka tribe. I am Cenarazh, the Mhezhen – that is the leader of the tribe. To my left is Terath, our loremaster, that is, he who retains the knowledge and history of our people. Please be seated.'

Servants, whom Morgan had not noticed before, placed some padded wooden chairs behind them. As he sat, he noticed that these, too, were beautifully carved. Carpentry was obviously a revered profession here.

'Satala, Mhezhen Cenarazh, Satala Terath, I am Cedric of Rossenwood, scholar – that is loremaster – of my people. With me is Morgan of Glaivedon, warrior of renown, and a man who tends to my infirmity. I come here partially seeking enlightenment from your people and also with a request from our Mhezhen, the Grand Duke.'

'Indeed, my daughter has already mentioned your imperfect health, something I can detect now you sit before me. Our people are blessed with a more robust constitution than yours and are far less likely to suffer from the plagues and agues that haunt mankind. Ironic, is it not, that I should be one of the few among my people to be afflicted with a canker of the leg? It will kill me eventually but I will resist it as long as I am able.' He clapped and the servants returned. *'Pileti ivvita hanara baramboros azhaza codarahenezharon zaikele frotan.'*

As Morgan tried to wrap his ears around the mellifluous complexities of the language, the servants departed.

'I am sorry to see that illness has impaired your abilities,' Cedric said. 'At least, unlike me, you have a son and daughter capable of assisting you with your onerous duties.'

'That is true. We have few children here and it is important that they fulfil the expectations we as parents have for them. Mine have done that and more.'

As he spoke, Itheya came and joined them. She had changed into a thin blue tunic just short of the knee, fastened at the waist with a belt whose buckle was encrusted with sapphires. She wore simple goatskin moccasins and with her calves exposed Morgan could see the tattoos on the back and sides of her legs, reaching down to her ankles. Morgan stood and offered her the chair, only for her to dismiss him with a flick of her hand. She went to her father and kissed him on the cheek.

'Satala, Foron, Canteleva zhasessa seatana.'

'Satala, Katyush,' he replied. 'Cantelevia zhasessa tafalle trezem.'

She went and sat on the floor next to Morgan with her knees drawn up to her chin. Morgan noticed casually that Dramalliel had not proffered such a greeting; he assumed it was because, unlike his sister, he had not left their home for some days.

Cedric spoke again, slowly and deliberately.

'I hope that during my stay here that we can learn a little of each other's ways and that, even if we are unable to help each other further, we both end up enriched by the experience. If there are any questions you wish to ask either of us while we are here, please do so, Mhezhen.'

'You speak well, Cedric. For many of us the only humans we meet are those who wish to despoil our lands or teach us of your religion. It will be refreshing to speak to a man of learning. My daughter speaks highly of you and she is a shrewd judge of people's hearts.'

As he spoke, a number of servants returned, one bearing a chair for Itheya, two carrying the trunk that had travelled so far with them, and others that set down a table before the two men and spread it with fruit, bread, strips of meat skewered on sticks, and clay goblets, which they proceeded to fill with a bright clear liquid. Morgan wondered if some formality had to be observed before they could begin, only to see Itheya fall on the food ravenously. Cedric followed. They had not eaten since early that morning, after all. Morgan ate some of the meat. It was spiced with something that gave it quite a heat. It tasted very nice but Morgan had to slake his thirst with the drink which tasted of elderflower. Itheya noticed his reddening face.

'We like our food to have some z'ezhel ... er... heat. You will get used to it.'

'Delicious!' said Cedric. 'I have already learned that you have a great culinary expertise here. I must take the recipe for this meat back with me.' He bathed in the approval he sensed in the room.

Once the food was cleared from the table, Terath carefully placed the artefacts upon it one by one. Once that was done, Cedric spoke.

'These were discovered by chance in ruins on our western coast. There are more of them that I was unable to bring with me, unfortunately. I am here because I wish to know more about them; they are such beautiful objects to my aged eyes.'

'They belong to a different age,' said Terath. 'An age when we lived on the plains, not the forests or on islands over the vast sea. They have religious significance for us, the four smaller objects depicting as they do some of Zhun's major spirits, embodiments of virtues we hold dear.' He held up the stag – 'Cuothos, pride tempered by humility' – then the beaver – 'Yeskila, hard work and industry' – then the falcon – 'Paskilan, the keen-eyed hunter, provider to his family, and lastly'– he held up the snake – 'Azzha, the wily opportunist who survives through cunning. They are all beautiful objects and fine examples of the skill of our ancestors. The ruins you refer to belong to the ancient port and city of Atem Sezheia, one of our oldest and greatest cities, used by our people to embark on the settlement of the western islands following our defeat in the human wars, the Vavanaa Kradascarusioc, as we call them. Even then, it was a city in decline and, once everyone who wanted to had left, it was abandoned, leaving as we thought an empty shell.'

Cenarazh then commented: 'But now we know that they left many things behind.'

Cedric proceeded to tell the story of how he had discovered the objects, though he glossed over the destruction of the sealed door. The four elves hung on his every word. When he had finished, the two older elves spoke to each other animatedly. Itheya looked intently at Cedric but did not speak.

'I have had but little time to examine these last two pieces,' said Terath. 'But I shall tell you what I have learned so far.

'The dragon is a representation of one of the first beings to inhabit this Earth, Azhanion, the Black Dragon, was the first, he was followed by the other immortal dragons, five in total charged with protecting all creatures on earth as Zhun created them. Once all life was created, they started to vie with each other for dominance. This was as Zhun wished, so he ordered the dragons to go to sleep, only to awake again if the Earth's creatures needed to be protected from destruction or if Zhun called upon them to destroy the life he had created if it had proved unworthy to his vision. This is a representation of Sistica, the Dragon of the Sea.'

'There are five other models back in Tanaren, one of them being two headed.'

'That would be Azhanion himself. Two heads in eternal conflict. These first dragons had many, many offspring; many different types of dragons came into this world.'

'But where are they now?' Morgan had not spoken before and his voice sounded husky as he asked the question.

'When winter comes,' said Cenarazh, 'the bear sleeps, emerging again only with the first shoots of spring. Dragons, too, sleep, but they reckon time like no other creature. A thousand years is but ten short breaths for a dragon. Ages of men and elves have risen and fallen while they barely stir deep under the mountains or in their caves beneath the sea.'

'Dragons can be awoken,' said Terath, 'but it requires the forgotten magic of the dragon stones. Did you find any of them? Like a ruby but larger.'

'No,' said Cedric, 'nothing of that nature.'

'Our ancestors hid them in our old cities on account of the possible destruction they could wreak. They set their locations down in a tome, *Za shtia neto nenneven,* but this was lost during the human wars. Which', he said, picking up the last artefact, 'brings us to the tooth.'

'Yes,' said Cedric. 'Itheya suspected that it may be a lot older than these other objects.'

'She is almost certainly correct. The first four objects date from around the time of the wars, making them some eight hundred years old. The dragon is older but the tooth is older still. We are talking of a time before even the southern human empire of Lileca rose to greatness.'

'Over three thousand years ago,' said Cedric softly. 'Tell me, is it the tooth of a dragon?'

'It is. The writing is in a dialect spoken by the Baetal tribe, a tribe long forgotten to us. It is also very formally structured and to date I have been able to translate but a little of it. However, it appears to contain lore relating to dragons and the dragon stones and discusses the summoning, binding and destruction of such creatures. It is frustrating, but I cannot be more specific than this at present apart from saying that we believe there were six of these created, one for each original type of dragon.'

'I would not like to have been the one extracting the tooth,' observed Morgan, smiling.

'True,' said Cenarazh. 'He may well have paid with his life.'

'Our forefathers set great store in the ability to ride and tame dragons,' said the loremaster. 'It is partly the reason why we were the first people, the first to spread over the face of the Earth before the humans came. This tooth is a link to that distant time. It is a relic beyond value.'

'Which brings us to the purpose of your visit to us,' said Cenarazh. 'It is not I feel solely to let us look at beautiful treasures from our past. Itheya has said so much already.'

Cedric sighed. 'You are right, of course. I truly wish it were not so but I am charged with a request from our Grand Duke. He wishes for you to send a contingent of warriors to fight in the war we are engaged in against our neighbours.'

'Ha!' Dramalliel snorted. His father looked over to him.

'My son holds strong views in this, and many other matters. Come, Dramalliel, say what you have to.'

'You know what I wish for – that the heads of these humans be returned to their Grand Duke and these objects kept in our possession. To deal with the *pekha* is to bring destruction on our peoples. Kill them both and send the message that to trifle with us only ends in death.'

'But death for whom?' said Cenarazh. 'A thousand years ago, when we dwelt on the plains, the Morioka could put out an army on its own of fifty thousand. Now, even if all our allies joined with us, we could not muster a tenth of that number. The death of which you speak seems to affect us far more than the humans, who breed quickly. Our isolationism has undoubtedly helped protect us but has not stopped our decline. What say you to this, my daughter.'

'Firstly,' she said, firmly, 'we cannot kill these humans after inviting them to our home – that would be the act of the savage. Secondly, these artefacts are just a small portion of the total. I do not like the way the others have been held back from us, although I believe that is not the fault of Master Cedric. But, if we wish to see all of them, we will have to negotiate for their return. As for us sending an army out of the forest, even if we were to agree, we would need the participation of the other tribes; we would have to call a krasa, a gathering, and discuss it there.'

'May I also say, before I forget,' said Cedric, 'you are being offered iron weapons in return for your support. I think it was a matter of fifty knives, a hundred spearheads and five hundred arrowheads, as an initial amount.'

'Noted,' said Cenarazh. 'As my son is aware, you cannot be killed after being invited into Zamezhenka; you will rather be treated as honoured guests while you remain. As for the krasa, riders have already been sent out yesterday inviting the tribes to meet; in six days it will happen. In the meantime I invite Master Cedric to aid Terath in the translation of the words on the tooth and to discuss human and elven lore together. Master Morgan is to be given the run of our home, providing he remains in the company of my daughter. In two days we have Armentele, a celebration of life as it prepares to sleep until spring, and you are both invited to observe that occasion.'

'I am honoured,' said Cedric.

'I shall retire now – rest is the prerogative of the elderly.' Cenarazh made to stand, wincing as he did so. Itheya ran to help him, as did Terath. Once upright, Dramalliel handed him a stick to lean on. It was not enough, though – for him to walk further support was required.

'Rest on my shoulder, Father,' said Itheya.

'No,' said Morgan, 'I am stronger; I will help you.'

Itheya assented and, leaning on the man and aided with his stick, Cenarazh started to make progress towards the stairs.

'Isn't it possible for someone to make a room for you up here?' Morgan suggested.

'The offer has been made, but I refused it. This is an audience chamber, not a hospital. If a room were put her, I might never leave it, and I would much rather end my days under the open sky.'

It took a long time but eventually Cenarazh reached his quarters on the second floor where his attendants took over. Dramalliel said his goodbyes and disappeared, while Terath led Cedric off down the next flight of stairs, already deep in discussion over the tooth. Morgan and Itheya were left alone. 'I will show you your room; it will be the one next to mine.'

She led him to a room opposite her father's, pulling back the curtain so he could enter. Inside, the first thing he noticed was that his pack had been taken there for him. There was a bed with white sheets and the ubiquitous detailed carvings on its frame and posts, and a small table under the window on which stood a pitcher designed to resemble a folding leaf and a bowl holding several of the strange warm, glowing stones.

'What are these?' he asked.

'Z'ezhalitha, heat stones or warm stones. They provide light and warmth without fires and the smoke that they bring. Terath and his assistants provide and maintain them.'

'Terath has magic?'

'We call it haraska, power. Power to shape the elements. All of us have a little of it but the loremaster is the one who understands it best.'

'So you have magic, too?'

'You might call it that. My power is minor and I barely use it.'

'So you won't set me on fire, if I annoy you.'

'If I could, I would have done so already.' She made to leave but stopped in the doorway.

'Thank you for helping, Father.'

'Oh, no need to do that.'

'Yes ... there is.'

'It upsets you, doesn't it, the way he is?'

'Of course, he is my father.'

'No ... I mean; I can see you are close.'

'We are, yes. I know we age slightly differently to humans but there are some years between me and my brother; for a while it was just me and father.' She stopped.

'What is it?'

'It is strange, confiding in a human. I should probably not be doing it.'

'Then I shall trouble you no further... So I have free access to your village?'

'No, that is not true. You go where I say and nowhere else without me, and you speak to no one unless I permit you to.'

'So what do we do now then?'

'I do not know. Father wishes for me to show you the island and the shoreline, if you wish.'

'That sounds fine to me.'

'Not just yet, though.'

'Why not?'

'First, I wish to see my brother.'

'Then I will wait here till you return.'

'Very well.'

'Just one more question before you go.'

She sighed. 'What is it?'

'The greeting you gave your father, what was it?'

'The traditional one – "Honour and peace be yours."'

'And how would I say it to you?'

'Satala, Itheya, canteleva zhasessana seatana.'

Morgan falteringly repeated the greeting to her; she gave a faint smile and replied.

'Satala, Morgan, canteleva zhasessa tafalle trezem, although, as I am going now, *moton at ate sheren* would be more appropriate.'

'Then *moton at ate sheren, Itheya.'*

She laughed softly. 'Stay here. I will be back shortly.'

She found her brother on the path outside the Zamezhenka, looking out over the lake. He heard her approaching but did not acknowledge her presence until she spoke.

'Are you trying to find new ways to anger me?'

He looked at her languidly. 'I thought I had discovered them all.'

Her breath hissed through her teeth. 'I really don't know where to start with you, little brother.'

His expression change, he was glaring now. 'I am a prince of the Morioka; you should not refer to me as "little brother" any longer. I am no longer bouncing on my wet nurse's knee.'

'If you listen to reason, then I might just do that.'

'What is it then, big sister?'

'Why did you talk about killing the humans in front of Father; you know the decision had already been made to let them live unless they themselves threatened violence. Are you angry because you were overruled? It made us look barbaric ... and divided.'

'The humans should know they are here under sufferance. We want nothing to do with them; it is they who need us, not the other way round. Besides, if they knew how you treated humans in the past, they might not be so trusting of you.'

'Why are you bringing that up now? Do not annoy me anymore, brother. Anything that happened in the past is just that, in the past. Besides, I had no choice with the incident you are thinking about, and they know they are here on our good graces; I have made it clear to them.'

'Have you? You seem very cosy with them, especially with that fighter.'

'You know nothing, and neither does your man, Tiavon. I want you to speak to him. He was extremely disrespectful to me in front of the humans; the older human knew exactly what he said.'

'I will speak to him but you know how he is – he thinks there is something between the two of you.'

'Well, there isn't. Make it clear to him.'

'I will.' Dramalliel looked back over the water. 'Father gets worse every day – can you see it?'

'I can. All the healers can do is try to ease the pain.'

'Are you ready to lead the tribe? You may have to soon.'

'You know that it is something I never wanted, but I will be ready, when the time comes; I have to be. And don't lecture me about succession not being automatic.'

'All the first families have to agree.'

'It is a formality, unless someone wishes to stir up trouble.'

Brother and sister looked at each other, looks that spoke a thousand words.

'I love you, brother, though you cannot see it.'

'I love you, too, sister, though you see it even less.'

She left him and walked back up the path.

32

Zerannon was a town first established to profit from trade with the elves. Many people had made a good living out of it. However, as relations soured between the two peoples, an alternative source of income needed to be found. In fact, three were tried. The first, fishing, paid poorly and was hard and dangerous work; the second, the export of gems trafficked in from Shayer Ridge and other towns, was more lucrative. The third, however, and the one that distinguished it from other towns in the region, came from the mineral-rich springs that opened out on the headland overlooking the sea. People started to report being miraculously healed by the waters and soon Saint Matha's spa in Zerannon drew the well-to-do from many miles around, all eager to experience its rejuvenating properties. The inner town was soon full of grand multi-storey stone buildings, large and airy, all commanding fantastic views of the sea through their expensive large glass windows. Soon, properties here were only second in price to those on Loubian Hill in Tanaren. A wall was built around it, not high enough on the seaward side to spoil the view, but enough to render Zerannon's inner city one of the best places to live in the entire country.

Haelward and his companions, however, were staying in the outer city.

The Spectral Goose was not a waterside inn where the straw on the packed earth floor stank of vomit and urine, and the only sober clientele were the cutpurses and the prostitutes who lured men into dark alleys, to be robbed at knifepoint; where the food was served in semi-darkness so the creatures crawling over the rotting vegetables could not be seen and the ale could not be distinguished from the storage vinegar. Rather, it was somewhere between that and the rarefied heights of the inner city. Halfway down the hill leading to the harbour, in the summer it would be full of merchants and tradesmen fresh from the market, but now in the late autumn it was winding down, the only traders present being ones who had had a poor season and were looking for one last transaction before the winter frosts settled in.

They had arrived earlier than expected and found the inn almost immediately. Ham was a large genial man who looked useful in a fight and probably had to be, given his profession. Haelward mentioned Morgan and the man smiled, took the coin and gave them three rooms for two months without asking any further questions.

They toured the town, which, apart from its nice views, was unremarkable (though they left the inner city alone, as most of the city watch seemed to be deployed there), after which they returned to the inn for a meal. It was simple fare – potage with a little meat, hard bread, cheese and apples washed down with ale only slightly watered down.

'Thank you, my dear,' said Samson, eyeing the comely serving girl.

'No standing on ceremony, let's tuck in,' said Haelward.

They ate in silence for a while, relishing the change from the iron rations they had lived on for the last two days. Then Leon spoke. 'So we just wait here for them to return? It could take weeks. And Artorus not let it be the case but what if they don't return at all?'

'I see it this way,' said Haelward, 'winter is coming, the pass is blocked already – to rejoin the army we would need to go around the mountains, which could take weeks. At least one of us has to stay here until they return, and we have the rooms for two months with an option to extend our stay, so, yes, we wait. If anyone has a pressing reason why they have to leave, just let me know. If Morgan and Cedric do not return, I intend to see out the winter here and return to the army in the spring.'

'From what I remember, though, Baron Felmere intended to fight through the winter; the army may need our help,' said Leon.

'The army assigned us to this task; we are already following their orders. In the spring the trade caravans start to go back through the pass; I was going to hire myself out as a guard and get back to the army that way, if Morgan no longer needed us.'

Leon nodded in agreement and continued devouring his potage.

The following day it rained, a fine driving rain blown in by the sea. It was the market day, though, so they went to take a look; the market, however, was barely a third full, with a dispiriting atmosphere in the wet, so they went to the theatre, which was performing Wharton's latest play,

Finovius, the Mad Duke. They paid a penny and stood in the pit, which was full of raucous drunks, women of questionable virtue and poor souls merely looking for a refuge from the rain. The performance was bawdy and enthusiastic, its gusto more than making up for its lack of finesse. They hissed when Finovius ordered his brother's death, laughed at Finovius's madness when he made his bear a seneschal, and cheered at the end when the Duke was finally cornered and executed by being crushed under a large bronze door, something which rather detracted from his moving final soliloquy. Thus heartened and with the light almost gone, they retired to The Spectral Goose for the evening meal.

They were discussing the play and wondering if they had already seen all the town had to offer.

'Boredom may become a problem here,' said Leon.

'Well, we could always try taking the waters,' said Varen. 'It may well be more expensive than the play, though – about a thousand times more expensive. Where is Samson?'

'Out by the stables rogering the serving girl. I knew she was doomed the moment he first saw her.'

'That might be a bad move. I heard she was one of Ham's nieces,' chipped in Haelward.

Leon laughed. 'Well, he needs teaching a lesson – as long as we have the coin to smooth things over with Ham if things get nasty.'

'I would rather spend it on something other than paying off disgruntled guardians. The brothel is just down the hill – why can't he go there?'

'Because the women are already available; all you need is coin. Samson likes the challenge of women who aren't so easy. That's why he ends up with so many married ones.'

Suddenly the door opened, causing a cold draught to billow around the common room. The lanterns flickered. A man covered in a weathered and sodden black cloak came in and strolled over to the bar to speak to the landlord.

'Foul night to be on a journey,' mumbled Varen into his ale.

After a minute or two Willem noticed something.

'Master Ham seems to be directing that man towards us.'

It was true – he was pointing in their general direction. The man in the cloak spotted them and began ambling their way. He was of medium height, quite young with a ruddy red face still wet with the rain.

'Who on earth knows us up here?' muttered Haelward.

'Good evening, gentlemen,' said the man briskly. 'I wonder if I might take up a minute of your time?'

Varen pulled a chair out for the man and Willem passed him some bread and cheese. The man thanked them and spoke.

'I have an ale coming in a minute and I certainly need it. I have ridden hard from Tanaren City looking for someone. The landlord says you may know of his whereabouts.'

'From Tanaren City?' said Haelward. 'I doubt that we are the people you seek; most of us haven't been there in years.'

'Ah, let me explain. I have been sent by a Professor Dearden, a scholar at St Philig's University. He is desperate to find a colleague of his, a Professor Cedric, who left for these parts on a business matter.'

Willem's eyes lit up. 'Professor Dearden wants Master Cedric? What on earth for?'

The man perked up at this. 'So I am talking to the right people, Artorus knows, I have travelled around asking in more taverns than I ever knew existed. The Professor wants your Master Cedric to go and help out a baroness no less; the details are here in this letter.'

He handed a letter to Willem who stared at it intently. As he did so, Samson returned with a big smile on his face.

'Nice out?' said Leon sardonically.

'The fresh air always works for me; you should all try it. I see I am the only one here with a smile on his face.' Behind him the serving girl came into the room, the lacing on her bodice sadly disarranged.

'This gentleman is enquiring as to whether we know the whereabouts of Professor Cedric,' said Haelward.

'Does anyone want to see this letter?' said Willem.

'My reading isn't so good,' said Leon. Haelward took the letter from Willem and scanned it quickly. He whistled.

'Cedric has been summoned by nobility,' he said. 'One of the Duke Hartfield's daughters wants to see him.' He read further down. 'What in the name of Artorus's holy boots is she doing in Osperitsan?' 'Where?' said Samson.

'It is an island out in the west; it looks like she has married someone out there. Why would that be, I wonder?'

Varen spoke to the messenger. 'We have bad news, I am afraid. Cedric is engaged on business in a place that is inaccessible to most of us. He could be gone for weeks.'

'Now that is a pity,' said the messenger. 'There is no way a message could be sent to him?'

'Not unless you want to visit the Wych folk, my friend.' Samson smiled at the girl as she set down fresh flagons of ale. She blushed before leaving them.

'I shall have to return to Tanaren then. Professor Ulian will be disappointed. Could I ask you to pass the letter on to Professor Cedric when he arrives?'

'Why Professor Ulian? Why would he be disappointed? The letter is not from him.' Willem frowned.

'Because the poor man has gone all the way out to Osperitsan to see them. Professor Ulian was hoping that Professor Cedric could go there to help him out. Instead all he has there with him is Cedric's young assistant.'

'Alys? You mean Alys?'

'Yes, the girl, the one who sketches for him.'

Willem was all agitation. 'I have to go out there. Tell Professor Dearden I will go and see them. I have Cedric's books. I should be able to do something.'

'Wait!' said Varen. 'Stop and think, how will you get out there? I know it is your lady and all that, but will you be able to help anyway?'

'Even if I can't, Professor Ulian can see Cedric's books; it sounds as though, whatever help this lady needs, the answer will be in them. A lot of them are about Wych magic.'

'He didn't burn them in the pass?' asked Samson.

'He only burned the basic reference books – things he had copies of, not the books he considered important.'

'But the journey will take weeks,' said Varen. 'A lot of it through bandit country and the Morrathnay Forest.'

'We are in a port,' said Haelward. 'If a ship can be found going that way, he could be there in a few days.'

'Then that settles it,' said Willem. 'I am going by sea. I will go down to the docks tomorrow, check to see if a ship is heading to ... to ... what is the place called?'

'Osperitsan,' said Haelward. 'I stopped there a few times when I was in the marines chasing pirates. Its bleak, but I quite liked it; I can't remember the Baron's name, though.'

'No disrespect, Willem,' said Leon, 'but you're not the most savvy person I know. Travelling alone with all that baggage, you are practically asking every low life on the high seas to stick a knife in your belly.'

'You are quite right, Leon,' said Haelward. 'And that is why I will be going with him.' He turned to the messenger. 'Tell your Professor that Cedric is indisposed at present; his assistant will be going in his stead and Cedric will be informed as soon as he becomes available. If I was you, I would eat up and get a room here; you look shattered.'

'You read me well,' said the man, 'I will make my way back in the morning with your reply. Right now I will take my leave and get my head down for the night. I thank all of you for your help and the coin I will pocket on my return.' He nodded, stood and left them.

'And I was just getting settled here, and I have instantly gone back on my word that I would stay here until Morgan arrived,' said Haelward with a smile. 'Willem and I will be up at dawn, then, looking for a ship. I can only ask the three of you to let Cedric know where we are when he arrives here.'

'I will stay,' said Varen. 'Samson and Leon, if you wish to leave or go elsewhere, you can do so. I have got my chair in the corner and am happily set for the next few weeks.

'No chance,' said Leon, 'As you say Haelward, the army is asking us to do this job and we will do just that, until our orders change. Besides,

Samson seems to have a ready-made supply of willing barmaids here and I would hate to make my cousin unhappy.'

'Do you think just the two of you going is enough?' said Samson.

'Oh, I am sure it will be,' said Haelward, smiling. 'It is a cushy job for me, keeping Willem out of trouble for a few days. He is the one having to do all the work. He may not have thought about it, but he is going to have to provide answers for a member of one of the country's foremost families. I would hate to get something wrong; it would probably mean six months in the Duke's dungeons licking moisture off the walls.'

'Lawks!' muttered Willem.

'Ignore him!' said Varen with a grin. 'He is teasing you. Come on, Willem, down your ale – who knows when you will get the chance of another?'

Willem did so, letting the ale swim round his head. He was regretting his brave words already.

33

The black-clad assassin stepped forward so Aganosticlan could see her properly. Her armour fitted her closely; it was obvious there was not an ounce of fat on her. It looked strange – it was metallic, but dull in colour and made no noise as she moved. Her pauldrons, elbow guards, vambraces and gauntlets were single pieces, the latter two sporting small but cruel outward facing spikes. She wore a small skirt of studded black leather strips over her mail leggings and he noticed her leg guards, like the pauldrons, carried similar spikes, a nasty surprise for anyone she kicked. She was covered in knives; he counted four at her belt including two thin, evil-looking stilettos as well as others strapped to her thighs and her boots. She bore no insignia, until he saw her face.

In another existence he would have called her beautiful, ash blonde, pale skinned with large sensitive deep-blue eyes; however, her hair was cropped short and gathered behind her head in a tight ponytail only a few inches long, her skin was as white as frost in a graveyard and any emotion in her eyes was hidden behind a veneer of sheer contempt and cruelty. He noticed a small tattoo, an 'S' shape, high on her right cheek.

'Your Majesty,' she said in a voice as cold and brittle as hoarfrost.

The King gave her a slight nod. 'Even here we have all heard of the reputation of the Strekha; I trust it is not a baseless one.'

Her expression changed slightly. She raised her thin eyebrow; she almost looked amused. He noted her thin, blood-red lips and it was as if a thin black glaze covered each eye. It was most perplexing.

'Your opinion of our reputation is immaterial,' she said. 'The Emperor has tasked me to perform two missions for you. You give me those missions. I perform them. Then I return to the Emperor's side and leave your dull, muddy little country behind for ever. I am sure we will both be a lot happier when that happens.'

Hem-Khozar broke in. 'As you can see, Your Majesty, the Strekha are not well versed in the art of diplomacy. They are highly educated in history, geography, the arts and sciences, as well as many other things, but to do their job they are required to be feared, not loved.'

Aganosticlan stood and faced her. She was taller than he; she could only have been a couple of inches short of six foot.

'But I am not sure I do fear her, Hem-Khozar. All I see is a tall but pretty girl in fancy armour. I could put one of my serving girls in the same garb; she would look impressive but would still be the same little bed-warmer under it all.' Hem-Khozar stood, nervously watching the girl's reaction. To his relief she did nothing.

'Do you wish for me to be your little bed-warmer?' The contempt she regarded him with when she first entered the throne room was replaced with something else. Amused contempt.

'Why not?,' said the King 'Everyone knows the Strekha are the Emperor's second harem, for when he requires a ... more challenging encounter.'

'I do not deny it.' she said, 'If the Emperor had told me to perform that service for you, then I would do it.' She grinned wickedly, looking down at this man who she obviously regarded as little more than something that might be found at the bottom of a pond. 'But he hasn't, so you are to remain forever disappointed. Let me do the other thing that I do best and content yourself with that.'

The two of them locked each other in a gaze, brown eyes against hellish blue. The King broke away quickly enough. He walked slowly to his display of arms.

'I thought all Kozeans were as dark-skinned as Hem-Khozar,' he said. 'Not as pale as marble, and your name, Syalin, is almost Chiran.' With his back to his two visitors, he removed a bejewelled throwing knife from his display, by the by noting how beautifully balanced it was.

'Ah you have forgotten,' said Hem-Khozar unctuously, 'when I introduced her I mentioned she hails from the foothills of the Gnekun Mountains, from Mount Kzugun itself. The people there are naturally pale. You forget Koze is an empire incorporating a thousand different peoples – the Empire of a multitude of cultures, languages and skin colours. Syalin is a Norvakkor; her peoples are divided equally between ourselves and Chira, hence the confusion in names.'

'Oh yes,' said the King. 'I remember now, but aren't the Norvakkor counted as one of your most rebellious peoples?'

'I was recruited aged ten,' said Syalin. 'My life before this is forgotten to me; I have no memory of whether my people were loyal or not.'

'And how old are you now?' Aganosticlan ran the knife against his thumb. It drew blood.

'My age is only counted from my recruitment. I am fifteen.'

'And how many have you killed?'

'I do not have the remotest idea. Everyone whom the Emperor has required me to kill has died.'

'And has anyone ever got close to killing you?'

'As a Strekha? Never.'

'Perhaps that might change.' With a swift movement, and he prided himself on his speed and dexterity, the King spun round and hurled the knife directly at Syalin's head.

With an action faster than the eye could see, faster than a cat pouncing on a mouse, faster than the wing beats of the iridescent blue marsh hummingbird, she brought both hands up in front of her. The knife was halted between her palms, its point not six inches from her face. She looked bored.

'Do you want me to throw it back to you?'

Aganosticlan breathed slowly, his eyes wide with astonishment. Slowly a wolfish grin spread over his face.

'It is true about you; nothing could have stopped that blade, nothing. How are you that fast?'

'A Strekha's abilities are enhanced with ... substances,' said Hem-Khozar. 'Chief among them is blackroot, which we find in our deep jungles and which is also found in the marshes just to the south of here.'

'Blackroot is a poison. It is known as widow's nutmeg – it kills anyone who swallows even the smallest amount.'

With a sense of theatre, Syalin pulled out a small pouch attached to her belt under her cloak. Opening it, she pulled out a small object that resembled a piece of fresh ginger in that it was bulbous, but, like everything else about her, was completely black. With one of her knives, she shaved off a small piece, held the knife and its shaving up to her mouth, and – with Aganosticlan watching wide-eyed – slowly and deliberately licked it off with her dark tongue. The King fancied he saw her pupils dilate ever so slightly and she definitely gasped, slightly but audibly. When, after a brief time, she gave no sign of dying she held out both arms as if to say 'I'm still here'.

'If used correctly,' she said, 'blackroot needn't be a poison. For us, it gives us our speed, strength and the ability to endure pain. It is what makes us so different to you. It also enhances the thrill of danger, heightens our senses and our libido. I have always thought that, if we were not burdened with our onerous responsibilities, we would be the most stimulating company.'

'And you are the best of the Strekha?'

'I am one of The Ten. We generally number between a hundred and a hundred and fifty. The Ten are personally chosen by the Emperor, so, as you say, we are the best of the Strekha. At least four of us are required to be by the Emperor's side at any one time; others can be assigned duties away from his person, as the Emperor wills. Generally for us to assist another requires the amount of coin most men can only dream of, but in his wisdom the Emperor has changed this policy, at least for now.'

'Fascinating,' the King said, stroking his beard. 'Two more questions, and then I shall stop annoying you and we can discuss your first mission.'

'Ask. Be brief.'

'How are The Ten selected, and how does your armour make no noise?'

'I can answer your second question easily, Your Majesty,' said HemKhozar. 'It is made from xhikon, "dull iron" in your tongue. There are only two seams of it known to man, both located deep in the mountain range from which Syalin herself hails. It requires extreme heat to shape, but when that is achieved it can be forged into tiny, powerful links of mail that are also almost noiseless, ideal for one who wishes to strike from the shadows.'

'It is obviously expensive then.'

'Indeed, Your Majesty, but in general the Strekha represent a colossal investment of time and resources on the Emperor's part.'

'What with the armour and the blackroot, you possess items that many would want to take for themselves.'

She looked at him – her disdain had returned tenfold. 'Do you wish to try?'

'As for your other question,' – the ambassador had returned to his seat – 'the Emperor chooses The Ten personally; he watches them train and fight each other with blunted weapons, fights that are still dangerous nevertheless. Our current Emperor also requires poise and intelligence in those he selects. If he chooses to replace one girl with another, the disgrace means that the one dismissed often takes her own life. Emperor Gyiliakosh has forbidden this practice; all Strekha can serve while they live.'

'Most interesting,' said the King. 'Now I had better start giving you details. My court is riddled with Chiran spies and I do not want word of our discussions to get back to Hylas.'

'Riddled, you say?' The assassin sounded curious. 'How is this so? Are you unable to control the loyalty of those in your presence.'

'Coin can purchase many loyalties, my dear.'

'But fear can concentrate those loyalties to whom they should belong. I tell you what – give me the names of those you suspect. When they start to die, their corpses prominently displayed, you will have the loyalty of your court, and no, this will not count as one of the Emperor's missions. I will do this as a favour for a beleaguered king and ally, and to keep me in shape; I am a little rusty and could do with the practice.'

'Very well, I shall have Obadrian draw up a list.'

'The people you consider as spies only, though, not those your man dislikes or people who slighted his wife or who accidentally ate his dinner. When I kill, it is for a purpose, not a whim or because of some person's idle fancy. If I am misled, it will be the writer of the list who suffers next.'

'Of course, it will be as you wish. I am grateful for your attention in this matter.' Despite everything, the King rather found himself warming to her. There was something about her though, in her eyes and her manner, that set him to thinking. He had seen similar things in other men before, those berserker mercenaries who drank blood before battle and who charged their enemies wielding a giant axe and no armour. The same men who would bite their arms or put glass in their mouths, so they could spit blood and terrify their foes. It was the demeanour of those who were not truly sane.

'Tell me, Syalin, does this blackroot have any other side effects?'

'No,' she said. 'None that matter anyway.' She actually smiled at him; she seemed almost coquettish 'Now, my dear king of the muddy fields, exactly who do you want me to kill?'

34

'Now, lean on me, take it slowly now... Good. How does it feel?' 'I am OK. I would be lying if I said it didn't hurt, but the strapping helps. Now perhaps I can leave this confounded tent.'

Leaning on Marcus, Cheris slowly but surely made her way around the tent. A lot of sleep and the firm bandage around her torso had strengthened her and made her feel a lot more confident. She had an invite to Baron Felmere's council in the manor house in Grest and was not going to miss it.

'What is the weather like?' She asked.

'Windy 'Marcus grunted 'And there is rain in the air.'

'Sounds lovely. 'She smiled her sweet smile 'Come on then Marcus, take me on a tour.'

With Sir Norton walking well ahead of them she ambled her way into the fresh air. As soon as she got outside she stopped to drink it in and feel the wind on her face. She shut her eyes feeling her hair being tugged by the breeze. It felt blissful.

'Are you all right?' Marcus looked concerned.

'Never better. Let's move on.'

The camp was a small tent city surrounded by a hastily constructed stockade, sitting directly under Grest Hill, right on the path leading up to the town itself. As she hobbled around she was noticed. Many of the soldiers engaged in running messages or making deliveries saw her. To a man they all either hailed or saluted her.

'See what I mean,' said Marcus. 'You are quite the heroine. Do you want to get on the carriage to take you up the hill?'

'I had better,' she said, 'before I get too sore.'

Sir Norton was already waiting for them on an uncovered wagon. Gingerly, she climbed up and sat next to him with Marcus sitting behind them. Once positioned, he tugged the reins and they were on their way. She felt a light smattering of rain and pulled her cloak tightly over her red robe. The wagon went over a stone, making her wince.

As they left the stockade, she had a bit of a surprise. Some two or three dozen men had collected either side of the path and as they rode past they loudly saluted her. She noticed a few ale jugs being bandied around, which obviously added to the general bonhomie. Not knowing how to react, she contented herself with smiling at both sides, a smile that quickly became a laugh as the gauntlet was run. Leaving the noise and the drunken cheering behind, they ascended the path. On the western side of the hill the trees and grass were dead and blackened, the ground scorched. Smoke was still rising from the cracked and scored earth, and the smell of burnt wood and resin was inescapable – it was a desolate scene. In a bizarre contrast, on other side of the path, the woods were untouched and were silently brooding, as if lamenting the loss of their comrades.

They approached the gates, both of which were open. The city walls themselves were not high, but sturdily built of large stones mortared together. Small wooden towers stood atop the walls either side of the gates, with a solitary guard in each. Both saluted them as they rode through and into the town.

Grest itself was not a big place. Small, closely packed thatched cottages pressed tightly against the narrow cobbled road they were progressing along. Being on a hill, there was no natural water supply, which came instead from wells and butts put out to collect rain. Consequently, sewage and other trash collected in trenches either side of the road. Now and then it would all be put into carts and dumped in the river, or put on to the fields, but not until it had reached an unpleasant level of putrefaction. It was Tanaren's poor quarter all over again.

The road opened on to the square. It was a motley affair – the largest building was the only one built of stone rather than being half-timbered. It stood at the other end of the square and she guessed correctly that it was the manor house. There was a house of Artorus and a tiny house of Meriel, with a statue of the goddess standing just outside the painted red and white door. All that, however, was incidental, for just to her left were a series of spears whose butts had been forced into the earth between the cobbles. Each spear sported a severed head; their white eyes stared glassily in her direction, and sticky blood coated the spear shafts and pooled over the ground. Carved into their foreheads, probably while they were still alive, was the word 'traitor'. In the stocks behind them were four young women, their heads shaved, all branded with the 'W' for whore.

And the executions had not finished. In the centre of the square was the executioner's block, black with the blood of its victims. A burly man stood close by, brandishing a colossal axe which he was using to make practice swings. A crowd was with him, goading him on, and, in a makeshift wooden cage not twenty feet from the executioner, were three men, bound and gagged and looking suitably terrified. A man in fine but slightly worn red robes appeared to be directing proceedings. Evidently the afternoon's entertainment was due to begin shortly.

'As you said, Marcus – reprisals,' Cheris said through gritted teeth.

'It is as I feared,' he replied. 'I hope the Baron calls a halt to this soon.'

He appeared to be getting his wish. A group of Felmere's soldiers moved across the square and started talking to the man in red. An argument appeared to break out between them. Were those men to be reprieved? Cheris wondered what they were thinking, imagining the hope flickering in their hearts. Alas, after a couple of minute's discussion the soldiers returned to their posts leaving the man to his bloody business.

Cheris felt deflated. So this was what victory was like.

'Ride on, Sir Norton,' she said. 'I think we have seen enough.' The manor house's main door was open, and guards clustered around it. Aided by Marcus, Cheris alighted from the carriage. The three of them passed the guards, who stood aside for them and went inside.

They entered a small reception room. It took a second for her eyes to adjust to the light but when they did she noticed that the carpet was torn and stained with dark patches that she realised were probably blood. A small bench to her right had been smashed; splintered wood lay around and about. She guessed the Arshuman garrison had made a stand here, one that hadn't gone well for them.

Sir Norton passed boldly through the arched doorway, and the mages followed, Cheris wishing for half of the knight's assertiveness. They were in the main hall. She looked about her – torch brackets were hanging off the wall, fragments of pottery were scattered over the floor, a painting lay drunkenly in the corner – it looked like somebody had put his foot through the canvas. What a party! she thought drily.

Directly ahead was the long table. It had been scored with knives and even partially burned, but it was a sturdy object and stubbornly remained in its original place. It was to the men surrounding it that her attention was drawn, though. She knew some of them – the knights Dominic and Reynard were there along with another whose breastplate sported a writhing green serpent. He was a rugged red-haired man with striking green eyes and a couple of days' growth of stubble on his chin. She saw Felmere sitting at the head of the table, right hand clasping a goblet, and next to him was Lasgaart and a craggy bald man in his sixties she believed to be Maynard. There were faces there she was unfamiliar with, though – a saturnine man scarred by smallpox, a boyish-faced blond who appeared to be fonder of the mirror than she, and a dashing dark-haired man of about thirty sporting a blue cloak emblazoned with crossed red spears. The cloak was stained with mud and grass, suggesting he had travelled a distance to get here. The other man whom she noticed among the crowd she found a little more disquieting. He was massively built, scarred and bearded, his eyes glittering with dark malice. When they entered the room all eyes turned to look at her, but it was only his gaze that she noticed.

Felmere got to his feet and raised his goblet. 'The mages!' It was a cry echoed by everyone there, except the big man who stared at them fixedly and with such intensity she briefly wondered if she had forgotten to put her robe on.

They were invited to sit at the bottom of the table, Cheris at the opposite end to Baron Felmere; there really was nowhere to hide here.

'Before we start,' Felmere said, 'I probably need to do some introductions and make an apology. These days I am so unused to female company you would at least think that, when I actually get to meet a woman, I would get her damn name right. The lady present and the architect of our victory is called Cheris, or, as the men are calling her, the

"Queen of Storms". It is good to see you feeling better, my dear. I formally give you the honorific "Battle Mage of Tanaren" and express the gratitude of myself and my soldiers for your contribution to our cause.'

He went around the room quickly spouting out names. Ulgar with the scars. The preening Fenchard. 'This,' he said, indicating the man in the blue cloak, 'is Esric Calvannen, Chief Prosecutor of the War in the South; he has left his army for a few days so information can be shared between us and we can make plans for the future. And this, for those few of us who don't know him, is Sir Trask, whom Fenchard has appointed to lead his men and give them the experience he lacks.' The big man gave no indication that he even knew his name had been mentioned.

'Finally,' said Felmere, indicating the red-haired knight, 'we have Sir Emeric of the Knights of the Serpent. They also fight mainly in the south, but maybe the time is coming for us to concentrate our efforts.'

'Now,' he continued, looking around the table. 'We have won a great victory. The scouts tell me that the enemy have withdrawn to Tantala, a small town on the Broken River. It is poorly fortified and they barely number a thousand men. These are the only substantial body of troops remaining in the north between us and Roshythe. And so we have our quandary – what do we do next? My plan at first was to rebuild the bridges here and gather the army for a major assault in the early spring, but it is so tempting, just so tempting, to try and smash them while they are demoralised and without a general. Heart and head are saying two different things, so I would like to hear your thoughts before we decide what to do. Firstly, Esric. I have heard little from the south in recent months – what are the enemy troop numbers like down there?'

Esric smiled, flashing a row of pearly-white teeth. 'Before I start,' he said, 'I would like to congratulate you all on your victory. The whole balance of power has changed and perhaps the end is finally in sight for us all. As to the south' – he paused and took a sip from his goblet – 'well, it has always been different for us in the south. For those who know little of our situation, I will give you a brief overview of our more recent travails.

'In the north you have the gem mines, tracts of arable land and large cities defended by walls of stone. In the south we have none of those things. The land can be fertile but is boggy and prone to flooding and our cities are smaller and defended by wooden stockades and ditches. When all my forces are summoned, I can at best put a thousand men into the field, backed by a hundred Serpent Knights. I myself am a baron in exile; our family's lands lie between the Broken River and the Helkus, an area we have not held in many years. As for our army, I took command after my father was killed in a skirmish three years ago. The enemy pressed us hard for a long time and our camp was riddled with desertions and treachery. Until recently things were as bleak as I have made them sound.

'Then I petitioned Lukas' – he indicated Felmere – 'for aid. He sent me a man who found our traitors for us. One of them was even the son of a baron, in the Arshumans' pay...'

'You are referring to Morgan,' said Ulgar.

'Yes, to be honest I half expected to see him here.'

'He is doing another job for me,' said Felmere. 'I do not know when he will return.'

'A pity,' said Esric. 'A good man. I was half hoping he could assist me with the new troops I have levied.'

'Not all of us,' Trask interrupted, his voice rumbling like a cave avalanche, 'have such a high opinion of the man of Glaivedon.'

Felmere smiled. 'Not you – I know, Trask,' he said. 'I know of your past run-ins but at least' – he looked at the man pointedly – 'he has always fought on our side.' Trask said nothing; he almost looked amused.

'He has insulted me and Ulgar, too,' bleated Fenchard. 'Personally I would have him whipped.'

'And I would have you whipped for having him whipped,' Felmere replied. 'He is not the matter here now; he is out of our sight. Carry on with your report, Esric.'

'As I said, our problem with the traitors was resolved, so I decided on a surprise attack on the main body of their forces. I hoped, seeing as they were still expecting secret reports from our lines that they would be complacent. And I was right. We moved swiftly, and hit them at dawn. Within the hour their camp was overrun and they were fleeing. The battle continued on the banks of the Whiterush. Boats were ferrying their men across it, so we kept at their rearguard. By late afternoon it was over. For the first time in four years they had no troops west of the river. Granted, they still hold some island forts on the Axe – that is the river that runs between the Vinoyen and the Whiterush – but hopefully we have time to take them at our leisure.

'But every pile of gold holds a copper. We drove them back but killed relatively few of them. Across the river lies the best part of two thousand men. I will bet you my daughter's first tooth that a thousand, maybe fifteen hundred, of them will be on the way to Tantala as we speak. You will not be fighting a thousand men there; it will be at least double that. Our scouts have all but confirmed this.'

'Would they leave the south so undefended?' asked Reynard. 'Wouldn't they be expecting you to attack them again?'

'The element of surprise has gone,' said Esric. 'They are dug in across the river. I could go north, cross the river at night and try attacking them in the rear, but it would be very risky; we could lose everything we have just gained.'

'You can bet their king will be sending reserves, or hastily pressed men, to bolster his army also,' said Felmere. 'Their quality may be questionable but the numbers alone will boost their morale. If it were just a thousand men we were facing, I would be hammering them right now with everything we have, but our men need resting, wounds need treating and supply lines need organising. We lost nearly a hundred men in the battle with three hundred carrying injuries of one kind or another. Digging in for the winter may be our best option.'

'Why not send a man to the Arshuman palace at Kitev to present their king with our terms?' Maynard, the eldest man there, was known as something of a pragmatist.'

'It is not my place.' Felmere drained his goblet. 'It is up to Duke Leontius and, as the possibility of total victory still exists, I doubt he will be interested. The next move is ours to make, unless he writes to me with different instructions, but I can't remember the last time that happened. Oh and Esric, well done, you learn fast!'

'Thank you, Lukas. I can even send you a small force to reinforce your army if required.'

'Thank you, but no. We are getting more men all the time. Fenchard has brought more as has Lasgaart. In fact, I am in a position to help you. Another mage is arriving. Leontius is pressing hard for victory. He will work for you when he arrives.'

'Who is this mage, Baron?' asked Marcus.

'He has been here before; you probably know him? Name of Mikel.'

Ha! thought Cheris. Bored with little Elsa already? Can't keep away from me, can you? She had to smile.

'That would be a bonus indeed.' Esric sounded elated. 'Perhaps I can attack them over the next few weeks, keep them busy, stop any further reinforcements coming north.'

'Perhaps,' said Felmere. He seemed to be thinking. 'The decision needs to be made. Consolidate over winter and attack in the spring, or attack in the next few weeks and try to drive them all the way back to Roshythe. Both arguments have their strengths and weakness.'

'I see no weaknesses in attacking now,' said Fenchard.

'There are many.' It was Dominic Hartfield's turn to speak. 'We have tired men and an injured mage; if we are driven back, it will boost their morale at a cost to ours. Even if we win, we will have to press on deep into the winter. We would have to camp by Roshythe and dig our own defences in the hard ground. Our supply lines would be stretched and we would be vulnerable to any counter-attack their king could muster if he didn't sue for peace.'

'Yet if we stay here we lose a golden opportunity for victory. Their king is a sybarite, but he is not stupid. He may well have no choice but to sue for peace.' Fenchard was animated, excited. Was he that desperate for glory? Cheris thought.

'What we are talking about is taking a risk to end the war quickly, or staying safe and prolonging it still further but at the same time securing our position. Fenchard, the men here have seen many more battles than you; it makes us more cautious. None of us want to lose more of our men than we have to.' Felmere sounded weary; his eyes were red and not only from drink. 'Perhaps you are all so used to war you cannot imagine any other life. Imagine, one victory, just one, could end this for ever.'

'I have heard that so many times,' said Maynard. 'And we are still here, still doing the same thing.'

'Ask the men,' said Fenchard. 'They have won a great victory. They would fight anyone, anywhere right now. We have mages and they do not. They have no leader and are disorganised.' His eyes blazed. 'It is within our grasp!'

'You speak well, Fenchard,' said Dominic. 'It is the duty of knights to seek glory in battle but not to throw lives away senselessly. We are in a much stronger position now than we were a year ago. We could advance in spring with all the dice in our favour.'

For the next half-hour the argument swung back and forth, from Fenchard's zeal to Maynard's phlegmatism, until the man in charge decided to intervene.

'We have reached an impasse,' said Felmere. 'Maybe we should have a vote, see which way the opinion sways. Mages, as this is purely a military matter, I will not include you in this.'

One by one the barons and other soldiers gave their yea or nay. Eventually only Trask, Fenchard, Lasgaart, Ulgar, Reynard and Felmere himself were left to vote, with the scores tied.

'I am obviously for an attack now,' said Fenchard, 'so count me as a yes.'

'I cannot disagree with the Baron ,' growled Trask. 'I am a yes also.'

'The yeas lead by two then,' said Felmere. 'Lasgaart?'

'It is difficult,' Lasgaart replied. 'I see Fenchard's vision but the winters here can be cruel; fighting through it is never easy. I will have to say no to this.'

Cheris saw Fenchard blanch slightly. He was counting on Lasgaart's vote, she thought.

'I am a no also,' said Reynard. 'I am standing with Dominic in this.'

'We are tied again,' said Felmere. 'Ulgar, it is just you and me.'

'Fenchard is a lad I have taken under my wing,' the scarred man said. 'I have tried to mentor him in his responsibilities; he is a man with much promise. Haslan Falls is thriving under his leadership; as you can see, he has brought a thousand men to the battlefield, nearly as many as you, Lukas, and more than me.' He turned directly to his protégé´. 'I can certainly see your arguments, Fenchard' – he sighed – 'but no, son, I cannot agree with you – war is not a game of chance. You only ever attack when you are certain of victory and too many things can go wrong here. I am sorry.'

Fenchard looked at Ulgar; his face looked as if it was set in frost and granite, his eyes flared with suppressed anger.' The boy has a temper, Cheris thought.

'It is up to me then,' said Felmere. 'The nays lead by one but I have the casting vote if there is a tie. If I vote yes then we will have a tie so then it will be solely my decision.' He sighed and put his head in both hands. When he looked at his audience again, he appeared to have aged ten years in a second.

'You know, gentlemen, if you had put this to me at any time in the past ten years, except now I would have no hesitation in saying we consolidate, bide our time and wait. When this war started, my boy, Kraven, was one year old. Now, he is eleven and sits with his stepmother in the castle in Felmere knowing nothing of peace. If we play the cautious game, maybe in two or three years we can claim victory, but then again maybe we won't. Maybe we never will. I feel that to win this cursed war someone has to take a chance, risk all in a game of hazard. If we lose, we fall back to Grest and see out the winter anyway. If we win though, if we could kick their arses all the way to Roshythe or Kitev, maybe we are just one winter away from victory, or a peace negotiated on our terms and in our favour.' He hesitated going over things in his head one more time.

'Artorus help me, but we will attack them at Tantala! We need some time for injuries to heal and for further drafts of men to arrive. I also want those two bridges built over the river under the hill. Two weeks should be enough. Two weeks, no, make it ten days, gentlemen, and we move on Tantala. May Mytha grant us victory and a final end to everything we have worked for. The decision is made.'

Cheris noted the mixed reaction in the room from Fenchard's exultant face to Dominic's worried frown. Only Sir Trask was completely unreadable and there was something about that that unsettled her even more.

The barons started to get up and mill around informally, chatting with each other; the meeting was obviously at an end. She wondered why they had to attend in the first place as their contribution had been nil (Marcus would explain later that it was protocol owing to the mages' unique status), but it had been nice for her to get out, notwithstanding the grisly scenes in the square. She wondered if they would be leaving now when she saw Baron Esric heading towards them. He smiled warmly at them.

'It is a pleasure to make your acquaintance,' he said to them. She got the impression he would be far more at home dancing the terrastep with the elegant perfumed ladies of the court at a formal ball than slogging over a muddy battlefield spattered in blood and covered with wounds. There would be no shortage of elegant ladies wishing the same, she was sure. She returned the smile while Marcus replied.

'It is a similar pleasure for us; you remind me very much of your father. I did actually fight by his side in the earlier days of the war when, if I recall, you were training with the Silver Lances in Tanaren. He was a generous man and is a grievous loss to us all.'

'Yes, he was,' said Esric. 'But miss him though we do, the present is all that matters. Tell me, do either of you know this mage who will be joining me?'

'Mikel?' said Cheris. 'Yes, he is a very good friend...' (Did she hear Marcus snigger?) 'He is nearer my age than Marcus and will not let you down. Unlike me, he has some experience of war already. When you see him, tell him I send my fondest wishes and ask him, who is feeding the cats.'

'The cats?' Esric frowned. 'You obviously do know each other well, I see. Fear not, I will convey your message word for word when I see him.'
'Oh and if you have a sister, keep her at a safe distance.'

Esric laughed. 'I have two sisters actually, back in the southern capital, Sketta, and I doubt either of them would be too displeased at any close attention from a handsome man.'

'Then they are little different to most women of my acquaintance, and I had probably better include myself in that assessment. Is that not the case, Marcus?'

'I dare say,' said Marcus. 'But do not listen to her; she is teasing you. He will greatly aid your cause in the south.'

'Tell me, Baron Esric,' Cheris asked, 'why are there two separate wars going on in the north and the south?'

'Oh you can blame the Arshumans for that!' said Esric. 'When they first attacked us they made a two-pronged assault into our lands, a large army in the north and a smaller one in the south. No doubt their intention was to meet in Athkaril, having swept past all of the Seven Rivers. The northern army nearly succeeded but we blocked off the southern one before they could cross the Vinoyen. And there have been two wars fought here ever since.'

'So few people seem aware of this, though.'

Esric laughed, 'Indeed, if the whole of the Seven Rivers are embroiled in a forgotten war, then we must be fighting the forgotten, forgotten war. It is not a heartening thought but at long last the Grand Duke seems to have taken notice of us. Perhaps the Gods are swinging our way at long last.'

'We can but hope,' said Marcus.

Suddenly through the door came another figure. It was Anaya. She looked a little red in the face and her robe was dishevelled. She came up to her fellow mages.

'Sorry for bothering the two of you. I do not normally come to these meetings but I need to ask both of you as well as Sir Norton and Baron Felmere something.' Her breath was short, as if she had been running and her clothes were wet. The rain had obviously broken outside.

'It seemed a good idea to catch you all in the same place while I could. Tell me, what has been decided here?'

'A further attack on the Arshumans in ten days or so,' said Marcus. 'Are you able to patch up the wounded in that time?'

'Ten days.' She looked thoughtful. 'Um, most but not all, Marcus. It is not a major problem really.'

'Well, come on,' said Cheris with a grin. 'Out with it, what is it you wish to ask?'

'Magical business,' said Esric. 'I will take my leave and hope to speak with you another time.'

After he left, Anaya spoke. 'As you know, I have been away from the college for many years. It has left me a little … rusty, with some aspects of the theory and practice of our art. Having the two of you here is an opportunity from the Gods.'

'So what is it you wish from us?' asked Marcus.

'Baron Felmere has kindly loaned me a small house. It is only an hour or so from the town of Shayer Ridge as the crow flies but on this side of the river. It is also just a day's hard walk from the town of Felmere itself and about two to three days' travel by horse from where we are now. I have a couple of tomes there and made some notes last winter that I would like to discuss with you both. A kind of a symposium, I suppose; it would just last a day or two then we could return here. My patients will be fine with the nurses for a few days. What do you say? Are you agreeable?'

She seemed so keen, so eager, that there was only one answer they could possibly give.

'Of course,' said Marcus. 'I am sure both Cheris and I would be happy to attend. You will need to speak to Felmere, though, and Sir Norton.'

'Yes,' she said, 'yes, I will do that now.' She left them and headed for Sir Norton, who was speaking to Emeric.

'It will be a change of scene, if nothing else,' Marcus said to Cheris.

'Like being back in one of your lessons again,' she groaned. 'I am not a natural student.'

'Well, as if I hadn't noticed that before,' he laughed. 'Just be grateful you have natural ability. I am sure you slept through most of my tutorials.'

'Marcus,' she asked, her voice lowered, 'if we had been given a vote over this battle, would you have been a yea or nay?'

'A nay,' he said. 'It is probably my age but I think this course of action could be rash.'

'Then, if it had been up to us, there would be no battle in ten days. Why is it I feel we are underestimating our opponent?'

'Because we are,' came the succinct reply.

Anaya was speaking to Felmere now; with him were Fenchard and Lasgaart. At length she returned to them. She was smiling.

'The Baron agrees,' she said. 'As long as we are back within ten days. I have some matters to attend to first, so maybe we can leave the day after tomorrow.'

'We are at your disposal,' said Marcus. 'I doubt that either Cheris or myself has any matters stopping us from attending.'

'If nothing else,' said Cheris, 'it will alleviate any boredom. Is this house in those woods under the mountains?'

'Yes,' said Anaya, 'It is a pretty place.'

'Good. I would like to see woods. Shall we leave here now?'

Sir Norton was coming towards them. After saying their goodbyes, they left the house leaving the barons to their machinations.

It was raining heavily. The square was now free of people, well, living ones anyway. She saw the cage was empty and that there were more heads on spears than there had been earlier in the day. She dully remembered during the council hearing cheers coming in through the open doorway; she assumed it was one cheer per lopped head. After getting in the wagon they rode back through the street, the rain increasing the pungency of the refuse in the open sewer. She would be perfectly happy if she never entered Grest again.

After passing through the walls, the wagon slowed; the dirt path was rapidly turning into mud. Pulling her hood tightly over her head, she thought through the events of the day. More mud and war seemed to sum it up. Getting off the island had seemed like a great opportunity at the time, but now with all her heart she knew she would have been quite happy to return there.

35

There was an hour, maybe an hour and a half, of daylight left when Itheya returned to him. WIth a gesture for him to follow, she led him out of the Zamazhenka and turned east, following its wall. Curious to see where she was going, he willingly followed. They were at the side of the lake now; the wind had picked up again and was playfully tugging at the hem of her tunic. She stopped and waited for him.

'There,' she said, pointing, 'we will take a boat; I will show you the lake.'

Ahead, the shore of the island curved around a little, following its line in a semicircle, and lying at rest in the tiny harbour it created were a number of small sailing boats. They were colourfully painted, mainly in yellows and blues, and all had carved figureheads depicting birds or fish or snakes. She skipped playfully across to the first boat and hopped in. It was only big enough for two people. Morgan followed her a lot more gingerly.

'Won't you be cold?' he asked.

She looked behind him. Morgan turned and saw one of the people who had served him food earlier in the day running up to the boat. He passed her a black cloak, which she arranged over her knees. She smiled at Morgan. 'Do you wish for one, too?'

'No thank you; I have my own cloak.'

The servant released the rope and handed the end to Morgan. Taking a paddle, Itheya gently steered the boat out of the harbour. Once there, she hoisted the sail; it was a lemon colour, a shard of brightness in the deepening gloom. Within seconds the wind caught it and they started to skip over the lake's surface.

'I will only be able to show you a little of the lake now. We may have time to see more another day, but I doubt it. We have Armentele coming up and then the krasa and I have to watch you and perform my other duties.'

'What about tomorrow?'

'Maybe. I will be dancing in the festival and will need to practise with the other women. While I am doing that, you will have to stay in your room – unless Father wishes otherwise.'

'You will be dancing?'

'Yes, is that so strange?'

'No. I suppose not. So you are a warrior and a dancer? Any other skills?'

'I sing, too, and I am required to know the history of my people over the last five thousand years as well as many other things that I will not bore you with.'

'And you sail. Are all elves this talented?' Morgan was smirking and, although her head was turned in the direction she was sailing, Itheya seemed to be perfectly aware of his expression.

'I may do all these things. But I excel at none of them. It is just that I am a Mhezhen's daughter. All these things are expected of me. Humility is important, too, as well as the ability to entertain unwanted guests.'

They had reached the middle of the lake and the light was beginning to turn as the sun began its long descent behind the clouded sky. Skilfully, she steered the little craft towards the eastern shore and followed its course in a northerly direction. They passed another glade full of tents; this one much was larger than the first one Morgan had visited, stretching back at least half a mile from the shoreline. Once they had left it behind, he saw many other wooden houses secreted tastefully behind the trees.

'You see,' she said, 'there are many more of us that you thought.'

'Does your tribe live around the whole lake?'

'In clusters, yes. We are one of the largest and most powerful tribes in the forest. Many smaller tribes owe us their loyalty. We have ties with most of them going back many centuries.'

'What about rival tribes?'

'There are several; most, though, are much deeper into the forest than ourselves. Our chief rival, the Ometahan, live just to the south, on terraces carved into the shoulders of the mountains.'

'What about war? Do you ever fight?'

'Yes, but it is not as you might see it. We are few in number and have fewer children, so if a dispute cannot be resolved peacefully then, yes, we fight, but we try to avoid excessive loss of life.'

'How? And how do you fight among all these trees?'

'We do not. Inside the forest are some wide open spaces, fields large enough to hold armies. We arrange a date and a time and meet there. The battles themselves are quite formal. Bow, spear and horse are all exercised, but each tribe's Mhezhen watches carefully. As soon as it is obvious which side has the advantage, the losing Mhezhen concedes and the battle ends. An agreement to end the dispute is then made to the winner's advantage, with the loser making concessions determined by both parties before the battle. It is a sensible system that keeps both tribes at near full strength. See, we are here.'

They were at the northern shore of the lake. The light was rapidly dimming. Itheya steered the boat on to the muddy bank and the two of them got out and hauled it on to the ground. Leaving her blanket behind, she said, 'Follow me,' and disappeared into the trees.

He did so, keeping track of her by watching her white arms and legs. After some five minutes she stopped and spoke to him.

'Between the mountains and the sea the ground slopes gradually. The Taethan enters the sea over the lip of a high cliff, falling into its waters as a fine spray. Mostly the slope is not noticeable but there are places where it falls steeply. We are at one of those places now. Can you hear the water?'

The sound of water rushing over stone was easy to hear, overpowering as it did the sad sigh of the trees and the early calls of a solitary owl. Itheya turned from him and disappeared down a steep defile in the earth, which appeared before him as though Artorus himself had thrust a colossal knife into the ground. Looking down, he saw steps had been carved into the stone under his feet. They were not steep but he still hesitated as they were all shrouded in darkness. He saw Itheya's white face turning to look at him.

'I see the brave human warrior has finally met his match, terrified as he is by a few steps.

'I cannot see them, you must have much better night vision than

I.'

She climbed back towards him. 'Take my hand.'

He grasped her hand. It was like clutching warm gossamer. Gently she led him through the defile until they stood on a stretch of leaf-covered earth.

'This way.'

A right turn and a brief walk, and the source of the noise was revealed to him.

This was obviously the point where the water left the lake and headed towards the sea. He stood before a waterfall, but it was so much more than that. Over a series of broad stone shelves the water danced, the slope of the ground gentle enough for the water to proceed serenely, falling over a low stone lip into a small pool, then over another lip and into another pool. There were many of these lips interspersed at irregular intervals along these broad falls. The water itself never got to more than a few inches deep and Morgan could see figures above him standing in its midst. He wondered why anyone would do such a thing with evening pressing on. Then it became obvious.

They were lighting lamps.

Posts had been fixed into the stone somehow and atop them flames flickered and danced. The flames in each lamp were of different colours – some were pale blue, some a rich green, or corundum, or sunflower yellow. There were dozens of these lamps spread up and down the falls as well as some thirty feet below him, arranged in a semicircle around the night-dark splash pool. From somewhere opposite him, across the falls, he started to hear singing, the voices of men and women meshing into something ethereal. He had never heard the celestial choir at the Grand Cathedral of Tanaren but he reckoned they would be hard pushed to come up with anything as mellifluous and dulcet sweet as what he was hearing now. Itheya, next to him, stood rapt, her eyes closed, swaying gently as the music possessed her. Morgan did not shut his eyes, for in the light of the lamps, the water was changing colour as it flowed downhill, so that the whole waterfall now resembled a shifting kaleidoscope of iridescent hues. He stood in silent wonder, letting it all wash over him, it was almost like a waking dream.

The night had fully arrived when the singing stopped and Itheya opened her eyes. 'Let us return,' she said softly to him.

The same sort of lamps now lit up the defile, so climbing back was easy and they were back into the boat and on to the lake in no time. As Itheya pushed the boat into the lake, Morgan rubbed his eyes. 'Am I seeing things?' he asked.

'No,' she said. 'Z'ezhesheken, fireflies.'

Across most of the lake he could see the flickering lights of the small creatures. Some were close enough for him to discern the wing beats. As with the falls, there was a shifting panoply of colour – yellow, red, green and white. It was enough to make him laugh out loud.

'Is something wrong?' she asked.

'No, this is just quite the spectacle. I am used to brown and green and grey, not this variety of colour. With this and the falls I have had my eyes opened.'

'You enjoyed the falls?'

'Indeed. I thank you for taking me there.'

'Elemassena, we call them. The "Singing Falls". In daylight they are equally beautiful; you can just sit, shut your eyes and listen to the cascade. It is easy to fall asleep and have nothing but the gentlest of dreams there.'

'The choir, what were they singing?'

'It is a different song every night. Tonight it was a song of remembrance, of the times when we lived in the plains. Such songs educate our children. They will be singing it at Zamezhenka when we return and at other places along the shore.'

She moved the tiller slightly and the wind caught the sail. As they moved through a cloud of fireflies, she started to sing softly:

> 'Azhai olenke eona keonon mar feno
> Sasara cerena olenres sha resklo
> Sasa fisken cothonda tulo sefel vocrezha
> Merenklay ul sessha cot sylvco sylvezha
> Ara vanionon xenestran vuzazha nesteran vuto cobera

vuto cobera vuto cobera
nesteran vuto cobera

Ten desenda uzhcothon pelevaa colzhava
Ten desenda groscothon tuto zenta sheniva
Flentesben remotho crata oleneklo
Tafalantesh zai tonos ezhint netarasglo
Ara vanionon xenestran vuzazha nesteran vuto cobera
vuto cobera vuto cobera
nesteran vuto cobera

Fen hassan zai neaniath in birra cot blere
Isisesh zhai thenestra enteriz olentere
Fen voto hashara voto cellenta hashera
Ara vaniona toluno fliazhintra hurbera
Ara vanionon xenestran vuzazha nesteran vuto cobera
vuto cobera vuto cobera
nesteran vuto cobera

Coth olea dromea onati frozomel
Coth olea dromea onati entracel
Ara vanionon xenestran vuzazha nesteran vuto cobera
vuto cobera vuto cobera nesteran vuto cobera

Ara vanionon xenestran cober'

'And you have a beautiful singing voice as well. We have a saying about the people of Tanaren in the south; it goes: "The only thing wrong with the southerners is that they are perfect." I get the impression that saying could equally apply to you.'

She coloured slightly, though he could not see this in the murk.

'I know your humour by now, so I am aware you are not being serious.'

'I was when I mentioned your voice. Tell me, are all your songs sad and melodious, relating melancholy stories from the past?'

'Well, that one is, and I only sang a small portion of it. What is love without loss? What is love without pain? As we remember our ancestors and their life on the plains. We have happier songs, for other occasions. Here is one.' She started to sing again but this one was much livelier and half shouted. He guessed it was one to sing after too much zhath.

> *'Xe ate holosh, em meon uven rotosh*
> *Plefennia manosh! Plefennia manosh!*
> *Toro meon crefer egia vono cramata*
> *Bromosi eontra ve nestero fezhaya!'*

'And what is that one about?'

'It is sung at Dromeantele, a spring festival for the young. You may hear it at the end of the evening. It has instructions from a woman to a man on how exactly he should please her. Do not ask me to translate it and do not tell Father that I sang it to you.'

'I take it that it is what we would call a bawdy song.'

'Yes, and not one a Mhezhen's daughter should be singing to a human.'

'Have you ever sung it to another elf?'

'Yes, and he obeyed the instructions, too.'

Morgan laughed. 'I guess he would.'

The island was coming into view. He already could see it was lit up from one end to the other, and as he got closer he could see how. All of the banner poles and flag poles thrusting up from the ground were blazing with the blue fire he had first seen on the statue when they had summoned the elves. None of the flags or banners was burning, though, even though the flames were licking at them. Also hanging between the houses were small crystals glowing intensely with a pure white light; he hadn't noticed them earlier. He hadn't looked up he supposed; there must have been several attached to a series of thin chords and tied to the various roof posts between buildings. As they got closer, the singing came to him again, drifting from the Zamezhenka across the gentle waters of the lake.

Itheya moved the tiller a little and, as the boat started to angle sharply towards the island, she spoke again.

'In the forest we have large shaggy beasts, horned – you would call them cattle, I suppose. Our name for them is strugo. They eat the leaves no other creatures can; they can also eat bark, moss, lichen; some even say they can eat the wood. They wander the forest in family groups between ten and twenty strong. Each small tribe is allowed to kill one a year, the larger tribes two. These creatures are quiet, stoic and dependable. They are strong but hardly ever use their strength. When one is killed, the others, instead of charging the hunter, surround the fallen one and refuse to move away from it. We have to leave and come back a day later for the body. They mourn their fallen; it says to me that the differences between ourselves and the beasts around us are smaller than we like to think.'

She stopped a second to check their course, then continued.

'Do not take this in a way it was not intended, but you remind me of such a creature. You seem strong, gentle even, but I know I would not like to face you in battle.'

'You are saying I remind you of a cow.'

She giggled, a sound almost as musical as her singing. 'No, I was taking some aspects of an animal's manner and comparing it to some aspects of yours. That is all. But I have a problem. I have known few humans, but those I have met have either been here to harm my people in some way, or, worse, have betrayed us; betrayed me! The strugo are never false; their hearts are always true and dependable. That is where you differ. I want to trust you Morgan, you and Master Cedric, but I do not know if I can.'

'What of the man who taught you our language?'

'He was not my only teacher. Father could speak your tongue long before he appeared, but, yes, he betrayed us and his betrayal was great in the end. All the humans I have known thus far have proven false. I do not wish it to happen again.'

'Which is why your brother is the way he is?'

'Partly. He also resents being the younger of the two of us. I am the one born to rule, the first in everybody's thoughts. I will speak at the krasa not he; it is I who lead the forest patrols, who will preside over the festivals when Father ... is not here. He is strong and clever, skilled with spear and bow, but nobody ever notices, and his resentment only increases over the years.'

'Itheya,' – Morgan leaned forward so he could see her face clearly – 'I cannot speak in absolutes here but with every fibre of my being I will never try to betray you. I have no designs on your people; my only job here is to protect Cedric. Really, if I am being honest, you are wasting a lot of your valuable time on me. If you have better things to do tomorrow, I will happily stay in my room under guard.'

'The tribe, including Father, wanted to allow Cedric in and only Cedric. It was I who wanted you here, which is why I stood surety for you. I was curious about you. You had an interesting smell, metal and leather and sweat, and I liked your eyes; they are deep, they tell many stories. So you are not wasting my time, not at all. Of course, you will be on your own tomorrow while I practise for Armentele. Then there is the krasa, which no outsiders may see. You will be sick of your room by the time this is over.'

At last, the boat glided into the harbour. She secured it and together they returned to the Zamezhenka. The roof sections were closed now and the light of the glow stones reflected warmly off the tiled floor. Small groups of elves huddled there, listening to the music coming from the top floor. Itheya led him to the second floor where a circular table was laid out at the centre and was laden with spiced rabbit, eggs cooked in a fiery red sauce, apples and blackberries, as well as a large pile of flatbreads. The elderflower drink was there as well as a sweet mead and a spiced drink of dark berries. Morgan sampled as much as he could. Cedric was there with Terath, as well as Dramalliel and Tiavon, but Itheya's father was not to be seen.

'He eats alone these days,' she said. 'All these people can be too much for him.'

Cedric came over to him. 'I have had the most stimulating day,' he said. 'I will never be able to set it all down in writing, I am bound to forget something.'

'Learned anything new?' asked Morgan.

'Well, I can awaken a dragon, maybe even control one, and then send it back into its slumber.'

'You can?'

'Well, no. But we are getting there. That tooth is the key; if only I had brought the other one. I have given Cenarazh these pieces unconditionally and in perpetuity. I am sure the Grand Duke will not mind.'

'Well, you know him better than I.'

'As in, not at all, I know.'

Dramalliel came over to them both. 'Well, humans, what are you planning to do tomorrow?'

'Oh, I will be with Terath all day probably. Your father hopes to join us if he is able.' Cedric struggled to talk and swallow some fruit at the same time. 'That is good. Keep exchanging your ideas; it is always good to know your enemy, so I am told. As for you, warrior, what does my enchanting sister want to do with you?'

'Very little. She is practising for the festival. I daresay I will have to remain in my room.'

'You will go mad with boredom. I have an idea. sister, come here I want to ask you something.'

Itheya came over. 'Yes, brother.'

'You are leaving the poor human in his room all day tomorrow. What kind of host will he think we are?'

'It will only be while I rehearse; maybe one or two hours.'

'Why don't you leave him with me for that time. I have an idea or two to keep him amused.'

'No. I know what you will do. He is my responsibility, not yours.'

'And what exactly do you think I will do to him?'

'You will try to fight him; maybe even try to kill him. I know you, brother; you see it as a test.'

'I give you my word, Itheya; I will not kill him.'

'The answer is still no.'

'Do I get a say in this?' Morgan asked quizzically.

'You do not.' Itheya was pouting.

'Just let me go out for one half-hour. Nothing bad can happen in that time.'

'Yes, it can.'

Cedric intervened. 'What if I go with him, and Terath. I get a chance to see outside this building and our two older heads can keep any hot-bloodedness in check. We can also make sure it is no more than half an hour.'

She raised her eyebrows. 'Menestron! Very well, but if there is any trouble or bad blood, I will not be forgiving of anyone.'

Dramalliel smiled at everyone. He looked utterly charming 'Till tomorrow, warrior Morgan. I will see you before noon.'

As he left, Morgan noticed Itheya's troubled face. 'Don't worry!' he mouthed to her. He knew he should have declined, but he also knew Dramalliel would keep sniping and sniping until he got what he wanted. Better to get any trouble over and done with. He only hoped that she would not see this as a betrayal – breaking his word in less than two hours was a record even for him.

36

He watched the mass of tousled brown hair spread out over the pillow as its possessor slept, peaceful at last. He had not slept since he had seen her, veins running with fire, her nightdress blackened. Little unnerved him at his age, but to see her vindicated in such a terrible way was something he would not forget easily.

Ebba joined him about an hour ago and, like him, was sitting in a chair looking at the girl intently. 'What can we do, my Lord?' she had said to him when he had told her of the night's events. Any answer totally eluded him.

He had retrieved the stone from the pitcher earlier and spent some time studying it. He saw the strange movement of its viscous centre but aside from that there seemed little to note about it. Holding it, he half expected to see visions of soaring dragons breathing fiery doom from the sky, but there was nothing. Absolutely nothing.

'Call me when she wakes,' he said to Ebba and left the room.

In the main hall a handful of people, guards and tradesmen bringing in provender were having breakfast. So, too, were Ulian and Alys. He went over to them and told them the events of the previous night as well as relating the tale of the fishermen at Oxhagen.

'What is it you want to do?' said Ulian, with a worried frown that seemed to knit his eyebrows together.

'I don't know. All I want to do is get rid of that cursed stone.'

'You want to take it back into that labyrinth? To face these spirits? Peasants can see phantoms in any shadow but there is obviously something in this tale. People died there – do you wish to take such a risk?'

'Well, we cannot let the current state of affairs continue. As it stands, I propose paying a couple of my more trusted men a lot of money to go with me. If these ... things see I have something they want, hopefully it will go well for us.'

'You have no successor, have you?'

'No, it is something I should consider. I had better get something legal drawn up.'

'It is not really my business, my Lord, but do you know who would inherit your estates if, Artorus help us, something terrible did happen to you?'

'It is no secret, at least not to the people that know me. A quarter of my lands that border Einar's go to him; the rest goes to the Hartfields. I have done that, because to bequeath it to my wife alone, would put her life in danger. There are many barons around here I trust little enough, but the thought of dealing with an army from the capital should rein in their ambitions nicely. No one would dare back-stab a Hartfield.'

'Do you think she is capable of ruling alone?'

'She has Bruan. And Einar. She has taken petitions on her own and done well. I have no concerns on that score.'

'May I go and see her, my Lord?' asked Alys.

'Of course, though she is asleep at present.'

After Alys had gone, Ulian wiped some gravy from his mouth. 'Very tasty. I commend your kitchens most highly. I will, of course, be coming with you; there may be something I can do to help.'

'No. It is too dangerous. You have told me everything you know; there is no need for you to make the journey.'

'I disagree. If I go there, into these tunnels, I might just see something important that you may not recognise as being so. If these are Wych tunnels, it is something I have more knowledge of than, with all due respect, you. ' 'You think you can navigate them?'

'I don't know till I get there, but I at least have as good a chance as you.'

Wulfthram thought for a moment. 'I will think about it.'

'Good, when are we, I mean you, leaving.'

'The weather is foul at the moment, not a good time to put to sea, but, assuming it does improve, I intend to leave as soon as I can – hopefully in a couple of days.'

'Have you told your wife you are not taking her?'

'No,' he groaned.

'It is just that she seems quite stubborn of mien; she might...'

'Yes, she might. I will speak to her when she wakes up.' At that point Ebba entered the room and came towards them.

'My Lord, her Ladyship has just woken. You asked me to let you know...'

'Right, fine, right. Run along, tell her I will be there presently.'

As Ebba did as she was bid, Wulfthram stared at the table, perfectly aware of the steady gaze Ulian was giving him. At length he stood, looked like he was about to say something, then sat down again calling for one of the servants.

'You know, what you said about the kitchens has made me quite hungry. I may just help myself to some breakfast first.'

Ceriana sat on the edge of the bed, running a comb roughly through her hair. Her skin was a sickly white colour and there were dark grey circles under her eyes. Alys was sitting next to her holding a hand mirror; she seemed pretty reluctant to hand it over, something the other girl obviously noticed.

'Do I look that bad? I can take it, Alys. Hand it over.' She took a quick look and groaned. 'Elissa's eyes, am I dead?' She handed the mirror back. 'Sorry, Alys, I was wrong. Is there anywhere I can get a new head? A prettier one that doesn't look like it died a week ago?'

'You don't need a new head, my Lady. We just need to sort this problem out, so you can recover yourself, get your health back as it should be.'

'I could take the waters at Zerannon,' she laughed. 'I have heard that mentioned by some. No, I need to do something with that infernal stone. I know what I have to do but my husband and others may be ... resistant.'

'Why not just throw it into the sea?'

'What? Hop in a ship, find the deepest ocean I can and just throw it over the side?'

'Well yes, my Lady.'

'It sounds tempting, doesn't it, but the dragon is awake now; if the stone is the key to returning him to his slumber, having it at the bottom of the ocean is not a particularly good idea. Besides, the link between the two of us is there now and I don't feel putting distance between myself and the stone will help anymore. There has to be another way.'

'What about trying to smash it? There must be a sledgehammer or something powerful enough to crush it into pieces.'

'But that might kill me!' She ran her hands through her hair. 'By the Gods, what a mess! Alys, talk to me about something else. I am sick and tired of thinking about the damned thing. Tell me about your man, or life at St Philig's, anything. You assisted some washerwomen before Cedric took you under his wing, did you not? What was that like?'

'Hard, my Lady, but we were a big family and it helped put food on the table. I have been working for Master Cedric for three years now, it is a lot more enjoyable than my former employment even though he cannot afford to pay me much of a stipend.'

'And your man?'

'Willem? He is the only person I know who is shyer than me. He came to St Philig's on a scholarship from a monastery. At first I avoided him thinking he was probably very religious.'

'Would that bother you?'

'Not in itself, no; it is just that religious people can talk down to you so. To be honest, my faith isn't that strong. I have seen both a brother and a sister lose their lives in a harsh winter, neither of them being any more than babes. If the Gods can take innocent children so easily, are they really worthy of our respect? Do we worship them out of fear in case it is us next?'

'The church says their motives are beyond our capacity to fathom. It is a question that has troubled me in the past, too.'

'Anyway, my Lady, Willem is a good disciple of the church but he has never spoken of his faith to me. We share an interest insofar as we are both keen to learn and are grateful for the opportunity Master Cedric has given us. He is kind, considerate and funny. There is the problem of him being a church scholar and so not permitted to marry, but Cedric has told me not to worry over such things and that ways can be found to get around this matter.'

'It is a barrier, though,' said Ceriana. 'I will help, if I can; if a letter to his monastery is needed, I will be happy to send one. I have sworn to help Ebba marry and it would be wonderful if I could help you, too.' At last, she thought, something to take my mind off recent events, to get me to stop thinking of just myself for a change.

'I am grateful, my Lady. Perhaps if Master Cedric manages to get here, the two of you could discuss the matter.'

'A splendid idea; I do hope he manages to get here soon. I suppose I had better get dressed and washed for breakfast.'

Just at that moment the door opened. She knew who it was as everybody else knocked. 'Yes, my husband?'

'You might want to come to the main hall.'

'I will – just let me get washed and dressed first.'

'Get dressed by all means, but you might want to leave your grooming till afterwards.'

She turned to face him, a perplexed expression on her pale face. 'Why? What in Elissa's name has happened?'

'We have ... visitors.'

She stood up; she and Alys became all bustle and animation. 'Is it the scholar? Has he arrived here?'

'No. It is not the scholar. They are in the main hall being watched by all the guards I have available.'

'Stop teasing me, Wulf. Who by all that's holy are they?'

'There are three of them. Their leader says his name is Luto; he says he wishes to help you if you return what has been taken from him.'

Realisation slowly dawned in her thumping head. 'You mean...?'

'Yes, Ulian's black priests; they are waiting to talk to us.'

She nodded slowly and started to pull on some clothes. For one of the first times in her life she neither saw nor cared about what she was wearing, or about make-up, or jewellery, or even washing.

It was as he said. In front of the high table, surrounded by guards whose halberds formed a ring of steel around them, stood three of the black priests.

To Ceriana, they barely seemed human. With their shaven heads and identical garb they looked as though they had hatched from the same egg or burst from the same seed pod. Their faces were devoid of expression, blank and inscrutable. They stood, awaiting their audience with a certain calm serenity, as though they had all the time in the world. The leader of the three, though, was a little different. His cheeks and eyes looked as though they had partly sunk into his face and his forehead was high and domed. He was also impossibly tall, Ceriana reckoned he could not be far short of seven foot in height and he stooped slightly with his shoulders pointing forwards, hunching slightly over his torso. Ulian was waiting there on the other side of the table, looking extremely discomfited. Wulfthram, however, gave no sign of being at the least troubled by the bizarre sight ahead of him. He walked to the table and sat down with all the self-assurance in the world, Ceriana and Alys followed behind in a much more timorous manner. When they were all seated, Wulfthram beckoned for their visitors to do the same. They remained standing. The tall man finally spoke.

'It is not for us to be seated and comfortable in the house of one who has wronged us.'

'I see.' Wulfthram spoke as if he were hearing the hundredth petition that day between farmers squabbling over the tiniest portion of land. 'And how exactly do you feel you have been wronged?'

The tall man's steely gaze alighted on Ceriana. 'The woman. She knows. She knows what she has taken.'

Ceriana squirmed in her seat. Wulfthram barely glanced at her. 'Oh you mean that stone. You are mistaken, my friend; she found it on a beach. She has stolen from the fish, the crabs, and the seaweed – no one else – and if you wish to accuse my wife of theft, you had better have some evidence to back this up otherwise I deem a flogging might be in order.'

The man's expression hardened, if that was possible. He spoke again, his accent thick, guttural. It required full concentration to understand what he was saying. He was obviously not speaking his native tongue.

'We came here to collect a precious object. We found it. It is now in the possession of that woman. For that wrong to be righted, it has to be returned.'

Ceriana realised that one of the men standing behind the spokesman was the same one she had seen when out riding in Thakholm. Plucking up courage and in a thin raspy voice, she asked the next question.

'If this stone was returned to you, what exactly would you do with it?'

The man met her stare; it took her all her willpower not to flinch, but she held firm.

'It is not your business to know this. We, of the Order of the Draigo, obey the will of the Ancient One. What that will is we have spent centuries discerning. How can I explain it to you in one afternoon?'

'You will have to try. Otherwise, you will have no chance of seeing the stone.'

The man smiled, a cruel smile. 'Are you so eager to accept the changes that the stone is working upon your body? Do you know how it will end for you? We can read the stone, we can locate it, we can see you are sensitive to its call. If you persist in keeping it, with communicating with the being you are linked to, then the stone will be lost to us; we will be unable to bend it the way we wish, but the cost to you will be a lot worse than that. You are young, your life could be long and happy, but retain this object in your possession and it will be anything but. A lifetime of pain and isolation in a body that is no longer fully human – that is what awaits you. We are prepared for this change – for us the transformation is a glorious one – but are you?'

Ulian had a book open in front of him. He asked the next question as Ceriana pondered the man's words, trying to fight the chill that was gripping her throat and stomach.

'It says in this book that your order was founded in imitation of the dragon worship common in elven societies about a thousand years ago. It also says that you wish to control dragons and use them to purge this world of the unworthy, so a new order can be brought about. Can you tell us exactly who the unworthy actually are?'

'That will not be for us to decide; the creatures that have been awakened will choose. The wisest ones, the Aelva, will be spared – that we know – but, apart from that, the will of the oldest creatures is closed to us.'

Ulian cleared his throat. 'What you are saying is that you wish to awaken these monsters and let them loose to wreak havoc upon the world. What if they deem you unworthy and set about slaughtering you?'

'Then we will accept our fate and commend our unworthy spirits to the Ancient One. Death holds no terrors for us.'

'Don't believe him!' Ceriana said to her companions. 'They can control the dragons through the stones. They are hardly going to attack their own people.'

'No,' said the man. 'Not if the will of the creature proves stronger. When one of our priests fuses with one of the Oldest Ones, it is never certain who will emerge the more dominant of the two.'

'How many of these stones are there?' asked Wulfthram.

'There are descriptions of each of them,' said the man, 'and their location, in ancient works of the Aelven, which were granted to us by them as reward for our long and trusted friendship. They were, however, written in cypher; it has taken us a millennium to decrypt but part of these writings. There could be hundreds of these stones. The unencrypted writings were carved on dragons' teeth, bound in gold and kept in the great Aelven cities. Each tooth contained a portion of the writings found in the entire book; all six of these, however, have been lost over time.'

The man behind him whom Ceriana had recognised earlier spoke: 'None of this is important. We have come here for the stone. Will you give it to us, or do we leave empty-handed? If that is to be the case, let us warn you – we will bide our time and take it back when we can, by force if necessary. Not to do so would dishonour our god.'

'That depends,' said Wulfthram. 'Tell me, is there any way this stone can be neutralised? Its power drained? Do your Wych tomes cover that at any point?'

'There are ways,' said the tall man. 'But we will never do this. It is to defy the will of the Ancient One to do such a thing. And' – he leaned forward, looking intently at Wulfthram – 'we will never tell any other of the way it is done either.'

Wulfthram spoke airily. 'Beneath this mansion there is a small dungeon; I use it rarely – only for the most heinous of criminals and egregious of offences. There is a man I can engage in the town, an expert on hot iron brands, a man thorough in his work pulling teeth or nails, turning the thumbscrews, fixing the bridle, that sort of thing. Do you wish me to employ him now? It is cold and damp down there. Wounds will never heal; rather they will fester, fill with pus; maybe an amputation would be necessary; we have the saw and the rag to put between what is left of your teeth to do such a thing. It would be easy for us to arrange it. So I ask again: how do you drain the power of this stone?'

The tall man smiled mirthlessly. 'We have come here voluntarily to request the return of our property and you threaten us with torture and mutilation. I doubt that the Oldest Ones would find you worthy. However, we were expecting such an eventuality and have not come unprepared. Our temple is close to the great jungles in the south. Many toxins thrive in these conditions; some, when mixed together, can produce unusual effects. Before leaving our ship this morning the three of us drank such a substance. If we do not return by noon on the morrow, its poison will kill us. The neutralising substance is with my brothers on the ship.'

'Noon tomorrow,' said Wulfthram. 'It still gives us enough time to persuade you to talk.'

'Our deaths will be assured, but so may yours. The substance we have imbibed is corrosive and unstable. Before we die we will sweat profusely as our organs start to break down. Any man nearby who touches us will contract the poison and suffer the same fate. It is an agonising way to die. The longer we are away from the antidote, the greater the chance of this happening. Your torturer is as unlikely to see noon tomorrow as we.'

'So I should tell my man to wear gloves then?' Wulfthram was unmoved.

'You are glib but this poison needs but the barest contact to work on another. Say your man wipes his brow, scratches his ear. That is all it would take.'

'Pah!' said Ulian. 'He is bluffing; no such substance exists.'

'Maybe in your little world, but there are so many things out there you have never seen. Do you wish to take such a risk?'

The other black priest spoke again: 'Will you give us the stone?'

Ceriana spoke in the most even voice she could manage. 'If we do, you will use it to control a dragon, which may well be turned against our own people. Surely you can see that we could never agree to such a thing.'

'Then we have nothing more to say to each other. We will take the stone for ourselves when you least expect it. However,' – he reached behind his neck and unclasped a thin chain from which hung a small disc of black metal – 'before I go I give you this.' He handed it to Ceriana. 'It is an amalgam of dull iron and sky metal, fallen from the heavens. Wear it under your clothes, close to your heart. While you have it your fusion with the creature will be held in abeyance. Nothing more will happen to you. We want the stone before it becomes irretrievably yours, so it is as much in our interest as yours to stop any further changes in your body. If you remove it at any time, though, what has been held in check will resume at some pace. So do not take it off. Ever! When we take the stone, then the intended fusion with the real dragonlord will begin.'

The priest behind the tall man smiled and Ceriana knew: he was to be the one to join with the dragon and, if he could take control of it, the first place he would come to, to judge the unworthy, would be here.

'We have no real quarrel with you,' the tall man resumed. 'The circumstances of our meeting are unfortunate. The next time we meet things may be somewhat less civil. I, Luto, and my brother priests, Dravan and Melnikor, bid you farewell.'

He turned to leave, but as he did so the three of them were faced by a row of halberds, their cruel head spikes pointing at the men's midriff.

'It is all right; let them go.' Wulfthram raised his hand to the guards, confirming his order. They sat down and watched as the three of them slowly left the room. After they had gone Wulfthram signalled to Bruan, who came over to him.

'Follow them.'

As Bruan was about to leave with his men, Wulfthram called him back.

'The Vesper of Kibil is in the harbour. It is a fast caravel with an experienced crew. If they take to sea, follow them at a safe distance. Do not engage them, unless you have to. Report back to me as soon as you are able.'

After Bruan had gone, he called for food for Ceriana who was pensively toying with the medallion.

'It is a dull thing, is it not?' she said absently, half to herself. 'Are you going to put it on?' he asked her gently.

'I suppose I had better; it looks harmless enough, I suppose.'

He helped her fasten it around her neck. When that was done, she pushed the metal disc under the front of her dress so that it was both against her skin and obscured. Servants placed some bread and cheese before her, along with a couple of pies and a warm posset. She ate slowly, completely unaware of the others watching her.

'What is the plan now, my Lord?' Ulian asked.

'It is unchanged. I will sail to Oxhagen within the next few days. Farnerun knows of my intentions, so hopefully he will have men at the town to assist when I arrive. I will engage one of the exiled fishermen to serve as a guide.'

'And if you succeed in returning the stone to its place of rest, what is to stop the black priests from reclaiming it as they have already done once before?'

'Guards. I have asked Farnerun to consider posting a garrison at the place – a matter I will pursue when I get there. I just want shot of the damned thing, so my wife can get back to a normal life.'

His wife was quietly nibbling at a large chunk of bread. 'Wulf,' she said.

'What is it?'

'You know I will be going with you when you sail, don't you? And I don't want any arguing to the contrary; no one is more involved in this matter than I.'

'But you heard the fisherman's story. This could be dangerous.'

'And you heard the black priest. According to him, I am changing in some way and my life could be incredibly short. What more possible danger could I be in that I am not in already?'

'The lady has a point,' said Ulian with a wry smile.

'But the dangers we may face are unknown ones – spirits or worse.'

'Then swords and force of arms are pretty much useless, don't you think? You will be in as much danger as I, maybe even more so. Can swords defeat spirits? Or will they merely make the bearers targets? I am going; you cannot deny me this.'

'I think I should go, too,' interrupted Alys.

'Artorus's eyes, this is not a scenic cruise followed by a picnic on the beach. None of us may come back alive! Do you really think it wise for both baron and baroness to go and risk their lives simultaneously?'

'Bruan will manage your lands, our lands, perfectly well on his own. He has done this many other times, including when you left here to come and marry me.' She pouted at him in such a way and with such firmness of expression that he knew the argument was already lost. He had never seen such resolve in her eyes and had to admit he was quietly impressed by her.

'Very well, Ceriana, I will cede to you just this once. But do not think I have become every inch the compliant husband.'

'I will believe that when the Gods come down from the heavens and start playing tag in the courtyard. Anyhow, I would much prefer you stubborn and unyielding to being a scold's lapdog. It makes our disagreements far more stimulating.'

All this time Alys looked like she wanted an opportunity to speak. Eventually Ceriana noticed her.

'What is it, Alys? What are you trying to tell me? Do I need a bath?'

'No, my Lady! I mean, well maybe, just a little. No, it was something that man said earlier.'

'Go on.'

'Well, he said they had writings from the elves that they had been deciphering; he was a bit vague when saying exactly what these writings talked about, but it all seemed to revolve around these stones. He also said they knew how to drain the stones of power, so presumably that crops up in these writings somewhere.'

'All fine and well,' said Ulian. 'But, unless we had these tomes in our possession, there is little we can do about it.'

'But we have!' Alys beamed. 'Some of them, anyway. He said the unencrypted versions were written on dragons' teeth and bound in gold. Well, when Professor Cedric uncovered that secret chamber of the elves on the coast here....'

'...He found two of them!' Ulian said quietly.

'You are saying, we may know how to drain these stones? That we could already have this information?' Ceriana looked hopeful.

'Possibly,' said Ulian. 'But it is a remote chance. The language they were written in is so archaic it might as well be cypher. Cedric has taken one to the Aelthenwood to see if the Wych folk can fare better with it. The other resides in the Grand Duke's treasury in Tanaren. I could write and request its release.'

'No,' said Ceriana, 'I will do that. I will also write to Father so I can explain its importance. Maybe your Cedric will return with the knowledge required to translate such an artefact; we lose nothing by trying, surely.'

'No, my Lady, we lose nothing at all, and thank you for remembering, Alys. The memory of an old man has even more holes than his socks.'

Ceriana walked over to the north wall, where the tall, mullioned windows overlooked the courtyard. The rain was coming down vertically; she watched it bouncing off the stone flags or splashing into the wide puddles that had formed on the uneven ground. The drainage channel looked like a miniature river Erskon and sporadic gusts of high wind tore at the canvas sheeting of the covered supply wagons standing stoically against the outer wall. A solitary crow hopped mournfully over the mossy stones, its glossy feathers still pristine, and under one of the wagons she saw two of the manor's cats, mousers both, who had abandoned their day's work and had gone to seek shelter – too late, as both were soggy and bedraggled.

'Well,' she said, 'we are not sailing anywhere with all this going on outside.'

Just as soon as she said those words, one of the doormen entered and approached Wulfthram. He had evidently been outside as his black-and-grey surcoat was stained with water.

'My Lord, there are people here who wish to speak with you.'

Wulfthram groaned. 'Do they wear black? Are they threatening to sweat and poison us all?'

The man looked confused. 'No, my Lord, they say they have come in response to a messenger seeking out a Master Cedric.' Alys looked up.

'Send them in,' Wulfthram said.

The two men that entered looked as though they had just taken a fully clothed bath. Water plastered their hair and their weathered cloaks and boots were sopping. They both laboured under heavy packs and, as the smaller man threw back his hood, Alys gave a small squeal of delight.

'My Lords, Ladies and Professors of the court,' said Haelward, 'you would not believe the journey we have had to get here. Talk about the god of storms!'

Willem smiled beside him. Soaked he may have been, but suddenly he had never felt warmer.

BOOK ONE: AUTUMN
37

The river coiled ever southward like a menacing black snake, its surface mottled with green and brown leaves fallen from the many trees overhanging its darkly sinuous form. It was silent, powerful, respected. Everyone knew the river; everyone deferred to it. It wasn't even given a name round here; it was just 'The River' such was its silent omnipotence.

Which, ruminated Whitey from his perch on the walkway overlooking it, was just exactly how he wanted to be. His entire life he had been shunned by his peers – from the moment he left his mother's womb, his pink eyes sending the midwife screaming, through his childhood spent cutting purses on the streets of Sketta, to his adulthood as a thug for hire, serving every erstwhile crime lord in the south at some point or another. The Book of Artorus had a famous passage referring to Keth's pale demons rising from the bowels of the earth to plague mankind for a thousand years, and so, being an albino, things were never going to be easy for him. He had spent his entire life avoiding the authorities, constantly fighting hunger or manacled to the walls of a cell or sleeping on excrement-covered stone floors, only waking sporadically to kick away the rats as they nibbled at his toes and fingers.

Now, however, things were different; now he was on the right side of the law for the first time in his life. Well, in a manner of speaking anyway. It had all come about through his meeting with Gorton. Meeting was perhaps not the right word; he was actually caught cutting his purse. As he sat in the stocks for the thousandth time covered in the refuse donated by the locals, Gorton, a merchant with a large round belly barely concealed under his green tunic, its gold buttons straining hard against the forces of nature opposing it, had come up to him with a member of the local watch.

'I am looking for a business partner,' he had said, as the watchman released the lock on the stocks. 'And I imagine you, sir, will be happy with employment of any kind, judging from your present predicament.'

And that's how it had started. The nature of the 'partnership' was unclear but he would have agreed with almost anything to get away from that village. It turned out that Gorton was a well-connected man who knew a large number of well-to-do merchants and minor nobility covering an area of hundreds of miles close to the war zone. He also knew when these people would be away from home and that's where Whitey came in. Armed with a map of the property, and cloaked in black, he would break in, steal a few key items selected by Gorton, and make good his escape. Whitey knew the right fences to use and the two men pocketed a fortune; to cap it all, Gorton had made him a junior partner in his legitimate import–export business. Whitey had started to call himself a merchant.

There were numerous side-lines to get involved in, too, and this was why he was here, staring at the river in a remote part of the country. It involved buying up a lot of cheap tat, glass beads, dull knives, coarse linen garments, soft metal arrowheads, and trading them with the strange Marsh Men that came here about once a week. In return, they would receive spices, herbs, drugs and poisons worth over a hundred times their initial outlay. The Marsh Men in their mud huts had no Artoran tongue in their head and were as easy to fleece as a six-year-old child. Until meeting Gorton, Whitey had no idea how many ways there were to make easy money. Now he wore an expensive silk shirt, fine leather breeches and a ring studded with small pearls, and he received unlimited attention from the whores in Sketta, women who just two years ago used to spit on him as he walked past them.

Anyway, to business – Tath Wernig, the trading post they had lived in for the last week or so, was not a place to linger long in the memory. The long road from Sketta ended here; there was nowhere else to go for to the south, the land was too boggy for anybody but the peat diggers. Just over a dozen buildings were built either side of this half forgotten cul-de-sac, including a sad little inn, all fleas and straw pallets, where they had the misfortune to be staying at the moment, and a decrepit house of Artorus bereft of windows, whose priest spent most of the time comatose with an empty flagon in his hand and vomit down his smock. There was a blacksmith-cum-cooper-cum-wheelwright and a building euphemistically called the manor house on account that it had a couple of extra rooms and housed four or five soldiers and a magistrate all in the pay of Baron

Eburg, who was fortunate enough, or maybe unfortunate enough, to hold suzerainty over the town.

And it had, of course, a trading post, a long, low building built on a platform overhanging the river and with a jetty pointing out into the gently churning waters. Whitey (he was never called by his real name; he barely could remember it himself) was standing on it now, looking southwards, waiting. They had already seen two Marsh Men this week; one more and all their goods would be gone and it would be back to Sketta to sell on what they had received in trade and so fill their purses.

He heard Gorton's heavy tread on the planking.

'Anything?'

'Nothing, Master Gorton, what do you think? Shall we give it one more day?'

Gorton broke wind loudly; he did this quite often. Whitey reckoned it was something to do with his weight; even the planking on the jetty creaked under it.

'Actually, I am rather tempted to leave now. There will hardly be any traffic up here what with winter coming, and there are some good opportunities coming up in Sketta. Filton Ottermore of the Vintners' Guild is taking his family to Tanaren City till the spring; his house will be guarded but I know of a side entrance that they won't be watching. Also the house of Meriel needs some torinbalm; they use it as a soporific and we have got plenty here.'

'Why don't we come here in the summer?'

'It is full of merchants then; they all compete with each other and the Marshies get a far better deal. This time of year they are much more desperate; if you can stand Tath Wernig for a week you can clean up here. Come, let us go; there will be nothing more here this year.'

'Wait,' said Whitey, pointing downriver. 'I can see something.'

Both men shielded their eyes against the glare of the river and slowly Gorton could see that Whitey had been correct. There it was, blacker against black, a tiny speck heading their way. 'By all the Gods, Pink-eye, you have a demon's vision.'

'Years of practice in avoiding the town watch,' Whitey said with a smile. 'Are you armed? Can't trust these Marshies not to cut up rough if they think they are being done over.' He lifted his faithful purse-cutter up for Gorton to see.

'I lack your ability with the blade but, yes, I am prepared.' He opened his cloak to show Whitey a stiletto that he had strapped to his waist. A woman's weapon, Whitey thought. Gorton rarely had to do his own dirty work; he hired lackeys for that – lackeys or Whitey. Whitey grinned at the thought.

The boat came closer. It was a small circular boat with a single occupant; the Marsh Folk usually came in twos or threes, so both men were further encouraged. This will be easy, Whitey thought.

They watched the man pull up to the jetty, clamber out and secure his boat. Once this was done, Gorton approached him, smiling broadly, trade goods carried in a large leather satchel. Whitey thought the man was a typical Marshy, dark, weather-beaten, and wearing a woollen tunic and leather breeches. He had a metal knife, which wasn't such a good thing, and there was something about the way he looked at them that made the albino think that perhaps this wasn't going to be as easy as he thought.

'Hail, friend from the marsh,' Gorton effused. 'I take it you have come to trade. If this is so, you are a lucky man indeed. Please look at the goods I have to offer.' He opened the satchel and started to lay the various pieces of junk out on to the jetty.

Whitey looked into the man's boat. In it was a covered basket far larger than the others he had seen before. Was it full of merchandise? Getting the man's attention, he pointed to the basket attempting through improvised sign language that he would like to see inside it.

'I am not here to trade with you. I am here to see your elder.'

Gorton was open-mouthed. 'You speak our language! Artorus above, I have never heard of such a thing. Allow me to introduce myself. I am Gorton the merchant and this strange fellow beside me is Master Whitey, my partner in business. Please, peruse our goods at your leisure.'

'As I have said, I am not here to trade. I would like to know who is in charge here; my elder wishes me to converse with him. The matter is very important.'

'Important, eh?' Whitey spoke. 'You look like you're here to trade to me. Look at that goods basket; you're not telling me it's full of apples.'

'No, it is not, but I will discuss its contents only with your elder, or baron. Is baron the right word?'

Gorton smiled, all jowls and brown teeth. 'With all due respect. my friend, the baron here – Eburg I think his name is – is not going to spare a swamp creature like yourself ten seconds of his time. Why should he? What could a hut dweller possibly have or know that would interest a baron?'

'Because his lands are in danger; I come to warn him of this.'

Whitey sneered at the man. 'You are not threatening to attack us, are you? A whole two dozen of you with your pointy sticks and woolly armour.' He smiled at Gorton who shared the joke and spoke again to the Marsh Man.

'Look, my friend,' – he put his arm around the man's shoulder – 'no one gives a wren's beak for your problems up here. If I were to take you to the Baron, we would as likely be flogged for our temerity in thinking he would design to see us, let alone you. Now, be reasonable; you have bought goods with you, that we can both see; now, why don't we barter a good deal for us both? Then you can go home and tell your elder the audience you sought was refused but, that on the other hand, you have traded for some quality goods from myself and my colleague. What say you, eh?'

The Marsh Man poked the merchant's wares with his foot. 'Even if I were to accept what you are saying, these are hardly "quality goods". Other tribes may be grateful for this rubbish but not mine. Is that where your baron lives?' He pointed to the magistrate's house.

Whitey was about to reply in the negative but Gorton spoke before him.

'I see you are far too clever to fall for my salesman's talk. I tell you what, I will send my colleague to the nobleman's house to see if he will grant you an audience, but' – he drew breath loudly – 'in order to do that we will need to see the goods that you bring; otherwise you will just get the door slammed in your face.'

Behind him, outside the inn, two of the magistrate's men leaned by its door, flagons in hand, while a third one was relieving himself against the wall; they were watching the proceedings at the trading post with a studied disinterest. The Marsh Man stared back at them; he was considering the merchant's words.

'Very well,' he said. He reached into the boat and pulled out the basket.

Uncovering it, he showed its contents to both men. Gorton looked appraisingly at the display then cleared his throat.

'Please, just give us a minute, I just need to confer with my colleague.' He beckoned Whitey to follow him and took a few steps away from the Marsh Man before whispering: 'Did you see all that! There is at least ten times what these people normally bring. We are made I tell you, made!'

'The house of Meriel will pay a fortune for this,' said Whitey, grinning.

'Forget them! See all that blackroot. Think what the gangs in Sketta will pay for that! You've got the connections. What would the Fists of Guerric or the Nemesis gang give us? We could sell half to each of them and watch them kill each other. Your old firm, the Dead Hand, could take over! This, my friend, is that house on Loubian Hill I have always dreamed of!' he chuckled softly.

'There is only one small problem,' Whitey looked at the Marsh Man. 'Mmmm,' said the merchant. 'Are the guards still watching us?' Whitey nodded.

'Do you think,' the merchant said slowly, 'that it would be a terrible thing if this man had an accident and fell into the river, or perhaps even fell on to your knife first? Could such a thing be contrived, I wonder? We could tell the baron's men he went for us; what say you?'

The two men exchanged a knowing look. 'Stand between me and the guards; we will have to do this quickly.' Whitey silently loosened the knife at his belt and strode forward, failing to notice the sweat beading on Gorton's brow.

'What are you two talking about,' said the Marsh Man suspiciously.

Whitey moved towards him, trying to look as friendly as he could.

'It is just that carrying all those expensive items, and on your own...' He put a confidential arm around the man's shoulder. 'Don't you think that perhaps that might be a little bit ... dangerous.' And with that, and swift as a snake, he went to slip the knife between the man's ribs. Unfortunately for him, Cyganexatavan knew exactly what the man intended.

He had been to this place many times before and had met many traders from the northern lands, so much so that he could read most of them pretty easily. There were honest ones and then there were ones like these two. The second he had opened the basket and saw the greed shine in their eyes, he knew what was going to happen. And so as Whitey thrust his blade towards him, he turned his body in the same direction, so that the knife cut his tunic and scored the flesh over his rib but did no real damage; then he grabbed the off-balance albino and smacked his head against one of the jetty posts. The man's legs turned to jelly and he screamed as he pitched downwards on to the planking. Cygan kicked him hard in the ribs and turned towards Gorton.

The man's face had turned as pale white as Whitey's and broke into a full sweat. The stiletto he held in his right hand was shaking wildly as he held it outwards towards Cygan.

'Put it down and get out of here,' Cygan said, walking firmly towards him. Gorton started, stepping backwards away from the man, but was so panic stricken that he paid no heed to where his feet were landing.

'No, Marsh Man, no, get away from me!' and with that he took a step too far in the wrong direction. His right foot contacted nothing but air and with a womanish shriek he toppled off the jetty into the river. There was a violent splash and he vanished under its black surface, his heavy clothes pulling him into its invisible depths.

Cygan noticed the soldiers by the inn had been alerted and were coming towards them. He then heard a scream behind him and turned to see Whitey barrelling his way with his knife held high and a bloody bruise on his forehead. Cygan drew his knife, crouched low, and slashed the man's chest, letting Whitey's own momentum carry him onwards until he slammed into the wall of the trading post. He got up quickly and turned to see Cygan staring at him, knife in hand.

'Guards!' he called, almost hysterically. 'The Marshie is trying to kill me!'

Two of the guards were nearly with them, halberds pointing ahead of them. Whitey, panic-stricken, saw a dark shape rise in the river, quite a distance away from where he was standing.

'Gorton! Gorton!' he called as the shape disappeared under the water again. It started to dawn on him how much he was dependent on the big man and how his new-found status in life was in jeopardy. 'Gorton!' He started to run along the bank, giving no thought as to how he was going to affect a rescue.

Then Gorton emerged, his pudgy white face a mask of pure terror. He was at the far bank among the reeds, his arms thrashing desperately. He managed to grasp at a branch of an overhanging willow.

'Help me!' he croaked desperately.

'Gorton! Just hold on. Just hold on!' Whitey was close to him by now, suddenly aware that there was a whole river between the two of them. Hearing a noise, he looked back towards the jetty.

The Marsh Man was in his boat again, coming towards them; the branch on to which Gorton was clinging was bending horribly; Whitey could see it slowly slipping through Gorton's wet hands.

'Hurry up, Marshie; he can't hold on much longer.'

But the man was there. He positioned his boat so that the current would pull Gorton towards him and with a little difficulty got him to grasp the side of the boat with both hands. The boat listed dangerously but the Marsh Man knew what he was doing. With deft strokes of his paddle, he cut against the current and steered the little craft towards Whitey. Arriving at the bank, the two men conspired to haul the sodden mass of the merchant on to the damp grass. Gorton was worryingly still.

Whitey started pressing the man's chest, imploring him to start breathing.

Cygan, though, stood apart from the two of them; the outcome was already obvious to him. He let Whitey carry on desperately for a little longer, then spoke.

'He is gone. His heart must have stopped in the water.'

The albino stopped his pummelling of the dead man's chest. Visions started to swim before his eyes, of his new life vanishing like mist. He saw himself back in the stocks again, or being flayed raw at the whipping post. He saw his old gang members walking past him, pausing only to spit in his direction, followed by the ladies of the brothel he had only just started to feel comfortable in, then the local magistrates; they all started to laugh, cold, cruel, mocking. He could hear them saying, 'The demon pink-eye thought he was human, thought he was like us. How ridiculous of him! Put a rope around his neck and make him dance, throw him a penny for livening up a boring afternoon.'

Suddenly he felt the wound on his chest smart, and the bump on his head throb. He looked down at the dead man's face and felt the shadow of the guards fall over him.

'It was him!' he cried to them, pointing at Cygan. 'He killed him, he wounded me – all for no reason at all!'

Cygan looked at the two guards and saw he had no choice. He held out both arms and let them take him without a fight. His fate was with the spirits now.

Or rather, with Magistrate Onkean, who was now sitting in the main room of his house behind his dining table, Cygan standing in front of him flanked by the two guards. Whitey, who had reason enough to be nervous around officialdom, was cringing in a dark corner. The magistrate drained his ale and took a bite out of a slice of bread before speaking.

'So a man is dead, you say, drowned in the river after an altercation with this marsh fellow.'

'Yes, sir,' said the guard. 'We saw the three of them at the trading post and the next minute a man was in the water, with this man' – he indicated Whitey – 'screaming his lungs out for us to come and help. The Marshie fished him out of the water, but he was already dead. He was a fat man and the shock stopped his heart. After that, though, we saw the wounds on the pink-eye and realised there must have been a fight of some sort. Then we found this.' He put the basket on the table. 'Look inside – there's enough stuff there to leave any merchant sitting pretty.'

The magistrate did so, his expression grave.

'You! Pink-eye, did you fight over his merchandise? And don't lie to me or I'll have your ears nailed to the stocks.'

Whitey feigned a low bow and wiped the sweat off his face.

'There was a misunderstanding, sir. We offered the man a fair price for his goods but he wasn't interested. Called the stuff we had to barter with rubbish and pulled a knife on us, he did. Poor Gorton was so afeard he fell overboard and I got slashed by him. Them Marshies have their own rules, they do; they just don't know how to behave in civilised lands, sir, so they don't.'

'I see,' the magistrate growled.

'It is not as this man said.' Cygan decided to speak. He had no idea of the protocols involved here but obviously this man passed as important.

'So, Marsh Man, you speak our tongue. Then tell me why, within five minutes of your arrival, a countryman of mine is lying cold on a table in the inn. Coincidence, maybe?'

'No. I came here with a message from the Elder of my tribe for your baron. The goods I brought with me were to be used as a gesture of goodwill and to ensure that our words were heard. The dead man and his ... ally' – he nodded towards Whitey – 'saw an opportunity to enrich themselves to the endangerment of us all. They attacked me and in the fight one of them fell into the river. I tried to rescue him but was too late.'

'How is it that this man is wounded and you are unscathed?'

'Actually, he did catch me a blow. Ten years ago he wouldn't have got near me.' He showed the magistrate the hole in his tunic and the strip of dried blood underneath.

Another mouthful of bread later and the magistrate spoke again.

'We have a classic case here. Two witnesses whose accounts differ and no one else around to corroborate either story. What am I to do?

BOOK ONE: AUTUMN

Eburg town is but less than ten miles away and a man is dead. A report has to go up there and any judgement I make the Baron will hear of. The last thing I want is for him to come down here with a load of his men undermining my authority. So, punishment has to be meted out.' He brushed some crumbs off his sleeve and gazed steadily at Cygan.

'I am sorry, Marsh Man, but a merchant is dead. Though I am far more inclined to believe you over the snivelling little shit in the corner, the villagers here, and the people at Eburg, will never accept the innocence of a non-Artoran barbarian against one raised under the Divine Pantheon. Take him out and hang him.'

Cygan's eyes blazed; his mind raced as to how he might attempt a desperate breakout when his guard spoke.

'If I may be so bold, sir, the people here rely on the Marshies and the trade and people they bring in. To execute one of them here, well, it could threaten the trading post. The Marshies could go further upriver instead, to Eburg, or further on.'

'I cannot let him go, my man. Do you have a suggestion?'

'Yes, sir. Send him to Eburg for judgement. They will probably decide the same as you, but, at least to the Marshies, it isn't us that has made the judgement. Besides, if the Marshy has a message for the Baron, at least he'll be closer to him. He just has to hope the Baron visits the dungeons from time to time.' The guard laughed at his joke.

'You have a point. I will prepare a written deputation and you two can shackle this man and take him to Eburg on the wagon. You can leave within the hour.'

'You are a fool,' said Cygan. 'You have to listen to what I have to say or you are all going to die. My people first, yours second.'

The magistrate gave him an icy stare. 'I will put your request in my deputation. If you are genuine, then pray to your gods that the Baron reads it. Take him away.'

The two men led Cygan away, out of the manor house towards the smithy. He didn't struggle; it was the Baron he wanted to see, after all, and to resist here would be a futile gesture.

The magistrate and Whitey were left alone in the room.

Onkean started scribbling, writing his deputation. Only the sound of the quill scratching the parchment could be heard. After a couple of minutes Whitey plucked up the courage to speak.

'Sir, I was ... er ... wondering as to who had the rights to the goods on the table. I was wondering if I could take some for ... um ... Gorton's widow, seeing as she will need providing for now her husband has gone. Any proceeds I make will go to her, I swear.'

Onkean was dismissive. 'This is all going to the Baron, as it is evidence in this case. You should go, too, as you are a witness, or would you rather I wrote down your evidence here rather than have you face the Baron yourself?'

'No sir, I am happy for you to write on my behalf.'

'Good. Now as you have no further business here, I suggest you settle your account at the inn and leave our village behind. You have the merchant's widow to speak to and his business interests to settle. I imagine you will be a busy man for a few weeks, will you not?'

'Of course, sir, as you command.' Whitey bowed and beat a hasty retreat from the room. He had the money from the transactions earlier in the week, so the trip had not been a total loss. Gorton was unmarried, of course, and Whitey knew nothing of his business interests other than the work he had put Whitey's way. So it was a case of take the money and run. Today had been a disaster but there were things that could be salvaged from it. He would decide what to do next when he was back in his room in Sketta.

Behind him Onkean continued writing. He looked up at the guard.

'That albino.'

'Yes, sir.'

'Make sure he leaves promptly. A man like that around brings bad luck to us all. Beat him out of town if you have to; his sort makes my flesh crawl.'

The man left and Onkean was alone. He finished his deputation with a sense of satisfaction. After sealing it, he sat back in his chair, smiled, and lifted the covering off Cygan's basket.

38

Morgan had slept well. The bed was one of the softest he had known and the gentle warmth of the glowstones suffusing the room had left him feeling more relaxed than perhaps he had ever been. For a while he had heard Itheya in the next room talking softly with someone in her own language, before she, too, had fallen silent and he had been left with the sounds of the wind gusting over the lake, the snapping of the banners outside his window and the soft lament of the trees as they shed their leaves in the face of the oncoming winter.

When he awoke, he saw that someone had been in his room leaving some bread and fruit and a large vessel containing water for him to wash with. Itheya had told him he could not leave his room, unless she was with him, so he accepted his benevolent incarceration and remained where he was.

He was not to remain alone for long. He had just devoured the last of the food when a shadowy figure appeared at the doorway.

'Good morning, Dramalliel. I take it you wish to be my escort for an hour or two?'

'Indeed,' the elf said with a smirk. 'Your fellow human and Terath are already on the shore waiting for us.'

And so they were. Morgan acknowledged Cedric who was swathed in a dark-green elven cloak that Terath had obviously given him. He leaned on his stick and was presumably feeling the drop in temperature. A small but curious crowd dressed in similar cloaks had gathered to watch them. Morgan, too, felt the late-autumnal nip in the air, pinching his nose and cheeks.

'Hello, my boy. I have some interesting news. Terath is going to attempt a scrying ritual using information gleaned from the tooth. It may give us the location of some of the dragon stones. Granted, none of that is of any practical use to us at the moment, but to the people here it is significant. It strengthens the ties between me and you and our hosts, and what with their gathering taking place a few days from now it can only be helpful.'

'Good,' said Morgan. 'Now if I can only get through the next hour unscathed, it will make for a perfect day.'

'Don't worry; Terath and I will keep an eye on him. The young elf is quite the hothead, or so I've been told.'

Dramalliel was joined by Tiavon and a couple of other elves, all carrying spears. He looked at Morgan, excitement in his violet eyes.

'It is this way. Follow, please.'

He led them along a narrow but well-defined track leading in a southerly direction away from the tented lawn. Morgan could hear the waters of the lake lapping at the shore to his left, barely fifty yards away; apart from that he was surrounded by the ancient woodland – trees sporting beards of lichen, overhanging banks of lime-coloured grass, and clumps of bracken. After a few short minutes the trees opened out on to a broad green sward that was actually sunken into the earth; it was bowl shaped and surrounded on all sides by high banks of trees. As Morgan looked around, he could see it was some sort of a training area; he saw some archery targets made of wicker, racks of spears, some hurdles, dummies and other unknown contraptions partially hidden under thick cloth covers.

'This is where the foot warriors train,' Dramalliel explained. 'With Armentele happening tomorrow no one is training today. However, I thought maybe I could show you how an elven warrior fights. Do you wish to test yourself here?'

'And what if I said no?'

'It is your decision, of course. Though rumours of the cowardice of humans might start to spread through our village.'

'And no one wants that, do they?'

Dramalliel smiled back at him. He called to Tiavon, the two of them spoke briefly, then Tiavon walked towards one of the racks of spears.

'I take it you have something in mind for us?'

'I do. Come with me.'

He walked towards one of the covers and with a flamboyant gesture pulled it back. Underneath it were two raised wooden rails running parallel to each other, some two to three feet apart. The rails themselves were narrow, barely an inch wide, and stood over what seemed to be a bed of smooth pebbles. No, they weren't pebbles, thought Morgan, they were glowstones. Tiavon then returned to the group carrying two spears, both of which had their heads covered with some soft cloth.

'Allow us to demonstrate what we do here,' Dramalliel said to Morgan, and with that he leapt cat-like on to the rails, balancing himself on them with ease. He was barefoot, Morgan noticed. Tiavon then hopped on to the rails to face Dramalliel, the two of them some four feet apart. Another of Dramalliel's cronies passed a spear to each of them.

'The first to fall off the rail loses the round. We either compete for an hour or until somebody wins a set number of rounds. Observe.'

Both elves adopted a crouching position, spears held in both hands as they shuffled forwards and backwards along the rails in their bare feet. Morgan could see that the object of the contest was to use the haft of the spear to unbalance the opponent and cause them to fall on to the stones beneath. He saw Tiavon try to hook his spear behind Dramalliel's right leg, only to see his effort blocked as the princeling executed a lightning-fast riposte – causing Tiavon to spring backwards, gazelle-like, and reposition himself on the rails. 'Little physical contact, blunted spears... I am wondering what all the fuss was about,' said Morgan wryly.

'Perhaps having Terath and myself here has calmed things somewhat,' Cedric replied.

'It's just as well, I haven't got a fool's hope against those two; I can't even balance myself on a horse.'

Suddenly, after many feints and bluffs, Dramalliel launched a full-scale assault on Tiavon, aiming his spear low as he tried to hook Tiavon's legs from under him. Tiavon blocked the first attack, then the second – on the third he actually jumped clear of the rails and the low spear blow, but the fourth caught his right ankle as he landed. With the dexterity of a mountain goat he managed to stay on his feet, but he was in no position to defend himself as Dramalliel leapt high, spun a full one hundred and eighty degrees and upended Tiavon's left leg, causing him to topple over and crash painfully on to his back on the stones.

Terath, Cedric and Morgan applauded the two men as Dramalliel helped his defeated opponent on to his feet. They both bowed to each other and Tiavon went to join his two other companions some distance away. Dramalliel came towards Morgan, holding one of the spears out to him.

'Fancy a trial? I promise I will go easy on you.'

Saying nothing, Morgan kicked off his boots, feeling the cold damp carpet of grass beneath his feet. He took the spear and gingerly stepped up on to the rails. They were smooth, but hard on his soles; he saw Dramalliel's feet were angled inward slightly and so copied him. He soon realised that finding a secure balance that he felt comfortable with was an art in itself.

'*Vitremon!*' Dramalliel called to him, holding his spear across his body in both hands at a forty-five-degree angle. Morgan nodded at him and did the same.

'Tell me,' he said. 'Are there any rules regarding the parts of the body I cannot hit?'

'Convention dictates that we target the legs to unbalance the opponent, but it is only the head that you are not allowed to hit. Allow me to demonstrate.'

With that, he attempted to hook Morgan's left leg away. Morgan saw it late – the elf certainly was quick – but he managed to block the attempt with the spear shaft. It was little more than a feint, however, for Dramalliel thrust again, fast as quicksilver, catching Morgan's right leg just above the ankle and hooking him off balance so that he stumbled to his knees on to the unforgiving stones.

'Nice block,' said Dramalliel. 'You get the idea now?'

Without speaking, Morgan got to his feet and repositioned himself on the rail, adopting the attack stance the elf was using.

Five more times they duelled and five more times with the exact same result. Dramalliel was plainly enjoying sending the human on to the stones, giving him bruises and grazes, but Morgan did not give up – every defeat was teaching him something. Dramalliel was flamboyant for one thing; he would never go for a conventional blow when he could leap into the air and assay a full turn before driving his spear at Morgan's toes. He was overconfident, and so his concentration was suspect. Morgan still couldn't land a telling blow on him, however. Dramalliel was as fast as a hummingbird around a flower.

'You have the basics now, human?' said Dramalliel with a malevolent smile.

'I suppose I do, after a fashion.'

'Good! And so it is now that the real contest begins.'

The elf passed his hand over the stones, whispering quietly under his breath. With a slight twinge of alarm, Morgan saw the stones begin to glow, first a deep red, then turning whiter; even at a distance he could feel the warmth on his face.

'Dramalliel! Fezhaye al ukellusha!' Terath shouted at him.

'No, young man,' Cedric joined in, 'this is not an acceptable development.'

Dramalliel, still smiling, bowed slightly at the older men.

'I apologise profoundly for offending both of you. I will nullify the haraska of the stones immediately, as I obviously had too elevated a view of human courage. All Morgan the warrior has to do is agree with the two of you and the matter will be closed.'

Morgan looked at the young elf with a little admiration. If he agreed with Cedric and Terath, he would look a coward in the eyes of the elf warriors present – something that no doubt would sweep through the village in no time – but if he didn't agree he risked having his feet turned into the sort of burnt offering the priests of Mytha still specialised in.

'Cedric, Terath,' he said. 'Thank you both for your concern – it is appreciated – but I will play the elven prince at his game; not to do so, after all, would be discourteous of me.' Offering a quick and silent prayer to Artorus and St Berris, patron of the true-hearted and those who insist on doing the right thing no matter at what cost to themselves, he hopped back on to the rails and held his spear in readiness.

Dramalliel faced him. Morgan could feel the heat from the hundreds of stones under him making his feet slippery; obviously glowstones could get a lot hotter than the ones in his room. He concentrated, not on Dramalliel himself, but on his spear and his feet splayed on to the rails. He blocked the first blow, then the second; he even managed a quick counterthrust causing Dramalliel to jump clear of the rails, though the elf landed sure-footed as ever.

Morgan was getting to be able to read Dramalliel's attack patterns and his blocking tactics, so far, were excellent. He was being forced backwards, though.

Then it happened. A quick thrust from the elf that he didn't fully block, and the butt of the spear caught him full on the shin, forcing him backwards as he winced with the pain. Dramalliel's next thrust he barely blocked but stepped backwards again, trying to right his balance on the rail.

But there was no rail there...

...His right foot landed on to the stones. There was a soft hiss and an unpleasant smell of burning, then the pain hit him, forcing him to call out and fall backwards, clear of the stones and on to the grass. His spear rolled away from him, stopping at Dramalliel's feet.

'Well fought, human.' Dramalliel helped him up; he sounded conciliatory. 'For someone who had not even seen the zezheflenta an hour ago you performed admirably. Our warriors will respect you, now that your bravery has been proven.'

Morgan gingerly put his full weight on to his right foot, brushed some grass off his leather tunic, and looked the elf in the eye,

'Best of three.'

The elf looked firstly astonished – this was something he certainly wasn't expecting – then, however, a thin smile spread over his handsome features. He nodded slowly at Morgan, handed him his spear and leapt over the stones on to the rail.

'Morgan,' called Cedric, 'desist from this; it is achieving nothing.'

'No, my friend,' Morgan said slowly, 'it is achieving a lot more than you realise.' And with that he climbed back into his position on the rail.

'*Vitremon!*' called Dramalliel and launched a ferocious attack on Morgan's legs. There was no holding back now; it was a fight he wanted finished and quickly. Morgan, however, was holding his own – he blocked all of the elf's initial blows and then, as Dramalliel swept his spear around in a wide arc, he too leapt clear of the rail, landing sure-footedly, as the elf paused for breath. Then he countered – three successive low blows designed to hook his opponent's legs from under him. Dramalliel defended all three but for the first time Morgan saw the uncertainty in his face. Back and forth the two of them went, thrusting and blocking, the elf faster and more experienced, the human more powerful, his defensive blows sapping his opponent's energy. The small audience watched open-mouthed. This duel was far more finely poised than any were expecting.

Then, however, as with every time before, Dramalliel caught him, on the instep this time, causing him to sway unevenly. Smiling, Dramalliel aimed for the same spot again, aiming to topple him on to the stones and finish what he had started. This was supposed to have been a spectacle to put the humans in their place – to show them as fumbling, clumsy and inferior – but Morgan's stoicism and determination had all but put pay to that ambition. Seeing this, Dramalliel just wanted to finish things as quickly and expediently as possible. He swung his spear, waiting for the impact on Morgan's leg that would give him his triumph.

But no contact was made. As Dramalliel was aiming his final stroke at the man's legs, Morgan thrust the butt of the spear, full length, into the elf's solar plexus.

'You said no head contact. You said nothing about the chest.'

Dramalliel toppled backwards, landing full on his back on both rails. He dropped his spear, which rolled clear of the stones, smoking as it did so, and his long hair started to hiss and burn underneath him.

'Concede?' Morgan offered him his hand, noting the barely suppressed surprise, shock and anger in the prince's eyes.

'*Cothoza prushu olea pritutazho!*'

He recognised the voice. Coming into the glade, flanked by two warriors and with a face that was all cold fury, was Itheya.

'Am I surrounded by fools? Is every man here a savage? How is it I leave all of you for less than two hours and you end up at each other's throats?' Morgan helped Dramalliel up.

'Really, Itheya, it is nothing like as bad as it might seem. Your brother was showing me how your warriors train. I have to say I am impressed.'

She appeared to be partly mollified, but only partly. 'It was still not a good idea, especially the decision to fire the stones. Were either of you hurt?'

'Not too badly.' Morgan tried to pay no heed to his sore foot. 'We actually still have to fight the decider.'

'The human is clever, and unorthodox,' said Dramalliel, rubbing his chest. 'Ask the others – no one lost honour in this fight.'

'Well, there will be no decider,' she said. 'I have finished preparing for the festival, so Morgan is returning with me. Come.'

She was wearing a long white cloak that covered her completely and dragged on the ground behind her, its hem stained with grass. Morgan followed, feeling a little like a trained poodle. Terath and Cedric came behind. Dramalliel remained with his followers; they appeared to be continuing with their training.

Back in his room, Morgan sat on his bed and wetted the sole of his foot with some water from the pitcher. He hadn't been on his own long when Itheya came into the room unannounced.

'Did you have to fight him? Couldn't you have declined?'

'No. Your brother has been desperate to try something since he first saw me. I figured better to let him get it out of his system rather than let things fester. I think the two of us understand each other a little better now.'

She appeared to accept what he said, nodding slowly. 'Very well, I will not admonish him; perhaps the matter is best left buried. Father needn't know of it.' She noticed his bare foot. 'Did you fall on to the stones?'

'Yes, it is not too bad. I will be fine in a little while.'

'Let me look. Burns from the stones can be nasty. I should know; I have had enough of them over the years.'

'No really, I'm fi...'

'Shut up and hold your foot out. You do not refuse a princess of the Morioka in her own home.'

Feeling like a naughty child, he complied; she got on to her knees and took his foot in her hands.

'It is blistering already; if you are to attend Armentele tomorrow you will need a poultice and a bandage, or' – she sighed heavily – 'I could use haraska.'

She placed her palm gently against the sole of his foot and spoke softly under her breath. Suddenly he felt something akin to a cool blush pass into his leg; it felt like being washed by a gentle wave on a beach of soft, cool sand. She seemed to be drawing the heat out of his body into her own. When she stopped after a few minutes, the pain had all but stopped. She, however, looked a little grey and tired.

'It wearies me, doing that. Rest your foot for the afternoon; you should be able to walk on it without pain by this evening.'

'Thank you. Your magic is of a healing nature?'

'As I said before, it is not strong. I can help with minor wounds, warm the stones and such things. I rarely use it. Tell me, you were going to fight my brother one more time, weren't you? The decider, you called it.'

'Yes, we had won a duel each; I burnt my foot when I lost to him.'

'Then I will fight it for you, when I have the time.'

'Really? I have seen you with a bow and knife but I have no idea of your abilities in combat. I wondered if they were just ceremonial.'

She laughed; there was a note of incredulity in it. 'I have led my tribe in battle,' she said. 'It is true I cannot stand toe to toe with the likes of you for long – you are too strong, after all – but there is no better archer in the tribe than I and no one faster with a spear. I have fought my brother many times over the firestones and lead him by quite a margin. He will be annoyed when he finds out I have become your champion.'

'I will leave it in your hands then. The important thing for me was that I wasn't humiliated and that I did not embarrass you. Hopefully I managed to achieve that.'

'I think you did. When I leave you I will hear from others about your performance, but I am not worried about it. Most people are too excited about Armentele to think about anything else.'

'When does it start tomorrow?'

'Early. Terath will fetch you and Cedric. There is a ceremony to herald the end of the harvest and greet the onset of winter, but after that it is a case of feasting and drinking jenessa, the spiced berry drink you had the other day. It ends as the sun goes down; there is a procession with torches back here to the island. There is a lot of singing and dancing. I am sure a warrior like yourself will find it all beyond tedious, guest of honour or no.'

'On the contrary,' said Morgan with a smile, 'I am looking forward to it, especially to the dance of the princess of the Morioka.'

She smiled, almost shyly. 'You will be underwhelmed, I am sure. I will leave you now. Rest your foot, otherwise you will see nothing tomorrow apart from these four walls.'

She left him and he fell flat on the bed, still feeling the soothing waves of energy pulse through his foot. It felt so soothing he was asleep in minutes.

The following morning he found himself sitting on the grass with Terath and Cedric. The Mhezhen was there, too, though he had to be carried there on a litter. He was the only one seated, for his throne had been brought here, too – the grass had to do for everybody else.

They were some two miles from the island, between the lake and the sea. It was another place where the land dropped sharply; there was a sheer rock face on the south side covered in moss, creeping vines and lichen. Through a cleft at its centre was another waterfall, this one falling in a sheer drop of some fifty feet, throwing up a cloud of fine spray from the dark pool under it. The water continued as a narrow river, dancing and babbling over copper coloured stones as it wound through the glade and into the woods to the north. The other main feature of the glade was sitting right beside the pool. In times past, a large section of the cliff face must have split off and crashed to the ground. There it lay, a vast slab of grey, nearly ten feet high and around a hundred feet across. It was perfectly flat, and ideal, as Terath had explained to them, for a stage. And it was facing this monolith, on both sides of the river, that everyone was sitting.

'Armentele is an occasion where we say farewell to the abundance of summer and autumn and prepare for the onset of winter. Fire is the symbol we use, the guardian against the frost and snows that await us,' Terath said solemnly.

As he spoke, figures appeared on the great stone slab; they were carrying buckets or similar containers and were pouring some viscous-looking substance on to its surface. When that was done, other men put torches to it. Immediately the substance ignited, great sheets of flame roaring skywards from the rock, all at least ten feet tall. The flames themselves were a variety of colours; Morgan almost expected this by now. As well as the reds and blues there were greens and pale yellows, all the colours constantly shifting. There was little breeze in this dell, so the flames were not buffeted by wind, keeping their shape – high walls of incandescence, crackling and reverberating – the noise of the fires echoing against the cliffs behind them. Musicians started to play. Two girls strumming an instrument similar to a harp played a haunting introduction, before the drummers and flautists joined them. Shortly afterwards, the singing started; a choir had joined the musicians at the back of the 'stage' and their voices melded with the instruments to produce a song of great complexity, its cadences rising and falling in time with the rumbling falls and the swaying fingers of flame.

Food and drink was put out before the watchers. The meat was spicier than he had tasted before and the spiced berry drink went down a treat in the fresh air, despite the early hour. Cedric, who had spent a lot of his time indoors with Terath, seemed to be relishing the change of scene, smiling beatifically as he watched the performance.

And then the dancers arrived. Men and women in shimmering white robes appeared leaping through the walls of flame. The men would pick up the women, hoisting them high as they stretched languidly, moving and swaying their arms with a gentle grace. Their costumes reflected the colours surrounding them, so that it was something like watching a thousand shifting, moving rainbows against a background of frowning cliffs and dark imperturbable trees.

And then he saw Itheya. Given her status, it was no surprise to see her at the centre of the ensemble, moving or being lifted and carried from one dance partner to the next, her long ponytail almost dragging on the floor as she stretched her graceful limbs behind, in front of and through the fire. Like the other elves, she had an almost feline poise; it was almost like watching a ballet performed by hunting animals, lithe and hypnotic, sinuous and elegant. Like the remainder of the audience, Morgan found himself almost being drawn into the performance – the trees, the damp grass, the sound of the shallow river were all forgotten as the dancers wove their exquisite tapestry. Time passed unnoticed and the fitful sun was a distant memory as the swaying dancers twirled and spun rhythmically. Morgan yet again felt as if he was in a waking dream.

And then it was over. The audience got to their feet, raised their arms to the stage and called, *'Satala, zana teripeto! Satala zana elethena! Satala za fimaremi!'* As they stood and watched, the fires died, the last of the musicians picked up their instruments and the choir solemnly ended their song. Within a minute the stage was empty.

'It is always important with our people that the successor to the Mhezhen participates in all aspects of our society. With human lords, I believe this is seen as demeaning, but that is not the case here.' Cenarazh was smiling, proud of his daughter's performance.

Everyone was feasting now, the spiced meats, the fish flavoured with herbs and wild garlic, hard cheeses and flatbreads all washed down with the jenessa. Morgan had the elves figured as quiet respectful people, but that was hardly the case today – people were laughing and gossiping, some were dancing with each other, a crowd of young elf children had climbed on to the stage and were attempting their own imitation performance, watched and cheered by their families.

'May I humbly ask where your son is today?' Cedric enquired of Cenarazh.

'Patrolling our border. Either he or Itheya usually lead these patrols. We have to be constantly watchful; we have humans to the west and tribes that have little love for us elsewhere. Our vigilance is necessary, if unfortunate.'

'I have often wondered,' said Cedric, 'whether the outcome of the tragic wars between our peoples might have been different if your tribes had been more unified.'

Cenerazh smiled. 'Our disunity has always been our greatest folly, one further compounded by our inability to learn from past mistakes. In my youth, I dreamed of uniting the tribes, moulding our people into a force again, but I soon learned it would be easier to touch the moon; I do not know what it is like in human society but with us every facial gesture is an imagined slight, every misplaced word an insult. The older one gets, the more wearisome it becomes.'

As he spoke, Itheya joined them. She still wore her white tunic and her thin torque, removed for her dance, was back around her neck. She greeted and kissed her father then came over to the humans and sat beside them.

'Did you enjoy what you saw? Or did it send you back to your slumbers?'

Morgan realised from her excited face that she was actually seeking their approval. He realised that he still couldn't work her out.

'I found it utterly hypnotic,' effused Cedric.

Her brow wrinkled. 'Hypno...? It is not a word I know.'

'He said he found it entrancing,' said Morgan. 'As did I.'

'Thank you. I am not sure I believe you, but thank you anyway. I need to sit with Father now, to discuss the krasa. Enjoy the festivities; I will speak with you later.'

And enjoy them they did. They ate and drank till they were fit to burst and then, as the sun receded over the lands of the humans, they joined the slow torch-lit procession back to the island and Zamezhenka. The singing and music accompanied them all the way and, after attending the feast that continued on the third floor, Morgan retired to his room with a feeling of tired elation. He was beginning to feel that he would be quite happy to stay here and never go back to the Seven Rivers – to war, cruelty and death, blood and loss. As he shut his eyes to sleep, he saw his wife's face for the first time in years, only briefly, but it jolted him like a kick from a horse. He sat upright in the bed, sweating, but could only see the light of the glowstones and hear the sounds of muted passion coming from Itheya's room. She had obviously found some company for the night.

'Ah, Lis,' he whispered softly, 'where are you now, I wonder? The Gods watch over you, always.'

With that he lay back on the bed and, with the wish that Itheya would just get on with it, finish with the fellow and give him some quiet so he could rest properly, he drifted off into a slumber full of dreams, but little peace.

39

The two-masted ship bobbed at anchor as it was slowly enveloped by mist. Within the narrow confines of its cabin were sitting Ceriana, Wulfthram, Ulian, Alys, Willem and Haelward. Ceriana had forbidden Ebba from coming and, for the first time she could remember, she had no handmaiden but she was coping manfully with the loss. She rather enjoyed the independence, in fact, and having her husband to help dress her had provided some of the more comedic moments of the past few days.

They were aboard the Arnberg, a caravel sporting two lateen sails and one of the fastest vessels in the Baron's small navy. Built for speed, it had little room for luxury, hence the single cabin with its solitary bench-cum-bed used by Wulfthram and his wife, who had spent the nights on board clinging to him, desperately trying not to fall off. The weather had been cold, with a persistent fine rain that had only ceased with the arrival of the mist, so the other four voyagers had been allowed to sleep in the cabin, too. This in itself was something of a triumph of ergonomics as there was barely enough room for a man to stand and walk five full paces without bumping into the lowhanging lantern or the creaking timbers of walls and door. The captain and crew, who were also few in number, slept outside, finding shelter where they could.

Not that Willem was complaining. For the first time he could sleep with Alys in his arms, her hard little head on his shoulder and her soft breath caressing his ear and cheek. He had told her of Cedric's proposal to pay for his education personally; she was thrilled but also concerned – how could such a great debt ever be repaid? He told her to speak to Cedric about it; the man had an amazing ability to allay any fears about any subject and Willem had never seen him lose an argument, even against his fellow professors.

Now, however, they were all awake, sitting around a low table that held Cedric's books. Night was approaching and there were no crying gulls or cursing sailor to break the sounds of the soft waves, the groaning of the ship's beams or the sigh of the slightest breeze coming in through the cabin's tiny half-open window.

'Now,' said Wulfthram, 'tomorrow when this mist clears we will arrive at Oxhagen. I will send my men out to ask around for someone who knows the location of this tower. As you know, the fishermen who fled to Osperitsan refused to return with us.'

'That augurs well,' said Haelward.

'Whether they were too afeard to return or just did not want to risk losing the foothold they had gained for themselves, I do not know,' said Wulfthram. 'Anyway when a guide has been secured, I, Haelward, Ulian and my men Strogar and Derkss will take the stone to the tower; the others will remain here with the ship's crew.'

'Nice try,' said Ceriana, 'but do you really think I am going to remain here?' She held out the stone. It had been enclosed in a silver fitting and chain which she proceeded to put around her neck.

'I could take it from you by force.'

'In front of all these people? With me all screaming and helpless?'

He sighed, smiling ever so slightly. 'Very well. I cannot stop you from coming, but do not go anywhere on your own. We have come here to protect you, after all.'

'I can accept that,' she said. 'Being surrounded by strong muscular warriors has its compensations.'

'And by me,' said Ulian.

'Of course, every expedition needs its brains.'

'Speaking of which,' said Ulian, 'I have been searching these books, the ones Willem brought here, for some reference to the "guardians" your fisherman referred to in the tunnels.'

'And?' said Wulfthram.

'Well, I have found something.'

'Yes?'

'It isn't good.'

'Just tell us.' The Baron sounded exasperated.

'The Wych folk, the elves, that hid this stone in these tunnels, if that is what they did, must have been desperate to protect their secrets. Let us try and imagine what it must have been like nearly eight hundred years ago. They had just been utterly defeated by the humans; thousands, maybe hundreds of thousands, of them had been killed or enslaved over the previous century. And the humans were coming; maybe they were only days away. These ruins and the others on the coast were once called the City of Light. At its peak it had hundreds of tall white spires each connected by elevated walkways over which were strung a series of delicate silver chains that held dozens of tiny silver crystals. These glittered by day or night and could be seen by sailors many miles from shore – that was how the city got its name. But, even as the refugees fled here, the city was declining, many spires were in ruins and its population had shrunk to about half of what it had been at its zenith. At this time the headland extended further into the sea and it had a wide shallow harbour. This would have been full of ships, each of them packed full of elves desperate to flee and start a new life on distant shores. Imagine now that the ships had nearly all gone, that only a few were left, but still the refugees kept pouring in. What were they to do? Not everyone would get a ship and what of the city's many secrets and treasures? Some tribes resigned themselves to their fate and fled to the Aelthenwood, where they would eventually settle, but still many more remained. Some terrible decisions needed to be made.'

Silence. Outside a thin sliver of moonlight broke through the mist and shone a sickly yellow on Ulian's pale face.

'It is not clear what exactly happened in these books, but by piecing the fragments of information that we have, comparing and cross-referencing them, I can only conclude that, though the women and children were excluded, lots were drawn for the men to determine who would leave and who would remain. Those that remained were charged with protecting the treasures of the city. Treasures that presumably included the very stone the Lady Baroness is now wearing.'

There were goblets of weak ale on the small, book-covered table. Ulian took a long draught for his dry throat and continued.

'I discovered an account written by an elf called Senathion. It is in the ancient Elvish tongue, but I have managed to translate it, well most of it. I have transcribed it here. He held up a scroll, written in his firm bold hand, and began to read:

'The scouts have returned and they are barely two days distant. The city will burn, this much we know. There are not enough of us to even defend the citadel. The last ships have left; at least I know my beloved Erethe is safe along with the child she carries, one I will never see. Dureke, our leader, has called a meeting – we will know our fate when it is over.'

Ulian paused and looked at his attentive audience. The sea was calm, the ship barely moving. 'He carries on after this meeting; he says:

'We are charged to protect the artefacts of our people. The humans see these objects of gold, ones that our finest craftsmen have taken years to create, and they hack out the gems and melt the gold into ingots, to present to their emperor, who by now must be sitting on a pile of them a mile high. We will not let this happen here.

'Some of the catacombs will be guarded with traps and poison. For others there are creatures that can lie dormant for centuries, only waking when the doors are breached. The draigolitha [er, that is the dragonstones] we will guard ourselves. We then asked Dureke how they would be guarded after we die? Then, finally, our doom was outlined to us.

'Dureke knows of a magic that will keep us forever vigilant, beyond death; we will trade our souls to do our duty for eternity. For that we have to take our own lives, with a knife of silver after drinking a bitter brew Dureke will prepare for us. After death he will make us the guardians, commanders of ice and frost, eternal enemies of the humans. We can be fooled, however – xhikon will hide living blood from us, the herb culestrak we will find repellent and the blue fire of Istraek will mark an enemy as friend – but what human will know any of this?'

Ulian stopped reading. 'Xhikon is dull iron; it is in that amulet the black priest gave to your Ladyship. I can only assume it is what they used to hide themselves and steal the stone. I do not know of this herb or the fire. Anyway the elf's account is nearly finished:

'We have made our final prayers and shortly will descend below the earth one last time. I have written this for our people to remember our sacrifice and to record the names of those who will still be watching long after the Empire of the humans has been cast to the four winds.'

Ulian put the scroll down. 'He then names every elf who presumably took part in this ritual. There are over a hundred of them.'

'It is ironic – don't you think?' said Haelward, '– that they took their own lives and were subjected to some unholy ritual so they could guard this stone for ever, and the first bunch of humans that try to take it stroll in and out without so much as a second thought.'

'But they knew what to do,' said Ulian. 'They have access to many elven writings and must have discovered it there somehow.'

'That's as maybe,' said Willem nervously, 'but these guardians are awake now, and alert.'

'But we have an amulet of dull iron and the stone they were guarding. It is obvious. I should go alone into this place as I am the only one guaranteed to be protected.' Ceriana's jaw was set firm, aware of the arguments that would follow.

'I seem to recall,' said Wulfthram, 'when you first arrived in my home, you got lost walking from your rooms to the great hall. How then do you think you will fare in a labyrinth?'

Her resolve was punctured immediately; she hated to admit it but he had a point.

'I will go with you if no one else. I am your husband and could do no less.'

'And I too,' said Ulian. 'The Wych folk used to put signs on their streets and temples so they could be navigated easily. When the wars started, they changed them into forms and letters they thought humans would not understand. I, however, have deciphered a few and Cedric many more, I have written them all down here; after all, would it not be too fanciful to think they may have done the same with the tunnels?'

'Very well,' Ceriana sighed. 'So much for my moment of heroism.

Anyway, we can't go anywhere with this fog sitting around us. Can someone close the window, please? There is something about it that unnerves me.'

Willem, who was nearest, complied. 'I am sure the fog will be gone soon,' he said.

But it wasn't gone by the morning. As everyone was slowly stirring, Wulfthram opened the cabin door to find he could barely see the ship's prow. It had got thicker if anything.

'It's a right one this, my Lord,' said the ship's captain, all wrapped up in a thick coat and gloves. 'We get them now and then around the coast here, but this is as thick as any I have seen before. Some of the boys are offering prayers to Hytha, hoping he will disperse it so we can get moving.'

But Hytha did not answer, at least not immediately. While the crew could spend the day scrubbing decks and attending to the forgotten jobs around the ship, the passengers could do little more than huddle in their cloaks and stare gloomily at the enveloping white swirls as they reached out with their icy tendrils to brush their noses and ears. They could do little more than wait.

Morning became afternoon, and, just as Wulfthram decided to go below decks for some potage rustled up by the ship's cook, he felt something pull at his hair and the hem of his cloak.

'The wind!' the captain called. 'The wind is picking up! That will drive this fog away. Hytha has heard us, after all.'

And he was right. The breeze became stronger and, as he peered over at the sea, he realised, with difficulty at first but then with increasing conviction, that the stifling white blanket was dispersing. Suddenly he had to cover his eyes as a shaft of pure sunlight broke through the miasma to illuminate the frowning grey sea.

'To work, lads! Get the sails hoisted! We can be away in minutes,' and then to Wulfthram: 'We will be in Oxhagen by nightfall, my Lord.'

He was as good as his word. In no time at all the twin sails were catching the prevailing wind and the Arnberg was skipping lightly over the white foam, breaking through the last feeble remnants of fog. Ceriana mounted the stern quarterdeck, peering to the port side with a sense of relief. Alys was with her and, as she shielded her eyes against the elements, she said to her excitedly:

'Look, the land, can you see?'

'Yes, my Lady, and there is the ruined city.'

They were drawing closer and Ceriana could see the truth in Alys's words. The sea, buoyed by wind and tide, was crashing against a rocky headland crowned with green, on top of which were fragments of white stone, some of it approximating a wall, but a wall reduced to rubble rising never higher than a few feet. After Ulian's description of the city she felt a little disappointed that more didn't remain. She expressed this to Alys.

'I think this is but the northern portion of the city; it continues for some distance along the coast and the ruins become more substantial the farther south we go. The part of it I visited with Master Cedric was much more substantial than this.'

Ceriana continued to watch, despite the cold that was numbing her fingers and toes. Sometimes the ruins would disappear entirely for a distance, only for a cluster of ruined white towers, little more than bases surrounded by tumbledown stone, to spring up like mushrooms from the ground. Gradually, though, the ruins grew more defined, just as Alys had said. The walls increased in height and the towers became more recognisable as such. She became aware of the sun against the back of her neck and realised it was beginning to drop beneath the horizon. Her husband joined her with a blanket, which he put over her shoulders.

'If memory serves me right, just behind this rocky outcropping we have...' He paused as the Arnberg swept past the high stones and bore eastward. There, as the shore grew closer than ever, she saw a series of towers hiding behind white walls perched on the cliff top, the largest she had seen so far. South of them the cliff dropped substantially and she saw where it bottomed out a series of small sandy beaches; and, at the southern headland where it pushed into the sea like a broken finger, she saw at last a group of huddled buildings clinging around a small harbour. One building had a tower and another, the largest there, was surrounded by a wall with battlements.

'Oxhagen,' he finished, smiling.

The sun was dropping fast now, the lateen sails casting triangular shadows over the sea. But something odd was happening for the little harbour was suddenly becoming more and more difficult to pick out, as if it was being covered in a ghostly shroud.

'Well, what have we done to the Gods today?' Wulfthram hissed under his breath.

It was unmistakeable now – not just Oxhagen but the elven towers – the very shoreline – were becoming indistinct. The fog was returning.

There were no oars on the Arnberg. It was a ship built for speed, after all, and as a result the captain was keen to weigh anchor again but Wulfthram was having none of it. After a brief but futile protest, the captain assented. One of the sails was pulled down and the vessel approached close to the shore. Periodically, great dark shoulders of rock would loom out of the mist, lowering and threatening, but the captain was skilful, the Arnberg never getting too close to danger. Up in the crow's nest one of the more experienced sailors kept calling down, instructing the captain as to the safe distance to keep from the shore, while another was dropping a line into the sea keeping track of the depth. In the mist the voices of the sailors were amplified, echoing off the rock, hollow and ghostly. The waves, too, were the same; it sounded almost like they were in a watery cave with the briny splashing around their very ears.

Everyone was on deck, the slow progress of the Arnberg and the close proximity of the cliffs and the town they were destined for meant nervous tension was passing from person to person like a virus. No one said a word; Ceriana clutched the port rail, her knuckles getting whiter by the minute.

Suddenly they all felt a sense of space as if the cliffs had crashed to the ocean floor. The man in the crow's nest called out 'Cove; keep the course steady ahead.'

The Arnberg continued forward. The cliffs might have disappeared but no one was fooled; everyone waited for them re-emerge to hover over them once more, but before that happened the man called out again: 'Ship! There is a ship in the cove!'

Ceriana squinted. The fog seemed to be affecting her breathing; she coughed slightly, putting her hand to her chest where she felt the amulet against her skin. So far it had worked; she had not experienced anything untoward since she had put it on – no dragons, no transformations. For a second her thoughts flew to the sepulchral black priest who had given it to her, and then ahead of her the mist cleared briefly but just enough to reinforce her belief in fate and the capriciousness of the Gods.

Only the outline of the other craft could be seen. It bobbed silently and impassively in the murk, –there was no movement on its decks, no lights, no flaming torches. As the Arnberg inched onward, the full length of the other vessel came into view, its prow at last becoming visible.

Its dragon-shaped prow.

Ceriana cried out as her heart flew into her throat.

Wulfthram heard her. 'Is that...?' he asked.

'Yes. They are here.'

Haelward was standing close by. After getting some clarification from Ulian, he came up to the two of them.

'If these are the people who want to take that trinket by force, then you will need some steel in your party. Supernatural foes may be beyond me, but men, armed or otherwise, are a different matter. I will come with you, if only to keep them off your back.'

Wulfthram nodded slowly, his gaze not leaving the other vessel until finally the Arnberg had cleared the cove and the high rock of the cliff face had returned.

'I couldn't see any of them on deck,' he said.

'They are not here just to bob around on the water,' said Ceriana quietly. 'They are waiting for us – or, rather, me. This amulet will protect me from the guardians but not from them. That was one of the reasons they gave it to me. The rest of you can be thrown to the mercies of whatever is waiting for us as far as they are concerned.'

'Well, we know they are here now. We can hole up at an inn or even stay on board this evening before climbing the cliff tomorrow. I would rather face them in daylight.'

'You don't understand.' she said. 'They are protected from these spirits; they will all have the same amulet as I have. They may be in the labyrinth already, waiting for us. They will let the guardians get the rest of you then move in on me. They are nothing if not patient. It has taken them nearly a thousand years to trace these stones remember. Like a dragon, they see a millennium as just another timespan to be endured.'

'These priests,' said Haelward, 'are they as unsettling as they sound?' Ceriana looked at him, a look that needed no words of confirmation.

'I thought as much, my Lady,' the deflated soldier replied.

They sailed on for another few minutes until the announcement came: 'Oxhagen harbour ahead!'

The mist was getting thicker, but there was no mistaking the shoulder of rock coming into view ahead of them. At its crest the outline of buildings could be seen, Ceriana could make out what looked like a statue of Hytha, standing proudly at the harbour's head. Inland, further blocky shapes could be seen, silhouettes of buildings large and small.

There was something odd, though, something intangible; she couldn't put her finger on it until finally her husband articulated it for her.

'Where are the lights?'

'You are right,' she said. 'There is not a single one.'

The mist lay heavy on the city; twisting ropes of it wound over the cobbles of the street on the harbour front but everywhere was in darkness. No flaming torches flickered in their brackets on the harbour wall and every window in every cottage, tavern and shop was a dark, eyeless void. There was no one out on the street and the whole town seemed to be smothered in a blanket of silence. All there was were the gentle sounds of waves lapping against rock and the groaning of the Arnberg's hull in the shallow waters. The captain came up to Wulfthram, his consternation written all over his face.

'What shall we do, my Lord? The whole town seems deserted.'

'Drop anchor in the harbour. Some of us will take the skiff and see what is going on here.'

'As you wish, my Lord.'

Within a very short time the Arnberg was sitting in the harbour, listing slightly as the outgoing tide tugged gently at its moorings. The skiff was readied, a small oar-powered vessel capable of holding around eight people.

'Before you say anything,' Ceriana told her husband, 'I am going with you. Do not make a final attempt to stop me. I know...'

'That's fine,' he replied, cutting her short. 'I was just about to ask you to take your seat. I will not ask you to row, though; I cannot see my wife with callouses on her palms.'

'I am probably not even strong enough to lift an oar; fortunately, I am surrounded by lots of strong men who can do all the hard work for me, which is exactly how I like it.'

Ignoring his sideways look, she took her place in the boat.

Wulfthram sat in a rowing position as Ulian took his place alongside Ceriana. Wulfthram's men, Strogar and Derkss, took up the other rowing positions along with Haelward. Willem called out to Ulian. 'Shall I come as well?'

'No, my boy, stay here with Alys and the books. If we are not back by the morning, well, I am sure you will know what to do.'

'We will be back long before then,' said Wulfthram. 'I am not trying those tunnels until I know what is going on here. Captain Devin, keep a watch out and the ballista manned. No one sleeps tonight, at least till we return.'

And with that the crew lowered the skiff gently into the water. After a few awkward seconds when the oars got tangled and the little craft turned a full circle, they finally got their orientation correct and were headed towards the town, a town in which there was nothing but silence.

40

'What in the name of Artorus's balls is going on here!'

Baron Lukas Felmere was not a happy man. He was standing on the riverbank in the pouring rain, watching his engineers' pathetic attempt at a bridge get washed away piece by piece. In all fairness to them, the weather had been absolutely atrocious and the river was swollen to the point of bursting its banks. The earth under his iron-shod feet squelched as liquid mud came up almost to his ankles.

Delays, delays, delays. So much for attacking the enemy within ten days! It was nearly two weeks since his army's triumph and they were still stuck here, bogged down on ground beginning to actually liquefy under their feet. The problem with being so close to the mountains was that any weather front heading up from the south tended to drop any precipitation that it carried either over the mountains or directly over their heads. And now it was over their heads. They could not proceed without the bridges to secure their supply lines and to carry the army over the river in safety, but safety was the last word that sprang to mind in the face of the raging torrent before him. On top of all this there had been an outbreak of dysentery in the camp, laying many a man low; the healing mage had been working all hours trying to combat the illness until she had collapsed with exhaustion. The outbreak was under control now and he had sent her away with the other mages for this conference she was so keen to have, and for the rest she needed if she was to be of any further use to him. They had left that very morning with instructions to return within five days. If the army was not ready to move by then, the whole plan of attack would have to be abandoned for the winter.

And it had got worse. With thousands of men frustrated by their inability to engage the enemy and virtually confined to their camp, petty quarrels became disputes and disputes became arguments; arguments that eventually found recourse in violence. The historical animosity between Lasgaart's and Vinoyen's men had expressed itself in a succession of bloody brawls, until eventually a man had died. The perpetrators had been swiftly executed but the simmering bad blood remained. Grest itself had seen problems, too; its bars and brothels had been too great a temptation to some of the men and, following representations from the magistrate, he had had to impose a curfew and restrict visiting rights to the town. He pictured the gods Artorus and Mytha sitting either side of a chequerboard, moving and toying with its pieces and laughing uproariously as they did so.

Reynard Lanthorpe was speaking to the engineers. He hadn't approached them himself for fear his own volatile temper would rise to the surface; he didn't want morale to drop further. His stomach had been playing him up lately, too; the constant burning had even caused him to give up the drink ... well almost.

Lanthorpe came up to him. 'They are telling me that it isn't as bad as it looks; the piles are there under the water, so it is just a question of getting a break in the weather. If they get that, they reckon they could have one bridge operational in a couple of days at the most.'

'And what do you think?'

'I see no reason to argue with them; all we need is a day with no rain.'

'Is that all?' Felmere laughed bitterly. 'Tell me, do you think the Gods are pissing over us because they have drunk too much, or because they can't stop themselves from laughing at us?'

'The Gods gave us victory less than two weeks ago, Baron. That is something we shouldn't forget.'

'Well, it might be a next-to-meaningless victory if the rain doesn't stop. Three days I am giving it, three days, and then we keep a garrison here but disband the troops until spring. We don't have enough food here to keep a full army for more than a week or so.'

'Hello,' said Lanthorpe slowly, 'is that a scout, or an Arshuman deserter?'

Across the river a horseman was approaching the small staging post the engineers had built there. As they watched, he dismounted, briefly spoke to one of the men, and the two of them clambered into a small rowing boat before pushing off into the ferocious torrent. It carried them downriver quite a way until they appeared as little more than a speck. Eventually, though, they made land, pulling the boat up behind them. Some soldiers went to speak to them.

'To be honest,' Felmere said, 'I won't be too disappointed if we have to cancel the attack. The fire of battle was in me when I committed to it, so maybe the Gods are just pointing me in the right direction. It will be nice to go and see my boy soon if we do have to abandon things till the spring.'

'It would be worth it just to see Fenchard's face,' said Lanthorpe, laughing, 'and Trask's, for that matter.'

'How many have we seen, Lanthorpe, fresh-faced barons eager to make their mark only to wind up dead within a week. I fear young Fenchard will be joining an ever-growing list soon.'

'I am not so sure,' said Lanthorpe. 'There is something a bit different about our Fenchard. Hiring Trask was a smart move for one.'

'A move that might well come back to bite him on the arse. Trask is loyal to one man and one man alone. That's why no one else will touch him with the tip of a pole arm.'

'He has fought for both sides, hasn't he?'

'In a manner of speaking. After the Serpent Knights kicked him out, he joined a bunch of mercenaries fighting for coin – the only thing that matters to him. Both sides hired him in the early years and he fought against us at Axmian. He has ... qualities, though, so he is generally forgiven for his eccentricities.' He sneezed into his hands. 'Artorus's teeth, they are bringing that man here – what has happened now?'

Two guards were approaching, with the man they had seen earlier walking between them. His boots were caked with mud and his hair and dark cloak were saturated with rain. He bowed slightly before he spoke to them.

'Baron Felmere, Sir Reynard, my name is Roden. I am one of your own scouts, my Lord, and have been in the lands of the enemy these past ten days.'

'Good man,' said Felmere. 'Give us your report and you can go into the town for a bath and an ale.'

'Thank you, my Lord. It has been dangerous work out there. Many of their light cavalry were scattered after the battle here and keeping out of their way has been Keth's own work, let alone getting to Tantala to gauge the strength of their forces.'

'But did you get to Tantala?'

'I did, my Lord. There are a few low hills in the area covered in trees and I concealed myself in one of them.'

'And what of his strength?,' said Reynard. 'Could that be gauged?'

'Growing by degrees; firstly with stragglers returning from the army we defeated, then a contingent arrived from the south, bringing their total to well over two thousand men. They are getting more organised every day. They have constructed catapults and dug a ditch around the town, but that is not all.'

Felmere shook his head. 'More and more bad news; every day we are delayed strengthens them. Well, my man, what is your other news.'

'Well, my Lord, not two days ago, just as I was about to leave, more men came up from the east. Some heavy cavalry but mainly infantry, mercenaries by the look of most of them – maybe a thousand in total – but it was not that I came to tell you.

The last contingent to arrive were Arshuman, well-armed and drilled. The thing was, though, my Lord: they marched under a black-and-yellow banner with a red sun at its centre. I have not seen it before but I am pretty sure it is the banner of...'

'The King!' said Felmere. 'King Aganosticlan's banner.'

'Keth's blood,' hissed Reynard through his teeth. 'He never leaves his palace. What by all the Gods would he be doing here? Are you sure it wasn't a ruse? Are you sure he was with them?'

'I cannot be certain, sir, but there was a man there being carried on a litter and surrounded by staff, servants, courtiers or what have you. I was pretty sure it was him.'

'He knows this is his last throw,' said Felmere hungrily. 'His general is dead so he has come to inspire his men. It sounds as if they will almost match us in numbers, but if we could get at their king it will hardly matter. By all the demons of the furnace, we have to bring them to battle now; we are so close to outright victory.'

As he spoke, Reynard looked up to the heavens. To his surprise, he felt nothing, no rain on his face, nothing stinging his eyes. As he watched, the incessant grey blanket of cloud, solid and unbroken for nearly two weeks, was finally pierced by a solitary shaft of light, pushing through it like a sword thrust and hitting Reynard square on the face. The sun's sudden warmth was like remembering an old friend and for the first time that day the lyrical call of a solitary songbird sounded in his ears.

'Get the engineers working,' said Felmere triumphantly. 'They have two days to build a bridge.' He turned to face Reynard. 'Well, my friend, perhaps the Gods do listen to us, after all.'

Oh, the indignities one had to bear if one was king. Not only had Aganosticlan had to endure the bumpiest and most uncomfortable of journeys perched atop his litter for all to see, like one of the exotic birds in his private zoo, but it had rained incessantly the whole time. Granted the litter had a roof, carved and gilded, but it would have looked so much more glorious in sunlight, and besides it did not protect from the damp and the chill airs that made him sniffle constantly and also made his joints ache first thing in the morning.

Still, it was over now; they had arrived at camp beside a poxy, flea-ridden village that could have been little more than the white tip of a pustule on Artorus's divine backside. Was ten years of war really for the likes of this? Of course, it wasn't! He looked north, to the mountains and its gems and other things of beauty. This village merely provided the labourers who would extract this wealth for him, nothing more. They had carried his throne all this way for him; it was his second throne, made of a carved dark wood found in the southern jungles, and usually resided in his palace in Arshuma's second city, Bect, which nestled in the foothills of the eastern Derannen Mountains. He was sitting in it now, sheltering in the royal pavilion, a vast lemon coloured affair that housed many of his staff and the barely clad serving girls of which he was so fond.

Obadrian stood before him, along with the local commander, General Terze, a surprisingly young man – well, perhaps not that surprising considering the mortality rate of his generals, especially of those that displeased him.

'Well, Obadrian, I am here just as you wished it. Do you think the Tanaren spies would have noticed my presence by now?'

'In all probability, Your Majesty, and I am sure it will soon have the desired effect.'

'You mean it will force them to attack against their better judgement?'

'Yes, Your Majesty, this weather could well have meant they abandoned their plans and remained where they were, which was the last thing we wanted, but with your royal presence here it should goad them into thinking they could take you and win the war in a stroke. I believe this is what you wanted them to think, Your Majesty?'

Aganosticlan did not answer. Instead, he left his throne and walked over to an armour stand close by. It was displaying a suit of garish and utterly impractical armour that looked as if were made out of solid gold: the helmet bore two golden bird wings sweeping majestically backwards; the cuirass bore the emblem of a golden sun; its pauldrons, vambraces and gauntlets had patterns of running flames, as did its greaves and sabatons, which, like the helmet bore wings sweeping backwards from the ankle. A couple of seasoned mace-wielding warriors would have carved through it in a minute, but that was not its purpose. This was the armour of a king.

'General Terze, you have found a man to wear this?'

'Yes, Your Majesty. We had many volunteers but have selected one that approximates closely to your size and build.' He did not mention how the threat of a flogging had exponentially increased the number of 'volunteers'.

'Good, but school him in the ways of a noble. He is supposed to be me, after all; the last thing we want is for him to start picking his nose on the battlefield. Obadrian, are my evacuation plans ready?'

'Yes, Your Majesty. Should the battle seem to be going amiss, you will be taken downriver by boat for a few miles where a fast carriage awaits. The ambassador is also on hand to carry our terms of surrender to their general.'

'Your Majesty,' General Terze said hesitantly, 'you surely do not think we could lose this battle?'

'Of course not!' snapped the King. 'But you may come to realise one day that it is well to be prepared for every eventuality. Now, give me the troop numbers.'

'We will have over four thousand men, Your Majesty,' said the General. 'The levies and mercenaries that arrived with you have greatly boosted our morale and fighting capabilities, almost as much as Your Majesty's presence here.'

'You are to be congratulated, Obadrian, I did not expect you to raise so many troops in so short a time. And for so little money at that.'

'The heavy cavalry were expensive, Your Majesty,' Obadrian intoned solemnly. 'But I had two factors in my favour.'

'And what, my dear chamberlain, were they?'

'The main body of mercenaries are fighting for plunder only; they have been recruiting heavily in Arshuma but their core is from Tanaren. They have a grudge against Baron Felmere and are more interested in vengeance than anything. They call themselves "The Vipers", Your Majesty. The second factor is far more down to Your Majesty's own cunning. The local nobility have been much more interested in spending their own money and levying troops since some of their number have started to fall victim to um...'

'Mysterious deaths? Assassination without motive?'

'Exactly, Your Majesty, speaking of which I wonder as to the location of that particular ... gift that you received.'

'Leave us, Terze. Tell the troops I will be inspecting them in the morning – ten royals to the most outstanding and ten lashes for the least. You understand?'

'Indeed, Your Majesty.' The general bowed low and departed.

'Obadrian,' the King said quietly. 'I trust you and my household staff – you have all signed declarations to say you will have your tongues removed if you speak falsely to me after all – but my generals, well, I am not so sure about them. I purge them from time to time but little seems to work. Never mention again that we have a Kozean assassin within our midst in front of them. The information would get back to Hylas in no time, or over the river into Tanaren.'

'I understand, Your Majesty, and ask you to forgive my impropriety.'

'Forgiven as always, Obadrian. As for where she is now, I am damned to the furnace if I know. She has been given her mark and I haven't seen her since. At a guess I will see her once more when her job is done and once again to be given her second task, and I would imagine that would be it. Her loyalties are not with us, after all.'

'Of course, Your Majesty. If I may confess, I always found her presence somewhat unnerving.'

'Then she is doing her job. In her homeland her function is to terrify and cow populace and nobility alike. Did she complete all the names on your list?'

'Indeed, Your Majesty. There were five names and none of them lived more than a week once she knew them.'

'Excellent, Obadrian. I think we can trust her to take care of business at her end; all we need do now is concentrate on the Tanaren army, I expect them to be here by the end of the week.'

Obadrian did not reply. Rather he looked nervously at the floor and shuffled his feet. Aganosticlan could read the signs perfectly. There was little about the chamberlain he didn't know, especially concerning his night visits to the good-looking young men of his court.

'What is it, Chamberlain? I see something is concerning you.'

'Well, Your Majesty, it is just that our army may well match the size of our enemy's, but ... they have mages and we do not. When we lost that last battle it was the mages that landed the decisive blow. We were holding them until they sent down terrible bolts of lightning from the sky.'

The King resumed his seat on the throne. He fixed Obadrian with a wicked smile.

'I have it on very good authority that any mages they have will not be taking to the field against us again.'

'You mean they will be taken care of? What authority do you have exactly, Your Majesty?'

'Very good authority. There will be no mage left alive to face us in battle here, take my word on it.'

BOOK ONE: AUTUMN

41

The caravan was moving again. Over an hour ago it had become stuck in an old water-filled wheel rut, and as the horses had tried to pull it free all it had done was turn the churned-up mud into a liquid morass that clung tightly to the caravan, sucking it downwards and holding it firm. The Knights of the Thorn had poles out, trying to ease the wheel free, but it had been lengthy and back-breaking work, by the end of which their fine white tabards were covered in water and filth.

Cheris and Marcus had offered to help but Sir Norton firmly and politely turned them away. She realised that she had no magic to aid in extricating wheels from quicksand; a pity, it would have made her a fortune, if she did. Instead, she sat next to Marcus in the self-same vehicle they had taken from Tanaren. Her head was buried in a book but she wasn't reading.

Her thoughts were with Anaya, who was fast asleep on the other seat. She had been excited about taking the two of them away to her cottage for a couple of days when a bout of illness had struck the army. Tired as she was dealing with the injured from the battle, she was in no shape to cope with a new wave of casualties. She had been treating a couple of new arrivals when she had collapsed. Her nurses diagnosed exhaustion and ordered her to rest. Cheris and Marcus tried to act as her locum but their rudimentary understanding of healing magic aided the nurses very little. Baron Felmere himself had stepped in and told them to take her away for a few days, as the army was bogged down with no prospect of leaving soon. And so yesterday they had left the camp. Sir Norton knew the way and had told them that they would arrive either later that day or early the following day. They were allowed just one full day in the cottage before they had to return. Cheris doubted that it was long enough for Anaya.

'She has slept all day,' Cheris said to Marcus. 'Poor lady, she has been taxed beyond endurance.'

'I have written to the college asking, no, insisting that they cancel her tour of duty and send someone else in her stead.' Marcus gloomily cupped his face with his hands. 'I will be having strong words with the Magisters' Council on my return. They have broken so many protocols and just because it is far easier to keep her here than replace her. Someone really should answer for it.'

'And we have another battle to go back to in a few days and I am hardly in great shape myself.'

'Your rib?'

'It is a lot better but I still get a twinge from time to time, if I get up too quickly or laugh too loud. Fortunately out here there is little chance of the latter happening often.'

'Tired of the outside world already?'

'Yes and no. After the battle it felt like a kick in the teeth seeing the villagers kill their own people and brand women just for sleeping with the wrong man; I mean why fight to try to end the war, if the victors are so excited by violence they just want more and more of it.'

'You have never lived under oppression. The people of Grest lived in fear of the Arshuman overlords and of those of our people who collaborated with them. If a people are kept at heel with violence, then at some point they will mete out the same in return. I am not agreeing with it, or condoning their actions, but it is the way it always has been and probably always will be, unless something drastic happens to human nature and men are turned into beatific purveyors of wisdom and mercy.'

'Stop sermonising. Just say that people are generally horrible and leave it at that.'

'Very well, Cheris. People are generally horrible and beyond redemption. Feel better now?'

'Nobody is beyond redemption. If they were, then there would be no need for the Gods. If people cannot be steered in a direction that could change their morality, then the Gods have no purpose.'

Marcus laughed. 'You are not having a theological discussion with an Artoran priest here. I know you have doubts about the Gods, as do I. But be aware that we are in a tiny minority and to say such things out loud on the mainland is close to heresy, a crime punishable by a very nasty death.'

'I don't know, Marcus.' She sighed. 'My beliefs change with the weather. I see something to make me doubt their existence, then ten minutes later I see something that reaffirms their existence. It is something for which, however long you go looking for an answer, a definitive one will never be found. Faith is of the heart, after all, and is not something that can be quantified in a dusty old book. It requires neither proof nor disproof. It just is. Like the standing stones at the college – however much you push at them, they will not move either way.'

'But the stones exist; we can all see and touch them. Belief, however, is amorphous and invisible and is never the same from person to person. Does faith even require definition? As you say, you can dance circles around the question till the day you die and never come up with an answer.'

'The day you die is the day you finally receive proof, of course. If Xhenafa stands before you and takes your hand to lead you one way or another, then you have your answer. If only it could be communicated to the living.'

'Then all priests would be out of a job and begging on the streets.'

'And all their buildings could be sold along with its gold and the poor need never go hungry again. Praise Elissa for miracles that will never happen.'

'And may the Gods protect us from blasphemers and those cursed with the gift of magic.'

'As it must be. For ever. Fancy a pastry? Sir Norton picked a few up in Grest. I was going to surprise you with them.'

'Keeping secrets from your mentor? You wicked woman! Place them in my custody immediately.'

They ate the sweet cakes discussing this and that. The weather became a topic, as this was the first day in a long time absolutely free from rain. They both recalled some of the dazzling electrical storms they had witnessed on the Isle of Tears. Cheris remembered the first one she saw, aged twelve.

'People were terrified,' she said. 'I had never seen people run to their cells so quickly. But it was different with me. It must have been the first time I realised I had an affinity, an empathy, with such power. I felt no fear at all, just excitement. I crept up to the balcony. It was completely deserted. It was strange; I felt like something was willing me on, compelling me to open the door. There was no one to stop me, so that is what I did.

'The shock when that door opened was incredible. The wind was pinning me against the wall and I could barely shut the door again. And the rain was so fierce that the balcony was nearly ankle deep in water, even with it pouring out of the drainage holes. But then I looked about me. Oh, Marcus, it was beautiful, to see the night clouds backlit with coruscating fire, watching as it struck from the skies into the boiling sea – it was vibrant, primeval. I had never felt my senses tingling like that ever before. I watched the storm move over the clouds, the crashing of the thunder getting ever louder and then, and I probably shouldn't tell you this, I took off my robe and stretched out my arms to the storm; I was gasping with the excitement. I stayed like that until the storm began to move away and the noise and light went north to Tanaren. Then I dressed in my sodden clothes and rushed back to my cell. No one ever knew, not till now anyway.' She saw Marcus's quizzical look.

'What? I was twelve years old. My body was changing. You know how sensitive girls are to mana at that age. It is why we are so much better at our art than men.' She set her chin defensively while wishing she had been a bit more discreet.

'When you return to the college and start mentoring others, will you advise all the young ladies in your charge to do the same thing?' She saw his barely suppressed smile and realised he was teasing her.

'Why not?' she smiled. 'Perhaps naked lightning worship is the future of our art.'

They laughed together softly, two old friends sharing a joke, when suddenly the prone form on the bed opposite started to stir.

'I have been asleep, haven't I?'

Cheris got up and moved over to her, crouching on the floor next to her bed.

'You could say that – you have slept all day. According to Sir

Norton, we are not far away from your house.'

A strange expression briefly crossed Anaya's face; it was almost one of dread as if it was the last place on earth she wanted to get to. But it passed almost instantly. She smiled at Cheris. 'I didn't realise it had been that long.'

'How do you feel?'

'Oh the sleep has helped definitely. I feel a lot stronger now.'

'Have a pastry. I hid this one from Marcus. The man is a wolf around sweet cakes.'

'Thank you.'

She ate it hungrily then swung her legs over and sat upright, inviting Cheris to sit next to her. 'When do we have to return?'

'We will only have one day at your house. Felmere wants us back quickly in case he can still attack the enemy.'

Anaya sighed resignedly. 'I suppose it was inevitable. It will be a long winter.'

'Maybe not for you Anaya.' Marcus stretched his legs out and yawned. 'What do you mean, Marcus?'

'I have written to the college. If they listen to me, and I see no reason why they shouldn't, then they will be recalling you and sending another in your stead.'

She stiffened, her eyes wide. 'No, no, you cannot do that! I have so much to do here; there is a system in place. Someone just can't walk in and take over. I, I swore to myself that I would stay here till the war ended. If I go back now, I would have achieved nothing.'

Marcus leaned forward, his eyes scanning her shocked face. He spoke firmly. 'Anaya. You are not well. You have done a world of good in this place, but you have to return before you become the war's latest casualty. I would not normally interfere, but Cheris and I are very concerned for you.'

Anaya's eyes were wild. 'I have no say in this? Neither of you know what you are doing; you cannot just walk in here, spend a few weeks and hand out orders to me. Surely I outrank both of you?'

'It is the Chief Magister's decision, not mine. Remember, I have been here a few times and each time I have found that your condition has deteriorated a little more than the time before. You obviously cannot see this; sometimes it takes a detached mind to see what is right and what is wrong.'

Cheris put her arm around her. 'It is for the best, believe me.'

Anaya started to cry, hiding her face with her hands. Cheris kept her arm around the woman, trying to comfort her as best she could. Eventually she stopped and wiped her reddened face. 'Very well, Marcus, then I will have to accept it.'

The silence that followed was awkward. Cheris decided to try to break it.

'I bet you have forgotten what the college is like after all this time; I have only been away just over a month and it seems like a distant memory to me. There are a lot of good things about it, the weather for one; have you forgotten what the sun looks like?'

'Not quite!' Anaya smiled wanly, blinking away her tears. 'I do remember it could get very hot in the summer; if you went outside for too long your face would be burnt red by the wind, and who was that old man who would sing those terrible songs on festival days? People would indulge him because he was so old, but I have carried his thin reedy voice with me to this day.'

'Oh Elissa preserve us, you are talking about Brother Rebdon. I had rather blotted him out from my mind.'

'He is not still alive, is he?'

'Very much so,' said Cheris, 'and still singing.'

'He must be a hundred if he is a day.'

'I believe he is ninety-two,' said Marcus. 'He was a Chief Magister some forty years ago. Of course no one remembers that now; just his warbling interrupting you when you are trying to eat.'

'What was that song he always sang every summer? The one about how awful it was being a mage? It used to have me gnawing the table.' Anaya was perking up now.

'You mean "A Mage's Lot", don't you?' groaned Cheris. 'He has sung it so many times I know it off by heart.' She started to sing, affecting the burr of Brother Rebdon's south-western accent. Anaya joined in shortly afterwards.

> 'Oh a mage's lot is a terrible thing
> So hearken ye all to the song I now sing
> As a child other boys would keep well away
> For with a click of my fingers I would make them obey
> But alas I was caught when I burnt a boy's hair
> As a knight clipped my ear with nary a care
> On a boat I was put and sent forth to an isle
> And was told that my stay would be for more than a while
> It was books, a hard bed and rules upon rules
> And stern teachers who would thrash you for acting like fools
> And slowly years passed and a long beard I did grow
> A part of this isle am I, never to know
> How the world moves far away from its shores
> And...'

The two women looked at each other, realising that they didn't know any more of the words and simultaneously they both burst out laughing. Marcus looked bemusedly at both of them until they had stopped.

'Brother Rebdon regards it as his finest work.'

They both looked at him, trying to look serious, but seconds later they were off again collapsing into fits of hysterical laughter that seemed to go on for ever. Marcus sighed and picked up the book Cheris had been reading. 'Women!' he said exasperatedly to himself.

The following morning, not long after dawn, with a thousand songbirds greeting the new day from trees almost denuded of leaves, they arrived at their destination. Sir Norton hammered at the door to wake them all and, grumbling and mumbling to themselves, they clambered out of the caravan into the weak sunlight, their breath frosting in the brittle air.

They had been climbing slowly up a narrow country path barely wide enough for the caravan, but finally it had come to a dead end in a small forest clearing strewn with leaves. Ahead of them was a shelf of rock into which some stone steps had been crudely carved. A narrow, barely discernible path led from it northwards, heading further towards the mountains.

'You have a half-hour walk,' said Sir Norton. 'Just follow the path. I and the other knights will be here and will see you when you return tomorrow morning.'

'I didn't know I would have to walk,' grumbled Cheris.

'Stop moaning,' said Marcus. 'You are the youngest person here.' And with that he followed Anaya up the stone steps and into the forest.

Before being exiled to the Isle of tears, Cheris had been a city girl. She remembered loving what the city had to offer, a feeling that had been partly recaptured in her ever so brief stop in Tanaren. A forest was to her an environment as alien as the surface of the moon. She pulled her cloak close to her body, as though every one of its unseen noises, the crack of dead wood, the rustle of wind in the ferns, the groaning of the swaying trees constituted an invisible threat of some sort. She could see its beauty and its serene tranquillity – it was a timeless place after all, a place where monks and priests would come to meditate on the nature of eternity and their own place in the divine plan of the Gods – but she could not bring herself to trust it.

Ferns and shrubs pressing close to the narrow stony path pulled and tugged at their garments, leaving them damp and sticky against their bodies. Despite the cold air, Cheris was feeling warmer and warmer as she walked. She was starting to have fantasies concerning hot baths perfumed with herbs and scented oils when Anaya stopped in front of her.

'Here we are,' she said.

It was an unprepossessing little cottage, standing in a small clearing in the trees. It looked like the sort of place a woodcutter would have once lived in before conflict drove him to the slums of Athkaril. The thatch on the roof looked like it would soon need replacing and there were cracks in the wattle and daub which would also soon need looking into. Nevertheless, Anaya seemed happy enough to see it.

'An hour's work and it will soon be a little palace.'

It had three rooms: a main living room with a small fireplace and a wonky wooden table with chairs placed neatly around it; a tiny bedroom with one bed, a straw pallet, and a chest of drawers stacked with books; and at the other side an area for preparing food, not that there was any food in the place. Sir Norton had given Anaya a pack that presumably had some, before they left him. It had a besom, though, and Cheris busied herself with sweeping the floor while Anaya put fresh coverings on the bed (she and Cheris were to share it, she said) and then went to unload the food from her pack. Marcus went to draw some water from the small well outside, before collecting some firewood, which he ignited just by pointing his finger and uttering a couple of words of power.

By noon it was a pleasant little habitation. They sat and ate lunch, warming themselves next to the fire. Once that was done, the table was cleared and Anaya went to get a couple of books from the chest of drawers. 'Now, I have a couple of questions concerning the theories in these books. I believe they have been discredited by more recent discoveries but I need clarification on a few points.'

And so the main business of the day started; ideas were passed back and forth and developments in magical theory discussed. Anaya was animated and curious the whole time while Marcus, as ever, was happy to dispense what knowledge he had. Cheris was the least involved of the three; she had heard so many similar debates between crusty old academics before and repeatedly found herself drifting. She did wonder as to the importance Anaya attached to the whole thing, though; there was nothing that couldn't have waited a month or two when the land would be in the grip of winter and soldiers would be far more interested in keeping warm than in killing the enemy.

After a few hours they broke for a brief and light dinner. Through the slatted window Cheris could see the light outside begin to descend into the gloom of an early dusk. Marcus sat back in his chair while Anaya popped into the bedroom. When she didn't return for a while, and when she felt that she could no longer bear sitting on the hard chair, Cheris went to see if there was anything wrong.

To her surprise, she saw Anaya leaning at the bedside silently praying. Cheris decided to leave her to her devotions when Anaya heard her feet shuffle on the earthen floor. She turned to face the younger women and Cheris saw immediately that she had been crying again. 'Is everything all right?' she asked.

'I am wrestling with a question,' she replied. 'I hoped the Gods could guide me but they are silent on this issue.'

'Then what is the question? Perhaps I can help.'

'I am just wondering if it is justifiable to commit a small evil that would ultimately result in achieving a much greater good. Are acts of questionable morality allowable in such cases? What do you think? I must admit I have wrestled with this for a long time.'

'It would depend on the scale of the evil, I suppose, and this good you speak of, would it truly be worth achieving? Would the price truly be worth paying?' There was something about the question Cheris found disturbing.

'Oh yes,' Anaya smiled sadly. 'It really would, more than anything.'

'Then I suppose the answer is yes. Did I not kill men so that Grest could be taken? I suppose that is one example.'

Anaya stood and brushed her knees clean. 'I suppose so, although Grest could easily be lost again, in which case what you did in the field merely furthered the futility of this war.'

'Are you saying I committed an evil act?'

'No, my dear, for you acted with a pure heart and entirely altruistic intentions, though I have seen so many before you do the same thing with little good resulting at the end. Come, let's get back to things; we have plenty more to get through.'

She took her place at the table and continued talking to Marcus. It was soon dark and Cheris busied herself lighting candles and closing the shutter on the window. After what to her seemed an age the two older mages finally seemed to be bringing things to a close.

'I have learned much,' said Anaya. (Had she really? thought Cheris. The practice of magic changes little over centuries let alone the few short years she had been away.) 'You forget so many things, so many things, when a library is no longer close at hand.'

'True,' Marcus replied. 'But for you in a few months that will no longer be a concern.'

'You mean when I go back to the island? You are right, of course.' She paused, and brushed a loose strand of hair from her face. 'I tell you what, Sir Norton has given us a bottle of wine. I have no idea how good it is. Let me go and prepare a warm posset for us, something to celebrate our all too brief time here.'

'Do you need a hand? It is quite dark, is it not?' asked Cheris.

'No, my dear, I will be fine. There is actually a lantern out here; I will light it and bring it in for us.'

After she left, Cheris looked at Marcus and yawned, 'Elissa preserve me from academics,' she said with a smile.

'Just be grateful your natural ability more than compensates for your reticence at study.' Marcus seemed in a good mood, as he always was after a productive teaching session. 'Though Anaya has forgotten more than I thought possible. I even wonder if she is pretending not to know certain things; some of the basics seemed to elude her, even though she has been practising magic constantly ever since she left the college.'

'But why would she do that? It makes no sense.'

'Indeed. Put it down to the paranoia of a man just past his middle years. Perhaps she feels sorry for me and saw feigning ignorance as an opportunity to flatter me on my depth of knowledge. I did enjoy myself, after all.' Cheris looked at him archly. 'Just past his middle years?' Marcus glared at her.

Shortly afterwards Anaya returned bearing goblets from which steam was rising.

'Magic is great for heating drinks. It should never be used in so trivial a manner but out here I think I can be forgiven.' She handed a mug to each of them.

It was warm spiced wine and tasted delicious. Cheris drank hers in no time at all and Marcus was only just behind. 'Thank you, Anaya; that was lovely,'

Cheris told her. 'I will sleep the dream sleep of Xhenafa tonight.'

'Indeed, you will, my girl; indeed you will.'

She stared at the yellow glow of the lantern. It was strange but it appeared a bit fuzzy to her, clear then hazy, and then clear again. Surely, the alcohol couldn't work that fast?

'I am so unused to wine, I can feel it affecting me already. With your permission I will take my leave and go to bed.' Cheris went to stand but found her muscles completely unresponsive; her head was spinning in circles. "Lissa's blood, Anaya, what was in that drink?'

'A concoction known only to healers and surgeons. I would stay in that chair if I were you; you will never make it to the bedroom.'

'By the gods, woman, what have you done!' Cheris heard Marcus say, his voice full of anger and confusion, but he sounded as if he were about a mile away. There was a noise. She realised Marcus had fallen off his chair and then briefly saw Anaya's face looking closely at her, lantern held high, but she was so blurred that Cheris could not gauge her expression. She tried to speak to her but only the tiniest gasp came out. Then she was gone, as a void of inky darkness swallowed her whole.

There was a voice – female, clear and pure. It entered her head like the ringing of a cluster of tiny silver bells. She could not understand the words; it was a strange language she had never heard before, or had she? No, there was something familiar about it; she was finding it so difficult to think. Her brain was still a fog but the voice was close, very close.

Cheris's eyelids slowly fluttered open. By the Gods, even that was an effort. She realised as her vision slowly began to clear that she was completely immobile, that she could neither move nor speak.

She was still in her chair and there was a dark shape slumped in the one opposite her. Marcus. He was staring fixedly ahead and she realised that this strange paralysis was affecting him also. It was difficult but she managed to twist her eyes towards the fireplace in the direction Marcus was staring.

And there, illuminated by the lantern now hanging from a ceiling beam, was Anaya. She was standing in front of another low table, one she must have dragged from the kitchen, and on it was a large bowl filled with a liquid from which steam was rising. A book was opened before her and she appeared to be following its instructions intently. Eventually she caught the whites of Marcus eyes and looked up at him.

'Hello, Marcus,' she said absently, then resumed whatever she was doing.

Cheris could see Marcus straining with effort. His mouth moved noiselessly, a line of dribble ran into his beard. Suddenly words came, choked and strangulated.

'What ... are ... you ... doing?'

Anaya paused for a second. 'I suppose I do owe you both an explanation. I am sorry for what I have done to you, but please understand I wish you no harm; I just knew you would try to stop me and so had to act the way I did. You have both been given a very strong soporific. Poor Cheris's dose is even higher than yours, Marcus; I do not know if you see it but she is so much more powerful than you – than both of us. She will be the perfect bait.' Marcus's breathing was heavy and ragged as he spoke again.

'Bait? ... why?'

'I have to do this now. I had changed my mind but you are sending me away after all and I will have no other opportunities to do what I must.' She left the table and came over to him.

'You see, Marcus, this war has to end. You cannot imagine what I have seen. Not just the mutilated and the dead but the transformation it wreaks on normal men; you see the fire die in their eyes being replaced by cold anger and hate, and now you have brought a sweet girl like Cheris with you, to turn into another butcher. I will not permit this to continue. I will not!'

She turned to Cheris next. 'It was our little discussion, my dear, that set my course in stone – a lesser evil to further a greater good. What I am doing now may be seen as evil but, if I succeed, this war will end, hundreds of deaths to prevent thousands. Is that not a good thing?' She returned to her table and picked up the book; it was not the thickest of tomes, but sizeable enough.

'Some few winters ago I was lucky enough to be given permission by chief butcher Felmere to study at St Delph's library in Tanaren. They have terrible security there and quite a few forbidden books. It was easy to smuggle this one out of there ... easy!'

She walked back to Marcus and held the book up to the light so that he could see it clearly. Despite his paralysis, his eyes widened with horror.

'Yes, Marcus. It is so. The Arshumans have but one army left – destroy that and the war is won. Felmere cannot do this; he might push them back, but then months will pass, they will push him back and the whole sorry mummers' play continues. What I am about to do will annihilate the Arshumans and make peace the only possible solution. You will look at me as a saviour when this is done.

'I came to this cottage last winter and went over and over the ritual in my head, but for it to work I needed a beacon, a magnet of magical power to draw my quarry to me, and now this year you two came. It is as if the very Gods are on my side. Tonight it is then. I am well into the ritual already. I just need some blood from the two of you and I can start the final incantations. And when they are done, Marcus, when they are done, there will be four of us in this room, us three and the demon. The demon I will summon to finish this war for good.'

BOOK ONE: AUTUMN

42

Thunder clouds sat heavily over the southern mountains and thin strands of mist wound their sinuous path between the trees overhanging the dank, still waters of the silent lake. It was a chill dawn, the sort in which Morgan always tried to grab an extra few minutes under the blanket before anyone noticed him. But not today; today he was stomping round his room stretching his muscles over the radiating warmth of the glowstones. It had been a couple of days since the festival, days in which he had been largely confined to his room, Itheya being busy with other duties. She did eventually get round to see him the evening before, just as his confinement was beginning to gnaw at him and the view from the window had long since lost its novelty. She had walked in as though he should have been expecting her.

'Are you bored to insanity yet?' She was wearing a simple green tunic patterned with broken black stripes, rather like the markings on a cat.

'You have cut your hair,' he said. It was true – her ponytail, though held high on her head, barely fell down below her shoulders.

'If I am to go into battle, long hair is just a hindrance. It grows back very quickly, far quicker than it does in humans. Tomorrow I leave for the krasa. I have been with Father most of the last couple of days; he is unable to attend himself so I must represent him. We have decided it is silly for you to stay here all day, so Terath will watch you when I am gone. He is performing some ceremony tomorrow regarding that tooth, so you and Cedric can attend with him. I will return in two or three days.'

'Slow down – that is a lot of information in a short time. So I am going with Terath tomorrow.'

'Yes. Early. He will take you to the cave in the morning. He is trying to locate a dragonstone; he has already said he does not expect success but he has to try.'

'And you? What will be happening with you?' She sat on the bed and sighed.

'I wish you and Cedric could come, but no humans are allowed. I will be meeting with the heads of the other tribes to tell them of your proposal. I will try to persuade them but you have no idea how difficult these gatherings can be, especially as I am not even the Mhezhen.'

'You have said that none of you get on with each other. How many tribes will be there?'

'All the western tribes will be there, tribes affiliated to our own – the Etutha, the Panugraic, the Cephellan, the Atagon, the Denussi and the Gapharan. Then there will be our chief rivals, the Ometahan, and their allies – the Chuchethen, the Boia, the Atrebenes, the Syrta and the Leretel. We may see the deep forest tribes – the Rengereth, the Coul and the Brantha – but we definitely will not see the tribes from the deep valleys carved into the mountains, tribes like the Obrosh and the Kesta, for they bother with no one but themselves. Even though I mentioned that tribes are affiliated to us, they are under no obligation to agree with me in this instance.'

'Do you end up having a vote on this?'

'Yes, but it is not straightforward. The Morioka have ten votes as befits their status – all will be in favour of joining you – other tribes have different numbers of votes – the Denussi have four, the Atagon five, for example. But not all those votes need go the same way, so the Atagon may have three votes for and two against, depending on the way their leaders feel. And this does not take into account the deals the tribes will do on the side or the fact that, even if there is a clear yes or no vote, tribes are still free to act independently if they so desire.'

'So you mean, even if the krasa votes no, some tribes may still decide to join us?'

'Yes, but if things go badly, they cannot call a krasa for aid, for none will be given.'

'It sounds extremely complicated; no wonder I haven't seen you for two days.'

'It is. I am sorry I have been away. but there has been much for me to take in. Since Armentele my head has been pounding with the things I have to remember. This is the first krasa I have had to take myself. It is an onerous responsibility; I must not let Father down.'

BOOK ONE: AUTUMN

'You don't get much time to yourself, do you?'

She did not answer; instead she put her head in her hands, drawing her knees up to her chin.

'Itheya? Are you all right?'

'I am fine,' she said. She stood and came up close to him; her strange eyes had an anguished look to them. She whispered softly, 'Father is very ill; the last two days have been ... difficult. Just talking to me tired him out, and his pain never ends despite the healing magic. There are times...' – she stopped and looked at the floor. 'There are times when I just want to get on my horse and ride until I am completely alone, just surrounded by trees and birds, no one to talk to or to remind me of my responsibilities. I confide in you because I cannot confide in my own people. I am their leader; I cannot be uncertain or weak in front of them.'

He put his hands on both her arms, gently pinning them to her side. She was wiry and strong and did not resist him.

'You must be prepared for the worst with your father.' She nodded slightly. 'There is no easy way to say it. I am sorry you feel alone, but if you need to talk to me, then I am going nowhere; I will be here for you.'

'Thank you.' she said. 'I still like your smell.'

'Stop flirting,' he said, smiling. 'I am human remember.'

'I remember,' she said sadly, 'I never forget. I must go now. I will see you in about three days.'

To his surprise, she leaned forward and kissed him softly on the cheek. *'Moton at ate sheren, Morgan.'* Then, without another word, she turned and left the room.

That was yesterday evening and by the time Terath called on him she had already gone.

And then it was into the woods again. This time Terath, Cedric and Morgan took a boat to the lake's farthest shore, on the east. Two young elves, one male and one female, accompanied them, steering the boat and assisting Cedric when it was time to walk again. Terath introduced them.

'This is Dirthen and Astania, my assistants; they have a little of your language, but are not confident with it. They help me prepare the glowstones and the lights and flame you see around the village, but they have many other duties as well that you probably have not seen.'

The two younger elves, both dark with vivid blue eyes, led the rest of the group into an area of woodland that was darker and wilder than any Morgan had previously seen. The trees here were truly ancient, twisting into many tortured shapes with great roots springing from the earth and winding around each other like mating serpents. Great trailing beards of lichen hung from the low overhanging branches, which interlocked with those from other trees to such an extent that they formed a great roof-like canopy peppered with crows and jackdaws, denying light to the forest floor. The five travellers were locked in a permanent twilight where flashes of moss and fern provided the only real colour.

After travelling with difficulty over the uneven surface for about half a mile they came across a narrow stream that cut across their path. It could be crossed easily with an elongated step, but instead the elves turned towards the mountains and started following its course. They had not gone far when the land dropped sharply. Cedric stumbled and almost fell as the sharpness of the incline caught him by surprise; his feet kicked up loose mud and shale as Dirthen and Morgan struggled to keep him upright. Once he was steady again, they continued downhill.

They were surrounded by high ferns that closed in around them, eventually reaching over their heads the farther they travelled. The air was still, close and stifling, and the smell of dank vegetation was overpowering. The two men were concentrating fully on not stumbling, though Morgan had awareness enough to notice that the elves had far less difficulty in navigating the treacherous path than he.

After what had seemed an age the ground levelled out and they came upon a flat stretch of muddy ground clear of vegetation. Ahead of them was a high bank of earth and loose stone, and at its centre, fringed with tree roots, like a single black unblinking eye, was the mouth of a cave. The stream merrily ran ahead of them and disappeared into it; they could hear it echoing as it plunged downwards once inside.

'We are here,' said Terath. 'This cave has great magical power; it comes in through the stream and the roots of the trees. The stones in the cave pool have the most power of all. Come with me and you shall see.' 'Is it an easy climb?' asked Cedric cautiously.

'Yes, there are steps, look.'

He pointed. Next to where the stream entered the cave was a broad flat stone. As they approached it, they could see it was but one of a series that descended into the darkness. They could see it wasn't a straight climb down; rather the stairs wound to the left the further down they went. Terath plunged into the darkness, brimming with enthusiasm. Morgan entered a lot more slowly, followed by Cedric and the two young elves.

As Morgan made his way carefully down the steps, he kept expecting the darkness to engulf him. That it didn't happen seemed rather confusing. Then, after over thirty steps, he reached the hard earth floor and could look around him properly.

He hadn't realised how far down he had climbed. He was confronted by a high-ceilinged cave; it was not large but broad and circular with many tree roots punching through its earthen walls. The stream fell in showers of rain on to a bed of large flat pebbles before running gently back the way it had come and emptying into a clear shallow lake. At its centre, reached by a narrow causeway of loose stones, was a circular island of dark earth, Morgan could see it had low benches and a large stone bowl at its centre. Surrounding the island, placed carefully at its edges, was a series of wide flat glowstones, whose warm crimson light reflected off the lake and on to the cave ceiling, but they were not the only light source present. As Morgan looked fixedly at the lake, he blinked uncertainly, before realising that the bottom of the lake was covered with pebbles all of which were marbled with an iridescent sapphire blue – it was this that was giving off a pale light making the waters shine like the iris of an elven eye. So that was it – the cave roof glowed a warm red and the lake an icy blue, between them illuminating every nook and cranny of Terath's grotto. The two young elves busied themselves with lighting a series of candles perched on stones or natural ledges and before long the faint citrus smell he was now so familiar with added its own ambience to the surroundings.

'This,' said Terath, 'is Haraskolon, the cave of power. This is where the glowstones are prepared, the source of all magic for the Morioka. It is the perfect place to try to perform the ritual inscribed on the dragon's tooth.'

Terath walked along the causeway, beckoning them to follow. Cedric spoke to Morgan:

'We have deciphered – well, Terath has deciphered – about a third of the inscription. The writing on it is tiny and in an obscure dialect little known by modern elves but Terath is working through it slowly. This ritual is one of the first things mentioned; its purpose is to detect any dragonstone within a reasonably close proximity.'

Cedric took a seat on a bench, Morgan sitting beside him. They watched as Astania filled a jug with lake water and poured it carefully into the large stone bowl at the island's centre. She did this three times until the bowl was three-quarters full. Terath then produced from his robe a large dully coloured red stone which he dropped into the bowl's centre.

'These dragonstones are of similar composition to that corundum,' Cedric explained. 'It is all about establishing a connection between us and them. They will also need some dragon's blood and some herbs and toxins found in the forest.'

'Two questions, Cedric.' Morgan replied. 'First, is that a real unpolished ruby?'

'Yes.'

'You could pretty much buy a baronetcy for that.'

'It has far more value here, don't you think? It is not healthy to see everything in terms of crowns, ducats and pennies, and it will not avail you here.' Cedric looked at Morgan closely.

'I agree, Cedric; I have seen what money can do to people.'

'Good,' said Cedric, his voice echoing in the hollow surroundings. 'And your second question?'

'Dragon's blood. Where by all the gods does one obtain dragon's blood?'

'I shall answer that,' said Terath. 'When we moved to Seyavanion eight hundred years ago we brought with us many magical components, often collected at great cost. Many of these components have perished over the years, despite our best efforts, but the dragon's blood, powdered as it is, has survived all this time; we should only need a small amount hopefully.'

Dirthen and Astania were adding further items to the bowl – dried leaves and some clear liquids poured from small stopper-topped bottles. A light steam started to rise from the bowl. Terath then stood over it and pulled out another bottle from the folds of his robe.

'Here it is – the blood of a dragon.' He shook the tiniest amount of red dust from the bottle on to the water's surface. As Morgan watched, the surface of the water turned the deepest scarlet, and the steam coming from it intensified.

'Now we are ready,' Terath whispered.

The three elves kneeled around the bowl and started to slowly chant. Morgan looked across at Cedric, to see if he understood any of it, but was met by a shrug of incomprehension. The chant was slow and sonorous, echoing off the cave wall like the drone of some giant bee. It seemed to gain in volume and power, as though it was not being chanted by a mere three elves but by a whole choir, full voiced and throaty. It was starting to make his head sore when, suddenly, the ruby at the centre of the bowl started to pulsate a deep throbbing crimson. Terath stopped chanting.

'It has started. I am unsure as to what happens next but at least one of you keep an eye on the lake!'

Morgan craned his neck to look but saw nothing on its shimmering surface. Cedric stood, so he could see the entire vista, but he, too, gave no indication of anything untoward.

This continued for some time, the deep chant, the ruby throbbing like a beating heart, steam from the bowl rising as a column up to the cave ceiling, but there was nothing to observe, either on the lake or elsewhere. Itheya said they did not expect success, he thought. Then, though, Cedric gave an excited squeak.

'Look! Over there!' he pointed at the lake's surface. Terath followed the man's finger, as did Morgan.

He saw nothing at first; the shine on the lake meant his eyes were constantly readjusting. But then there it was, like a painting, a painting that moved. It was a man's open hand, and at its centre was a red stone, pulsing just as the one in the bowl was. The vision moved, pulling away from the hand and turning until the face and upper body of the man could be seen.

'Ugh,' said Morgan. It was a horrible sight. The man wore a tattered black robe and his skin was waxy and pale. His open mouth appeared to be black inside and Morgan could not see any teeth or tongue. It was the eyes that drew him, though – they were enormous lifeless orbs of pure darkness, without whites or iris, and appeared to be weeping a substance from the corners which ran freely down over the waxy skin.

'What, by all the Gods, is that?' breathed Cedric.

The vision pulled backwards further and further till the man creature was but a tiny distant feature. They were looking at a wide lake, its impenetrable waters whipped by the wind and glittering in the winter sun. Beyond the lake lay miles and miles of reeds and rushes covering a land bereft of hill and mountain, in which only rare clusters of trees broke up the level horizon. Then from the lake rose a great beast, a colossal serpent bearing the tiniest of wings, putting Morgan immediately in mind of the golden dragon they had presented to Cenarazh about a week ago. It plunged again, disappearing beneath the surface and leaving a colossal wave in its wake that broke over the reed beds, briefly submerging them and sending the water birds into the air eager to escape the inundation. Then the vision disappeared.

They waited a little longer for something else to happen. Eventually another image appeared; this one, however, was too dim to make out clearly. 'Something is blocking it,' muttered Terath.

All they could see was shadow. There was the vaguest outline, a woman maybe, but it was very indistinct.

With a frustrated growl Terath removed the stopper from his bottle and added another pinch of red powder to the bowl. He and the other elves restarted their chant, increasing the power of their voices. As Morgan and Cedric watched, a clearer picture started to appear. It was a girl, thin, lightly freckled with long light-brown hair and large sensitive eyes. She wore an expensive dress and a beautiful green brooch pinned at her bosom. The vision swung to that of a great grey cliff crested with scores of ruined stone towers.

'The City of Light!' breathed Cedric.

They were looking at the girl again; she was looking puzzled and put her hand to her chest. Morgan made a mental note of every detail of her face and clothing, then the vision started to fade, becoming shadowy and indistinct again, until finally it was gone. They kept looking and looking but nothing returned. Terath and the elves stopped chanting and the pillar of steam petered out. Morgan looked at the bowl. All it contained were a few dried shrivelled leaves, everything else, including the ruby, had completely disappeared.

'Well, what do we make of all that?' asked Cedric. It was a half-hour later. All five of them had left the cave and were eating a lunch of flatbread, berries and jenessa in the small clearing outside.

'I think we have been successful,' said Terath. 'Unfortunately we have been far more successful than we had a right to be. Everything that we saw in the lake indicates a terrible truth.'

'What truth is that?' said Morgan. 'We saw a man creature and a snake dragon on a lake, and a young girl and this ruined city Cedric knows so well. What does that tell us?'

'The ceremony was designed to locate a dragonstone; we thought it would not succeed because the stones are dormant and we could locate them only at a relatively short distance anyway. The strange man we first saw was holding one in his hand. It was an active stone, Morgan, and he has raised a dragon with it.' Cedric sounded concerned. 'The only question is where?'

'The only landscape like that around Tanaren would be in the Endless Marshes. There are other marshes in the country but those seemed to be going on for ever. It could be nowhere else. Perhaps that is why we have heard nothing about it so far.'

'The other vision of Atem Sezheia and the girl was strange. Something was blocking it. I needed to draw on more power to make the image clear,' said Terath.

'But the City of Light is at the other end of the country to the Marshes, if the Marshes it were,' said Cedric. He scratched his head.

'Then there are two stones,' said Terath. 'We saw no dragon with the second set of images, so the process must be at an early stage. Remember the face of the girl, but for the time being it is the Marshes that are our immediate concern. Your war is not important compared to what we have seen. There is a raised dragon; it could kill more than the greatest army you could muster. No matter the result of the krasa, we three will ride with you when you leave. This creature has to be stopped and the answer to how this can be done lies in the script on the tooth; I am convinced of it.'

'So only we can stop it?' said Morgan disconsolately. He continued to eat the bread but, despite its freshness and the delicacy, it tasted like wood pulp in his mouth.

In the midst of the Aelthenwood, almost at its geographical centre, was a tall hill. No trees grew upon it; rather it was covered in long sweet grass from its base to its crown. It was flat-topped and, if one stood atop it, the entire Aelthenwood could be surveyed – east and west an unbroken line of trees with the jagged snow-capped mountains to the south and a grey swathe of sea to the north. It was a view with no equal in the forest but to its inhabitants it held a far greater significance. It was the political heart of the country of the elves.

The location of the krasa.

In total some fifteen tribes, their leaders and retinue had gathered there. It was the morning of the second day and the tribes were voting. It had been an exhausting time for Itheya and her brother, who had accompanied her. She had opened the debate with a long and impassioned speech and, once that was over, had spent the rest of the day and half of the night going from tribe to tribe – cajoling, persuading, bullying, haranguing and begging – in an attempt to sway them all to see her point of view. Now she was to find out if her efforts had been rewarded. At the centre of the hill was a large stone plinth which had been carved with many figures of beasts and birds with elves pursuing them with bow and spear. Time and the elements had worn many of these figures almost smooth and many of the subtleties of design created by the original craftsmen had been destroyed. Its function then as now, though, had remained unchanged. For at its centre was a hole under which was a deep bowl-shaped recess and it was into here that the votes had been cast. The elves used wolf claws and teeth as tokens, claws being yes votes and teeth no votes. The man to count them was a member of the Rengereth tribe, deemed to be as neutral in this case as it was possible to be. Itheya had expected her brother to argue against casting all ten of their votes in favour of the proposal but he had not said a word against it.

'In this, I shall not stand against you. I know how much it means to you, even if it does look like you stand foursquare with the humans.' This was in the hour before dawn when she had just finished speaking to everyone and was hoping for an hour or two's sleep. She was just grateful for his response and could not be bothered asking for the reasoning behind it.

Now, however, the counter of the votes was about to start. As he pulled each token out of the small pit, he would raise it and show it to each tribe in turn before calling out the result. This was to ensure no cheating could take place. It also meant that, with close to eighty tokens, to be counted, it was rather a slow and tortuous process. 'One tooth, a no,' he would call, before showing it to all and sundry. 'Overall total: six to four against.

Itheya was sitting on the grass next to her brother pensively watching the man. She noticed Cullenan, Mhezhen of the Ometahan, with his son Culleneron. Both were looking at her. The possibility of her marrying Culleneron at some point was one that had been long mooted.

'One claw, a yes,' called the man. 'Overall total: fifteen to twelve against.'

It was not going well. She consoled herself with the thought that she and her tribes had voted first so many claw tokens would be at the bottom and the last to be pulled out.

'What will you do if it is a no?' her brother asked.

'There is nothing to do. We return home and the humans leave unmolested.'

'You could still go with them; many riders would follow you.'

'Father wishes me to respect the vote and I agree with him.'

'Will you not miss the two humans? You seem fond of them.'

'My feelings in this case are not important. They rarely are.'

Dramalliel smiled. 'My poor sister, the reluctant queen.'

She shot him a fierce look. 'Say rather that I am one who fulfils her duty.'

'That I do not doubt, sister; I never have.'

'One tooth, a no. Overall total: twenty-three to twenty against.'

'How many votes are there, sister?'

'I believe seventy-eight.'

'Then there could be a tie.'

'If there is, then the proposal is defeated. We need a majority.'

'Then start praying for claws; numbers are running out.'

'One claw, a yes. Overall total: thirty-three to thirty-two against.'

'Careful, sister, your nails, you are digging them into your arms; you could draw blood.'

'I will draw blood if you are not quiet.'

'Votes are starting to go in your favour.'

'Our favour.'

'Of course, I misspoke.'

'Where did you learn to be so glib?'

'You and Father taught me; I had to do something to counter such righteous earnestness.'

'I swear by Zhun we cannot be of the same blood.'

'That is just wishful thinking on your part.'

'Then I shall keep wishing.'

'One tooth, a no. Overall total: thirty-nine to thirty-eight for. One vote remains.'

BOOK ONE: AUTUMN

Her brother said something but she didn't hear him. He was right, though – her nails had drawn a trickle of blood on her arm. Her jaw was locked solid with the tension.

'One claw, a yes. Final vote: forty to thirty-eight in favour. The proposal to send warriors into the human lands is accepted.'

A cry rang out from the assembled tribes; Itheya closed her eyes and whispered a silent prayer of thanks. When she opened them again, she saw Cullenan coming towards her with his son. She rose to meet them.

'Congratulations, Itheya' he said. 'Rarely has one so young carried a vote at the krasa. Granted the influence of your tribe helped greatly and the good wishes we all bear your father, who is respected by all here, but your achievement in this place stands on its own.'

'Thank you, Cullenan. So it is to be as we agreed.'

'Yes, I and my affiliates will supply two hundred horse, as will you and your allies. The deep forest tribes will supply a further fifty. Both you and Culleneron will jointly lead, commanding fully on alternate days. We will all meet at the agreed rendezvous at dawn three days from now. This agreement will last a year and will be conditional on the humans supplying us with iron and the release of further artefacts; a further krasa will be called in one year to see if this agreement is to be renewed. Zhun protect you all.'

Within the hour Itheya was speeding back to her people. It was not as many warriors as she had hoped and co-leading with Culleneron was bound to be problematic, but she had to be content with the result – it was a victory after all.

Her victory.

Back at the island, there was a whirlwind of meetings in a very short time. After Dramalliel had left to muster the horsemen, she saw her father, then Terath and Cedric, and learned about the rebirth of the dragonstones. She saw Morgan, who confirmed he would ride with them and act as their guide and escort, and then, after several other meetings to discuss logistics, supplies and other details, she retired to her room, exhausted. She had not been there long though when a servant brought the message. 'My Lady, your father wishes to see you.'

It was quite late. There were few people around as she strode, barefoot, into her father's room. He lay on his bed, his foot resting on a high stool. Two attendants were with him constantly but he dismissed them as she entered.

'You wished to see me, Father.'

'I did, yes. Come closer, I cannot see you.' She went towards the bed and knelt in front of him.

'That is better, my daughter; you will not have much time to yourself now and I needed to speak with you.' He swallowed loudly, 'First, I wanted to congratulate you on winning over the krasa; few here thought it could be done.'

'It was hard work, Father.'

'Nothing of worth can be achieved without hard work. Your success, however, will bring about problems of their own.'

She wrinkled her eyebrows. 'Whatever do you mean?'

'You will command the warriors jointly with Culleneron; this means you will be gone for some time – a year, maybe more.'

'Yes, Father. Culleneron is a fine warrior, though like many young men he is prone to foolhardiness and rash decision making.'

'I am sure you will manage him. My point, however, is when you leave here you will not see me alive again.'

She got to her feet. 'You cannot know that, Father. I...'

He raised his hand. 'No protests! We both know in our hearts this to be true.'

She choked slightly; her throat had dried.

'Now this is the problem, child. With you gone and me dead, your brother will command until your return, but – and I have my spies so I know the truth here – he will try to assume full power in your absence.'

She found her voice again. 'He would not dare! We are not back-stabbing humans. He would never have the support.'

'Did he object to you putting all ten votes towards your proposal at the krasa? I thought not. He wants you out of the way. He has many of the younger warriors on his side and few of them will be riding with you. He will seize power by force, if necessary, see you exiled and possibly plunge our tribe into a civil war that could severely damage our status as the pre-eminent tribe in the west.'

'No, I do not believe he could be so stupid and destructive.'

Cenarazh propped himself up on his pillow. 'He is not your little brother anymore; he is a man consumed with jealousy and ambition. With your duties taking you away from the island so frequently, you have not seen him change. As I have got worse, so the likes of Tiavon have been whispering poison in his ear. When you leave, the temptation will surely be too great for him.'

'But, Father, I have to lead the warriors; I cannot lose face like this.'

'Of course you must go, but there is a solution.'

She looked at him dumbly. 'What?'

He propped himself up on his elbow and pulled out the bolster cushion that he had been resting on. 'That you are named Mhezhen before you leave.' Itheya wrinkled her forehead and squinted at her father. 'How can that possibly be? I will be gone in under a day.'

Cenarazh spoke slowly. 'You can be named such if I am no longer here to hinder your progress.'

She was scornful now. 'Father, you are not going to die before I leave, the healers are sure of it.'

'No, I am not, not without assistance from a third party.'

Itheya switched from scorn to alarm in a trice. 'What are you saying, Father? What exactly are you implying?'

Cenarazh indicated the cushion he was holding. 'That I am no longer of use to the tribe, that it is time to pass the leadership on. On to the rightful heir, Itheya, on to you. Take this cushion and place it firmly over my face. Do not lift it until I stop moving.'

It took a second to register with her what he was suggesting. She took a couple of steps backwards, her face a mask of horror. 'No, Father, no! I cannot.'

He leaned forward a little, his pale face no longer shrouded in gloom. 'Listen to me, child. I love you. You are the finest daughter any man could have, but I cannot describe to you the pain I am in. When I rest it is dull, persistent, like I am being gnawed by rats in a dozen different places. When I move, it is as though my veins are liquid fire. The pain never stops, never eases. I am dying in agony, Itheya. I merely propose that you end my pain for me, that you release my spirit to Zhun and grant me peace. The fact that you will become Mhezhen is merely serendipity. Terath will be called to verify my death and he has been told to say there are no suspicious circumstances. There is no man more loyal.'

Itheya was rigid, her eyes wide, despite that she took the pillow from her father.

'You will never perform a greater, kinder duty than this,' he said to her.

Her voice was a strangled gasp. 'You ask too much, Father, I cannot destroy that which I love.'

'What you love is a husk, child, a shell. I am no longer the one that raised you, much of that person has gone already, eaten away by pain. Your thoughts must be with the tribe now, what I am asking you to do is for the benefit of our people, the people that we both must serve.'

She continued to resist. 'No. Even if I were to agree with you and were happy to let your spirit fly this world I could not do it by my hand. Why could not others perform this task or you yourself for that matter, why should it be me?'

Cenarazh coughed, a hacking cough that briefly coloured his yellow skin. 'I am too weak, child,' he finally said. 'Otherwise I would have already done so, and as for letting another end things for me, would you let them if you knew? Would you seek vengeance against this perpetrator? Would you believe him if he told you that I had commanded such a thing? Besides, as I have said, it would be an act of love, of mercy on your part. Please do not force me to order you to do it, for order it I will if I have to.'

She swallowed, her mind was racing, her throat dry. 'You would command me? You truly want this so badly you would order your daughter to...?' He nodded. She swallowed again. 'Very well, Father, if it is what you truly wish.'

'With all my heart,' Cenarazh whispered quietly.

She clutched the pillow firmly, her arms shaking. 'Father, I ... I still have so many things to say to you, so many things to discuss, to learn. I am not ready to command, I will be bereft...' She choked back a sob, her usual eloquence had deserted her.

'You have been ready for a long time,' he said. 'Now, please, prevaricate no longer, do what has to be done.'

He lay back and spread his arms wide. She placed the pillow over his face, it was almost as if somebody else was working her body, surely she could not be doing this?

But she was. Trying to steel herself, she pressed the pillow down firmly, trying to clear her mind, trying to ignore the choking sounds he would soon make.

She saw herself as a child riding her first horse, with him there smiling, encouraging her, always encouraging. She saw him again, holding her as she cried as the horse was put to sleep after breaking its leg. She saw him watching proudly as she sang and danced at her userazha, her ceremony to mark her passage into adulthood, and here she was now choking the very life out of him...

She abruptly hurled the pillow against the bedroom wall. He started gasping, dragging in great lungfuls of air. She buried her head on his chest, soaking it with her tears.

'I cannot, Father, I cannot. Forgive me, but I cannot do this.'

He gently put his hand around her head. 'It is all right, Itheya. I understand. Thank you for your loyalty, and your love.'

They both took a minute to compose themselves. When this was over she gently placed the pillow back under his head.

'You will be leaving tomorrow?'

'Yes, Father, we are all to meet at the Pass of the Knife the following dawn.'

'Then allow me to wish you the very best. May Zhun watch over you and bring you back safely.'

'Thank you, Father.'

'You had better go now.'

'Of course, Father. Sleep well.'

'I will try, my dear. Now get some rest; you will need it.'

She bowed low to him, kissed him on the forehead, and left the room, knowing deep in her heart that it was as he said – that she would never see him alive again.

BOOK ONE: AUTUMN

43

Ahead of them was a small island covered in trees and brush, sitting in the midst of a sluggish river that wound lazily eastward as if it could barely muster the effort. The land either side of it sloped gently to the water's edge; it was mainly grassy downland, broken up by the occasional tree or stand of bushes, a gentle valley amid the low chalk hills. The ground was heavy after the recent rains, the smell of sodden mud and grass was inescapable, and the horses threw up great clods of turf as they trotted over it.

At last, though, their hard ride northwards was over. A group of horsemen sat watching the island right now, the flanks of their steeds were steaming and white with sweat, testament to a hard ride. At their centre was Esric Calvannen, Baron and Chief Prosecutor of the War in the South. Next to him was the red-haired Emeric, leader of the Serpent Knights, and making up the rest of the group were Esric's chief allies, his fellow southern barons, Garal, Eburg, Josar and Spalforth. There was one other figure, too, a ruggedly handsome dark-haired man with pale-grey eyes, dressed in a black cloak.

Esric turned to Emeric, though his question was directed to all present. 'How many of them are there, do you think?'

'About fifty I would say,' said Emeric. 'They are dug in, won't move and are refusing to surrender.'

'I suppose the Gods could not accept all the islands surrendering to us. They had to leave one Arshuman curmudgeon refusing to accept our terms. Well, who are we to deny the Gods their sport, their daily ration of bloodletting? Remember though, take this island and the river Axe is fully under our control for the first time in years. It is quite an incentive. Are the boats ready?'

'Yes, Baron,' said Spalforth, a man with a beard so long he could tuck it into his belt. 'Twenty boats, each of which can carry eight to ten men. They are moored just over a mile away.'

'Very well, this is no encounter for horse. Josar, this is your land; you can join the landing party with me. In the meantime have the archers soften them up. Tell them to be careful, though; I want no wasted arrows.'

'Yes, Baron,' said Emeric. He put a horn that he always carried in his belt to his lips and sounded it.

'Mikel,' said Esric, 'can you do anything to flush out these men?'

The cloaked man pushed his horse forward so that Esric could hear him better.

'I could set a fire in the trees but that will hamper you and your men just as much as them. I am generally a practitioner of more subtle magics than that. Leave it with me. By the time you arrive their appetite for resistance will hopefully be greatly reduced.'

'Get to it then. Josar, come with me.' He spurred his horse onward, followed by the other barons. As he did so, the field behind him was filling with many lightly armoured men all of whom carried bows.

As he was told, barely a mile upriver he came to the boats; they were propelled by oar with three rowlocks either side. Nearly two hundred men armed with mace or sword and mainly armoured in mail or leather were waiting there for them.

'You know, Esric,' Josar said to him as they got near to the boats. 'There is no need for you to risk yourself in this skirmish. Leave it to me; we will soon flush these rats out.'

'No, my friend. The Grand Duke named me as Chief Prosecutor of the South; it is my duty to lead these men.'

'You are exposing yourself to unnecessary risk this way. You have proven your worth in battle many times; you can't seriously believe the men still call you the "Poet Baron" after all this time?'

'If I sit back and let others endanger themselves in my stead, then the name would be justified.' He lifted his helmet visor and stopped to inhale the sweet air off the river.

'Besides, Josar, there is more than a grain of truth in the name. I am a man who far prefers the indolent life of court to the shambles that is the battlefield. Can I help it if I prefer the lute and the muse, the company of educated women and the finest wines of Tarindia and Svytoia? The Gods have been cruel indeed to cast me from such a life.'

Josar laughed out loud. 'There are times, my dearest Baron, when you sound like a Lilac Palace eunuch, only a little more effeminate. Besides, I have read your poetry and believe me, having you thrown into battle and cast away from your pen, has been a blessing for us all. The Gods may have been cruel to you, but to us they have been merciful.'

Esric smiled. 'Emeric did once say that to make a prisoner talk all I need do is read to him one of my sonnets.'

'Keep doing that, Baron, and this war will be won in a week.'

They both laughed as they dismounted from their horses. Josar, a muscular fair-haired man with a week's growth of stubble, and the smaller, more intense Esric had been friends from childhood and constantly indulged in their favoured pastime of putting the other man down. After leaving the horses with the ostler and stable lads, they gave the order for the soldiers present to get into the boats.

'Six men rowing, one or two upfront holding their shields high, and one or two in the stern to steer and balance out the weight. They will try peppering us with arrows, so keep your heads down and when we get to the island try to beach the boats simultaneously. If we land piecemeal, then they can pick us off one at a time.'

'Calvannen!' the men shouted. 'Calvannen and Tanaren!'

Twenty boats pushed off from the bank trying to maintain spacing so that the enemy archers had more difficulty finding a mark. Slowly they rounded a bend and, once they had negotiated that, the island stood ahead of them in the distance.

Calvannen, in the lead boat, could see the sky was dark with arrows flying in both directions. He saw shadowy figures on the island ducking under the cover of the trees. His men on the bank were more exposed and he could see some casualties had already been suffered. This decided his next course of action.

'Speed up, lads; let's get to the island as fast as we can!'

All around him he could hear the grunting of men as they strained at the oars, putting the effort in to close the gap between them and their destination. There were inevitable collisions and much suppressed swearing as the small craft arrowed through the water, churning up wakes that caused the boats behind to lurch drunkenly as they rocked back and forth helplessly. Despite the chaos, though, progress was swift. Esric saw the men in the trees pointing frenziedly and knew they had been spotted. 'Heads down, prepare for their arrows!'

Even as he spoke, he heard the whistling of one such shaft as it skipped off his boat's hull and vanished under the water. More followed. Men were holding up shields to block them, but many shafts avoided them and landed inside the multitude of small craft. He could hear shouts and screams as arrows pierced arms, legs or more fatal areas. The man ahead of Esric looked up to see what was happening, and as he did so an arrow shot into the boat hit him square in the face. He dropped his oar and screamed, putting his hand to his face. As he writhed, the boat listed dangerously. Esric had already seen another capsize as the wounded tried desperately to escape their torment. The man ahead of him continued to thrash around in his agony; the arrow had entered his right cheek and its head had punched through the skin and was jutting out under his jaw. Without the rower, the boat had stalled and was heading towards the bank.

'You!' he said to the man next to him 'Sit on this fellow, try breaking the shaft and pull it out. If he doesn't stop thrashing around, kill him or we will all be going into the water.' With that he took the vacant oar space himself. He could hear the man behind trying to calm the stricken man, whose mad frenzy was weakening. The island was close now. The first of the boats had already landed; two now had capsized on the approach.

'My Lord!' the man behind him spoke. 'This fellow has died.'

'Xhenafa bring him safely to Artorus's side,' said Esric, pangs of guilt hitting him as he thought of his last order to the man. 'But we must complete the task in hand.'

With that, the boat slammed on to the low bank of the island. The men dropped their oars and, with a furious call upon the favours of Mytha, plunged into the trees. Esric followed, his sword drawn.

Once his eyes had adjusted to the twilight under the trees, he could see a savage broil going on barely twenty yards away. About twenty men from each side were desperately hacking away at each other. As he leapt to join them, he heard the crack of bone and an Arshuman fell backwards, his face a mass of blood and pulp – a Tanaren mace had done its worst. More of his own men landed and pushed under the trees. The Arshumans were surely doomed, though he had decided to show mercy should any of them surrender. He faced up to an Arshuman warrior, in a shirt and coif of mail, shield held low, sword held ready, obviously an experienced man.

They traded blows and both shields did their work. These Arshumans are stubborn fellows, thought Esric. And indeed they were holding their own, despite being outnumbered. The man assayed a vicious swipe to his head, but he ducked under it, countering with a savage thrust that the man barely parried. The noise of battle filled his ears for the thousandth time.

Then something strange happened. Before his eyes he saw what appeared to be wisps of black smoke, wrapping around the trees, wafting over the combatants. It smelt of nothing, though, and was not following the direction of the wind; it was almost as though he was dreaming it.

The effect on the Arshumans, though, was electric. The man facing him dropped his guard. His sword fell from his nerveless fingers, his mouth opened and closed, his eyes became the size of dinner plates. Esric realised his expression was one of pure unalloyed terror.

The man was too horrified to scream. Instead, he dropped his shield and fled directly away from the strange smoke, his countrymen following. Some slumped at the base of a tree trunk, covering their face with their hands and screaming as if in the grip of a primeval fear. Most, however, jumped straight into the river, trying desperately to get away from the smoke. Weighed down as they were with their heavy armour, none made it to the far bank. His own men stood dumbstruck at the bizarre turn of events. Josar, his face spattered with other men's blood, saw him and came over.

'See the benefits of having a mage? I have heard of such spells. He has conjured phantoms of pure terror for these men while we see only smoke. Congratulations, Esric, another fine victory.'

Esric appeared to overcome his surprise and decided to shout out a few orders.

'See these survivors are gathered together and bound. Strip them of equipment while I go and proffer thanks to the learned Mikel.'

'We all have our own specialist fields of expertise, Many of them overlap with other mages; sometimes, though, they are unique. I personally like to dabble with illusions, to confuse and obfuscate my victims. I shrouded those poor fellows with visions of their own worst nightmares. I have to confess I hoped they would collapse to their knees, not plunge into the water and so to their own deaths.'

'Indeed, many of them reacted as if they had seen Josar's wife for the first time.' Josar said nothing; he did not appear to disagree.

The brief and bloody skirmish had concluded about an hour ago and the barons and the mage were back on the riverbank evaluating the results – six dead and a dozen wounded to incapacity compared with at least thirty dead of the enemy with fifteen prisoners taken. All in all, a highly successful outcome.

'Oh, I have a message for you mage.' Esric had taken off his helmet and was letting the cool breeze dry his sticky hair. 'The lady Cheris in the north wishes you well and asks after who is feeding her cats? I hope this makes sense to you.'

Mikel smiled warmly. 'Ah, so you have met the divine Cheris herself, have you? She is a different sort of mage to me. In battle, whereas I tease and confuse my enemy, I would imagine she is far happier making them explode; and if she were here I would tell her that Elsa is feeding her cats and that they have very much taken to her. With any luck, though, I will see her myself before too long, so I can explain this to her personally.'

'It is strange how we are awash with mages at the moment. We have four with us now, I believe.'

'Yes, four it is,' Mikel replied. 'The college does not let us go cheaply. I imagine Leontius is spending a pretty hefty amount of coin on four at once.'

'He wants this war won and over with,' said Esric. A servant had brought him a goblet of thin ale which he drank greedily. He does not want it hanging over his tenure at the Ducal Palace. He is an ambitious young man who obviously has his own plans for his reign.'

As he spoke, a tall cadaverous man came to speak with him. He was thin as a lath and his ill-fitting mail shirt swung loosely at his sides. He wore a deep-blue surcoat bearing the emblem of a golden heron.

'Many salutations on a fine victory, Baron,' said the man. 'The river Axe is now under your sole control; things have not looked so promising in the south for many years.'

'Thank you, Eburg.' Esric acknowledged him with the tiniest of bows. 'But you know I am a naturally cautious man and will not rest easy until the entire south is free from the enemy; and that..., – he paused for effect – 'depends on occurrences in the north over the next few weeks.'

'As you say, Baron, and now, with your permission, I would like to take twenty of my men back home with me. I have many matters to attend to there and with winter coming I do not expect too many military developments to press into my, I mean, our time.'

'Of course, Eburg, but be ready if I call upon you.' 'That I will, Baron.' The man bowed and left them.

Josar watched him go, then spoke to Esric.

'You have told him nothing of your meeting with Felmere?'

'No, it is still too early, and I cannot yet trust him properly.'

Mikel broke in. 'Apologies if I appear impertinent, but am I missing something here?'

'That, my friend,' said Josar, 'is Baron Eburg of the town of the same name. Nary a few weeks ago his wife's son by her first marriage, his adopted heir, was discovered passing information to the Arshumans.'

'He was caught totally red-handed, in a secret meeting with their spies.' Esric continued. 'It cost him his head, which we sent to his mother. Eburg himself, it seems, has not been blessed by the Gods when it comes to fertility and has no natural progeny. Since that particular episode he has been at pains to ingratiate himself with me. He is terrified of losing his baronial seat.'

'It is a justifiable terror,' said Josar. 'We have many candidates, which Esric here, as Southern Prosecutor, has the legal right to raise to the status of Baron. Eburg is on shiftier ground than the marsh his town is built on.'

'I will be watching him keenly. Let it remain at that.' Esric turned and started off to the army's camp. When he arrived there he was saluted with much cheering and clashing of weapons on shields. As Josar had told him correctly, he was the Poet Baron no more.

44

Echoes. What was it about fog that caused every footstep, every breath, to resonate so starkly, so clearly, that it felt to Ceriana that she was on a stage with nowhere to hide. The harder she tried to hush her footfalls and control her breathing, the noisier she seemed to become and, in this town of absolute silence, the last thing she wanted to do was draw attention to herself.

The six of them had left the little boat at the pier, climbed the steep steps of the harbour wall, crept past the statue of Hytha, and were now standing on the street facing out to the sea. Even the sea made no noise here – there was just fog above them, below them and about them, enfolding them with its icy fingers, shortening their breath and making Ceriana's heart thump so violently she half expected it to see it explode out of her chest.

Wulfthram was in the lead, with Ceriana following closely behind him, as they walked slowly past dark lifeless cottage after dark lifeless cottage. Then he stopped.

'A tavern,' he said. 'If we are going to find anyone in this place, surely it'll be here.' Even he was trying to speak quietly.

They all looked at the gloomy two-storey building in front of them. The sign, displaying some sort of jolly fisherman, hung limply without moving over the dark oak door. There were two bowed thick glass windows that reflected no light in front of them. Ceriana tried peering through but could see nothing. 'Who's going in?' she asked.

'It's black as pitch in there,' said Haelward. 'It looks as deserted as every other place we've seen.'

'Hand me the lantern,' said Wulfthram, 'Strogar, Haelward, come with me; you three wait here; I reckon we will only be a minute.'

The door was not locked. As Wulfthram pushed it, it creaked slowly inwards, a noise that seemed a violation to the all-pervading stillness around them. Wulfthram looked at Strogar, who was a bull of a man, who in turn looked at Haelward, who in turn looked at the three people behind him. He raised his eyes, making Ceriana smile back at him.

Then the three of them disappeared into the tavern.

Ceriana looked around her. The moon was casting a ghoulish light on to the cobbled street and making both her and her companions faces look as white as a death mask. Derkss, a thin-faced man with a full growth of beard, held the remaining lantern. He looked as discomfited by their surroundings as any of them.

'Are you all right?' Ceriana asked him.

'Of course, my Lady; it is just that I am a simple enough man who would much prefer a stand-up fight to all this creeping around. And this place ... can't you feel it? It is as though it has been forsaken by the Gods.'

'Forsaken by the Gods!' Ceriana whispered to herself. 'Perhaps I am in the right place, after all.'

Ulian padded softly to the water's edge. The outline of their ship could barely be seen. After a little while, though, he asked out loud, 'Do you think this is a natural fog?'

'Why wouldn't it be?' Derkss replied nervously. 'These parts have many heavy sea fogs.'

Ceriana did not reply; the same thought had already occurred to her. What if the fog was the cause of everyone's disappearance? And here they were trapped in the middle of it. It was cold, too. Her cloak seemed to be doing nothing to protect her; the fog seemed to be passing right through it, her dress, her very skin. Her very soul seemed frozen by it.

The three men came out of the tavern. 'Nothing,' said Wulfthram. 'It looks like the place was full of people who for no reason at all decided to get up and leave. Mugs of ale not fully consumed, plates of half-eaten food, crumpled bed sheets. It is so strange.'

'The ale was still there, though.' Haelward was holding a bottle. The men passed it round, each taking a swig. Wulfthram passed it finally to Ceriana. 'Go on,' he said, 'show me how northern you have become.'

Without hesitating, she took a draught. By Elissa, it was horrible, but she was determined not to show it. She wiped her lips, gave the slightest feminine burp and handed it back to her husband.

'Have you nothing stronger than this pond water?'

There were laughs all round, and the laughter seemed as

incongruous as it was possible to be, given their surroundings. 'Let us check the town square,' said Wulfthram. 'Then we can return to the boat and leave further investigations till the morning.'

There was a narrow side street next to the tavern that led uphill towards the square. Its buildings were squeezed so closely to the roadside that it felt like they were deliberately hemming them in. The men drew their blades as the fog thickened the further they progressed. Finally, the street ended, the climb finished and they were on the level ground of the town's square.

It was a fairly nondescript square, cobbled and with a house of Artorus at its far end. The buildings here were taller, two-storey townhouses and warehouses with dark leaded windows; it was a place for the better-off people of the town, or at least it had been.

At the centre of the square was a fountain. In the height of summer it would have been a lovely place to sit, maybe to run one's fingers through the waters or feel the light spray caress one's cheek. None of the six people looking at it felt anything like that now, though.

For the fountain was frozen.

The air around them was cold but not freezing, certainly not cold enough to freeze moving water, but there the fountain was, its jets paralysed, twisting like frosted white chains, entwining but never reaching the unmoving pool underneath.

Wulfthram and Haelward moved towards the fountain; they started to walk around it but both stopped simultaneously when they saw what lay behind it. 'Mytha's claw!' breathed Haelward.

Lying on the ground behind the fountain were close to a dozen people. They were all dead; they were all frozen. All of them were holding their hands to their faces as if to ward off some unseen terror. Fear was writ large on all of them, their eyes wide, their mouths open as though their paralysis had started long before the frost overtook them.

'They are all men,' said Haelward as the others joined them. 'I wonder if they had sent the women and children away somewhere and decided to stay and fight for their homes.'

'But to fight what?,' said Derkss. 'What in this world can do this to a man?'

Nobody answered him. Wulfthram continued to walk the square and when he got to the house of Artorus he called the others to him. Ceriana walked up to him, expecting the worst.

She was not disappointed.

Pews and benches had been put behind the doorway in order to reinforce it, but both doors had been torn off their hinges and lay where they had been thrown, in the square about ten feet from the holy house. Some benches had been smashed into matchwood; others had been ripped in half as though they were made of paper. They slowly eased their way past this destruction and stood on the tiled floor at the centre of the church.

Against the far wall, all huddled together, were at least two dozen more people, all frozen in their death throes, many of them holding each other as though seeking comfort. It was as if the certainty of their fate was already apparent to them. And these were not young men. They were mainly women and children; some of the children were little more than babes in arms. They could not run, so they came here, hoping the Gods would protect them; but it was as Derkss said – the Gods had already forsaken this town. Ceriana choked back a sob. These poor people – none of them deserved this!

She turned and left the building. From this side of the square it was easy to see the hill and cliff top where the ruins stood. And now it was her turn to notice something. She waited for the others to join her and pointed up the hill.

Despite the fog and the darkness, the dark outlines of some of the nearer ruined towers could be seen, but it was not at these that Ceriana was pointing. Somewhere up the hill, amid the smoky white blanket shrouding the land, was a light. It was a sickly green in colour and it pulsated slowly, in a similar way to the stone at her breast sometimes did. She could not tell how far away it was, but every instinct told her that it was in that direction they should be heading.

Wulfthram evidently felt the same. He stood next to her, looked at it for a moment and said:

'Well, my dear, I don't think we need bother hiring a guide after all.'

And with that he starting walking, heading straight towards the hill. After a deep breath Ceriana touched the amulet of dull iron and followed. Behind her, she heard Haelward mutter: 'I hope the Gods are watching tonight. Artorus help us, have I ever done anything braver?'

No, she thought, none of us have.

45

There was a grille in the roof of his cell. Cygan knew he was underground and that the grille opened out on to the stone floor of the courtyard of this baron's enormous house, but for Cygan it was the only source of light in this cramped miserable little chamber. Moisture dripped through it – where it slid down the walls the stones were streaked with moss and where it pooled on the floor it stained the already-filthy straw black.

He wasn't quite sure how many days he had been here. He thought back to when he was bundled into the wagon, his hands and feet shackled, and the short journey along the river's edge to the town where he was now being held. The trading post had been the only settlement of the Taneren he had ever seen and his shock at seeing this much larger city, with its smells of leather, horse, and dung and the press of unwashed citizens, had been great. He was, of course, something of a curiosity to them and it was almost a relief when they passed through the great gates of this mansion and he had left the wide-eyed and pointing populace behind. There he was handed over to a large slack-jawed hulk of a man named Cornock, who had thrown him into this tiny cell, though not until after he had spat on him, called him a murderer and remarked on how much he was looking forward to see him dance at the end of a rope. And here he had remained. The cell stank, the door had only been opened once a day for feeding purposes, and he had seen and spoken to no one in all this time.

Which brought him back to the grille and the small square of light that it cast on to the stone wall in front of him. He would watch it move as the day progressed, from dawn – when it would appear on the cell door – to nightfall – when, if there was no moon, it would disappear on the wall against which he now sat. He tried to keep focusing on it, thinking of the freedom that it represented, a freedom he was not likely to experience again. He deliberately did not think of his wife and children, not while hope still remained. To dwell on his wife's dark, intelligent face and his children, laughing and shouting as they played outside their home, would be to weaken him, to make him think of what he had to lose – and right now he was still alive and charged with a mission from the Elder. However remote the possibility of him discharging his duty, while the possibility remained, then his duty was all that mattered and he had to be strong for that.

How or what he could do to accomplish it, though, was another matter. He knew a little of the society of these people from snippets of conversation picked up at the trading posts and with conversations held with the more amenable merchants there. He believed the Baron would look at the details of his case and pronounce judgement, and that he had the right to speak before him before sentence was pronounced. It was likely to be his only chance to warn these people of their folly; if they ignored him, the Malaac would be here soon enough. What would happen to his village and his people, though, he did not want to think. He had no real inner conviction that Cerren's brave sacrifice would grant the protection the Gods had promised.

Suddenly the silence was broken. He heard the sound of a bolt being drawn back and the key being turned in the lock. He went and stood with his back to the far wall as the door was slowly opened, its hinges groaning in protest. In the doorway stood Cornock, his forearms bare, his mouth open in a sneer that showed his blackened teeth. He came into the cell followed by two other men Cygan had not seen before. He noticed, though, that they were both almost as muscular as the jailor.

Cornock folded his arms. One of the men behind him was holding a flaming torch. It gave off little light but made the jailor's black eyes glitter like two pits of obsidian. Cygan noticed the man dribbled slightly; maybe his teeth were giving him problems.

'Well, Marsh Man,' he said, 'we have just had some good news, good for us that is. A herald has just arrived to say the Baron will be here tomorrow. Apparently, he has business to attend to.'

'Yes,' laughed one of the men behind him, 'the business of hanging you.'

Cornock said nothing. Instead, he started pulling the fingers of his left hand, clicking each knuckle in turn.

'It is true – holding the local justice hearings is one of his chief duties. Magistrate Onkean has written the deputation in your case; I am sure he will hear it in the next few days.'

'Then I will be brought before your baron?' asked Cygan. 'I will be able to speak with him?'

Cornock sniggered, then without warning he back-handed Cygan across the face. Cygan did not fall but stood to face the man almost immediately, a thin line of blood trickling from the corner of his lip.

'And what exactly do you think our baron' – he emphasised the last word – 'would want with a barbaric little sewer rat like you. You think you have rights here? You are not even a citizen of the country; an Arshuman dog is more important than you to us. Just because you have managed to stop scratching the fleas on your arse long enough to speak a civilised language does not make you a human being and that' – he stopped to clean some wax out of his ear – 'is exactly how Baron Eburg will see you.'

'He would be a fool not to listen to me.' Cygan stood tall and unflinching, matching Cornock's stare. 'His people are in as much danger as mine. That includes you. You would be a very tasty meal for the creatures that are attacking us, and...' – he paused to let the words sink home – 'if they were to feast on your corpulence, it would be the first thing I could give them credit for.'

Cornock glowered menacingly. 'See, boys; what we have here is an uppity Marshie, one as thinks he is as good as us.' He moved closer to Cygan, close enough for his fetid breath to be smelled. 'Just be grateful that we need no information from you, boy; otherwise there would be nothing to stop me from applying hot brands to your scaly marsh flesh. One thing though' – he moved backwards a couple of feet so the men behind could hear him clearly – 'you really should not have tried to escape; using force to restrain you should never have been necessary.'

Cygan quietly flexed his arms; he could see where this was going. He could see the man with the torch fixing it to the wall bracket so that he was now unencumbered. He had to say it. 'But I have not tried to escape.'

'Is that right, Marshie? Even with the door open and just me between you and freedom?'

As soon as he said the last word he swung a powerful fist straight at Cygan's face. The Marsh Man was too quick for him, though, ducking under the blow and landing one of his own straight into Cornock's stomach, winding him. The two other men piled in and Cygan bloodied them both before numbers took their toll and he was overpowered. Cornock kicking him viciously to the ground.

The three men stood over Cygan for a second, breathing heavily and feeling their bruises. Then, all together they started, kicking and punching the prone man again and again and again. When they had finished, they stopped for breath, their knuckles bruised and bloody. And then they started all over again. And over them, through the grille, the moon rose, its pallid light the only witness to the three men, who all laughed as they continued the work they relished.

46

Cheris had never felt so completely and utterly terrified. She was lying back in her chair, able to move nothing except her eyes. The drug she had been slipped was still having a powerful effect on her; she should really be feeling woozy and tired but the presence of a madwoman just a few feet away, calmly preparing to commit an act of pure horror, meant that, if nothing else about her was working, her mind was racing like one of the Grand Duke's thoroughbred racehorses.

She saw Marcus sitting opposite her. Unlike Cheris, he had some limited movement of his hands and mouth. If anything, he looked even more frightened than she did.

'Anaya,' he croaked. 'Do not do this. Only a handful of people have ever succeeded at doing what you are trying to do. Think hard and see; you have neither the strength nor the ability.'

Anaya stopped what she was doing for a second and looked up, annoyed at the break in her concentration.

'That remains to be seen. Nevertheless, I have to try.'

Marcus sounded desperate. 'You are exhausted; you will never control the powers you want to unleash.'

'I should have given you a stronger dose, kept you as quiet as the girl. I am not stupid. I will be summoning a minor demon only; it should be sufficient for my plans. As soon as it is here, I chant the words of binding and he is mine. Now, let's take some blood from you both.'

She went up to Marcus with a small but sharp knife and a metal bowl. Lifting up his sleeve she cut him across the arm, holding the bowl under the wound and catching his blood, almost black in colour as it dripped freely. This done, she put her hand over the cut saying a few soft words. When she took her hand away the bleeding had stopped. She then turned towards Cheris who stared at her imploringly.

'Now, my dear, it is your turn; your blood is very important for the ritual.'

She lifted Cheris, sleeve up and repeated the procedure. Cheris could hear her blood dripping into the bowl but felt no pain; the drug had numbed her too much.

Anaya returned to her table and stood behind the bowl at its centre. She poured the blood into it then ran the knife over her hand, adding her own blood to the mix.

'The blood of three mages, Marcus; what demon could possibly resist that?'

She then turned the pages of her book until she found the required passage, somewhere near its end. After scanning its words briefly, she started to chant – not the formal arcane language they learned at the college but something older. It had its similarities, though, and Cheris could recognise parts of it. She could certainly feel its power – the air around them started to crackle like wood in a fireplace.

Marcus was getting more feeling back in his hands; he could almost move them freely now, though his arms still resisted him. Cheris saw that Anaya had not noticed this and started to hope that Marcus would be able to use his magic again very shortly. She tried moving her toes but it was like trying to push back a mountain. The air at the room's centre between Anaya and herself was shimmering now and the temperature was rising. This and her own fear were making her sweat; she could feel it on her face and under her robes, trickling down her legs and between her breasts. A droplet then fell off her nose. Elissa help her, but it was getting hot as a furnace.

Anaya continued to chant but Cheris noticed a high-pitched edge of excitement to her voice, obviously what she wanted to happen was not too far away. Marcus tried pleading with her one last time.

'Desist, Anaya! This is madness. Please, before it is too late!'

Anaya ignored him and continued chanting; she was speaking faster and faster now and from the bowl in front of her blue flame was now licking at its edges.

Cheris continued to watch her but then realised something else was happening. A shape, a very dark and as yet amorphous shape, was beginning to materialise at the centre of the room, between Cheris and Anaya. As yet it had no form, a whirling mist of midnight black, but Cheris could feel its power, its malevolence, its anger.

And it was growing. As Marcus and Cheris watched, as helpless as children, the shadow grew taller; it was a darkness reaching past the beams to the very roof and they both knew it could get taller still. Anaya stopped chanting for a second and laughed.

'Do you see? Do you see? It is a demon of fire, and it is coming!'

Fire, thought Cheris dully. She then realised her body allowed her to do one thing. She felt the wetness on her face and realised she was crying.

The black shape continued to gather form. Cheris suddenly understood that it was not the demon itself; rather it was the void between the two planes that Anaya had created. The demon was still being pulled from its home and when it arrived here it would inhabit the space she had prepared for it, a space not six feet away from her. Ten foot tall, she reckoned, maybe six broad – it would be a pillar of living flame. Cheris had dreamt fancifully before of her final hours, in which she lay abed surrounded by friends praying for her. What would she be thinking? she had wondered. Would she be ruminating on the nature of the Gods? Would she have any regretful feelings? And now here she was, never closer to her doom, and she saw that her terror had driven any real thought processes away. She was frightened and helpless and right now didn't give a fig for the Gods. And what was Marcus doing? He must have regained some feeling in his legs and feet for he appeared to be trying to upset the chair on which he sat. Was he trying to escape? Was he going to leave her? The thought made her choke.

And then she saw what he was doing. Behind him, against the wall, leant their staffs. If he could just get his hands on one, maybe, just maybe, he could do something to save them. She started willing him on desperately, but then she afforded a look to her left, at the void of blackness.

Except it was a void no longer. As she watched, she saw red and white flame start to appear inside it, barely a flicker at first but getting ever larger. Marcus saw it, too, and his scrabbling with the chair became ever more frantic. It started getting warmer again, her robes feeling ever more uncomfortable against her skin. As Anaya had promised, the demon was coming.

Anaya herself had never seemed so animated. As the whirling column of flame grew before her she seemed impervious to its heat; rather her face shone with excitement, her skin flushed pink in the glow of the creature before her, her eyes wild, like a child witnessing the sea for the first time.

And then it was here. To Cheris it appeared as little more than a roaring column of flame, but she knew it was so much more than that. It had intelligence, a powerful will, and, most of all, a seething wrath against its summoner, the being that had sucked it into this dry plane, like a shark in a desert. It knew it was doomed here, in a world nearly devoid of the magical forces it needed for its survival. All it could do was feed on the little energy available, and the mage that had called it forth would be its first victim.

Helpless and terrified, all Cheris could do was watch the events play out before her. She heard a crash and realised that Marcus had fallen off the chair and was slowly but frantically trying to pull himself towards his staff. She looked at Anaya, a tiny figure before the burning demon. She was attempting the binding ritual Cheris realised, the attempt to subjugate the creature to her will. However, Cheris could see that the presence of the writhing twisting pillar of fire just a few feet away from her was proving unsettling. After flicking desperately over a few pages of the book, Anaya started to speak the ritual, but her voice was faltering, hesitant, unsteady. Then Cheris heard the voice. The demon was a magical creature and could enter the heads of those with a similar sensitivity, and it was there she could hear the voice; it was all fury, all hatred.

'What is this? Who has called me to my doom?'

Anaya did not answer but continued to read from the book; the heat was affecting her now all right, rivers of sweat poured down her nose, off her brow and into her eyes, making it ever more difficult for her to read without making mistakes.

'You are too late, flesh creature; your words cannot have any effect on me.'

Still she ignored the voice, she had nearly finished, she was nearly there, the demon would soon be hers to control.

'And still you try. Tell me, creature, how can you read without your eyes?'

Cheris whimpered softly at this. Despite all she had done, Cheris felt desperately sorry for Anaya, but she couldn't look away; she couldn't avert her eyes as a gout of near-white flame shot forth from the demon straight into the other woman's face.

With a piercing scream Anaya collapsed behind the table. The demon slid forward towards her. The table ignited and Cheris saw the roof beams beginning to blister and smoke. Her lungs and throat became dry and choking; she hoped the smoke would kill her before the flames could. She almost willingly inhaled their acrid poison. Let it be done with, there was no escape after all. She commended her soul to the Gods.

There was more terrible shrill screaming. Cheris's stinging eyes watched as the demon moved back to its original position. This time, though, at its burning heart, suspended several feet above the ground by forces she didn't comprehend, was Anaya.

Or rather the thing that had been Anaya. Cheris beheld it as its screams ceased. She watched as hair and flesh blackened and melted to nothing. She watched her face, bereft of eyes, liquefy and evaporate away from the skull, the mouth open in noiseless agony; she saw her robes burn off her and the tallow under her skin ripple and slough off her bones. The smell of burnt flesh, like a spitted pig, made Cheris gag, bringing bile to her throat. Finally, it was just the bones that remained crackling and popping in the flames, flames that turned whiter and burned hotter as then, in one final dramatic flourish, the skeleton disintegrated, imploding in on itself, fragments of bone no larger than dust particles floating up to the roof where the thatch had started to burn.

Then Cheris realised the demon was slowly moving towards her.

She was beyond terror now, gibbering like a child, the Gods a distant memory. She felt the thing's heat, her robe soaked with sweat, her hair glued to her face. She tried moving and for the first time her toes and fingers responded, they moved slightly. But it was a pathetic, futile gesture, too little too late.

BOOK ONE: AUTUMN

The vast tower of flame was almost upon her. She looked up at it, and in its fire she thought she could see the outlines of a face or, more accurately, a skull of death. It regarded her for a second through two empty pits that could have been eyes. She looked back at it, unsure if terror was making her hallucinate – demons were not supposed to have eyes. Behind and above it the roof blazed; she could even see a couple of night stars.

'Your power is mine, surrender to me, be as fuel to my great majesty, let it be the purpose for your brief and futile existence.'

Cheris was weeping now, but the tears dried in the heat before they could run down her face. Anaya had visited Keth's furnace upon them, a veritable vision of the underworld. She swore softly to herself as the hem of her robe started to smoke, and then start to crisp at her feet, with the slightest flicker of a blue flame beginning to catch at it. 'Oh fuck, fuck, fuck,' she quailed.

Just in front of her face she saw the wall of flame bulge slightly. From the body of the demon an appendage of pure fire emerged slowly, about the same dimensions as a human arm. It obviously knew of her helplessness, for it seemed to be toying with her. It stopped about eight inches from her face and started to wave and twist in front of her. Then, at last, Cheris found her voice, dry and raspy with the heat and her fear.

'Just do it you bastard, just do it, you filthy ... abomination!'

The demon paused for a second as though surprised; the flame on Cheris's robe crept a little higher as smoke rose from the rest of the garment and her hair.

Then there was another noise. Slowly and uncertainly, like a new-born deer, Marcus rose to stand unsteadily before the monster, one hand leaning on the table, the other clutching his staff, which shone like a shard of ice in his hand.

'Leave the girl be and face a man, why don't you?' His voice was strong, firm and commanding.

The demon stopped again. The arm of flame remained perilously close to Cheris's face, but, for a few seconds, was completely still.

'Tenetrej pulo ataralius,' said Marcus, raising his staff.

There was no response from the demon. For one second, maybe less, all was still. Cheris heard her pounding heart and saw Marcus standing proud before the monster. Then, without warning, the arm of flame shot forward to cover Cheris's face, upper body, and finally her legs, clothing her in white immolating fire.

How the girl screamed – she did not realise the power in her lungs. All of her terror, her fear, her pain was released in that scream. She saw the flames licking over her; she could hear their gleeful crackle surrounding her. It was the ghastliest doom she could imagine.

Then the flames were gone.

Then the flames were gone and she was still sitting there, hot but untouched. Her flesh had not melted from her bones; her eyes had not liquefied. Even the flames on her robe were no more. She looked at Marcus, who looked back at her with the gentlest and saddest of smiles.

'Be strong, Cheris! Be the mage I know you can be. Know that I love you, as a father loves his daughter.' He then turned from her and faced the demon whose howls and snarls resounded in her head.

'Come on, you vile spawn of Lucan. Let us return to the void together!' And with that his staff blazed white, and a bolt of pure magical frost shot forth at the demon's heart. Its white flame turned a cool blue and Cheris recognised a change in its howling. It was in pain.

The blackened beams of the cottage suddenly started to collapse as clumps of burning thatch started to rain down upon them. Marcus's robe was on fire, and his hair was starting to burn. She began to realise the nature of the spell he had put on her, a protective spell; she could not cast or even move while it lasted but it was an impervious layer, a second skin. It could resist flame, falling beams and thatch, anything that would threaten her. It would last too, maybe for hours, even after the death of its caster. Exactly as Marcus must have intended.

Marcus and the demon circled each other even as the flames consumed the cottage. The timbers of the walls were burning now, the daub blackening and disintegrating. Marcus stopped, held his staff up high and cried out.

'Stoviatum clamelis san drekovium!'

BOOK ONE: AUTUMN

He was still swaying on his unsteady legs but with that last cry he summoned the last of his strength and leapt straight at the demon, disappearing into its fiery heart. The demon roared again; it was in terror this time, though, and, as Cheris watched, its flame cooled, white to red, red to blue, and then from its base up to its tip, a full ten feet, it started to freeze. The flame stopped dancing and flickering and within seconds it had become a column of pure blue ice, completely solid. Like the great ice pillars of the north that the sailors told fanciful tales of. All around it, though, the cottage burned, the fires glittering on the many facets of the silent demon.

And then the demon exploded.

Shards of pure ice shot everywhere, bouncing off her protective skin, flying into the sky, where a great pillar of smoke was forming, and hissing into the flames. She half expected to see Marcus appear at its centre, smiling at her or scolding her for some minor misdemeanour, but he was nowhere to be seen.

Her mind was too active to digest this fact properly, but as she lay in the midst of it all the entire cottage finally collapsed. A great roof beam fell towards her but bounced off to land a couple of feet away. The walls either side of her crumbled, the thatch, glowing and smouldering, flew into the night air and finally she was smothered by a pall of smoke, dust and mortar. It continued to burn on top of her and, though still protected, the drugged wine and heightened terrors of the evening finally did their work and she passed out of consciousness, into a dream of pure darkness.

She was woken by the dawn chorus. It was a harsh noise as the trees around her appeared to be dotted with crows. There was a foul taste in her mouth and she spat out a mouthful of dust and ash. This caused a fit of choking and her nose and eyes ran black. Carefully she got to her feet, brushing off dirt, burnt wood and daub, emerging in a billowing grey cloud. All about her was a scene of utter devastation. She stood at the centre of what was once a cottage but was now nothing more than a pile of still-glowing embers amid piles of black-and-grey spoil. A smouldering tower of black smoke rose into the air before being picked up and dispersed by a brisk northerly wind. She stood and tried to walk, grimly aware of the picture she painted.

Her hair, face and clothes were filthy, coated in grey and black powder which she felt she would never wash off. She slowly made her way out of the confines of the cottage, climbing over the charred remains of what was once a door. Once she had done that, she turned and looked about her, the import of last night's events slowly creeping into her consciousness.

Marcus was dead. Anaya was dead. Marcus had died to save her, she thought; he could have placed the protective field around himself but had chosen not to. She thought of his final words to her and choked back a sob; he had been with her throughout all her time on the island. She could not remember life without him. How shall I tell Gilda? she thought to herself. As for Anaya, she had obviously toyed with this plan for a long time, probably with no real intention of following it through, until her exhaustion and threat of recall to the island had pushed her over the edge. Cheris hadn't known her that well – she stayed mainly on the Isle of healing after all and Cheris had only been in her early to mid-teens when she had left – but she had seemed a good person, if too strained and driven. Anyway, no one deserved to die like that. No one.

She spent a little while scrabbling through the ruins; she wasn't quite sure why. Perhaps she was looking for signs of Marcus, anything, something she could mourn properly, but it was a fruitless search. She did find a couple of things, though. First, her staff and its blade, both untouched by the flame. She had expected no less. Magical staffs, after all, had all sorts of protective charms woven into them. Anaya's staff was there, too, but she left it untouched. She would tell the knights about it when she saw them.

The second discovery was a little more surprising. One of the few features of the house still standing was the stone fireplace. Close to it, under a pile of ash, she saw a shape that intrigued her. She kicked the detritus away, first with her foot and then with her hand. How in the name of Keth had that survived? Leaning forward, she put her hand in the dirt and pulled out a book. It was Anaya's book, the one that had so terrified

Marcus. There was something disquieting about its binding; it felt like a thick hide or skin and was yellowish in colour. Inscribed on it in a flowing hand was the title *'Shtia Demontia nenneven azhatrneko'*. She opened it and scanned its hand written pages briefly.

She wondered at the language Anaya was speaking last night. It sounded similar to Elvish, but the dialect was unfamiliar to her. And now, in front of her, was the corroboration. It was a form of Elvish, as she had suspected. All mages had to have a working knowledge of the language; magic was originally learned from the elves after all. No doubt that, after a little hard work, she would be able to understand it, but that was obviously out of the question. It was a book concerning demonic secrets and their summoning after all. She would take it with her and give it to Sir Norton.

And what would she tell the knights when she saw them? She did not want to tell them of Anaya's folly but after a quick study of the facts she saw she had no choice. She couldn't leave the book lying around and she was just too tired and fragile to think of concocting some feeble lie which no doubt would be torn to shreds by the knights in seconds. Anyway, it was damning evidence against the complacency of the college in keeping someone here for far too long. No, the truth was the best policy here.

She walked up to the well, drew some water and emptied the whole lot over her head, washing the grime and filth off her face and hair. The shock of the water made her shudder, snapping her out of her tiredness, if not her sadness. Her robe, its hem torn and burnt, the rest of it coated in grey-and-white ash and black soot was beyond redemption. She hoped the knights had a spare one for her. She shivered in the morning air; hopefully, they would have a cloak for her, too.

Carrying the staff and book she went towards the woodland path, heading southwards back to the knights. Before she started off she turned for one last look at the scene of the previous night's tragedy. She started to think properly about what had happened and for the first time a deep sense of loss started to hit her. Her heart started to flutter up into her throat and her eyes brimmed with tears.

'Goodbye Marcus,' she whispered hoarsely, then without looking back she turned and headed down the path.

She had not gone far when she stopped. Was it her or did she just hear a twig break? She waited, still as a statue, straining her ears for the slightest sound. If only she could tell those birds to shut up for a second! Nothing came to her, though; she must have imagined it. After scanning the trees one more time she carried on.

She was half expecting to meet the knights on the path. Surely they had seen the smoke and would have come to investigate? She kept rehearsing what she would say to them when she did see them; she was already resigned to bursting into tears. On her own, she could be fairly self-contained, but in front of others her emotions would be laid bare; she knew everything would come welling to the surface and she hoped she could at least retain an element of self-control. It then dawned on her that she would be expected to fight in battle a few days. The thought chilled her to her marrow. Even this walk was tiring her out – how could she be expected to take on an army in her current state? Perhaps Felmere would excuse her this time. Knowing his eagerness for this battle, though, somehow she doubted it.

At long last she espied the clearing and the silhouette of the caravan close to the stone steps leading down from the path. She felt relief washing over her. Being on her own felt strange, disturbing. Years and years at the college living cheek by jowl with so many other people meant that she was used to noise, gossip, friendship and arguments. Her trips to the sea rose garden were one of the few times she could have time on her own, almost. And right now the thought of seeing a familiar face felt like a balm to her shattered nerves.

She reached the steps and climbed down them, casting about for a sign of one of the knights. She saw no one, though. After leaning her staff against the side of the caravan and placing the book next to it, she walked around the clearing, fully conscious of what a sight she must be.

There was no one there.

'Sir Norton?' she tried calling out but her voice was still croaky.

The remains of the knights' fire was there and their tents, but she could see the fire had died hours ago.

'Sir Norton!' she called again, firmer this time; she felt her nerves tingle slightly and tasted bile in her throat. Her damp hair made her shudder slightly.

The clearing and campsite were deserted, that much was clear, so where could they have gone? She had not passed them, so they must be further down the road. And where were the horses? They would have kept them tethered surely? Unless, of course, they had to ride off somewhere. Biting her lip slightly she passed the clearing and continued onwards down the southward path. It was much wider here, and muddier, she had to pick her way along the path to avoid the water-filled wheel tracks and other muddy pools that dotted it. Eventually she gave up; seeing there was a high kerb of grass to the right she clambered up it and continued slowly on her way.

She had not gone far when she saw something through the trees; the pale sun had caught something white making it flash like a star – only for a second, but a second was enough. She climbed down from the kerb, crossed the path and went to investigate.

She stumbled on a tree root and was whipped by some trailing nettles, stinging her hand. She stopped and sucked her wounded fingers. She had had enough of woodland to last an eternity. After a silent curse to herself (Elissa help her, her language was appalling these days; it must be being around so many soldiers), she continued onwards.

She broached another tiny clearing and stopped dead in her tracks, her eyes like saucers. The white flash through the trees had been a cloak, one of the knight's cloaks. Not ten feet away from her, in a neat row, lay all the knights, all of them dead and spattered with blood. A quick perusal showed that they had had their throats cut, and from the way the blood had run it appeared that this had been done when they were lying down, in their sleep maybe. Sir Norton was there, his eyes wide and glassy and the fear, which she had held in abeyance for a few hours, returned to her tenfold.

And then it was that sound again, the breaking twig, immediately behind her. She whirled around, ready to raise her hand and use the force spell on any assailant, but she was far too late. Three men had crept up behind her almost noiselessly. Two of them grabbed an arm each and one placed a hand firmly over her mouth. She tried kicking out, but a moment later was lifted clean off the ground. They were all so much stronger than she was, though it didn't stop her wriggling and struggling, however fruitless the end result.

There were a couple more figures in the trees coming towards her. One was slight and looked no more than a boy. The other was the exact opposite, a hulking man, broad-shouldered and powerful. The sun shone in their faces, meaning she couldn't see them clearly, but there was something familiar about the big man. Then he spoke and her worst fears were realised.

'I told you, boys, she was a feisty one. I am glad she survived; she will entertain us all for the next hour or two.' Sir Trask stepped forward into the clearing and stood not five feet from her, stroking his bald head. He had forsaken his mail and wore riding leathers like the other men. Behind him was a boy, maybe fifteen or sixteen years old. He looked like he didn't even shave. Trask turned to him.

'Bring the horses up to the clearing, and don't look so frightened. Today is the day you lose your virginity after all. You three, gag her and tie her hands; without them she is just another woman.' Then at last he spoke directly to her.

'We followed you last night,' he said with a smile. 'We were going to cut your throats as you slept, just like we did with these knights, but then you went and started your little bonfire. So we had to wait and watch for survivors, to ambush you before you could fry us. I would like to thank you for doing two-thirds of the job for us; it means we can take more time with the remaining third. And, believe me, we will take our time – weeks in the field have made the boys ... hungry, if you know what I mean, and a delicate little specimen like you is just the perfect answer.'

He turned and started to walk away. 'Bring her to the clearing and keep her angry; it's all the better when they wriggle.'

They started to carry her, like a sack or piece of baggage, laughing as they went. Cheris felt empty, a hollow vessel. Nothing more could be done to her surely. She just hoped they killed her quickly; she realised dully that there was nothing else she wanted, nothing she wanted at all anymore. Just death and eternal sleep.

47

'Right. So what do we do know?' Ceriana hunched her shoulders and stared straight ahead into the gloom.

The climb up the hill had taken about half an hour. There was a path cut through a narrow defile in the hillside with room for two people to walk abreast. This they had followed until it had opened out on to the grassy hilltop. At last, she saw they were among the ruins. And, despite the fog shrouding everything, she could tell immediately that these ruins were not of human origin. Architecture in Tanaren was square or rectangular – large functional blocks of stone put together to make buildings in which practicality was all. There were exceptions, the Grand Cathedral, the Ducal Palace, but in most cases aesthetics were a secondary consideration. Obviously, the Wych folk had seen things differently. The towers that had not collapsed were tall and elegant, reminding her rather of delicate ladies' fingers. They were circular in design and she noticed, at least in one tower where the wall had partially collapsed, a narrow but elegant spiral staircase. Fragments of marble still covered some of the steps, though most had long been stripped off by looters. There were graceful colonnades holding up long-vanished ceilings, floor mosaics all broken up and obscured by grass, and fragments of high walls and parapets with fluted walkways. At its peak, the city must have been a joy to behold. But its peak was long ago and, of course, its destruction had been partly due to her ancestors carving out their own territory on the backs of this now long-departed people.

Her companions were not in such a reflective mood, except perhaps for Ulian, who stopped briefly to contemplate the wonder still visible in the murk.

'If only circumstances were different and I had more time,' he said. 'Cedric did invite me to come with him on more than one occasion, but fool that I am I always declined. I have never been one for travel.'

'All my life I have lived in castles and palaces, surrounded by cities that are little more than shanty towns, but this is an entire city built like a palace – it goes on for miles and miles.' Ceriana spoke in hushed tones, the fog still oppressed her.

'And the others are leaving us behind,' he replied quickly. 'Come, let us not get lost in this mist.'

They quickly caught up with the others, who had struck a path towards a cluster of three small and crumbled towers surrounded by an encircling wall that was pierced by a single delicate archway, narrow and slender. It was through this that the strange light shone. The wet grass soaked the hem of Ceriana's thick velvet dress and her thin shoes, already derided by her husband as utterly impractical, offered her no protection from either wet or cold. She drew her cloak closer around her.

'Footprints,' said Haelward. He indicated a patch of grass bruised by several booted feet. The grass was springy but had not yet recovered from its trampling.

'Recent, too,' said Wulfthram. 'And we can all guess where they lead.'

Ceriana followed them, knowing full well that they would lead to the archway. And so it proved. Once they got there, the prints proceeded inside, clustering around the central tower. The whole enclosure was a mass of tumbledown stone. Very little remained of the integrity of the towers, but any rubble obstructing the route to the central tower had recently been cleared away. It was here where they now stood contemplating the next move.

'We have to go in,' said her husband.

'I thought we were waiting till morning?' Ulian asked.

'Day and night are the same in a tunnel and we have the lanterns. We are here now; there is no point going back. Let's get this finished.'

'I am unsure,' said Ceriana, 'about the rest of you coming with me. With this amulet I am theoretically protected from harm, but no one else here is.'

Wulfthram gave an exasperated sigh. 'Not this again. Are you protected from the creators of these footprints? Is hiding in the town any safer than being here? If anyone wishes to go back to the ship, they are welcome to do so, but from what I have seen there is no sanctuary to be found, not even there.'

'None of us is going back,' Haelward said softly.

'Then let us press on.' With that Wulfthram strode towards the ruined tower, Ceriana following close behind.

A series of wide and steep black steps led downwards close to the entrance to the tower; at their foot she expected to see a floor with some sort of doorway, but no, the steps just went down and down straight into the bowels of the earth through a circular hole in the ground. It was not a haphazard construction, lined as it was with smoothed and rounded stone. And it was from here that the green light emanated before being trapped and reflected by the fog swirling about them.

'The steps are damp and slippery,' said Wulfthram. 'Take them carefully; if you slip who knows how far down you will fall.'

He took the lead, holding a lantern before him, although the green light provided plenty of illumination, Ceriana followed him closely. It was a difficult climb, for the steps were steep and she was the shortest person there. She put her hand into her husband's and he assisted her firmly but gently as they made their way downhill. They passed the stone-lined underground entrance, which was not much more than a glorified hole in the ground. The sickly green light revealed a narrow shaft, walled with bricks covered in mossy green and smelling of damp and earthy decay. Ceriana still could not see how far it descended. They pressed on; time passed and the steps continued. Ceriana's thighs were aching in protest at their forced exertion. Her feet were wet and cold, and there was a dewdrop hanging miserably from the end of her nose. The strange light still had no visible source. Then Wulfthram stopped so suddenly, she bumped into him.

'Well, here we are,' was all he said.

She realised with some relief that they had cleared the last step and were standing on a small uneven landing before a great arched opening in the wall. It would have been another delicately tapered entrance but the weight of the earth above it had cracked and buckled it and the tallest among them would have to stoop slightly to pass through. The strange green light seemed to stop here. The tunnel ahead was swathed in total darkness. The small party exchanged nervous glances.

'I lead with one lantern. Strogar, bring up the rear with the other. Ulian, keep next to me with your scroll; anything you can see that can point the way for us, just shout out. Ceriana, just stick behind me. Maybe your amulet will help those stood close to you.'

'You do like shouting out your orders, don't you?' she whispered in her husband's ear.

'I do. They always appear wasted on you, though.'

'Then I will obey this time – just this time.'

Wulfthram grunted and strode forward, his lantern casting wild shadows on to the narrow walls.

The heavy boots of the soldiers echoed on the uneven stone floor. Every sound was amplified tenfold in this confined space. Ceriana felt as though her breathing sounded like that of an exhausted, panting dog, and every time she looked up she half expected to see a strange wraith-like phantom waiting for them at the edge of the darkness, beckoning them to their doom. So far, though, there was nothing except the drip, drip of water leaking through the cracked ceiling and running in rivulets down the dank green walls. Her feet were certainly getting no drier.

Then came their first dilemma. Ceriana felt a draught tug at her ears and realised that there was a shaft to their left. Wulfthram stopped and held the lantern up to it.

'Another passage,' he said. 'This was bound to happen sooner or later.'

'Hold the lantern here a second.' Ulian was fumbling for something in his pack. He produced some parchment and started scribbling on it with a piece of graphite. 'It's as good a time as any to start a map.' 'But which way do we go?' Ceriana asked. 'We could split up,' suggested Haelward.

'Probably to never see each other again, to get lost and hunted down in the dark, forgotten by everyone until we are nothing but bones and shadows.'

Haelward looked at Ceriana. 'Bad idea, then?'

'She is right,' said Wulfthram. 'We do not separate down here.'

'I'll say it again.' said Ceriana. 'Which way do we go?'

Ulian was peering at the archway in the dim light when he suddenly gave an uncharacteristic whoop of triumph. 'Here, bring the lantern here ... No, lower ... That's it, now what do we have here.' He put down his ad hoc map and pulled out one of his many other scrolls. Everyone crowded round him so closely he had to shoo them away.

He indicated the third stone of the arch on the right. Ceriana had keen eyesight but even she couldn't make it out at first, but then there it was – a series of elegant fine white scratches carved by a strong hand.

'By Elissa, how did you see that?'

'Years of deciphering spidery scrawls in many books. It gives you an eye for this sort of thing. Now hopefully I have the pattern written down somewhere.'

Drip, drip, drip. Ceriana shuffled from one foot to another waiting for the scholar to pronounce judgement. After an age which soon became an eternity, Ulian spoke again.

'I do not find an exact reproduction here, but I have found something that is a close approximation – three cross strokes, a diagonal and that pattern there. The closest I have is the symbol for home. It is to home that this passage leads, whatever that means.'

'Home,' said Wulfthram. 'Well, I had rather it had said the place where the red stone belongs, but I suppose it will have to do.' 'Towards home then?' asked Ulian.

'Towards home. It sounds like the place we should be heading. Unless there are any objections?'

There weren't. Wulfthram ducked under the narrow arch and carried on.

Shortly after, they came to a junction, and then another. Each time this happened Ulian would amend his map and look for the tell-tale symbol. Fortunately, he found it on each occasion. And so they continued, into this dark forgotten place where time did not seem to exist.

They came to a flight of broken steps; there weren't many but it helped reinforce an impression Ceriana was getting.

'We are going ever deeper,' she said. 'The passage was sloping downhill already. Did anyone notice? And it is getting warmer and drier;

my feet aren't nearly so cold.'

There was an air of agreement among her companions, though no one actually spoke. As they continued along the passage, Ceriana listened to her companions' rhythmic breathing – Ulian's was thin and wheezy; Strogar's deep and sonorous; Derkss's fast and short; her husband's deep and assured; Haelward hardly breathed at all... And then she heard something else; it sounded like breathing but, no, it wasn't; it was more like whispering. There it was again, like a soft freezing wind passing over jagged shards of ice. It was barely perceptible, more like a gentle hiss, but for all that a hiss cloaked in threat and menace, a dagger in a velvet scabbard. And there were words there; she couldn't understand them but there was a form to the noise that had to be language of some sort.

'Did anyone hear that?' she asked.

Ulian stopped and looked at her. 'No. What did you hear?'

'I don't know,' she said. 'But I think something is watching us.'

Wulfthram's face was a warm orange under the lantern. 'What exactly do you think it is?'

Ceriana said nothing, but her expression gave her thoughts away.

'The guardians,' said Ulian. 'If they know we are here, why aren't they attacking us?'

'Perhaps they are curious about us? Perhaps they want to see why we are here first?' Ceriana sounded hopeful.

'Well, concealment was always going to be unlikely down here,' said Wulfthram. 'Come on, let us continue while the lanterns burn.'

Ceriana felt the amulet against her skin. She had thought that the heat of her body would take the coldness from it and make it barely noticeable, but this had never happened –it was always cold as a winter lake, a constant reminder of her predicament and of the life she had lost after that fateful day on the beach. A fleeting memory of Doren and her family made her stop and swallow sadly. Then she composed herself once more; feelings of loss and regret were entirely inappropriate at this time.

Not twenty steps further on and they all stopped almost in unison. There was a swirling draught and a sense of space about them. And above them. The lanterns gave little away, except to show that the walls had disappeared. 'A cavern?' asked Haelward.

'If it is, it is one without a floor.' Wulfthram stepped forward and by the light of the lantern they saw the dead drop ahead of them. The ground disappeared over a wet stony lip and into a chasm of pure darkness. Ceriana sighed in disappointment, thinking it was journey's end, but then saw that this was not the case. A thin finger of stone, a pathway maybe five feet across, extended in front of them. It was not like any bridge she had ever seen before, for it twisted like a fast-moving snake and seemed to extend downward into nothingness. As to where it ended or led, the lantern's small light could give no indication.

'Be very careful, everyone,' said Wulfthram. 'Take your time; I want no one falling here.'

With some trepidation, Ceriana followed Wulfthram and Ulian on to the strange structure. She looked up, left and right, but there was just blackness.

She decided to concentrate on her feet and ignore everything else. The air was getting warmer and more stifling; she was beginning to feel uncomfortable in her cloak and her dress felt prickly on her neck and back. And then the strange whispering returned, clearer this time, a language she did not understand spoken by someone who felt as if he was standing right on her shoulder. She swung round to confront the tormentor but there was nothing but the eternal night around her.

'Are you sure none of you can hear that?' she hissed. Her voice barely carried in the dead air. Heads were shaken and so, with a sigh of nervous frustration, she carried on.

Eventually (and she couldn't even to begin to guess the time in the world above ground) the strange pathway ended in a broad landing, which produced a collective sigh of relief. Wulfthram, however, afforded himself little time to gather his thoughts and continued to press forward. Ceriana found herself rather admiring his singular determination. She was not sure if it was driven by concern for her or just a desire to get out of this place as soon as possible, or maybe a little of both, but whatever was driving him on she was grateful for it.

'Ulian,' he called, 'we have more than one entrance here. Come and look.'

With his lantern held high, Ulian walked the length of the broad face of rock in front of them. He passed one archway, then another and another. In total, there were five such openings facing them, five unblinking eyes, darkness within darkness; it was difficult not to feel lost and completely helpless within such stifling confines.

Ulian and Wulfthram started to check each entrance in turn. Ceriana watched them in an almost disinterested manner, noticing how each arch had buckled over time on account of the vast weight of rock pressing down on them. She wondered if the tunnels beyond were equally damaged and, if so, whether they were navigable or not. It would be beyond infuriating to find their progress stopped by something as mundane as a rock fall. Maybe they would not even get that far, as Ulian appeared to be having problems.

'There are no symbols anywhere that I can find,' he was saying, plainly agitated. 'Nothing. I wonder if it was deliberate, a final protection against the likes of us, outsiders who have deciphered the symbols. Those that mattered would know the correct way in. The other four tunnels are probably dead ends, beset by traps of some sort. There are other examples of the Wych folk doing such things in antiquity.'

'Well, that is no help at all.' Wulfthram sounded exasperated .'So we have a four in five chance of stumbling on some trap or other. Were these traps ever of the lethal kind?'

'Oh without exception,' said Ulian glibly.

Ignoring the ironic laughter and groaning from his companions, Wulfthram slowly went and sat on the stony floor.

'Let's rest for ten minutes and have some food and water; we all need to think as to what to do next.'

Ceriana sat next to her husband and nibbled a piece of dried bread without enthusiasm. She took her husband's arm.

'I want to thank you,' she said, 'for coming here, for doing this when you really didn't have to.'

'Oh but I did have to,' he replied. 'The current state of affairs cannot be left to continue. Whatever possesses you has to be driven out somehow.'

'The way I see it is that there are three possible outcomes. The best one is that we return the stone, go home happy and resume our lives as we should. The second is that all of this is some mad and pointless enterprise; we are in the wrong place and so we go home with nothing changed.'

'And the third?'

'We die!' she said with a soft laugh. 'It would be an outcome of sorts.'

'Other things may happen.'

'Such as?'

'The amulet protects you and the rest of us die.'

She stirred uncomfortably. 'That will not happen; I will make sure of it.'

'Will you?' he smiled. 'You had better know: you and your family will take over the majority of my lands on my death. Marry wisely when I am gone; I would not have Osperitsan in the hands of some drooling idiot.'

'You will not die here, not if I can help it.' Her chin was set firmly. 'And as far as marrying a drooling idiot is concerned, I will just stay clear of the Grand Duke's court.'

Wulfthram smiled. 'Have you heard the rumours about him and you?'

Her back stiffened. 'What rumours?'

'Surprised that I have ears in the court in Tanaren City? There are a few actually. One is that the two of you were and still are lovers, though how you can carry on from a distance of hundreds of miles is a mystery to me. Another is that you both share the same father, the former Grand Duke having had an illicit tryst with your mother. and yet another is that, once your inheritance is secured in my will, the Grand Duke will use his prerogative to divorce the two of us and take you for himself. That is the only rumour I do not have difficulty disbelieving.'

She stared at him and, despite her best efforts, her large eyes were shot through with guilt. She hoped the darkness would help hide her embarrassment.

It didn't. 'Ah, so you did know something along those lines?'

'He told me at the feast, at Erskon House, after the wedding,' she stumbled. 'He is the Grand Duke and swore me to secrecy. Believe me when I say it has been an agony for me. I am sorry. My loyalty is to you first and foremost, I swear it.'

He put his arm around her briefly. 'It is not your fault. He put you in an invidious position. If those are his plans, though, I hope he is aware that there would be many ramifications up here. As you now know, we in the north are not easy to forget or forgive an insult.'

'No, it is a folly of his. When my father comes here I will speak to him. I swear I will fight any such move all the way.'

'You would refuse the Grand Duke for me?'

'It is the principle. I will say it again, I am a Hartfield and for us duty always comes first. I am your wife and as you are my husband my loyalty will always be to you no matter what the sacrifice. One day maybe I will get to prove this to you.'

Wulfthram looked impressed. 'Thank you, my Lady. Are you sure you have no northern blood?'

She grinned, thankful for his response. 'The only part of the north I have ever had in me belongs to you, my Lord. Now to the present: we have no idea at all which tunnel to take?'

'None at all.'

'I will go and take a look at them.'

'As you wish.'

Taking one of the lanterns, she moved towards the nearest entrance. Why on earth had she said that to him? What could she possibly see that Ulian couldn't? She moved from one tunnel to the next, realising with a heavy heart that they were all near enough identical. This is it then, she thought. The journey ends here.

She was at the fourth tunnel now. She stared at it. It stared back. Her shoulders slumped. She went to move on to the final tunnel when like a wisp of bitter frost floating about her ears the voice came to her once more. It was little more than a soft echo but there was something in the voice that froze her to the core. It was not anger or even hostility; it was a voice that spoke of suffering, of an eternity of tormented loneliness, a soul confined to the utter dark unto infinity, never to find peace or a sweet release.

'It is this one,' she said, indicating the tunnel. 'Do not ask me how I know; just understand that I do know.'

'Then it is through here that we must proceed,' Ulian said, giving her an understanding smile.

The tunnel itself was lower and narrower than its predecessors. Its floor was littered with loose stones and rubble, causing many stumbles, bruised toes and suppressed curses. There was also an all-pervading musty smell to it, whether due to age, decay or something else Ceriana did not know. There were also signs that some of the heavier piles of spoil had been partially cleared and moved to the sides. No one spoke about it but it brought the image of a sepulchral shaven-headed man in black straight to the front of her mind. Ceriana wondered where they were hiding.

Suddenly Wulfthram turned to the others. 'Strogar, put out your lantern.' 'Are you sure, sir? Will we have enough light with just your lantern?'

'Probably not. I am putting mine out as well.'

Strogar looked at his baron as though he had lost his mind. But he obeyed his order and his face was lost to the darkness as his light went out.

'Now to see if I am right,' said Wulfthram and followed suit.

Momentarily they were plunged into a blackness deeper than anything Ceriana had ever experienced before, something that she imagined existed at the very depths of the ocean floor. Perhaps her husband had gone mad after all; she put her hand in front of her face expecting to see nothing. But she could see it! It glowed a faint mustard colour, almost as if it was luminous. Then she looked up.

Above her the entire roof of the tunnel was coated in something glowing a fluorescent yellow. There were patches of darkness here and there, usually circular in shape, but they were surrounded by something that reminded her of a macabre type of seaweed. It extended partway down either wall and continued before them for some considerable distance. The soft light emitted meant they could see far ahead of them and there, maybe a quarter of a mile ahead, was a small black rectangle which could only be an exit from the claustrophobic space they now inhabited.

'A bizarre type of phosphorescent fungus,' said Ulian. 'I have heard of such things but have never seen anything like it myself before. And look, it is moving – ever so slowly – but if you watch carefully it is inching down the walls. What a strange thing it is.'

'It is a living thing then,' said Ceriana. 'I do not know why, but somehow that makes me feel quite uncomfortable. Let us leave this place behind.'

They picked up speed; everyone, it seemed, was of a like mind. Ceriana stubbed her toe on a loose rock and for the thousandth time cursed her foolish choice of footwear. From behind her she heard Haelward make a sound of disgust. It was so strongly expressed she turned around to see what irked him so.

She hadn't been looking up but realised that had been something of a mistake. From the strange mass above them tendrils were dropping – thin milky strands bulbous at their end. They were brushing the hair of the taller men at the back of the party; Strogar, especially, was shaking his head as these dangling filaments stroked his face and shoulders.

'Artorus's beard, these things are sticky.' Haelward spat his distaste, holding his arm to his face and hair to ward off the assault.

'Keth take me but they burn!' Strogar had a note of panic in his voice.

Wulfthram had seen enough. 'Run!' he shouted.

Heads held down they bolted as fast as they could, all thoughts focused on getting out of the place. Ceriana stayed close to her husband who held one arm over her. Her eyes were fixed on the ground and she saw with a sense of shock that it was neither stones nor rubble she was disturbing with her feet.

It was bones.

There were many small animal bones that she kicked or crushed underfoot in her haste, but for all her mind's attempts to deny the truth before her there were also much larger bones among them. And then she saw her first human skull. A thrill of fear passed down her spine.

'Hurry everyone, hurry!' she shouted, feeling more panicky with every passing second.

She kicked up a cloud of dust as she ran, spitting as it went up her nose. They were nearly out now and she put on an extra spurt to get there. The exit from the tunnel she could now see was backlit with a flickering red glow. Fire? she thought, Before she could dwell on this further, though, a bellow of fear behind her caused her to twist her neck backwards.

Strogar had been completely enveloped. An enormous man-sized polyp had descended from the roof swallowing him whole. He had been lifted from the ground as the yellow sac slowly heaved itself upwards again. The strange growth was changing colour, too; a livid green fluid was streaming through it, all of it being pumped into the sac which was now nearly full of it. Inside she could see Strogar struggling to free himself. He had his short sword out and was stabbing at the thing enclosing him with completely unsuccessful results. The thing was translucent and she could see his wide-eyed desperate face – the green fluid was up to his eyes and appeared to be choking him.

Drawing his sword, Haelward roared and thrust at the sac, shield held over his head as he held off dozens of other tendrils as they whipped at him, trying to force him backwards. Derkss drew his sword but immediately it was caught by the spidery growths, leaving him unable to swing it either backwards or forwards. In frustration, he released his grip whereupon the weapon was lifted to the roof and absorbed under the strange shifting mass above them. Haelward, meanwhile, had managed to force his blade partially into the green sac only to find it had become stuck. He was unable to pull it free until Wulfthram joined him and the two of them grasped the sword's hilt and pulled together. Finally, as both men groaned with the exertion, it came free, causing the two of them to fall to the floor. A spurt of green liquid followed it, splashing to the ground where it smoked and hissed and sent forth a noxious steam.

Haelward's sword was smoking, too, and they watched as the tip of the blade started to dissolve in front of their eyes. Inside the sac, Strogar was motionless now, the green fluid over his head. They saw the sac's contents darken as streams of black blood started to fill it. With mounting horror they saw that Strogar's face had started to melt. His eyeballs had gone and blood flowed freely from the empty sockets. The skin had started to shrivel and peel back from his mouth and cheeks, exposing more and more of the dead man's skull. Above them the yellow growth was darkening as the man's life juices were sucked from him, and the bulging sac was now nearly black in colour as the digestion process continued.

As one, the rest of the party ran, Haelward leaving behind his shield and now useless sword and pulling out a long stabbing knife instead. Wulfthram had his sword drawn and Derkss, like Haelward, was reduced to carrying his hunting knife. Ulian was in the lead and it was he who first burst out of the tunnel into the next chamber. Ceriana was right behind him.

Straight away she sensed they were at journey's end. They were in a large circular chamber in which visibility was not a problem, for the walls were lined by many flaming torches. It had a high ceiling, very high – were they really that far underground? The ceiling was tiled in white and bore a strange geometric pattern but there were so many cracks and gaps in the tiles that its meaning was beyond ascertaining. The floor was not tiled, but even if it were they would not have been able to tell for it was covered in bones. At least a hundred people must have died in this place – without wind or scavengers to disturb them they were lying pretty much where they had fallen, inside their rusted armour with their weapons lying close by. One could not take a step without crushing something underfoot.

They huddled together, not wishing to disturb their grisly surroundings. In front of them was a raised circular plinth with a lip at its edge. Contained within this plinth were dozens, maybe hundreds, of beautifully carved objects of gold, silver and bone, all of them, it seemed, depicting some type of animal and nearly all studded with gems – rubies, sapphires, emeralds and diamonds. There was more wealth in front of them than was held in the Grand Duke's treasury, but none of those present were thinking of that at present. For in the midst of the plinth was a throne. It was carved in onyx or a similar hard black stone and on it sat a figure. It was clad in full armour, bright silver in colour, and its pauldrons, gauntlets and high conical helmet glittered with tiny diamonds. Without the armour the figure would have been near invisible for its skin and flesh were almost transparent, a ghostly pale shade of tremulous silvery white through which phantasmal blood vessels and bones could be seen. The skull was clearly discernible, a thin pale cranium like a waning moon part obscured by cloud. The only clear feature was its eyes, large and flaming red, and they now seemed to be gazing at the intruders as a master chef might have looked at a cockroach in his kitchen.

But he was not alone. Surrounding the plinth were a ring of similar phantoms. They bore no armour and their full skeletons were clearly visible, clothed under transparent flesh. Unlike the seated figure, their eyes were an icy pale blue and burned with a hostile intensity. Ulian stepped in front of the others.

'Only I here can speak some of their language. Perhaps I should converse with them.'

'Perhaps not!' came a voice from the shadows behind them. 'Perhaps you should just give us what we want. We may even allow you to leave this place alive.'

Three figures strode forth and stood before them, paying no regard to the bones they crushed as they walked. Ceriana took an involuntary step backwards, hiding behind her husband. For the black priests had made their move and were here to reclaim what they believed was rightfully theirs.

BOOK ONE: AUTUMN
48

Dawn rose, crisp, clear and cold. The forest mist, such a pervasive feature of the Aelthenwood, licked around the fetlocks and haunches of the horses as they stood impatiently in the grassy clearing. They were standing on a high plateau that overlooked a virtually unbroken vista of trees to their north; many of these trees were clad in their solemn late-autumn colours of russets, buttery yellows and browns; only the stands of evergreens, such as the pine forests that hugged the foothills of the mountains, defied the overall tone.

Morgan, perched as indelicately as ever on his patient piebald mount, watched a skein of geese pass high overhead, flying away to the south and west where the weather was warmer and feeding easier. He was musing on how much easier things would be if he had a pair of wings himself when Itheya rode up alongside him. She was back in her dark leathers and was equipped again with her bow and long knife. She followed his eyes to the distant geese, which were growing smaller by the second.

'If I had more time, I would have taken you to the northern cliffs overlooking the sea. This time of year they are packed with seabirds ready to journey south. For the young, it is the first time they fly. If they do not make it to the sea, the foxes will get them. Then on the water there are many schools of whales coming close to the shore picking up the last remnants of the available food. We do not see them during winter. As a child, I used to spend many hours watching both whales and birds; to see the fledglings struggle so hard is quite an inspiration, even if they do not all make it. It is Zhun's way – the death of some means survival for the foxes – and just as many birds return here the following year.'

'Will you ever get the chance to see it again? You strike me as someone who needs time for quiet reflection. It sounds quite a sight, but will you ever get the opportunity to be alone with your thoughts, given that you may be leading your tribe fairly soon?'

She smiled sadly. 'Probably not – my duties consume my time more and more. Maybe when I am old and toothless I may get the chance to return there – but not before.'

'Responsibility is a burden on us all. It is like a growth on your face; you can ignore it for a while but it never goes away, and sooner or later you have to deal with it, take a hot knife to your face and grit your teeth against the pain.'

'Speaking of such things, Master Cedric does not look too well. Yesterday was quite a hard ride even for me; we want to be across the mountains in two days and I am not sure he can do it unassisted. Come with me.'

She rode slowly up towards Cedric, who was hunched stiffly over his small horse. He had not spoken to anyone for a while and his tremor was as pronounced as Morgan had seen it.

'Master Cedric,' – Itheya slipped gracefully off her horse – 'will you do me the honour of riding with me for a while; it will rest your horse for when she is most needed and I can answer any questions you may have about the next stage of our journey.'

'You are very kind, my Lady, but I do not know how I will get on to your horse.'

'Morgan and I will help you. Come.'

Morgan dismounted and the two of them managed to ease Cedric off his horse. Itheya then helped give him a leg up and Morgan practically lifted the exhausted man on to her steed.

'Terath,' she called, 'can you do something here?'

'No, no, I am fine,' Cedric interposed. 'I'm just feeling the early-morning cold.' He seemed eager to draw attention away from himself.

'Terath can help with that,' she said dismissively. 'When we ride, hold on to me; you may even sleep if you are tired.'

'I feel a terrible fraud here. You have far more important things to attend to than my welfare.'

'The welfare of everyone under my command is important to me, and right now you are the one requiring attention. Let Terath attend to you, then you will be not be such a pressing concern.'

'Strnavi, Itheya, z'ometahan zhai ne an tafallazho.'

One of the elves at the other side of the camp was calling her. He had raised his spear to attract her attention.

'He has seen the Ometahan,' she said. 'I had better go see.'

She dismounted and left them just as Terath arrived, he immediately started to lay his hands on Cedric's arms and hands before chanting slowly. Morgan watched for a minute and noticed some colour return to the old scholar's cheeks.

'I am sorry, Cedric, I should have noticed; I have been so wrapped up in this journey and I keep thinking you are indestructible. Shout out next time you feel ill.'

'You forget, Morgan, that these people can sense infirmity, and what's more they can do something about it. I can feel Terath's power helping me already. I will be fine. Besides, I am rather keen to see this pass of theirs. Can you imagine – there is a path through the mountains we know nothing about?'

'They go to great lengths to conceal it from us, I believe, and it is so narrow, it is not easily spotted anyway. I still feel bad leaving Haelward and the others.'

'What? Safely ensconced in a tavern for the winter, rather than on the front lines? I am sure they will curse you when they rejoin the army in spring.'

'They will probably think we are dead and the mission a failure; it is a pity we could not get a message to them somehow.'

'But you will, my boy. When you get to Felmere or some other town over the mountains you can send a messenger their way. They are soldiers; they will understand.'

'Sometimes, Cedric,' said Morgan with a smile, 'you sound like the military veteran and I like the crusty scholar... Oh and by the way, this is for you.' He put something into Cedric's hand.

Cedric opened his palm. 'Six pennies. You see, I only pretended to lose at dice because I knew the money would be coming straight back to me. Now I have some days to think how exactly I can spend it. Console yourself with the fact that I will have my hands on the Lady Itheya for the next few hours.'

'Don't squeeze too hard or she will feed you to the bears.'

Terath laughed. 'You can see why our Lady is so loved by her tribe; she can be as brittle and threatening as a winter frost and as warm as blue fire at one and the same time. Once she has seen into your soul, though, and has read your heart, there is no one as loyal as she. She, of course, will expect the same loyalty in return and has no tolerance for those who transgress or deviate from her own standards. It is a lesson worth learning. How do you feel now, Cedric?'

'Like a new man!' Cedric did seem to have a bloom in his cheeks, which had been an ashen grey not ten minutes before. 'Thank you, Terath.'

'If you feel poorly later on, then I will send Dirthen or Astania to do the same for you. It will be good practice for them, too.'

Terath left them and Morgan clambered back on to his mount. 'This never gets any easier,' he moaned to Cedric. 'I will always be a foot soldier.'

'Unlike the people of this forest,' said Cedric. 'It looks like the other contingent has arrived.'

Morgan looked over the clearing. Up on to the plateau other horsemen were arriving. As with the contingent of Morioka warriors, he noticed that over a quarter of their number were women. Their leader was speaking with Itheya now; it was as she had told him yesterday – intermarriage occurred between the tribes but so few children were born different racial characteristics between them could be striking. The Morioka were dark-haired with blue or violet eyes; the Ometahan seemed to have flaming-red hair with eyes green as emeralds. Itheya and the man she was speaking to, who happened to be one of the tallest elves Morgan had seen, came over to see them. Itheya climbed on to her horse, being careful not to hit Cedric who leaned backwards to give her room.

'This is Culleneron,' she said, a little breathlessly. 'We will share leadership of this expedition; he speaks a little of your language but a full conversation may be difficult for him. I will translate where necessary.'

'*Satala, Culleneron,*' said Cedric. '*Ve ne Cedric, al e olem Morgan. Ema olem trnacantele tafalinkare teo.*'

The red-haired elf bowed slightly. '*Azha ve ate.*'

Itheya turned her head slightly and spoke to Cedric.

'Hold me here.' She placed his hand at her waist. 'If you tire, inform me.'

Once he had done this she kicked the horse and rode to the centre of the clearing. *'Tafalavons Aelvena!'* she called in a clear high voice. Culleneron joined her and shortly after the two elves found themselves surrounded by a circle of horsemen all within hearing of the two commanders. Morgan stayed just outside the circle as Itheya addressed them.

'Hrtena azha trneka. Atekele zhucetheku ze'a zhutesse se'atan craba. Tafashen hanza spetu eonameon brataspako vo'voe tafasiol. Votodane altafa havysk'ara basekykal azhatafa hawritu ar'vekleno nesprta za hemenest. Voto ne an caltazha heten tafinezho. Cotho voto nean spesa tafadane xexenesh nesptru Araelva. Cantele azha vaveress wyathan! Tafalla siol Aelvenna!'

('Brothers and sisters. You have been chosen as the elite of your tribes. Together, for the first time in generations, we go to war. We do this to reclaim our heritage and to reaffirm our identity among the humans. We are proud and bow to no one. What we are about to do will resonate among our people. Elves, to war!')

The company raised their weapons and shouted. Culleneron then said something similar and with the same response. Morgan noticed flasks being passed around the circle; one of the elves noticed him and handed him a flask. Morgan took a drink and handed it back before he sputtered and embarrassed himself. Zhath.

And then the elves formed into a loose column and headed northwards into the trees. Itheya hung back and waited for Morgan.

'Culleneron commands today. He will lead us into the pass and I will lead us out. Humans do not know what they have called upon. There are fewer than five hundred of us but we are the finest horse in the world. We are an alliance, Morgan; you do not command us. We will fight where we deem it the most appropriate. You can request our presence in battle but we make the final decision.'

The excitement among the elves was infectious and it had

definitely caught Itheya. Her violet eyes shone radiantly and there was a bloom on her pale skin. Morgan suddenly noticed a tattoo on her neck that he was sure he hadn't seen before. He pointed this out.

'Yes, it is new. Only elves at war with peoples other than ourselves can wear it. It is Vewhenesha, the hunting wolf. The elves are hunting, Morgan; it is time for the humans to fear!'

And with that the elves at the head of the column started to call, an eerily pitched noise not unlike that of a vast pack of baying wolves. It was taken up by the remainder of the elves, nearly five hundred howling voices calling for blood, and for the first time in days Morgan was reminded of the alien and savage nature of the people he had been living among. Even the trees seemed to tremble as the host plunged forth; birds scattered from the trees; deer and even bears dispersed at their approach – nothing stood before them. And still the elves called until the encroaching mountains called back to them. Morgan half expected the very stone to part at their approach.

'What have we unleashed here?' he kept asking himself. And he had no answer.

After just under an hour's riding they stood before a great shoulder of rock. At its base it was surrounded by pine trees with straggly patches of grass clinging to its heights. Culleneron at the head of the column disappeared into the trees, plunging downhill along a narrow path. The other elves followed.

'Where are they going?' Cedric asked. 'I can't see any way forward.'

'It is Bleneshea Axenat,' Itheya replied. 'The Pass of the Knife. Never has a place been so aptly named.'

They were near the rear of the column but eventually it was their turn to begin the climb downhill. The path was stony and lined with bracken, meaning Morgan had to concentrate on keeping control of his horse. When he did look up he started with surprise. It could not be seen at a distance but now he could see that the rock ahead was riven in two by a fissure that extended its full length but never at any point exceeded ten feet across. Itheya noticed his expression.

BOOK ONE: AUTUMN

'Some say long ago a bolt of lightning greater than one ever seen before or since struck this mountain side, splitting the entire range in two. Others say it was a rare example of Zhun himself acting to change the world while others say it is just the action of water or of extreme cold on vulnerable rock. I have no answer; I leave it to the likes of Terath to explain such things. This pass, however, crosses the entire range and never gets wider than that you can see here.'

'Where is the entrance on the other side of the mountains?' Morgan asked. 'I have lived around the Seven Rivers all my life and know nothing of this pass.'

'As it should be.' Itheya looked at him, obviously pleased with the ingenuity of her people. 'The cleft on the other side is concealed as this one is. We patrol it regularly and make it appear to humans that it is blocked, should any of you notice it and try to enter. I will have to ask the two of you to swear never to reveal its location for there have been occasions when a curious human has wandered into it and we have either had to drug them and release them far away or, as a last resort, kill them. As to where it exits, it is close to a river and waterfall; the river runs for some miles before it passes through a large human city, full of stone and no trees. It then joins a larger river after entering the woods to the west. The city has a high wall and a plateau at its centre on which is built a large fortification or dwelling; I do not know the difference.'

'Felmere? It sounds like Felmere. So this exits near the Fel. I have travelled there many times and never knew of this place. No wonder some of us call you the Wych folk.'

'It is not a name we like. We are not witches. But then we have worse names for you, so we cannot claim the high ground here. Stay close, Morgan. I hope you do not mind confined spaces.'

She led her horse into the cleft with Morgan following close behind. He felt he was being swallowed by the mountain, delving into a river of stone. He looked up at the tiniest strip of light, a sliver of radiance in the gloom around him. The only sound was the heavy breathing of elf, man and horse and the clopping of a thousand hooves echoing and resounding off the unending cliffs.

THE FORGOTTEN WAR

'We get trolls here occasionally,' said Itheya in hushed tones. 'They try to pick off any stray elves or horses. They are unlikely to attack such a large group but we cannot afford to let up our guard.'

'Why is there no snow overhead?' asked Cedric 'We fled Claw Pass just as the snows were getting heavy there. The pass is closed now.'

'Terath can explain. It has something to do with the stone raising the temperature here; you will notice the cliffs are very wet, as is the ground under us. Snow becomes water – see our breath is steaming. All our bodies will make it humid for us; see how sticky and uncomfortable our clothes will become.'

'Do you know Culleneron very well?' Morgan asked .'Can you trust him?'

She craned her neck to see Morgan. 'Yes, he can be trusted. He is a brave warrior, although he could use this' – she tapped her head – 'a little more. It is perfectly likely that we will wed at some time in the future. I will make sure that it is a long time in the future if I can.'

'Will that mean the end of any post-festival trysts? I could barely sleep for your noise that night.'

Her eyes narrowed. She was the ice queen again. 'That was the dancer who helped me during Armentele. It was an easy way to thank him. Other than that, it is no business of yours. I had thought that you had drunk enough not to be wakened by me; otherwise it would not have happened. Anyway, you woke me enough that night with your shouting.'

'What shouting?'

'You were dreaming, obviously. You kept shouting out Lisbeth all the time. Is this a human name? Your wife perhaps?'

'Yes to both questions, if you must know.' It was Morgan's turn to be defensive.

'I didn't know you were married.' Cedric sounded surprised. 'You have never mentioned her before.'

'She is dead. Therefore it is not worth mentioning.'

'Oh my boy, I am so sorry. I should not have been so glib.'

'That is all right, Cedric; you were not to know. I am one of many anyway. You should know, Itheya, that you are entering a country of widows and widowers; my situation is hardly unique there.'

Her expression had softened. She said nothing, though; it was as if she could not find the right words. She contented herself with a slight nod, which he returned. She then continued on her way, her back high in the saddle, Cedric gripping on to her, Morgan following on behind.

The hours passed. A human party would have stopped for a quick lunch but there was no sign of this with the elves. The stone floor of the pass was wet and covered in loose shale chippings, slowing their progress but not prohibitively so. Morgan could tell they were proceeding much faster than they had on the equivalent journey north where the ettins had ended Rozgon's life.

The light, or what little there was, was starting to fade. He was expecting torches to be lit among the procession; indeed, some were but most of the elves had glowstones which they held tied on to their spears. The humidity Itheya had spoken of became a lot more noticeable once these were illuminated. Morgan did feel sticky and uncomfortable; he wondered how they were all going to sleep in this narrow cleft. He decided to ask Itheya; the first time they had spoken in hours.

'It is not easy,' she replied. 'We tend to sleep on the horses but they need rest, too, so we stay on the horses for some hours then stand in the wet to give the horses sleep. It will not be restful but it will be our only night here so we make the best of it that we can.'

Morgan grunted. 'I see.'

'Cedric is asleep,' she said. 'At least he is rested.'

'Good,' said Morgan. 'If anyone needed it, then it was him. Thanks for being so attentive with him.'

'He has much ahead of him, and he is the oldest one here, except maybe for Terath.'

Morgan did not reply. They continued on for a little while when she spoke again.

'I mentioned earlier the human city that this river runs through.'

'Felmere.' Morgan replied.

'Felmere. What is it like living in such a place, surrounded by stone and dead wood, full of dirt and little clean water?'

'Bear in mind, I am a country dweller myself. I grew up on a farm close to a small village. I have visited places like Felmere many times, though, and have little love for such places if I am being honest. There is dirt, a press of unwashed bodies, piles of dung and other spoil. All of it causes a miasma that you would find very displeasing, I am sure.'

'But why do your people choose such a life?'

'Many reasons. There is more money in cities; better opportunities to get rich. In bad years people in the country can starve – I should know. Both have their strong and weak points. Personally, though, a nice country house by the river with apple trees and abundant fish would be close to paradise for me. Maybe one day.'

'Your people do not store food for the bad times?'

'In a ten-year war such reserves were used up long ago. It is down to the local baron. Some are wise and store grain; others sell the excess for whatever reason. As I say, there is no easy or simple answer to any of your questions; there are as many answers as there are people.'

She ran a hand through her hair. 'I am sorry for being flippant with you earlier – I mean about your wife.'

'No need. As I recall, I was the flippant one; you simply gave as good as you got.'

'Do you miss her?'

'Of course. The passage of time helps but I will always miss her.'

She stopped her horse to let him move alongside her; there was just enough room.

'My father I love, of course, but I have never loved a man in the way you obviously loved your wife. As you said earlier, maybe one day, but it has not happened for me yet.'

'I am sure it will, Itheya. What restricts you, I suppose, is your status and your duty. You cannot form friendships as most of us do and when you do marry; it is as likely to be for the good of the tribe as anything else.'

Her voice was barely a whisper. 'You are right. of course, but my duty has brought me close to someone I have started to care about a great deal.'

BOOK ONE: AUTUMN

She pressed her face to within inches of his. her lips close to his ear.

'Nothing can come of it, as you well know; it is little short of treachery for a princess to consort with one not of her kind. If the barrier did not exist, though, then at least on her part she would be happy for things to get as close as they were possible to get.' She gave a quick look round, ensuring no one could see her in this darkness, then leaned forward and kissed him gently on the cheek. She was as soft as goose down and her warm breath smelled like a light floral wine.

'Your destiny is to lead your tribe,' Morgan replied as quietly as he could. 'It is something I could never be part of.'

'I know,' she whispered back, 'but I felt it was for the best if I told you the way I feel. I do not know if you share these feelings and I suppose it is not important either way, but you know my heart now for good or ill. I will not mention this again.'

'Thank you for your honesty. For my part, let me say that you are a princess and it would be presumptuous of me to declare such high feelings for you. Let me also say, though, that since I lost my wife I have never felt as close to someone as I have with you. I was actually jealous that night after the festival when I heard you with someone else, but, as you say, this goes no further. It ends here and I will speak no more of it either.'

She smiled slightly; it made her lip slightly crooked. 'As we are being honest, here I must confess that my capricious nature overtook me that night. Part of me wanted to incite such feelings in you; another part of me took this man to my room to stop me from doing what I really wanted.'

'And what was that?'

'I was a little affected by the drink and I wanted to come to your room that night. I wanted you, Morgan, Zhun help me. The scandal would have ruined me, so instead I collected this man and used him instead.'

'You could not just have slept alone?'

She sounded surprised. 'Alone? No. I like sex too much. All of my people do. I know it is not the way with your people and your religion would chastise me for my morals, but fortunately for me mine says otherwise. Maybe it is because we have so few children that we see things differently, I hear humans can have vast families, so I can understand disapproval of such behaviour, but I still feel sorry for you. You miss out on so much.'

'You learned this from the missionary you held here?'

'Yes, he was always criticising my flighty behaviour, which only made me behave even more appallingly.'

'How did he betray you?'

Her expression changed; she became sombre as well as sad. 'That is you being direct again. I will tell you, but not now; it is not the time and it is not a happy tale. I thank you for your honesty tonight; I feel the better for it. But now the army is stopping and it is time to get what rest we can.'

The evening passed just as she said it would. The elves appeared to sleep on their horses without difficulty, their heads bowed, their breathing low and steady. Itheya slept in that manner even with Cedric slumped on to her back, his snoring booming off the high rock. For Morgan, however, sleep was a completely unattainable ideal. He was saddle-sore enough as it was and did not have enough confidence not to think he would fall off the saddle as soon as sleep took him. Eventually he got off the poor old horse and tried sleeping while leaning against the mountain. Exhaustion led him to have little cat naps; he would suddenly come to, to see that he had slumped part way down the rock and had to stand up again. In this way a long, sticky and uncomfortable night passed. At one point, he saw Itheya climb off her horse, make sure Cedric was comfortable and lean against the mountain just as he had done. At another he caught her looking at him; they both smiled at each other but nothing more was said.

At long last a thin sliver of blue-grey light appeared in the world high above them. Instantly Itheya was awake; she gave Morgan a gentle slap to wake him, then tugged Cedric's sleeve before hopping on to her horse.

'I lead our forces today. Come with me.'

There was barely enough room to squeeze past the other elves, who were either still asleep or just beginning to stir and check their mounts and equipment. Fortunately the pass widened for a brief period, enabling them to speed up a little. Morgan wondered if the stop here was deliberate, so that any emergency redeployment could be affected with minimum fuss. In no time at all they were at the head of the column. Terath greeted them warmly and Culleneron was already sitting stiffly on his horse. After a brief verbal exchange he rode back down the column to take his place with the Ometahan.

Cedric spoke to Itheya. 'It is for you to lead today, my girl. The last thing you need is some dull old cripple hanging on to you. I feel a lot better today so give me my horse and let me ride alone.'

She twisted her neck to see him. 'Are you sure? It is no trouble for me really.' Despite her protestations, there was the slightest tinge of relief in her voice.

'Yes, your horse needs a rest from me, if nothing else.'

As they waited for Cedric's horse to be brought up, Terath spoke to Cedric.

'I could not sleep last night, so I ended up studying the tooth inscriptions by the light of a glowstone.'

'Figure out anything new?'

'A little more, though it just confirmed what we already have discussed. Dragons, or at least summoned dragons, do not come alone it seems. Each type has at least one ... um ... what it calls a thrall, an under-species, creatures that follow the dragon and protect it and may even do its bidding. And for the first time I read something about how the creatures might be killed. It mentions the use of "opposite force", whatever that means, and suggests that the death of the summoner, the breaking of the bond, will drive the creature away, panicked and desperate – either that, or turn it into a crazed monster desperate for vengeance. The script is often a little ambiguous!'

'I would call that a very good night's work,' said Cedric. 'At last things become clearer. We still have a strategy to plan to deal with these creatures, though.'

'If I am able,' Terath said, 'I will head south to these marshes. I would hope for an escort at least, but that is up to our commanders.'

'Of course, you will have an escort,' Itheya snapped, 'but now is not the time to discuss the matter. We are ready to move. Prepare yourself. No one wants to stay in here longer than they have to.'

No one disagreed with her and very shortly they were on the move again.

Itheya was in the lead, accompanied by a couple of young warriors whose names Morgan didn't know. Now and then she would give her orders to them and they would drop back to convey the orders to the column. The two humans, along with Terath, Dirthen and Astania, followed closely behind. The path was fairly clear and progress was good, but Morgan had never wanted to feel a breeze on his face more than he did now. The air was cloying and still and sweat ran down everybody's faces, backs and legs like a river. Cedric was beginning to flag and Astania who was closest to him laid her hands on him, perking him up a little. It was obvious, though, that he was in poor shape; he was stooped over his horse and his tremor was there for all to see. Morgan came over to him.

'Quite the journey, eh,' he said. 'If the Gods are with us, we should be out fairly soon; here let me take your reins, you only need to concentrate on staying on the thing then.'

Cedric gladly assented and on they went. Morgan guessed they were quite a way past noon when the ground started to get more uneven. There were slopes and dips and a fair bit of scree scattered everywhere. Morgan's heart started to sink when he saw this, but Itheya was strangely encouraged.

'We are close now; maybe an hour at the most.'

Her enthusiasm seemed to pass down the line and Morgan noticed everyone seemed to put a spurt on. Half an hour passed when they came to the highest slope they had seen so far, fairly steep and maybe twenty feet high, directly in front of them. Itheya's horse practically skipped up it and, when she had reached its highest point she stopped and called to all those behind her. *'Drese za Tanteshfor!'*

Looking behind him, he saw the elves raise their banners. Unlike the broad rectangular banners he was used to seeing these were more like large pennants, triangular and held on very high poles. He saw the green-and-gold Morioka banner and at least a dozen others. Most had a plain but brightly coloured background with an animal as the emblem. He saw a bear, a fox and osprey, several other birds, and even an enormous silver fish. Itheya looked at him. She was smiling.

'For the first time in many generations our banners will be seen south of the mountains. *'Za Aelvetheth!'*

It was a cry taken up by the whole host. *'Za Aelvetheth! Za Aelvetheth ne an tafalna!'*

Itheya sped on, the host following closely. As Morgan crested the hill he saw it, a narrow aperture with a flash of vivid green behind it. The elves started their wolf call, as Itheya, at their head, disappeared through the gap into the outside world. Morgan, still holding Cedric's reins, was a little slower but still by his standards almost at a gallop when he, too, finally broached the clearing. He was in a dip surrounded by brush, a thicket and many tall broad-leaved trees, their branches now almost bare.

'Give me the reins, my boy; I can take it from here.' Cedric was smiling with relief. Together the two humans climbed the underbrush and found themselves in the high, mainly pine woodland that clothed nearly all of the foothills surrounding the Derannen Mountains. Morgan stopped and let the keen breeze cool his face and freeze his undershirt to his back. 'Home,' he said quietly to himself.

Itheya was at the head of the host with her standard-bearer next to her. She broke through the last of the trees and found herself on a broad expanse of grassland, a high shelf with a sheer drop to the rolling blanket of trees underneath. To the west, maybe a mile away through a high gorge in the mountains, spilled a fast-flowing waterfall. A cloud of fine spray cloaked much of it, including the closely huddled pine trees among which it plunged. A shimmering silver ribbon of a river then sped away through the woods heading away from them. It broke into a clearing and ran a winding course across a green plain, and, there it was, encircled with a ring of grey stone crowned with battlements. A great human city. Close-packed houses roofed in thatch and slate took up every inch of space within its encircling wall, except at its centre, where there stood a flat-topped hill with the river dividing and encircling it. On this hill was a great castle. A high tower stood at each corner and at its centre was a square keep. Unusually for the region it sported a thin central tower, crowned by a conical roof finished in terracotta. From this flew a great flag bearing the emblem of a brutal-looking mace. After encircling the hill, the river continued on its journey, exiting the city through a large culvert in the western wall. From there it continued across the plain, before plunging into a dense woodland and disappearing from view. Morgan knew, of course, that after a few miles it would merge with the slower, darker waters of the Vinoyen before journeying far to the south, past Tetha Vinoyen and Haslan Falls and then into the southern lands, past Sketta and Eburg, before joining the Endless Marshes on its way to the sea.

Gradually the clearing filled with horsemen, banners held proudly aloft. Overhead, the sun broke through the clouds and on to the host of warriors as they assembled together in their tribal group. The mood had palpably lifted; they were glad to see the daylight once more.

'Felmere,' said Morgan, 'the biggest city in these parts, the biggest in the disputed lands, except perhaps for Roshythe. It is hard to believe that at the outset of the war it actually fell to the enemy. The gates were open and barely guarded and they just rode in and sacked the place. The occupation barely lasted two days before they fled with their plunder and the city was retaken. Lessons were learned and the walls strengthened. Since then it has been the bastion against the enemy, the rock on which armies dash themselves. Without Felmere the war may well have been lost years ago.'

'I did not expect it to be so grand,' said Cedric. 'Granted it is much smaller than Tanaren City, but then so are most places. This is where Baron Felmere is based then?'

'Yes, but he is in the field most of the time these days. His family is there, including his boy, Kraven, and his second wife, Mathilde.'

'His first wife died, I believe,' said Cedric.

'Yes, about three years ago, of a sickness. He remarried almost immediately; she is a Lasgaart. There is a disputed town the other side of the river, not Shayer Ridge, but a place called Skandun and it was deemed the best way to solve matters. They barely see each other because of the war but I think they are perfectly happy with the arrangement.'

Itheya rode over to join them. 'Well then, guide, whither now? Are we allied with that city, as I believe?'

'Yes,' said Morgan, 'that is Felmere, the place I spoke of yesterday. We cross the plain and head into the woods opposite. There is a road there that leads to the places where the army is encamped. I have two camps in mind and Baron Felmere could be in either. We will learn of the current situation there.'

'How long before we get there?'

'The way you lot ride maybe two days to the first camp, three to the second. When I left he was planning to attack a town on the next river, so I need to learn how those plans went before I can give you any more specifics.'

'And what of Terath and his journey south?'

'I cannot answer yet; I might ask you to divide your force in two, or perhaps he need only have an escort. Let us get to the camp first. There is maybe an hour of daylight left. Let us get down this hill and camp at the edge of these woods tonight. Tomorrow we can ride past the walls of the city and give them something to talk about until spring arrives.'

Itheya laughed. 'Those are my orders to give, but I agree with your assessment. We will sound the horns and move on.'

And so they did. There was a steep path to the west of the clearing and this the horses made light work of. They followed the speeding river, passing a couple of woodsmen burning charcoal who stared open-mouthed at their passing. As the sun went down, they rested up at the edge of the forest looking at the lights of the city, waiting for the dawn when the elves would truly be riding to war.

49

Baron Zlaton Eburg was a fastidious man. He sat behind his high table dabbing his mouth with a thick white cloth, wiping away the residue from the goblet of highly watered wine from which he had been drinking. A pewter plate sat on the table where he had pushed it; a few thin bones and a film of sticky gravy were all that was left from the meal he had just enjoyed. His ghostly white face, now clear of any cloying foodstuff, regarded his retainers, servants and soldiers, who, like him, had finished eating and were waiting for any instructions he might give them.

'As you know, I have been away a while. The good news is that the military campaign has gone well, better than at any time in the last ten years. This means I have an opportunity to attend to more domestic matters for there is indeed much to attend to. You may all return to your duties except for Seneschal Carey and Captain Jeffen who will brief me on what needs to be done here. And you, of course, Mother, you always have a place at my side.'

Sitting to his left, clad in layers of black velvet and buried under an enormous felt hat of indeterminate shape, was a woman of greatly advanced decrepitude. Her face seemed minute under her clothing and was a sea of wrinkles broken only by two sunken black eyes and a wafer-thin line of painted red that approximated to lips. She put a withered hand to her mouth to stifle a yawn.

'Yes, my dear; we always help each other when we can.'

The crowd gradually dispersed until just a handful of people remained. Eburg surveyed those present then beckoned to a nearby servant.

'Send in Brother Cornelius, so that we may have spiritual guidance in our sundry deliberations.'

A short while later the brother arrived. Some two hundred years ago a split had occurred within the Artoran Church. A group of priests in Chira, seeing the current church as decadent and self- absorbed, hailed the formation of a new organisation, the Fellowship of Righteous Adherents to the Church's High Tenets. The FRACHT, or the Frach

BOOK ONE: AUTUMN

Brotherhood as it was called, was initially denounced as heretical, but given the phenomenal number of converts in its first twenty years of existence the sheer impracticality of burning thousands and thousands of ordinary people led the official church to swiftly realign its position. As a consequence, the Brotherhood was given official status, allowed to preach the words of the Divine Pantheon and build its own places of worship. Within fifty years there was little to differentiate it from the main church and the same accusations of decadence and indolence were beginning to be levelled at it, too. As far as Tanaren was concerned, the new church found its most receptive ears in the east of the country. From the monastery of Frach Menthon it preached its values of piety, humility and self-sacrifice, winning many converts in the area, although whether these ideals were actively practised by the congregation was arguable. The distinctive features of the Brotherhood were the tonsured head and the all-white hessian robe. All new brothers were required to hand-inscribe their own copy of the Book of Artorus which they were then to wear fixed to a chain around their neck for twenty-three hours a day. Many of them went further, showing their piety by binding their books in iron and making them as large as possible. Brother Cornelius was a case in point – his book was encased in metal with a bulky lock, causing him to walk with a permanent stoop. He also affected a shuffling gait, such also being seen as a sign of humility.

    He stood next to Eburg now, reciting the Prayer of Artorus, one slightly adapted from the official prayer, something the Brotherhood was wont to do. Once he had finished the Baron and his mother, along with Carey and Jeffen, seated themselves at the great table. Cornelius remained standing; he would only sit for a maximum of one hour a day, slept on a bed of stone and once a week would flagellate himself with birch branches. The Book of Artorus made no reference to the virtue of pain and suffering but it had never stopped the Brotherhood from seeing permanent discomfort as the state best suited for bringing one closer to the Gods.

    Eburg said his own silent prayer then addressed his audience.

    'It is good to see all of you again. As you know it has been a difficult few months for us. My good lady wife still wears black and refuses to leave her room and I am still excluded from Baron Esric's more secret counsels. I have determined that the best course of action for all of us is to draw as little attention to ourselves as possible; maybe some months in the future the transgressions of my son may be forgiven and things can return to as close to normal as is possible in such straitened times.'

'He is a savage! A barbarian, I tell you! No man of Artorus would send the head of a woman's own son to his mother. It is the despicable act of a coward to do such a thing.' Eburg's mother was suddenly very animated.

'Nevertheless, the boy was shown to be disloyal.' Seneschal Carey, a silver-haired man of iron who had seen most things in his life, spoke in gravelly tones. 'You may argue that their actions were overzealous or excessive, but the boy was caught dealing with the Arshumans. That is something we cannot dispute. This followed a period of defeat after defeat where the enemy seemed to be aware of our every move before we had even committed ourselves. It is a tragedy for your family, my Lady, but all we can do is pray to the Gods for wisdom and continue to serve Baron Esric as best we can, however much it sticks in the craw.'

'Well, young Esric will learn. Eburgs always have their vengeance, however long it takes.' Lady Eburg smacked her thin lips with relish.

'What we are talking about here is nothing less than the loss of my baronetcy. Esric has that power, he could freely hand my lands over to whichever of his lackeys he chooses. My lands!' Eburg thumped his hand on to the table with alacrity. He was as pale as a ghost, his eyes lined with red. 'Enough, we are not here to discuss our greater problems; the ordering of my lands are the priority here. Jeffen, brief me on the state of the villages and the farms. Has there been any sedition in the country?'

His captain then embarked on a detailed, drawn-out account of the situation in the further-flung parts of his baronetcy. There had been discontented rumblings in many villages – the treachery against Baron Esric, a substandard harvest caused by heavy rain and some overzealous judgements by local magistrates had led to a lot of stored-up resentment and anger. Jeffen's fear was how this might manifest itself.

BOOK ONE: AUTUMN

'A harsh winter and shortages of food could lead to revolt in the villages; starving people with nothing to lose can be as dangerous as a wounded boar.' 'And what do you suggest we do about this problem?'

'My Lord, our grain stores are low. Petition Baron Esric for a loan of grain from Sketta; let the villages know we are providing for them – the goodwill engendered alone should stave off any threat to us.'

Eburg snorted. 'Brother Cornelius, the thoughts of the holy church, please.'

Cornelius stooped even lower.

'The church will always put those with the least first. The prospect of any worshipper of the Divine Pantheon struggling for food this winter is not one of which the Gods would approve.'

'Then let the church feed them.' Eburg's mother sounded shrill. 'We are not begging Esric for charity, not after his crimes against us.'

'Mother is right,' Eburg said. 'Have I not said we do not attract attention to ourselves at this time? I will get the magistrates and local nobility to pay a tithe to you, Cornelius; you will see that your worshippers are provided for.' Captain Jeffen bowed silently, as did Cornelius. The matter was closed.

An hour or so passed with such discussions and there was a collective sigh of relief when Eburg seemed to wind things up. He took a long drink from his goblet.

'Now, the petitions. I am in the mood to dispense some summary justice.'

'Are you sure you or your mother do not need a rest before we proceed? 'Carey sounded hopeful.

'No, we are both fine. We will continue until it is dark. Arrange the petitions for us.'

And so the afternoon continued. Eburg mediated in several interminable disputes as to who owned this hedge or that hedge, this hen or that hen, who had property rights in this village, who owned the contracts to trade silks in the town, which wainwright should supply wagons to the militia and so forth. Carey and Jeffen advised where they could and Eburg insured Cornelius had a say on each case before he made his decision. Eburg's mother also chipped in frequently. She obviously felt her advice was indispensable, and this indeed seemed to be the case, for Eburg rarely, if ever, went against her wishes.

Civil disputes over, it was time to move on to criminal matters, something Eburg was much more interested in. The brutal jailor would haul the poor alleged miscreant in front of the Baron; the seneschal would give a brief rundown of the facts of each case; the Baron would briefly peruse any written evidence; witnesses and the defendant would be questioned, and the Baron would pronounce sentence. In this manner justice was dispensed in a brutally efficient manner.

One twenty-two-year old man caught stealing apples from a farmers orchard – a night in the stocks; one eighteen-year-old man caught poaching the Baron's deer (accomplices escaped) – death by hanging; one thirteen year-old boy, part of a gang cutting purses in the market – ten lashes; a hired thug, age unknown, numerous crimes including murder, theft and assault – death by hanging; and one prostitute and her accomplice guilty of assaulting and robbing clients – ten lashes for her and a branding, thirty lashes for him. One man was found innocent, a businessman accused of arranging the murder of a family residing in a building he wished demolished and replaced with a property built for the more genteel. He was excused on condition of making an increased contribution to Eburg's war chest.

'One more case, my Lord,' said Carey, 'a slightly unusual one, a man from the Endless Marshes accused of the murder of a trader in Tath Wernig. Magistrate Onkean has written a deputation here and in here we have some evidence, medicines, poisons and herbs the man had brought to trade.'

'Bring him in,' sighed Eburg, picking up then speed-reading the deputation. He had a look at the basket. 'All that is worth a fair bit, is it not?'

'Yes, my Lord,' said Carey. 'If you have the right connections, this could set your average country merchant up prettily.'

'Enough to kill for?'

'Indeed, my Lord.'

BOOK ONE: AUTUMN

The Baron switched his attention back to the missive in front of him as, under guard, the next man was brought in. After finishing his reading he looked up at the accused. His mouth opened slightly in shock.

In front of him stood a man, who from his woollen garments, ceremonial scarring and ruddy complexion was definitely not from the locality; that was no more than Eburg had expected. However, he had definitely come off the worst in some brawl or other. His right eye was ringed with yellow, puffy and partially closed; his nose had been broken; there was livid purple bruising on other parts of his face and neck, and his lip was swollen and split. Despite this, and the heavy shackles that he wore, he held himself proudly, tall and erect. There was always a certain bearing about the Marsh Men that disturbed him. Eburg addressed the jailor.

'Cornock, how did he end up like this?'

'Oh my Lord, we were cleaning out his cell (the Marsh Man snorted) when he made a break for it. It took three of us to restrain him, fought like one of Keth's demons he did, a marsh demon if you like. My Lord, these folks are savage when roused, marked us all he did.' Cornock disconsolately stroked a bruise on his jaw.

'Very well, good work. It says here there was a skirmish over the river with two traders. One fell in and died ... My my, the information here is scant. Is the surviving trader here?'

'No, my Lord,' said Carey, 'By all accounts he was a bit of a dubious character with an um... distrust of authority. I believe Onkean transcribes his statement in his deputation.'

'He does. They argued over these trade goods and this man attacked them.

There...'

'I did not,' Cygan said quietly.

Eburg looked at him. 'You understand us marsh fellow? Good. That will make things easier. You, however, need to learn that you speak only when I say. I am Baron here and you are lower than the humblest peasant. Speak again and this jailor needs no excuse to strike you further.'

Cygan glowered at him. Evidently he had no idea of Eburg's

importance, the Baron thought. He rubbed his cheek with his hand.

'The guards saw nothing, the magistrate saw nothing, our witness has disappeared... It is one word against another; the whole thing is as murky as the depths of the Vinoyen. What do we know of the dead man?'

'A trader of some repute,' said Carey. 'He had a broad network of associates and was pretty well spoken of; some of his methods were apparently dubious, but we could say that about any merchant that ever lived. His standing in Sketta was pretty high.'

'Was it? Was it?' Eburg suddenly felt tired. 'That complicates things. It says here Marsh Man that you have something to tell us, something you feel is important. Speak.'

'I can talk now then?' Cygan's tone was sardonic.

'Don't be impertinent! Did I not just say so?'

'With you people, what is said seems to rarely match what is meant. It is not like that where I live – we are plain-speaking folk and have no need to cloak our intentions behind falsehoods and duplicity.'

'Do not try my patience, marsh savage. If you are as plain speaking as you say, then tell us why you came here.'

'Very well. I was sent here by my Elder. Our lands are threatened by a danger unleashed by outsiders. We do not know who these outsiders are or why they have done what they have; I have come here to try to find out.'

'What sort of danger?'

'An ancient race,' – Cygan was having difficulty speaking through his busted lip – 'one that has been confined to a distant lake for aeons but which now has started to spread, to attack our people. They are aquatic, they hide in water and they attack at night. They are almost impossible to stop. And once they have destroyed us they will come for you, your lands being nearest to ours. And that is not all. They are led by Ventekuu, the Great Worm; I know for I have seen it myself. It could swallow this town whole such is its colossal size. My advice to you is to find out who has called this creature from its home so that it can be stopped before it is too late for us all. I am here to warn you; you would do well to heed my words.'

BOOK ONE: AUTUMN

Eburg looked grave. He appeared to be carefully weighing up what this strange man was saying. His reverie, though, was broken by the contemptuous snort of his mother.

'Superstitious claptrap! Why are we even countenancing the words of this foul pagan? His very sight, his very smell, is an assault on my most delicate sensibilities. Come, I hunger for my dinner. Let us swiftly dispense justice on this savage and get the kitchens to attend to us.'

'Wise words, my Lady.' Cornelius was bowing so low his head was almost at the level of his knees. 'Baron, this creature is not one that recognises the Divine Pantheon, and as such our normal rules of justice do not apply. Pagans who murder those blessed by our Gods deserve only one type of justice. This creature, remember, does not even have a soul.'

Eburg twiddled his thumbs. 'Carey?'

'Personally, my Lord, I feel that, while his warnings sound fanciful, we cannot wilfully ignore them. I would put him back in his cell and get Calvannen's advice on the matter. That would help us gain favour with him and, if anything were to happen to us on our lands as this man warns, then it cannot be said we ignored advice given freely.'

'And yet I cannot be seen to favour the rantings of a Marsh Man over one of our own people.' Eburg indicated the basket and looked at Cygan. 'What was the purpose of bringing this with you?'

'We understood that you would not listen to me alone. This gesture, most of our remaining stock, was meant to be a gesture of goodwill and to show how important your response is to us. Hopefully, this Calvannen fellow will have the sense to respond. By the way, there was much more in that basket when I left my village.'

Lady Eburg was piqued. 'The arrogance of the creature! To presume that you are in capable of understanding the situation for yourself!' She called over a servant. 'Get the kitchens moving, I require sustenance. Gentleman, I am leaving now; I will promenade in the courtyard and breathe some unpolluted air.'

With much kerfuffle and aided by a handmaiden Lady Eburg left the room. Her son stood, too, and stretched his back and legs.

'These trade goods are now the property of the baronetcy. I will write to Onkean to enquire as to the missing items. Captain Jeffen, double the river patrols; we have to at least give the impression of responding to this man's warnings. As to my decision on this case...' He returned to his seat, his face ashen grey.

'Mother is right as always, a pagan barbarian cannot stroll in and slaughter a trader of repute in Sketta and escape unpunished.'

'But we have no evidence that that was what he did.' Carey spoke gravely.

'We do, Carey – it is written down here from a witness who worships the divine Artorus. We have two executions to arrange already; it is time to make it three. The prisoner is to be hanged; there is nothing better to improve the morale of the townsfolk than a multiple execution. Arrange for the three of them to be hung in the square; tell the market traders they can trade that day also.'

Cygan fought against his chains. 'You are a fool! You have to listen! The Malaac are coming for you, they eat those they kill... You will all be next, all of you!'

'Take him away, Cornock.' Eburg sighed wearily. 'Do not harm the prisoner. The execution of an exotic will draw a crowd; he needs to be fit enough to resist and struggle on the way to the gallows.'

The jailor bowed and, aided by two guards, led the Marsh Man away.

Eburg got up and made to leave. 'Jeffen, how long before the executions can proceed?'

'Two days, my Lord. They will be dancing on a rope at noon the day after next.'

'Good. Come with me, Jeffen. I think I will join Mother in her promenade.'

The two men left the room, leaving Carey all alone. He looked around to check he wasn't being watched, then hastily put pen to parchment and scribbled a brief letter. After folding it, he placed the note in a pouch at his waist and also left the room.

Sketta was less than ten miles from Eburg. Unlike the smaller town on the river, it was located inland, away from the marshier climes. Having said that, many years of local peat diggings had created many quiet water-filled channels that both surrounded and ran through the bustling, picturesque town. It was a town the Arshumans had never come close to capturing in the last ten years and so its populace lacked the fearfulness of the other towns of the Seven Rivers. There was a casual relaxed confidence to the place. Many exiled nobles lived there including Baron Esric Calvannen, Chief Prosecutor of the War in the South.

The town's manor house was a long, grand affair, rendered in stone, itself a rarity in these parts. Its banqueting hall was vast, its floor covered in cool grey flagstones covered by thick, luxurious red carpet. From both flanking galleries hung many lavishly woven tapestries depicting many of the wars and battles that had shaped both the area and its peoples over the centuries. The galleries were full of musicians playing to entertain the elegantly clad dancers below. It was a ball, held ostensibly to herald the end of autumn, but it was just as much to celebrate the Baron's return and the end of the fighting season as anything else. Esric himself sat watching the dancers; he himself had not danced here for many years. Clad in a velvet tunic and black leather breeches, he watched the elegantly swaying participants with an air of studied nonchalance.

His sisters were as usual the main attraction. There was but a year between them; they were as close to being twins as it was possible to be, hair black as ink cascading over shoulders white as marble – the very epitome of Tanarese beauty. It was Esric's job to marry them off, but he was fond of them both and there were no outstanding candidates for their hands, so he had let the matter rest. His time was filled with far more pressing matters, after all. They had spent most of the evening dancing with the knights, who were always in demand on occasions like these. When they weren't dancing they seemed to be enjoying the company of Mikel, the mage, who was obviously quite the raconteur; Esric remembered the warning he was given about his womanising and allowed himself a wry smile.

A servant approached him and whispered something quietly in his ear. He nodded at the man, made his excuses and followed him out of the room. From there it was through a dimly lit corridor, down a flight of stairs and into a small windowless anteroom lit by a single sputtering torch. There was a man waiting there seated quietly on a bench. The servant left the two of them alone and Esric, after blinking back a tear, caused by the smoke, spoke hoarsely.

'You have news for me? Baron Garal cited pressing domestic matters as his reason for not attending tonight.'

The man was hooded and his features could be barely seen in the semidarkness. 'Arshuman money is changing hands in the east. I have seen Garal's seneschal's picked men doing deals in dark alleys. I cannot confirm that he is definitely in the pay of the enemy; rather, I feel he is keeping in the good graces of both sides, waiting to see in whose favour the wind blows. It is not my place to advise you, my Lord, but keep him away from your most private counsels. He is also corresponding with Eburg. Give me some time and I should be able to intercept his messengers and get my hands on one of these letters. And there is another thing.'

Esric raised an eyebrow. 'And that is?'

'Strange things are happening on Garal's southern borders. People are moving north, fleeing their homes. There have been dark rumours of attacks by strange creatures in the dead of night. Garal dismisses these tales as the ramblings of superstitious peasants, but I have spoken with some of them, solid men, farmers, and when they say they have seen demons, half-men covered in scales and slime rising from the river, and they say it without blanching, then I tend to think investigation is necessary at the very least.'

'Tell me more.'

'Some Marsh Men have fled their villages, too, and have set up a camp on Garal's lands. He has threatened them with eviction but they are too afeard to return home. It is a rum situation. Garal is far more interested in his own intrigues than in what is happening on his own borders.'

Esric nodded slowly. 'Return to his lands and resume your duty there. My man here will arrange your payment, and get me some proof of the treachery you speak of, if you can.'

The Baron left the room and climbed back up the stairs. Once in the corridor, he pulled out a piece of parchment he had been hiding in an internal pocket in his robes. Slowly he read and reread its words, words he was familiar with already. He replaced the parchment and rejoined the ball.

Enough alcohol had been consumed to loosen up the dancers' inhibitions. The stiff formality of the earlier hours had been replaced by the more frenzied reels. The musicians, knowing what was required, had stepped up the pace considerably; there was much laughing and joking; his sisters were swirling about the place, knights draped on their arms. Esric circulated, spoke to the people he had to, until finally he joined Josar in the shadows at the back of the hall.

'I need a favour from you,' he told his old friend.

'What? Someone needs beating up? A friendly word in a maiden's ear? Young Lady Selmia has kept her eyes on you all night.'

'No, I need you to stay here for a couple of days. I want you to travel to Eburg with me the day after tomorrow. My patience with the Baron is at the point of snapping.'

Josar raised an appraising eyebrow. 'And what exactly has driven you to this conclusion – one, I may add, that many of us came to a while ago.'

'You know his seneschal, Carey?'

'By Artorus yes, a good man, his boy, too; he was with us when we cleared the island on the Axe.'

'Exactly. You know I naively thought all the sedition and treachery we have had to face had been put to bed after Morgan's visit. He said not all the vipers had had their fangs drawn when he left and it appears he may have been right. Earlier on I received a missive from Carey; apparently Eburg is planning some executions in a couple of days and one of the victims is a Marsh Man. It is a matter he should have consulted me about but he has instead decided to press on regardless.'

Josar looked sceptical. 'But surely that is more a mistake on his part than out and out treachery.'

'I agree. Ordinarily, I would let the matter pass but according to Carey this Marsh Man has knowledge of a matter of a troubling nature about problems on our borders. Before you laugh, I have had corroboration from another source which more or less confirms that there is trouble in the Marshes, trouble that both Eburg and Garal are keeping from me – either through stupidity or malice, I know not. And then there is this...' He pulled the parchment out of his pocket and gave it to Josar. 'Carey found it on Eburg's desk and decided to let me look.'

Josar read the brief message. 'Border trouble my end. War on two fronts? Time to sit back and profit from the demise of the Prosecutors? Will write soon. G.'

Josar looked up at Esric. 'If he hadn't mentioned the demise of the Prosecutors, this would be ambiguous rubbish, but because he does this is treachery. And this was written by Garal to Eburg?'

'No,' said Esric. 'Firstly Garal doesn't sign it; it could be from anyone with a name beginning with G. I am having him watched anyway; maybe he can lead us to all those involved if there is treachery among the barons. Secondly, it was not addressed to Eburg.'

'Not Eburg? Then who?'

'I will tell you on the way there; I want no one overhearing.'

'Very well. One other question, why aren't we going tomorrow?'

Esric shook his head, affecting a world-weariness brought on by companions with no sense of subtlety. 'Josar, my friend, you have absolutely no sense of theatre. We will arrive unannounced an hour or so before these executions are supposed to commence; I want to see Eburg's reaction. Well no, perhaps all I actually want is to see him squirm.'

'Now that,' said Josar, draining his goblet, 'is something I wouldn't miss for the world. Now let me introduce you to Selmia, a lady whose only fault is a terrible taste in men.'

The two of them emerged from the shadows, their smiles showing they had not a care in the world.

It was dusk over Tath Wernig. Lights were beginning to appear through the windows of the inn, the magistrate's house and a couple of the smaller residences. Outside the smithy, several tethered horses were munching contentedly at their feed. Crepuscular shadows clung to the trading post and the houses close to it. The river, glittering like a studded leather belt, threaded its never-changing course southward. Outside the inn, two men hung around the doorway sharing a mug of ale and several fanciful stories. It was a scene of serene tranquillity.

Or maybe not. High among the twisted branches of an ancient oak, close to the magistrate's house and unseen by anybody was a crouched figure, swathed in black from his hood to his boots. Whitey was not a man who gave up easily.

The guards had run him out of town; he had only barely avoided a beating. Once he was clear of them, he returned to digs in Eburg, sat and pondered all the recent events in his life, and realised that without the big merchant his prospects were as poor as ever.

It was time for revenge.

The magistrate had kept the Marsh Man's trade goods for himself; he had taken his share and sent the rest to the Baron. They were gone now and there was nothing he could do about it. The magistrate's silver, though, was another matter. He had seen it when he was inside his house – candlesticks, plates, spoons – much of it just displayed on a dresser. And so he had returned. He had spent a day or so casing the place. There were two guards at the front gate but no one at the servant's entrance at the rear. There was a seven-foot wall to scale and a lock to pick, but then he was in; it was child's play for a seasoned professional such as he. He would wait for the dead of night when everyone was asleep, including the guards (well, they had slept through their watch the night before), and the only noise was the sound of the owls and their victims, the river and the chill wind in the trees. He could be in and out in fifteen minutes. All he had to do now was wait.

A couple of guards were strolling around the village; one was by the waterside, the other was stroking the horses. It was just them and the two men at the inn, them and the rapidly receding light.

Whitey had great night vision and was watching the man at the river's edge. Boredom was always a problem with these jobs, keeping focused, not letting the mind w...

What in the name of Artorus happened there?

In the blink of an eye he saw something. Shapes, man shapes, emerging out of the river and smothering the man at the water's edge. Then they were gone, back into the river with a soft splash, leaving the bank clear. Then silence.

Had he dreamed it? Nobody else seemed to notice what had happened.

Were the Marsh Men attacking in vengeance?

Then at the very same place the river started to boil.

One black figure, its silhouette close to human, but definitely not human, leapt on to the bank. Then a second. And a third. Suddenly the bank was alive, swarming with dozens of these things. And then they started creeping into the village.

The guard could see them now. He bellowed a warning to the other men and ran forward, his halberd lowered. The men raised a hue and cry in the inn and several of their companions emerged bleary and confused.

The black figures started to attack them. There were shouts and screaming from the men and suddenly from their assailants a blood-curdling unearthly howl. From the house he had been planning to rob the magistrate emerged with a dozen or so armed guards. They joined the fray outside the inn.

It was a terrible battle. These creatures were unarmed but were biting and clawing there victims; blows were struck on them but seemed to make little impression.

Artorus's divine bollocks, thought Whitey, the Marsh Man was right!

Ever the one for executive action Whitey made a decision. It was time to flee. He gracefully swung out of the tree and landed softly on the muddy ground. Quietly he made his way to the smithy. The horses were rearing and white-eyed but they were not being bothered at the moment. He always had an empathy with horses and managed to calm one sufficiently enough to lead it away from the others. Eventually it was still enough to mount. He swung his leg over it and started to ride it into the trees.

Suddenly from nowhere one of the creatures leapt in front of him. He saw it only briefly – its strange, lizard-like eyes, its sharp white teeth, its coat of wet glistening scales – before his horse reared in terror. Whitey clung for dear life to its neck barely staying on but he had lost complete control of it. In its terror to get away, it rode at full pelt towards the inn.

It was all a whirl of lightning-fast images, brief impressions gleaned from the back of a panicked horse for Whitey now. The sound of these creatures devouring the other screaming horses, the slick of slippery blood at the inn door, the sight of them carrying the dead and dragging the wounded towards the river, the crunch of his horse's hoof on one of these monster's skulls as it ran in front of him. As helpless as a baby, Whitey held desperately on to his mount as it plunged through the carnage at the inn. Women and children were fleeing into the woods; a small knot of desperate men, halberds in hand, thrust and stabbed at the ever-increasing enemy trying frantically not to be swarmed. They were far too preoccupied to notice Magistrate Onkean, blood masking his horrified face, as he punched weakly at two of his assailants, before being dragged bodily under the river's foaming surface.

But Whitey was gone, plunging down the road to Eburg, clinging with all his strength to his crazed mount, leaving behind the scene of irreparable carnage that was once the village of Tath Wernig.

50

Sir Trask got to his feet, adjusted his breeches and smacked his lips lasciviously.

'See, as I told you, no pillars of fire, no explosions, no shards of ice, nothing. Tie her up and gag her and she is no different to any camp whore.' He turned away from the subject of his discourse and walked towards the horses picketed by the south road.

The girl he walked away from lay on her back in the tattered remnants of her robes and stared blankly at the slate-grey sky.

She was beyond anything now – pain, suffering, fear, all had melded together into a melange of unending agony, leaving her empty, devoid of everything that had made her human, stripped of everything that once was Cheris. All that remained was nothing more than what she actually physically was – skin, blood, hair and bone. She had nothing more that they could take.

They had hauled her up the road kicking and struggling every inch of the way. Once they were back in the clearing, she managed to wriggle free of her captors and made a desperate bolt for freedom, towards the path that lead to what was left of Anaya's cottage. The three men caught her just as she drew alongside the caravan; she was pushed against its wooden panelling and went crashing to the floor sending her staff rattling to the ground from where it rolled into the shade under the caravan's chassis. Then they all started to kick her, steel-capped boots finding many a soft mark. Bound and gagged, she still managed some muffled screams, her only outlet for the hurt they were causing her.

Then Trask arrived and they stopped. They were all obviously as frightened of him as she was. Although she knew what was to come, she had no idea of how it would feel. Mikel had been her only long-term lover, following a series of frantic fumbles in her teens with other similarly inexperienced initiates – the blind leading the blind as it were. Mikel knew what he was doing, though, was expert and attentive, and her times with him had always been passionate, energetic and fun. What had just happened to her here was about as diametrically opposed to that as it was possible to get. Trask's body was a muscular, crushing weight, squeezing the air out of her and reigniting the pain in her damaged rib. When he forced himself into her he seemed to delight in the way she winced; it seemed to encourage him, to make him try to find new ways to hurt. An inner conflict raged in her mind as she fought against the pain and revulsion: she wanted to remain stiff as a board, be utterly emotionless, to give him no gratification at all; she also wanted to break into floods of tears, to beg him to stop, to plead for her life, for his mercy.

Ultimately, she did neither. She gauged him to be a man utterly without pity, so sobbing like a child would not avail her; neither could she remain still under him – every thrust was a spear of agony and her body's instinctive reaction was to move away from the source of the pain. It was a mistake, for every tic of her body seemed to excite him, but one she could not control. He took an age to finish with her; he found every entrance that she had and when he finally spent himself on her, she had to fight hard to control the shaking convulsions that shock had induced in her. Eventually she resorted to digging her knuckles hard into her back and biting her own tongue as a distraction, tasting the coppery blood as it ran down her throat.

He looked at her for a while, as a cat watches a mouse, curious as to the way she reacted in her fear. She could not meet his gaze, steeped as it was in malice and sadistic pleasure; she stared at the sky, fighting to control her trembling, taking an age to succeed. Finally, when she had regained some composure, he decided it was time to leave. His companions watched the whole thing, adding comments, encouragements and suggestions that only added to her trembling nausea. The younger lad, however, remained with the horses; his stomach was obviously not strong enough for what was going on before his very eyes.

'I have to leave now.' Trask took the reins the boy handed to him. 'Fresh horses at regular stops mean that I should be back in Grest by the morning. No one is looking out for you lot, so make your way back when you have finished with her.'

'And what do you want us to do with her in the end, sir?' The soldiers seemed to regard Trask with awe.

'She is a witch, is she not? I thought in these parts any witches the knights didn't get you burned. How you kill her is not important to me as long as you do kill her – oh and let the boy have a go at her next. Don't worry about violating an innocent, son; I got the impression she has been ridden more times than Felmere's charger. Can't blame her, though – entertainment must be sorely lacking trapped on an island for years on end with nothing but books to read. Do your job, lads, and when I see you next we can celebrate our upcoming triumph.' Trask whirled his horse around and was gone, riding as quickly as possible over the mud-churned track.

While they were talking, Cheris managed to crane her neck to her right. She saw, under the caravan's wheels, her staff lying unnoticed among the dead leaves. She could also see its blade; it had come free of the staff and was lying close to the front left wheel. Tantalisingly, it was only a few feet away from her but she was trussed up like a joint of meat and had no way of moving there unseen. Even when talking to Trask, at least one of the men always kept his eye on her. Frantic and hopeless, she looked to the heavens again. Blood was congealing on her thighs and the stabbing pain in her womb never relented. What hope was there for her?

With Trask gone, she became the centre of attention again. All four of the men came and stood around her. Her robe was bunched up at her waist and she had no way of concealing herself from them, her dry eyes stung with tears at what was to come next.

'Did you see Trask?' one of them was saying. 'Hung like a prize stallion. Hey, missy!' He prodded her with his boot. 'None of us can rip you apart like he did, not that it will stop us from trying. Sam boy, you heard the man; it's your turn next.'

The boy's voice betrayed his nervousness. 'Could I be left alone with her. Having you all watching, well, it might just put me off.'

'Ah, you big milksop. Have it your own way; we will be the other side of this wagon... Oh and if you lose the desire, just give her a squeeze; I am sure you know where.'

Laughing among themselves, they moved out of sight behind the caravan. The boy started fiddling with his clothes. How old was he? Fifteen? Fourteen? He had a feeble attempt at a moustache and was obviously not shaving yet, she thought. He moved into position on top of her. Unlike Trask who kept his head high, eager to see her discomfort, the boy lay full on her. He was taller than her but not by much. He kept his head close to hers; she could smell his damp clothes, his sweat, feel his breath on her cheek. He had difficulty finding the right place and manoeuvring into a comfortable position, but once he had got going it was all over in less than a minute. Unlike Trask, she had barely noticed him. Once he was done, he put his head next to hers and in the tiniest voice he could manage whispered into her ear.

'I am sorry.'

As he dressed himself, she could hear the other men discussing the best way to kill her.

'Trask wants her burned; that was what he said.'

'Don't be a fool! The smoke could attract anybody. The wood here is damp and hard to light; it would take hours to do the job properly.'

'You want to hang her then?'

'We could, but I really want to be out of here as soon as possible. The quicker we do it the less chance she has to use her witch tricks on us. When we are done with her as Trask wants, let us just cut her throat and leave her for the wolves and crows.'

The boy had gone back to his horses and suddenly Cheris realised that she was on her own. For the first time she was alone. Her torpid acceptance of her fate, the one which caused her to lay motionless and unfeeling under the boy, was replaced by a spark, the barest flickering of hope in a dark place. Making as little noise as she possibly could, she wriggled so that she was plumb next to the wheel on the caravan, the one which was barely a foot away from her staff's blade. She swivelled and sat up, her head and upper shoulders resting uncomfortably against the main body of the caravan next to the wheel. Her hands started to scrabble among the leaf litter reaching for the blade.

Too late, she realised. From behind the caravan one of the men came, his tread sure and steady. He was the one she thought to be the leader of the men that remained – balding with a moustache, a slight beard and several missing teeth. He obviously interpreted her movements as another feeble attempt to escape.

'Less of that!' he growled at her before back-handing her face with a stinging blow. She tasted blood on her lip – how much blood did she have left in her?

He pulled a dagger on her, a long cruel blade, razor-sharp. He held its point against her eye before moving it down slightly and pricking the orbit under her eyeball. The tiniest drop of blood ran down her cheek almost like a tear.

'Any attempt at being clever and I stab your eyeball until it bursts.' He pulled her gag down and free of her mouth. 'Open it!' he ordered her. 'Let's see if you can take it like a tavern slut, five pennies a go.'

With the knife less than an inch from her eye Cheris opened her mouth. She could smell him, a soldier that hadn't washed in weeks. She fought hard to keep the disgust from rising in her, to stop her from gagging. He was exposed now and forced himself into that place he wanted to go.

He grunted as she choked, his blade started to wander. Looking up she saw he was not really looking at her, that his eyes were half closed. He was thrusting so violently he did not notice as her hands dug into the soil behind her. There was earth, leaves and more earth, filling her fingernails. And then there was something else, cold icy cold. She remembered the cold metal of her staff and knew it was the blade she was touching. She felt its edge, it cut her hand but she didn't care. Desperately hoping he would not finish too quickly, she worked the blade until she held it in her right hand. She had been cut several times and felt the warm blood oozing over her palms and fingers, but it was a minor pain compared to what had gone before, easy to ignore. She had little room to move her wrists, but little was enough, just enough. She felt the rope start to give as she sawed the blade across it.

The man gave out a load groan as his release came. Cheris, her eyes watering at his aggression already, fought against every instinct to stop herself spitting and retching as she tasted him. He pulled out, his eyes once again fully focused on her. 'Swallow it all.'

Meekly, she complied and did not struggle as he pulled the gag back over her mouth. Then he looked away from her as he endeavoured to push his flaccid member back into his breeches. He did not notice at first as Cheris slowly got to her feet. He swore, his laces were all tangled, he still swung free in front of her.

Then he looked up.

Cheris stood before him in her tattered robes and, as he watched she put her bloodied hands, now free of cords, to her mouth and pulled down her gag. She hawked and spat the residue of the man's semen on to the ground. 'You really are a very stupid man,' she croaked hoarsely.

Dagger in hand he went to thrust at her vitals but the fear in his eyes was easy to see.

She read him all the way. Before he could get near her she held out her hand, palm outward, and said the softest of words under her breath. The same words she had used against the horse beater in Tanaren, but this time meant with much more force and power.

The man was lifted into the air and propelled backwards at a ferocious velocity. He flew some twenty, maybe thirty feet, crying in terror until he impacted against the gnarled trunk of a giant oak tree. She heard his back snap, and the dull crack of his skull against wood, then he slid like a ragdoll down the length of the tree before slumping lifeless at its roots, his trousers loose around his ankles.

Cheris walked slowly around the caravan, every step an agony. The two men stood looking at her, their faces pale with fear. The boy had left the horses and was standing just behind them.

'The Gods help us!' whispered the young one.

There was a second of pure crystalline silence, as the four protagonists beheld each other. Then as one the three men bolted towards the southern road as though the demons of Keth were at their heels.

Cheris watched them run as though weighing in her mind whether she should show them mercy. Then she spoke, her voice regaining some strength, words the men would not recognise but the ones that spelt their certain doom.

    Once that was done, she spoke again.

    'There are no gods,' she said.

    As soon as the fireball was released she turned her back on them. She knew its aim was true and there was no escape for her erstwhile murderers. She heard the crash of flame and the nigh-on feminine screams of the men as they were engulfed. She heard the horses cry in terror, pull up their pickets and bolt into the woods. It didn't matter; she could not ride anyway. She tried walking to the caravan's rear entrance but stopped after a few strides. The pain was too great – walking had never felt so difficult. She slumped against the caravan's wheel, sliding down its length before curling up at its base in a foetal position. The birds were singing. She heard several deer breaking through the underbrush; it was as though nothing untoward had ever happened here. Numb and exhausted, with the smells of earth and blood in her nostrils, she drifted, her mind, normally so active, frozen and incapable of putting anything coherent together. Cheris Menthur, eyes glazed and lifeless, passed out, her senses in shutdown, all in denial of what had been done to her.

    She did not know how long she had lain upon the ground – an hour, maybe less than that, maybe a lot less? Something had made her come to, though – a noise? Yes, it was a noise.

    There it was again. It sounded like a mewling infant, a feeble barely discernible whimper. She forced herself to stand, finding her staff she leant on it, using it for the first time like an old man's prop. There was the noise again. She hurriedly scanned the clearing but there was nothing, just the caravan, the abandoned tents of the knights and the dead man next to the tree.

    The noise was coming from the southern path, from where she had directed the fireball.

    Slowly and with an indefinable sense of dread she hobbled in the direction of the noise. It was as if a fire had been set in every private place below her waist. Her hands were numb and throbbing, still coated with her own blood; her mouth stung from where the man had struck her, and the bruises on her torso where she had been kicked roared their protest as she moved. Gritting her teeth, she reached the path and made her way towards some blackened shapes where the crows were clustering.

There were two bodies in close proximity to each other. Both were smoking and charred from head to toe and were barely recognisable as human. The crows scattered and flew as she approached them. They had been busy. In several places on both bodies the blackened skin had been opened, revealing the pulpy red flesh underneath; strings of it had been pulled out and decorated the corpses like some ghastly spring festival rosette. The noise had definitely not come from these two.

She scanned the road ahead. It was all water and mud; she felt it squelch underfoot. Then the noise came again and this time she homed in on it.

There was a prone figure less than a hundred yards ahead sheltering against the verge on the eastern edge of the road. With her feet and staff sinking into the morass she made as good progress as she could until she was just a few feet from the figure. Then she caught her breath.

She realised dully that of the dozens of men she must have killed at Grest she had seen none of them close to hand. She had heard screams and cries of pain but they could have been caused by anything. She had had an almost antiseptic detachment from the misery and suffering she must have caused. Not this time, though. This time the evidence was there before her.

It was the boy, of course. It had to be. The fireball could not have caught him properly. His back was to her and he seemed unaware of her presence as he whimpered again. His legs, and even his trousers, were barely scored by flame and he was using these to push himself slowly along the muddy ground. His back, though, was scorched black; she could see where his shirt had melted and fused with his flesh along his shoulders. His hair had partially burned away and the exposed skin on his scalp was viscous, almost liquid. The one ear she could see had all but gone, leaving a gaping hole in the side of his head. The acrid smell of his partially cooked body stuck at the back of her throat. He must have heard her for slowly he rolled on to his back screaming hoarsely at his torture.

His hands were little more than fused stumps of flesh and bone; his face, however, was almost intact, although one eye was white and blind. His torso, though ... just the sight brought a croaking gasp to her throat.

The fire had burned through his clothes and crackled and shrivelled the skin on his right-hand side. She counted four mud-covered ribs, all blackened and exposed by the hole where his diaphragm had once been. Under the ribs were the pinkish tinge of his organs; they seemed intact and healthy, though, if truth be told, she looked away from them as soon as she possibly could.

'How is it you are not dead?' she said aloud, as much to herself as to him.

His mouth opened. His face was covered in mud and soot, but the expression in his one good eye spoke more eloquently than a thousand words could.

'Please,' he said, his voice cracked and thin. 'Please.'

Cheris fought to regain control. 'I, I cannot do anything for you. I am not a healer and, even if I were, I doubt, I doubt you could be saved. All I can do is ease your passing, end it quickly. Is this what you wish?'

The boy gave the tiniest of nods; he whimpered one more time.

Cheris's eyes were stinging. This boy had raped her – why was she feeling so ashamed?

'Very well. May Xhenafa bring you to the Gods for judgement. What you did ... what you did... I know you were forced... Maybe they will show you mercy, I do not know.'

Her magic was draining her already exhausted body, but she forced herself, just one more time. She had to. Pointing at the boy she spoke again, a thin bolt of cerulean leapt from her finger straight at him. There it became as dozens of small charged snakes covering and encasing his spasming, writhing form, crackling as the smell of ozone filled the air. In a few seconds it was over. The boy lay still, his scarred face revealing a semblance of peace. Turning slowly away from him, Cheris doubled over and emptied the scant contents of her stomach into the mud.

It took an eternity for her to get back to the caravan; her pain had become omnipresent. She could barely remember a time before she had had it. It controlled her. It was who she was. The blood coating her thighs, buttocks and hands had congealed; she could still taste it in her mouth where she had bitten herself in her torment.

With her remaining strength she pulled open the rear door, clambered inside and slammed the bolt home. She staggered to her couch. Sitting on it hurt her so she attempted to lie full length on it. Eventually she found a tolerable position. Quietly she tried to let sleep take her.

It couldn't. The second her eyes closed there he was, pressing on her, crushing her, hurting her, his eyes burning through into her soul. He smelled clean, cleaner than the other men; he even sweated less but his breath was toxic. At one point he dribbled, his spittle dropping on to her forehead. She lay stock still, not daring to blanch. And then he licked her face, just to see her be repulsed. She sat upright on the couch and screamed her hurt and frustration.

For a second she wondered what she looked like. Her mirror was in her trunk; she was always using it. Perhaps she should get it out and see. See what, though? An ugly violated creature? A dirty cheapened thing? She remembered the way he had described her, ridden more times than Felmere's charger. There it was again, Cheris the slut. That was how they saw her here; perhaps that was what she was. Perhaps they thought they weren't even hurting her. Perhaps they thought it was the way she liked it, the way she wanted it. Maybe they thought they were doing her a favour. She was obviously asking for it, a woman alone in an army of men with her eye make-up and her hair just so; she was practically leaving the bedroom door open for them.

No, she did not want her mirror. She eased herself off the couch and dug around the storage compartments for food. She found a small flask of water, which she drank greedily – anything to take away the taste of that last man, and some small hard flatbreads which she bit into, risking her teeth. She seated herself on the other couch to finish her meal and remembered the last time she had sat there, whom she had been talking to.

Marcus. She had almost forgotten. Her face reddened with grief and tears finally came. For five minutes or so she sat there silently weeping for her mentor ... her friend. The man who had saved her life. Again she thought of Gilda and how she would speak to her and what exactly she would say.

The light was beginning to fade in the windows. She shuttered them both up; she wanted no reminders of the world outside. And at last she confronted it. The thought that had been floating around her head from the moment she first saw Trask gazing balefully at her next to the body of Sir Norton.

The men that had done this to her, that wanted her, the other mages and the knights all dead were her allies. She may well even have fought with them at Grest. What had turned them so? What did they want to achieve? It all begged many serious questions.

It also meant she could not stay here. Something was afoot and people needed to know. And only she, barely able to walk herself, could tell them. She did not know how far she had to go or whom to speak to; all she knew was that she had to follow the broad southern road until she got to ... somewhere. Then again were these men her only enemies? She could not tell just anyone. She had to be careful; treachery could be widespread here after all. She sighed. She still knew so little of the situation, the politics in this country.

Outside in the far distance a lone wolf howled. Cheris shivered. She felt her shock start to return and she just sat there, knees drawn up to her chin, trembling and shaking, small and very much alone. She had always seen herself as a strong woman, opinionated and as well capable of reason and well-constructed arguments as any man. She had always felt a little sorry for the gentler girls at the college. Girls like Elsa, all sweet smiles and artlessness. Yet here she now was herself, all tears and helplessness, hating her own vulnerability. She was all front, all façade. Underneath it all, when it all really mattered she was as quivering, spineless and terrified as the meekest, mildest wallflower.

And so it continued as night drew on – her mind did not stop. It circled and circled endlessly around itself, loathing and disgust still going hand in hand with the throbbing pains in her body. Eventually, she exhausted herself beyond any further emotion. She returned to her own couch, lay full length on it, threw a blanket over herself and slept instantly, in a place too dark even for dreams.

She woke only once. A noise outside the normal night sounds of the forest caused her to snap out of her sleep immediately. It sounded like hands or claws scrabbling or digging into the earth and was accompanied by another sound, a low growling noise made by two or three voices. Was it wolves? She raised her aching body on to her knees on the couch and as quietly as possible slid back the shutter on the window. Little could be seen by the light of the pale moon; it was a still cold night with nary a cloud under the expanse of shimmering stars. Her breath was starting to frost the window and she was about to pull the shutter to when she saw movement. It was over by the tree where she had flung that man, near to where his body lay. She couldn't quite make it out. It didn't look like they were wolves; the shapes seemed too small and almost humanoid. Then she remembered Roland and his tale of ghouls feasting on the flesh of the dead. She had given it little credence at the time but at that time she had not been alone, and afraid, and in the middle of a forest. She closed the shutter, checked the bolt on the door, resolved to blast anything that tried to get through it, and was asleep again in seconds. She never found out exactly what it was she saw but in the morning, when she stepped outside, all of the bodies were gone.

It was a chill morning. Frost lay heavy on the ground, coating the dead leaves and freezing the tiny puddles of standing water. She emerged wearing Marcus's cloak, which she pulled tightly over her rags and shivered. The intensity of the pain had receded to be replaced with a persistent throbbing ache. Her torso was sore with many tender spots where her bruises had come into their own overnight. She had her staff with her but no longer needed it to help her walk. She still shuffled slowly, though, lest the pain started to flare inside her again.

She cast around the knights' tents looking for food that hadn't been nibbled by rats, voles and other small furry forest creatures. Eventually she found some bread and fruit that had been wrapped securely enough to foil any would-be raider and three flasks of water, one of which was stained with dark blood. Two of the flasks were half full and, without knowing why exactly, she emptied both of these over her head. It gave her a couple of seconds of feeling cleansed and refreshed, followed by many minutes of feeling absolutely bitterly cold. Idiot, she thought to herself.

Back in the caravan she had an idea. She opened the trunk and pulled out the simple serving girl's dress she had purchased through Sir Dylan. Tossing away her rapidly disintegrating robes, she changed into it. She had taken an empty pack from the knights' camp and proceeded to fill it with the food, her personal knick-knacks including her mirror (though she did not look into it) and her book. Then she had another thought. Stepping outside the caravan, she scanned the frozen leaf litter till she saw it. Gingerly bending over, she picked up Anaya's book. She did not really want to keep it but it was too dangerous to leave lying around. After deliberating for a few seconds, she hastily stuffed it into her ever-heavier pack.

She kept getting flashbacks, mainly of Trask, but at some point or other all of the ordeals of the previous two days popped into her mind. She kept thinking that for quite a while it had driven her into a sort of tacit acceptance of her fate, almost as though she was happy to die. This had never been her way before; nothing had ever crushed her spirit like that – ever. She was angry. Angry at herself and angry at those who had defiled her, and of them only one remained. It also occurred to her that, if Anaya had not lost her sanity that night, then she would be lying in the cottage with her throat cut and Trask and his cronies would be drinking to a successful enterprise, Anaya's crazed delusions had indirectly saved her life.

So finally it was time to move. She left the clearing and started down the road. She was drained, still tired and hurting. Now and then she would see Trask on top of her and stop, brushing her hand over her face as she tried to fight the waves of nausea and disgust that kept washing over her. When she regained herself, she continued to walk the road south, wondering how her composure would fare when she finally had to talk to somebody. She had to keep alert as well. If she heard horses on the road, she would have to hide until she knew that the travellers were not Trask's men. She felt too weary to use magic today and did not know how much fight she had left in her.

She had walked a couple of miles when she espied something close by through the trees. Entering the dense woodland, she walked towards it knowing already what it was – a small but deep pond. It had been dammed by a beaver lodge and was still and wide; a couple of ducks swam along its further reaches, arrowing away from her. Setting down her pack, she undressed and, oblivious to any risk or harm she might do to herself, she jumped right in.

It had warmed up a little since the frosty dawn but the shock on her naked bruised skin was still enough to take the breath from her. She bobbed to the surface like a cork, but that was not what she wanted. Filling her empty lungs she submerged herself completely, washing away the dirt, the remaining flakes of blood, the scent of the men who had abused her. She popped up again and repeated the procedure. After the fifth submergence she felt cleansed enough; she knew in her heart that she would never feel wholly clean again, but at least now she was physically purified, if not spiritually. She clambered out of the pond and the chill air felt invigorating on her open pores. She stopped, raising her arms to the weak sun until she was as dry as she was ever going to get here. She dressed slowly and rejoined the path.

No, she would never be clean again ever. She did not know if she could even be close to a man again. Right now, the thought repelled her. It was Trask's fault, she thought. He had taken something honest and true-hearted, if not totally pure, and despoiled it, broken it, turned it into something rotten. There was only one way she could help herself get back to what she had once been, to find redemption after the horror she had endured, to become Cheris again.

Sir Trask had to die, and die by her hand alone.

51

No one moved. Wulfthram and his companions stared at the black priests, who stared right back at them. The phantoms also remained in place, a coldness radiating from them that made Ceriana shiver. At last the great silver-clad figure rose slowly from his throne, the phantoms parting to let him pass. Before they could divine its intentions, Ulian decided to speak, praying silently that his mastery of their tongue was sufficient for the task.

'Hail to the guardians of Atem Sezheia! I am Ulian, a scholar of the humans travelled here along with their nobles to address Dureke, your leader, on a matter of importance to us both.'

At the mention of the name the creature stopped. No words came from it yet they all heard them, and somehow understood them. It was the glacial, disdainful whisper Ceriana had heard several times earlier that night, only this time it carried the potency of a striking snake, venomous and charged with hostility.

'How does a human know my name?'

Ulian continued nervously, and as he did so the phantoms approached him and began to move around him. As they did so, some raised their arms and brushed him with their spectral fingers, and every time he was touched it was though a shard of metallic cold steel was thrusting deep into his skin.

'As I say, I am a scholar and have learned your name through research, although I have heard nothing of the necromancy you must have practised on your companions to raise them in such a form as this.'

A phantom stood directly in front of him and stopped; he could discern features in the near transparent flesh covering the skull. Its eyes had the blue of a mountain lake and were looking at him more with curiosity than hatred. 'We have had access to many arts you savages could never learn or master.

Tell me, how long is it since we made our home down here?' Ulian swallowed; the phantom in front of him had not moved.

'Over seven hundred years.'

BOOK ONE: AUTUMN

The expression of the phantom gazing at Ulian changed; he could see the weariness of an eternity of waiting in its eyes. The suffering caused by lifetimes of nothing but stillness, down here in the dark, watching and watching, and then failing in its duty to protect the items placed in its trust.

'Is it really that long?' Even Dureke sounded weary. 'It has passed so quickly. Tell me, human, why have you come here? Are you the thief who has taken the stone?'

'No.' Ulian could think of nothing else to say. The phantom moved and he could see Dureke regarding him, and those with him.

'I thought not. Then why are you here?'

'We have come to return that that was taken from you.'

Dureke remained motionless. Then he reached over his shoulder and slowly pulled forth a blade that must have been strapped to his back. It was possibly the largest sword Ceriana had ever seen, a full six feet of frosted white metal. The blade steamed as he held it, a steam of intense cold.

All this time the black priests stood and watched, not saying a word. Now, however, the tall man – Luto, if Ceriana remembered correctly – nodded to his companions and one of them, the man she had seen in Thakholm all that time ago, moved slowly away from them. He went and stood by a small barrel placed under one of the torches. She spotted another three of these barrels located at equal distances along the wall.

'You are saying that you have the stone?' Dureke's voice seemed to take on an ever-deeper, more menacing tone.

Ceriana stepped forward, fighting against all her natural instincts that were telling here to turn and run and not to stop until her lungs burst.

'I have the stone, right here.'

The reactions of the blue-eyed phantoms were extraordinary; they started to move, to swirl around her and the room. They did not walk as such; rather, they floated or hovered, the pale light of their legs and feet either not touching the ground or actually descending into it. could they move through stone walls? Ceriana wondered. How could one combat such spirits? Wulfthram spoke guardedly to her, not looking at her, his eyes fixed on Dureke in front of him.

'You are wearing the amulet; they cannot see you, though I think they know you are here.'

Dureke hissed and raised his sword with his mailed hands.

'We sense the presences of others, the wearers of xhikon. It is a metal that negates magic; it makes its wearer unclear to us but we know they are here. When the stone was taken from us we slept, unaware of what was happening. Now we have awoken, we search for the stone and slay those who stand before us.'

'Including the people of the village? They were all innocent in this affair.' Wulfthram held his sword in front of him, pointing it at Dureke.

'Humans that dwell within or around the confines of Atem Sezheia cannot be called innocent. Our people died so they could seize our lands and settle here. And unless you have the stone, it is now your time to die.' He stepped towards them, hefting his mighty sword; alongside him the phantoms started to close in around them.

'Wait!' Ceriana shouted, not knowing if they could hear her or not. Without thinking of any consequences she pulled the amulet off her neck and handed it to Wulfthram. Then, holding the stone in the upturned palm of her outstretched right hand, she walked towards Dureke.

Within seconds her mind was alive with images – a gargantuan yellow eye, slitted like a lizard's, the dusty floor of a great city of stone, the hoarse clipped cries of dozens of winged shadowy shapes swooping low over her head. Her hand holding the stone started to glow, her veins, arteries and the blood pumping through them visible to the naked eye. Luto the priest started towards her but the blades of Wulfthram and Haelward blocked his path. He stared at the warriors with a cold ire.

'Can you drain the power of this stone?' she asked plaintively. 'Free me from the grip it exerts?'

Dureke lowered his sword until its point touched the ground. He held out his other hand to her, palm upturned. Understanding, she placed the stone into the mailed nothingness that his hand had now become.

'Put the xhikon back around your throat' was all he said.

Wulfthram handed it to her and she took it swiftly, placing it back in its original position. The second she took it from him, her hand returned to normal, pink skinned with a tiny wrist and thin delicate fingers.

Dureke, with all the delicacy of a mother cat carrying its infant in its jaws, returned to his throne with the stone. As they all watched, the silver chain and fitting in which it was housed appeared to turn into vapour and disappear; soon it was only the stone that remained There was a socket at the top of the throne's high back. He placed it in there where it fitted perfectly. It ceased to glow and looked little more than an enormous ruby, secure in its housing.

Dureke sat back on his seat.

'I know how the stone's power can be drained,' he said, 'but it will not avail you. Zhun has determined your destiny already. You, human child, are a prodigy. You have a sensitivity to the stone's power that I have seen only in a very few of my own kind. It is too late for you; the bond between you and Draigezhed, the Fire Dragon, is so strong, you no longer need the stone for it to continue. It can only be held in check; it cannot be reversed. Wear the amulet every day for the rest of your life or you and the Draigezhed will become a symbiote, two bodies with a single spirit. It will become more like you; you more like it. You will cease to be truly human.' Dureke rested his head in the palm of his right hand.

'You can no longer be considered our enemy. The stone has been returned. You may leave with your companions. The siselo, the creature you passed to get here, has fed, and will not trouble you again.'

'Then there is nothing that can be done for her? Nothing at all?' Wulthram spoke, his voice sounding both frustrated and concerned.

'Nothing.' Dureke sounded emphatic. 'Among our people she would be revered, one with a direct contact with Zhun's first creatures. For us it is a great gift, not a curse. We honour her.'

Ceriana looked at the ground. A single heavy tear fell and exploded among the dust at her feet.

Wulfthram spoke. 'We cannot leave just yet. Your stone is not safe here. The people who removed it in the first place will do the same again. They are here waiting to do just that.' He had noticed that the black priests were all wearing the same amulets that Ceriana wore, so after speaking Wulfthram took two steps backward, grabbed the priest standing next to Luto, tore the amulet off his neck and threw it to Haelward, who caught it deftly. He then threw the man to the ground.

The man got to his feet, his hand clutching his throat, feeling for the protection that was no longer there. His eyes fully expressed the dawning horror of his predicament. He turned towards the tunnel and started to run but only went a couple of steps before stumbling and falling. He had got back on to his knees, his mouth wide open in fear. Then the phantoms struck him. One passed right through his body leaving a frosty rime on his face, hair and cloak; he stood and tried to run again but another phantom went through him and another and another. Each time this happened the phantom's body would pulse a blood red colour, just once, just briefly, but each time this happened the man got whiter and whiter until finally he stopped moving completely. Dozens of phantoms continued to run through him until finally he could no longer be seen and just a column of glistening white frost remained where the man had once stood.

'So you see, Dureke,' Ulian said. 'These people will never give up. The stone must be drained; unless it is the case that, now that the lady has used it, it cannot be used again.'

'Ordinarily it would be so. But the child possessor is so powerful she no longer needs the stone. Another could use it; another creature could be found and bonded with.'

Luto smiled knowingly. He seemed unconcerned at the death of his colleague. The object of his quest was but a few feet away from him, and he had all the time in the world.

'Then,' said Ulian, 'its power must be drained, if that is at all possible.' Dureke stood again and came slowly towards them.

'It can be done,' he said, 'but its power can only be drained into a living vessel. The two opposing life forces in one body neutralise each other, destroying both of them. The body dies and the stone is drained simultaneously.'

Luto's smile grew broader. 'You are saying,' said Wulfthram, 'that someone has to die?'

'Indeed,' said Dureke 'It is the only way.'

Luto spoke slowly. 'We knew this of course. Do any of you wish to trade your life to stop me?'

'How is it they cannot hear you?' Ceriana asked him shrewishly. 'I have not revealed myself to them, unlike you. Everything I do is shielded from them. They know we are here. You are speaking to us, after all, but we are as easy to trace for them as smoke in the wind.'

It appeared that he was speaking the truth. The phantoms were passing around him, even through him, but they seemed to have no idea where he was; unlike Ceriana, who felt their blue eyes piercing her like a lance. She reddened slightly and in a tiny voice that she felt was not even her own she said.

'I will do this ritual. My life is blighted for ever anyway. Wherever this stone is it will be my curse until I die. The Gods appear to have deemed it so, and my life seems to be forfeit to them. I am ready for this.'

'Artorus's holy teeth you are!' Wulfthram interposed himself between her and Dureke. 'Say that again and I will send you to Xhenafa myself!'

'I don't think any of us would accept that, my Lady,' Haelward said quietly, keeping his knife firmly pointed at Luto. 'If you go through with this then we have all failed you.'

'It would not work with the girl. ' Dureke said. 'She and the stone are as one; her soul is not an opposite force and could not negate its power. If she has offered herself for the ritual then her bravery and willingness to sacrifice herself to protect others again marks her as special. I suspect that the blood of our people flows in her.'

'Perhaps,' said Ulian, 'no sacrifice needs to be made. Maybe these priests can be prevailed upon not to try and seize the stone.'

'You mean,' Wulfthram said with a wolfish smile. 'We should kill them. I have no problem with that, though they be unarmed.'

'I was thinking rather that we should try to reason with them,' said Ulian sheepishly. 'Though you obviously have the final say in the matter, there must be something that can be offered to them to make them cease this mad enterprise.'

'There is nothing,' said Luto. 'We live for one thing and only one thing, to bring the ancient gods of the elves back to this Earth, for them to pronounce judgement on the foulness and decadence of its unworthy populace, to purge the realms of men, to cleanse them and let them be reborn under the rule of their new gods, pure and unsullied. Our lives are secondary in all this. By all means kill us here, but there will always be others to follow us; as long as the stones exist we will pursue them. We have taken nearly a millennium to start locating them and this age will be our age – the time of the return of the true gods and the end of the empires of men and their false religions. Make no mistake, we will take this stone eventually, even were it buried under an eternity of stone. I will tell you this: one of our brethren has already raised a dragon in the east of your country, and shortly he will purify the lands there. We will raise a dragon in the west. Whether we do it today or next year, or the year afterwards, is immaterial. It will happen and when the Great One destroys the undeserving in your lands the slaughter will be terrible. We will watch with joy as it feeds, devouring the filth infesting your lands, sparing neither children nor the infirm nor the elderly. And we will worship the Great One, praise him for his divine justice and rebuild the new country he has made.'

'We have our answer,' said Wulfthram. 'Derkss, Haelward, kill that fellow lurking over there with the torch; I will take the tall one. They cannot leave here alive. If you cannot kill them, remove their amulets and let these guardians do their work. Show no mercy. They are fanatics and would think nothing of seeing you and your families dead if it furthers their cause.'

At this Luto nodded at the other man, who was standing by one of the barrels holding a torch he had removed from its bracket on the wall. Straight away he lowered the torch, putting it to a length of rope fixed to the barrel. He started to run, and before the two men could get to him, he had moved to the next barrel, and the next, lighting them each in turn. Luto laughed.

'Did I not say we would collect the stone whether it was here or buried under tons of rock. You have decided – it is the latter course for us!

We can all join our gods together.'

Wulfthram looked at the flames licking up to the barrels, back at Luto's serene face, at Dureke standing motionless before him, then back at the barrels. He remembered stories of his childhood, of the exotic warriors of the south and of the blasting powder they used to demolish the walls of the cities that opposed them – technology now known only to a few. Without knowing for certain that he was doing the right thing, he called out at the top of his lungs.

'Into the tunnel, everyone! Now!'

Ceriana saw the grave look in his eyes and repeated the call. The two of them hurtled straight towards the tunnel, Wulfthram propelling his wife by the shoulder. Haelward and Derkss abandoned their pursuit of the black priest and followed closely after them. Back in the chamber, Luto and his companion shut their eyes and slowly removed the amulets from their necks. Luto flung out his arms in a cruciform shape embracing the guardians as they finally saw him and came towards him eager to punish the one who had violated the sanctity of the chamber. Within seconds all that remained of the two men were two tall white columns of bitter frost, with a steaming mist swirling around them. The chamber was now clear of all living creatures.

All except one. Ulian had made to follow the others as they fled, but, once they were in the tunnel, he turned and walked back to Dureke.

'Do the ritual,' he said, choking slightly but with a firm resolve in his eyes. 'I am the one you should use. I have few enough years left as it is.'

'Come forward then,' the armoured figure replied. 'It will be as you wish.'

Ulian approached the throne. Dureke placed one steel hand on the stone and waited for Ulian to come closer. When he was close enough Dureke placed another hand on Ulian's forehead. The shock of the spirit's icy fingers caused him to convulse but he stood his ground.

Dureke started to chant, a deep slow sonorous chant that rumbled through the dust and stone of the floor. And all the time the rope fuses burned.

The stone started to flare, a brilliant scarlet red reflecting off the white steel of Dureke's armour. The guardians surrounded the two figures and started their own whispering, a hundred hissing sepulchral voices, their sound reflecting off the walls and rising towards the chamber's high roof. The brighter the stone flared, the paler Ulian grew; he seemed fixed to Dureke's hand and shuddered and convulsed at the spirit's touch. Then Dureke himself started to glow and, as he did so, the light of the stone started to recede, to diminish. Dureke's chant grew louder, as did his followers', and now he blazed like a flaming torch, the light casting high shadows in this darkest of places. The torches on the wall gave off no illumination now. Dureke was the sun and the chamber his universe, the guardians his satellites, beholden to him for their long existence. Then the light of the stone snapped off completely; it became dark, dark as obsidian, a blacker eye in a sea of blackness. It seemed to absorb what little light surround it, to devour it, to feed on it. And Dureke, even as he shone like the brightest star in the cosmos, was plunged black into darkness. The flame he had drawn into himself was released from his spectral form and instead flew upwards to the chamber's roof, where it blazed brightly for less than a second and was gone.

Back on the floor, next to the throne, Dureke finally released Ulian from his grip and the scholar, who loved his desk and his books and his lectures and who hated travel so much, slumped to the ground. It was as if all of his blood had evaporated, such was the paleness of his skin, whiter than candle wax or the virgin snow in a winter's field, even the irises of his now-sightless eyes seemed devoid of colour. A man whose sacrifice would be known by so few people but mean so much to thousands of others, though they knew it not.

And, as the power finally left the stone of the dragon, the flames that had been creeping slowly along their fuses finally found their mark.

Ceriana and her companions had almost cleared the tunnel when the barrels finally did their work. The creature on the roof did not move as they passed it; it was now a sickly luminous green with a dark, nearly black polyp forming at its centre. They tried not to think about Strogar; it was their own survival that was imperative now. Wulfthram had snatched a torch as they fled the chamber and this was their only source of illumination as they ran. Until the explosion.

The first Ceriana knew of it was the noise, a dull muffled rumble that made her ears pop. Then came the red fire, briefly lighting up the tunnel as though they were running from Keth's infernal furnace itself. She choked and spat out a mouthful of black dust. And then came the sound of avalanche, of tons upon tons of rock and earth pouring into the void, she turned her head quickly and saw a great spume of coal black dust roiling along the tunnel, heading for them at such a velocity there was no way to escape it. Behind this noxious cloud was a lick of crimson fire, swiftly extinguished as the tunnel began to collapse in on itself.

'Run, everybody!' She could barely get the words out through the choking fog. She felt the dust fill her lungs, her hair; she felt it stinging her eyes and blocking her nose. But she did not stop running. She did not dare. And suddenly there it was, a cold air hitting her full on the face, a sense of space to her left and right. She suddenly remembered there was a precipice close at hand and stopped her running, flinging herself to her left as the tunnel behind her collapsed, shooting forth a midnight cloud of debris, a jet of filth and spoil that covered all of them in such a thick film of grit and residue that she felt a swim in the Western Ocean, so close to them, would not even remove it all.

As the cavernous echo of the collapsing rock behind them began to recede, Wulfthram was the first to get up. His torch was still lit, though it was sputtering alarmingly.

'Here, the land bridge over this gorge – it is here. Hurry, we do not know if the earth above us has ceased collapsing.'

'Where is Ulian?' asked Haelward. It was the first chance they had to take stock of their surroundings. In the chaos no one had seen what he had done. Except Ceriana. She had sensed it, felt it when he made his sacrifice.

'He is gone,' she said, 'and the stone is drained. I don't know what else to say.'

It took a second for the words to sink in. Haelward, his face looking unearthly in the light from the torch, was about to speak again when there was an ominous rumble from almost directly above their heads.

'Later,' said Wulfthram. 'For now, we move.'

He led the way along the narrow stone bridge as it wound its way over the abyss to their left and right. Despite the precariousness of the traverse it seemed to Ceriana that they crossed it in no time at all. Behind her she could hear the hollow sound of dust and light earth falling into nothingness as the ground above them continued to settle itself.

'Which way now?' asked Wulfthram. 'Does anybody remember?'

'I do,' said Haelward. 'Follow me.'

'I am glad one of us has a sense of direction.'

'Oh, I don't really,' replied the smiling soldier, 'but I do have a strong sense of self-preservation, especially after all we have seen down here.'

They followed him through the tunnels. As they went Derkss piped up.

'What by all the Gods caused that collapse? Did the priests summon Keth's demons?'

'Nothing as dramatic,' Haelward replied, 'though no less effective. I should have realised what they were doing, but I have only witnessed such things at first hand myself twice. Those barrels they ignited, they contained a powder that just explodes in a ball of fire once a naked flame is put to it. When I was in the marines some Kudreyan pirates got hold of some; they started hurling these small metal globes on to our ship. They had a lighted wick, like the barrels we saw. Well, we were all laughing at them as though they had lost their senses; people were calling over to their ship asking if Uba, god of fools, was steering their vessel. Well, suddenly the cursed things just went up – a gout of flame and a wave of force that could knock a man over. Closest I came to death in that war it was; I was a fool to have forgotten about it. It is to the right here, my Lord.'

Ceriana followed them, feeling a sense of familiarity as they entered tunnels where the rock was damp and moist. One more turning and in front of them was a passage ending with a low roof beyond which was a steep step illuminated by a small well of light, projected through the earth by the late autumn sun, an object Ceriana had all but forgotten about.

'Praise Artorus and the Gods for daylight!' sighed Derkss. 'We may abandon them, but they never abandon us.'

Allowing herself a brief moment of blasphemy to wonder what Strogar would think of such a statement, Ceriana braced herself for the steep but welcome climb, and so it was that shortly afterwards they emerged, blinking, filthy and as black as coal miners, into the fine mid-morning sunlight. Their surroundings looked so much more benign without the mist and the night surrounding them. If she wasn't so choked and emotional, she would have loved to have taken her time to wonder at the people who had created this city of ruins. According to Dureke, she had some of their own blood in her. She knew for certain that there were many gaps in her family tree; it could be traced back over a thousand years after all. Who could say who had filled them, especially in the early days of the invasion of the land that would become Tanaren. As they walked slowly back towards Oxhagen, they noticed a spiral of dust less than a mile away, a plume reaching for the thin white clouds above from behind a stand of trees to their east.

'I imagine there is a fair old crater there now,' mused Wulfthram as he stopped to clear his throat and lungs of the tar-like substance clogging them.

'Yes,' said Haelward. 'After all that has happened I can content myself with the thought of those damned priests scrabbling through the earth for months on end only to find their precious stone is no use to them.'

'No,' said Ceriana sadly, 'they will know it no longer has power. Ulian has ended the threat they posed to the west and north, at least for now.'

'The university needs to know,' said Wulfthram. 'Both of his loss and the reason for it.'

'There is something else,' Ceriana said while wiping her face with her hand, trying and failing to make a clean patch 'That priest Luto said they had raised a dragon in the east. It may be that they are all too aware of it already, but if not, they should be warned. My brother is out there; perhaps I should write to him.'

'It sounds like,' said Haelward, staring wistfully at the sea through a gap in the collapsed city wall, 'it is time for me to travel again. I can escort Willem and Alys back to Tanaren City and carry on back to the east. I can take your letter, though a professional travelling through the coaching inns would probably be swifter.'

'Yes,' said Wulfthram, 'it is time for the two youngsters to go home. The next port Eltlo is some ten miles down the coast; we can take you there. I don't know if you can find a ship that can take you all the way to Tanaren, but there should be one that takes you most of the way at least.'

They were starting to go downhill and Oxhagen lay huddled around the bay before them. Their ship lay at the harbour and the sun glinted off the flecks of white foam that dappled in the grey-blue sea to the west. It was an idyllic scene, as far removed from the circumstances of their arrival as it was possible to be.

A horseman was riding up the path from the town; he appeared to be purposefully heading towards them. The bedraggled group stopped and waited for him to get to them.

'Hail, Baron Wulfthram!' the man saluted them. 'The men of your ship told us where you were. I see the landslip caught you in its midst. Anyhow, Baron Farnerun waits in Oxhagen for you with the rest of his men. He is at the manor house where you can bathe and hopefully accept his hospitality.'

'I would be delighted,' Wulfthram replied, 'but is there any news of the people of the town? When we travelled through it earlier only the dead remained.'

'Indeed, my Lord, most of the people fled to Eltlo and to other nearby villages. It was their calls to the Baron and your letter that prompted him to journey here. He is not allowing them to return until the strange threat to them has been dealt with.'

'Then he can recall them. The danger has passed here.'

'That is joyous news indeed. Please, my Lord and Lady, remain here while I go and sort out horses for the four of you; it will be but a few minutes before my return.' With that he turned and headed back down the path.

    Ceriana sat on the wet grass, her head spinning with the night's events. At long last tiredness was beginning to stretch its fingers over her and she nodded, resting her head against her husband's shoulder. Much had changed for her, and also little, but she was too tired to take stock now. Instead, she gazed blearily at the sea, the sea that had brought the stone to her in the first place and she wished she had never decided all that time ago to head for that picnic on the beach.

52

The square was busy for the time of year. Perhaps this was due to the fine crisp late-autumn sunshine; perhaps, rather, it was the presence of the market stalls squeezed around the square's periphery, their vendors hoarse with cajoling, begging and charming the apathetic locals into parting with their modest savings in return for the best bargains this side of the river Kada; or perhaps it was the looming presence of the three gallows positioned at the square's west end near the town gates, their silent brooding presence eliciting feelings of both anticipation and dread.

Baron Eburg and his mother were there seated in style at a raised, cloth covered platform at the opposite end of the square to the gallows and thereby afforded the best possible view of proceedings. A couple of senior retainers and Captain Jeffen were with them, keeping a stern eye over the local guardsmen secreted among the villagers. Never a man at ease, he was one to see sedition everywhere and in the current climate he was barely able to keep his seat.

They had arrived early, wrapped up against the cold. Really it was probably too early, for located in the narrow streets directly behind them was the town's shambles and the slaughter of the pigs for market had not been completed. So they had to endure an uncomfortable period where Lady Eburg had to stop her ears against the almost human screaming of the doomed animals. Although most of the blood was collected for sale, the narrow gutters surrounding the square still filled with the stuff for a while before draining through the grilles into the river.

Eburg drained his posset, fortifying himself against the chill that was stiffening his fingers and numbing the extremities on his face. He turned to Jeffen.

'It is far too cold for Mother out here, Jeffen; can't we speed things up a little? The square is full; I don't see the problem with starting things earlier than anticipated.'

'As you wish, my Lord; I will have a word with the jailor and executioner.'

Jeffen left them to do just that. Eburg enquired as to his mother's health.

'Never better, my boy You could have told Jeffen that it was you feeling the cold not I. I have never been troubled by the inclemency of the weather and personally find it rather bracing. The freshness of the air is ideal in dispersing any of the fetid vapours that cling to a city so.'

'Yes, Mother, but you have not spent months in the field as I have. The allure of a quiet room and an open fire cannot be understated to a man wearied by the grind of life in the saddle.'

'Nonsense, my boy. Hardship and privation are what makes a man a man. Your father could endure any weather. I do not know how he begat such a weakling as yourself.'

'Well, he could endure anything but the cholera; that was what saw to him in the end, was it not?'

'Do not be so disrespectful, child! He was your father, though you knew him not; a fine man and capable steward of his lands.'

'Implying that I am not so capable, Mother?' Eburg said wryly.

'Not at all – he did not have all the obstacles to sound rule that you have had to endure; no Prosecutors looking over his shoulder constantly, waiting to leap on the tiniest mistake. You need to be ever more the diplomat than he had to be.'

'I thank you for that, Mother. I do feel sometimes that the Gods pull me in a dozen different ways at the same time. I will be happy to see these executions go smoothly so that maybe I can relax for a few days before Winter Feast.'

'Indeed, Zlaton. Just let thoughts of spiced wine and fowl with berries content you over the distant and trivial concerns of war and your uncertain tenure over your lands.'

Eburg hissed with exasperation. 'Mother! Stop vexing me so!'

'Very well, I will do so. If you need time to relax, then take it. Leave everything to me. It is usually the correct thing to do. Mother will see that things are done appropriately.'

Eburg did not reply; his earlier, brighter mood was fading fast. He gazed at the gallows standing before him. Crows had gathered and were perching on them, pecking tentatively at the ropes knotted around the top bar of the gallows frame. They had been built on to a wooden scaffold on which now stood one man alone. The executioner. He was wearing his traditional conical black hood and robes and was clapping his hands together to keep the blood flowing. Once that was over, he set himself to checking the ropes. As he tugged at them, the crows scattered, their noisy protest drowning out the general hubbub of the crowd below.

A short ladder gave access to the platform and up it now climbed Brother Cornelius, followed by three bound and hooded men. They were encouraged in their progress by halberd-bearing men-at-arms who thought nothing of giving the prisoners a quick jab, a reminder that their mortality was at hand and there was nothing they could do about it. Once they were all assembled on the scaffold, the prisoners positioned under their own noose, Cornelius strode forward and addressed the crowd.

'Brothers and sisters, if I may just call you forth from your perusal of the goods of the market, goods provided unto you by the bountiful Gods themselves, I would like to say that we are here also to witness the demise of three souls. No; three men and two souls found to be unworthy of the Gods' mercy. Crimes they have committed, and death is the sentence pronounced by the temporal justice of these lands. Before we proceed, let us just say the Prayer of Artorus and help commit the souls of those poor unfortunates behind me to a higher judgement than any that can be found here on this Earth.'

Everyone stopped what they were doing, including Eburg, and recited the prayer they had all learned before they were out of swaddling clothes. That done, Cornelius recited the Prayer of Xhenafa while his audience remained with their heads bowed, showing their supplication to the Gods.

'Divine Xhenafa, whom we shall meet once and once only, I commend the souls of the condemned to Thee. Guide them safely to the seat of the Gods and forgive them the sins of their miserable lives. Let them be judged fairly and, if they are required to labour in Keth's furnace for eternity, grant them the forbearance and endurance required for such a task. As it must be. For ever.'

The executioner went to each prisoner in turn removing their hoods. Eburg saw with satisfaction that the young poacher was crying like a child – in all fairness he was little more than one anyway. Still, he was old enough to choose his friends and it was for this lack of judgement that he was being punished. The thug was smiling grimly; obviously he had known of this possible outcome of his life for years and was amply prepared for it. Only the Marsh Man was a disappointment. Eburg had hoped that, being a savage, he would struggle and scream, drawing opprobrium from the crowd – something that would culminate in a large cheer once the trapdoor was opened and he was jerking and kicking on the rope. Unfortunately, though, he seemed to be facing his end with the calm stoicism one usually only saw in priests. Eburg wished he was close enough to get one of the guards to jab him with his pole arm, anything to elicit the desired reaction. So this one was a noble savage, after all.

Cornelius went up to the blubbering lad.

'Do you accept that you will be judged by the Gods, that your soul will be held in their hands and that you have to give a fair account of both the good and evil that you have committed in your life. Do you wish for your soul to be blessed by the holy church and for that blessing to be conveyed by Xhenafa to the very seat of Artorus himself?'

Through his choking sobs the boy managed to say the words, 'I do, Father.'

'Then, son, I bless you in the name of the holy church. May you pass into the divine realm in the sure and certain knowledge that you have been born and raised under the tenets of the Pantheon and that, but for a few wayward steps, you still adhere to the values as espoused in the Book of Artorus. The church therefore commends your soul to Xhenafa. May the Gods be merciful to you.'

Cornelius moved on. He asked the same questions of the thuggish man in the centre. This time the man gave a brutish snarl of a laugh.

'There are no Gods, priest.'

Cornelius gave the man a resigned look, as though he had heard similar remarks from such strata of society many times before.

'Nevertheless, as you were born under the Divine Pantheon I still commend your soul to Xhenafa and request that the Gods show you what mercy they can.'

The man was still smiling as Cornelius left him and moved towards Cygan. His expression changed from one of beatific generosity to frowning disapproval.

'I cannot confer the blessing of the Gods upon your heathen soul, if soul you have. You are already condemned in their eyes. That is, unless you agree to undergo the rite of purification by earth and water that all our new-born go through.'

Cygan just glared back at the priest. Cornelius shook his head and walked quietly away without another word.

The executioner placed the rope around the boy's neck, then the thugs and finally Cygan's. Cornelius stood at the edge of the scaffold and prayed loudly enough for everyone to hear. Once this was done he stepped down from the scaffold, his job done. All that remained now was for the executioner to place the condemned men over the trapdoors and pull the lever to open them. Eburg and his mother edged forward in their seats.

Without any warning a blast from a cornet resounded over the square, causing Lady Eburg to clutch at her heart and her son to catch his breath. A gaudily liveried herald, clad in quartered red and blue and carrying a colossal similarly coloured banner, rode his horse past the scaffold and into the square where the crowd parted before him like a sea. He slowed to a trot and rode up to Baron Eburg's platform.

'Hail to Baron Eburg. I have come to announce the arrival of my Lords Baron Calvannen and Baron Josar Trevok here to commence their visits to all the southern baronetcies standing firm against invasion by the foul Arshumans. I have ridden on ahead but they will be here in a matter of minutes to discuss any matters of mutual concern to both your noble houses.'

Eburg stared blankly at the man as his horse fought against the reins, eager to start galloping full pelt again. His mother, however, found her voice rather more easily.

'Esric is coming here? Without announcement? Does he not know any of the protocols?'

'Indeed, he does, my Lady. However, he felt in these circumstances, given the close relationship he holds with both of you, that such pettifogging details need not apply here.'

'Is that so?' Eburg finally spoke. 'Please return and tell him that he will be as welcome as ever and will be invited into my humble home as soon as the current business here is attended to.'

The herald frowned. 'Oh, that is the other thing, my Lord – he requests that any on-going business you may be conducting at present be held in abeyance until his arrival. He has matters to discuss with you concerning them.'

'I see.' Eburg felt his mother squirming in her seat in annoyance.

'Then that is what we shall do. I hope he arrives swiftly in order that the suffering of these men is not unduly prolonged.'

The herald bowed as low as his horse could let him and rode off, scattering the throng in the square hither and thither. Many started to leave, detecting a change in the weather, and soon the crowd in the square had reduced by over half. Lady Eburg could not conceal her agitation.

'We should proceed with these executions anyway. Who does he think he is to so wantonly interfere in our affairs?'

The executioner was looking at the Baron, waiting for the signal to proceed. Eburg, however, shook his head and instead signalled with his hand that the man should stand down, at least for the present.

'He is here for a reason, Mother. We should at least wait to find out what it is.'

He did not have to wait long. After less than ten minutes the trumpets started to sound again, matching the pounding of hooves on cobbles. The market-stall traders started to pack up and the few remnants of the crowd started to make their way home.

Esric on his black charger led the horsemen into the square. Josar, a man Eburg never felt comfortable around, was with him. Behind them were at least thirty horsemen and heralds, the men-at-arms bearing shield and spear, their silver helms burnished in the sun. Further behind, another hundred or so footmen armed with sword and shield, all clad in the blue and red of Calvannen's house started to spill into the square. Against them Jeffen's twenty or so men seemed anaemic in comparison. Esric called out to his fellow baron.

'Well met, Baron Eburg, and you too, Lady Eburg; it is good to see you both in such rude health enjoying this bracing morning; and I see' – he looked behind him at the scaffold – 'dispensing some of the Grand Duke's justice to your people.'

'Thank you, Esric; you are always welcome in my humble home. Perhaps you would like to join me on the platform here to watch the proceedings unfold.' Eburg stood to welcome the only man in the south that had authority over him.

'And who exactly is on the receiving end of your judgements here?' Eburg narrowed his eyes. Why would Esric want to know?

'Well, there is a boy who was part of a gang making a business out of poaching my deer; a professional killer guilty of many major transgressions of the law, and finally a more exotic creature, a man from the Endless Marshes found guilty of killing a prominent merchant in Sketta.'

Esric smiled, a smile that usually had a devastating effect on any lady who should witness it. Lady Eburg, however, was immune to such things and sat there, lips pursed, nose held high, as though having to tolerate an unpleasant odour.

'A Marsh Man? How interesting. What evidence condemned this man exactly?'

Eburg did not reply immediately; he seemed to be going over his judgement in his mind. Finally he seemed ready to speak but it was a response that never came.

There was a commotion in the square behind them. Several of Esric's men-at-arms seemed to be struggling with another man. He was kicking and pushing at his erstwhile captors attempting to break free of them. Finally he managed to push his head above the arms and bodies encircling him and shouted at the top of his lungs.

'Stop the executions! The man is innocent. Death is coming to us, they are coming! They are coming!' He disappeared under a sea of arms.

BOOK ONE: AUTUMN

Esric watched the struggle a little longer then said quietly but firmly.

'Bring him before us.'

Eburg sat back down, aware that he had lost all control of proceedings; his mother seethed quietly beside him.

Esric's men half carried, half pushed the man towards him. The man ceased his struggling and allowed them to do what they wished. Finally, weapons pointed at him, the men fell back leaving the man standing alone before Esric. Esric and Eburg both choked back exclamations of surprise.

For the man was an albino.

He cringed slightly at the stern expression of the powerful baron on his horse. He was bathed in sweat; his clothes were of decent make but were stuck to him; his hair was also plastered to his forehead. His breath came in short ragged gasps.

'Well, my man,' said Esric. 'You have caused quite a perturbation in the square. I hope the explanation you are about to give me is a plausible one, for your own sake.'

'It is, my Lord.' The man was breathing heavily, doubled over. Esric waited patiently, giving him time to compose himself. Finally he spoke again. 'My Lord, I have run nearly all the way from the trading post in the south; my horse threw me almost as soon as I escaped.'

'Trading post? You mean Tath Wernig?' Eburg knew immediately this was the man mentioned in the magistrate's letter.

'Escaped? What do you mean escaped?' Esric grew sterner.

'Yes, my Lords, Tath Wernig was attacked late last night. All the horses were killed; I don't know about the villagers ... I barely got out with my life; they were dragging people into the river.' The man looked over at the self-same river, just visible behind a row of wattle-and-daub buildings that huddled close to it and recoiled, almost as if it was about to come alive and strike him like a snake.

'Who were dragging them into the river, man? Who?' Esric's tone was harsh.

The albino gasped, his voice barely a whisper. 'Monsters, my Lord, just as the Marsh Man said. He is innocent, my Lord; my partner, Gorton, tried to rob him and fell in the river. It was not his fault. He tried to tell us, he did, but we wouldn't listen – we just wanted his trade goods, Artorus forgive me.' Eburg stood again, affecting all the outrage he could possibly muster.

'You are the albino Onkean mentions in his deputation, are you not? You are saying that you lied to my own appointed official? That you perjured yourself before him in order to condemn an innocent man? Then it is you that shall replace him on the gallows! Take him to the scaffold, Jeffen!'

He forgot himself for a second. Jeffen and his men, heavily outnumbered, were standing some way from proceedings and did not move at his command. Esric raised an admonishing hand.

'Patience, Eburg. This man could have fled into the country, never to be seen by us again. Instead, he came here and is plainly terrified. I am inclined to believe him. Do any of you men here know him?'

One of his men at arms, halberd pointed at the albino, spoke.

'Yes, my Lord, he is well known in some parts of Sketta; we come from the same district. He is a slippery customer, always a step ahead of the law. He runs with the gangs by the river and among the warehouses. Whitey, we all call him.'

'Whitey,' Esric murmured quietly. 'Tell me, Dennick,' he said to the man-at-arms. 'You were once with the gangs, were you not?'

'Yes, my Lord, a lot of us were, but we are all your men now – those days are long in the past.'

'Yes,' said Esric, 'I know. Tell me, Whitey, do you believe in redemption? That a man can undo all the wrong in his life by turning from the road he has journeyed since his birth and serving the cause of justice?'

Whitey looked at the ground, clasping his hands together.

'Of course, my Lord.'

'Then I give you a choice. You can submit to Baron Eburg's justice and dance on the gallows for the entertainment of the mob or you can submit to my justice. Which would you prefer?'

'I, I do not wish to hang, my Lord.'

'Very well,' Esric said briskly. 'Dennick, induct this man into the guard, give him a uniform and his basic training, and before anyone says anything I do not wish to hear that superstitious claptrap about pink eyes being bad luck, understand?'

The men mumbled their assent, not necessarily wholeheartedly.

'And as for you, Whitey, I will be watching you carefully. If one weapon vanishes from the armoury, one joint of pork disappears from the kitchens, one silver button goes from my sister's jewellery box, then it is to you I shall turn. Understand?'

Whitey gulped. 'Yes, my Lord.'

'As to the matter you have reported to us, I will question you further presently. Expect to be assigned to the troops designated to defend us from this strange new threat. Captain Jeffen!'

Jeffen looked at Eburg, who opened his hands in supplication, then to Esric.

'My Lord.'

'There will be no hangings today. Return the two prisoners to their cells and bring the Marsh Man to the manor house. Baron Eburg and I have matters to discuss over dinner.'

He spurred his horse towards Eburg's home, leaving its owner to catch up behind him. Josar, riding next to him, spoke as quietly as he could.

'You rather usurped Eburg's authority there; it was boldly done indeed.'

'I am weary, Josar,' Esric replied, not caring who heard him, 'of having charge over barons who are bound and determined to ignore everything I command. It stops here. A man could have hanged today, a man who knows something of whatever unholy dangers threaten our southern borders, even as the Arshumans press us to the north. And I will do whatever it takes to have everyone here put their own petty ambitions to one side until this war is over.'

'Whatever it takes?' Josar said wryly.

'Whatever it takes.'

Shortly afterwards, in the courtyard of Eburg's walled estate, Esric and Josar had dismounted and were facing the Marsh Man and Captain Jeffen. Eburg and his mother had retired to the dining room to ensure that the kitchens were doing their duty and able to feed extra mouths that day.

Esric noticed Cygan's injuries.

'They worked you over pretty thoroughly, did they not?'

'Indeed.'

'Allow me to introduce myself. I am Baron Esric Calvannen, Chief Prosecutor of the War in the South. I am the man in authority here and the one to whom you shall speak on the matter of these creatures and how best to combat the threat they present.'

'And I am Cyganexatavan of the Black Lake, sent to tell you of the danger on the threshold of your home.'

'Well met, Cyganexatavan. We shall speak at length shortly. First of all, though, do you think it wise to send some troops to this trading post to gauge the import of the events two nights ago?'

'Yes, of course, though it is not for me to tell you what to do with your men.'

'No, it is not. Captain Jeffen, take twenty of your horse to Tath Wernig, search for survivors and see how the village can be best defended in the future. Twenty of my horse will accompany you, report back to me.'

'To you, my Lord?'

'Yes to me. Now go – it is your people being threatened after all.'

Jeffen bowed and left them. The courtyard was empty bar the three men and a few troops milling around idly.

'Now to speak to Eburg.' Esric turned towards the manor house.

'If it is all right by you,' said Cygan, 'I will join you later; I have some small business to attend to first.'

Esric nodded and he and Josar entered the manor house. Cygan watched them go, then turned in the opposite direction. In the high stone wall encircling the estate was a black space, an entrance that opened on to a flight of steep, dark, slippery steps, leading down into a darkness lit only by a couple of flickering torches, and it was to this entrance that he was now heading.

BOOK ONE: AUTUMN

It was not the food, but the atmosphere, that could be carved with a knife in Eburg's dining hall. Eburg himself was sitting ashen-faced, distractedly pulling the meat off a pigeon; his mother, who normally devoured everything within an arm's radius, could barely force down a piece of dried bread, and their staff and retainers appeared similarly affected by their Lord's parsimonious approach to his vittles. Esric, however, was ravenous, appearing to devour his own weight in food and sending to the kitchens for more once his plate was cleared. At last, the staff of the household returned to their duties elsewhere and it was not long before it was just the two Eburgs, Seneschal Carey, Josar, Calvannen and half a dozen guards, representing both Houses, left in the hall.

Esric took a draught of watered wine. 'I heartily commend your kitchens, Eburg. If only my own had the same delicacy of touch; every pigeon I have been given lately is as black as a lump of Derannen coal.'

'Thank you, Esric,' Eburg smiled nervously. 'Mother vets every member of the kitchen staff personally, from humblest scullion to grandest chef; it is an obsession of hers, to see that I am well provided for.'

'That is good to hear,' said Esric heartily. 'Where would we all be without the care and attentiveness of our mothers?'

'Mine died when I was but a child,' said Josar. 'Though my father remarried it was hardly the same. The Gods have smiled on you, Eburg.'

'Yes, in some ways they have.'

'And now, Eburg,' – Esric wiped the last of the gravy off his chin with a white cloth – 'I suppose you are wondering what brought me here unannounced, in breach of the usual protocols, which is certainly not something I would normally do.'

'Yes, Esric, I did wonder.'

'Good. What would a man be without his natural curiosity? Coincidentally, it was curiosity that has driven me here – curiosity as to how the lands closest to the Endless Marshes were being administered; curiosity as to the quality of the kitchens in houses other than my own, one I may add that has been sated most satisfactorily, and curiosity as to why the baronial House of Eburg keeps receiving seditious letters, ones that speak with the most earnest anticipation of my forthcoming demise.'

Eburg almost choked. 'What? W...Whatever do you mean, Esric? I know nothing of such letters.'

'Worry not, Eburg; I am reassured as to your ignorance of such matters. However, I would like to address this matter to your mother, to whom all the intercepted correspondence has been addressed.'

Eburg stood up in shock. 'Now, Calvannen, you have gone too far. This is my house and you cannot enter it and fling about baseless accusations at members of my own family. I think it is best that you leave these premises and do not return until I say that you can, or at least until you have some hard evidence you can put before my eyes.'

Esric watched him, his eyes keen and determined. 'I do have some. Lady Eburg?'

Eburg's mother writhed in her chair as though engaged in some inner conflict. Eventually though she slowly turned her head to Esric, the malice in her eyes enough to make a weaker man quail.

'You are an arrogant presumptuous child, are you not? Quite how Duke Leontius named you as Prosecutor is a mystery, even to the wise among us. A dissolute wine-drenched boy, idling his days writing tawdry poetry and bedding the cheapest, disease-riddled flea-bitten whores that could be found in his city – this is the man chosen to lead our resistance to the invaders? A cheap joke! And how you dare to step under the roof of the house of the woman whose only son you mutilated and to whom you sent such a grisly token of his terrible demise, Uba knows! You, sir, are not fit to lead a carnival of drunkards. Motley should be your raiment and juggling coloured balls for your betters your occupation. Was I party to the plot against you? Did I encourage my adopted grandson to stir for your untimely removal? I most definitely did so. My only regret is that you are still here, a festering tumour at the heart of the lands of the south, the finest, most desirable lands in Tanaren. Mark my words, boy, the Gods will see to you. I and others will do their work for them, have no fear of that!' She stood and spat at Esric's feet, her wizened face contorted with malice.

Eburg was as white as a sheet. He slumped over the table, head in hands and gasping the single word 'Mother!'

Esric did not move. He fixed her with an icy stare. Josar had drawn his sword and was standing, waiting for the word. Lady Eburg saw this.

'And now you would torture and slay me, an old woman. Let everyone see the justice of the Calvannens and make their own judgement upon them.' Her voice was getting shriller by the minute.

Esric waved at Josar to sit.

'Thank you for your opinions, Lady Eburg, and for your full confession to your crimes. I actually only had the scantest evidence for them, so your confirmation is most welcome. I was advised that not every traitor had been caught the last time.'

'Traitor!' she spluttered indignantly. 'You would call me traitor!'

'I would. What other word would you use for those that deal in secret with the Arshumans? And now I suppose it is time for you to hear the justice of the Calvannens; I fear that the opinions of others regarding it will be completely immaterial to you. Seneschal, place this woman under arrest.'

Along with a guard, Carey, somewhat shamefacedly, moved towards Lady Eburg. Once they had reached her, though, Esric signalled for them to stop.

'Eburg,' he said, 'just as with the albino earlier I am going to give you a choice; you can decide your mother's fate, at least to a degree. Are you prepared to listen to me?'

Eburg looked to have aged years in minutes; he looked almost as old as his mother. Wearily he nodded at the Baron.

'Very well. Your mother is guilty of treason and I am perfectly justified in putting her head on the block. However, owing to her age and reported infirmity, I am willing to explore other possibilities. Your House, Eburg, is fatally compromised and your tenure as baron in question. I have many candidates for this baronetcy and am inclined to offer it to one of them. This is the choice you have. I have a cousin with estates near the Morrathnay Forest. There is an unused house there with some lands in a secluded spot. Renounce your baronetcy and I will permit you, your wife and mother to go and live there unmolested. You will have a small income and a cook and a couple of servants. You will, of course, need to sign the official papers for this to happen, but, if you agree to this, you may live there in peace till the end of your days. Your mother will have freedom to do whatever she wishes as long as she never meddles in politics again.'

'I see,' said Eburg quietly. 'And my other choice?'

'You keep your seat here. I am satisfied as to your innocence in this affair and am prepared to let you stay. However, for this to happen you have to denounce your mother for the crimes she has committed. She will spend the rest of her days in prison in Tanaren City. She will be given a dry room and kept in such comfort that circumstances will allow. But she will never see the sun again and the two of you will not be allowed to correspond nor will visits be allowed. You will be informed when she dies, but that is all.' Esric stood and produced a letter from his belt.

'I will give you some minutes to decide. In the meantime one of your men can take this to your wife. It contains my apologies for the manner in which she was informed of her son's death and my willingness, when she is ready, for us to meet face to face to discuss whatever matters she deems appropriate. Josar, let us walk in the courtyard for a few minutes while the Baron talks matters over with his mother.'

The two men left the room, leaving behind the cadaverous ghostly figure of Baron Eburg, a man appearing to have the weight of several worlds on his shoulders and his mother, who for the first time that her son could remember wept openly before him.

Jailor Cornock turned the key on the cell door and swore quietly under his breath. The day had not gone well for him at all. He had had to return two prisoners to the cells, prisoners who should have already choked on the end of the rope by now, and as for the third, well unbelievably he had been given his freedom. He had done what he could to prepare the prisoners. The crowds love a crier so he had applied a flaming brand to the boy's chest earlier that day, but all of it was for naught. His baron, too, he could see was under pressure; the men that Calvannen had brought weren't just there for show. All in all, a disappointing day.

Once the prisoners were back in their cells, he returned to his own small room next to them. It was little more than a cell itself, dark and dank with little light. The only thing different about it was the lack of a door and the presence of some simple furniture including a low table lit by a single candle and a rickety wooden chair. Into this he now slumped. He reached for a dirty sack-cloth bag on the floor and pulled out a substantial lump of dried bread, which he started to devour with some relish.

Lost in his thoughts, he suddenly snapped to. What was that noise? It was coming from one of the cells, a scraping sound like a stone being dragged over the floor. He gave an exasperated bellow, put his food on to the table and picked up a brutal-looking wooden cudgel. Stepping out of his room, he started to follow his ears.

He heard some low sobbing coming from the boy's cell to his left. The noise wasn't coming from there. He stopped and listened again. It was coming from the end cell where the door stood open, the cell that had once held the Marsh Man. Gripping his cudgel as tightly as he could, he inched towards the door. It stood half open; he would need to push it to get into the cell. Slowly, he forced the door open, causing it to creak noisily on its hinges.

The grille in the roof shone a patch of light on to the floor of the cell. And on to a man's foot. Smiling, his cudgel giving him a boost to his confidence he stepped fully into the cell part pushing the door to behind him. 'Come back for more, have you, Marsh Man?'

Cygan stepped forward to face him directly, dropping the stone he had held in his right hand.

'I wanted to see if that was fat or muscle. I think it is fat.'

Without warning, Cornock hefted his cudgel, aiming to bring it down sharply on to the man's temple. Before he could, though, Cygan grabbed the man's arm firmly and slammed his fist into Cornock's stomach. Winded, the man doubled over, giving Cygan enough time to twist the man's arm behind his back, forcing him to drop his weapon. Cornock pushed back on his heels, using all of his bull-like strength to try and topple his assailant. He did not succeed, though. A brawl developed as Cornock tried to turn and face his man while Cygan attempted to get his forearm around Cornock's throat. They crashed into the cell walls several times as they wrestled, but Cygan inexorably gained the upper hand, finally locking the man's neck in a deadly embrace. Cornock fell to the ground, kicking out behind him as he tried desperately to dislodge his enemy – the man proving to be far stronger than he had imagined. He started to choke and a line of spittle ran from the corner of his mouth. Panic-stricken, he flapped his arms, clawing at Cygan's face, but the Marsh Man was remorseless. His arm lock was as strong as iron and his determination like granite. He held on as Cornock's struggles became weaker and weaker. Eventually, after an eternity they ceased altogether.

Cygan kept gripping him for a further minute or so, just to make sure, then, satisfied, he stood, letting the body of the dead man flop to the ground. 'It was fat then,' he said grimly.

Leaving the body where it fell, he strode to the jailor's room. Scanning it briefly he located the keys left on the table. Up until recently, he had never seen such a thing as a key, now though he knew exactly how they worked. He went from cell to cell, unlocking them all except for his old cell, which he locked firmly. That job done he threw the keys back into the small room and scaled the stairs into the outside world.

He was not a man used to confinement and fancied a sight of the land. Locating the nearest flight of stairs, he climbed the wall of the manor house and looked about him. There was no view of the countryside, just the town. He could just make out the square and the scaffold, their redundant nooses swinging forlornly in the breeze. For now there was a breeze. It had become warmer and closer, too, and as he looked at the sky he could see the heavy black clouds moving north from his homeland. A storm was brewing.

Esric and Josar stepped into the courtyard and smelled the change in the air. Silently they strolled around the side of the house, quietly amused as the servants went to great lengths to get out of their way. Finally Josar broke the silence.

'Are you satisfied with what happened in there?'

'Yes,' Esric replied, 'I had not expected the old hag's confession, but obviously her hatred for me drove her into indiscretion. I suppose she played right into my hands so, yes, I am satisfied. There is no pleasure to take in this outcome, though. There is still a network of people who wish to bring me down, just as Morgan warned. I am unsure of their captain for a start. That was why I sent him away; the last thing we need is fighting in the streets between our own men and Eburg's.'

'Poor old Eburg!' Josar said wistfully. 'I almost feel sorry for him. What do you think he will do?'

'Oh, I think we will be installing Carey as the new Baron Eburg soon enough. The current incumbent will never abandon his mother. Carey is a loyal man and has been angling for this for a while. His son will become a noble and can join the knights, too, so there are several good things to come out of this.'

They turned and made their way back to the entrance of the house. A lone figure stood out against the sky on the low battlement of the encircling wall. He appeared to notice them and climbed down the steps to join them.

My business is complete,' said Cygan. 'I do not understand your peoples disdain for the open sky; you seem to enjoy creating places to shut it off. It will be good to return to my people, though we have much to discuss first.'

'Yes, we can talk on the way to this trading post. I will then have to prevail upon you to return to Sketta, my town, with me while I decide upon a course of action with the other barons. After that you are free to go your own way.'

Cygan followed them through the door of the manor house. They had not yet reached the dining hall when they heard a piercing scream from somewhere ahead of them. Running, they burst into the hall, where a serving girl was crying hysterically.

'By all the Gods!' Josar said quietly.

Lady Eburg sat back in her chair, her arms hanging limply at her side. Across her throat was a thin red line from which ran several narrow streaks of blood. The front of her dress was soaked in crimson and her small black eyes stared glassily ahead of her. Her son was slumped over the table, one twitching hand dangling over its edge. The white tablecloth was soaked in blood which was pooling above the stone steps that raised the table above the rest of the room. Under Eburg's hand on the floor, in the midst of the sticky mess, lay a knife, one that had obviously fallen from the man's fingers as the feeling drained from them.

'I didn't think they had enough time to do such a thing!' Josar muttered. 'They chose the third option then.' Esric sounded resigned. 'I suppose this is what you get when you try to be merciful.'

Outside through the windows came a dull and distant rumble of thunder as a smattering of rain struck the glass.

BOOK ONE: AUTUMN

53

'There is no sight likely to stir the blood and fire the senses more than that of an army arraigned for battle. To see the banners raised, to hear the cornets sound and the hoarse cries of the captains exhorting the men to ever greater feats of valour. To witness the sun glint off polished armour, off burnished shield, off the fierce eyes of the warriors is to be born anew, purified in the blood about to be shed, the blood of the brave. How humbling it is to see spears raised in unison, ranks and ranks of disciplined and determined men march with one step, one heart, one soul under the Gods. Even I, as a humble priest, could not fail to feel the lust of battle pulsing through my unworthy body; 'twas almost as if I, too, wished to fling myself at the shields of the enemy crying 'Artorus! The Gods! And the joy of war!'

Father Edforth Crebinus, Chronicle of the Emperors and the Downfall of the Knights of Rumil.

Baron Felmere gazed at his full goblet of wine. It was nowhere near noon yet and he still felt like he needed it. Knights Dominic and Reynard stood before him and their news was not good.

'So the mages have not returned and the enemy is on the march.' He sounded almost matter of fact.

'Yes, the Arshumans have surprised us. The scouts say they are but a few hours away.' Reynard had a bit of a cold and snuffled his words.

'And the mages? Mytha's bloody wounds, they were supposed to be back this morning. I knew I shouldn't have let them go.'

'No sign, Lukas. I have sent a knight along the road to look for them, but if you remember their instructions were to be back today and it is still but morning. We expected to attack the enemy at our leisure; no one expected them to move on us.'

Dominic was already fully armoured, his helm pushed back to reveal his sharp grey eyes.

'Well, no matter what, we need to mobilise pretty sharpish. What of their numbers?'

'That is what makes it such a bold move. They have fewer men than us – maybe not even five thousand including mercenaries and fresh troops unproven in battle. Their king rides at their head in his golden armour; you know how the Arshumans love their pointless displays of ostentation.' Reynard looked tense.

'Well, as Dominic says, we need to go out and face them. You don't know the country round here, do you, Hartfield?'

'No, Lukas, but once you've seen one muddy field...'

'Perfectly true. Now, if you leave the tent and look out from the camp you will see a high ridge lined with trees on the eastern horizon. Beyond that is a low plain that extends for some miles. It used to be prime farming country, lots of hamlets and villages, it also used to be very pretty in the early autumn – golden fields and sheep and cattle grazing in the sunset. Now, of course, no one lives there. The buildings are empty or destroyed and it has a new name, after the only creature that wanders there now.'

'Wolf Plain,' said Reynard.

'Yes,' said Felmere. 'It is their country now, especially in winter when the land is covered in snow. It is but a couple of hours' march away. That is where we shall meet them. The generals and signalmen can stay on the ridge and try and direct things from there. We need to move fast; I want us up there ready and deployed before they get here.'

'And the order of deployment?' asked Reynard.

'Yes, send the light cavalry and archers on ahead to keep their skirmishers busy, then the infantry can march unmolested. We will deploy with Lasgaart on the left, then my men, then Vinoyen; after all the trouble between those two contingents I want my men to keep them apart. Then we can have the Haslan Falls and Maynard's men on the right. You have heard about Wyak and the Athkaril men, I take it.'

'Some sort of trouble back home, I understand.' Dominic knew far less of the local political situation than the other two.

'Athkaril has been ready to ignite for some time now. Too many refugees short of food and too many supercilious townsfolk seeing themselves as better than them. And now there are riots there and reports of the town going up in flames. Wyak has taken the men he can trust back with him and left the rest here. They will fight with my men. Despite that, we should still have nearly a thousand more men than the enemy.' Felmere stood and drained his goblet. 'Despite these setbacks, we can break them here, scatter them to the four winds and win this war by the spring. Keep that at the front of your minds as we march. They are being bold but they are there for the taking.'

From outside the tent the trumpets sounded the call to mobilisation. The three men strode into the open air. Conditions were changing. A bitterly cold dawn was giving way to a close, warmer middle day as heavy black clouds started to come nearer and nearer. Felmere looked to the heavens. 'Not more damned rain – just as I thought things were getting drier!'

The camp they were in was a hastily constructed tent city on the eastern bank of the Whiterush. Over the other side of the river they were overlooked by the hill with the town of Grest perched at its crown. Two wooden bridges had been constructed over the river; one of the reasons the army had moved was to protect both of them. Felmere's tent stood close to the riverbank, bordered as it was with high reeds and the occasional stunted tree. The camp itself was surrounded with a hastily constructed ditch lined with sharpened stakes.

As Felmere wished, mobilisation was rapid. After just over an hour the army was marching eastwards, banners unfurled with many of the men gloriously singing the 'Battle Song of Mytha' and clashing weapons on shields. Overhead a couple of harrier hawks hovered over the proceedings and the trees on the ridge they were approaching were black with crows, collecting there in anticipation of a feast to come. Felmere was at the head of his men, riding up and down the line exhorting them, telling them that this was the battle, the decisive one, the one to end the entire war. He offered fifty crowns to the man who brought down the fop in the golden armour and seemed inspired by the enthusiasm he engendered. And on they marched, as the clouds gathered and the first heavy drops of rain fell on metal helms and unprotected heads. Everyone there knew that within the next few hours battle would finally be joined and there seemed to be none among them who did not relish the prospect.

It had been quite a morning for the inhabitants of the town of Felmere. Shortly after dawn, as a cold sun started to pick out the flecks of frost on the grass that flowed up to the city walls, a rumour spread like wildfire among the market traders, the good wives, the men-at-arms, the customers at the taverns, the merchants and their caravans, even the whores and cutpurses that clung to the dark alleys. An army was assembling on the plain.

People fought for vantage points on the walls; the gates were closed against attack even though this mystery force was definitely not from Arshuma. From the high towers of the house of Artorus, priests and choirboys squinted for a better view and from the keep of Felmere's grand castle the lords, ladies and servants chattered in breathless excitement. Just who in the name of the Gods were these people?

It was an army consisting entirely of horse. At dawn it emerged from the woods to the east, trotting at a steady pace. Gaudy, unfamiliar pennants raised high in the air. It drew closer and closer to Felmere. The town guard were getting nervous; crossbowmen jostled locals out of the way on the city walls and readied themselves; halberdiers congregated at the gates, packing closely together. Then the new rumour started. 'The Wych folk, the Wych folk are coming!'

Reactions were electrifying. Many on the walls fled to their homes terrified, the places they vacated being taken up almost immediately by other braver souls. None present had ever seen one of the Wych folk and for many curiosity overrode the deep-seated fear that all the good people of Tanaren held for such savage, alien creatures.

Morgan, of course, guessed the reaction of the townsfolk perfectly. 'Gallop past with horns blaring and banners raised. They will be terrified and excited at one and the same time.'

Culleneron had charge of his people for the day. Itheya rode with him, though, and once they judged they were within hearing distance of the town they gave the word. Long thin silver horns, all antiques from an older time, sounded in unison. Their high fluting sound flooded the plain and caused many a townsman to stop his ears in trepidation. Then they started to gallop. No man could ride at that speed for so long. Morgan and Cedric soon found themselves adrift of the last man, but, at the same time, they could not but help admire the artistry of the horse folk ahead of them. Spears lowered, they sped past the walled city, the hooves of their steeds thunder on the plain. Clods of earth flew hither and thither as they sped past the city gates, leaving the human onlookers slack-jawed with awe. Raising their banners and spears to salute the people of Felmere, they rushed passed the town leaving behind memories that would never fade. The people watched as they crashed into the trees to the west and were lost from view, and within seconds every tavern was heaving with astonished and thirsty people eager to recount the time they saw the Wych folk ride to war.

Cheris, sore and tired, had at least got into some sort of rhythm with her walking. She did not know how far she had gone though she suspected it was less than she hoped; she wasn't even certain she was heading in the right direction but she continued to walk, plod, plod, plod, pumping her legs as solidly as she could, ignoring the internal pains and discomfort it was causing her. Meriel's benison but she would feel it tomorrow! But she could not stop; Trask's treachery had to be told to someone. The most upsetting thing was the flashbacks. Coming completely unbidden into her mind, a sharp memory would stab her behind the eyes – the flaming demon about to fry the flesh from her bones; Trask's breath, his weight, the things he did to degrade her further; what she had done to that boy. It was the rape that kept coming to her most frequently; a brief picture would appear in her mind of her being squeezed, pawed, licked; she felt again the violence of the way he had parted her legs and had a good look, calling the others over for the same purpose. When this happened she would stop dead and cry out 'No!' or just emit a choked sob and cover her face with her hand. She felt a burning shame, even if she kept telling herself she had no reason to.

She had met no one on the road. A small flock of deer had run front of her, spooked by some phantom threat. And she had seen through the trees not long ago some wild boar grubbing among the tree roots. But people? There was no one. War had cleared these lands years ago.

The weather was changing, too. Her bathe in that pond had felt good at the time but during the first half-hour of her walk afterwards she could not stop shivering. For some time, though, she had felt warm and clammy. At first she had thought the change was due to exercise but now she knew otherwise. Her head was throbbing and she could taste the air. It was close, almost humid. A storm was on its way. Would she see lightning? She did not know but the tingling in her fingertips told her it was a distinct possibility. Of course this meant rain and a wet and uncomfortable night in the woods. She had already been fretting about sleeping among wolves and ghouls, and had even contemplated climbing a tree for safety, and now the thought of a torrential rainstorm dampened her spirits further.

What would her friends at the college think to see her walk like this? Exercise was difficult to find on such a small island. Many there had joined societies dedicated to keeping fit and healthy. There were dedicated walkers and runners who would do several circuits of the island, along the narrow coastal path, every day. There were sports teams, too – stone ball, high mark and tag teams played each other regularly and with a high degree of competitiveness. Cheris, of course, belonged to none of these teams. She loathed exercise with a passion and had said this to many people on many occasions. And now here she was clumping along a dirt road like a farmer's wife. How they would laugh!

At least she was going downhill. She knew eventually the path would level out, the trees would reduce greatly and become a broad expanse of tussock-heavy grass. She would have to be careful not to turn her ankle or catch herself in some hidden rabbit hole. She was sore and wounded in enough places already.

From behind her came the noise of dozens of birds taking flight. Not just crows but many other types. She turned and saw them rising, like some shadowy cloud floating into the darkening sky, calling out their indignation.

Had something disturbed them? Feeling suddenly wary, she climbed off the path and secreted herself behind the largest tree she could find. She could hear something. Was it thunder? No. It felt as though it was the very ground that was reverberating under her feet sending dull throbbing waves of sound up her legs into her cranium, making her head pound. It was getting louder, too, and she realised that it was not one noise but many. Horses, dozens and dozens of them. She had passed several side roads in her walk and they could have joined the path she was walking at any of these points. What should she do, she wondered? Trask was not a cavalry man, but she had to be sure before she could show herself. There was something else, too. She realised that she did not want to face anyone at this juncture. It just felt too soon. How could she talk with any degree of eloquence after what had happened to her? Her walk had helped keep her upset and emotional state in some degree of abeyance, but hearing the horses getting nearer by the second she felt her face redden and her nose start to run. She sniffed loudly and ran further into the trees. By Elissa there were hundreds of horses, hundreds! She couldn't face so many, she just couldn't. Not now, maybe never. She saw a high bank of earth flanking a ditch covered in bracken. She made herself small and hid behind it waiting for this mysterious cavalry to pass. Strangely she felt no urge, no curiosity to even try and look at them. She just wanted them to go so her walk could continue in peace.

The elves were in good spirits. Their ride past the city of stone and the cowed awestruck nature of their reception had them laughing and singing for some miles now. Itheya had dropped back through the ranks, waiting for Morgan and Cedric to join her.

'You are so slow, hemenestra!' she laughed. 'You are riding visloyi not strykera!'

'Is that so? If I had any idea of what you were talking about, maybe I could even answer you.' Morgan smiled back at her.

'We are riding horses not oxen,' explained Cedric. 'Visloyi is one of the many words they have for horses; it refers to the special swift and brave war horses peculiar to their people. I assume they were bred to be exactly that centuries ago.'

'You are as wise as the warrior is ignorant, Cedric.' Itheya leaned over and gave Morgan's ear a playful tug. 'It is a sad circumstance that we did not meet years earlier; with Morgan, of course, it is a sad circumstance that we ever met at all.'

'Bear in mind that I am supposed to be guiding you here; it would be a shame would it not if this road led to a sudden quicksand or the bottom of a deep dark lake?'

'Ha! It is a road. We follow it southward. What more do we need to know?

Besides, what sort of guide rides at the rear of a column?' 'One that cannot ride a horse?' Cedric chipped in.

'I see,' said Morgan. 'You are both turning on me. I had kept some rations back, intending to share them with you this evening, but alas, I suddenly feel an extra hunger come upon me. Still, you can enjoy nibbling grass stalks like a rabbit while I tuck into the delights of soft bread and berries.'

'Now if you had said roast boar with cherries,' said Cedric, licking his lips, 'I could not have apologised fast enough.'

'Maybe we will catch some later,' said Itheya. 'We will send hunters out when we camp. I think we are too late for cherries, though.'

They continued along the road, the horses churning up mud as some parts of it resembled a quagmire. The initial impetus of the gallop past Felmere lost, the horses slowed to a more sedate pace, allowing Itheya and the humans to pass through the column and join Culleneron at its head. No one mentioned the weather. The low scudding thunderheads inching closer towards them were obvious to all.

'Are we far from this camp?' Itheya asked as noon passed them by.

'No,' said Morgan. 'Maybe we will get there late this afternoon. I had underestimated the speed at which you travel.'

'You are not Aelthen.' Culleneron spoke haltingly, wrestling with the alien tongue. 'How could you know of the speed of our people.'

Suddenly, with no warning Itheya, raised a hand and called a halt. Within seconds the entire column obeyed, almost like a single sentient creature. She looked to her right at the trees and said quietly to Culleneron. *'Danete crthelema? Spashiyi mandaran zafle. Spashiye grna.'*

'Kerfel vsehur?' Culleneron replied, a little louder.

'In, em olea tef grnosh azhasclova, vexevoe azhesse.'

Culleneron seemed slightly put out by her response. *'Ve mezhino! Vexhesse!'*

Itheya cocked an ear to him; there was a playful disdain in her voice when she answered: *'Zuke teo sast altafal bebrnoze kemhezho orfea ketrxa meon o victrex, dane zeate satsal.'*

Culleneron looked slightly sheepish. He just nodded in her direction, as though passing some responsibility to her.

'Carac! Mhevhillo! Tafalonat vonsa!' She barked an order then came up to Morgan.

'Something disturbs the undergrowth, something large and clumsy. From what I hear it can only be human. Come with me; you may be of use. When we get near to it, hang back until my signal. You are too noisy and ride a horse as a cow would.'

She headed off the path, two other elves followed her closely, arrows nocked. As soon as he had a chance, Morgan whispered to her.

'Isn't Culleneron in charge today? Should he not be doing this?'

She looked at him with a degree of exasperation. In a barely audible whisper she replied.

'I just had this conversation with him. I told him he would look a fine leader emerging from the trees in front of his men holding aloft a rabbit in triumph. He backed down then. Men do so hate to look foolish.'

She put a finger to her lips and bade him stay behind them. Like ghosts, the three elves dismounted and melted into the trees; their leathers, coloured in dull greens, brown and grey helped them disappear instantly. Morgan stayed with the horses, feeling exactly like the cow she had described him as.

Itheya was hunting. Crouching low, she listened intently, her head almost on the ground. She did not have to wait long. A loud crack of a broken twig pinpointed her quarry. Silently she moved towards the source of the noise, her two companions moving out wide to flank her. There was a low shelf of earth ahead of her coated in ferns, bracken and dead wood; it was definitely in there. She inched herself forward, pushing her head ever so slightly through the covering undergrowth, and she saw what had drawn her to this spot.

A human woman crouched behind the ditch, obviously thinking herself hidden. She wore a simple grey-brown dress whose hem was stained with mud and grass. Her hair was raven black, not unlike Itheya's, but it was cut short, to the neck. What drew Itheya's attention though were her wounds – her hands were ribboned with nasty red cuts only just beginning to heal. Her face was bruised and red from crying. There was more, too; she could sense that she had been hurt in other ways, but until Itheya could get closer she could not be more specific. And then Itheya saw the staff and sensed the power within her. It was like a bloom around her – there was far more power than Itheya had sensed in anyone before, even Terath. This girl was dangerous.

But not threatening. Itheya sensed the girl's fear; as long as she did not exacerbate those feelings then she felt conversation was possible.

Both her companions were close by, ready to fire. Waving them to stand down, Itheya stood up slowly, lowered her bow and stepped carefully towards the troubled girl.

'May I ask politely what exactly a human woman is doing here, alone in these dangerous woods.' She spoke slowly, clearly, doing everything she could to calm the fear she sensed in this strange girl.

It did not work. She shot up in alarm, blue-grey eyes flecked with terror.

'Stay back!' she called. 'I know not what you are but you can die as easily as all the others!' She held her hand out, palm thrust towards the elf.

Itheya dropped her bow and raised both arms above her head.

'You see – I mean you no harm. Notice I have two companions with me; we could have killed you before you noticed us. But I would much sooner we talked. May I come towards you a little?'

The girl hesitated, unsure of herself. 'Very well, but beware, I have enough magic to kill you.'

'I can see that, but I want neither of us to die today.'

She approached Cheris, who slowly lowered her hand and looked with not a little wonder at the taller woman facing her. The distance between them was only a few feet. Despite herself, she had to ask.

'Are you ... an elf?'

Itheya laughed 'Of course! My name is Itheya. These lands are new to me, though not so different to my home.'

'Cheris,' the girl replied. 'My ... name is ... Cheris.'

Itheya came close to her, sniffing her slightly – much to the girl's alarm. She raised a hand and put it close to her face then lowered it down to her belly then lower again. Her expression changed to one of sad pity.

'You poor child, what by the spirits has happened to you?'

Cheris looked into the elf's strange eyes. She did not expect to see pain and compassion in them, so when that was exactly what she did see she had no prepared defence. As she feared she would do, she broke down, her face a livid scarlet, tears flooding down her cheeks, her shoulders shaking.

'There is nothing to fear, child. You are safe now.' Without thinking Itheya embraced the poor tortured girl, letting her work out her tears, as they stained the leather of her jerkin.

And that was how Morgan found them. He had received no signal from Itheya but sufficient time had elapsed for him to decide to investigate. The two other elves had returned to the horses so he saw no reason to stay with them. He strode into the ditch, crunching wood and bracken beneath his feet.

Cheris started and pulled clear of Itheya.

'Who are you?' she rasped. 'Do you work with Trask?'

'Trask?' Morgan questioned. 'What about him?'

Cheris backed away 'You do know him!' she shouted, hysteria in her voice. 'You bastard, you are not going to get what he took from me. I will kill you first!'

Morgan spoke again, as softly as he could. 'Whoa, please, not so hasty. I do know Trask, yes, but I do not work with him. Rather, we dislike each other intensely. What do you know of him?'

'Morgan,' Itheya said softly, 'this lady is called Cheris. She has haraska, magic – a lot of it in fact. And she has been badly used, as only a man can use a woman. Recently. And more than once.' She looked at Cheris. 'Come with us. We have people who can help with the pain.'

Morgan's jaw set firmly at what she told him. He looked at Cheris, who was choking back sobs again. 'Was it Trask?'

She nodded. They could tell she wanted to speak but no words could come. Both waited patiently, not wanting to hurry the girl. At last Cheris regained a measure of composure, her breathing was still ragged but words came falteringly.

'They tried ... to kill me ... once they had finished. Two other mages ... dead. Trask fights with ... with our army ... but ... but ... he is a ... .traitor.'

Morgan's face looked hewn from stone. 'Where is Trask now?'

'Back with the ... army. Baron Felmere does ... not ... know.'

He looked at the ground, then to the heavens where the clouds were almost black. 'Shit!' he said softly. 'Mytha's bleeding stools!'

Itheya looked between the two humans. 'I am not sure I understand. This Trask is not a man to trust, I take it?'

'Yes, my Lady, this is bad news. When I left here to see you he had disappeared for a while; I had hoped he had gone for ever. The Gods, you see, love chaos and he is their instrument. A renegade knight, I have fought both with him and against him. He has his own code of honour, far removed from most other people's. He loves instilling fear in his enemies and taking what they have for his own. Raping the enemy's women is a favourite trick of his. I am sorry, Cheris, but you weren't the first or the hundred and first, and you won't be the last either. I wonder which lord he fights with now?' Cheris pinched her nose, trying to stop it running.

'Fenchard,' she said. Morgan nodded his head slowly. 'Of course. Why did I have to ask?'

Itheya continued to look puzzled. 'He fights for you, for us then. Then why do what he did to this girl, why try to kill her?'

BOOK ONE: AUTUMN

Morgan looked at the elf's pale face, his world-weariness writ large in his dark eyes. 'I think I have mentioned this before. Whereas you people argue constantly with each other and deal with all your disagreements face to face and honestly, with humans saying one thing and doing another is an art. Men of power do it all the time – it is what power does, what it is. Trask seeks to betray us somehow, probably for a large amount of gold, it being the thing he values above all others. I need to get to Baron Felmere before they fight the enemy again.'

Cheris had regained herself a little. 'I, we, were due back at Grest with the army today. He was going to march against them on our return. I am supposed to be fighting for him.'

'Then we have some little time. I take it Trask thinks you dead?' Cheris nodded.

'I congratulate you then. Most caught in his schemes do not survive the experience. My manners have deserted me also. Forgive me, Cheris, my name is Morgan, a soldier serving Baron Felmere and Tanaren. You are in no shape to fight. I will tell him that when I see him. He can be a little overeager sometimes, but the two of us go back a long way. He will listen to reason and you will be spared the next battle. In fact, it may be a good idea for you to return to your island and another mage sent, if that is what you wish.'

'Thank you, Sir Morgan,' Cheris said quietly, 'but right now I do not know what I wish. I am having trouble thinking clearly.'

'Of course you don't!' he said briskly. 'Right now is not the time. Ride with us for now and make your decisions later, when we return you to the knights.'

'If any are left,' said Cheris wistfully. 'Trask killed those that accompanied us.'

Itheya shook her head. 'Your ways are strange to me. Traitors, that is zavuyugon in our tongue, are so rare in our history as to be almost unheard of. The punishments for ones such as they are ... terrible.'

Morgan cast around him, looking for something. He strode forward, crouched low and stood up again, holding a low, flat stone covered in dried mud at one edge. He held it up to both women.

'Do you know what this is?'

Itheya laughed, a short, sharp exclamation. Morgan looked at Cheris; even she was smiling slightly.

'Are stones so rare this side of the mountains? Perhaps you use them as jewellery here.' Itheya picked up her bow.

'You are right, of course; it is a stone but, more importantly, it is a Tanaren stone. Now, it has not been always thus. Over the last ten years, by my calculation, it has been Tanarese four times and Arshuman three, such are the amount of times this land has been passed back and forth between us. This does not count the other times where skirmishers or raiders have held this ground for a day or two. Now, in order to get possession of such an important piece of rock, our opposing forces have met in two to three great battles a year, along with hundreds of smaller conflicts involving under a hundred men or so. People have been skewered, burned, had their faces and limbs hacked off, been castrated and left to swing from a tree on innumerable occasions just for this stone.

'Sorry to tell you this, Cheris, but thousands of women have been raped and hundreds of bastards fathered owing loyalty to no one but themselves. I have seen children tied to poles, covered in pitch and used as flaming torches in the early years, when terror could still shock. It has worked, too. I see myself as a reasonable man in most things, but I would kill an Arshuman soldier in cold blood without a second thought, such are the things they have done to us. No one knows why we are fighting anymore – for honour, I suppose – yet I doubt there are a dozen men in these lands who could tell you exactly what that word means. And now we have to ride with the speed of an arrow to Grest to warn Felmere not to commit an act of folly and trust a man for whom all of this is as the meat and drink of the Gods. Without this war, Artorus only knows what he would be, a drunk in a forgotten tavern somewhere, I suppose, or a sellsword wielding his blade in the far south. I can cope with his mercenary ways as long as it is a long way from here. Come, ladies, we have delayed long enough.'

He dropped the stone and headed back towards the horses. Itheya looked at Cheris and smiled. 'Come, ride with me.'

Cheris thanked her and followed the elf in the same direction as Morgan. As she did so the first rumble of thunder sounded, followed shortly by scores of large heavy raindrops, filling the muddy hoof prints on the path before washing them away completely.

54

The army was deployed; the line was set. Rank upon rank of pale grim men stood behind their shields, their spears held aloft, gazing through the rain at the approaching enemy. Thunder rolled across the plain, turning the grass grey and ashen. Prior to this cloudburst, the opposing sets of light cavalry had been chasing each other over the open field, exchanging bow shot and insults. It had been entertaining but totally inconclusive, and once the rain started they had withdrawn back to their comrades. Baron Felmere trotted up and down the line making sure the men could see him; the rain was a good thing for him, for the enemy's light cavalry would be slowed and the effectiveness of the archers reduced. He shouted this out to his soldiers time and time again, hammering home that they had superiority in numbers and troop quality and that this was the time to grasp the nettle and send the yellow demons to the furnace. His job done, he returned to the far left of the line where the knights were stationed.

'Well, Reynard' he said bluffly, 'you know how bad my eyesight is. How is the enemy looking?'

'They are nearly deployed; the jester in the golden armour is at their heart with their first unit collected around him. Take them out of it, though, and it looks like they have just three units of regular troops. I am guessing, too, that many of them are newly enrolled. There are, however, a couple of blocks of mercenaries, the Vipers, the Mailed Hand, Menneken's Spears, and others. They are lining up to their right, opposite us; get among them early enough and they will break easily.'

Overhead there was a flash of lightning, the first Felmere had seen. Thunder followed shortly afterwards, intensifying the rain, making it even more difficult to see clearly.

'Artorus's eyes, damn this weather,' muttered Felmere. 'Still, let's not give them time to catch their breath. Let's get the advance sounded and get this done with.'

The word went out and, shortly after, a blaring of trumpets jolted the troops into action. Following their drummers each unit started to march slowly, closing the gap on the enemy which currently stood at about a mile. Felmere watched them. Lasgaart was on the far left, a mounted man among infantry, his sodden banner dripping on to his helm. Then came his own troops, the largest group, a thousand war veterans under his captain, Mirik. After this the green of Vinoyen – Ulgar was there, his scarred face clothed in steel. Felmere heard his barked commands, as he got his drummer to increase the marching speed. Then it was Haslan Falls, a large group again, expensively clad though mostly untested. Fenchard himself sat atop a white charger, a preening peacock of a man undaunted by the drenching he was receiving. Felmere saw Trask at their head, by the banner; he seemed twice the size of the men around him. Finally, to their right, was Maynard with the lesser barons, each represented by a banner. Light cavalry flanked to the left and right in the traditional formation with a thin line of archers to the fore; they would melt back through the ranks once their job of disrupting and unsettling the enemy formation was done. When he was satisfied, Felmere nodded to both Reynard and Dominic, spurring the knights forward. They had noticed a low hill on the plain a quarter of a mile away and he had decided to observe proceedings from there, so that they could better judge the time to send the knights in when their charge would be at its most devastating.

    The men were becoming subdued. Rain tended to do that. Summer was the true fighting season when a man could fight the enemy rather than the elements and wounds would bleed fast but heal quickly. Despite Felmere's best efforts, the news of the absence of the magical healer had spread among the men. That, together with the march to battle coming without any time for the customary prayers and blessings, had caused much muted grumbling among the rank and file. The Baron let them moan; once battle was joined, no one would be thinking of such things.

    He gained the hill and remained there with the knights, watching the infantry progress towards the enemy. The Arshumans had finished deploying and were waiting, stock still, for their foes to come to them. Their king in his ridiculous armour had found his own high ground and looked down upon his charges as they unfurled their yellow banners defiantly against the storm. The mercenaries, a mishmash of weapons and armour waiting under banners of simple cloth, stood slightly apart from the Arshuman troops. Lasgaart would engage them, Felmere thought, and he already had the mind to send the Silver Lances crashing into their flank once they were engaged. If they broke their formation, it would compromise the Arshumans defence considerably, it would give his men some impetus, maybe then they could roll across the Arshuman line, putting the untested troops under pressure. Hopefully, it would break their will and put them to flight. The battle would be won then; it would just be a matter of time.

'How much did you offer for the King's head?' Dominic Hartfield asked him. As with the last battle, Felmere stayed with the Silver Lances, leaving Reynard a little further forward ready to charge in if something went amiss.

'Fifty crowns if we win the battle; ten if we don't. I will obviously still need the money then.'

'Mytha's spear, that is a fortune! More than many of these fellows see in a lifetime!'

'It is supposed to be an incentive.' Felmere reminded him.

'It is their king, I suppose; his death would probably end this war in a trice. Why would he show himself in battle at this hour, I wonder?'

'Desperation, hopefully; maybe an attempt to shore up the morale of his men – that is, if they haven't got some poor soul desperate for coin to run around in it while the real king sits in Roshythe surrounded by all the serving girls his appetites can handle.'

'I had thought that, too.' Dominic's face was grim, not that Felmere could see it; conditions were getting wetter by the minute. 'What do you think the chances of it being the case are?'

'Evens I daresay. Still, we have to treat him as though he is the King; it is important we take him here, alive or dead. Just getting his armour would be worth it; we can send it to Leontius. The new Tanaren high fashion. When you return there you will see everyone wearing a suit.' Felmere chuckled at his poor joke, not realising how accurate their conjecture was, for King Aganosticlan was many miles away, at Tantala, secure from the predations of his enemies.

Dominic did not reply; he was staring at the advancing row of men.

'Our line is getting a bit ragged – it must be the weather – we need to signal them to tighten things up a bit.'

Felmere sheltered his eyes with his hand. What the knight had said was true – the right flank in particular was looking pretty uneven with Fenchard's men dropping rapidly behind Vinoyen's, and Maynard's men, unsure who to align themselves with, just drifting between the two.

Felmere cursed and passed a message to the flag-bearers and musicians to get them to order Fenchard and Maynard to speed up a little. That done, he grabbed some bread off one of the foot messengers; he hadn't eaten that morning as his stomach was playing up and he suddenly felt desperately hungry.

There was about a quarter of a mile between the opposing forces. Arrows were flying between them but were having a negligible effect in this weather; cavalry sorties were also going on but they seemed equally half-hearted. And still Haslan Falls were behind the line. If anything the gap had increased, their front rank now being behind Ulgar Vinoyen's final rank. Maynard's men had pushed on and were holding the correct position again, so if Baron Fenchard's men fell back any further then the opposing cavalry could fill the gap and fire arrows at the exposed flanks to their left and right.

'What by Artorus's bollocks is he playing at?' Felmere shouted in frustration.

'I will send a man up to them,' Dominic replied.

He did so and within the minute a knight of the Silver Lances was barrelling towards the Haslan Falls banner with all the speed he could manage over the soft ground.

The gap increased still further. There was clear daylight between Haslan Falls and Vinoyen. The men of Ulgar's Company were turning to them, though whether they were exhorting them to push on or just shouting obscenities, Felmere could not tell. Ahead of them Reynard broke rank and started spurring his horse towards Felmere, who waited for him with curiosity. The storm was nearing its full fury now; it was not long after noon but the land was steeped in a grey murk, enlivened only by a coruscating flash of lightning that illuminated the toiling soldiers for less than a second, freezing them in Felmere's memory, and still Haslan Falls were behind the others.

Reynard pulled his visor back, his eyes looked slightly panicked, something Felmere was not used to seeing.

'Baron,' he said, 'I don't know if this is important but Trask vanished for a couple of days in the last week, only returning yesterday. When I asked him where he had been he made up some story about visiting a prostitute. I didn't believe him then and...'

'By all the Gods,' said Dominic softly, his voice reflecting Reynard's concern, 'you don't think...'

Felmere wasn't sure what the two men were trying to say, but the problem with the advance needed resolving immediately. He called over to the musicians at the top of his lungs. 'Sound the halt ... now!'

The response was instant. The signal sounded, clear as crystal through the rain, yet again Felmere felt proud of the iron discipline of his men as they stopped their march almost in unison.

All except one.

Haslan Falls men continued forward. At first Felmere was pleased, thinking they would plug the gap in the line. Instead they started to veer to the left, putting them on a collision course with Ulgar Vinoyen's men. From the Arshuman line cornets blasted a single piercing note, the signal for them to start their march.

'The mages aren't coming back,' said Dominic ominously.

'What do you mean?,' said Felmere. His patience with the two knights' evasiveness seemed to be running out.

Reynard looked at Dominic and they both understood each other. Dominic spoke again: 'Baron, we need to withdraw.'

'Withdraw?' roared Felmere with some anger. 'Battle is about to be joined; we have the advantage. What milky-livered womanish cowardice is this? The battle is ours to win.'

'Because we are being betrayed.' Felmere's jaw dropped like a stone.

Up ahead, Dominic's knight reached the Haslan Falls banner. They saw him speaking to Trask, with Fenchard now alongside him. Dominic looked on in anguish because he now knew exactly what was coming next and could not do a thing to stop it.

As the knight leaned forward on his horse, neck craned to listen to the man on foot, Trask swung his arm around the man's throat and dragged him off his horse. They could not see the denouement of this act but didn't need to. The horse ran off as it no longer had a master to serve.

And then came the next stage in the proceedings. To Felmere, it seemed to take an eternity, as though every protagonist was wading through bone glue. As he watched, already aware of the horror about to be enacted, the men of Haslan Falls lowered their spears, broke into a well-coordinated run, and charged Ulgar Vinoyen's unit in its unprotected rear.

Chaos would be the only word to describe what ensued over the next hour. Immediately, Felmere saw that this was not a battle to sit back and direct calmly. Spurring his horse, he and the other knights charged towards the turncoats of Haslan Falls.

It was patently clear to all concerned that this was going to be a disaster of some scale. Fenchard's men outnumbered Vinoyen's by two to one and had already scattered most of the surprised and panicked troops. Baron Maynard on the far right was left isolated and the Arshumans had sent all their light cavalry to surround him and pepper his men with arrows. So effectively, after a matter of minutes, the army of Tanaren was reduced to two units. Baron Lasgaart was engaging the mercenary force on the left and Felmere's own men, along with the men of Athkaril, were fending off two units of the enemy who had just crashed into them, spear against shield. The shock of the impact could even be heard above the thunder.

'For Tanaren!' roared Felmere and along with the other knights he slammed into the rear of Fenchard's men, in a frantic attempt to stop their inexorable progress through the remnants of Vinoyen's forces and into his own soldiers' unprotected flank.

It worked to a degree – blood and confusion reigned. Felmere ran his spear through the innards of one man before he could ready his shield. His horse crunched into the men immediately behind, hooves snapping bone and raking flesh. Felmere swept out his sword, cleanly parting another man's head from his shoulders. As he killed, though, he couldn't help thinking, 'By all the Gods, these are my own men.'

Dominic and the Silver Lances to his left and right were doing similar grisly work. A wedge had been carved into Fenchard's men, leaving many dead and dying, but they were prepared now. The impetus of the charge had gone and the danger now was that they would be surrounded. The knights, visors down, blood spattered over their shining plate mail and soaked into the barding of the horses, faced the enemy, who had backed away, leaving a space of some yards between the two of them. The Baron looked at these men carefully for the first time – many had brands, the mark of a criminal, and there were some swarthy-faced men, skin burnished by the sun almost as if they were born and raised in sunnier climes than here. Before they could counter-charge, though, Felmere sounded the retreat and the knights pulled free of their treacherous foes.

Reynard's men were engaging the mercenaries along with Lasgaart's infantry and were holding their own despite being outnumbered. Unlike the regimented appearance of the Arshuman regulars, no two of the mercenaries looked the same. Some had shields; others eschewed them in favour of colossal double-headed axes or giant six-foot swords needing two hands to wield. Others carried little more than brutal-looking cudgels; some were clad in leather armour, others in chain with enclosing helmets, and yet more wore little more than brigandine. They held a much looser formation, though, and would charge. ferociously grabbing their opponents' spears and cleaving through their shields. The fighting degenerated quickly into brutal close hand-to-hand combat – maces pounding into skulls and crushing bone and brain; short swords hammered into ribs or through the mouths of the screaming enemy, shattering teeth and punching clean through to the other side, causing blood to spray like rain; and long swords, the ultimate slashing weapon, slicing through scapula to coccyx, spilling pale intestines and other scarlet, pulpy organs like some demonic butcher's yard. The agonised high pitch screaming of the wounded mixed with the concentrated grunting of the hard-pressed defenders and the battle cries of warriors sensing victory. Black blood and faeces covered the churned-up mud underfoot, and the relentless rain, washing everything into soggy shallow pools, caused the stink to rise. The true stench of death.

Elsewhere in the field, Felmere noted that his archers had nearly all been run down and scattered and that the light cavalry, though fighting gamely against a more numerous foe, were no match for their Arshuman equivalent. They had fragmented and had not even the loosest formation to speak of. His army consisted of two poorly protected units of infantry and a small number of brave, but outmanned, knights. And still not all of the opposing troops had been committed.

Then Maynard's men, alone and tormented by arrows, broke and started to run back towards the ridge and the camp. The true slaughter in a battle comes not from determined men facing each other sword against shield; it comes through fear and panic. As Maynard's men turned to flee, their backs were turned to the enemy horse and any semblance of a disciplined formation was lost. The enemy trumpets sounded and their small unit of heavy cavalry advanced ready to mow down and slaughter those whose courage had failed them. Men tried desperately to dive out of the way of the thundering hooves bearing down on them, falling to the earth covering their heads with their hands, only to be pounded, pummelled or run through with lances or spears.

Seeing this, Felmere called Dominic over. 'I need to get to Reynard!' he shouted hoarsely. 'Take your knights and get among their cavalry. Try to save some of those poor bastards and stop them attacking our rear. I need to change things here.'

As the Silver Lances galloped off to do what they could, Felmere galloped around the rear lines of his forces to where Reynard had disengaged and was trying to gain some respite, regain his breath. About a quarter of his men were missing.

'We cannot stand up to them; we need to withdraw, but slowly and in formation. When Lasgaart's forces separate from the enemy, get them into a circle; I will do the same with my men. Our job then is to get everyone out of here without them getting surrounded and destroyed.'

Reynard nodded. 'Baron Ulgar is dead. I saw Trask pull him down myself, though Fenchard landed the killing blow.'

Felmere whistled through gritted teeth. 'Maynard, too; his men broke when an arrow caught him. We need to pull back over the river and destroy the bridges to buy some time. There are not enough of us to defend Grest. I want you to evacuate the city; you know what Arshuman retribution is like.'

'As you wish,' said Reynard, 'though I would sooner try and put Trask's eyes on a stick and roast them over a fire.'

'His bollocks, you mean. And Fenchard's, too, if he has any. Go and see Lasgaart; we have little time.'

The battle had been raging for under an hour, but the next phase of it lasted much, much longer and was infinitely more gruelling. As Felmere ordered, the two remaining units of infantry reordered themselves into circles, spears facing outwards. In this way they could not be flanked, though they could no longer muster a decisive charge. Fresher men could replace tired ones easily and both units could be much more durable. Marching in coherent formation was difficult, however, and the retreat was painfully slow. Time and time again Arshuman arrows fell among them, the wounded stumbling and falling, their comrades trying to lift them and keep them moving. Anyone who could not move would have to be left behind – and no mercy was shown to stragglers, who would be clubbed to death, or have their throats opened with dagger thrusts, blood spraying on to the face of their killer.

The Arshuman infantry was relentless in their pursuit, attempting to encircle the men of Tanaren entirely, a circle they could then close slowly, crushing the surrounded units in a vice of steel. Felmere remembered his tutor as a child, telling him stories of the great battles of the past; he thought of the Battle of Oro-Califan when a Kozean army, though outnumbering their enemy greatly, was destroyed in a similar manner. Men were pressed so closely together in that terrible conflict that they could not draw or swing their weapons, or breathe properly, or control their bladders. To stop this from happening here, he, Dominic and Reynard led their exhausted cavalry in charges to drive back the foe. It worked, too – no encirclement was made and the will and strength of the Arshuman footmen and their quislings was slowly drained.

After three exhausting hours they made the ridge bounding Wolf Plain, and Felmere heard with relief the brass trumpets of his enemy sounding the withdrawal. The Arshuman army, and their gold-clad "king", too, needed some time to rest up before pressing onwards. It was a window of time Felmere had to use to his advantage.

He looked at his exhausted men. An army of nearly six thousand had marched from camp earlier that day and now they would be returning with little more than a third of that amount; granted a thousand of the starter force had turned traitor and many men had fled and scattered, but it was still a terrible reverse. Every face he looked at was pale, tired and bloodied; many were badly wounded. The auxiliaries with stretchers who would normally ferry the injured back to the healer's tent had been attacked themselves, so Felmere had dismissed them for their own protection. It was a battle with few prisoners taken; the Arshumans' thirst for vengeance after the Battle of Grest had been more than sated.

After clearing the tree-lined ridge, though, they could now see the river and the tented camp this side of it. Heartened, their pace picked up a little and they closed the distance quite quickly. All kept looking back, though, expecting at any minute ranks of grim mailed warriors, grouped under banners of yellow, to appear atop the ridge, bent on revenge.

The rain stopped and it started to get cold again, numbing fingers and toes and causing spirits to drop even further. It was a thoroughly demoralised army that limped back into the camp, a place of refuge, but they had no time to rest their tired muscles. Immediately Felmere called the remaining generals and nobles to his tent.

He had had no time to dwell on the ruin of his hopes and dreams. The despair he was gamely fighting back into the darker recesses of his mind would get full vent over a bottle of vinegary wine later; now, however, he had to pick up the shattered pieces of this debacle.

'We can discuss what happened today later,' he said, his voice thick with disappointment. 'But now we have to get everyone out of this camp and destroy the bridges. It will buy us time and give us a chance to get everyone out of Grest who wants to leave.'

'Fair comment, my Lord,' said Tomak, a veteran general of his own House. 'But what happens after that? If we are abandoning Grest, how far back do we retreat?'

'Winter is coming. There will be little more campaigning this year,' said Felmere. 'With Ulgar dead and Haslan Falls betraying us, the entire region is threatening to break up into a patchwork of separate strongholds with Tanaren controlling little of it. We need to get word to Esric and secure Tetha Vinoyen, though I am sure Fenchard has already stolen a march on us there.

We retreat to our fortified camp in the plain; thereafter, I don't know – we will have to see. Right now, though, Reynard, take your knights up to Grest and start getting the people out of there. Tomak, Mirik, I want a hundred volunteers to be last over the bridges and to destroy them as they cross. Get the civvies over the bridge first. Now, all of you, move – we have little time as it is!'

Everyone beat a hasty exit except for Dominic Hartfield. Felmere didn't seem to notice him at first, lost as he was in a reverie. Dominic had to call him by name before Felmere responded.

'The Silver Lances. What do you wish of them? Shall we escort the civilians to the camp?'

'Yes, by all means,' the Baron replied absently. 'And take this with you.' He handed Dominic a small chest, about the right size to store documents. It was locked, so Felmere handed him the key. Both men knew of its contents.

'Ulgar and Maynard are dead,' he said. 'Their wills are in there, along with those of all the other nobles. Once your escort duties are done, take it to my city; it needs to be kept safe. I would have gone if the battle had gone well, but now I will be staying on the front lines until this mess is sorted.'

Dominic bowed. 'Of course, Baron, but once that has been

arranged I will fight alongside you.'

'As you wish. I am grateful.' Felmere watched him leave, his face blank and expressionless. Dominic ducked out of the tent, leaving Felmere alone for a second.

He cursed softly to himself and strode through to that part of the tent partitioned off for his sleeping quarters. A servant was there packing a trunk; everything else there had been already moved out. He could smell the river, swollen with the rain. It was only a matter of yards away, concealed by high rushes. The light had almost gone and the lanterns had been lit, their soft red light suffusing the confined space with its warmth.

'Have you nearly finished?' he asked the sweating man.

'Yes, my Lord, I will only be a few minutes then I can load it on to the wagon.'

'Good. Get yourself over the bridge as soon as you can. The enemy could be here at any time and I don't want you caught up in that.'

'Thank you, my Lord, but I will be done here very quickly.'

Felmere left him and strolled back to the main part of the tent. Wearily, he unstrapped his breastplate and lowered it to the ground, all the better for his slightly overweight frame to breathe properly for five minutes. It felt strange being on his own; it happened so rarely. Being alone with his thoughts was something he wasn't used to and after the disasters of the day he wasn't sure it was something he wanted either. The Gods had truly forsaken them. Not having the morning devotions had obviously been a terrible mistake. He would have to see the Artoran priest, to ask what public penance he should undergo to gain their forgiveness in the eyes of his men. When would he see his family again?

He could hear the servant packing the trunk, heavy footsteps along with the muffled sounds of clothes, scrolls or other bric-a-brac being stowed hastily with scant regard for order or tidiness. He was about to leave the man, to check whether the Arshumans had been sighted when he heard a heavier thump. Had the man dropped something? No matter, given the haste required, mistakes could be forgiven. He waited to hear him start work again but there was only silence. Strange, he thought. He called out the man's name. There was no response. He called again with the same result. Damn the man to the furnace, what was he up to? With an exasperated sigh he barged back into the sleeping quarters, his face reddening slightly. 'By the furnace and the saints, my man, what exactly is going on he...?' He stopped dead in his tracks.

Slumped over the trunk, limp and lifeless, was the servant's body. For a second he entertained the notion that the man had collapsed drunk; something he dismissed just as quickly. He put his hand to his sword ready to draw it, an occurrence that was never to happen.

He felt it, of course, if only for less than a second, a sliver of cold icy metal, both freezing and searing hot, thrust with a calculated precision into his back just left of his spine. There was no time to feel pain – the blade entered his heart much too quickly for that. And then ...nothing. Was he now seated at the great table of the Gods, supping with divine Artorus and Camille, talking freely with Elissa and Mytha? Was he joined again with the spirit of his first wife, a lady for whom he had more affection than he had ever let show? Unfortunately, these were things that humble mortals would never know. Felmere was dead long before his body slumped to the ground.

The only person left alive in the room, cloaked and hooded in midnight black, wiped the blade on the grass before slipping it back into her belt. Fortune had smiled on Syalin these last couple of days – the camp moving, Felmere pitching his tent right next to the river, things couldn't had fallen easier. She knelt over the fallen body and gently prised the man's signet ring from his middle finger. She was glad she didn't have to cut the finger off; carrying such a thing round with her was always mildly irritating. Ducking down low, she looked under the tent flap. It was dark now and the coast was clear. Noiselessly, like a spirit of air, she left the tent and headed for the river. She stopped for a second, looking and tasting the breeze. Then she slipped down the bank and into the reeds where she disappeared from view completely.

Shortly afterwards she emerged again, in a small round boat of the kind so beloved of the Marsh Men. It had been expertly concealed in the reeds for a couple of days as had she. The rain had been troubling; as the river rose, her hiding place had been compromised, but fortunately no one was minded to be vigilant in these terrible conditions and the darkness had come early, shrouding her from view again.

She did not use the oar; rather she let the river take her. She left the camp behind just as she heard the panicked shouts of men and the subsequent hue and cry, indicating her handiwork had been discovered. She continued to drift downriver; the temperature on a river was always so much colder than the land surrounding it, she thought. She drew her cloak around her, annoyed at the weakness she showed in feeling the damp chill. Eventually, after travelling a mile or more she came to a knot of trees on the eastern bank. Steering the little boat patiently, at long last she pulled it over among a clump of reeds and tied it up against a tree root. Now it was just a case of waiting till the morning.

She looked up at the early-evening stars, the beautiful, beautiful stars. For a fleeting second she thought of her home. Her first home before her rebirth as a Strekha. On the foothills of the mountains could be seen stars like no others. Why did man crave diamonds when the bejewelled majesty of the night sky was there for all to see? Her fellow species, as always, remained a mystery to her; their priorities were not her priorities. As a child among her barbarous people, all that mattered was a good hunt and food on the table. Then, as a servant of the Emperor, want was not a concept that ever arose – how strange it was, then, to see the merchant class of Koze, fat men spending their lives acquiring coin they could not spend. All it made as far as she could see was enemies and she had killed enough of them to know that to be the truth.

She left the boat and sat on a tump of thick grass next to the bole of a tree. From a small pack at her waist she pulled a hard circular biscuit, which she nibbled fastidiously. That eaten, she took a bare sip of water from a small hip flask and swallowed a tiny sliver of blackroot. Sitting cross-legged, her hands in her lap, she entered a light trance. In such a state she could not feel cold, or damp and pain, and discomfort could be ignored. Her mind went back to her home, the swaying palms sighing over a languid river, the orange groves within the white walls of the palace of the sages with the sharp tang of citrus in the air. The high alabaster towers topped with gold shimmering in the midday heat haze and the small monkeys bold enough to steal dates from the harvest baskets of the nut-brown villagers. She knew those people saw her pale skin and white hair as something of a marvel, but none would dare approach her to ask about it.

Other memories came to her then, unbidden ones, the type she could usually shut out; she did not know why they flashed through her mind now. She was about twelve. Her wrists were secured with manacles attached to a chain that was pulling her nearly off the floor. She was nearly naked, bathed in sweat; fear, such a rare feeling these days, was coursing through her, causing tears to drip heavily on to the stone floor over which the rats scurried. A hulk of a man stood over her brandishing a many-thonged whip. She remembered to this day the noise it made, the swish as he swung it left and right, and even now she flinched at the memory. Of course, she knew now that he had no intention of using it on her – her skin was to remain as unblemished as possible in case the Emperor wanted her to satisfy himself – but back then she was terrified of it. Something else she was to learn was that there were ways of inflicting the most intensely cruel pain imaginable without breaking the skin.

'Say it again,' the man said to her, 'And get it right this time.'

The small girl she once was held back her sobs, not daring to get it wrong again.

'The Emperor is the father of Koze; the Emperor is therefore my true father. I have no family but the Strekha and the Strekha are the Emperor's most beloved children. He is the light that fills me. His love is the only true love; any other is false and ephemeral, devoid of substance. My body is his to command and my will is his will, my desires are his desires, and my hope is his hope. I have been reborn as his greatest thrall, a golden butterfly from an ugly white grub crawling through the dirt. Without the Emperor I am nothing, for I was nothing until my choosing. My life will be lived through his glory and will end at his behest when my purpose has been fulfilled.'

'Better,' said the man. 'Now, say it a hundred times over, with no mistakes and I can finally let you down.'

BOOK ONE: AUTUMN

'The Emperor is the father of Koze, the E...'

Something broke into her memories, a bright-yellow glow further up the river. It reflected off the tree-covered hill on which the city stood and caused the river to gleam darkly in the distance. She sighed slightly, a sigh that was little more than a murmur, then took another biscuit out of her pack and nibbled it like a mouse. The bridges were on fire.

55

The elves were at camp. They had gathered much dead wood and piled it into a large bonfire. Though most of it was damp and hard to light, the judicious application of several of the ubiquitous glowstones soon had it roaring heartily, if a little smokily.

It had been a day of hard riding in frequently terrible conditions. Cheris and Cedric were soaked through in no time and both had spent a good part of the day sweating at their exertion and shivering at the cold, especially after the storm had moved on to the north and west and the late-autumn chill had returned.

Still, progress had been good. They were now within half a mile of Baron Felmere's forward camp just an hour or two away from the town of Grest. Morgan, eager for information, had left them earlier to go there in search of news. They were expecting him back at any time.

Cheris and Cedric were sitting together around the fire. Terath was next to them with Itheya a little further away, where she was issuing orders and talking with her people. Earlier that day, during an ever-so-brief pause to eat during a lull in the rain, Astania, a small, pert dark-haired elf with haunting sapphire-blue eyes, had approached Cheris.

'I am to help you,' she said haltingly. 'Let me touch you; it will be good.'

Cheris assented and watched as Astania passed her hand over Cheris's diaphragm, over her bruised torso and still-sore rib, and lower, over her womb and the top of her legs. Lastly she took Cheris, hands in her own, grasping them firmly but gently. And all the time she slowly chanted, soft words that Cheris herself partly recognised as a litany of healing. It worked, too – everywhere her hands passed Cheris could feel the pain being drawn from her, the soreness and dull throbbing aches becoming more muted. She felt a new vigour inside her; even her sadness and the nagging sense of humiliation she had borne all day seemed to be allayed. She watched Dirthen, the male healer, do something similar with Cedric. Cedric was a man Cheris did not know, but they exchanged smiles at the shared experience. They had been talking comfortably together since camp had been made.

The elves started to sing. Cheris had heard the mages, choir singing songs of devotion many times and thought it quite grand, if a little pompous and self-important. This was different though, men and women combining voices in a soft lament redolent with feeling and a yearning for times long lost. Though she could only make out some of the words, its melancholy beauty tugged at her heart in a way she could not describe.

Ay alune memero, ay alune memera
Gaterian azhuntath, ser froto res hetha
Ke brako smeshen, sea issa von brogo
Za brnathare sealve, coz omo terefogo
Ser res hetha, ser res hetha
Frot o eonona, frot o eonona

Ay alune memero, ay alune memera
Sezheia za sasha, seser froto res hetha
Danara lutelere, hassadesh zamon brako
Cot dane za hemenes, benremath strakafanto
Ser res hetha, ser res hetha
Frot o eonona, frot o eonona

Ay alune memero, ay alune memera
Ess azhuntath siono, forgor nestro siona
Cotholi omerme, cotholea stref tishi
Amanza trenexmrsha, coth hashara varverissi
Ser res hetha, ser res hetha
Frot o eonona, frot o eonona

There were many more verses and soon she was struggling to catch up with her translation. They spoke the language far more quickly and in a much more relaxed manner than anyone at college did, even her tutors. She gave up eventually and chose the lazy option, quietly asking Cedric what he knew.

'Oh, I lost it a while back,' he said. 'I know they are singing about Roshythe, though.'

'Res hetha, that is "cloud spire". Is that Roshythe then?'

'Yes, it is an important city and has a great emotional attachment for all bar those who occupy it at the present.'

'It was an elven city,' she said earnestly. 'Taken over by Tanaren but not destroyed.'

Cedric laughed silently. 'It is nice to speak to someone who knows their history. You are right. When Tanar, the first Grand Duke, came to the river, the first human to set eyes upon it, he saw Roshythe on the lake and thought it the fairest place on earth. He forbad siege towers or catapults to be used against it, lest the walls be damaged and instead surrounded the city, letting no one in or out. Eventually, after much privation and suffering, the elves sent a deputation to him. Many women and children were dying, so they offered him the city as long as they were allowed to leave in peace to seek their brethren on the isles. Tanar agreed to this and the humans watched as a column of elves miles long exited Roshythe along the path by Lake Winmead.

'But some men saw the gold they were carrying on them and grew covetous. Greed overtook restraint and elves were attacked and killed, their possessions seized. Seeing this, the elven leader called a halt and commanded those of his people still inside the city to destroy it. One of the high towers they started to dismantle stone by stone. Tanar was furious and was going to slaughter every elf until he saw the attacking humans. At this point and for the only recorded time in the Elven Wars he begged forgiveness of the elves. The miscreants were crucified along the lake, and their possessions returned. The elves departed out of history, at least for many centuries. Then Tanar took the city, passed a decree that no stone was ever to be changed there, and named it his new capital.'

'But it was not the capital for long, was it?'

'No, within a century of Tanar's death, there was a new city, a port, big and brash, chaotic and badly ordered, rather like humans themselves, I suppose. The eighth Grand Duke, Tamas, named Tanaren the new capital – they say, because he liked the vices that it offered –and it has been thus ever since. Then, just two hundred years ago, Grand Duke Eginvald, a greedy, vain man who had never been to Roshythe in his life sold it to Arshuma. Their king took control in a lavish ceremony and promised to uphold the decree never to change the place. Such was the outrage engendered by the transaction that both their king and Eginvald were assassinated within the year. The Arshuman king has never lived there since; rather they use it as a trinket to dangle before the men of Tanaren, to infuriate them.

So you see, for both us and the elves, Roshythe is a symbol of loss. The elves feel shame for not defending the city more strongly and we feel shame for handing the city over for a few cheap gold coins.'

'The elven tribe that lived there – who were they?'

'Two tribes shared the city, controlling it on alternate years. The tribe that surrendered it to the humans caused a deep-seated animosity with the other, one that persists to this day.'

'But how do you know this, if they went over the sea?'

'Because they didn't. They could not. They arrived at Atem Sezheia to see it in chaos, partly destroyed and boats leaving every hour. Rather than play the game of chance that they could find ships to take them, they turned back eastwards, to the Aelvenwood, where they live to this day.'

Cheris lowered her voice to a tiny whisper. 'So they are here then?'

'Yes, the princess of the one tribe you have shared a horse with today; the prince of the other is the red-headed fellow who keeps looking at you suspiciously. One tribe rides under the green and gold banner, the other under the banner of the hawk with open wings. Actually it is a kite, not a hawk, with feathers almost as red as their hair.'

'So which tribe abandoned the city?'

'That I do not know; the records name the tribes but say no more than that. I think the reason for them singing the song together is an attempt at both forgiveness and understanding between them. I hope that is the case anyway.'

Cheris looked deeply into the fire; its warmth had never been more welcome. 'This friend of yours, Morgan. Can I trust him?'

Cedric looked surprised at the question. 'Bear in mind I have known him for a fairly short period myself. Saying that, though, in that time we have been through a lot together and, yes, I think it would be fair to say that I trust him like I trust few other men. You need have no fear of him, really.'

'I am sorry if my question seems impertinent; it is just that after what happened to me I think I will be wary of any man, at least for a while.'

'You are not wary of me, are you?'

She laughed. 'No, with all the respect in the world, you seem a little too old, even for me'

Cedric grunted. 'So, I am safe then.'

'Yes, Cedric, you are safe.'

There was a commotion behind them, causing both Cedric and Cheris to look round. Through the darkness striding up to the fire was Morgan. As he warmed his hands over the blaze, both Itheya and Cedric could see his face was drawn and anxious. Itheya walked up to him.

'What news? Is it not good?'

'No,' said Morgan, 'not good at all. The battle may have already been fought. I need to leave now to see what news of it I can find.'

'Then we need to be quick. I will go with you.'

'Very well. Bring a few of your brethren – not more than a dozen – just in case we run into trouble.'

Cheris stood, a little unwillingly. 'Shall I come? You might need me.'

Morgan glanced at her. 'No, you will need time, I feel. It may be a good idea for you to spend the winter at Felmere Castle. It is as safe as any place here and your body can heal at its own pace. When it gets warmer you can then decide if you want to return to your island or not. Thank you for the offer anyway.'

Within a few minutes he was mounted again alongside Itheya and eight other spear-and-bow armed warriors.

'I go to find news,' he said. 'What we all do next depends on what we hear. Expect us back not long after dawn. If we do not return, then you must decide among yourselves what to do. Fare you well.'

They rode towards the east, soon striking a path leading from the human camp. Itheya had not seen him looking so tense.

'Why do you think battle has been joined already?'

'Felmere, the commander of the army, has moved his forward camp to the other side of the river. The place I have just left was practically deserted, but there were enough people there to say that Felmere has scented blood and is eager to engage the enemy quickly. And why wouldn't he? He had the advantage in numbers and morale and was blithely unaware of the snake in his midst. I hope we can get there in time to warn him.'

Within the hour, though, they had their answer. Itheya, inevitably, heard it first.

'Heavy traffic,' she said, '– carts and wagons – on the road.'

They picked up speed and soon even Morgan could hear them. A vast convoy was coming towards them. Not quickly – there were too many of them for unbridled haste – but steadily and methodically.

'It is not an army,' said Morgan. 'Civilians of some sort.'

The night black sky was changing to a deep blue. Dawn was not too far away and there was the faintest light now to ride by. It was still too early to douse the flaming torches they all carried though. But ahead the outline of carts and tumbrils could be seen. Morgan and Itheya rode ahead, eager to talk with their riders.

They were village folk, cloaked and booted against the cold; the women inside the wagons wore shawls.

'Where are you folk all going on such a cold unfriendly night?' Morgan asked them in a clear voice.

'We were told to.' Morgan could see no faces but the voice belonged to an old man. He realised wryly that they would not see Itheya was an elf. At least it will stop a panic, he thought to himself. The old man continued. 'Late afternoon, early evening, a group of knights rode into the town telling everyone to pack up and leave. The Arshumans were coming, they said. Of course, not everyone fled; those whose loyalties were to the other side were more than happy to stay put. If the knights hadn't have been there, there would be many among us murdered in their beds this past night.' Morgan let them on their way.

He wore his sense of dread about him like a cloak. Itheya turned to him, appearing equally concerned.

'This is bad for us, yes?'

'Well, they would not evacuate the city without good reason. I am sorry, you appear to have joined our cause at a difficult time.'

'We can return home any time we choose. But somehow I do not think we will.'

'Why would you think that exactly? This is not your war; you have said it many times yourself.' Morgan was frowning.

Itheya smiled softly in return. 'Did you not see us passing your stone city? We have spent all our lives in the forest seeing nothing else, living in a self-inflicted prison, and now we have been released. We were discussing it this evening, the sense of freedom, the sating of our curiosity regarding the wider world. And there is something else also. You defeated us in a great war; we have always felt some chagrin, some sense of humiliation about that – whether you outnumbered us or not, whether you exploited our differences for your own ends. Well, this is a chance to redeem ourselves for our people. What care we about iron weapons when we can show how elves truly fight. There is no shame in dying, Morgan, but there is in living on your knees. We are the first siolesta – that is, war band – to fight this side of the mountains in generations and we will not return skulking and cowed.'

Morgan looked at her slyly. 'I have yet to see you fight.'

'I am afraid it sounds like you will get your wish granted very soon now.'

Morgan did not answer. He trotted past the evacuees, who were sweating and grumbling as they drove their carthorses slowly forward. Grinding his teeth, he stared ahead, trying to pierce the darkness, to get the answers he needed. In a matter of minutes, though, Itheya behind him hissed softly.

'Horses ahead, armoured men on horses. Is this what you seek?'

'Quite possibly!' Morgan replied. 'Let us find out shall we?'

Even he could see them now. Dawn was near and thin tendrils of early morning mist were rising from the damp ground. They, too, saw him in return and rode towards him – knights clad in full plate bearing lances and shields of silver, riding under the banner of Tanaren. Their leader, riding bareheaded, had close-cropped dark hair and steely determined eyes. He hailed Morgan gruffly.

'Who in the name of the Gods are you and why are you riding in the wrong cursed direction?' He did not seem in the mood to brook any nonsense.

Morgan raised an appraising eyebrow. 'My name is Morgan, once of Glaivedon and envoy to Baron Felmere. I come here with the siolesta, a war band of elves who have graciously decided to join our cause. It looks to me that you are the head of the Silver Lances, bodyguard to the Grand Duke, and I hope you can give me some news as to what is happening here. I have been away for some weeks after all.'

The knight stopped. He looked shocked, though Morgan did not have the first idea why.

'The ways of the Gods are mysterious indeed,' he replied. 'You are the person I am bound to seek, though I have never met you and have only descriptions of your appearance. Your scar confirms it to me.'

'I am sorry,' said Morgan, puzzled, 'but you are speaking in riddles.'

The man pulled himself out of his distracted state. 'Forgive me, I shall explain. I am Dominic Hartfield, commander of the Silver Lances here, as you said. Yesterday was a calamitous day for us all...'

'You fought a battle and were betrayed.'

Dominic nodded gravely, showing no surprise at Morgan's prescience. At that moment Itheya rode forward to be beside Morgan, causing Dominic to start slightly.

'I am Itheya, commander of the elves here. Please tell your tale.'

Composing himself, Dominic recounted the events of the battle, the betrayal of Fenchard and the deaths of Ulgar and Baron Maynard. 'I noticed when we charged them, they had prisoners, foreign sellswords, all kinds of detritus in their ranks. Now, of course, we know that Arshuman money was paying for his ever-growing army; it was just that none of us ever suspected that a baron would sell out his country for his own ends.'

'Fenchard has surprised me, too,' said Morgan. 'I thought he had neither the wit nor ability to commit an act of such audacity. What is the situation now?'

'The Arshumans are on the other side of the river. We have burned the bridges but that will not hold them for long. By this time tomorrow their cavalry could be within spitting distance of Tetha Vinoyen; we have precious few men to stop them.'

'Perhaps it is not men that we need. Itheya, the Arshuman light horse have been a curse to us for many years. Do you think they are a match for you?'

Itheya gave a musical laugh. 'Is that a challenge?'

He returned the smile, 'Time to prove yourself, my girl. Seriously, though, the people we passed earlier and others like them need time to find what refuge they can. You can give them that time. You cannot stop the yellow advance – there are not enough of you – but you can harass them all the way, make them pay in blood for every yard gained, and save many of my countrymen's lives. I just hope I don't slow you down.'

Dominic coughed politely. 'You may have other things to consider.'

'Such as?'

'You were close to Baron Felmere, I believe. I am sorry to tell you that he is dead.'

It was Morgan's turn to look stunned. 'In battle?' he said quietly.

'No, in his tent, at the end of an assassin's knife.'

'Xhenafa carry his soul safely.' Morgan's voice sounded thick. 'Was this assassin caught?'

'No, we think he escaped downriver; probably one of Haslan Falls men and certainly a professional job. If it is any consolation, it was a knife in the heart, instant and painless.'

Morgan turned to Itheya. 'I am sorry but I will have to leave you here. I will need to get to Felmere Castle to speak to his wife and boy. Dominic, is there anyone who can guide these folk here; they do not know the country.'

Dominic nodded. 'Reynard has completed the evacuation of Grest.

He will be here shortly and will be happy to help the lady.' He swallowed. 'Morgan, there is one more thing – one that implies that Felmere Castle is just the place you should be headed.'

Morgan spoke wryly. 'What can that be. I am going to see his boy Kraven, unless someone else wishes to do so in my stead.'

'No, Morgan, it is a job for you. You see, once we knew of his death, we had to read his will. The north is without a Prosecutor of War and his son is not yet of age. Fortunately his will was clear. It names the man to be both guardian of his son until he does come of age and, by default, ruler of his lands and the new Prosecutor – that is, until the Grand Duke names another.' Morgan looked askance. Surely he could not mean...

'Yes, Morgan, it is you he names. Reynard was too young and would have to give up his position with the knights. He wanted a man who has raised a son, a shrewd man and a good judge of character. These are all his words by the way. He named you to rule his lands and to recover the mess we are now all in. May Artorus help you.'

Morgan was dumbstruck. Finally he turned to Itheya, who wordlessly handed him her flask of zhath. He took a mouthful, wishing it was something even more poisonous. What in this world of horror and wonder had the Gods done to him now?

…

END OF BOOK ONE

BOOK ONE: AUTUMN

Printed in Great Britain
by Amazon